The
Ski Slope Mystery

Nancy pushed off and glided down the hill. As she reached the bottom, she aimed the tips of her skis together to make a wedge. It was hard to keep her feet pointed the right way, but she did it. She stopped perfectly and smiled.

Then she heard a scream.

Nancy twisted around, being careful not to cross her skis.

George was speeding down the hill right behind Bess.

"Look out, Bess!" George screamed. "I can't stop!"

The Nancy Drew Notebooks

Available from MINSTREL Books

#16

THE NANCY DREW NOTEBOOKS®

THE SKI SLOPE MYSTERY

CAROLYN KEENE

Illustrated by Anthony Accardo

A MINSTREL® BOOK

PUBLISHED BY POCKET BOOKS

New York   London   Toronto   Sydney   Tokyo   Singapore

A MINSTREL PAPERBACK *Original*

 A Minstrel Book published by
POCKET BOOKS, a division of Simon & Schuster Inc.
1230 Avenue of the Americas, New York, NY 10020

Copyright © 1997 by Simon & Schuster Inc.
Produced by Mega-Books, Inc.

ISBN: 0-671-56860-4

First Minstrel Books printing January 1997

10 9 8 7 6 5 4 3 2 1

Cover art by Aleta Jenks

Printed in the U.S.A.

1

Hot Fudge
and Cold Snow

Race you to the hot fudge," George Fayne said to her cousin Bess Marvin.

"No way." Bess pushed her blond hair behind her ear and picked up her dish of chocolate ice cream. "I don't want hot fudge today. I'm having caramel."

Eight-year-old Nancy Drew smiled as she sprinkled chopped nuts over her strawberry ice cream. The three best friends were at a make-your-own-sundae party at the Snowshoe Mountain Ski Lodge.

Nancy's father had brought Nancy, Bess, and George to the resort for a three-day weekend. The girls were going to take skiing lessons at the Snowshoe Lodge ski school. The school had classes for everyone, from beginners to experts.

"I still can't believe we're really here," Nancy said to her friends. She glanced around the large, wood-paneled dining room. All around her, people were helping themselves to ice cream and toppings. Outside the window, snow was falling gently as the sun set behind the tall peak of Snowshoe Mountain. "I've always wanted to learn to ski."

"Me, too," Bess said.

"You'll love it," George promised. George liked all kinds of sports. She had been skiing a few times before.

The girls walked across the crowded room to the table where Mr. Drew was drinking coffee. "Do you think all these people are here for ski school?" Nancy asked her father as they sat down.

"I hope not," George said. "I want to spend the weekend skiing, not waiting in line."

"Don't worry, George." Mr. Drew smiled. "I'm sure you'll be able to do all the skiing you want."

"That's right," Bess said. "Your lucky necklace won't let you get stuck in line."

George scooped up a bite of her hot-fudge sundae and nodded.

"You mean the necklace your parents just gave you?" Nancy asked.

George swallowed her ice cream. Then she reached up and touched the pair of little silver skis hanging from a velvet ribbon around her neck. "It's my good-luck charm."

"It's great," Nancy said, looking at the tiny skis.

"Look, girls," Mr. Drew said, nodding toward the small stage at one end of the room. "They're going to make an announcement."

The girls turned and saw a man with short, sandy hair stepping up to a microphone on the stage. "May I have your attention, please?" he asked.

Nancy, Bess, and George stopped talking. But the two boys at the next table weren't paying attention to the man. They kept laughing loudly. One of them picked up a spoonful of ice cream and flipped it at the other.

The second boy leaned to the side, and the ice cream went flying past him—straight toward Bess!

Bess saw it coming just in time and ducked. The ice cream landed on the floor behind her.

"You creeps! You almost got ice cream on my sweater!" Bess cried.

The boys stared at her. They looked exactly alike. Even their clothes were the same. The only way to tell them apart was by the hot-fudge mustache one of them had on his face.

"Look, they're twins," Nancy said.

"Twin creeps, you mean," Bess said, frowning at the boys.

The boy with the fudge mustache stuck out his tongue. His brother

picked up another spoonful of ice cream and aimed it at Bess.

"Don't even think about it," Bess warned.

Mr. Drew turned and saw what was happening. "That's enough, boys," he said.

Both twins turned and faced the stage.

"I want to welcome everyone to Snowshoe Mountain," the man on the stage said. "I'm Bob Murray, the director of the ski school. How many of you are here for our ski school weekend?"

A lot of people waved their hands and cheered, including Nancy and Bess. George put two fingers in her mouth and whistled.

Bob Murray smiled. "I know you'll all have a great time and learn a lot. Now I'd like to introduce our instructors."

The ski instructors all wore black ski pants and bright red jackets.

"I love their outfits," Bess said. "They're almost as cute as my new pink ski jacket and hat." Her jacket was hanging on the back of her chair, with the pink hat tucked into the pocket.

"When you've finished eating, feel free to explore the rest of the lodge," Bob Murray said. "There's a game room across the hall, and a fireplace in the lounge. I hope everyone has a great weekend!"

"Let's go check out the game room," Nancy said to her friends. "Can we, Dad?"

"Okay," her father said. "I'll come to get you in a little while."

Nancy, Bess, and George quickly slurped down the rest of their ice cream. They picked up their jackets and hurried across the hall and into the game room.

"Looks like they're showing some cool skiing videos." George pointed to a big-screen television by the windows.

"Hey, maybe they have Star Quest," Nancy said when she saw the row of video games along the wall. The game was based on one of Nancy's favorite movies. "Let's go see."

As the girls headed toward the games, Nancy heard the sound of running footsteps. Then someone pushed Bess—hard.

She stumbled and almost fell into a table. Nancy grabbed her arm at the last minute.

"Bess, are you okay?" Nancy asked.

"My new ski hat," Bess cried. "Those twins just grabbed it out of my pocket!"

2

Double Trouble

Hat, hat, who's got the hat?" the twins chanted. They were standing behind Nancy and her friends. The twin holding Bess's new hat threw it into the air.

"Give it back!" Bess shrieked. She grabbed for the hat.

The other twin got it first. "Pink stinks, pink stinks." He threw the hat, and his brother reached forward to catch it.

George jumped up and caught the hat before the first twin reached it. *"Twins* stink," she said to the boys.

The twins stuck out their tongues

and laughed. Then they ran past the girls to the video games.

"Thanks, George," Bess said, stuffing the hat back into her pocket.

"Tim and Tom are such creeps," a girl's voice said.

Nancy turned and saw a girl about their own age standing in the doorway to the game room. She had short, smooth black hair and green eyes.

"Do you know them?" Nancy asked.

"They were in the beginners' class with me last year." The girl walked over to where Nancy, Bess, and George were standing. "They were always getting in trouble."

"*Double* trouble, I bet," George said.

The girl looked at George. "I like your necklace," she said.

George touched the tiny silver skis. "Thanks. It's my new good-luck charm. I won't ski without it."

"Are you a good skier?" the girl asked.

George shrugged. "I've only been skiing a few times. But I like it. I can't wait for ski school to start."

"I'll be in ski school, too," the girl said. "My name is Kelly Allen." Just then a girl with two long brown braids came into the game room and stood beside Kelly. "This is my little sister, Jennifer," Kelly said.

"Hi," Jennifer said, smiling.

Nancy smiled back. "Hi. I'm Nancy, and these are my friends Bess and George."

"Come on, let's watch the ski video," Kelly said. She led the way over to the big couch across from the TV.

As the girls sat down, Nancy looked at the skier on the screen. He was skiing around some orange flags. "I don't think I can do that yet," she said.

Jennifer laughed. "Me, either. I'm a beginner. I didn't get to come with Kelly last year because I had the flu."

"Bess and I are beginners, too," Nancy said. "Maybe we'll be in the same class."

"What about you, George?" Kelly asked. "Which level are you in?"

"Intermediate," George said, her eyes glued to the skier on the screen. He was gliding down a wide mountain trail, swooping back and forth to avoid rocks and trees.

"Me, too," Kelly said. "Every year there's a contest to choose the best skiers in each class. This year I know I'm going to win the award for best skier in my group."

"Who cares about winning a stupid skiing contest," a boy's voice said loudly.

The girls turned as a boy walked up to them. He had short black hair that stuck straight up.

"Skiing is *so* dumb," the boy said.

"It is not!" George said angrily.

The boy scowled at George. "Is, too."

"If you think skiing is dumb, why are you here?" Bess asked.

"My parents made me come," he said.

"Will," a woman called from the doorway.

"Coming, Mom!" the boy yelled. He stomped away without saying goodbye.

"There are *a lot* of creepy boys around this lodge," Bess said.

"He's probably just afraid to ski." George touched her necklace. "Maybe he needs a good-luck charm like mine."

"Does that really bring you luck?" Kelly asked. "Can I try it on?"

George didn't move for a moment. Nancy could tell she didn't want to take off her silver skis. But George untied the velvet ribbon and handed the necklace to Kelly anyway.

"Thanks." Kelly tied the ribbon around her own neck. "Maybe wearing it for a minute will bring me luck, too."

Nancy saw her father come into the room. "Time to go, girls," he called.

Nancy, Bess, and George put on their jackets. They said goodbye to Kelly and Jennifer and started to follow Mr. Drew out of the room.

"Oops! I almost forgot my necklace," George said.

Kelly took off the necklace. "Do you want me to tie it on for you?"

George nodded and pushed her dark curls out of the way. She smiled and touched the silver skis when they were back in place.

Bess, George, and Nancy followed Nancy's father out of the lodge and into the cold, starry night. So did Jennifer and Kelly.

"Bye!" Jennifer called from the doorway of the lodge.

Nancy turned and waved to her new friends. Jennifer waved back. But Kelly didn't see Nancy. She was busy looking at the glistening snow.

"I hope it's not this cold tomorrow," Bess said. She pulled on her pink hat.

"I don't care how cold it is," Nancy said, swishing her boots in the snow on the path. "We're going to have fun!"

It only took a few minutes to get to the apartment they were staying in for the weekend. From the living room window they could see the brightly colored gondola cars. Each day the gondolas carried skiers to the restaurant at the very top of the mountain.

It was chilly inside the apartment. Nancy quickly changed into her warm flannel nightgown and brushed her teeth. The bedroom she was sharing with Bess and George had two sets of bunk beds. She jumped into the lower bunk of one of the beds and snuggled under a cozy yellow- and white-striped comforter.

Bess came out of the bathroom and hopped into the other lower bunk. "Brrr," she said. "Hurry up and brush your teeth, George. Then you can tell us what skiing is like before we go to sleep."

"I'll be right out," George promised, rushing into the bathroom.

"I wish Chip was here," Nancy said. "She could keep my feet warm."

Chip was Nancy's Labrador retriever puppy. Her full name was Chocolate Chip because she was a chocolate brown color.

Suddenly George came racing out of

the bathroom with toothpaste foam around her mouth. She was waving her toothbrush.

"George, what's wrong?" Nancy asked.

"My necklace!" George cried. "It's gone!"

3

Beginners Only!

Nancy jumped out of bed, forgetting all about the cold. "Maybe it fell off while you were brushing your teeth."

"I looked," George said. "I couldn't find it anywhere."

"Let's look again," Nancy said.

They went into the bathroom and searched. The charm wasn't there.

"When do you remember having it last?" Nancy asked.

George shrugged, then looked under the sink again. "I remember Kelly tying it on in the lodge. After that, I'm not sure."

She stomped back to the bunks and

climbed the ladder to the bed above Nancy's.

"I might as well stay right here for the rest of the weekend." She flopped onto her bed. "I can't ski without my lucky charm."

"Nancy will help you find your silver skis," Bess said. "She can find anything."

"It's no use," George said.

Bess looked at Nancy but didn't say anything else. She climbed into her bunk as Nancy turned off the light.

Nancy lay down in her bed and closed her eyes. She couldn't fall asleep right away. Where could George's necklace be?

"Wake up, sleepyheads!" Nancy's father said the next morning as he poked his head into the girls' room.

The girls got dressed and then went into the kitchen. "Something smells yummy," Bess said. "What is it?"

Nancy sniffed. "I can solve *that* mystery right now," she said. "Pancakes!"

"Case closed, Pumpkin," Mr. Drew said. "It's my special recipe, so dig in."

Nancy noticed that George hardly ate anything. She knew her friend was still upset about losing her necklace.

After breakfast they all headed for the lodge to rent skis. Nancy walked slowly, looking carefully at the path. Maybe George lost her silver skis while we were walking home last night, she thought.

When she didn't see the necklace, Nancy had another idea.

"Can Bess and George and I stop by the game room for a second?" she asked her father. "We want to look for something."

Her father nodded. "Meet me at the ski shop to pick up your boots and skis."

When they got to the game room, Nancy told Bess and George her idea.

"Do you really think it might be here?" George asked.

"There's only one way to find out," Nancy said.

The three friends searched the whole room. The necklace wasn't there.

"I'm sorry, George," Nancy said. "I hope you didn't mean it when you said you wouldn't ski without your necklace."

George shrugged. "I guess I'll ski," she said, trying to smile.

At the ski shop, Mr. Drew and the girls put on their ski boots and picked up their poles and skis. The clerk wrote Nancy's, Bess's, and George's names on pieces of tape and stuck them on each ski.

"This way you'll be able to keep track of whose skis are whose," he told them.

The girls thanked the clerk and followed Mr. Drew out of the shop. It was hard to hold on to everything as they clomped in their heavy ski boots. Bess giggled every time her poles slipped out of her grasp.

"You're supposed to meet the other students over there," Mr. Drew said when they got outside. He pointed to a

21

large group of kids gathered around the ski school instructors. "I'll be skiing on the regular trails. Let's meet back at the lodge for lunch. Have fun!"

The girls hurried to join the group. Bob Murray looked up their names on his list. "Nancy and Bess, you're in Alexandra's Bunny class," he said. He nodded toward a tall woman with blond hair. Several other kids were already standing with her.

"What about me?" George asked eagerly. Nancy was glad George wasn't too worried about her necklace to have fun.

"You're in the Jackrabbit class. Hector is your teacher," Bob Murray said. He pointed at a man with shaggy brown hair, wearing wraparound sunglasses.

"Cool," George said. She grabbed her poles and skis and hurried over to Hector.

Nancy and Bess walked toward Alexandra. "Oh, no. Look who else is in our class," Bess whispered. "It's that grumpy boy from last night."

Nancy saw Will standing next to Alexandra. "It's cold," he complained.

"Let's just ignore him," Nancy said to Bess.

"We'll start our lesson just as soon as Jennifer arrives," Alexandra told the Bunny group.

Nancy looked around for Jennifer. She saw her talking to Bob Murray. Jennifer put her hands on her hips and shook her head. Finally she turned and walked toward them.

"Is something wrong?" Nancy asked.

"I wanted to be in my sister's class," Jennifer said, looking over at the Jackrabbits.

"But you told us you don't know how to ski," Bess said.

"Kelly says it isn't that hard," Jennifer said. "*You* might not be able to do it, but *I* could."

Jennifer isn't as nice as she was yesterday, Nancy thought.

Alexandra called the Bunny class to attention. She tightened all their boots and showed the students how to put on their skis. "Now we're going to practice walking," she said.

"I *know* how to walk," Jennifer snapped. She took a few steps on her skis, lifting her feet and keeping them straight.

"This is boring," Will complained.

Nancy hoped Jennifer and Will weren't going to be like this all weekend.

Alexandra smiled. "Don't worry, Will, you won't be bored for long."

The Bunny class practiced walking. Then they practiced turning around.

When Will tried to turn, he crossed the tip of one ski over the other. His skis made a big X in the snow.

"I'm stuck!" he cried.

Jennifer rolled her eyes and sighed while Alexandra helped Will get unstuck.

"Now we'll walk sideways up this little hill," Alexandra said after everyone was able to turn around.

Bess giggled as they clomped sideways up the hill. "This isn't so hard."

But when they stopped and looked down the hill, it seemed much bigger and steeper than it had from the bottom.

"Now what?" Bess asked nervously.

"Now we ski down," Alexandra told her.

"I'll break a leg," Will said.

"Keep your knees bent and your weight over the tops of your boots," Alexandra explained. "Like this."

She pushed off with her poles and glided down the hill. "Nancy, you try it," she called when she reached the bottom.

Nancy stuck her poles in the snow and pushed off, just as Alexandra had.

The air rushed past her cheeks. Her skis seemed to fly over the snow. When she reached the flat part at the bottom of the hill, her skis slowed to a stop.

One by one, the rest of the class skied down the hill.

"No problem," Jennifer said. As she reached the bottom, she turned her skis so the tips faced each other.

"Watch out," Will said nervously. "Don't make an X."

"That's how you stop, stupid," Jennifer said. Then she turned to Alexandra. "Now can I switch to Kelly's class? I know how to stop, and no one else in this class does."

"Jennifer just showed us how to stop," Alexandra said to the rest of the class. "It's called making a wedge. Let's all walk up the hill again and try it." She looked at Jennifer. "You, too."

"I'm tired of walking only partway up the slope." Jennifer pointed to the chairs hanging from a cable above them. "When can we ride the ski lift to the top?"

Nancy looked up. She saw George and Kelly sitting in a ski lift chair. It was carrying them to the top of the slope.

"Hector's class is going to ski down part of the trail and meet us at the top of this hill," Alexandra said. "Later we'll take the rope tow up the beginners' slope."

"I thought this *was* the beginners' slope," Bess said.

"It's the *baby* slope," Jennifer said.

Alexandra led the Bunny class back up the small hill. Hector and the Jackrabbits were waiting for them.

"Hi," Nancy said to George. "Are you having fun?"

"Yup," George said. "The only bad thing is those twins are in my class."

Nancy looked and saw Tim and Tom standing in the group of Jackrabbits. One of them saw Nancy looking and crossed his eyes at her.

"I'm glad they're not in our class," Bess whispered. "It's bad enough we have to listen to Will and Jennifer all the time."

"Okay, skiers," Hector called to the two groups. "Line up. We'll go down the hill one at a time."

Nancy was first again. "Good luck," Bess said. She was next in line.

Nancy pushed off and glided down the hill. As she reached the bottom, she aimed the tips of her skis together to make a wedge. It was hard to keep her feet pointed the right way, but she did it. She stopped perfectly and smiled.

Then she heard a scream.

Nancy twisted around, being careful not to cross her skis.

George was speeding down the hill right behind Bess. "Look out, Bess!" George screamed. "I can't stop!"

4

Out of Control

Bess looked over her shoulder. The tips of her skis crossed, and she fell.

George tried to turn, but it was too late. One of her skis went underneath one of Bess's. George tripped and fell right on top of her cousin!

Nancy turned her skis sideways and climbed up the hill toward her friends as fast as she could.

Some of the Bunny and Jackrabbit students waited as Hector and Alexandra skied down the hill toward Bess and George. Kelly, Jennifer, Will, and a few others skied down behind the teachers.

Alexandra and Hector arrived beside Bess and George, tossing up fans of snow as they stopped. Hector helped the girls stand up.

"Are you guys okay?" Nancy cried when she finally reached her friends.

"They're fine," Hector said. "Just a little shaken up."

Then they all skied down to the bottom.

"Who did that?" George asked when they got there. She was covered with snow.

"*You* did," Bess said. She sounded just as cross as her cousin. She was covered with snow, too.

"Okay, girls, settle down. We have to help the others down the hill," Alexandra told them.

"So don't move," Hector said to the group. "We'll be right back."

The two instructors skied off.

"What happened?" Nancy asked when the adults were gone.

George narrowed her eyes. "Someone pushed me," she said.

"That's what everyone says when they fall," Jennifer said. "Right, Kelly?"

Kelly shrugged. "I guess."

Bess dug her ski poles into the snow and straightened up. "If my cousin says she was pushed, she was pushed."

"I told you skiing was stupid," Will said to George.

George ignored him. She still looked angry. "I bet this wouldn't have happened if I still had my good-luck charm."

"Did you lose it?" Jennifer asked.

George nodded.

"That's weird," Kelly said. "You said you couldn't ski without it. And you fell."

"I was *pushed,*" George insisted.

By now the rest of the students had reached the bottom of the hill. "Okay, people, time for lunch," Hector said.

"Maybe after lunch George and I should switch classes," Jennifer said to Alexandra. "I didn't fall once."

"No, Jennifer, I don't think so," Alexandra answered.

Nancy and Bess took off their skis.

As they carried them to the ski racks outside the lodge, George walked ahead of them.

Bess leaned close to Nancy. "Poor George. First she loses her silver skis. Then someone pushes her. Why would anyone do that?"

"Maybe they didn't do it on purpose." Nancy frowned. "But then why didn't whoever did it just apologize?"

"Maybe they're chicken. Or creeps like the twins," Bess said. *"They* didn't apologize when they almost got ice cream on my sweater last night."

George had leaned her skis against one end of a ski rack right outside the lodge door. "Hurry up," she said. "All that skiing made me hungry."

Nancy and Bess leaned their skis against the rack, too. They looped the straps of their poles over the tips of their skis.

Then they all clomped into the lodge in their ski boots. Nancy liked walking in her ski boots. It was hard, but it made her feel like a real skier.

Kelly and Jennifer were standing in the hall outside the dining room. "Are you sure you guys are okay?" Kelly asked George and Bess.

"Yeah," George said. Bess nodded.

"Sometimes when people fall, it scares them," Kelly went on. "It makes it harder for them to ski again."

"I've fallen before," George said. "It's no big deal."

"Kelly, you promised to help me practice," Jennifer said. "We have to hurry. I don't want to have to stay in the baby class *forever*."

The sisters hurried away.

The girls found Nancy's father waiting for them just inside the cafeteria. "How'd it go, girls?" he asked.

"Great," Nancy said.

"Except someone pushed me," George added.

"I bet I know who, too," Bess said. "I think it was—"

Suddenly Bess's voice rose to a shriek. "Tim and Tom!" she cried. "You creeps!"

5

Sticky Skis

One of the twins had snatched Bess's pink ski hat off her head, while the other had jammed his own red stocking cap over Bess's ears.

Bess yanked the stocking cap from her head. "They stole my hat again!"

The twins raced across the hall into the game room. The girls chased them.

"Give that back!" Bess shouted.

"Finders keepers, losers weepers," the first twin said as he jammed Bess's hat onto his head.

Bess reached for her hat. The twin ducked. "Catch me if you can!"

He started to run out of the room.

When he reached the doorway, he bumped into Mr. Drew.

"Oops," the twin said, looking up at Nancy's father.

Just then a woman appeared next to Mr. Drew. "Tom, Tim, did you forget?" she asked. "We're having lunch at the Mountaintop Café today. We're going to ride the gondola."

"Coming, Mom," the twins said at the same time. The first twin took Bess's hat off his head and tossed it toward her. The other twin grabbed the red stocking cap out of her hand.

"Wait," Nancy said to the twins. "Have you seen a silver pendant shaped like skis?"

"Yeah, right." The second twin laughed. "That's girl stuff." Then the boys left the room with their mother.

"Maybe they'll get stuck in a gondola and never come down," George said.

Mr. Drew laughed. "Come on, girls," he said. "Let's have lunch."

Soon they were all back in the cafeteria with steaming plates of food in front of them. "Now, tell me about your latest mystery," Mr. Drew said to Nancy.

"How did you know about the mystery, Daddy?" Nancy asked. She reached for her water glass and took a sip.

Her father smiled. "You aren't the only detective in the family," he said. "I heard you question the twins in the game room just now. And I remembered you were looking for something this morning."

"My necklace," George said. "I lost it last night."

"Don't forget, someone pushed George down the hill," Bess said. "Maybe the same person took her silver skis!"

"Do you think that's what happened, Daddy?" Nancy asked her father.

"You know, Nancy, it's important to get all the facts first," her father said, leaning back in his chair. "Did someone really push George on purpose? Or was it an accident?"

Nancy took a small blue notebook and a pen out of the inside pocket of her ski jacket. It was her mystery note-book. She wrote about all her cases in it.

She turned to a blank page and wrote "The Silver Skis Mystery." Under that she made a list:

1) George's lucky necklace is missing.
2) Someone pushed George down ski slope (on purpose or accident?).

Nancy started a second list. At the top she wrote "Suspects." Then she stopped writing.

"So, who are your suspects?" her father asked, looking at the page.

"The twins, Tim and Tom," Nancy said. "I can't tell them apart, so I guess they're both suspects. And they both could have pushed George." She wrote down the twins' names.

"Why would they do something like that?" Mr. Drew asked.

"They're boys," Bess said. "They don't need a reason to be mean."

Mr. Drew smiled. "Are they your only suspects?"

"What about whiny Will?" Bess asked.

"Well, he was there," Nancy said. "And he hates skiing. So I guess he could have pushed George to try to make the class end earlier." She wrote Will's name down, too.

"Anybody else?" George asked.

"Jennifer and Kelly were nearby when you were pushed," Nancy said.

"Why would they push George?" her father asked.

Nancy thought for a minute. "Jennifer wants to be in the Jackrabbit class instead of the Bunny class," she said.

"She thought the instructors would make us change places if I fell," George said. "She even said so."

"But what about Kelly?" Nancy said. "Would she push George to get Jennifer into the Jackrabbit class?"

"Well, it's a detective's job to find the truth," Mr. Drew said.

"I know," Nancy said. She wrote down the sisters' names. Then she put her notebook away. "We'll have to keep our eyes open for new clues during class this afternoon," she said to her friends.

"Don't worry," George said. "We will!"

After lunch the girls said goodbye to Nancy's father. Then they clomped down the hall toward the door leading outside.

George stopped. "Hey!" she said. "What are my skis doing in here?"

George's skis were leaning against the wall just inside the door.

"Are you sure those are yours?" Nancy asked.

George pointed to the strip of tape with her name written on it. "See? Definitely mine."

"Maybe someone took yours by mistake and left them here," Nancy said.

"Or maybe it was the twins playing another dumb trick," Bess said, looking around. The twins were nowhere in sight.

"Oh, well," George said. "At least my

skis are safe." She picked up her skis and poles and followed Nancy and Bess outside.

Nancy and Bess found their skis where they had left them. The three girls put on their skis. They saw Alexandra and Will standing at the bottom of the beginners' slope. Hector was nearby with Kelly, some of the other Jackrabbits, and Jennifer.

Will waved when he saw Nancy and Bess. "Hurry up. I'm freezing!"

"See you later," George said as she pushed off with her poles.

But she didn't budge.

She pushed again, harder.

Still nothing.

"Something's wrong with my skis," George cried. "I can't move!"

6

Dirty Trick

George took off her skis. She turned them over. The bottoms were covered with lumpy, bumpy ice!

Alexandra skied over to the girls. "What's the problem?" she asked.

George showed the instructor her skis. "Did you leave your skis inside the lodge during lunch?" Alexandra asked.

George shook her head. "No, but someone moved them inside."

"That explains it," Alexandra said. "Your skis got warm inside. When they touched the ground out here, they melted the snow. Since it's so cold outside, the water refroze. That's why there's ice on the bottom of your skis."

"I can't ski on these," George said. "This is the worst luck ever!"

Hector, Kelly, and Jennifer skied up behind George.

"What happened?" Hector asked.

"George's skis are all iced up," Alexandra said.

"Someone put them inside while we were having lunch," Bess explained.

"Gee, that's too bad," Jennifer said. "I guess you'll have to miss your class, George. But I can take your place."

"That won't be necessary," Alexandra said firmly.

"Right," Hector agreed. "I'll take George to rent another pair of skis." He took off his skis and headed inside with George.

All during class Nancy kept thinking about George's frozen skis. Was this more bad luck? Or was someone out to get George?

By the end of the afternoon, the Bunny class had learned how to use the rope tow and had skied down from a higher part of the mountain. Nancy had a lot of fun. But she still couldn't stop thinking about the mystery.

"I'll see you all at the snowman-building party," Alexandra said when class was over. "There'll be plenty of hot chocolate for everyone."

"I don't like hot chocolate," Will said. "I always burn my tongue."

"Building snowmen is for babies," Jennifer muttered.

"What a couple of party poopers," Bess whispered to Nancy as they went to meet George in the lodge.

The locker room was crowded with Jackrabbits, Bunnies, and kids from the other classes.

"Wow, I'm tired," Bess said as she put on her regular shoes.

"Not me," Jennifer said. "I could ski all day and night."

Jennifer held up her shoes. They were tied together by the shoelaces. She gave one of the laces a quick pull, and they came apart.

"How'd you do that?" Bess asked.

"It's a slip knot," Jennifer said. "Kelly showed me how to do it."

"It's a good trick to know when your fingers are cold," Kelly explained.

"But you have to be careful," Jennifer said. "Or the knot could slip loose when you don't want it to."

Nancy's father was waiting for the girls outside the locker room. "How was skiing this afternoon?" he asked them.

"Okay," George said. "But I bet I would have skied better if I'd had my good-luck charm."

"You would have had better luck, too," Bess said.

Nancy told her father about George's frozen skis.

"That *is* bad luck," he said.

"I think it's another clue," Nancy said. She pulled out her notebook and wrote it down.

Then they headed outside to the snowy field behind the lodge. When they arrived, it was full of people.

"Have fun, girls," Mr. Drew said. "I'm going to get our skis and stuff and take it all back to the apartment. I'll see you in a little while."

"Okay, Daddy," Nancy said.

"Let's build a snow dog," Bess said as Mr. Drew walked away.

"Like Chocolate Chip," George said.

"No fair!" Nancy heard Jennifer shout. Then Jennifer laughed as she scooped up a snowball and threw it at her sister.

Kelly ducked behind the snowman Tim and Tom were building. The snowball hit its head and knocked part of it off.

"Sorry," Jennifer said.

"No problem," one of the twins said. "Tom and I are making a snow monster. It only has one eye anyway."

"And a long monster nose," Tim added. He stuck a stick in the monster's face.

Kelly scooped up another snowball and threw it at Jennifer. It missed her.

"Ow!" Will said. He had just joined

the party and was brushing snow off his coat. "That does it. I'm not building any stupid snowman!" He stomped away.

I guess Will's not having a very good time, Nancy thought. She started to roll a snowball for the snow dog's body.

"Here's a monster nose ring," Nancy heard one of the twins say. She looked up.

One of the boys put something on the snow monster's stick nose.

Nancy's eyes widened. "Where did you get George's necklace?" she shouted.

"Hey!" George cried. She ran to grab her necklace.

But Tom grabbed it first. "Hey, Tim! Catch!" He threw it to his brother.

"Oh, no! Not again," Bess said.

Tim caught the necklace. When George tried to get it, he threw it back to Tom.

But Kelly jumped in and caught it before Tom.

"Good catch, Kelly," George said.

"I'll tie it on for you," Kelly said.

"Tie it tight," George said. "I don't

want to lose it again." She touched the silver charm.

As Kelly tied the ribbon around George's neck, Jennifer giggled. "Better not tie a slip knot, Kelly."

Nancy turned to the twins. "You said you didn't have George's necklace."

"They took it!" Bess shouted.

"We did not," Tom said. "We found it."

Tim pointed to the ground by the side of the lodge. "It was lying in the snow."

Nancy looked where Tim was pointing. There were lots of footprints in the snow—too many to tell who had made them.

How had George's necklace gotten there? she wondered. Someone must have dropped it. Kelly and Jennifer's snowman was nearby. So was the twins' snow monster. And Will had just stomped through there.

Nancy sighed. She had found George's necklace. But the mystery was more mysterious than ever.

7

No Clues

That night after dinner Nancy curled up on her bunk and opened her notebook.

Bess sat down next to Nancy. "I bet the twins moved George's skis today."

George sat down on Nancy's other side. "It couldn't have been the twins," she said. "They had lunch at the Mountaintop Café."

"Maybe they moved them on their way out of the building," Bess argued.

Nancy shook her head. "They were with their mother, remember?"

"Well, they probably took George's necklace," Bess said. "They keep taking my hat."

"Maybe," Nancy said slowly. "But *three* bad-luck things have happened to George. I bet one person did all three." She crossed the twins' names off her suspect list. "That means Tim and Tom couldn't be the ones."

George looked at Nancy's suspect list. "Kelly, Jennifer, and Will were all near me when I was pushed."

Nancy studied her notebook. "Kelly and Jennifer had gone out to practice before the next class," she said. "They could have moved George's skis."

"Will was already waiting for class to begin when we got outside," Bess remembered. "He could have come out early and done it, too."

Nancy looked at the names on her list. Jennifer didn't want to be in the Bunny class. Could she have moved George's skis? Would she have pushed George down the hill just to get into the Jackrabbit class?

Maybe, Nancy thought. But Kelly could have moved the skis and pushed

George, too. Maybe she had done it to help her sister.

"But why would *Will* move your skis, George?" Nancy wondered aloud.

"I don't know," George said. "Maybe he hates skiing so much that he doesn't want anyone else to have fun doing it."

Nancy sighed and closed her notebook. "We still haven't solved the mystery."

George touched her necklace. "But you found my silver skis," she told Nancy. "At least my bad luck is over."

"I hope so," Nancy said. But deep down inside, Nancy had a feeling more bad luck was coming.

Bess looked down at her feet dangling over the edge of the ski lift chair. She quickly leaned back. "Oh, boy. It's a long way down."

The Bunnies had practiced all morning. Now they were riding on the ski lift for the first time.

"This isn't so bad," Nancy heard Will

say to Jennifer. They were in the chair behind Nancy and Bess.

"It's just a chair lift," Jennifer said.

Wow, Nancy thought. Jennifer is cranky about *everything*.

When they reached the top, Nancy and Bess raised the safety bar, stood up on their skis, and slid off the lift. They made a wedge and stopped by Alexandra.

"Everybody ready?" Alexandra said when the whole class was there. "Good. Let's ski!"

"Um, can I *walk* down?" Bess asked.

"You can do it, Bess," Nancy said.

"Just remember not to cross your skis," Will added.

Jennifer pushed her way to the front of the line. "I'll go first. I don't want any of you falling in front of me and making *me* fall."

Alexandra shrugged. "Fine, go ahead."

Jennifer smiled and pushed off down the hill.

When it was her turn, Nancy took a

deep breath and pushed off. She was going so fast! For a moment she was almost afraid. But she had learned a lot this weekend. She turned her skis into a wedge and slowed down. This is fun, she thought.

They practiced skiing down the slope for the rest of the afternoon.

"You all did really well," Alexandra told them when class was over. "Tomorrow morning is the skiing contest. After that there will be an awards ceremony at the Mountaintop Café."

"Thanks for the lessons," Nancy told Alexandra. "They were fun."

"Yeah," Will added. "Skiing isn't as dumb as I thought."

Alexandra smiled. "My pleasure. See you at the skating party by the pond tonight." She pointed to the pond in the distance. "And good luck tomorrow!"

Jennifer dug her poles into the snow and pushed off. "I don't need luck," she said over her shoulder. "Because I'm

57

going to win. And that makes you all losers!''

That night when the girls arrived at the skating party, George quickly put on her skates and hurried off to play ice hockey. Nancy and Bess took their time lacing up their skates.

Nancy noticed Jennifer standing alone by a table with drinks and snacks on it. "Let's set a trap for Jennifer," she whispered to Bess,

"How?" Bess asked.

"If she moved George's skis, that means she knows what they look like, right?" Nancy said.

"That makes sense," Bess agreed.

Nancy stood up. "Come on. I've got a plan." She skated toward Jennifer.

"What plan?" Bess whispered, trying to catch up with her. "What do we do?"

"Just play along," Nancy whispered back. She stopped by the table. "Hi, Jennifer!''

Jennifer had just finished drinking a cup of hot cocoa. "I'm glad you're here,''

Jennifer said. "Kelly's playing ice hockey, and I'm bored. Come skate with me."

"Hey, Jennifer, Bess was thinking about buying some skis," Nancy said as the three girls slowly skated around the pond.

"I was?" Bess said. Nancy elbowed her. "I mean, yes, I was."

"She wants some like the first pair of skis George rented," Nancy continued. "They're good skis. Don't you think so?"

Jennifer shrugged. "I guess. I really didn't notice them."

Nancy studied Jennifer's face. She looked as if she was telling the truth.

The trap hadn't worked very well. Nancy decided to try something else.

"Do you still wish you'd been in the Jackrabbit class?" she asked.

Jennifer laughed. "I was so silly," she said. "If I was in Kelly's class, I'd have to ski against her tomorrow. Kelly's a better skier than I am. But this way, I can win in my class and Kelly can win in hers."

"Someone else might win, you know," Bess said.

Jennifer laughed again. "Now *you're* being silly," she told Bess.

"Jen!" Nancy heard Kelly shout. "Come on. We need another player to win."

"Okay," Jennifer called. "See you later," she said to Nancy and Bess.

Bess glared after her. "That Jennifer thinks she's so great," she said.

"Yes," Nancy said. "And she's still a suspect—even if our trap didn't work."

After breakfast the next morning, Mr. Drew, Nancy, George, and Bess headed for the ski lodge. All three girls were excited about the skiing contest.

They had just reached the front steps when Jennifer came hurrying out. "Hi," she said breathlessly. "We're supposed to meet by the pond this morning instead of the usual place." Then she ran off.

"We'd better hurry," George said. "It's a long walk to the pond."

"I'm going to go find a good place to

watch the action," Mr. Drew said. "Good luck, girls!"

The three friends changed into their ski boots. They carried their skis as fast as they could down the path toward the pond.

"I wonder where everyone is," George said when they arrived.

A woman polishing a snowmobile near an equipment shed looked up. "Are you girls lost?" she asked.

"Isn't this where we're supposed to meet for the skiing contest?" Nancy asked.

The woman shook her head. "The contest is back there." She pointed toward the bottom of the beginners' slope. "It looks as if it's about to start."

George's eyes flashed angrily. "Wait until I find that Jennifer!"

"Come on," Nancy said quickly. "If we run, we might make it."

"We can't run in ski boots!" Bess cried. "We'll never make it in time. It's hopeless!"

8

Winners and Losers

Sounds as if someone played a dirty trick on you," the woman said. "I'll take you over on my snowmobile."

Nancy, Bess, and George put their skis in the sled behind the snowmobile. Then they climbed onto the snowmobile seat. A moment later they were zooming back toward the slope.

"Thanks," Nancy said when the snowmobile came to a stop. She jumped off, grabbed her skis, and raced toward Alexandra. Bess was right behind her.

George rushed past them to the lift. The rest of the Jackrabbit class was already riding up the hill.

"You're late," Alexandra said. She was frowning.

"It wasn't our fault," Bess said. "Someone told us to go to the pond." She glared at Jennifer. But Jennifer wouldn't look at her.

Nancy and Bess put on their skis and got on the ski lift. As they rode to the top of the hill, they saw George skiing down. Nancy thought she skied well.

Kelly skied down a moment later. She's good, too, Nancy thought. Almost as good as those skiers in the videos.

Finally they reached the top, and it was time for the Bunny class to ski.

Will fell halfway down the hill, then slid the rest of the way to the bottom. But when he got up, he was laughing.

Then Jennifer dug her ski poles into the snow and pushed off hard—so hard she fell right over the front of her skis! She stood up and pushed off again. This time she finished the course perfectly.

"That was brave of her," Nancy said. "She didn't quit just because she fell."

"She's still a sneak," Bess said.

Nancy was next. She took a deep breath and pushed off. The wind rushed past her. She pointed her skis into a wedge and zigzagged down the snowy trail.

"That was great!" George said when Nancy reached the bottom of the hill.

"Thanks," Nancy said. "You were great, too." She glanced over at the people watching and saw her father waving at her and grinning proudly.

Nancy and George watched as Bess skied down the hill. Bess went very, very slowly. But she didn't fall once.

Nancy and George cheered as Bess crossed the finish line.

"I *knew* it was Jennifer!" Bess crowed at lunch. "Her mean trick almost made us miss the contest. That proves it!"

Nancy reached for her notebook. She crossed off Will's name. He liked skiing now, so he wasn't a suspect anymore.

That left Jennifer and Kelly. And

Jennifer had lied to them about meeting at the pond. That meant she must be the one.

Something isn't right, Nancy thought, putting her notebook away. But she wasn't sure what was bothering her.

Nancy was still thinking about the mystery that afternoon as they got ready to go to the awards ceremony.

"Why would she do it?" Nancy muttered under her breath on the way to the gondola lift.

"What?" George asked.

"We thought Jennifer did everything because she wanted to be a Jackrabbit," Nancy said. "But then she decided she didn't. So why would she *keep* doing mean things to you, George? It doesn't make sense. Unless . . ."

Nancy saw George reknot the velvet ribbon of her necklace. The silver skis caught the late-afternoon sun and flashed brightly.

Just then Nancy remembered that Kelly knew how to tie a slip knot. And Jennifer had told a joke about Kelly tying George's necklace on with a slip knot, too.

"That's it!" Nancy said. She looked ahead at the gondola line, then turned to her father. "Can we ride the gondola with our friends?"

When he nodded, Nancy grabbed George and Bess. She pushed through the line until they were standing with Kelly, Jennifer, and their parents.

When the next gondola came, Nancy led George and Bess onto it, right behind the sisters. The gondola was full.

"You'll have to catch the next one," the gondola operator told Kelly and Jennifer's parents.

The gondola lifted them higher and higher up the side of the mountain.

Nancy faced Kelly and Jennifer. "Kelly, I know you're the one who's been doing mean things to George."

Kelly shrugged and stared out the window. "I don't know what you're talking about."

Nancy looked at Jennifer. "Kelly

made you tell us to go to the pond, didn't she?"

Jennifer glanced at Kelly. "No," she said. "I really thought we were meeting there."

Nancy wasn't going to give up. She moved closer to Jennifer. "Kelly *told* you that, right? We know, because we know it was Kelly who stole George's good-luck charm and pushed her down the hill."

"You can't prove that," Kelly burst out. "Anyway, what makes you think I took her stupid necklace?"

"The slip knot," Nancy said. "You used that kind of knot on George's necklace. Am I right?"

For a minute it looked as though Kelly was going to deny it. Then she glanced at her sister and sighed. "Yes," she told Nancy quietly. "I tied the ribbon with a very loose slip knot so it would come off. I saw it fall outside the lodge and I picked it up."

"Then you dropped it by accident and the twins found it," Nancy said.

Kelly nodded. "That's right. I did all the other things, too."

"Why?" George demanded.

Kelly met George's eyes. "Last year at the contest I fell and didn't finish. Everyone laughed at me. I wanted to win this year. No one laughs at a winner."

The gondola bumped to a stop at the top of the mountain. Kelly jumped out and started running.

Jennifer got out, too. "I'm sorry," she said. Then she ran after her sister.

The Mountaintop Café was buzzing with excitement as Alexandra announced the award winners in the Bunny class.

Bess won an award for being the skier with the most style. Will won for having the most improved attitude.

Even Jennifer won an award. It was for being the bravest skier—because she finished the contest after she had fallen.

"Finally, the award you've all been waiting for," Alexandra announced.

"For the best overall skier in the Bunny group, our award goes to Nancy Drew."

Nancy smiled proudly as she shook Alexandra's hand.

Nancy noticed that everyone in the class had received an award. No one was a loser.

But she couldn't help holding her breath when it was time to announce the awards for the Jackrabbit class.

"Everyone worked hard," Hector said. "But we think the most promising skier is Georgia Fayne."

George made a face at hearing her whole name. But she grinned as she went to get her award.

Tim and Tom got awards for being the fastest twins on skis. They ran up to get their awards and ran back to their seats.

"And the best all-around skier in the Jackrabbit class is Kelly Allen."

Nancy clapped politely as Kelly got her award. Bess didn't clap.

As Kelly walked by their table back to her own, George jumped up and stuck out her hand. "Congratulations, Kelly."

"You mean it?" Kelly said.

"Sure," George said. "Even though you tried to cheat, you won the contest fair and square. You *were* the best skier."

Kelly shook George's hand. Then, in a low voice, she said, "I'm really sorry, George."

"It's okay," George said. She grinned. "Just don't try anything like that next year!"

That evening Nancy finished packing before Bess and George. She took out her notebook and sat on her bunk.

She turned to the page headed "The Silver Skis Mystery." At the bottom she wrote:

I learned to ski this weekend, and I won a prize for it. I solved a mystery, too. When I solved the mystery, I learned something important. Winning is fun, but not if all you care about is winning. And if you have to cheat to win, you haven't really won at all.

Case closed.

TAKE A RIDE
WITH THE KIDS ON BUS FIVE!

Natalie Adams and James Penny have just started
third grade. They like their teacher, and they like
Maple Street School. The only trouble is, they have
to ride bad old Bus Five to get there!

#1 THE BAD NEWS BULLY
Can Natalie and James stop the bully on Bus Five?

#2 WILD MAN AT THE WHEEL
When Mr. Balter calls in sick,
the kids get some strange new drivers.

#3 FINDERS KEEPERS
The kids on Bus Five keep losing things.
Is there a thief on board?

(And coming soon)
#4 I SURVIVED ON BUS FIVE
Bad luck turns into big fun
when Bus Five breaks down in a rainstorm.

BY MARCIA LEONARD
ILLUSTRATED BY JULIE DURRELL

A MINSTREL® BOOK
Published by Pocket Books

1237-03

FULL HOUSE™
Michelle

#1: THE GREAT PET PROJECT 51905-0/$3.50

#2: THE SUPER-DUPER SLEEPOVER PARTY
51906-9/$3.50

#3: MY TWO BEST FRIENDS 52271-X/$3.50

#4: LUCKY, LUCKY DAY 52272-8/$3.50

#5: THE GHOST IN MY CLOSET 53573-0/$3.99

#6: BALLET SURPRISE 53574-9/$3.99

#7: MAJOR LEAGUE TROUBLE 53575-7/$3.50

#8: MY FOURTH-GRADE MESS 53576-5/$3.99

#9: BUNK 3, TEDDY, AND ME 56834-5/$3.50

#10: MY BEST FRIEND IS A MOVIE STAR!
(Super Edition) 56835-3/$3.50

#11: THE BIG TURKEY ESCAPE 56836-1/$3.50

#12: THE SUBSTITUTE TEACHER 00364-X/$3.50

A MINSTREL® BOOK

Published by Pocket Books

Assessment of Exceptional Students

Educational and Psychological Procedures

THIRD EDITION

RONALD L. TAYLOR
Florida Atlantic University

ALLYN AND BACON
Boston   London   Toronto   Sydney   Tokyo   Singapore

This book is affectionately dedicated
To my parents, Ron and Juanita, to my wife, Yvette,
and to my sons, Michael and Daniel.
Thanks for always being there.

Series Editor: *Ray Short*
Series Editorial Assistant: *Christine Shaw*
Production Administrator: *Susan McIntyre*
Editorial-Production Service: *Ruttle, Shaw & Wetherill, Inc.*
Cover Administrator: *Linda Dickinson*
Composition Buyer: *Linda Cox*
Manufacturing Buyer: *Louise Richardson*

Copyright © 1993, 1989, 1984 by Allyn & Bacon
A Division of Simon & Schuster, Inc.
160 Gould Street
Needham Heights, MA 02194

Library of Congress Cataloging-in-Publication Data

Taylor, Ronald L.
    Assessment of exceptional students : educational and psychological
    procedures / Ronald L. Taylor.
        p.   cm.
    Includes bibliographical references and index.
    ISBN 0-205-14142-0
    1. Handicapped children--Education--United States.   2. Handicapped
children--United States--Psychological testing.   3. Educational
tests and measurements--United States.   4. Special education--United
States.   I. Title.
LC4031.T36   1992
371.9'0973--dc20   92-15195
                                                                                   CIP

Printed in the United States of America

10   9   8   7   6   5   4   3   2   1   96   95   94   93   92   91

____Contents_____

Preface

Assessment is an area that is constantly changing. New laws, philosophies, and assessment instruments and techniques make information in this field obsolete very quickly. A tremendous amount of change has occurred in the four years since the publication of the second edition of this book. This third edition includes information that reflects those changes. Specifically, this edition includes:

1. A separate chapter on historical, philosophical, and legal factors affecting assessment;
2. A separate chapter on curriculum-based assessment;
3. Separate chapters for both infant assessment and early childhood assessment;
4. A separate chapter on vocational/transitional assessment;
5. Descriptions of over 15 new tests and 15 revisions of older tests;
6. More emphasis on academic testing;
7. An update of the review of relevant research for the instruments discussed;
8. More emphasis on error analysis and other informal techniques;
9. A major reorganization and expansion of materials including approximately 350 new references. An expanded instructor's manual with test questions is also available.

Obviously, other changes have also been made and many of the procedures or instruments that are outdated have been eliminated (or greatly reduced if they are outdated but still used). The third edition has, however, kept most of the general features of the previous editions. The following description provides information regarding the organization and content of the third edition.

The text is divided into six major parts. Part One, entitled, "Introduction to Assessment: Issues and Concerns," begins with a chapter that traces the historical, philosophical, and legal foundations of assessment. The second chapter serves as a general introduction to educational and psychological assessment. It poses several questions that must be answered prior to assessing any student, and it also proposes an assessment model. Chapter 3 addresses practical considerations that should be taken into account during the assessment process, whereas Chapter 4 focuses on the controversial area of labeling and classification. The second part, "Informal Procedures: Basic Tools for Teachers," includes chapters related to observation (Chapter 5), criterion-referenced testing and error analysis (Chapter 6), and curriculum-based assessment and measurement (Chapter 7).

The third part, consisting of Chapters 8 through 11, provides a discussion and overview of the instruments and procedures most widely used to assess an individual's underlying *abilities*. This includes chapters on the assessment of intelligence (Chapter 8), adaptive behavior (Chapter 9), emotional/behavioral status (Chapter 10), and language (Chapter 11). The fourth part focuses on the assessment of *achievement,* including general academic areas (Chapter 12), reading (Chapter 13), and mathematics and spelling (Chapter 14). The following format is used to describe the instruments in these two parts: A general description is followed by a more specific description of subtests or other components of each test; a discussion about how the scores are interpreted; a subsection focusing on technical characteristics, including standardization, reliability, and validity, and a review of the relevant research (discussed later). Finally, for each test described, an overview box summarizes the information and suggests uses for the test.

The Review of Relevant Research section for each test is a feature unique to this textbook, and it describes the literature that practitioners will find useful for test selection, administration, and interpretation. Specifically, these reviews highlight studies dealing with the reliability and validity of the instruments, as well as their use with special education students. The research studies were located by a computer search. The information yielded by the search was cross-checked against the following periodicals: *Diagnostique, Learning Disability Quarterly, Remedial and Special Education, Journal of Learning Disabilities, Journal of Special Education, Exceptional Children, Psychology in the Schools, Journal of School Psychology, Education and Training in Mental Retardation, Mental Retardation, American Journal of Mental Retardation, Gifted Child Quarterly,* and *Educational and Psychological Measurement.* For the third edition, literature from 1987 through 1991 was updated.

The fifth part, "Special Assessment Considerations," includes a description of assessment procedures and instruments relevant for infants (Chapter 15), early childhood (Chapter 16), and older students with vocational/transitional needs (Chapter 17). The book concludes with two case studies in which the assessment process is followed from initial identification through the development of an Individual Education Program (IEP).

The third edition has kept a number of unique features:

1. A pragmatic approach to assessment is emphasized.
2. A summary matrix is provided for most chapters. This matrix presents information about specific instruments and techniques in a format that allows easy comparison of the instruments for suggested use and target population. The matrix also includes a statement of any special considerations of which a user should be aware. Finally, for each instrument or technique, the matrix gives the educational relevance for exceptional students. The matrices are directly related to the assessment model proposed in Chapter 2.
3. Both informal and formal assessment procedures are included, with emphasis on how each kind of procedure fits into the assessment process.
4. A thorough review of relevant research is provided for each norm-referenced instrument. The review emphasizes the use of the test with exceptional students.
5. An overview box is provided for each test. The overview summarizes the age range, technical adequacy, and suggested use for the test. This feature adds to the value of this book as a reference text.
6. The book examines instruments and techniques both for mildly and moderately disabled students and for severely and profoundly disabled individuals. The two case studies in Part Six reflect this emphasis.

Needless to say, many individuals deserve my sincere appreciation and thanks. Although many provided feedback and suggestions, several deserve specific acknowledgment. My thanks go to Steve Richards and Rod Van Dyke for their contributions to Chapter 17; to graduate students Mary Schroeder, Jamie Schick, Pegi Davis, and Kim Denault for their assistance in compiling information; to Sherié Campbell for her perseverance in putting "just one more thing" on the computer; and to my family, for always being there when I put the manuscript down.

PART ONE

Introduction to Assessment: Issues and Concerns

Assessment is a critical component of the educational process. It allows educators and other professionals to make relevant educational decisions. Some individuals downplay the importance of assessment, believing that time spent *assessing* would better be spent *teaching*. If, however, appropriate assessment procedures are conducted, the information obtained can be used to enhance the teaching process.

In this section, several issues important to the establishment of appropriate assessment procedures will be discussed. The potential uses as well as the limitations of assessment will be considered. Assessment does not occur in a vacuum; neither is it left totally to the discretion of the assessor. Many important historical events and philosophical movements have shaped the assessment procedures found in today's schools. Similarly, there have been significant court cases and legislation that mandate certain assessment practices. These areas, discussed in Chapter 1, will provide the reader with the *historical framework* for developing assessment procedures.

Assessment should also be practical and efficient. One very important issue is knowing *when* to apply *what* assessment procedure. This requires, among other things, understanding the types and purposes of various assessment sources. Such information will be provided and an assessment model will be presented in Chapter 2. This will give the reader a *conceptual framework* for developing assessment procedures.

Assessment certainly is more than the simple administration of a test. Nonetheless, testing is an integral part of the assessment process. Because tests supply only a *sample* of a student's behavior, it is important to understand all the variables that can affect test performance. More importantly, these variables must be considered when making decisions based on that test performance. These *practical considerations* related to the testing process and tests themselves are discussed in Chapter 3. One of the most controversial uses of assessment information is to make *labeling and classification decisions.* Chapter 4 is devoted to a critical discussion of this very important area.

After reading Part One you should be able to:

1. *Identify historical events, philosophical movements, litigation, and legislation that have had an effect on assessment procedures in today's schools*
2. *Identify important questions that should be asked before initiating any assessment, resulting in a more efficient and practical process*
3. *Identify factors that can affect assessment results, including those related to the examiner, the examinee, and the test itself*
4. *Identify the important issues and problems related to the use of assessment information for labeling and classification purposes*

1

Assessment: Historical, Philosophical, and Legal Considerations

AREAS INCLUDED

HISTORICAL EVENTS

PHILOSOPHICAL MOVEMENTS

RELEVANT LITIGATION
- Bias in Testing
- Appropriateness of Assessment Procedures

RELEVANT LEGISLATION
- P.L. 94-142
- P.L. 99-457
- P.L. 101-476

Assessment refers to the gathering of relevant information to help an individual make decisions. The educational and psychological assessment of exceptional students, specifically, involves the collection of information that is relevant in making decisions regarding appropriate goals and objectives, teaching strategies, and program placement. The assessment process should include the regular-education teacher, special-education teacher, school psychologist, specialists, therapists, and any other individual who is involved in a student's educational program. Assessment should be an active, ongoing process that has a clearly specified purpose. Further, it can and should be an individualized process, as individualized as instructional strategies are. Not only is it inappropriate, but it is also practically impossible to use the same group of tests with all exceptional students; by definition, this population has unique characteristics and concerns that require an individualized approach.

Although educational and psychological assessment has been considered to be synonymous with testing, it involves much more than the simple acts of administering and scoring tests and reporting test scores. It includes the careful analysis of the information provided by various instruments and techniques (including tests), which should result in functional, relevant, appropriate decisions. The choice of which instrument or technique to use and the decision about which method of analysis or interpretation is best largely depends on the goal or purpose for the assessment. This textbook focuses on this pragmatic issue that emphasizes the app*ropriate* use of various instruments/techniques, depending on the specific purpose for the assessment.

Before addressing these pragmatic issues that will shape the assessment process, it is important to discuss other factors that have had, and will continue to have, an effect on assessment policies and procedures used in the schools. These include historical events/philosophical movements, court cases (litigation), and legislation that directly or indirectly affect assessment practices. In this chapter, a chronology of the historical, philosophical, and legal events that have influenced assessment practices will be presented, followed by a summary of the legislation that has led to, or has been a result of, those events.

HISTORICAL EVENTS/ PHILOSOPHICAL MOVEMENTS

Early Twentieth Century

Before special education became a formal field, most assessment issues were related to the measurement of the areas of intelligence and personality. This reflected the beginnings of the special education field with its roots in medicine and psychology. Alfred Binet perhaps had the first major impact on the use of assessment instruments with exceptional individuals. He and Theodore Simon were asked by the Ministry of Education in France to develop an intelligence test that could be used to differentiate normal and mentally retarded individuals. Their test was translated into English in 1908 and was later revised by Terman in 1916 and called the Stanford-Binet. This marked the first formal attempt to provide an objective measure of intelligence.

1920s–1950s

Attempts at measuring personality characteristics and emotional status were popular over the next three decades using a variety of different types of instruments tied primarily to the fields of psychology and psychiatry. These included the development of projective tests such as the Rorschach Ink Blot Test (Rorschach, 1932), thematic picture tests such as the Thematic Apperception Test (Murray, 1943), and personality inventories such as the Minnesota Multiphasic Personality Inventory (Hathaway & Meehl, 1951). These tests are still used today, although their relevance in education has been questioned (see Chapter 10 for a discussion). Also during this period, there was increased interest in the measurement of achievement. Many group achievement tests such as the Metropolitan Achievement Tests were developed over fifty years ago and continue to be revised as the educational demands and curricula in the schools change.

1960s

In the 1960s, the role of assessment, particularly standardized testing, became increasingly popular. This also mirrored the coming of age of the field of special education itself. When the term "learning disabilities" was coined in 1963, the door opened for the development of tests that went beyond the measurement of intelligence, personality, and achievement. During this period, primarily as a result of the application of the medical/neurological model, "process testing" became very popular. This included perceptual-motor tests and other instruments designed to measure how a student processed information. Examples of such tests are the Illinois Test of Psycholinguistic Ability (Kirk, McCarthy, & Kirk, 1968) and the Developmental Test of Visual Perception (Frostig, Lefever, & Whittlesey, 1966). Appendix A provides a brief description of several instruments that have been used as process tests. As you will see, the overemphasis on perceptual-motor testing, in particular, had quite an impact on the field of assessment.

Misuses of perceptual-motor tests

Perceptual-motor theorists such as Kephart, Cratty, and Frostig were partially responsible for the movement toward perceptual-motor testing during the 1960s. These theorists emphasized the importance—in fact, the necessity—of perceptual-motor skills in the acquisition of academic skills. The problem was that many professionals stressed perceptual-motor development to the exclusion of academic-skill development. In other words, people assumed that development of perceptual-motor skills would "generalize" to academic areas, since such skills were considered a crucial component of the academic skills. Historically, this movement led to (1) the use of perceptual-motor tests to predict achievement; (2) the use of perceptual-motor tests to help determine "modality strength and weaknesses" for teaching purposes; and (3) the development of remedial programs specifically designed for perceptual-motor skills. Each of these purported uses is discussed separately.

Use of tests to predict achievement

In general, the research on the use of perceptual-motor tests to predict achievement was disappointing. At best, most tests showed moderate correlations with achievement. Hammill and Larsen (1974) reviewed more than thirty research studies investigating the relationship of auditory-visual integration with reading disability. They concluded that "apparently a large percentage of children who perform adequately on tests of auditory perception experience difficulty in learning to read; and an equally sizeable percentage who do poorly on these same tests have no problems in reading" (p. 434). Similarly, Larsen and Hammill (1975) reviewed more than sixty studies of visual perception and school learning and found no support for the relationship between tested visual-perceptual problems and academic achievement.

Use of tests to determine modality preference

One of the least-understood issues in the area of special education is that of "modality teaching." According to proponents of this model (for example, Johnson & Myklebust, 1967; Wepman, 1967), children should be classified as primarily auditory or primarily visual learners, according to their scores on certain tests. The children should then be taught through their strong modality (for example, phonics for auditory learners; sight-word for visual learners). Although this approach might have intuitive appeal, there has been very little empirical evidence that the model is a valid one. In a careful analysis of the existing literature on the subject, Arter and Jenkins (1977) found that only 1 of 14 studies supported the modality-teaching model. That study (Bursuk, 1971) differed from the others in that secondary-level students were used and reading comprehension was the dependent measure (all the other studies used elementary students and tested beginning-reading skills). Arter and Jenkins (1977) gave several possible explanations for the general lack of support for the modality-preference model: (1) Modality strength may be an irrelevant factor in teaching; (2) other uncontrolled factors may conceal the effects of modality teaching; (3) the instruments used to determine modality preference are ineffective and technically inadequate; and (4) the criterion measures used to determine learning might be insensitive. Whatever the reason, little empirical evidence has supported this widely used model. It does stand to reason, however, that using an indirect measure (such as a perceptual-motor test) to determine modality preference for *academic learning* is not the best way to find out the desired information. Why not determine modality preference directly, by measuring the effects of various instructional procedures on learning rate?

Use of perceptual-motor training programs

Research in this area has been fairly straightforward. There is little or no evidence that perceptual-motor training improves academic ability

(Hallahan & Cruickshank, 1973; Hallahan & Kauffman, 1976; Larsen & Hammill, 1975). In fact, Kavale and Mattson (1983), using a metaanalysis procedure, found that perceptual-motor training was not an effective intervention technique for improving academic, cognitive, or perceptual-motor skills. They titled their article "One Jumped Off the Balance Beam: Metaanalysis of Perceptual-Motor Training" as an analogy to "One Flew Over the Cuckoo's Nest," the Ken Kesey play in which mental patients endured the harsh, and usually illogical, authority of the head nurse until one patient finally rebelled and escaped. Kavale and Mattson comment: "Perceptual-motor interventions are not effective treatments for exceptional children. Perceptual-motor training results in little or no improvement for trained subjects but will probably continue until its apparent futility becomes recognized and one falls off the balance beam" (p. 171). Interestingly, there has been some official movement to deemphasize the use of perceptual-motor training. In 1986, the Council for Learning Disabilities published a position statement that opposed the measurement and training of perceptual and perceptual-motor functions as a part of learning disabilities services.

Early 1970s

Partially as a result of the backlash against perceptual-motor testing, the 1970s brought a somewhat negative view of standardized testing in special education. This negativism was fueled by court cases accusing the schools of discriminatory use of assessment information and charging that many of the tests themselves were discriminatory (discussed later in this chapter). Also at this time, the behavioral model became prominent; included in this model was an emphasis on observation and a de-emphasis on the use of test data on which inferences had to be made. Indeed, there was almost a moratorium against the use of many standardized tests in special education; certainly there was a widespread acknowledgment of their limitations.

Late 1970s and Early 1980s

To further cloud the issue, the passage of P.L. 94-142 (discussed later in this chapter) mandated certain assessment procedures (e.g., nondiscriminatory evaluation) and implied the need for various types of assessment procedures. For example, P.L. 94-142 required that students receive a specific label in order to receive funding; this implied the need for standardized norm-referenced tests. (Chapter 4 addresses the important issue of labeling and classification.) Further, the requirement of an Individual Education Program suggested the need for more precise informal measures. Suffice it to say that in the late 1970s and early 1980s there was a shift in emphasis to more informal assessment tempered by the realization that more formal assessment procedures would need to be used as well. The philosophy stated in the next chapter and applied throughout this book is that *both* types of assessment procedures can and should be helpful. The appropriate use of both types occurs when the purpose for the evaluation is matched to the type of assessment procedure and when the strengths and limitations of both approaches are recognized.

Mid 1980s–Early 1990s

In the mid-1980s, a major philosophical movement affected the field of education and its assessment practices. In an article entitled "Educating Children with Learning Problems: A Shared Responsibility," Madeleine Will (1986) summarized several reasons why and how the concept of special education might be changed. Will, who was Assistant Secretary of the Office of Special Education and Rehabilitative Services in the U.S. Office of Education, was in a unique position both to evaluate the state of special education and to suggest any necessary changes. She noted, for example, that the current system separated regular and special education, stigmatized certain students as being handicapped, and addressed failure of students rather than prevention of problems. She also noted that whereas approximately 10 percent of the school population might be eligible to receive special education, another 10–20 percent had significant problems in school yet did not qualify for special education. Her recommendation was to have regular educators and special educators "collectively contribute skills and resources to carry out individual educational plans based on individualized educational needs" (p. 413). Specifically, she suggested that assessment and intervention strategies be employed before the referral for special education to try to prevent the identification of a child as handicapped. Figure 1-1 shows a model for prereferral intervention that emphasizes the amount of assessment and intervention that should take place before a referral is made. She also suggested that we needed to emphasize the *curriculum-based assessment* procedures discussed in Chapter 7.

This *Regular Education Initiative* (REI) was implemented on a trial basis in a number of states and local school districts. Although the pros and cons of the initiative are still being debated, there were many changes in assessment practices as a result.

RELEVANT ASSESSMENT LITIGATION

The majority of the court cases related to assessment practices, particularly the earlier ones, focused on the discriminatory use of tests with ethnic minority children. Many of these cases also helped lead to the nondiscriminatory evaluation clause of P.L. 94-142, discussed later in this

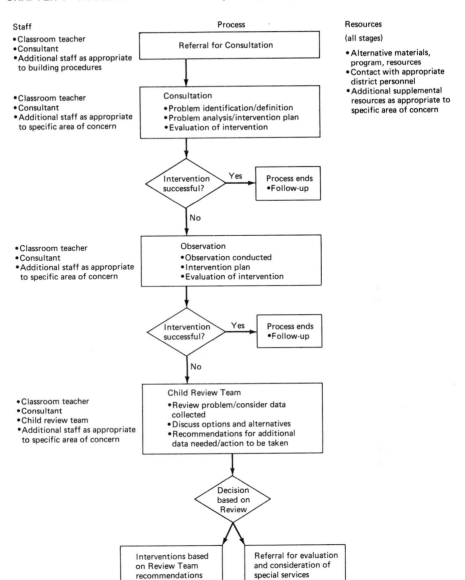

FIGURE 1-1   A Model for Prereferral Intervention

From J. Graden, A. Casey, and S. Christenson. Implementing a Prereferral Intervention System: Part I. The Model. *Exceptional Children*, 1985, *51*, 380. Copyright © 1985 by the Council for Exceptional Children.

chapter. Those cases included *Hobson v. Hanson, Diana v. California, Guadalupe v. Tempe, Larry P. v. Riles, PASE v. Hannon,* and *Marshall v. Georgia.* Later cases focused more on assessment *practices* such as the timely delivery of assessment procedures. These included *Jose P. v. Ambach* and *Luke S. & Hans S. v. Nix et al.* Each of these cases is summarized next.

Hobson v. Hanson (1968)

This was the first major case focusing on the misuse or discriminatory use of test scores. The plaintiff charged that test scores were being used to "track" minority students, particularly black students, into the lower track of the educational programs. The court found the grouping of students for tracking purposes to be unconstitutional due to its discriminatory nature.

Diana v. State Board of Education (1970)

This case was filed in California on behalf of nine Spanish-speaking children who were placed into classes for mentally retarded students based on their scores from intelligence tests administered in English. Among the consent decrees from this case, several had particular relevance: (1) there should be assessment of primary language competence, (2) there should be subsequent administration of tests in the student's primary language, (3) there should be more emphasis on nonverbal measures for students whose primary language was not English, and (4) there should be appropriate reevaluations of the students who were misplaced.

Guadalupe v. Tempe (1972)

This case was very similar to the *Diana* case with very similar conclusions. In addition, however, this case noted the importance of evaluating adaptive behavior before labeling a student as mentally retarded. (Adaptive behavior is discussed in Chapter 9.)

Larry P. v. Riles (1971)

This is perhaps the best-known and certainly the most complex court case that has dealt with assessment issues. In fact, the case has surfaced and resurfaced for over fifteen years in appeals and was the basis for another court case, *Crawford v. Honig* (1988). There are purportedly over 10,000 pages of transcripts related to the case (Reschly, Kicklighter, & McKee, 1988). The *Larry P.* case was first filed in 1971. There were several injunctions imposed until 1977, at which time there was an eight-month trial. Finally in 1979 Judge Peckham reached the following conclusions: (1) intelligence tests are biased, (2) the use of intelligence tests to classify black children as mentally retarded was prohibited, and (3) the over-representation of black children as educably mentally retarded must be eliminated. The state of California appealed the decision, but it was upheld by a 2 to 1 vote in 1984. In 1986, the *Larry P.* plaintiffs again went to court charging that the over-representation of black students had not changed markedly since the early 1970s although the label had changed to "learning handicapped" (Reschly, 1991). The result was the complete prohibition of intelligence tests for the purpose of identifying or placing black students into special education. Further, an intelligence test could not be used with a black student *even with parental consent*. This last point is the basis for the previously mentioned *Crawford v. Honig* in which black parents argued discrimination because their children *could not* be evaluated using an intelligence test. One can clearly see the impact that the *Larry P.* case has had on assessment procedures overall and in California in particular.

PASE v. Hannon (1980)

Ironically, another court case almost identical to the *Larry P.* case was heard in the state of Illinois with the opposite conclusions. Provided with very similar evidence, Judge Grady ruled that intelligence test bias had an insignificant influence on psychoeducational assessment and that the over-representation was not regarded as discriminatory (Reschly, 1991). Clearly, this confused the overall issue of test bias. It did, however, help formulate the professional question of whether or not the right issue is being debated. Is it the tests that are biased or are tests being used in a biased fashion (Taylor, 1990)?

Marshall v. Georgia (1984)

In a related case, the plaintiffs alleged that over-representation of black students in special education was caused by violations of procedural regulations and improper interpretation of state and federal guidelines regarding classification and placement. Although the issues of intelligence tests and IQs were discussed, they clearly took a subordinate role (Reschly, Kicklighter, & McKee, 1988). Again in this case the defense of the school district was supported, although procedural violations were acknowledged and prereferral intervention guidelines were established (Reschly, 1991). It would appear that, for the most part, the specific allegations against test bias will probably be debated in a different environment than the courtroom in the future.

Jose P. v. Ambach (1983)

This suit filed against New York City was concerned with the appropriate delivery of services. Specifically, the plaintiffs noted the delays in providing services to students referred for special education. The judge sided with the plaintiffs and, among other things, charged that the district must provide a *timely evaluation* after a student was referred. This was defined as a minimum of thirty days from referral to evaluation.

Luke S. & Hans S. v. Nix et al. (1982)

This case was similar to that of *Jose P.* There were estimates that as many as 10,000 students were not being evaluated within the sixty-day period after referral noted in Louisiana's guidelines. The court agreed with the plaintiffs and noted that the state should provide greater assessment *before* the referral is made (prereferral assessment). It also resulted in more training of both regular and special educators in the area of assessment.

SIGNIFICANT LEGISLATION

Along with philosophical movements and litigation comes legislation. Interestingly, while in some cases the philosophical movements and litigation have led to legislation, in others the legislation has led to philosophical movements and litigation. Among the relevant legislation that has an impact on assessment practices is P.L. 94-142 as well as various amendments to that law, including P.L. 99-457 and P.L. 101-476.

Public Law 94-142:
Education for All Handicapped Children Act

The law that has had perhaps the most impact on the field of special education is the Education for All Handicapped Children Act (P.L. 94-142). Regardless of any future changes in legislation, and the fact that federal legislation cannot override state laws, P.L. 94-142 has had a profound effect on assessment practices in special education. The law emphasizes the following six principles (Federal Register, 1977):

1. *Zero reject:* All handicapped children should be provided with a free, appropriate public education.

2. *Nondiscriminatory evaluation:* This principle is defined as avoiding discrimination in the

   . . . procedures used . . . to determine whether a child is handicapped and the nature and extent of the special education and related services that the child needs. The term means procedures used selectively with a child and does not include basic tests administered to or procedures used with all children in a school, grade or class (Federal Register, p. 42494).

   This definition implies that the principle of nondiscriminatory evaluation covers classification as well as the determination of the most appropriate educational program.

3. *Individual Education Programs* (IEPs): All handicapped students must have an IEP; among other components, IEPs should include (1) documentation of the current level of performance; (b) annual goals; (c) short-term objectives; and (d) evaluation procedures and schedules for determining the mastery of short-term objectives. Other requirements include documenta-

tion of the type and duration of the planned services, and information related to the extent of regular-education programming.

4. *Least restrictive environment:* This is perhaps the most publicized and least understood principle of P.L. 94-142. Although it implies that handicapped children should be educated with nonhandicapped children to the maximum extent possible, it is not synonymous with mainstreaming. The idea of the law is that, ultimately, a handicapped child should be mainstreamed; however, the law does not require that a child be mainstreamed if the type or severity of the handicap precludes the child's successful performance in a mainstream environment.

5. *Due process:* This principle refers to a system of checks and balances that seeks to ensure the fairness of educational decisions and the accountability of both the professionals and the parents who make those decisions (Strickland & Turnbull, 1990).

6. *Parental participation:* This principle ensures that parents are informed of decisions made about their children and encourages their participation in the decision-making process.

In reality, all of these principles addressed by P.L. 94-142 indirectly affect or are affected by assessment. The two principles that have direct relevance are *nondiscriminatory evaluation* and *parental participation.*

Nondiscriminatory evaluation

Although it includes no suggested procedures or specific definition of nondiscriminatory evaluation, P.L. 94-142 does outline acceptable assessment guidelines in considerable detail. Six points were included in those guidelines.

1. *Tests and other evaluation material*

   a. *should be provided and administered in the child's native language or other mode of communication, unless it is clearly not feasible to do so.* Considerable research points to the unfairness of using inappropriate tests with certain populations. Examples include using intelligence tests requiring motor responses for cerebral-palsied individuals, or tests using visual input for partially sighted children, and auditory input for hard-of-hearing persons. Similarly, using tests in English for children whose primary language is not English is no longer considered appropriate. Although these examples are obvious, they demonstrate the need to ensure the measurement of skills through the dominant mode of communication.

   b. *should have been validated for the specific purpose for which they are used.* The validity of tests and other assessment materials is an absolute prerequisite for a meaningful evaluation (see Chapter 3).

c. *should be administered by trained personnel in conformity with the instructions provided by the producer.* The American Psychological Association's *Standards for Educational and Psychological Tests* (1985) includes a number of guidelines for test administrators. At the very least, persons involved in evaluation should be thoroughly familiar with the instrument used and should be knowledgeable about the general area of assessment. The degree of expertise necessary, at least in terms of test administration, depends somewhat on the test used. To administer some tests (such as the WISC-III and the Stanford-Binet), certification and licenses are necessary. The amount of preparation required to administer most tests, however, is left to the examiner's discretion. Such factors as test length, type of test, and degree of subjectivity in the scoring criteria should be considered in determining when an examiner is considered to be trained. Because of differences in length of administration and sophistication of scoring, for example, it will take more preparation to administer a test such as the Differential Abilities Scale than to administer the Wide Range Achievement Test-Revised.

2. *Tests and other evaluation materials should include instruments tailored to assess specific areas of educational need, and not merely instruments designed to provide a single general IQ.* This simply means that the bottom line is the individual's actual educational ability or disability. Procedures aimed at determining those needs, therefore, become the core of the evaluation. Intelligence testing alone is not considered sufficient to determine a student's educational status.

3. *Tests should be selected and administered so as to best ensure that for a child with impaired sensory, manual, or speaking skills, the test accurately reflects the child's aptitude or achievement level or whatever other factors the test purports to measure, rather then reflecting the child's impaired sensory, manual, or speaking skills (except where those skills are the factors that the test purports to measure).* This point essentially means that the test results should not be affected by the child's handicap. For instance, a child with a reading problem should not be given a written math test stressing word problems to determine arithmetic achievement.

4. *No single procedure should be used as the sole criterion for determining an appropriate educational program for a child.* Again, the obvious implication is that a child can no longer be placed according to the results of a single instrument. Several of the previously discussed court cases focusing on the use of a single IQ to determine placement helped lead to this mandate.

5. *The evaluation should be made by a multidisciplinary team or group of persons including at least one teacher or other specialist with knowledge in the area of the suspected disability.* One important component is the inclusion of the teacher or other professional who has the most knowledge of the disability. This requires the teacher to become an active part of the assessment process. The multidisciplinary approach also requires communication among the evaluators to avoid replication of test procedures and to enhance interpretation of the results.

6. *The child should be assessed in all areas related to the suspected disability, including, where appropriate, health, vision, hearing, social and emotional status, general intelligence, academic performance, communicative status, and motor abilities.* This point again emphasizes the multidisciplinary approach to assessment.

The search for nondiscriminatory evaluation procedures has been frustrating. Duffey, Salvia, Tucker, and Ysseldyke (1981) identified eleven proposed solutions that had been tried. Among these were development of culture-fair, culture-free, or culture-specific tests; translation of existing tests; alteration of administrative procedures; and a moratorium on testing. Unfortunately, none of these approaches has been a panacea. As an example, Padilla and Garza (1975) noted that difficulties are encountered when tests are translated from one language to another. One example is an intelligence test item in which the examiner shows his or her thumb and asks, "What do you call this finger?" They point out that the formal word for thumb in Spanish is pulgar, but that this word is rarely used; most Spanish-speaking children would probably respond "dedo gordo," a common colloquial phrase meaning "fat finger." This answer would be scored as incorrect, according to the scoring criteria in the manual.

Parental participation

P.L. 94-142 specifies that parents must be kept informed about, and give their consent to, any evaluation of their child. The parents should receive written notification that includes the following types of information:

1. The reason for the evaluation and the person(s) who requested it.
2. The evaluation procedures and instruments that will be used. The parents have a right to evaluate those instruments.
3. A statement that they have the right to refuse the evaluation, but that an impartial hearing might be necessary to determine the outcome.
4. A statement that they have the right to an independent evaluation (usually paid by the parents).

In addition, schools must allow parents to inspect their child's educational records (including assessment information) and provide them the opportunity to question the appropriateness of any of the included material. In general, this part of the law establishes that parents have the right, if not the obligation, to be aware of all steps in the special education process.

Public Law 99-457:
Education of the Handicapped Act Amendments of 1986

Although there have been several amendments to P.L. 94-142, the one that perhaps has had the greatest impact on the area of assessment has been P.L. 99-457. Among the recommendations in this amendment was the need to identify and establish programs for handicapped infants and toddlers (children from birth to age two). Specifically, P.L. 99-457 states that there is an urgent and substantial need

1. *to enhance the development of handicapped infants and toddlers and to minimize their potential for developmental delay,*
2. *to reduce the educational costs to our society, including our Nation's schools, by minimizing the need for special education and related services after handicapped infants and toddlers reach school age,*
3. *to minimize the likelihood of institutionalization of handicapped individuals and maximize the potential for their independent living in society, and*
4. *to enhance the capacity of families to meet the special needs of their infants and toddlers with handicaps* (P.L. 99-457, Sec. 671; 1986).

The amendment defines handicapped infants and toddlers as children from birth to age 2 who are experiencing developmental delays, as measured by appropriate diagnostic instruments and procedures, in areas such as cognitive development, physical development, language and speech development, psychosocial development, or self-help skills. The law goes on to state that others who might qualify are those children who have a diagnosed physical or mental condition that has a high probability of resulting in developmental delay or children who are at risk of having substantial developmental delays should early intervention not be provided. The inclusion of "at-risk" children is up to the individual state's discretion, however. P.L. 99-457 also mandates that all states applying for P.L. 94-142 funds must serve all children aged 3–5 who are handicapped. In fact, considerable fiscal support is available for the preschool population.

This increased emphasis on early intervention has created a need for more and improved diagnostic procedures for young children from birth through age 5. This has resulted in the development of new developmental tests and the revision of several older ones. Chapters 15 and 16 address the areas of infant and early childhood assessment.

Public Law 101-476:
Education of the Handicapped Act Amendments of 1990

In 1990, President Bush signed the Amendments to the Education of the Handicapped Act that changed its name to the Individuals with Disabilities Education Act (IDEA). All of the references to *handicaps* noted in P.L. 94-142 and subsequent amendments were replaced by the term "disabilities." For example, the phrase "handicapped infants and toddlers" was replaced with "infants and toddlers with disabilities."

Although the most sweeping changes in P.L. 101-476 dealt with the authorization of grants for special programs and services (Maroldo, 1991), a few of the changes do have some impact on assessment practices. Among them are an emphasis on transition services that includes vocational evaluation (discussed in Chapter 17) and a requirement that a statement of needed transition services be placed in a student's IEP by at least the age of sixteen. Another change was the inclusion of traumatic brain injury and autism as separate categories of disability.

SUMMARY

A number of historical, philosophical, and legal events have played an important role in shaping the assessment policies and procedures that are used in the schools today. Historically, interest in the development and use of standardized tests, particularly in the areas of intelligence, personality, and achievement, grew in the first half of the twentieth century. In the 1960s, with the development of special education as a formal field, the interest in standardized testing increased, particularly in tests designed for use with students with learning disabilities. The 1970s, however, brought a somewhat negative attitude toward testing, partially as a result of discriminatory test practices and the overreliance on certain types of standardized tests (e.g., process tests). In the mid 1980s, proponents of the Regular Education Initiative re-emphasized the limitations of standardized testing and stressed the importance of informal measures, particularly curriculum-based assessment. Currently there is a general agreement that both types of assessment have their place if used appropriately.

Legally, the area of assessment has been affected by both litigation and legislation. Most court cases have dealt with the discriminatory use of tests (e.g., *Diana* and *Larry P.*) or with timely delivery of assessment services (e.g., *Jose P.*). The most relevant legislation has been P.L. 94-142 with its specific requirements for (among other things) the development of an Individual Education Program, the use of nondiscriminatory procedures, and the delineation of parents' rights in the assessment process. Other legislation that has affected assessment are P.L. 99-457, which increased emphasis on infants and preschool children, and P.L. 101-476, which emphasized the importance of the assessment of a student's need for transitional services and added the categories of traumatic brain injury and autism.

2

The Assessment Process: A Proposed Model

AREAS INCLUDED

WHY ASSESS?
HOW IS THE PROCESS INITIATED?
WHAT PROCEDURES SHOULD BE USED?
WHO SHOULD ASSESS?
WHEN SHOULD ASSESSMENT BE CONDUCTED?
WHAT SHOULD BE DONE WITH THE RESULTS?
AN ASSESSMENT MODEL

Before any assessment procedure is initiated, the prerequisite questions listed above must be addressed. The answers to these prerequisite questions serve as a basis for an assessment model discussed later in this chapter. A discussion of each of these questions and possible answers follows.

WHY ASSESS?

Any person who is involved in the assessment process should know why the assessment is being conducted. There are many purposes for assessment, and with careful planning more than one purpose can usually be addressed. Among the many purposes for assessment are (1) initial identification or screening; (2) determination and evaluation of teaching programs and strategies; (3) determination of current performance level and educational need; (4) decisions about classification and program placement; and (5) development of Individual Education Programs (including goals, objectives, and evaluation procedures).

Initial Identification (Screening)

Typically, individuals who might require special services or special education are initially identified through assessment procedures. These can be either informal procedures (such as observation or analysis of work products) or more formal procedures (such as achievement or intelligence tests). In other words, assessment can be used to identify individuals who warrant further evaluation.

Assessment can also be used to screen individuals who are considered to be "high risk" for developing various problems. These individuals do not yet demonstrate deficiencies requiring special attention, but they do demonstrate behaviors that suggest possible problems in the future. Identification of such individuals allows the careful monitoring of those potential trouble areas and occasionally implies the use of a program designed to "prevent the problem." For instance, children who lag behind in language skills prior to entering kindergarten might be monitored closely after they enter school to make sure that they do not fall behind in language-oriented areas. It might also be possible to initiate a language-stimulation program prior to kindergarten as a preventive measure.

Assessment for initial identification purposes, therefore, is used to identify individuals who might need additional evaluation or who might develop problems in the future. It is also possible to use assessment to identify those students for whom some type of immediate, remedial program is warranted. In other words, assessment can be used to determine those students for whom prereferral intervention is necessary.

Determination and Evaluation of Teaching Programs and Strategies

One of the more important roles of assessment is to help determine appropriate teaching programs and strategies. For this purpose, assessment information can be used in four ways. First, prior to a student's receiving special education, it can be used to assist the regular-education teacher in determining what to teach and the best method for teaching it. Second, assessment procedures can also serve as a method of evaluating the effectiveness of the particular teaching program or strategy. Many times a formal referral for special education can be avoided if assessment information is used in this way. In other words, assessment data can be used to develop and evaluate prereferral intervention programs. Suppose, for example, that a teacher, Ms. Jones, had a student, Jim, who was performing very inconsistently in the area of spelling. The teacher, prior to referring Jim for possible placement in a resource room for learning disabled students, decided to assess him informally. On the basis of the assessment, she determined that Jim was sounding out and spelling words purely on their phonetic representation. For instance, "decision" was spelled "dasishun," and "enough" was spelled "enuff." Ms. Jones then initiated an appropriate remedial program that, among other things, emphasized spelling rules. She reevaluated Jim periodically and determined that her teaching program had been effective, thus avoiding an unnecessary referral for a learning-disabilities program. In a survey of state departments of education, Carter and Sugai (1989) found that the majority strongly advocated the use of prereferral intervention and noted the crucial role played by the regular educator.

Third, in determining appropriate programs and strategies, assessment can provide prereferral information to document the need for a formal referral. Suppose, for instance, that the remedial program in the preceding example did *not* work. The documentation from that experience could be used to help justify a referral for possible special-education services. Fourth, this information can be incorporated into the individual education program for students who are eligible for and who ultimately receive special education. Particularly relevant would be information that documents which teaching strategies or approaches have been used, both successfully and unsuccessfully.

Determination of Current Performance Level and Educational Need

Since the mandate of P.L. 94-142, students who receive special education must have a clearly identified need that is not being currently met by his or her program. This is accomplished by evaluating the student's present level of performance and could involve, among other things, the measurement of preacademic, academic, or social skills. By using information for this purpose, the teacher or examiner can document the subject(s) and/or skill(s) for which the student needs special assistance. This information would also include the student's strengths and weaknesses and possible teaching strategies. In other words, assessment data for this purpose are used (1) to identify general areas in which the student needs additional help; (2) to identify both strengths and weaknesses of the student; and (3) to determine possible teaching strategies and remedial approaches for the student.

Decisions about Classification and Program Placement

The use of assessment data for classification purposes is controversial. Theoretically, individuals are classified to indicate similarities and relationships among their educational problems and to provide nomenclature that facilitates communication within the field (Hardman, Drew, Egan, &

Wolf, 1990). Except for minor exceptions, at the present time it is also necessary to classify in order to receive federal funds for special-education services. On the negative side, attention has focused on the stigmatizing effect of such labels and the disproportionately high number of minority students labeled. (The important area of classification and labeling is discussed in depth in Chapter 4.)

At the time of classification, a placement decision is usually made, and assessment data are used to help make that decision. As noted previously, P.L. 94-142 required that individuals be placed in the least restrictive environment. While this is often interpreted as mainstreaming, it suggests that students be placed into as "normal" an educational setting as is deemed appropriate, that is, one that provides optimum chance for success. This has traditionally resulted in a decision (using assessment information) to determine which "least restrictive" placement would be best for a child on a continuum from, for example, separate school, self-contained classroom, resource room, to regular classroom. The emphasis has been placed on the student and the determination of the setting in which the student will best learn and perform. In the mid 1980s, emphasis shifted to investigating more creative settings that might be appropriate for students with different ability levels. One example was the *Adaptive Learning Environments Model* (ALEM). This model, developed and field tested at the University of Pittsburgh, contained twelve design components that allowed (1) early identification of learning problems through diagnostic-prescriptive monitoring, (2) description of students' needs in instructional rather than labeling terms, (3) the development of individually designed educational plans, and (4) the teaching of self-management skills (Wang & Birch, 1984). To meet these objectives, the ALEM does such things as involving the family, encouraging multi-age grouping of students based on instructional needs, and changing staffing patterns to provide an interface between regular and special education. Unfortunately, the research on the effectiveness of the ALEM has been criticized. Bryan and Bryan (1988) noted, for example, that there was a general lack of control subjects. Similarly, Anderegg and Vergason (1988) pointed out that ALEM was subject to problems in personnel, funding, and practical application. Wang and Zollers (1990) argued that ALEM was effective but acknowledged that it required systematic staff development and organizational support.

Development of the Individual Education Program

If a student receives formal special-education services and receives federal funding, he or she must have an Individual Education Program (IEP), another requirement mandated by P.L. 94-142. Even if the law changes regarding requirement for delivery of special-education services, the IEP should still be considered as best practice and should not be eliminated. The IEP functions like a "contract" to identify goals, objectives, and timelines for delivery of services. More recently, legislation has led to a trend to develop Individual Transition Programs (ITPs) and Individual Family Service Programs (IFSPs). ITPs are designed to assist students in the transition from school to the working world, whereas IFSPs have been used to assist families who have a disabled child.

For an IEP, the following information must be included:

1. Documentation of the student's present level of performance
2. Indication of the specific services and type of program to be provided, including the timelines for delivery of services
3. Annual goals
4. Short-term objectives
5. Procedures and schedules for evaluating goals and objectives

The first two requirements were discussed earlier; the other three requirements are extremely important and will be discussed as separate purposes. Also note that if you use assessment data for these five purposes, you will meet the legal requirement for the development of IEPs.

Determination of Goals

Assessment data can help determine realistic goals for students. Typically, the goals identified for students are annual; that is, they project approximately one year in advance what a student should be doing. Goals are, as a rule, fairly general; they more or less delineate those major areas for which more specific and short-term objectives will be identified. An example of a goal might be, "Student will correctly add two digit numbers with carrying."

Determination of Objectives

Assessment data are also important in determining appropriate objectives for students. The objectives that are identified for exceptional students are a sequential breakdown of those skills that provide a link between the student's current performance level and the projected annual goals. Assume, for instance, that a student can only add one-digit numbers with a sum of less than 10 (current performance level); using the goal cited in the preceding section, it might be possible to identify two objectives that are the necessary steps to reach the goal. These objectives might be (1) student will correctly add one-digit numbers with a sum greater than 10; and (2) student will correctly add two-digit numbers without carrying.

Objectives are usually thought of either as *general* (projecting where a student will be performing in approximately three to six months) or *short-term* (stating the immediate objective on which the student should be working). Figure 2-1 shows the progression that is followed in the IEP process and the way that the objectives fit into that progression.

To ensure that goals and objectives are appropriately determined, Tymitz-Wolf (1982) developed a checklist to serve as guidelines (Figure 2-2). Many assessment instruments and techniques are developed by following a sequential framework and are particularly relevant for identifying specific objectives. In reality, goals and objectives are usually determined simultaneously, using the same or similar assessment data. It is possible, however, that the information for goals and for objectives could come from different sources.

Evaluation of Goals and Objectives

An often-overlooked area in which assessment plays a major role is that of *program evaluation;* this refers to the constant monitoring of the appropriateness and effectiveness of the goals and objectives designed for each student. The evaluation of goals and objectives has three major aspects: (1) the determination of objective criteria; (2) the determination of appropriate evaluation procedures; and (3) the determination of evaluation schedules (Strickland & Turnbull, 1990).

The *determination of objective criteria* suggests that the goals and objectives be stated in terms of standards of time and/or accuracy. The following example, for instance, clearly states the criteria: "Given a worksheet with 10 problems of two-digit addition (without carrying), the student will correctly solve the problems in 20 minutes or less with at least 90 percent accuracy." This aspect (determining objective criteria) can be addressed, therefore, by carefully writing the objective to include time and accuracy standards.

The *appropriate evaluation procedure* will depend on a number of factors. In practice, more formal procedures are used to evaluate goals and general objectives, whereas informal procedures are used to measure short-term objectives. In general, the schedule for evaluating goals and objectives should be determined when the IEP is developed. Also, it is helpful to determine what person is responsible for the evaluation. Table 2-1 gives a schedule that could be followed in evaluating an IEP.

Current Level of Performance	What the student can do currently
Short-Term Objective	What the student should be working on in the immediate future
General Objective	What the student should be able to do in three to six months
Goal	What the student should be able to do in a year

FIGURE 2-1   Steps in the IEP Process

1. Does the goal statement refer to target areas of deficit?	**OR**	Have I written a goal which is unrelated to remediation needs described in present level of performance and assessment information?
2. Given the assessment data, is it probable that this goal could be achieved in a year (i.e., annual period for the IEP)?	**OR**	Is the goal so broad that it may take two or more years to accomplish?
3. Does the goal contain observable terms with an identified target·area for remediation?	**OR**	Have I used words which fail to accurately describe the problem area or direction I am taking?
4. Have goals been written for each area of deficit?	**OR**	Do I have dangling data (data which indicate a need for remediation but have been overlooked)?
5. Is the scope of the objective appropriate?	**OR**	Have I written any objectives that encompass the entire year, thus making them annual goals?
6. Do the objectives describe a subskill of the goal?	**OR**	Have I failed to determine the hierarchy needed to teach the skill? • Did I simply rephrase the goal statement? • Did I describe a terminal skill, but only less of it?
7. Are the objectives presented in a sequential order?	**OR**	Have I listed the objectives in random order, unrelated to the way the skill would logically be taught?
8. Do the objectives show a progression through the skill to meet the goal?	**OR**	Do the objectives emphasize only one phase of a particular skill?
9. Does the objective contain an appropriately stated condition?	**OR**	Have I failed to describe the exact circumstances under which the behavior is to occur? • Have I described irrelevant or extraneous materials? • Does the condition refer to an isolated classroom activity?
10. Does the objective contain an appropriately stated performance using observable terms?	**OR**	Is the mode of performance (e.g., oral) different from the desired goal (e.g., written)?
11. Does the objective contain an appropriately stated standard?	**OR**	Is the standard unrelated to the assessment information and level of performance? • Am I using the performance statement as a standard? • Am I using percentages when the behavior requires alternative ways to measure? • Have I chosen arbitrary percentages?

FIGURE 2-2 Checklist for IEP Goals and Objectives

From Barbara Tymitz-Wolf. Guidelines for Assessing IEP Goals and Objectives. *Teaching Exceptional Children*, 1982, *14*, 200. Copyright © 1982 by the Council for Exceptional Children. Reprinted by permission.

TABLE 2-1   Schedule for Evaluating an IEP

COMPONENT	SCHEDULE FOR EVALUATION	PERSON PRIMARILY RESPONSIBLE
1. Short-term instructional objective	Daily or weekly	Teacher(s)
2. General objective	2 to 6 months	Teacher(s), parents, and other staff
3. Annual goals	Once a year	Representative of public agency, teacher, and other staff
4. Delivery of services	2 to 6 months and at least twice a year	Representative of public agency, teacher, and other staff

From: S. Larsen and M. Poplin. *Methods for Educating the Handicapped: An Individualized Education Program Approach* (Boston: Allyn & Bacon. 1980). Copyright 1980 by Allyn & Bacon. Reprinted by permission.

HOW IS THE PROCESS INITIATED?

After a student has been initially identified as having some type of problem or potential problem, decisions must be made about what to do next. As previously discussed, one option is to gather prereferral information and initiate a prereferral intervention program. In other words, the student is further assessed by the teacher who made the initial identification. In other situations, a formal referral will be initiated to obtain the necessary assessment service. Each school or school district has different procedures for referring individuals for assessment. All those involved in assessment should be thoroughly familiar with the referral procedures used in their school or facility and with the services that are available.

Two points regarding referrals deserve further comment. The first is that, as a rule, an individual should not be referred until preliminary assessment data have been collected. For instance, instead of simply referring a child who is "acting up" in class, the documentation should include information about the type of behavior, the frequency or duration of the behavior, and the conditions under which the behavior occurs (time of day, behavioral antecedents, and consequences). In other instances, however, more extensive assessment can be done, including academic testing. As previously mentioned, many times a formal referral might be avoided by collecting this prereferral information and implementing a prereferral intervention program. Usually the severity of the problem will dictate when and if a formal referral will be necessary.

In reality, students who receive special education provided by federal funds go through the formal referral process. The second point is that the referral should include the prereferral assessment data and other specific information such as the type and effectiveness of any prereferral intervention strategies. Nothing is more frustrating than to refer a student for assessment, wait months for a report of the results, and find that you only learned what you already knew, or that a program that you had already tried was recommended. This unnecessary situation can be avoided by carefully communicating what is already known about the individual and specifying clearly why you want the assessment. Figure 2-3 shows a referral form that might be more meaningful than many that are currently used. A referral form such as this can be modified to adjust to the needs of each school. Moreover, the time spent completing such a form will be well spent.

Please complete the following checklist if you need an educational assessment of a student in your class. This information will assist us in responding to your request. Please return the completed form to _____ (school psychologist).

Teacher: Referral Problem:
Student:
Date of Birth:
Date of Referral:
A. Priority for assessment
   _____1. *Urgent*—cannot program without further information
   _____2. *Important*—need information to develop most appropriate program
   _____3. *Useful*—need information to refine teaching program
B. Reason for referral
   _____1. To determine current level of academic functioning
   _____2. To compare with previous testing
   _____3. To establish educational objectives
   _____4. To determine student's learning style
   _____5. To consider student for possible special-education program
   _____6. To receive information regarding possible behavior-intervention program
   _____7. Other (Please explain)
C. Type of assistance needed
   _____1. Formalized objective tests, i.e., battery of achievement and diagnostic testing
   _____2. Classroom observation with formal and informal testing
   _____3. Classroom observation, informal assessment, and diagnostic prescriptive teaching assistance (involvement with child and teacher both in and out of the classroom)
D. Work products
   If the referral problem is in the academic area, please attach any examples of his/her performance.
   If the referral is in a nonacademic area, please include any relevant observational data.
E. Please attach any information regarding intervention/remediation strategies that have already been tried to deal with the referral problem.

FIGURE 2-3   Example of a Referral Form

WHAT PROCEDURES SHOULD BE USED?

Typically, people think of "giving tests" when they think of assessment. Although tests are typically included in the assessment process, the two terms are certainly not synonymous. Tests are merely a means of obtaining behavioral samples that give examiners a *quantitative* measure in a specific area. Thus, we might find out such information as John has an IQ of 102, Bill scored at the 3.6 grade level in reading, or Jane correctly completed 89 percent of her two-digit addition problems. In short, *tests are simply devices to which individuals are exposed that give a quantitative characterization of one or more traits of those individuals.* Nevertheless, tests are used extensively in the assessment of exceptional students. They can be classified in various ways. For educational purposes, however, three comparisons are most relevant. These are norm-referenced versus criterion-referenced tests, speed versus power tests, and group versus individual tests.

Norm-Referenced Tests

A *norm-referenced test* is one in which a person's score is compared to a specific reference group. The reference group is also called the *normative* or *standardization sample* and provides the norms on which to base the comparison. Norm-referenced tests are typically used when a person is interested in how a student performs in a certain area relative to other individuals. Since norm-referenced tests compare an individual's performance to those individuals in the normative sample, it is very important to know the make-up and characteristics of the sample. These tests basically address the question of *how much* rather than *what* a person knows or can do and are normed on either an age scale or a point scale. In an *age scale,* a person's performance on a test is compared to a typical performance by a person of the same age. This is determined by the percentage of individuals at various age levels who respond correctly to a test item. For instance, a particular test might be normed for three-through eight-year-old children. Certain items on the test will be scaled for each age level. Thus, for those items scaled for six-year-old children, some four- to five-year-old children should answer them correctly, most six-year-old children should, and almost all seven- to eight-year-old students should.

Point scales include test items that are of different levels of difficulty but that are not specifically tied to age-related percentages. In such a scale, items that are passed are added (this figure becomes the *raw score*). The raw score can then be converted to one of a variety of *derived scores* comparing the raw score to the performance of a group of subjects of known demographic characteristics, such as age, sex, and geographic area (Salvia & Ysseldyke, 1991). Thus, the derived scores give relative meaning to the raw scores. A number of derived scores are used in educational and psychological testing. The most common are age equivalents, grade equivalents, quartiles, deciles, percentiles, and standard scores. These scores are briefly defined in the next section. Other types of scores are defined in later chapters that provide descriptions of the specific norm-referenced tests.

Age and grade equivalents

Age and grade equivalents are both considered to be *developmental* scores. Both types of scores attempt to transform a raw score into the "average" performance of a particular age group or grade level. Age equivalents are expressed in years and months. For instance, suppose that during the standardization of a particular intelligence test, the mean (or median in some tests) number of correct responses was eighty for all individuals six years, six months old. Any person taking that test who obtained a raw score of 80 would have an age equivalent of 6–6.

Grade equivalents are expressed in years and tenths of years. The calendar year is actually divided into ten parts, nine of which represent the nine months of the academic year, and the last of which represents the summer months. Thus, a 7.2 would be interpreted seventh grade, second month. Like age equivalents, grade equivalents are based on the average performance of the standardization sample. Grade equivalents are often used inappropriately to measure gains in achievement and to identify learning-disabled and other exceptional students. For instance, a student with an average IQ in grade 6.7 who scores at the 3.2 grade level in achievement might be considered learning disabled. The use of grade equivalents has certain intuitive appeal, because educators often think in such terms regarding academic ability. This emphasis on grade equivalents (as well as age equivalents) has been seriously questioned, however. Burns (1982), for instance, noted that grade equivalents lack sensitivity, are based on extrapolated scores for upper and lower ends of most tests, and have different standard deviations for different age groups. Berk (1981) stated "there is no technically sound reason to justify their use in the identification, diagnosis, and remediation of learning disabilities" (p. 137). This statement is true for all special-education students as well. Green (1987) cautioned the use of these scores with secondary-level students in particular. The International Reading Association, in fact, encouraged a moratorium on the use of grade equivalents. Interestingly, however, Huebner (1989) noted that the widespread use and criticism of grade equivalents has increased evaluators' awareness and has led to their more accurate interpretation.

Quartiles, deciles, and percentiles

Quartiles, deciles, and percentiles are all indications of the percentage of scores (determined from the standardization sample) that fall below a person's raw score. Quartiles divide the distribution of scores from the standardization into 4 equal parts, deciles into 10 equal parts, and percentiles into 100 equal parts. Thus, for example, the first quartile (Q_1) is the point at which 25 percent of the scores fall below; the eighth decile (D_8) is the point at which 80 percent of the scores fall below; and the twenty-third percentile (P_{23}) is the point at which 23 percent of the scores fall below. In other words, if a person's raw score on a test was at the Q_1, D_8, or P_{23}, it would be equal to or higher than, respectively, 25 percent, 80 percent, or 23 percent of the scores on which the test was normed. Of these three types of scores the most widely used is the percentile. The score itself is often referred to as a *percentile rank*.

Standard scores

Standard scores are transformed raw scores with the same mean and standard deviation. The *mean* represents the average score, and the *standard deviation* reflects the variability of a set of scores. In the standardization of a test, approximately 34 percent of the subjects score within one standard deviation of the mean; approximately 14 percent score between one and two standard deviations; only 2 percent score between two and three standard deviations. Thus, approximately 68 percent of the subjects score between ± 1 standard deviations, and approximately 96 percent score between ± 2 standard deviations. For instance, assume that a test has a mean of 100 and a standard deviation of 15. This means that the average score of those subjects in the standardization sample was 100 and that 68 percent scored between 85 and 115. Similarly, 96 percent scored between 70 and 130. Because of its statistical base, standard deviation plays an important role in the determination of extent of strength or weakness in a student's abilities. Figure 2-4 gives a visual representation of the relationship of percentile ranks and a variety of standard scores with different means and standard deviations.

There are many types of standard scores, including z scores, *T* scores, stanines, and scaled scores. In general, standard scores allow for the direct comparison of raw scores of individuals of different ages (or other characteristics). Suppose, for example, that a scaled score for a particular test had a mean of 10 and a standard deviation of 3. Child A, aged 6-2, had a *raw score* of 15. Child B, aged 12-4, had a raw score of 32. It is possible (depending on the standardization) that both children would have *scaled scores* of 10 (representing the average performance).

Normal curve equivalents

Normal curve equivalents (NCEs) are, in a sense, a combination of standard scores and percentile ranks. It is expressed as a standard score with a mean of 50 and a standard deviation of 21.06. The atypical standard deviation results from dividing the normal curve into 100 equal intervals.

FIGURE 2-4   Relationship of Various Types of Derived Scores

SS = Standard score.

Scoring and interpretation of norm-referenced tests

The scoring of many norm-referenced tests can be tedious and frequently results in errors including computational errors and the misuse of statistical tables. For this reason, it is important that test examiners are properly trained and careful when doing mathematical calculations and using tables to convert raw scores to derived scores. It is also for this reason that computer scoring programs are available for many tests. For example, one test publisher—Pro-Ed—has a computer program called PRO-SCORE for many of its tests. This program provides a printout that includes background information on the child, raw scores, percentiles, standard scores, and descriptions of all the subtests, profiles of subtests and subtest combinations (composites), and significance testing of the comparisons of all the composites.

Simply reporting derived scores, whether they are determined through hand-scoring or computer scoring, is not sufficient. For example, suppose that a person obtained a percentile rank of 52 on a spelling test. This would indicate that he or she performed slightly above average in spelling compared to the normative sample. To really understand what that means, however, it is necessary to *consider the task demands of the test itself.* In other words, *what did the student have to do to score well on the test?* Did he have to orally spell words? Write words from dictation? Identify the correct spelling of a word from four choices? Each of these skills might be called "spelling"; it is possible, however, that one might make a mistake assuming that the student with a 52nd percentile rank was about average in the area of written spelling if the score was based on oral spelling. Often the name of a test or subtest does not imply the specific task demands. Frequently, in fact, the name of the test or subtest has little to do with what the examinee actually has to do. It is therefore imperative that those task requirements be determined and considered when interpreting the results.

Criterion-Referenced Tests and Curriculum-Based Assessment

A *criterion-referenced test,* as opposed to a norm-referenced test, does not specifically compare an individual's score to other people's scores. Rather, it measures an individual's mastery of content. For instance, instead of discovering that Joan scored at the 63rd percentile in math (norm-referenced test), you might find that she can add and subtract 1-digit numbers correctly 100 percent of the time, but can add and subtract 2-digit numbers correctly only 25 percent of the time (criterion-referenced test). In a criterion-referenced test you learn specifically *what a person knows,* instead of *how much a person knows compared to others.* Criterion-referenced tests are often "teacher made" and thus pinpoint the exact areas included in an individual's curriculum. In fact, many criterion-referenced tests are developed around specific educational objectives. This is accomplished by sequencing the objectives (task analysis) and developing test items that measure each objective (discussed in Chapter 6). There are also, however, a number of commercially prepared criterion-referenced tests that measure both academic skills and developmental skills.

For teaching purposes, the advantage of using criterion-referenced tests is that they usually provide more specific information about a person's ability level than do norm-referenced tests. In fact, individual education programs (IEPs) can usually be developed much more easily from criterion-referenced test data. The disadvantages of criterion-referenced tests are that you do not get comparative information, and unless you use a commercially prepared test, you must take the time to develop the instrument.

An area that has received considerable attention in the last few years is *curriculum-based assessment* (CBA). CBAs use the expected curricular outcomes of the school as their content. In reality, they are very similar in nature to criterion-referenced tests. If, for example, a school was using the Macmillan reading series, then CBAs would use the content of that series for the test items. A type of CBA, referred to as *curriculum-based measurement* (CBM), has also become popular. CBM includes a more standardized methodology and typically focuses on items representing an entire annual curricular area (Fuchs, Fuchs, Hamlett, & Allinder, 1989). Chapter 7 discusses CBA and CBM in greater depth and provides examples.

Power Versus Speed Tests

Norm-referenced and criterion-referenced tests can measure power or speed. A *power test* is one designed to measure a full range of skills or abilities without a time limit. In a power test you are more interested in *how much* a person knows than in *how fast* he or she can perform. Usually, test items are of increasing difficulty, so that a person taking the test will answer some but not all correctly. A *speed test* is one in which the time element becomes important. With speed tests, the examiners are more concerned with how many test items a person can complete within a specific time limit. Usually the level of difficulty for each item is such that given unlimited time, all the items could be completed. In reality, many tests in special education are a combination of speed and power.

Individual Versus Group Tests

Norm-referenced and criterion-referenced tests can also be individually or group administered. Certain advantages and disadvantages are inherent in each type of test. Group tests yield information in a shorter amount of time. For instance, it might be possible to obtain achievement scores for an entire class in two or three hours. However, you lose the opportunity to observe an individual's approach to a certain task. In short, group tests are usually administered for screening, and individual tests are administered for diagnostic, classification, and program-placement purposes. Certainly, both types of tests have their place in the assessment process.

Other Assessment Procedures

As previously mentioned, assessment involves more than simply the administration, scoring, and interpretation of tests. Any and all *relevant* information about an individual should be gathered. This information can be meaningful in its own right, and it can also help put the test data into proper perspective. Although the sources of such information are virtually limitless, several specific sources are frequently used in assessing exceptional individuals. They can be divided roughly into two categories: sources that directly involve the person being assessed and sources that do not actively involve the person in the assessment.

Procedures in which the person being assessed is actively involved include *inventories, checklists,* and *observation.* Both formal and informal checklists and inventories can be used to help locate behavior that can be observed later or assessed in depth. Observation is an invaluable tool that is always used, but not always systematically. (Observational assessment and its very important role in the overall process are discussed in Chapter 5.)

Many sources of assessment information, however, do not require the student to be an active participant. Among the more common are school records, discussion with parents and previous or current teachers, analysis of the home and academic environments, medical and developmental histories, and error analysis of specific work samples.

School records can and should be more than a collection of meaningless data accumulated in a file folder. They should contain relevant information about previous assessments, specific documentation of behavioral observations, and information relating to teaching strategies or intervention programs that have been implemented. This type of knowledge can eliminate a tremendous amount of duplication of services in two ways. First, it will help avoid a situation in which a child is overtested. For instance, in some schools the psychologist, regular-classroom teacher, learning-disability specialist, and speech therapist have all given the same test within a short period of time. That problem can be eliminated if the school records are used as a central data bank. Second, use of the information in the school records can help avoid a waste of time in recommending or implementing a program that has already been tried and been found ineffective.

Discussions with parents and teachers can also be helpful, although you should be aware of the possibility of biased information. In addition to obtaining valuable information about the specific nature of an individual's problem, you can also obtain an historical perspective. For example, you might discover whether there were any factors in the person's home life that suddenly changed. You might also find out whether the primary language spoken in the home was the same as or different from the one used in school. In addition, you can determine whether the child behaves differently at home than at school. If, for instance, a child has problems at school but not at home, certain conditions can often be identified in the home environment that can be replicated in the school environment.

It should be pointed out that discussions with parents and analyses of the home environment are sensitive areas. Care must be taken not to imply blame or in any manner make the parents feel threatened or uncomfortable. To avoid this, some structured approach is usually helpful. Also, you should avoid asking questions that are irrelevant to the student's problem or situation. Any information gathered should serve a useful purpose.

Another source of information is the medical and developmental history of an individual. Again, this is a sensitive area, in which only information that is potentially relevant to the assessment process should be obtained. Most medical and developmental histories are used in the early identification or prediction of some type of special problem, or in the search for a cause or prognosis for a particular type of problem (particularly, more severe problems). If one of these is the goal for the assessment, an in-depth evaluation of developmental milestones and pre-, peri-, or postnatal infections, intoxications, or other events might be relevant. You must keep in mind, however, that knowing the cause of a problem does not necessarily imply an appropriate treatment program. Also, asking this information of a parent of a seven-year-old child with spelling problems probably would be unnecessary and might cause undue anxiety in that parent. ("Why are they asking me these questions? Do they suspect brain damage or retardation?") In other words, collect the information if there is a reason, but do not collect it if you are not going to use it or do not know what to do with it.

One often-overlooked source of information is the work that is collected daily during routine class time. Work products, like test results, are samples of a student's behavior and can be analyzed and interpreted in much the same way. Careful analysis of the kinds of errors made on work products can provide invaluable information (error analysis is discussed in Chapter 6) Figure 2-5 provides examples of types of errors that could be made on a simple arithmetic worksheet.

The first problem in Figure 2-5 is an example of the use of a wrong operation; the person added instead of subtracting. The second example contains an obvious computational error. The third problem is an example of a defective algorithm; this means that there were procedural errors in an attempt to apply the correct process. The answer to the last problem

```
        38                      53
      − 21                    ×  2
      _____                  _____
        59                     116

  Wrong operation        Computational error


       685                     463
     − 497                    × 25
      _____                  _____
       212                     185

 Defective algorithm        Random error
```

FIGURE 2-5   Examples of Error Analysis in Arithmetic

appears to be a random error. Clearly, each of the types of errors would require different remedial strategies.

In summary, a number of techniques and types of instruments are available to assess exceptional students. In general, these approaches are thought of as being *informal procedures* or *formal procedures.* Informal assessment procedures include observation, teacher-made tests, and error analyses. Formal assessment procedures include norm-referenced tests, as well as commercially prepared inventories and criterion-referenced tests. The choice of which type of procedure to use will depend largely on the purposes for the assessment. Table 2-2 matches the purposes with recommended formal and informal procedures.

Three points should be made about Table 2-2. First, these are merely *suggestions* for types of assessment procedures that can be used for various purposes. There are times when other tests or measures would be more beneficial for the purpose stated. Conversely, not all the procedures mentioned need to be used in all situations. Second, you should determine whether to use informal procedures, formal procedures, or a combination of the two. For many purposes, either type will give the desired information. Third, there is a great deal of overlap in the types of procedures used; in other words, results from specific assessment procedures can often be used for more than one purpose. Acknowledging this point and planning the procedures in advance will result in a more efficient, more practical assessment.

WHO SHOULD ASSESS?

Answering this question is very important for several reasons. First, it can help avoid having more than one person administer the same test or

TABLE 2-2   Matching the Purposes and Types of Assessment Procedures

PURPOSE	TYPE	
	FORMAL	INFORMAL
1. Initial identification (screening)	Screening and readiness tests; achievement tests	Criterion-referenced tests; observation; curriculum-based assessment
2. Determination and evaluation of teaching programs and strategies	Depends on area of need	Criterion-referenced tests; error analysis; curriculum-based assessment
3. Determination of current performance level and educational need	Achievement or diagnostic academic tests; other tests (depending on area of need)	Criterion-referenced tests; observation; curriculum-based assessment
4. Decisions about classification and program placement	Intelligence, achievement, adaptive-behavior and classroom-behavior measures	Observation and criterion-referenced tests, used to supplement formal testing
5. Development of IEPs (goals, objectives, teaching strategies)	Commercially prepared inventories and criterion-referenced tests	Criterion-referenced tests; observation; error analysis
6. Evaluation of IEPs	Some norm-referenced tests	Criterion-referenced tests; observation

battery of tests. In addition, it makes a person think of why the assessment is needed and how the results will be used. As noted previously, assessment can and perhaps should be performed by everyone involved with the education or training of an individual. This might include regular-education teachers, special-education teachers, specialists, therapists, school psychologists, and parents. Each has a unique perspective that might prove invaluable. This does not mean that everyone should always be involved. There are times when a teacher's assessment in the classroom is all that is needed; in other instances, in-depth assessment by a number of professionals is indicated. Again, to a large extent, the purpose for assessment will determine who assesses.

It is certainly important to include the teacher (special-education, regular-education, or both) in the assessment process at all times. Teachers are perhaps in the best position to assess their students effectively. First, there is a strong rapport between the teacher and student that might bring out the student's best effort. Second, the student can usually be assessed in the classroom, which typically reduces the fear of testing that is often seen. Third, the teacher can assess at the most appropriate times and not have to wait for an outside evaluator who typically is working under a tight schedule.

WHEN SHOULD ASSESSMENT BE CONDUCTED?

Time of assessment will depend largely on the answer to the question, Who will assess? If the evaluator is someone other than the teacher or other individual who routinely works with the student, the issue of when to assess becomes one of scheduling. In other words, the student is usually pulled out of class and evaluated at a time that fits into both the examiner's and the student's schedule. Clearly, this is not always the most appropriate or beneficial time, but is dependent on a number of factors, such as case loads or priorities for assessment. For this reason, it is even more important that teachers use discretion in referring students for further assessment and that they help in establishing priorities regarding who needs assessing the most. If every child in a class is referred for assessment, chances are that many students who do not really need this service will be evaluated, whereas others who need it will not be evaluated until later.

If a student is evaluated by the teacher (who, as previously stated, should do at least some of the assessment), the issue of scheduling takes on new meaning. The student will not usually be taken out of the classroom, and so assessment time is either incorporated into or separated from teaching time. For example, it might be possible to administer an informal test to a student before and after group instruction in a certain academic area. It might also be possible to assess individually during the day when the rest of the class is busy doing some other type of assignment (such as individual seat work, workbooks, or small-group projects). As noted previously, one recent trend is to evaluate all of the students in the class based on the content of the curriculum (curriculum-based assessment).

One way of looking at assessment in the classroom (and anywhere else, for that matter) is to think of a filtering process in which you begin with information for a number of individuals and gradually collect more on those who need more assessment. For instance, a group-achievement test or curriculum-based assessment might be given as a first step to an entire class of 30 (Figure 2-6). The assessment at this stage could be incorporated into the teaching time. From these results, the teacher might identify 10 percent, or three students, who need further testing. As a second step, a more individualized achievement test could be given to those 10 percent to determine specific areas of academic strengths and weaknesses. This testing could be given while the rest of the class is working on other assignments. Suppose one person performed very poorly in math and another in spelling, while another had some minor problems in reading. As a third step, the teacher or other evaluator could then test the first two students' academic areas through diagnostic testing and find out what the student does and does not know within the area and possibly determine reasons why the student is having problems. This assessment

FIGURE 2-6   Example of a Teacher-Initiated Assessment

could be done either within or outside the classroom setting, depending on who assesses. For the third student, a prereferral intervention program could be initiated. Steps 1 and 2 could easily be administered by the teacher and, *if necessary,* by other professionals. It is at this point that the teacher typically makes the referral decision.

It is important to note that this is only an example of a sequence in which assessment might occur. Many times these specific steps will not be followed. If a teacher has a student who is clearly having serious problems—either academic, emotional, or physical—then a referral is usually made with observational and supporting data, but not necessarily with formalized test results.

WHAT SHOULD BE DONE WITH THE RESULTS?

In a certain sense, this should be the first question asked. If you cannot answer it, you probably should not initiate the assessment. Too much time and energy is wasted on testing students and writing reports that are filed in folders and never used. If assessment data are collected, there should be a clearly specified means of using the results. What you do with the results will depend largely on the purpose for assessment. For example, if you are assessing for initial identification purposes, the results might be used to determine the need for and type of further assessment, or to monitor certain kinds of behavior that are considered high risk. Conversely, data for classification and program-placement decisions might be used more formally, usually evaluated by a multidisciplinary team of professionals. Information for program planning might be used informally by a teacher to initiate or modify a teaching strategy, or it might be formally used to develop an IEP, ITP, or IFSP. Whoever is involved in assessment should take the time to learn the policies governing dissemination of assessment data in his or her school or other educational setting. Knowing this information can expedite the effective use of assessment data and can increase communication among the various professionals involved in assessment.

AN ASSESSMENT MODEL

Assessment should be a dynamic, continuous process undertaken with a clearly specified goal in mind. The process should be monitored and should be flexible enough to be modified if necessary. One way to view assessment is to break it down into two components: prereferral and postreferral (Figure 2-7). The goal of the *prereferral component* is to develop and implement a teaching or remedial program and to monitor the effectiveness of the program by observing the student's progress. Assessment in this component is conducted prior to making a referral for special education services and will hopefully result in no referral at all. This component is heavily weighted toward informal assessment procedures, such as observation, error analysis of work products, curriculum-based assessment, and teacher-made tests. Note that the *purposes* for assessment are closely tied to the assessment model. If the purpose is identified, the appropriate steps in the model can be followed. Norm-referenced tests are also used occasionally. The prereferral component is usually implemented by the teacher within the student's current educational setting.

The *postreferral component* includes the documentation of an educational need and usually results in decisions about classification and program placement. It also might result in the development of a formalized IEP that includes the goals, objectives, instructional strategies, and timeline for implementing and evaluating goals and objectives. This component includes both formal assessment (norm-referenced tests, also commercially prepared inventories and criterion-referenced tests) as well as informal assessment procedures. A multidisciplinary approach (including the teacher) is used during this component.

It is entirely possible that *both* components might be included in the assessment of a particular student. Where possible, it is better to go through the prereferral assessment first. In fact, this is a requirement in many states. Many times this will yield enough information to deal with the situation that required the assessment. If further assessment is necessary, important prereferral information can be incorporated into the assessment at the time of the referral. On the other hand, with certain

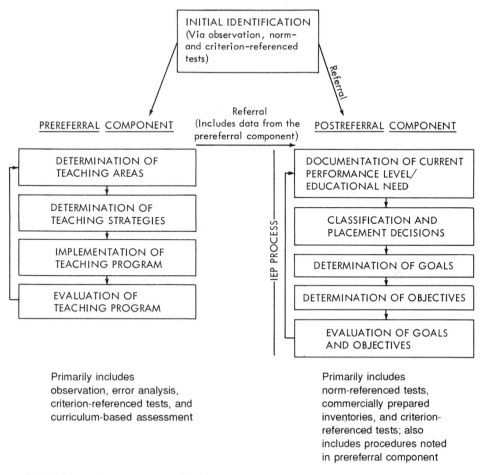

FIGURE 2-7   An Assessment Model

students, a referral may be justified as the first step, as soon as a problem has been identified. This is particularly true for children whose problems are severe and who definitely need supplementary or alternative programming. *Note that the procedures used and the information gathered in the prereferral component are of great value in the postreferral component.* In a sense, the entire prereferral component could also be considered as part of the postreferral component (particularly the documentation of educational need and IEP development steps).

SUMMARY

It is extremely important that the legal and philosophical factors that relate to special education be considered when planning assessment strategies. It is also important that several questions be answered before any assessment begins. These questions are (1) Why assess? (2) How is the process initiated? (3) What procedures should be used? (4) When should assessment be conducted? (5) Who should assess? (6) What should be done with the results? Answering these questions will save time and avoid unnecessary or irrelevant assessment. It is possible, and in fact probable, that the answers to these questions will change once the process begins. It is up to you to keep thinking about them *throughout* the process. One way to do that is to think of assessment as a continuous, dynamic process, constantly requiring monitoring and modification. When assessment is looked at in this way, who should be involved and how the results will be used will be clearly indicated. An assessment model was proposed that ties directly into this pragmatic philosophy. Once the specific purpose for the assessment was identified in the model, the procedures and steps to follow were delineated.

3

Practical Considerations

AREAS INCLUDED

FACTORS RELATED TO THE EXAMINEE

FACTORS RELATED TO THE EXAMINER

FACTORS RELATED TO THE EXAMINER-EXAMINEE INTERACTION

FACTORS RELATED TO THE TEST ITSELF

There are several considerations that must be addressed before conducting any type of assessment procedure. Although these considerations are relevant for all formal as well as informal assessment procedures, they are primarily related to norm-referenced testing. This relevance lies in the format and types of questions as well as in the kind of emphasis placed on the scores of norm-referenced tests.

FACTORS AFFECTING TEST RESULTS

Three principal classes of factors can affect an individual's performance on a test and can minimize the meaning of, and in some cases invalidate, the test results. They are (1) factors related to the person being tested; (2) factors related to the examiner and the examiner–examinee interaction; and (3) factors related to the test itself. Each will be discussed separately.

Factors Related to the Examinee

Anxiety and motivation

The first major potential source of error consists of factors related to the examinee. Among these are such obvious factors as anxiety and motivation. All of us have probably experienced test phobia or test anxiety and know how it can affect performance. Unfortunately, some attempts at reducing test anxiety have resulted in reduced anxiety but no improvement in test performance (Kass & Fish, 1991). There is, however, some evidence that eliminating time pressure reduces anxiety and improves test performance (Plass & Hill, 1986).

Similarly, lack of motivation may suggest that an "I don't know" response to a test question means "I don't care." Anxiety and motivational factors might be minimized by ensuring that a test environment is positive, supportive, and nonthreatening. Extra time spent establishing rapport might also help eliminate this source of error.

Test wiseness

Another factor that may influence the student's performance on tests is the effect of practice, that is, repeated administrations of the same test or same type of test. Practice can occur through routine test-taking or through coaching. Test wiseness has been suggested as an important consideration in the testing of both minority children (Dreisbach & Keogh, 1982) and learning-disabled students (Scruggs & Lifson, 1986), who have been shown to have deficits in their test-taking ability.

There is evidence suggesting that test performance can be improved through practice of test-taking skills (Dreisbach & Keogh, 1982). In fact, books and manuals including strategies and exercises for improving test-taking skills have been developed (e.g., Ciardi, 1990; Gall, 1990).

There are also some data to support the idea that certain types of test performances are more amenable to coaching than others. In a series of studies (Scruggs & Mastropieri, 1986; Scruggs, Mastropieri, & Tolfa-Veit, 1986), it was found that learning-disabled and behavior-disordered students improved more on tasks such as word-study skills and mathematical concepts than on reading comprehension after coaching (consisting of teaching them to attend to the appropriate stimulus, mark answers correctly, use time wisely, and avoid careless errors). They hypothesized that this result was due to two factors. First, the word-study and mathematical concepts have very complicated formats that would ordinarily confuse them. Second, their continued poor performance in reading comprehension was due to problems in deductive reasoning and other deficits that are not related to the coaching per se.

A "test to test test wiseness" was developed to identify students who lack test-taking skills (Parrish, 1982). The interesting question that must be asked is, "Should students be trained if they are identified as having these deficiencies?" On the one hand, if the goal is to get an accurate picture of how much a person knows, any disadvantage a person might have that is unrelated to the test content should be eliminated. On the other hand, training students might result in test scores that are not reflective of their true classroom performance. Scruggs, Mastropieri, and Tolfa-Veit (1986) discussed this issue and suggested the need for research to determine the best practice to follow. It would seem that, once again, the *purpose* of the testing is very important in that decision. Regardless of the purpose, the specific test items should not be taught; only instruction in test-taking skills should be considered.

Health and emotional state

Other factors that can affect the test taker's performance are health and emotional state. Time should be spent to determine whether a student is performing "typically" at the time of evaluation. A teacher is perhaps in the best position to make this judgment, and this is one of the many advantages of teacher assessment. If examiners other than the teacher (or other person familiar with the child) administer the tests, they should consult with the teacher to get this important information.

Factors Related to the Examiner and the Examiner–Examinee Relationship

Differences in administration and interpretation

The next major factor affecting test results relates to the examiner and the examiner–examinee relationship. One of the most common sources of error is differences in test administration and test interpretation. Assessment instruments, particularly norm-referenced tests, are designed to be administered in a standard, similar manner. However, many factors during the assessment process make this difficult to do. Examiners' personalities and methods of interacting with the examinees result in differences in rapport and amount of feedback given, both of which can greatly affect the testing situation. For example, differences in the amount of reinforcement and/or verbal approval might affect test scores, particularly for younger students (Bradley-Johnson, Graham, & Johnson, 1986. In one study, Breuning and Zella (1978) found that for an experimental group, individualized incentives increased IQ scores an average of 13 points over a control group. Marlaire and Maynard (1990) stressed that the entire process of testing is an "interactional phenomenon."

There are other factors that also should be considered regarding the effects of reinforcement on test-taking behavior. One factor is the *age* of the student being tested. Bradley-Johnson, Graham, and Johnson (1986) reported that almost all studies using rewards with early elementary-aged children have found increases, while those using students in the sixth grade or above have not. Other differences occur when test examiners are confronted with a unique, atypical, or ambiguous answer. Sattler, Andres, Squire, Wisely, and Maloy (1978) found that when examiners (regardless of their level of training) were asked to score "ambiguous" responses on the Wechsler Intelligence Scale for Children-Revised (WISC-R), there was considerable disagreement. Consider the following example of an interaction between the examiner and examinee on the comprehension subtest of the WISC-R:

> *Examiner:*   What are you supposed to do if you find someone's wallet or pocketbook in a store?
> *Examinee:*   I'd give it to the person behind the counter.
> *Examiner:*   What should you do if you see thick smoke coming from the window of your neighbor's house?
> *Examinee:*   Call the police and call an ambulance.
> *Examiner:*   What are some reasons why we need policemen?
> *Examinee:*   Because people are always fighting and there are drugs around here.

If these answers are scored according to the criteria stated in the WISC-R manual, the student would receive a 2 (indicating best response) for the first two questions and a 0 (indicating an incorrect response or no credit) for the last question. What if, however, the student comes from a tough neighborhood where fighting and drugs are associated with the police? Would you score the response as incorrect in accordance with the WISC-R scoring criteria? Would you give some credit because the response was correct, given the student's environment? No doubt, many examiners would respond differently to this example, depending on their philosophy of assessment and the reason for the evaluation. Because standardized tests imply a standard format for administration and scoring, violations result in invalid findings. One rule of thumb is to adhere strictly to the standard administration and scoring guidelines when possible and to state precisely why and where you differ if it is necessary to do so.

Differences of interpretation are especially obvious when more subjective scoring systems are used. In many situations, a question has no right or wrong answer, but the answers have varying degrees of correctness. The area in which interpretation of results varies the most is probably projective testing, which is discussed in Chapter 10.

Examiner bias

Another examiner-related source of error is examiner bias. This is not necessarily conscious bias. Depending on the information you have heard about a particular student, you might have a tendency to give the benefit of the doubt or to be somewhat more conservative with the scoring.

McDermott (1981), in reviewing the possible sources of "biasing cues," indicated that empirical evidence suggests that the evaluator's knowledge of special-education placement, race, sex, social class, and cultural background significantly affects diagnostic decisions. More recently, research has reinforced the bias factor, particularly related to special education placement. O'Reilly (1989) found that information related to reason for referral (gifted or learning disabled) resulted in significant bias regarding assessment and classification. One general guideline is to make use of the information that you have about an individual but make a conscious effort to avoid being biased. Also, it helps to be aware that some bias will probably still exist.

The reason for testing can also affect the scoring. If you know that good students are being routinely evaluated, there might be a tendency to give them positive scores for ambiguous answers. If, however, you know that the "class troublemaker" is being evaluated for possible special-education placement, you might not be as liberal in your scoring. Again, these are not necessarily conscious biases but, rather, biases that are tied into expectations. For example, Ysseldyke, Algozzine, Regan, and McGue (1981) found that many students are classified for and receive special education simply because they are referred. In addition, the decision regarding the *type* of test to administer can be affected by certain factors. Huebner (1989) found that school psychologists' decisions about further psychoeducational testing were affected by students' achievement test scores but not by their race or socioeconomic status. Previous test performance within a testing session might also bias the examiner. For example, if students were doing well up to a point, there might be a tendency to give them credit for answers of questionable quality later in the test.

Race of examiner

The racial differences between examiner and examinee have received widespread attention. For a number of years, it was assumed, for instance, that black children would score higher on tests if the examiner was also black. An analysis of the research, however, suggested that the race of the examiner does not have a significant effect on test performance. Sattler and Gwynne (1982a) reviewed 27 published articles in which the race of examiner was explored empirically; in 23 of the 27 studies, no significant effect was found. They concluded that "some writers have simply declared by fiat that white examiners impair the intelligence test scores of black children. Unfortunately, this declaration is not justified by the available research, as the present review and as past reviews have shown. In everyday clinical and school encounters, there are probably individual cases in which a white examiner adversely affects a black person's performance on intelligence tests, but the research suggests that these situations are infrequent" (p. 207). Similarly, Graziano

(1982) reviewed 15 years of research and found no biasing effect of examiner race. Fuchs and Fuchs (1989), however, found that *familiarity* with the examiner did have an effect on Hispanic and black children's test performance.

Culture and language of the examiner

Similarly, the cultural, language, and dialect differences of the examiner and the examinee have been explored to determine if they affect test performance. Padilla and Garza (1975) noted that "when a Spanish-surnamed examinee and a non-Spanish–surnamed examiner sit across from each other in a testing situation, there is often a wider gulf separating them than just the table. Typically, there is a linguistic, cultural, and socioeconomic gap between them, associated with their different sets of life experiences. An examiner who is not sensitive to these differences will surely have a negative influence on the outcome of the child's performance" (pp. 55–56). The available research suggests that the effect of the language differences of both the examiner and test diminishes as the Spanish-speaking child spends more time in English-speaking schools (Clarizio, 1982). More recently, Wolfram (1990) reported on the very important role of dialect differences and its biasing effect on testing.

Scoring errors

The last source of examiner error is scoring errors. Although this is an area in which extra care can and should be taken, scoring errors do exist. They can cause problems leading to incorrect educational programming and, in some cases, incorrect classification. For example, Sherrets, Gard, and Langner (1979), in a study of 39 examiners' scorings of 200 intelligence-test protocols, noted that 90 percent of the examiners made some kind of scoring error. The largest error would have raised the student's IQ by 9 points or lowered it by 7 points. Interestingly, 32 percent of the protocols included some type of simple addition error. Similarly, Hunnicutt, Slate, Gamble, and Wheeler (1990) found examiner errors on 83 percent of the intelligence test protocols they checked and found that the IQ should have been different in about 50 percent of the tests. The tendency to make scoring errors apparently begins early in a professional's career. Slate and Jones (1990) reported that students in a graduate course in assessment made an average of almost nine errors per test protocol; Giacobbe and Traynelis-Yurck (1989) found that when undergraduate students were asked to administer and score a vocabulary test, over 70 percent made some type of error. In addition, it appears that even tests that are relatively simple to administer and score are subject to scoring errors. For example, Peterson et al. (1991) noted that there were mistakes on 95 percent of the protocols for the Wide Range Achievement Test-Revised, a test that is widely administered.

Factors Related to the Test Itself

The last factor that can affect test results relates to the test itself. This involves the test's technical adequacy (for example, validity and reliability) or its possible bias against certain types of students.

Validity

Validity refers to the extent to which a test measures what it purports to measure. Three major types of validity are included in a discussion of assessment instruments: criterion-related validity, content validity, and construct validity.

Criterion-related validity refers to the extent to which a person's score on a certain test correlates with a criterion measure (usually that person's score on another test). The correlation coefficient that this comparison yields is called a *validity coefficient.* Correlation coefficients indicate the degree of relationship between two variables. They range from a −1.00 (perfect negative correlation) to +1.00 (perfect positive correlation). A +1.00 correlation means that as the values of the first variable change, the values of the second variable change in the same direction. Alternately, a −1.00 correlation means that as the values of the first variable change, the values of the second variable change in the opposite direction. Very rarely, however, do correlations reach −1.00 or +1.00. Usually, correlations are expressed as a positive or negative two-digit decimal, such as .63 or −.86 or .75. In assessment, positive correlations are used almost exclusively. In measuring criterion-related validity, the closer the decimal is to +1.00, the more valid the instrument is with respect to the criterion measure. No cut-off point exists that makes a test either valid or not valid; in general, however, a validity coefficient of less than .70 for individual tests and less than .60 for group-administered tests probably should be interpreted with caution.

An example of establishing criterion-related validity is shown in Table 3-1, giving the data from two intelligence tests.

By using the formula for determining correlation coefficients, you can determine that Intelligence Test 1 (test to be validated) correlates .86 with Intelligence Test 2 (criterion measure). This type of criterion-related validity is called *concurrent validity,* and it quantifies the degree to which a test correlates with a criterion measure administered at roughly the same time.

The other type of criterion-related validity is *predictive validity,* which refers to the extent to which test results correlate with a criterion measure that is given at some future time. To establish the predictive validity of the Scholastic Aptitude Test (SAT), for instance, the SAT scores (test to be validated) of individuals in high school might be correlated with these individuals' grade-point averages (criterion measure)

TABLE 3-1   Example of Criterion Related Validity

SUBJECT	INTELLIGENCE TEST 1 (TEST TO BE VALIDATED)	INTELLIGENCE TEST 2 (CRITERION MEASURE)
Ron	97	94
Roni	89	96
Muriel	109	113
Mark	78	85
Juanita	98	95
Ruth	116	110
Helen	93	89
Stuart	100	109
Jay	100	97
Sherri	84	89
Scott	97	99
Randi	98	104
Sonny	102	99
Michael	108	112
JoAnn	89	90
Daniel	93	98
Evan	87	85
Erin	97	107
Lauren	108	110
Eric	111	106

after their freshman year in college. The closer the correlation is to +1.00, the greater the predictive validity of the SAT.

Regarding criterion-related validity, it is important to be aware that a test is only as valid as the criterion measure. If authors report high correlations between their test and a criterion test that is not considered valid, this correlation does not make the authors' test valid. You must learn to look not only at the magnitude of the correlation coefficient, but also at the criterion measure itself. Suppose, for instance, that you were interested in establishing the validity of a new intelligence test. You chose as your criterion measure the Terrible Test of Intelligence, a technically inadequate test in its own right. A high correlation would indicate that the new test measures areas similar to those measured in the historically inadequate Terrible Test.

Content validity refers to the extent to which a test accurately measures the sample of behaviors under consideration. Salvia and Ysseldyke (1991) noted three factors that should be considered in establishing content validity:

1. Appropriateness of the test items (that is, are the items appropriate in age level and content?).
2. Completeness of the item sample (that is, does the test include a broad sample of tasks in the measured domain?).

3. Appropriateness of the way in which the test items measure the content (that is, the type of task required, such as multiple choice, fill in the blank, or true-false).

Suppose, for example, that a test was developed to measure spelling for students in grades 1–6. If the test had a number of extremely difficult items (for example, *pulchritude, unctuous*), it would not be *appropriate*. If the test only included simple two-letter words (for example, *do, an, of*), it would not be *complete*. If it required an examinee to indicate whether a word was spelled correctly using a true-false format, it might not be measuring spelling in an *appropriate way*.

Establishing content validity is extremely important, yet doing so is not as straightforward as determining criterion-related validity. One way to maximize content validity is to consider what needs to be measured and how it will best be measured during test construction. The determination of content validity usually involves some type of expert judgment. In the above example, a group of teachers familiar with spelling curricula might be asked to judge the content validity of the spelling test.

Construct validity has to do with the extent to which a test measures some type of theoretical characteristic or concept. Self-concept and reasoning ability are two examples of these relatively abstract constructs that are difficult to define and subsequently difficult to measure. In general, the establishment of construct validity includes the careful identification and definition of the construct and then the derivation and verification of hypotheses concerning test performance related to the construct (Gronlund, 1988).

Construct validity is usually established through careful empirical studies using certain statistical procedures. Two procedures are frequently used for this purpose. The first involves the intercorrelation among test items to determine if the test primarily measures a single construct. The second involves procedures to establish a positive correlation of the test scores with other measures that supposedly measure the same construct and a negative correlation with other measures that supposedly do not (Standards for Educational and Psychological Testing, 1985).

Reliability

Another important quality of a test is reliability. Reliability refers to the consistency of a test. If a test is not reliable, it is not dependable, stable, predictable, or accurate (Kerlinger, 1986). Lack of these traits is obviously undesirable in an assessment instrument designed to identify educational needs. If a test is not reliable, by definition it cannot be valid (Salvia & Ysseldyke, 1991). However, just because a test is reliable, it is not necessarily valid; in other words, results on a test could be consistent, but they could consistently measure the wrong thing. Four kinds of reliability are most commonly reported: test-retest, equivalent form, internal, and interscorer.

Test-retest is probably the most commonly used reliability, and it quantifies the extent to which results from a test remain consistent over time. Test-retest reliability is established by correlating the test results of a group of individuals with the same individuals' test results after a relatively short period of time (usually about 2 weeks, but time varies with the type of test). As a rule, when a reliability coefficient is reported without designation of the type of reliability, it is a test-retest coefficient. Table 3-2 gives hypothetical data demonstrating the test-retest reliability of an intelligence test. The resulting correlation coefficient is .92, a figure that indicates a generally high test-retest reliability. Usually, a reliability coefficient of at least .90 is desirable for individual diagnostic tests, .80 for group-administered tests, and .60 for screening tests (Salvia & Ysseldyke, 1991).

Equivalent-form reliability is established by using alternate forms of an instrument that measure the same skills. The correlation of scores quantifies the similarity of the two forms and gives some indication of the degree to which they are interchangeable. For example, two forms of a mathematics test might include different test items to measure knowledge of the same concepts. Equivalent-form reliability would be established by administering the two forms to the same population and correlating the resulting scores. In establishing equivalent-form reliability, it is important that the time between administration of the two forms be as short as possible. This eliminates the possibility that other factors might affect the test performances. Equivalent-form reliability is also referred to as alternate-form reliability.

Another method of establishing reliability that is, in a sense, a combination of the two previously discussed approaches is *test-retest* with *alternate forms*. This involves administering one form of a test to a group of individuals at a given time and then administering the alternate form of the test to the same group after a short period of time has passed. Many argue that this is the best method of estimating test error (e.g., Anastasi, 1988). One should note, however, that the resulting correlation coefficient is lower than those yielded by the test-retest or alternate form techniques.

Internal reliability is determined using a variety of procedures. This type of reliability refers of the internal consistency of a test and is computed using statistical procedures such as coefficient alpha and Kuder-Richardson formulae. Another procedure, called *split-half,* involves the correlation of one half of a test with the other half (for example, odd versus even items, first half versus second half). In a sense, this provides an estimate of the alternate-form reliability of the total test.

Interscorer reliability, sometimes referred to as interrater reliability, is concerned with how consistently a test is scored or a behavior is

TABLE 3-2   Example of Test-Retest Reliability

SUBJECT	SCORE ON INTELLIGENCE TEST (FIRST ADMINISTRATION)	SCORE ON INTELLIGENCE TEST (SECOND ADMINISTRATION)
Ron	97	89
Roni	89	87
Muriel	109	109
Mark	78	80
Juanita	98	96
Ruth	116	119
Helen	93	99
Stuart	100	103
Jay	100	100
Sherri	84	82
Scott	97	93
Randi	98	99
Sonny	102	105
Michael	108	104
Joann	89	90
Daniel	93	97
Evan	87	84
Erin	97	104
Lauren	108	110
Eric	111	107

rated by two examiners. In the first type, a test might be administered to a group of students and given to two individuals to score. The results of the two individuals' scoring of the tests for the student could be correlated to provide a reliability coefficient. In the second type, usually involved in behavioral observation, the percentage of agreement between two individuals observing the same behavior is computed.

Other technical characteristics

Another reliability-related characteristic that is often reported is the standard error of measurement (SEM). The SEM represents an attempt to account for the possible variability or error involved in the scoring and interpretation of a test. Because no tests are absolutely reliable, a person's *true score*—score on a test if the test were totally reliable—is never known. Individual scores on tests, therefore, can be thought of as estimates of true scores. The greater the reliability of a test the smaller the SEM (and vice versa).

The SEM is used to provide a range that more accurately reflects how closely people's scores on a test approach their true scores. For instance, if Bob scored 110 on a given test whose SEM was 2.4, then approximately two-thirds of the time his true score would fall somewhere between 107.6 and 112.4. In general, the lower the SEM, the more confident you can be that a person's score on a test is an accurate estimate of the true score. Conversely, the larger the SEM for a test, the less confident you can be. The SEM is extremely important when labeling and classification are considered.

Another type of technical information that should be considered is the nature of the norm, or population used to standardize a norm-referenced test. Because an individual's score on a norm-referenced test is derived through comparison with the standardization population, it is extremely important that the nature of that population is known. Are you comparing a student's performance to a random sample of children across the United States? Males from lower socioeconomic, rural areas? Severely retarded students living in institutions? Obviously, the score that the student receives needs to be interpreted relative to those who comprise the normative sample. An "average" score would be interpreted differently when compared to the three populations just mentioned, for example. It is best to have a representative sample that considers characteristics such as sex, race, geographic region, and parents' education. It is important to remember that the norm does not necessarily refer to normal but to the types of individuals included in the standardization sample.

Many tests also have basals and ceilings. Although not considered technical characteristics in a traditional sense, basals and ceilings are important to understand for both correct administration and interpretation. Basals and ceilings are used in power tests in which the difficulty level of the items progresses from easy to hard. The *basal* of a test is the point at which the examiner assumes that the student could answer easier items. The *ceiling* of a test is the point at which the examiner assumes that the student would miss more difficult items. The use of a basal and ceiling allows the examiner to save time by not administering items that are probably too easy or too difficult for the student. For example, suppose the basal rule of a test was three in a row correct while the ceiling rule was three in a row incorrect. You start administering the test at item 30 (as noted in the manual according to the age of the student). Items 32–34 were correct and items 41–43 were incorrect. You would assume that all items before 32 (1–31) are correct and all items past 43 are incorrect. Therefore, certain assumptions are being made about the student's performance.

Possible test bias

A test is often considered biased when individuals with certain characteristics (for example, different ethnic groups, geographic regions, economic levels, sex) consistently score differently when it is administered under similar conditions. For example, a test might be considered biased if, when administered in a consistent fashion, Hispanic students score lower than white children, males lower than females, or rural children lower than urban children.

There are actually several possible reasons *why* individuals with certain characteristics might score lower on a particular test. One explanation is that the differences in test scores are a result of bias in the test itself. Another explanation is that the differences in test performance reflect true differences and therefore are not the result of test bias. These differing interpretations of the same phenomenon have resulted in heated debate regarding test bias, particularly in the area of intelligence testing. Considerable attention was addressed in the 1970s to the bias of intelligence tests against ethnic minority students (see Hobbs, 1975; Mercer, 1972, 1973; Samuda, 1975). A number of court cases investigating the discriminatory nature of intelligence testing resulted from this attention. Unfortunately, the results from litigation have provided little additional insight into the issue of bias in testing. As noted in Chapter 1, in some cases, such as *Larry P. v. Riles,* (1979), the decision implied that there was bias in the tests, whereas in others (*PASE v. Hannon,* 1980), the decision did not support test bias.

What is evident from the history of contradiction regarding test bias is that there needs to be a clear definition of bias or at least a delineation of the types of bias that can be empirically explored. Reschly (1980) identified nine common definitions, four of which are particularly relevant to this discussion. These are mean-difference bias, item bias, psychometric bias, and factor-analytic bias.

Mean-difference bias is perhaps the most common definition of bias and is the one described in the previous discussion. It asks the question, Do individuals with different characteristics score differently on the same test? Because certain groups do score lower on certain types of tests, those tests have been considered biased against those groups. As discussed previously, the causes of those differences in scores are subject to considerable controversy.

Item bias refers to the situation in which specific items on a test are considered to be outside the life experiences of certain individuals. For example, a potentially biased item for a lower socioeconomic, rural child might be "How far is it from New York to Los Angeles?" (from WISC-R, one of the tests involved in litigation). Other items might be considered biased if a certain type of typical, stereotyped response is considered the correct answer. For example, one item that appeared in the WISC-R is, "What is the thing to do if a boy (or girl) much smaller than yourself starts to fight with you?" The answer that receives the most credit is to "walk away," although many individuals have argued that this would not be an appropriate response (or behavior) of an inner-city child.

Williams (1972) developed a test to illustrate the point that administering a test that includes items to which a person has not been exposed results in biased decisions. His test, called the Black Intelligence Test of Cultural Homogeneity (BITCH), includes 100 vocabulary words that he feels would be a better predictor of learning ability for black children than traditional intelligence test items. Figure 3-1 shows examples from this test.

The problem with deciding which items on a test are biased is that it requires subjective judgment, a problem that has resulted in experimental investigation and criticism. For example, when studying the performance of children of different ethnic groups, researchers have not found significant differences on items assumed to be biased (Sandoval, 1979). In addition, there is actually little agreement among raters on which items should be considered biased (Sandoval & Miille, 1980).

Other types of bias include *psychometric bias* and *factor-analytic* bias. Psychometric bias is determined by asking the question, Are the technical characteristics (for example, validity and reliability) similar for individuals with different characteristics? Factor-analytic bias involves the use of a statistical procedure in which items (or subtests) are grouped together because they correlate highly with one another and have low correlations with other factors identified by the same process. To determine this type of bias, one would see if similar or different factors on a test were identified for the groups of individuals under investigation. This type of bias is related to psychometric bias, because it essentially focuses on the issue of construct validity.

The controversy regarding the issue of bias in testing, particularly intelligence testing, raises important questions and, once again, should make us look very carefully at the uses and limitations of test scores. Perhaps educators should be less concerned about whether or not specific tests are biased and more concerned about the appropriate uses of the tests and the possible use of test scores for discriminatory purposes. Many

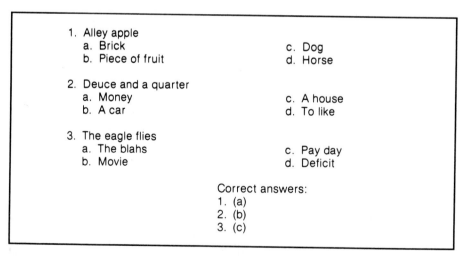

1. Alley apple
   a. Brick
   b. Piece of fruit
   c. Dog
   d. Horse

2. Deuce and a quarter
   a. Money
   b. A car
   c. A house
   d. To like

3. The eagle flies
   a. The blahs
   b. Movie
   c. Pay day
   d. Deficit

Correct answers:
1. (a)
2. (b)
3. (c)

FIGURE 3-1　Examples from the Black Intelligence Test of Cultural Homogeneity intelligence tests, for example, have been shown to be relatively good predictors of school performance (measured by achievement test scores), regardless of the ethnic background of the student (see Oakland, 1977; Reschly & Reschly, 1979). On the other hand, the results of these tests should not be overemphasized, and their use in major educational decisions should be avoided (Clarizio, 1982). Certainly, equating these scores with "intellectual potential" is inappropriate (discussed in Chapter 8). The Alliance of Black School Educators (1984) cogently reported their position on the use of "biased" tests:

> *Testing in order to rank children by intellect, to rank them by cognitive or behavioral style, or to rank them with "nonbiased" assessment procedures is malpractice, in our opinion, unless such practices can be demonstrated by valid research to result in significant and meaningful changes in achievement for our children. (p. 28)*

SUMMARY

There are several considerations that must be addressed during assessment. These considerations or factors pertain specifically to formal assessment procedures, although they can also provide guidelines for informal procedures.

The first factor that could affect test results is related to the person being tested (the examinee). Included in this category are such factors as anxiety, motivation, previous test experience, health and emotional status, and attitudes of the person being tested. The second major factor relates to the examiner. In this category, test administration and interpretation differences, styles of interacting with the examinee, bias, racial or cultural differences between the examiner and examinee, and scoring errors were discussed. The last major factor is in the test itself, including its validity, reliability, standard error of measurement, and possible bias. All three of these factors should be considered throughout the assessment. Acknowledging these factors will help in reducing some of the error and in putting assessment data into proper perspective. Specifically, these factors should be considered during test selection, administration, and interpretation. Such consideration should give a test user some idea of the limitations of assessment information and, when relevant, some idea of appropriate generalization of assessment data.

4

Assessing to Label: Issues and Caveats

AREAS INCLUDED

ISSUES
- Method for Obtaining Funding
- Minority Overrepresentation
- Possible Stigmatizing Effects

CAVEATS
- Sources of Error
- Changing Definitions
- Variability within Categories

The use of assessment data for labeling and classification is a controversial yet important issue in special education, and it is a crucial component in the postreferral assessment process. The pros and cons of labeling have been argued, debated, and analyzed for a number of years. The major goals and purposes of labeling and classifying in special education are to identify children with significant educational problems, to indicate similarities and relationships among the educational problems, and to provide information that allows professional communication within the field (Hardman, Drew, Egan, & Wolf, 1990).

In the 1970s and 1980s, however, the way was paved for noncategorical or generic approaches to classification. This development was primarily the result of pressure by critics who were highly vocal in their dislike of labeling. Among their criticisms were that the various handicapping conditions lacked acceptable definitions, that the number of minority students labeled was disproportionately high, that not enough appropriate, identifiable educational programs were available to prescribe after classification, and that labels had a possible stigmatizing effect. This last criticism was the most controversial and was the focus of considerable research in the 1970s and early 1980s. For example, several researchers (including Algozzine & Sutherland, 1977; Jacobs, 1978; and Taylor, Smiley, & Ziegler, 1983) found that when labels such as mentally retarded, emotionally disturbed, and learning disabled were used, teachers' expectations were lower and negative attitudes were developed. On the other hand, in what has become a classic review of the subject, MacMillan, Jones, and Aloia (1974) found no conclusive evidence that the label "mentally retarded" had any biasing effect. That review, however, was conducted two decades ago.

Apparently, labeling is a complex issue that involves both the label and the behavior of the labeled student (Dusek & O'Connell, 1973; Good & Brophy, 1972). Reschly and Lamprecht (1979), for example, found that teachers' expectancies of labeled students' behavior changed when they observed behavior that was inconsistent with the label. Undoubtedly, the debate over the effects of labeling will continue as long as labels are used.

Despite these controversies and the long history of research, labeling and classification have continued, primarily as a means of establishing priorities and obtaining funds for educational programming. Public Law 94-142, for instance, carefully defined those children for whom special education is warranted:

> *Handicapped children means those children evaluated as being mentally retarded, hard of hearing, deaf, speech impaired, visually handicapped, seriously emotionally disturbed, orthopedically impaired, other health impaired, deaf-blind, multi-handicapped, or as having specific learning disabilities, who because of those impairments need special education and related services. (p. 121a.5)*

More recently, P.L. 101-476, although changing the term *handicapped children* to *children with disabilities*, kept the categorical designations. P.L. 101-476 noted that the term *children with disabilities* means children with mental retardation, hearing impairments including deafness, speech or language impairments, visual impairments including blindness, serious emotional disturbance, orthopedic impairments, autism, traumatic brain injury, other health impairments, or specific learning disabilities.

It should be noted that the Regular Education Initiative (discussed in Chapter 1) and other, similar movements have suggested that labels should not be used in the identification of students who need additional services. However, if the labels noted in federal legislation are no longer used, other labels—either formal or informal—will undoubtedly take their place.

PRELIMINARY CONSIDERATIONS

The term *norm-referenced testing* is often thought of as synonymous with labeling. While labeling and classification usually require the administration of norm-referenced tests, these are certainly not the only purposes of such tests. Furthermore, because of several factors, the use of assessment data for labeling is anything but an exact science. Among these factors are those mentioned in Chapter 3, as well as the inexact and changing definitions of the various labels.

A number of other considerations should be kept in mind regarding labeling and classification:

1. In many situations, labeling and classification are not necessary. It is important to try to work with a student to see if a referral and possible label can be avoided (prereferral intervention).

2. The types of tests (and the tests themselves) used to label students differ from examiner to examiner.

3. The criteria used to determine various labels differ considerably from state to state. It is entirely possible that a student might receive one label in a particular state and another or no label in a different state. These different criteria also result in significant variation in the percentages of students who are labeled. Hallahan, Keller, and Ball (1986), for example, noted that the percentage of students labeled learning disabled ranged from 3.06 (Indiana) to 8.73 (Rhode Island). Similarly the percentages for mentally retarded and emotionally disturbed students ranged from .67 (three states) to 4.77 (Alabama) and .09 (Mississippi) to 3.45 (Delaware), respectively.

4. Although students are often labeled and classified on the basis of educational and psychological assessment, this is not always the most prudent thing to do. The advantages of using such an approach (for example, added services) must be weighed against the disadvantages (for example, possible stigmatizing effects).

PROCEDURES

Not all exceptional children are initially identified through educational and psychological assessment. Many children with disabilities such as those with orthopedic impairments, hearing impairments, or traumatic brain injury are identified through medical and other procedures. Even in these situations, however, assessment data are usually used to document the need for special education and to establish specific goals and objectives.

Classification on the basis of educational and psychological assessment becomes particularly important in situations in which the label or diagnosis depends primarily on the student's intellectual and academic skills or emotional and behavioral status. For example, learning-disabled, gifted, mentally retarded, and emotionally disturbed or behavior-disordered children are often identified through educational and psychological assessment data. It might be more appropriate to state that these types of students are determined to be eligible for special education using educational and psychological tests.

How can test data be used for labeling purposes? Usually, a battery of tests is administered to a student, and the results are examined for certain patterns. The same test battery, however, is not appropriate for all students. As mentioned in Chapter 2, individualizing the assessment procedure is extremely important. Although tests vary greatly, at least some measure of individual intelligence, achievement, adaptive behavior, and emotional and behavioral characteristics is usually obtained as a basis for classification. In general, although some informal and criterion-referenced tests may be used, norm-referenced tests are usually administered. After the selected instruments are administered and scored, the results can be used in deciding the possible classification, if any, of the student.

The following section reviews the definitions of the various labels used in special education and examines their implications for assessment. An *assessment profile* is mentioned for each type of exceptional student. This profile (which includes measures of intelligence, achievement, adaptive behavior, and emotional and behavioral characteristics) is meant as an example to demonstrate how data might be used. More important, the profiles are presented to show how difficult it really is to use assessment as a basis for labeling. As will be discussed, differences in definitions and eligibility criteria for various labels as well as the differences in characteristics of students with the same label make the formulation of a "typical" assessment profile very difficult.

Learning Disabilities

Since the term *learning disabilities* was introduced in 1963, professionals have disagreed about its definition. Of the many definitions available, the one proposed by the National Advisory Committee on Handicapped Children (1968) is accepted by many special educators and was only slightly modified by P.L. 94-142. That definition states:

> *Children with specific learning disabilities exhibit a disorder in one or more of the basic psychological processes involved in understanding or in using spoken or written language. They may be manifested in disorders of listening, thinking, talking, reading, writing, spelling, or arithmetic. They include*

conditions which have been referred to as perceptual handicaps, brain in-
jury, minimal brain dysfunction, dyslexia, developmental aphasia, etc. They
do not include learning problems which are primarily due to visual, hearing,
or motor handicaps, to mental retardation, emotional disturbance, or to
environmental disadvantage. (p. 34)

There is certainly not a consensus regarding the definition of learning
disabilities. In 1981, the National Joint Committee for Learning Disabilities (NJCLD) recommended a different definition. That definition reads

Learning disabilities is a generic term that refers to a heterogeneous group of
disorders manifested by significant difficulties in the acquisition and use of
listening, speaking, reading, writing, reasoning, or mathematical abilities.
These disorders are intrinsic to the individual and presumed to be due to
central nervous system dysfunction. Even though a learning disability may
occur concomitantly with other handicapping conditions (e.g., sensory im-
pairment, mental retardation, social and emotional disturbance) or environ-
mental influences (e.g., cultural differences, insufficient/inappropriate in-
struction, psychogenic factors), it is not the direct result of those conditions or
influences. (Hammill, Leigh, McNutt, & Larsen, 1981, p. 336)

The NJCLD definition was modified in 1987. That proposed definition was developed by the Interagency Committee on Learning Disabilities (ICLD), a group consisting of 13 federal agencies. The major modification proposed added social skills deficits as a possible characteristic of
learning disabilities and acknowledged that learning disabilities might
coexist with attention deficit disorder. The ICLD definition follows (with
parentheses and italics deleted to show the differences with the NJCLD
definition):

Learning disabilities is a generic term that refers to a heterogeneous group of
disorders manifested by significant difficulties in the acquisition and use of
listening, speaking, reading, writing, reasoning, or mathematical abilities,
(or of social skills). *These disorders are intrinsic to the individual and*
presumed to be due to central nervous system dysfunction. Even though a
learning disability may occur concomitantly with other handicapping condi-
tions (e.g., sensory impairment, mental retardation, social and emotional
disturbance) with (socioenvironmental) *influences (e.g., cultural differences,*
insufficient or inappropriate instruction, psychogenic factors), (and especially attention deficit disorder, all of which may cause learning problems, a
learning disability) *is not the direct result of those conditions or influences.*

Hammill (1990) reviewed 11 definitions of learning disabilities and
found that although there was considerable agreement among them, the
NJCLD definition appeared to include the best descriptive statements.
Regardless of which definition is used, one common diagnostic criterion is
the documentation of a discrepancy between expected and actual
performance. In a survey of the definitions used by all 50 states, three

factors emerged in 75 percent or more of their criteria for identifying learning disabilities. Those were exclusion (such as problems not due to another handicap) and language and academic problems usually expressed by some type of discrepancy formula (Mercer, King-Sears, & Mercer, 1990).

Historically, learning-disabled (LD) students have been assumed to have normal or low normal intelligence but have problems in at least one area of achievement. Heward and Orlansky (1992) noted that the most common characteristic of children with learning disabilities is a significant achievement deficiency in the presence of adequate overall intelligence (i.e., a discrepancy between aptitude and achievement). A number of aptitude-achievement formulae are being used to identify LD students. The formulae differ significantly, and their use can result in very different types of students being identified. For example, Reynolds (1985) noted that grade-level discrepancy criteria typically will deny learning disability services to students with IQs that are above average, while most standard score models will deny services to students with below-average IQs. In general, the entire area of aptitude-achievement discrepancies has been criticized because of their lack of empirical support and the statistical flaws inherent in many of the formulae. Evans (1990) reported that the regression model formula was the best although the issue of classification is still dependent on the tests used. In other words, it is possible that the same student could be given different batteries of tests resulting in different classification decisions using the same formula. In addition, Siegel (1989) argued that IQ should not be used in such formulae because they do not measure potential and are not independent of achievement. In fact, the Council for Learning Disabilities has recommended that the use of discrepancy formulae be abandoned; Wood (1991) also urged that *educational significance,* not just statistical significance, be considered when using the formulae. It should be noted, however, that discrepancy formulae are still being used widely; Hickman and Bevins (1990) for example, recently published a computer program to perform discrepancy analyses.

Because of the differences in definition and criteria used in the field of learning disabilities, it is difficult to identify a specific assessment profile for this population. A review of the characteristics of the LD population confuses the matter even more. As an example, Rivers and Smith (1988) reviewed the assessment profiles of 200 LD students and found that many had below average IQs and did not have aptitude-achievement discrepancies. The following profile represents a pattern of assessment results that *might* be found for an LD student. Note the variability in each of the areas included.

SAMPLE ASSESSMENT PROFILE: LEARNING DISABILITY (LD)

INTELLIGENCE: Average or low-average performance
ACHIEVEMENT: Variable or low-average performance
ADAPTIVE BEHAVIOR: Average or variable performance
EMOTIONAL AND BEHAVIORAL CHARACTERISTICS: Variable
  performance

Thus, if a student were administered a battery of tests and the scores resulted in this profile, this student might be considered learning disabled. Some regulations also require the assessment of deficits in information processing; such deficits are usually measured by specific perceptual-motor, aptitude, or language tests (see Appendix A).

Mental Retardation

Although a number of classification systems are still used for mentally retarded students, the most accepted system is the one proposed by the American Association on Mental Deficiency (AAMD) in its *Manual on Terminology and Classification* (Grossman, 1983). That definition states

> *Mental retardation refers to significantly subaverage general intellectual functioning existing concurrently with deficits in adaptive behavior and manifested during the developmental period. (p. 11)*

The AAMD further states that "significantly subaverage intellectual functioning" is defined by a score on a standardized intelligence test that is 70 or below, although it could be extended to 75 under certain circumstances. Although the criterion is specifically stated, the interpretation is not as straightforward. Wodrich and Barry (1991), in a survey of actual practices, found that over 25 percent of the school psychologists were flexible and would identify a student as retarded who had an IQ above the cut-off point. Table 4-1 indicates the range of intelligence test scores for the various levels of mental retardation according to the AAMD classification system.

It should be noted that the American Association on Mental Retardation (AAMR is the new name for AAMD) is currently revising the definition and subsequent criteria for mental retardation. That new definition eliminates the various levels of mental retardation and emphasizes adaptive behavior (discussed next).

TABLE 4-1   AAMD Levels of Mental Retardation

LEVEL OF RETARDATION	IQ RANGE
Mild	50–55 to approx. 70
Moderate	35–40 to 50–55
Severe	20–25 to 35–40
Profound	Below 20 or 25

From H. Grossman, *Classification in Mental Retardation,* 1983. Copyright © American Association on Mental Deficiency.

The other criterion stated in the AAMD definition is a deficit in adaptive behavior. Unfortunately, as is discussed in Chapter 9, adaptive behavior testing has many limitations, primarily because of the difficulty in defining what constitutes adaptive behavior. The age-specific and situation-specific nature of adaptive behavior adds to the confusion. The AAMD provides examples of adaptive behavior in such areas as sensorimotor, communication, self-help, and socialization skills (infancy and early childhood); skills making use of abilities involving learning processes (childhood and early adolescence); and vocational skills and social responsibilities (late adolescence and adulthood). The translation of the adaptive behavior criteria to practice is also somewhat problematic. For one thing, the score on an adaptive behavior test that is required to indicate a deficit is not clear. Wodrich and Barry (1991) reported that only 50 percent of the school psychologists surveyed used a cut-off of 70 (usually two standard deviations below the mean).

In achievement, mentally retarded (MR) students also perform significantly below their peers (e.g., Taylor & Sternberg, 1989). In general, achievement by MR students is consistent with their mental ages. For educable MR (mildly retarded) children, intellectual development is typically one half to three fourths that of their average peers (Robinson & Robinson, 1976); a similar lag in achievement might be expected.

Other than the individual differences noted in everyone, few patterns of classroom behavior are typical of MR students. Two that tend to surface, however, are lack of motivation (Balla & Zigler, 1979) and a poor self-concept (Robinson & Robinson, 1976).

A sample profile for an MR child, therefore, might look like the following:

SAMPLE ASSESSMENT PROFILE: MENTAL RETARDATION (MR)

INTELLIGENCE: Low performance

ACHIEVEMENT: Low performance

ADAPTIVE BEHAVIOR: Low performance

EMOTIONAL AND BEHAVIORAL CHARACTERISTICS: Variable
   performance

Emotional Disturbance and Behavior Disorders

Emotional disturbance is extremely difficult to define. In fact, there is little agreement about the term to use to refer to individuals with emotional or behavioral problems. Emotional disturbance, emotional handicap, and behavior disorder, among other terms, have all been used. There is also a considerable amount of subjectivity about what constitutes an emotional or behavioral problem. Indeed, there is no consensus and no universally accepted definition, although Bower's definition (1969) is the one most widely used by educators and is the basis for the definition used in P.L. 94-142. Bower (pp. 22–23) stated that an emotionally disturbed child is one who exhibits one or more of the following characteristics to a marked degree over a period of time:

1. An inability to learn which cannot be explained by intellectual, sensory, or health factors.
2. An inability to build or maintain satisfactory interpersonal relationships with peers and teachers.
3. Inappropriate types of behavior or feelings under normal circumstances.
4. A general pervasive mood of unhappiness or depression.
5. A tendency to develop physical symptoms, pains, or fear associated with personal or school problems.

As a basis for assessment, Bower's definition is frustrating because it is subjective. Individual interpretations of "inappropriate behavior or feelings," "unhappiness," and "depression" can be very different, leading to application of the emotionally disturbed classification to a wide range of children. Social, cultural, and situational expectations confuse the assessment even more.

Recently, in fact, a new definition has been proposed that was developed by the Task Force of the Mental Health and Special Education Coalition. That definition reads

Emotional or Behavioral Disorder (EBD) refers to a condition in which behavioral or emotional responses of an individual in school are so different from his/her generally accepted, age-appropriate, ethnic or cultural norms as to result in significant impairment in self-care, social relationships, educational progress, classroom behavior, or work adjustment.

This category may include children or youth with schizophrenia, affective disorders, anxiety disorders, or with other sustained disturbances of conduct, attention, or adjustment.

EBD can co-exist with other handicapping conditions, as defined elsewhere in this law.

EBD is more than a transient, expected response to stressors in the child's or youth's environments and would persist even with individualized interventions, such as feedback to the individual, consultation with parents or families, and/or modification of the educational environment.

The eligibility decision must be based on multiple sources of data about the individual's behavioral or emotional functioning. EBD must be exhibited in at least two different settings, at least one of which is school-related.

This proposed definition uses different terminology, although it still requires subjective interpretation.

The assessment profile of the individual with emotional or behavioral problems is also somewhat confusing. For example, documentation of a typical cognitive, academic, and behavioral performance is very difficult. By definition, intellectual deficits should not be the cause of an emotionally disturbed individual's inability to learn. This implies that to be correctly classified as emotionally disturbed, a person should score within the normal range of intelligence. Kauffman (1989) noted that as a group, emotionally disturbed children score in the low-normal range but that their scores have a wide range.

Kauffman further noted that low achievement goes hand in hand with behavior disorders, although it is not clear if the behavior problem causes the low achievement, or vice versa. In general, however, the achievement of emotionally disturbed students is as variable as their scores on intelligence tests. Tamkin (1960) found that in achievement, 41 percent of the disturbed children he studied were above grade level, and only 32 percent were below. Other researchers (including Motto & Wilkins, 1968; Bower, 1969) found that emotionally disturbed children were significantly below their peers in academic achievement. These apparently contradictory findings may derive at least in part from the variations in the type and severity of the problems that led to the classification.

Emotionally disturbed children have behavior problems that are usually demonstrated in the classroom. To a certain extent, they tend to have problems in adaptive behavior. Kauffman (1989) mentioned the following four kinds of behavior that are typically associated with emotionally disturbed children: (1) hyperactivity, distractibility, and impulsivity; (2) aggression; (3) withdrawal, immaturity, and inadequacy; and (4) juvenile delinquency and deficiencies in moral development.

Although it is very difficult to determine an assessment profile for students who are emotionally disturbed or who have behavior disorders, such a profile might look like the following:

SAMPLE ASSESSMENT PROFILE:
EMOTIONAL OR BEHAVIOR PROBLEMS

INTELLIGENCE: Average or low-average performance

ACHIEVEMENT: Variable or low-average performance

ADAPTIVE BEHAVIOR: Variable performance

EMOTIONAL AND BEHAVIORAL CHARACTERISTICS: Low performance

Gifted and Talented

In recent years, gifted children have been receiving more and more attention. In a certain sense, however, definitions of *gifted* are just as ambiguous as definitions of other exceptional categories—if not more so. The generally accepted definition was set forth in Section 902 of the Gifted and Talented Children's Act (P.L. 95-561) and reported in the *Congressional Record* (1978).

> *The term* gifted and talented children *means children and, whenever applicable, youth who are identified at the preschool, elementary, or secondary level as possessing demonstrated or potential abilities that give evidence of high performance capabilities in areas such as intellectual, creative, specific academic or leadership ability, or in the performing and visual arts, and who by reason thereof, require services or activities not ordinarily provided by the school. (H-12179)*

In general, a subtle distinction is made between the terms *gifted* and *talented*. Gifted often refers to cognitive and creative superiority in combination with strong motivation, whereas talented refers to a special ability, aptitude, or accomplishment (Hallahan & Kauffman, 1991). Kirk and Gallagher (1988), however, pointed out a substantial positive correlation between intellectual ability and talented performance.

Although superior academic achievement is common in gifted children, some professionals estimate that as many as 15 to 20 percent of gifted children do not achieve at their expected level (Kirk & Gallagher, 1988). Lack of interest, of motivation, or of self-confidence could all be contributing factors.

In terms of behavioral characteristics, Terman's longitudinal study (Terman, 1925; Terman & Oden, 1959) is perhaps the most exhaustive. Terman found that scores for gifted children were average or above average in virtually every character trait measured. An exception might occur in unmotivated or underachieving gifted students, who might demonstrate some inappropriate classroom behavior. In terms of adaptive behavior, the definition and description of gifted children implies that the majority are average or above. Exceptional leadership skills, for instance, are not uncommon in gifted students (Kirk & Gallagher, 1988).

The following profile is offered for gifted children:

SAMPLE ASSESSMENT PROFILE: GIFTED

INTELLIGENCE: High performance

ACHIEVEMENT: High or variable performance

ADAPTIVE BEHAVIOR: Average or high performance

EMOTIONAL AND BEHAVIORAL CHARACTERISTICS: Average or variable performance

---

Educationally Disadvantaged

Even though *educationally disadvantaged* is not an officially accepted classification for exceptional children, it is included here because many children who are classified as having mental retardation, emotional or behavioral problems, or learning disabilities probably should fall within this classification. Educationally disadvantaged refers to those students who are not doing well in school yet are not handicapped in the traditional sense. These children often come from low socioeconomic groups or non-Anglo cultures in which English may be a second language. The concept *educationally disadvantaged* does not imply that the students it refers to cannot be considered mentally retarded, learning disabled, emotionally disturbed, or be exceptional in some other way; rather, it means that they are often labeled as such when they should not be.

It has long been recognized that educationally disadvantaged students typically perform poorly on intelligence tests (Kaufman & Doppelt, 1976; Mercer, 1973). Since intelligence tests predict achievement fairly well (see Chapter 8), such children also usually do poorly on achievement tests. One striking difference between these students and MR students (who also score low on intelligence and achievement tests) is their behavior *outside the classroom.* Mercer (1973) distinguished between clinically retarded children (who have difficulties with day-to-day living skills) and quasi-retarded children (who get along well in the community, hold jobs, and develop social relationships with co-workers and friends). Analogously, the assessment profiles for educationally disadvantaged children resemble those for MR children, with the exception that educationally disadvantaged children have average scores in the area of adaptive behavior.

The profile for an educationally disadvantaged student might look something like this:

SAMPLE ASSESSMENT PROFILE: EDUCATION DISADVANTAGE

INTELLIGENCE: Low performance

ACHIEVEMENT: Low performance

ADAPTIVE BEHAVIOR: Average performance

EMOTIONAL AND BEHAVIORAL CHARACTERISTICS: Variable
   performance

CAVEATS

Many problematic issues must be considered when assessment data are used for labeling and classification. Table 4-2 presents an overall matrix for the test profiles of the exceptional categories discussed. It would be wonderful if the process were as simple and clear-cut as Table 4-2 may seem to imply. Unfortunately, this is not the case. As mentioned previously, some of the causes for the difficulty in using assessment data as a basis for classification are (1) the factors that affect test results; (2) the changing and variable definitions of the categories of exceptional children; (3) the variation among children within these categories; and (4) the different eligibility criteria used by different states.

Factors that Affect Test Results

Virtually all the factors that can affect tests results that were mentioned in Chapter 3 should be considered during labeling and classification. As much care as possible should be taken in eliminating, or at least minimizing, those variables. Proper test selection, adherence to administration and scoring criteria (or documentation of any modification), sensitivity before and during the testing session, and a full understanding of the limitations of tests—that is, their use solely as samples of behavior—are all necessary. Attending to all these factors might seem to be a formidable task, but careful planning and thought beforehand will make the procedure easier.

Problems with Definitions

The differing opinions on definition and prevalence of the various categories of exceptional students make labeling and classification even harder. Most definitions are subjective enough to allow a multitude of interpretations. Hence, a student might be considered learning disabled in one evaluator's opinion, but not in another's. Two other considerations also apply: (1) the periodic changes in definitions and terminology within the field of special education; and (2) the resulting confusion about which classification system to use. There are many examples of changing definitions and their subsequent effect on the use of assessment data for assigning labels. The previously discussed proposed definitions for learning disabilities (by the NJCLD) and emotional/behavioral disorder (by the Task Force of the Mental Health and Special Education Coalition) are appropriate. In addition, the American Association on Mental Retardation (AAMR)—the new name for the AAMD—is finalizing a new definition of mental retardation. The new AAMR definition provides more specific requirements for adaptive behavior deficits as well as other changes that might affect assessment practices.

The result of changing definitions was explored by Taylor (1980), who looked at the systems used in classifying mental retardation. He found that the AAMD classification system was used in only 28 percent of the articles in the journals published by the AAMD between 1973 and

TABLE 4-2 Test-Profile Matrix

	LEARNING DISABLED	MENTALLY RETARDED	EMOTIONALLY DISTURBED	EDUCATIONALLY DISADVANTAGED	NORMAL	GIFTED
Intelligence	A–LA	L	A–LA	L	A	H
Achievement	V–LA	L	LA–V	L	A	H–V
Adaptive Behavior	A–V	L	V	A	A	A–H
Emotional and Behavioral Characteristics	V	V	L	V	A	A–V

A = Average   L = Low   LA = Low-average
H = High   V = Variable

1979. In approximately 27 percent of the articles, the educational classifications *educable* and *trainable* were used, and in 40 percent, the subjects were simply classified as mentally retarded, with no mention of the classification system used. In a follow-up study, Taylor and Kaufman (1992) reported that the use of the AAMD system almost doubled during the decade of the 1980s, although no classification system was used for almost 25 percent of the studies.

Variability within Categories

The variability of test scores of individuals within each category also causes problems. While the matrix shown in Table 4-2 may show the typical pattern of the test scores, in reality, scores vary greatly within each category. For instance, regarding intelligence, learning-disabled students are often thought of as being average; their reported IQs, however, are often below 90. Similarly, emotionally disturbed students should have average IQs, yet as a group, they tend to score in the low-average range, implying that at least some of these students score below average.

Careful analysis of the research into the use of norm-referenced instruments with exceptional students, unfortunately, indicates that many of these instruments have definite limitations. Also, the severity of the children's handicaps obviously will affect their test performance. In general, the information in this chapter, particularly concerning mental retardation and emotional disturbance, relates to the assessment of mildly and moderately handicapped students. In most cases, children who are severely or profoundly retarded or who are severely emotionally disturbed (for example, autistic) are extremely difficult to test in the traditional manner and are usually identified through other means, such as medical diagnosis.

Differences in Eligibility Criteria

As noted previously, there is tremendous variability regarding the specific criteria used to identify special education students. The possibility of a student with a specific label losing (or changing) that label when moving to an area that uses different criteria is one to consider. The different aptitude–achievement discrepancy formulae used to identify LD students is a good example of this point. An individual might be considered LD using one formula and not LD using another, even though the same test scores are used. Another issue to consider is changes in criteria *within a specific* area. For example, Frankenberger and Fronzaglio reported that 40 percent of the states revised their guidelines for identifying LD students between 1988–1990.

Stability of Categories

Because of all the reasons previously discussed, it is very possible that a person's label might change even without differences in eligibility criteria. In a study designed to determine the stability of the categorical designations that an individual might receive, Wolman, Thurlow, and Bruininks (1989) followed over 500 special education students over the course of their school years. They found that approximately 25 percent had at least one change in their labels. They also found that the change was more likely to occur during the secondary years and was more likely to result in a change to a label that most considered to be a more serious handicap.

SUMMARY

Labeling and classification have advocates and critics. It is clear that in many situations the procedures are necessary in order to obtain proper educational services. They might also be viewed as techniques for assigning priority to those who are in need of additional help, although Will (1986) estimated that there are probably another 20 percent of the student population who are not labeled that do need additional help. On the other hand, there are also potential dangers in labeling and classifying children. The issues of overrepresentation of minorities and the possible stigmatizing effects of labels should be considered. Perhaps most important, it should be remembered that assessment for labeling and classifying is not an exact science—not only because of the limitations in the tests themselves, but also because of the ambiguity in the definitions of types of exceptional children.

Too often, people have taken an all-or-none approach to labeling and classification, either believing that any child needing additional help should be labeled, or that no child should be subjected to the process, regardless of the circumstances. Perhaps a more pragmatic approach is in order. If a student is initially identified as needing help, every effort could be made to provide this help by informally adapting the environment, curriculum, or materials (that is, by using prereferral assessment procedures). Doing so might even include consultation with the most appropriate specialists.

If this approach does not work, the teacher should be aware of the implications of labeling and weigh them against the potential value of the services available. In other words, the question, "Is it worth it to put a child through the referral and subsequent assessment process?" should be asked. At times the answer to the question will be yes, and at other times it will be no. The information included in this chapter should help in making those decisions. Figure 4-1 is a flow chart that summarizes the decision-making process involved in labeling and classification.

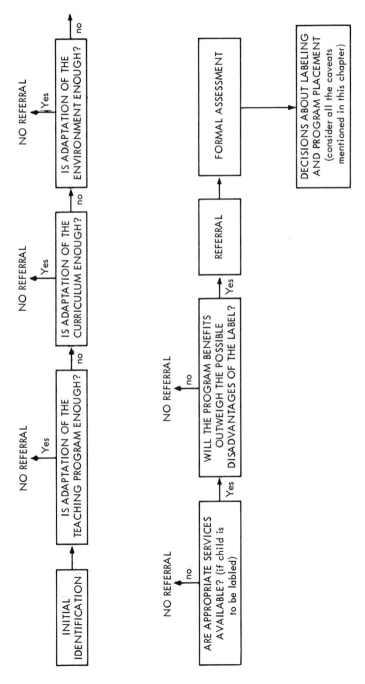

FIGURE 4-1   Steps in the Decision-Making Process

In the past, the terms *assessment* and *labeling* became almost synonymous. Confusing these terms, unfortunately, led to misunderstanding and a partial loss of interest in assessment. The final point in this chapter is to emphasize that labeling and classification are not the only use of assessment; they are, in fact, only a small part of the complete process.

Informal Procedures: Basic Tools for Teachers

Most assessment can and should be incorporated into the students' "routine" daily schedule. In other words, teachers should be aware of the importance of gathering information that is provided during the instructional process. In many cases, such data can be routinely collected through *observation* (discussed in Chapter 5) and *analysis of work products* (discussed in Chapter 6). In other cases, the teacher can use the curriculum or a student's Individual Education Program (IEP) to develop a *criterion-referenced instrument* (discussed in Chapter 6) or a curriculum-based assessment instrument (discussed in Chapter 7). The administration of these types of tests provides the teacher with relevant information on which to base instructional decisions.

As noted in Chapter 2, all of these informal procedures are important *throughout* the assessment process. They are crucial to the prereferral component and can provide much-needed information for developing prereferral intervention programs and/or documenting a referral of a student for special education. Conversely, these approaches are invaluable in developing and evaluating educational programs *after* a student has been identified as needing special education services (post-referral component).

For each technique described in this section the following information is provided:

1. A summary matrix that presents information about specific instruments and techniques in a format allowing easy comparison of the instruments for suggested use and target population. The matrix also includes a statement of any special considerations of which a user should be aware. In addition, for each technique, the matrix gives the educational

relevance for exceptional students. The matrices are directly related to the assessment model proposed in Chapter 2.

2. An introduction box for each technique identifying the suggested use and the suggested user.

After reading Part Two you should be able to:

1. *Identify the components involved in observational assessment, including the appropriate recording procedures*

2. *Identify the steps involved in developing a criterion-referenced test*

3. *Identify the steps involved in conducting an error analysis in the areas of reading, mathematics, and spelling*

4. *Identify the steps involved in developing a curriculum-based assessment instrument*

5. *Identify the similarities and differences between curriculum-based assessment and curriculum-based measurement*

5

Observational Assessment

INSTRUMENTS/PROCEDURES INCLUDED

STUDENT OBSERVATION—INFORMAL SYSTEMS
- Goals of Observation
- An Observational Model
- Other Uses of Data

STUDENT OBSERVATION—FORMAL SYSTEMS

OBSERVATION OF THE ENVIRONMENT

Observation is undoubtedly the most pervasive and widely used method of assessment. Virtually every second spent during a day in the classroom yields a tremendous amount of observational data. The key, however, is to use the observational data in a systematic and meaningful way. As mentioned in Chapter 2, the collection of prereferral information is important in determining the course and method of evaluation. Observational data certainly fit into this category of prereferral assessment. Such data can be used to determine and evaluate a teaching or behavioral program that in turn can be used to identify those students who will need more in-depth formal evaluation. Observation can also be very helpful in developing and monitoring Individual Education Programs (IEPs) for both academic and nonacademic behavior. On the other hand, observation of the educational *environment* can also provide important information for making educational decisions.

Observation is perhaps the most objective method of assessment. In fact, it is generally thought of as the most direct method of obtaining assessment data with the least amount of inference by the evaluator. Keller (1980) noted that "observation involves description of behaviors which requires little, if any, inference by observers. Further, the use of observation involves direct measurement of behaviors in settings of concern to the child being referred and of concern to the referral agent. The result of its use is a more direct and close relationship between assessment and intervention, with a minimum, or at least reduction, of inferential leaps relative to a reliance upon standardized tests solely" (p. 21).

When most people think of observation as an assessment tool, they think about observing student behavior to obtain information that will aid in educational decision making. However, as noted previously, observation of the educational *or* instructional environment can also provide valuable information.

Observational techniques can be classified as either formal or informal. Formal approaches include observational packages that usually include specific coding and scoring systems. Informal approaches—by far more commonly used—include observation with the observer already present in the setting; observation with an outside observer in the setting; and observation with the observer not present in the setting. These types of informal approaches are particularly relevant when student behavior is being observed.

STUDENT OBSERVATION: INFORMAL SYSTEMS

WHY USE?
Screening and identification; informal determination and evaluation of teaching programs and strategies; documentation of need for further evaluation or referral; development and evaluation of IEPs

WHO SHOULD USE?
Primarily teachers; also school psychologists and parents

In the most widely used of the three informal procedures, the observer is already present in the natural environment. In this approach, many times the teacher is the primary evaluator or observer. It is also possible that peers—or even the target child—could perform these observations. Theoretically, the primary advantage of observation by someone who is already present is that since no external observer is involved, the observed child should "act naturally." Observation of the child's behavior in the natural setting, with no changes in the schedule or routine or environment, should give a truer measure of the problem behavior. This procedure also has disadvantages. First, it is often difficult to manage (or find) the time to collect observational data. This is particularly true for the teacher. It is possible to have teacher's aides collect this information, but again, the time element is extremely crucial.

In the second type of informal procedure, there is an external or outside observer in the natural setting. The observer can be a psychologist, parent, volunteer, principal, or any school staff member who does not routinely work with the child in that setting (usually the classroom). The advantage of this procedure is that it allows the teacher to continue in the routine daily schedule. The observers can work at times that are appropriate both for the child and for themselves. The disadvantage of this approach is that it may cause reactivity (the effect of an observer on the behavior of the observed individual) that might bias the results.

Many researchers (including Boehm & Weinberg, 1987; Repp, Nieminen, Olinger, and Brusca, 1988) have discussed the issue of reactivity and its effects on observational assessment. Haynes (1978), in fact, indicated a number of ways in which reactivity could be reduced. These included decreasing the conspicuousness of the observer and minimizing the interaction between the observed person and the observer.

The third informal procedure involves an observer who is not present in the natural setting. This approach usually includes an artificial apparatus such as a one-way mirror or a videotape, or audiotape that can later be transcribed. The advantage of this approach is that no observer is actually seen by the child, so that reactivity becomes less of an issue. The apparatus itself; however, can have some reactive effect on the child (Boehm & Weinberg, 1987). Obviously, the less obtrusive the apparatus appears, the more "naturally" a child will behave. This approach can be time consuming (particularly using tapes) or restrictive (not every classroom has one-way mirrors).

With all these informal observation procedures, it is extremely important to obtain reliable, valid information. For maximum reliability in obtaining information, observers should use specific operational definitions and collect interrater reliability data—that is, more than one person should observe the behavior until all observers reach agreement. For maximum validity, information should be collected by observing the behavior in the environment in which it is a problem. Also, the observation must measure a representative sample of the person's behavior. In general, ensuring the reliability and validity of informal observation is often overlooked. This is an unfortunate oversight that could have a negative effect on the decisions made about the observed student.

Goals of Observing Student Behavior

Keller (1980) delineated four general uses of observation. Those were the direct assessment of problems in the setting of concern, the monitoring of an intervention program, a measurement of the effectiveness and generalization of an intervention, and the enhancement of collaborative consultation among school personnel. Cartwright and Cartwright (1984) outlined more specific uses of observation for educational decision making.

Those included (1) early detection of problems; (2) making decisions about entry behaviors; and (3) making instructional decisions. Another important goal of observation that really incorporates many of the previously mentioned uses is to provide a model to allow teachers to increase, decrease, or maintain certain academic or social behaviors of their students.

Early detection of problems

The use of observation to detect problems is an informal way of screening. It simply means that the observer notes that a student is starting to experience difficulty in some area. This observation is usually based on his or her knowledge of "typical" or "expected" development or on a comparison to other individuals who have similar characteristics (for example, same age and sex). This can lead to more formal assessment to determine the extent and possible cause of the problem.

Making decisions about entry behaviors

In a sense, making decisions about entry behaviors is similar to determining a student's current level of performance. In other words, it allows an observer to determine what behaviors in a given area a student already possesses. This requires that the observer must critically analyze the student's needs to determine which behaviors should be observed. This usually involves some type of ecological assessment, or the analysis of the environments within which the student exists or will exist to determine those behaviors that are necessary to function as independently as possible. These might be academic skills for younger, mildly handicapped students, more functional "survival" skills, such as recognizing danger signs or completing job applications, for older handicapped students, or independent living skills for students who have more severe handicaps. By determining a student's entry level in specified areas, the observer will have a good idea where to begin a more in-depth evaluation.

Making instructional decisions

Another use of observation is to help make instructional decisions. As Cartwright and Cartwright (1984) noted, "If you have been able to collect information about a child's history of successes with different instructional materials, then you are better able to select appropriate teaching methods and materials that can be used with some assurance of effectiveness with the child" (p. 17). Using observation for this purpose is very important to plan for prereferral intervention strategies.

Student Observation: A Model

One very important goal of observational assessment is to provide information that will enable a teacher to increase, decrease, or maintain specific academic and nonacademic behaviors. This can be easily accomplished if a fourstep model is followed. Those four steps are: (1) careful identification of the target behavior; (2) precise and appropriate measurement of the target behavior; (3) systematic introduction of a(n) intervention/remedial program; and (4) evaluation of the effectiveness of the program.

Identification of the target behavior

Chances are that the success of any program designed to change behavior will depend largely on how well the target behavior is defined. It is extremely important that behaviors be identified in terms that are precise, observable, and measurable. Terms such as "aggression," "hyperactivity," "poor self-concept," and "academically slow" are too vague and general to have any practical value. These terms also mean different things to different people, making it difficult to obtain reliable measurement. As Taylor and Marholin (1980) noted, "Behaviors presented in terms of traits, personality characteristics, and labels are too general and open to idiosyncratic interpretation to be of much value. If behaviors are defined objectively, few or no inferences are necessary to detect behaviors when they occur" (p. 273). For example, "aggression" might be defined as "strikes out at others with fists or objects" or "verbally abuses others by using curse words or a loud tone of voice." Similarly, "poor self-concept" might be defined as "makes negative statements about self," and "hyperactivity" might be considered as "gets out of seat at inappropriate times." In the above examples, the behaviors are precise, observable, and measurable; yet even these could be still further defined to include the setting and a clarification of terms. For example, it might be acceptable for a child to raise his or her voice on the playground. Or it might be necessary to indicate at which times or in which situations getting out of a seat is considered inappropriate. In every instance when the behavior is defined, the student, the situation, and the anticipated goal or outcome should be kept in mind. For every child labeled "distractible," the term "distractibility" might be defined differently. You should strive to be specific enough so that if other people were to observe and measure the behavior they would be able to obtain the same or similar results. It is also important to be aware of the possibility of "observer drift," a situation in which the observer gradually shifts from the initial definition of the target behavior (Alberto & Troutman, 1990; Repp et al., 1988).

Measurement of the target behavior

The accurate, careful recording of behavioral data is extremely important. Informal observational assessment requires the evaluator to develop and implement a unique measurement system. Typically, lack of time or misunderstanding of the importance of objective data leads to the use of some type of subjective system. Subjective systems include evaluations such as, "John seems to be doing much better in the area of self-help skills," or "Sally appears to be getting out of her seat less often than she used to."

Observational data are usually recorded as frequently as possible, ideally daily, thus giving the observer a much better idea of the changes in behavior as a function of environmental interventions and of the teaching program. The observational data are usually recorded on a graph or chart, thereby presenting a visual display of the change in behavior over time.

Initially, data are collected when no specific intervention program is in effect (or when the current, unsuccessful program is in effect). These preintervention data are called *baseline data* and correspond roughly to a *pretest* in traditional assessment measures. Usually baseline data are collected until they stabilize or show a consistent pattern. If a consistent pattern does not emerge, further definition of the target behavior might be necessary.

Before initiating an observational assessment, it is necessary to choose both the recording devices and the recording procedures that will be used. The choice of recording procedure is particularly important and is largely dependent on the type of behavior that is being observed. The general issue of recording devices and several specific recording procedures are discussed next.

Recording devices

Three basic tools are necessary to observe and record behavior: a timer, a counter, and a graph or chart. For all the observational approaches, the issue of time is important. Certain recording procedures, however, require more exact timekeeping devices. The most common are the stopwatch, the clock or watch with a second hand, and the calculator with a stopwatch or timer. Devices for counting behaviors include wrist counters, abacus beads, and the basic pencil-and-paper technique. The wrist counter is worn like a watch. By pushing a button on the counter, the observer keeps a cumulative tally. Abacus beads can also be worn on the wrist. They consist of rows of beads that represent place values (ones, tens, hundreds). Pencil-and-paper tallies are widely used. There are a limitless number of pencil-and-paper techniques, although Tukey (1977) developed a standard system. Alessi (1980) described Tukey's system:

> In this system, dots and lines are used to tally counts. The first count is represented by a single dot (.), the second by two dots (. .), the third by three dots (. :) and the fourth by four dots(: :). The dots are placed so as to outline a box. The numbers five, six, seven and eight are then represented by completing the box sides with lines, in any order: Five = **I :**, six = **L:**, seven = **LJ**, eight = **⊐**, nine = **◲**, and ten = **◲**. Fewer errors in both tabulation and summation are likely using this system as compared with others (such as 1, 11, 111, 1111). The dot and box system also takes much less space on the protocol. (pp. 36–37)

More expensive and sophisticated devices are also available. For example, Datamyte (Electro General Corporation) and MORE (Observational Systems, Inc.) are hand-held data collectors that include a measure of time and a counter. These systems also have solid-state memory and optional features that allow interface with a computer for data storage and analysis. These instruments are relatively expensive and overly sophisticated for everyday classroom use.

The last basic tool is the graph or chart, which offers a visual representation of observed behaviors. In the most common graph the data are plotted along a vertical line (ordinate) and a horizontal line (abscissa). The ordinate usually represents the unit of behavioral measure (such as frequency or percentage), and the abscissa represents the unit of time (Alberto & Troutman, 1990). Figure 5-1 demonstrates this approach. Graphs such as this are usually drawn on plain or graph paper. More sophisticated charts are also available. One example is the Standard Behavior Chart (SBC) that is used in precision teaching. The SBC is a semilogarithmic chart that is based on a ratio rather than an ordinal scale (Figure 5-2). Essentially, this means that the vertical axis is scaled proportionally so that, for instance, the distance between 1 and 5 is the same as the difference between 100 and 500. This allows the plotting of behavior that occurs as frequently as 1000 times per minute or as infre-

FIGURE 5-1   **Example of a Graph**

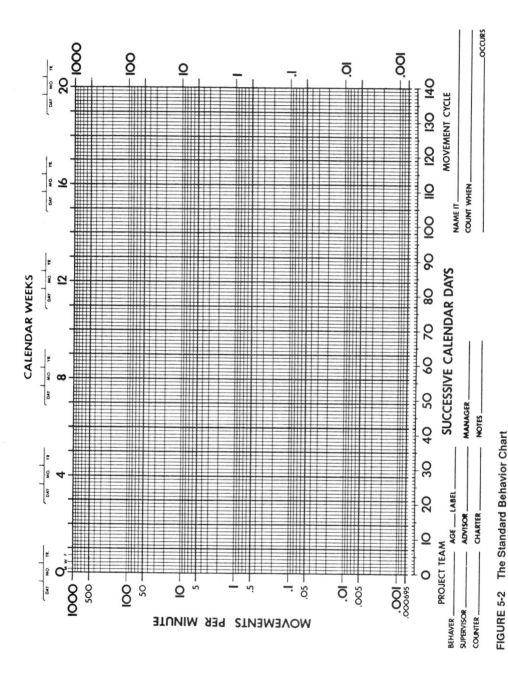

FIGURE 5-2   The Standard Behavior Chart

From Behavior Research Company, Kansas City, Kansas. Reprinted by permission.

quently as one time in 1000 minutes on the same 9 1/2-in. x 11-in. chart. The SBC uses *frequency* (defined as number of behaviors divided by number of minutes observed) as its primary measure. The advantage of a system such as this is that it is interpretable by all who are familiar with the chart (an advantage that is rare when individuals develop their own systems). The SBC also allows a standard measure of learning rate (called *celeration*) and variability (called *bounce*).

Recording procedures

One very important issue is the choice of recording procedures. Clearly, certain recording procedures are more appropriate for certain types of behavior. A description of each type of recording procedure follows, including examples of appropriate use.

Event recording.   Event recording, sometimes referred to as frequency recording, involves counting the number of behaviors that occur within a certain time limit—for instance, the number of times Bill gets out of his seat during a 50-minute science period, or the number of correct problems Alex completes during a 15-minute mathematics session. By including both the number of behaviors and the time interval, it is possible to convert the data to a standard period. This is accomplished by using the following formula:

$$\text{frequency} = \frac{\text{number of behaviors observed}}{\text{number of minutes or hours spent observing}}$$

This allows the observer to record for different time periods without misrepresenting the data. For instance, suppose a teacher noted that Karl was getting more aggressive because he kicked his playmate 7 times during recess on Monday and 10 times on Tuesday and Wednesday. If, in fact, recess was 20 minutes on Monday and 30 minutes on Tuesday and Wednesday, then Karl decreased, not increased, his frequency of kicking.

Event recording is best used when the behavior has a discrete beginning and ending and when occurrences can be easily counted, particularly if a permanent product is left (such as the number of windows broken or the number of words spelled correctly). It is not a good method to use if the behavior occurs at an extremely high rate (for example, pencil tapping) or for an extended period of time (for example, staring out the windows). The example of Sandy demonstrates the use of event recording.

EXAMPLE: SANDY

Mr. Harper, a third-grade teacher, is concerned about his student Sandy, who is constantly getting into trouble on the way to the lunchroom. Sandy will speak to anyone and everyone she sees, even though she has been told to remain quiet while in the hallway. Mr. Harper decided to implement a behavior-change program aimed at decreasing her talking episodes. The following preintervention or baseline data were collected:

	M	*Tu*	*W*	*Th*	*F*
Time observed (in minutes)	4	8	6	5	7
Number of behaviors	3	9	7	8	7
Frequency	0.75	1.13	1.17	1.60	1.00

Next, he implemented his behavior-change program, and the following data were collected:

	M	*Tu*	*W*	*Th*	*F*
Time observed (in minutes)	7	8	6	7	5
Number of behaviors	7	4	3	2	1
Frequency	1.0	0.50	0.50	0.29	0.20

Figure 5-3 is a graph of these data.

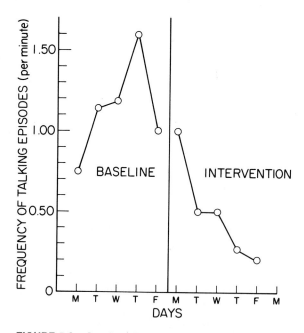

FIGURE 5-3   Graph of Event-Recording Data

Duration recording.   Suppose you had a student who would get out of his or her seat at the beginning of an instructional period and stay out until the end. In this case, the frequency of the behavior would be irrelevant, and event recording would not be the most appropriate method for measuring the behavior. For a problem in which the important factor is the amount of time a person spends engaging in the target behavior, duration recording should be used. Because duration measures require constant attention and monitoring of the time, a stopwatch or clock with a second hand is almost a must. This need for a constant monitoring of the time is a major disadvantage of duration recording, and it usually dictates that only one child at a time be observed. The example of Jimmy represents the use of duration recording.

EXAMPLE: JIMMY

Mrs. Lambert was concerned that her student Jimmy would frequently be off-task during individual seat work. Typically, he would start his work but lose interest rather quickly. At that point, he would tap his pencil, look out the window, or in some other way avoid completing the task. Mrs. Lambert decided to implement a program designed to increase Jimmy's on-task behavior. She decided to measure the amount of time Jimmy actually spent on-task. She defined on-task behavior as keeping his eyes on his paper. She decided to observe him for a 10-minute period each day. The following baseline data were recorded:

	M	Tu	W	Th	F
Minutes spent on-task	3	2	6	4	5

She then implemented her behavioral program with Jimmy, and it resulted in the following data:

	M	Tu	W	Th	F
Minutes spent on-task	6	7	9	10	10

Figure 5-4 is the visual representation of these data.

Latency recording.   Suppose you had a student who typically wandered around the room and visited with his friends even after the bell rang, signaling him to sit in his chair. In this situation, both event recording and duration recording would be inappropriate. Latency recording would be the recording procedure of choice. Latency recording measures the amount of time that elapses between the signaling of a stimulus (such as the sound of the bell) and the initiation of a behavior (sitting in a chair). Latency recording, like duration recording, has the basic disadvan-

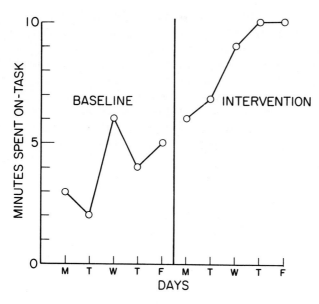

FIGURE 5-4   Graph of Duration-Recording Data

tage of requiring constant attention to the time. The example of Les demonstrates the use of latency recording.

EXAMPLE: LES

Mrs. Jones was concerned about one of her students, Les. When she instructed the class to begin solving written math problems, Les would drop his pencil, stare out the window, or demonstrate other avoidance behaviors. She wanted to develop a program to minimize the amount of time he took before he started writing his answers. She therefore chose a latency-recording procedure to measure the amount of time it took him to start writing after she gave the instructions. The following baseline data were collected:

	M	Tu	W	Th	F	M
Number of seconds elapsed	42	18	36	41	39	44

She then developed a program for Les and put it into effect. The following data were then recorded:

Tu	W	Th	F	M	Tu	W	Th
25	15	20	14	12	10	10	5

Figure 5-5 shows these data.

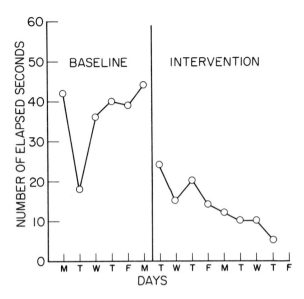

FIGURE 5-5 **Graph of Latency-Recording Data**

Interval recording.   Another useful procedure for recording observations is interval recording. Interval recording measures the occurrences
or nonoccurrences of the target behavior during specified time intervals
marked off within an overall observation period. This procedure is appropriate for behaviors that occur at a high frequency or for extended periods
of time, and it indicates the pattern of behavior. Suppose, for instance,
that Susan is off-task a considerable amount of time during her 5-minute
workbook session. Interval recording would make it possible to determine
if a pattern exists (such as primarily at the beginning or end of the
session) as well as to specify the percentage of off-task behavior. (Of
course, the term *off-task* would need to be carefully defined.) To set up an
interval-recording system, the overall observation period can be divided
into smaller time intervals. A 5-minute period divided into 15-second
intervals, for example, would yield 20 time intervals. The observer simply
indicates whether or not the behavior occurs during any portion of each
time interval. It should be noted that the length of the interval is important. For example, Repp et al. (1988) noted that smaller intervals are
more accurate than large intervals. Typically, a plus is given for the
presence of the behavior and a minus for the absence. In this example, the
target behavior (off-task behavior) was observed during the 1st, 2nd, 3rd,
5th, 6th, 7th, 18th, 19th, and 20th intervals:

+	+	+	−	+	+	+	−	−	−
−	−	−	−	−	−	−	+	+	+

These data indicate that the student was off-task during approximately 45 percent of the intervals, primarily during the beginning and end of the session.

Momentary time sampling.   Momentary time sampling is similar to interval recording. During momentary time sampling, the individual is observed at a given time (for example, every 15 seconds). The observer must indicate whether or not the target behavior is exhibited *at those particular times.* One advantage of both interval recording and momentary time sampling is that more than one child can be observed at one time. One potential disadvantage of both interval recording and momentary time sampling is that some type of cue must signal the time to record. A number of cuing systems are available, such as a kitchen timer or an audio tape with a signal prerecorded at certain intervals. Another disadvantage is that only limited conclusions can be drawn on the behavior recorded. For example, it might be possible that the behavior occurs frequently but not at the specific time that it was observed (Alberto & Troutman, 1990).

Introduction of intervention programs

As noted in the previous examples of Sandy, Jimmy, and Les, after a specific behavior or skill has been carefully identified, defined, and recorded, it is time to systematically introduce some type of intervention or remedial program in an attempt to change the behavior in the desired direction. Using whatever information is available, including observational data, the teacher (or other change agent) will make the decision on the nature of the intervention procedure. The key is to attempt to demonstrate that changes in the target behavior are related to the introduction of the intervention program. If an effective procedure can be found for a specific behavior for a given individual, that same procedure might also be effective for other behaviors in the same individual or for the same behavior with different individuals. It is for this reason that it is important to be specific and not attempt to change too many behaviors or introduce a "shotgun approach" to intervention. It is possible that changes in the behavior(s) might occur, but the value of the data for assessment purposes will be minimized.

Evaluation of the intervention program

This is a very important step in the observational model and, coincidentally, one that is often overlooked. It essentially involves recording (using the same procedures as were used in the collection of baseline data) to determine if the initiation of the intervention program had an effect on the target behavior. If change occurs in the desired direction, the information can be used to plan future instructional programs. If the behavior does not change, or changes in the opposite direction, it signals the need for trying a different approach, or perhaps the need to identify a different target behavior that might be within the student's behavioral repertoire. For example, it might be possible that a target behavior identified for a student might be too "difficult," and an "easier" or prerequisite behavior would be more appropriate as a target.

The previously described SBC is used in a system called *precision teaching* (Lindsley, 1964), a system that incorporates the four-step observation model to make instructional decisions. Precision teaching usually involves six steps. They are:

1. Pinpoint the exact behavior (academic or social) that you wish to change.
2. Record the number of behaviors observed and the number of minutes spent observing.
3. Calculate the frequency by dividing the number of behaviors by the number of minutes.
4. Plot these frequencies on the SBC.
5. Make a systematic change in the environment or instructional program.
6. Use the SBC regularly to observe the effects of the instructional or environmental changes on the pinpointed behavior.

Steps 1, 2, 5, and 6 are the same as those described in the four-step model of identifying the target behavior, measuring the target behavior, introducing the intervention program, and evaluating the intervention program.

Other Uses of Student Observational Data

Observational data can be used for a variety of purposes. In addition to those previously described, another purpose is to document that a problem exists. One procedure for this purpose is called the *referred-student/comparison-student* approach (as in Walker & Hops, 1976). In such an approach, data are collected simultaneously on the target subject as well as on a control subject who is the same age and sex and who is not experiencing difficulties. Such data collection can lead to the development of "local micronorms" that reflect the degree to which certain behaviors are considered acceptable by the teacher or other observer (Alessi, 1980). For instance, suppose a teacher was concerned about a student's (Karen) out-of-seat behavior. Using a momentary time sampling, it would be possible to observe Karen as well as another student to determine their percentages of out-of-seat behavior. It would also be possible to collect this data for the entire class (that is, percentage of children out of seat at any given time). The following data might be collected:

	OUT OF SEAT
Karen	85%
Control subject	5%
Class	3%

These data can be used to help decide the relative inappropriateness of Karen's behavior.

Similarly, Deno (1980) described a system using peer sampling. This system involved, first, the recording of four key behaviors (noisemaking, out-of-seat activity, physical contact or destruction of objects, and off-task activity) of a target subject and a peer and, second, a comparison of the data. In any approach such as this, however, the significance assigned to the magnitude of the discrepancy between the data for the target subject and the data for peers must be subjective.

STUDENT OBSERVATION: FORMAL SYSTEMS

In addition to the informal observation procedures that can be used to assess student needs and instructional programs, there are also more formal observational systems available. These systems usually include some type of coding or notational procedure so that behaviors can be categorized in some meaningful way. Many formal systems also allow for the coding of behavioral interactions rather than the behavior of the student in isolation. For example, the Behavioral Coding System (Patterson, Reid, Jones, & Conger, 1975) includes 14 behavior categories. In this system, numbers are assigned to the target child and those who interact with him. For example, 2YE*-1IG* might represent an interaction in which the mother yelled and the target child ignored the outburst. The advantage of formal systems is that they allow for greater communication among individuals observing a student. For example, if a student was being observed at home by his parents and at school by his teacher, the coded results would allow each of the observers to understand what was happening in the other environment.

Other systems have been developed exclusively for the school environment but retain the coding systems for behavior interactions. One example is the Manual for Coding Discrete Behaviors in the School Setting (Cobb & Ray, 1975). In this system, there are 19 behavior categories; both the behaviors of the target child and his/her peers are alternately observed in 6-second intervals. Figure 5-6 shows an example of the

Observer _____   Sheet No. _____ Subject _____

Date _____   Academic Activity _____

Structured _____ Unstructured _____ Group _____ Individual _____ Transitional _____

		Structured	Unstructured				Group					Individual			Transitional				
Subject	AP	CO	TT+	IP+	VO	AT	PN	DS	DI	NY	NC	PL	TT−	IP−	IL	SS	LO	NA	IT
Peer 1	AP	CO	TT+	IP+	VO	(AT)	PN	DS	DI	NY	NC	PL	TT−	(IP−)	IL	SS	LO	NA	IT
Subject	AP	CO	TT+	IP+	VO	(AT)	PN	DS	DI	NY	NC	PL	TT−	IP−	IL	SS	LO	NA	IT
Peer 2	AP	CO	TT+	IP+	VO	AT	PN	DS	DI	NY	NC	PL	TT−	IP−	IL	SS	(LO)	NA	IT
Subject	AP	CO	(TT+)	IP+	VO	AT	PN	DS	DI	NY	NC	PL	TT−	IP−	IL	SS	LO	NA	IT
Peer 3	AP	CO	TT+	IP+	VO	(AT)	PN	DS	DI	NY	NC	PL	TT−	IP−	IL	SS	LO	NA	IT
Subject	AP	CO	TT+	IP+	VO	AT	PN	DS	DI	NY	NC	PL	TT−	IP−	IL	SS	LO	NA	IT
Peer 4	AP	CO	TT+	IP+	VO	AT	PN	DS	DI	(NY)	NC	PL	TT−	IP−	IL	SS	LO	NA	IT
Subject	AP	CO	TT+	IP+	VO	AT	PN	DS	DI	NY	NC	PL	TT−	IP−	(IL)	SS	LO	NA	IT
Peer 5	AP	CO	TT+	IP+	VO	AT	(PN)	DS	DI	NY	NC	PL	TT−	IP−	IL	SS	LO	NA	IT

FIGURE 5-6   Example of Coded Behavior Interactions

interaction for the following sequence. (Note: IP– = inappropriate interaction with peers, AT = attending, TT+ = appropriate talking with teacher, LO = looking around, NY = noisy, IL = inappropriate locale, and PN = physical negative.)

Albert is a fourth-grade student in a self-contained learning-disability classroom with five other students. He is involved in a structured individual task of using the dictionary to define certain vocabulary words. The following sequence is observed during the 6-second intervals:

1. Albert is talking with a student about a television show. The student responds.
2. Peer 1 is looking at the dictionary.
3. Albert is looking at the dictionary.
4. Peer 2 is staring out the window.
5. Albert is asking the teacher about alphabetizing.
6. Peer 3 is writing a definition.
7. Albert is banging his dictionary on the desk. The teacher tells him to stop.
8. Peer 4 is reading the dictionary.
9. Albert leaves his seat to visit a friend. His friend gets mad and tears a page out of the dictionary.
10. Peer 5 is pulling the hair of his friend.

OBSERVATION OF THE ENVIRONMENT

WHY USE?
Analysis of instructional environment

WHO SHOULD USE?
Teachers

Although assessment of student behavior is the primary use of observational data, the assessment of the student's instructional environment is another role of observation. Both types of observation have a common goal of improving instructional practices that will positively affect the student.

According to Cartwright and Cartwright (1984), there are four components of the instructional environment that should be considered. These components (which actually interact constantly) are teacher behaviors, space and objects in the environment, time variables, and the management and teaching procedures that are used within the instructional environment. For example, it might be possible to observe teachers and provide feedback on their behavior. It might be observed that a teacher is inadvertently reinforcing a student behavior that is annoying by attending to it whenever it occurs. It might also be possible that a student is much more distractible when placed in an open classroom setting, thus implying that moving him to a more structured setting would be advisable. Time variables are important in setting up schedules that optimize the chance for student success.

While most observation of instructional environments is done informally, and sometimes inconsistently, there are a few formalized approaches/instruments that have been designed to achieve this goal. For example, the Stanford Research Institute Classroom Observation Instrument (Stallings, 1977) was developed to measure the relationship between the instructional environment and student behavior. Both the physical environment and the interaction between student and teacher is examined. More recently, Ysseldyke and Christenson (1987a) developed *The Instructional Environment Scale* (TIES), which is described as a comprehensive methodology for assessing an individual student's instruction. The authors state that TIES is not a teacher-evaluation tool, a norm-referenced test, or an instrument to compare schools or school districts (Ysseldyke & Christenson, 1987b). They further describe the 12 components that are a part of TIES. Information is gathered through observation of the student in a classroom setting and through interviews with the student and the student's teacher. The following is a list of the components and an example of the type of information that is evaluated:

Instructional Presentation—Instruction is clear and effective; directions are presented in sufficient detail.

Classroom Environment—Classroom is positive and supportive; time is used effectively.

Teacher Expectations—Expectations of student performance are realistic yet high.

Cognitive Emphasis—Thinking skills necessary to complete tasks are communicated to the student.

Motivational Techniques—Teacher uses good strategies to increase student interest and effort.

Relevant Practice—Student is given adequate opportunities for practice.

Academic Engaged Time—Student is actively engaged in tasks and is redirected by teacher if not.

Informed Feedback—Student receives appropriate feedback for correct and incorrect performance.

Adaptive Instruction—Curriculum is modified to meet student needs.

Progress Evaluation—Teacher uses direct and frequent measures of student progress.

Instructional Planning—Appropriate instruction is based on assessment data.

Student Understanding—Student knows what to do in the classroom.

SUMMARY MATRIX

The summary for all chapters that describe instruments or techniques will be in the form of a *summary matrix*. This matrix will allow the reader to compare and contrast the instruments or techniques in terms of their suggested use, target population, and relevance for exceptional students. The matrix includes the following specific components (and their definitions):

A. Suggested use
1. *Screening and initial identification (prereferral)*—use of assessment data to identify individuals who need further evaluation, remedial help, or both.
2. *Informal determination and evaluation of teaching programs and strategies (prereferral)*—use of assessment data (1) to assist the regular-education teacher in identifying and evaluating appropriate objectives and teaching strategies, (2) to help document the need for a formal referral, and (3) to assist in the development of IEPs for students who receive special education .
3. *Determination of current performance level and educational need (postreferral)*—use of assessment data to determine (1) general areas in which a student needs remediation or assistance, (2) strengths and weaknesses, and (3) possible teaching strategies and approaches.
4. *Decisions about classification and program placement (postreferral)*—use of assessment data to determine special-education eligibility and to identify the most appropriate program setting for the student.
5. *Development of IEP (postreferral)*—use of assessment data to identify annual goals.
6. *Objectives of IEP (postreferral)*—use of assessment data to identify appropriate objectives.
7. *Evaluation of IEP(postreferral)*—use of assessment data to monitor student progress toward meeting the identified goals and objectives.

B. Target population
1. *Mild/moderate*—refers to individuals whose special needs are usually met within a mainstreamed classroom, resource room, or self-contained classroom. This category may include mildly or moderately mentally retarded children as well as learning-disabled children and behaviorally disordered or other disabled individuals whose problems are not considered to be "severe."
2. *Severe/profound*—refers to individuals whose special needs are usually met within a self-contained classroom, special school, or residential setting. This category may include severely or profoundly retarded, multiply handicapped, sensory impaired (blind or deaf), or other disabled individuals who have significant impairments.
3. *Preschool*—includes individuals from birth through approximately age 5.
4. *Elementary age*—includes individuals from ages 6 through approximately 12 (kindergarten through grade 6).

     5. *Secondary age*—includes individuals from approximately ages 13 through 18 or 20 (grade 7 through grade 12).

     6. *Adult*—includes individuals who because of their age no longer receive public-school services (usually above 18 or 21).

C. *Special considerations*—includes a brief statement of any particular advantage or disadvantage, technical characteristic, or other consideration that is relevant to each instrument or technique.

D. *Educational relevance for exceptional students*—provides a rating of the relative applicability of each instrument or technique for exceptional students. The ratings are "very limited," "limited," "adequate," "useful," and "very useful." This rating is based on information such as the type of data yielded, the technical adequacy of an instrument, and research related to the instrument or technique.

| Instrument or Technique | Suggested Use | | | | | | | Target Population | | | | | | Special Considerations | Educational Relevance for Exceptional Students |
| | Prereferral | | | Postreferral | | | | | | | | | | | |
	Screening and Initial Identification	Informal Determination and Evaluation of Teaching Programs and Strategies	Determination of Current Performance Level and Educational Need	Decisions about Classification and Program Placement	IEP Goals	IEP Objectives	IEP Evaluation	Mild/Moderate	Severe/Profound	Preschool	Elementary Age	Secondary Age	Adult		
Event Recording	X	X	X		X	X	X	X	X	X	X	X	X	Use when the frequency of a behavior is important; behavior should have a discrete beginning and ending	useful
Duration Recording	X	X	X		X	X	X	X	X	X	X	X	X	Use when the amount of time during which behavior occurs is important; requires constant monitoring	useful
Latency Recording	X	X	X		X	X	X	X	X	X	X	X	X	Requires constant monitoring	useful
Interval Recording	X	X	X		X	X	X	X	X	X	X	X	X	Use for behaviors that occur at a high frequency or for an extended time	useful
Momentary Time Sampling	X	X	X		X	X	X	X	X	X	X	X	X	More than one person can be observed at a time; requires a cue to signal when to record	useful
Behavioral Coding System	X	X					X	X	X	X	X	X	X	Use in home and school; codes behavioral interactions; has a complex scoring system	adequate
Manual for Coding Discrete Behaviors in the School Setting	X	X					X	X	X	X	X	X	X	Use in the school setting; requires the observation of the target subject and control subjects	adequate
The Instructional Environment Scale		X						X			X	X		Provides qualitative evaluation of learning environment; also looks at teacher behaviors	useful

6

Criterion-Referenced
Testing and
Error Analysis

AREAS COVERED

CRITERION-REFERENCED TESTS
- An Overview of Principles
- Procedures
- An Example

WHAT TO TEACH VERSUS HOW TO TEACH
- Error Analysis

CRITERION-REFERENCED TESTS

WHY USE?
Determination and evaluation of objectives and teaching strategies; gathering of prereferral information; development and evaluation of IEPs

WHO SHOULD USE?
Teachers

When people refer to tests used in schools, they usually think of traditional norm-referenced instruments such as achievement tests or intelligence tests. These instruments can be very helpful in making certain types of decisions including screening, eligibility, and the determination of strengths and weaknesses. There are some shortcomings of these types of traditional assessment instruments, however (Gable, 1990). As noted in Chapter 2, norm-referenced tests (NRTs) show how an individual performs compared to others but provide little information that can be used for the development of specific instructional programs. The type of instrument typically used for those decisions are criterion-referenced tests (CRTs). Gronlund (1988) noted that whereas there are many similarities in the development of NRTs and CRTs, there are also some basic points of difference. For example, in an NRT the intended learning outcome may be described in either general or specific terms, while in a CRT the intended outcome tends to be described in more specific terms. Second, an NRT usually covers a broad range of areas with few items per area, while a CRT usually measures a more limited domain with numerous items per area. Finally, an NRT is designed so that the items can *discriminate* among students while a CRT is designed so that the items will *describe* student performance on specific learning tasks.

An Overview of Principles

CRTs are particularly helpful in determining *what* to teach. For this reason, they are frequently used to determine appropriate goals and objectives for a student. Many CRTs have been developed and published commercially and will be discussed elsewhere in this textbook. This chapter, however, will focus on the principles and procedures that teachers/diagnosticians can use to develop their own CRTs. As mentioned in Chapter 2, CRTs focus more on an individual's mastery of content (for example, John can complete 90 percent of his two-digit addition problems correctly) than on a comparison of that individual with others (for example, John is at the 63rd percentile in arithmetic).

By developing your own test, you can ensure that relevant objectives and items are included in the instrument. However, it is necessary to design and construct the CRT in a systematic, meaningful fashion. Gronlund (1973, pp. 3–5) suggested the following six principles to follow in developing a CRT:

1. Criterion-referenced testing requires a clearly defined and delimited domain of learning tasks.
2. Criterion-referenced testing requires that instructional objectives be clearly defined in behavioral (performance) terms.
3. Criterion-referenced testing requires that standards of performance be clearly specified.
4. Criterion-referenced testing requires that student performance be adequately sampled within each area of performance.
5. Criterion-referenced testing requires that test items be selected on the basis of how well they reflect the behavior specified in the instructional objectives.

6. Criterion-referenced testing requires a scoring and reporting system that adequately describes student performance on clearly defined learning tasks.*

Each of these six principles will be discussed in greater detail.

Principle 1—Clearly define and delimit domain of learning tasks

Criterion-referenced testing is most effective when it focuses on a specific set of instructional objectives. Identifying the skill or skills for which a CRT will be developed is simplest if certain procedures are kept in mind. First, certain types of skills are more amenable to this type of testing. Gronlund (1973) noted that the basic skill areas (for example, arithmetic) are easier to measure than loosely structured areas (for example, social studies). In either case, however, the skills should be broken down into manageable units. This is usually accomplished through a task analysis of the instructional objective to be measured.

Task analysis refers to the identification and sequencing of behaviors that are necessary components of the skill required for an individual to complete a task. Figure 6-1 gives an example of a task analysis. Note that each step is a prerequisite for later steps in the task analysis.

Two issues concerning task analysis should be mentioned. The first concerns the determination of how small or incremental the steps should be. For instance, it might be possible to have two equally valid task analyses, one with 100 steps and another with 10 steps. The choice of which task analysis you would use as the basis for a CRT would depend largely on the type of student for whom the test was designed. A profoundly retarded student, for example, might need a much more sensitive sequential breakdown than a learning-disabled student.

The second issue concerns the kind of skill for which a task analysis is planned. It is much easier to task-analyze nonacademic skills (such as tying a shoe or dialing the telephone) than academic skills (such as identifying words by sight or multiplying two-digit numbers). Lidz (1979) noted that in general there is little consensus on how to identify and sequence the objectives in a task analysis. Again, the choice of objectives or subcomponents might depend on the type of student.

Principle 2—Define the objectives in behavioral terms

This principle requires that an objective be defined in such a way that its mastery must be observed in student behavior. In other words,

---

*Reprinted with permission of Macmillan Publishing from *Preparing Criterion-Referenced Tests* by Norman E. Gronlund. Copyright © 1973 by Norman E. Gronlund.

Task Analysis of Objective: the child is able to alphabetize the follow-ing list of words, each of which has been placed on a separate card: stop, ask, dinner, name, boy

1. Child can write the alphabet in the correct order.
2. Given a stack of 26 flash cards, each containing a different letter of the alphabet, the child can place the cards in alphabetical order.
3. Given a stack of 26 flash cards, each containing a word beginning with a dif-ferent letter of the alphabet, the child can place the cards in alphabetical order *with* the help of an alphabet chart.
4. Given a stack of 26 flash cards, each containing a word beginning with a dif-ferent letter of the alphabet, the child can place the cards in alphabetical order *without* the help of an alphabet chart.
5. Given a stack of 15 flash cards, each containing a different letter of the alphabet, the child can place the cards in alphabetical order *with* the help of an alphabet chart (therefore, some letters of the alphabet are missing).
6. Given a stack of 15 flash cards, each containing a different letter of the alphabet, the child can place the cards in alphabetical order *without* the help of an alphabet chart.
7. Given a stack of 15 flash cards, each containing a word beginning with a dif-ferent letter of the alphabet, the child can place cards in alphabetical order *with* the help of an alphabet chart.
8. Given a stack of 15 flash cards, each containing a word beginning with a dif-ferent letter of the alphabet, the child can place the cards in alphabetical order *without* the help of an alphabet chart.
9. The child is able to alphabetize the following list of words, each of which has been placed on a separate card: *stop, ask, dinner, name, boy.*

FIGURE 6-1   Example of a Task Analysis

From A. R. Frank, "Breaking Down Learning Tasks: A Sequence Approach," *Teaching Exceptional Children,* 1973, 19. Copyright © 1973 by the Council for Exceptional Children. Reprinted with permission.

students must demonstrate that they have met an objective. "The student must complete correctly arithmetic problems involving the multiplication of three-digit numbers by two-digit numbers with carrying" is an objective that requires a specific behavioral performance. "Understands multiplica-tion" does not. Swezey (1981) further noted that a good objective should specify the conditions and standards. The condition refers to the situa-tions under which a student's performance is evaluated. The standard refers to the level of performance required (discussed next).

Principle 3—Specify standards of performance

One extremely important issue in the development of criterion-referenced tests is to determine what the criteria should be—that is, what criterion level a student must meet if an observer is to assume that the student has mastered that skill. Criteria in general tend to be determined arbitrarily. One teacher might feel that a student must answer 90 percent of mathematical problems correctly, and another teacher might feel 95 percent must be completed satisfactorily. One guide to use is to identify which students appear to have mastered a particular skill, and then to determine their performance level. This level could then be taken as a standard for mastery.

Another important issue is *maintenance* of the behavioral performance. Can it be assumed that a student has mastered a skill if he or she meets a 90 percent criterion for only one day? In defining mastery, it is also important to indicate how many times a student must meet the criterion level.

Principle 4—Adequately sample student performance

As a rule, the more items a test has in a specific area, the better picture the test provides of the student's true ability in that area. It is necessary to be practical, however, in deciding how many items to use. Several factors affect this decision. First, the number of test items will depend on the skill being measured. More items measuring the execution of simple addition could feasibly be included, for example, than items demonstrating the ability to handle money and make change. Second, for some skills, the complete sample of the skill can be described in the test items (Gronlund, 1973). These include skills such as identifying letters of the alphabet or writing numbers from 1 to 20. In general, it is advisable that at least twice as many test items are created as will actually be used in the test. If necessary, the extra items could be used to develop alternate forms of the test (Swezey, 1981).

Principle 5—Reflect in the test items the behavior specified in the instructional objectives

Criterion-referenced testing uses a direct approach in obtaining information. In other words, a specific instructional area is determined, behaviors are identified that are associated with that area, and test items are developed to measure those behaviors. In evaluating the test results, therefore, very little inference needs to be made. The test yields specific, relevant information, such as, "Trisha is having difficulty adding two-digit numbers requiring carrying, because she missed 10 out of 10 problems of this type," as opposed to general, relatively meaningless information, such as, "Trisha is having difficulty adding two-digit numbers because she is functioning at the 1.6 grade level in mathematics." Gronlund (1988) proposed eight questions that should be asked to determine if the test items have been properly constructed. These include, "Does each item present a clearly formulated task?" "Is the item free of extraneous clues?" and "Is each test item independent?" and "Are the items as a group free from overlapping?"

Principle 6—Include a scoring system that describes student performance on specific learning tasks

This principle incorporates many of the previously mentioned points. It means that a CRT should indicate, first, the area and objective to be measured, and second, the specific behavior to be measured, including the standard of performance required of the student. Conversely, the results of a CRT include the exact performance level of the student in a specific area.

Development of Criterion-Referenced Tests: Procedures

The following steps can act as guidelines for developing a CRT:

Step 1—Identification of skill to be measured

Problem. Determine the skills to be measured.

Comments. The skills that should be measured can be determined in a number of ways. Hopefully, a student's IEP will reflect his or her educational needs and will indicate those areas that need to be assessed. Therefore, if the student is not receiving special-education services and no IEP is available, a careful analysis of the areas covered in your curriculum will identify a number of goals. In some situations, school or district policy will determine the skills to be covered.

Step 2—Identification of objectives

Problem. Identify the specific subskills or objectives to be measured.

Comments. Again, objectives can be identified in a number of ways. If a student has an IEP, it will state the objectives. Unfortunately, many IEPs do not include good, sequential objectives. As a result it may be necessary to perform a task analysis of the skill.

Step 3—Development of test items

Problem. Develop materials and test items for each objective.

Comments. If the objective is associated with a finite, easily manageable number of behaviors (such as count from 1 to 10), *each* behavior can be included in the test. If this is not possible, the test should cover as many items as feasible. More test items can be developed for simple skills (such as multiplying three-digit numbers by two-digit numbers) than for more complex skills (such as reciting middle-English poems). In general the evaluator should ask several questions such as, "Are the intended learning outcomes stated in measurable terms?" "Is each test item relevant to an important learning outcome?" and "Is there an adequate number of items for each interpretation to be made?" (Gronlund 1988). If the answer is not yes to all the questions, the items should be modified. Table 6-1 also provides a series of questions based on the *type* of item that is developed. After the items have been developed, they must be put together in a meaningful way. Watanabe and Algozzine (1989) suggested that items should be grouped that measure the same skill or content area and should be placed in progressive order of difficulty.

Step 4—Determination of standard of performance

Problem.   Determine standard of performance.

Comments.   In developing a CRT, it is important to establish criteria to indicate when a student has mastered a particular skill. Although the criteria could be related to *speed* (for example, can read 20 sight words in 2 minutes), they usually involve accuracy, specifically the percentage of items passed. Although determining the criteria or the standard of performance is usually left up to the teacher's (or other testmaker's) discretion, certain standards are typically used more than others. Frequently, 90 or 95 percent of the items must be passed before mastery is assumed. As noted previously, however, there is a great deal of flexibility in determining those criteria. One should keep in mind that identifying a cutoff for mastery will impose "a false dichotomy on a continuum of proficiency" (Berk, 1984). In other words, if 90 percent correct is determined to be the criterion level for mastery, a person who correctly answered 89 percent of the items on a 100-item test would not have "mastered" the skill involved, whereas a person who answered one more correctly would have.

Gronlund (1988, pp. 119–120) noted that when a testmaker is setting the performance standards, several considerations should be taken into account. Those are:

1. Set mastery level on a multiple-choice test at 85 percent correct.
2. Increase the level if essential for next stage of instruction
3. Increase the level if essential for safety (for example, mixing chemicals).
4. Increase the level if test or subtest is short
5. Decrease the level if repetition is provided at next stage.
6. Decrease the level if tasks have low relevance.
7. Decrease the level if items are extremely difficult.
8. Adjust the level up or down as teaching experience dictates.

Standards can also be calculated empirically by determining the performance levels of students who, in the testmaker's eyes, have already

TABLE 6-1   Questions to Ask Before Developing CRT Items.

From Norman E. Gronlund, *How to Construct Achievement Tests,* 4th ed. © 1988 Allyn & Bacon. Reprinted with permission.

A. MULTIPLE-CHOICE ITEMS
1. Does the stem of the item present a single, clearly formulated problem?
2. Is the stem stated in simple, readable language?
3. Is the stem worded so that there is no repetition of material in the alternatives?
4. Is the stem stated in positive form, wherever possible?
5. If negative wording is used in the stem, is it emphasized (by underlining or caps)?
6. Is the intended answer correct or clearly best?
7. Are all alternatives grammatically consistent with the stem and parallel in form?
8. Are the alternatives free from verbal clues to the correct answer?
9. Are the distracters plausible and attractive to the uninformed?
10. Is the relative length of the correct answer varied, to eliminate length as a clue?
11. Has the alternative "all of the above" been avoided and "none of the above" used only when appropriate?
12. Is the position of the correct answer varied so that there is no detectable pattern?

C. TRUE-FALSE ITEMS
1. Does each statement contain one central, significant idea?
2. Is the statement so precisely worded that it can be unequivocally judged true or false?
3. Are the statements brief and stated in simple language?
4. Are negative statements used sparingly and double negatives avoided?
5. Are statements of opinion attributed to some source?
6. Have specific determiners (such as, always, sometimes, may) and other clues (such as, length) been avoided?

D. MATCHING ITEMS
1. Does each matching item contain only homogeneous material?
2. Is the list of items short with the brief responses on the right?
3. Is the list of responses longer or shorter than the list of premises, to provide an uneven match?
4. Do the directions clearly state the basis for matching and that the responses can be used once, more than once, or not at all?

E. INTERPRETIVE EXERCISES
1. Is the introductory material relevant to the learning outcomes to be measured?
2. Is the introductory material new to the examinees?
3. Is the introductory material as brief as possible?
4. Do the test items call forth the performance specified in the learning outcomes?
5. Do the test items meet the criteria of effective item writing that apply to the type of objective item being used?

F. SHORT-ANSWER ITEMS
1. Is the item stated so that a single, brief answer is possible?
2. Has the item been stated as a direct question wherever possible?
3. Do the words to be supplied relate to the main point of the item?
4. Are the blanks placed at the end of the statement?
5. Have extraneous clues (such as "a" or "an," and length of the blank) been avoided?
6. Where numerical answers are to be given, have the expected degree of precision and the units in which they are to be expressed been indicated?

G. ESSAY TEST
1. Is each question restricted to the measurement of complex learning outcomes?
2. Is each question relevant to the learning outcome being measured?
3. Does each question present a clearly defined task?
4. Are all examinees directed to answer the same questions (unless the outcome requires a choice)?
5. Has ample time been allowed for answering, and has a time limit been suggested for each question?
6. Have adequate provisions been made for scoring the essay answers?

H. PERFORMANCE TEST
1. Have the performance outcomes to be measured been clearly specified?
2. Does the test situation reflect an appropriate degree of realism for the outcomes being measured?
3. Do the instructions clearly describe the test situation?
4. Are the observational forms well designed and appropriate for the performance being evaluated?

mastered a particular objective. It is also a good idea to indicate how many times a student must reach criterion level before mastery is assumed.

Step 5—Administration of the test

Problem.   Administer the CRT.

Comment.   After the test has been developed carefully, it can be administered to the student(s) for whom it was intended. One frequently overlooked area has to do with ensuring that the student is given proper instructions on how to take the criterion-referenced test. Swezey (1981) indicated that general test instructions should include the following type of information:

1. The purpose of the test
2. The time limits for the test
3. A description of the test conditions (e.g., "You may use scratch paper if you wish")
4. A description of the test standards (e.g., "In order to receive credit you must get the exact answer")
5. A description of the test items (e.g., "Reduce fractions in your answers to the lowest common denominator")
6. The general test regulations (e.g., "Continue to the next page when you see a finger pointing at the bottom of a page; stop when you see a stop sign at the bottom of the page")

Step 6—Scoring of the test

Problem.   Score the CRT.

Comment.   After the test has been developed and appropriately administered, it is necessary to score the test. This usually will involve determining the number of correct and incorrect items for each skill area and determining the percentage of mastery. Obviously, the scoring of the instrument will be dependent on the type of items used and the purpose for the testing. For example, if rate were more important than accuracy it might only be necessary to count the correct responses (e.g., the number of words read in a 1-minute period).

Johnson and Harlow (1989) noted that the CRT model calls for a large number of items that go into depth and detail. Subsequently, there is a great deal of clerical work that is necessary. They argued that teachers should consider the use of computers to score, analyze, and profile the data obtained from CRTs.

Step 7—Interpret the test

Problem.   Interpret the CRT.

Comments.   Suppose that in the measurement of a specific skill, 10 subcomponents or objectives were determined. For each of these 10 objectives, 10 test items were developed, resulting in a CRT of 100 items. Is it necessary to administer all 100 items? Probably not. The goal of a CRT is to provide specific information for instructional purposes. Two approaches might be appropriate. First, on the basis of the information that is available about a student, (for example, work products, results of tests to document educational need), the test user might know that the student has mastered some of the earlier objectives and can therefore "skip" them. Another approach might be to administer the items for objective 10 (goal) first, and work backwards to the items for objectives 9, 8, 7, and so on. If a student reaches mastery for the items for objective 5, for instance, it could be assumed that the student also has mastery over items in objectives 1 through 4. Thus, a teacher might gain from the test an indication of the immediate short-term objective (objective 5) as well as a list of sequential objectives (6 through 9) leading to the goal (objective 10).

Development of Criterion-Referenced Tests: An Example

The following is an example of the development of a CRT:

Step 1—Identification of skill to be measured
Subtraction of whole numbers (with renaming)

Step 2—Identification of objectives

1. Given problems requiring the subtraction of numbers 1–18 from the numbers 1–18, the student will provide the correct answers.
2. Given problems requiring the subtraction of 0 from the numbers 1–10, the student will provide the correct answers.
3. Given problems requiring the subtraction of a one-digit number from a two-digit number without renaming, the student will provide the correct answers.
4. Given problems requiring the subtraction of a two-digit number from a two-digit number without renaming, the student will provide the correct answers.
5. Given problems requiring the subtraction of three-digit numbers from three-digit numbers without renaming, the student will provide the correct answers.
6. Given problems requiring the subtraction of a one-digit number from a two-digit number with renaming, the student will provide the correct answers.

7. Given problems requiring the subtraction of a two-digit number from a two-digit number with renaming, the student will provide the correct answers.
8. Given problems requiring the subtraction of a three-digit number from a three-digit number with renaming, the student will provide the correct answers.

Step 3—Development of test items

1.	18	8	13	7	11	14	4	17	9	15
	−9	−4	−11	−1	−10	−6	−2	−7	−3	−12

2.	9	5	3	8	1	4	7	2	6	10
	−0	−0	−0	−0	−0	−0	−0	−0	−0	−0

3.	17	14	26	48	79	23	65	89	55	96
	−5	−2	−4	−6	−3	−2	−1	−7	−3	−5

4.	28	39	45	13	86	64	78	57	92	40
	−16	−17	−22	−11	−45	−32	−23	−34	−81	−10

5.	865	752	279	370	143	666	478	607	191	754
	−652	−241	−124	−230	−121	−351	−352	−506	−180	−322

6.	18	55	62	27	76	91	36	44	82	17
	−9	−7	−8	−9	−8	−3	−9	−5	−4	−8

7.	84	28	31	82	65	97	56	33	41	92
	−35	−19	−22	−64	−17	−38	−29	−16	−25	−83

8.	985	257	381	973	444	543	674	278	626	552
	−796	−179	−193	−588	−255	−358	−596	−179	−337	−274

Step 4—Determination of standard of performance
The student must correctly answer at least 9 out of 10 problems (90 percent) before mastery is assumed. Further, the student must reach criterion level for 3 consecutive days before mastery is assumed.

Step 5—Administration, scoring, and interpretation of test
On the information gathered prior to the administration of the CRT (for example, test data to document educational need, work samples), the teacher was able to determine that the student knew his basic number facts and had no problems with one-digit numbers. Therefore, the criterion-referenced testing began with objective 3—subtraction of a one-digit number from a two-digit number without renaming.

FIRST ADMINISTRATION	SECOND ADMINISTRATION	THIRD ADMINISTRATION
1. Not administered (NA)	1. NA	1. NA
2. NA	2. NA	2. NA
3. 90%	3. 100%	3. 90%
4. 20%	4. 40%	4. 30%
5. 10%	5. 20%	5. 20%
6. 0%	6. 0%	6. 0%
7. NA	7. NA	7. NA
8. NA	8. NA	8. NA

These results suggest that the student has mastered objectives 1–3, is having difficulty and is somewhat inconsistent with objectives 4 and 5, and does not know how to do objectives 6–8. The immediate objective for this student would be to subtract multidigit numbers without renaming. The goal would be to teach the concept of renaming. The teacher would progress from objectives 4–8 and reevaluate using the CRT as skills are taught.

WHAT TO TEACH VERSUS HOW TO TEACH

Although CRTs are very helpful in determining students' performance in specific curriculum areas, they do have their limitations. For example, a CRT will tell a teacher *what to teach* but gives little information about *how to teach* that skill effectively (Cohen and Spruill, 1990). Put another way, most CRTs are more interested in measuring *product* rather than *process*. Swezey (1981), however, argued that CRTs could be designed to measure process as well as product. His distinction was that a product refers to something tangible that can be easily measured, whereas a process usually refers to the degree to which a student follows procedures correctly regardless of the outcome (e.g., did the student use the right strategy in solving a computation problem but made a mistake that resulted in the wrong answer?). The example below illustrates this point. The student knew to carry the one to the tens place but made an error in adding 1+4+9. This information would indicate that additional instruction in renaming might not be necessary but that addition of three one-digit numbers might be warranted.

$$
\begin{array}{r}
1 \\
48 \\
+\ 97 \\
\hline
155
\end{array}
$$

One method that can be used to help determine the process or strategies a student is using when engaging in academic tasks is *error analysis.*

Error Analysis

WHY USE?
Determination and evaluation of teaching strategies; gathering of prereferral information; development and evaluation of IEPs.

WHO SHOULD USE?
Teachers

A great deal of information can be determined from the type of error a student makes in routine school work products that are easily obtained. Similarly, when test results (CRT or NRT) are examined, the type as well as the number of errors can provide meaningful information. Suppose, for example, that in the previous computation problem the following solution was given:

$$
\begin{array}{r}
48 \\
+\,97 \\
\hline
1315
\end{array}
$$

This would indicate that the student *does* need instruction in renaming because he added the ones and tens column separately.

Gable and Hendrickson (1990) provided several suggestions for maximizing the usefulness of error analysis. For example, they suggested that at least five items are necessary for a given skill before error analysis is used. They also noted that as a first step, a teacher should choose one subject area and one student rather than attempting to analyze errors for an entire class. The following are specific guidelines for conducting error analyses in the areas of reading, mathematics, and spelling.

Reading

Error analysis in reading can focus on oral reading, reading comprehension, or both. A procedure called *miscue analysis,* for example, addresses oral reading, comprehension, and word analysis skills.

Oral Reading. The analysis of the types of errors made during oral reading and word recognition can provide important information that can be useful in developing instructional plans for students. For example, a student who substitutes a different word (e.g., suit for shout) might require different teaching procedures from a student who incorrectly sounds out phonetically a given word (e.g., tut for toot). Usually, error types such as omissions, substitutions, mispronunciations, repetitions, insertions, reversals, or hesitations are noted when conducting an error analysis of word recognition (Evans, Evans, & Mercer, 1986).

Morsink and Gable (1990) reported a four-step procedure for the analysis of word recognition errors. The first step involves the *actual sampling of the oral reading.* They suggest that the student should read from graded material from a basal series or other instructional material at a level at which the student can comprehend approximately 60 percent of the information. In other words, one should choose a reading passage that is not too difficult and not too easy for the student. The second step is *to identify possible error patterns and to confirm those patterns through retesting.* To identify error patterns, Morsink and Gable (1990) suggested that both qualitative information and quantitative information be gathered. A chart similar to that found in Figure 6-2 can help in determining the type of error pattern that exists. Retesting is important to determine if the problem is consistent or is due perhaps to other factors such as lack of motivation or inattention. It is also possible that retesting might help to determine other relevant diagnostic information. For example, Salvia and Hughes (1990) noted that it is important to distinguish between words that a student can read without time constraints and words that a student cannot read at all. This distinction is important because different teaching procedures are required for increasing word fluency and for teaching unknown words.

It is important that a consistent coding/notation system and perhaps a scoring system be used that allows for greater communication among those who see the error analysis (for example, the regular and special education teacher). Figure 6-3 is an example of a notation system that might be used for coding reading errors. Miller (1986) has suggested a scoring system whereby one point is deducted for an error that affects comprehension and one-half point is deducted for minor errors that do not affect comprehension. The points are totaled and divided by the number of words in the paragraph to obtain a percentage of correct words.

The third step is *to interview the student.* This involves asking the student what type of approach to reading he or she is using. For example, an incorrect word could be shown to the student, who is then asked, "Were you trying to sound out this word or were you trying to figure it out by looking at the other words in the sentence?" Information from these types of questions can provide very important insight into the method of read-

Student _____   Dates _____

Material/Level _____

	Error Type/Number	Prioritized Instruction	
Ignore Punctuation			Proficiency
Hesitation			Proficiency
Repetition			Proficiency
Insertion			Transition
Self-Correct			Transition
Substitution			Acquisition
Teacher Aid			Acquisition
Mispronounce			Acquisition

Number of readings _____

Average number of words _____

Average time of readings _____

Correct rate _____ Error rate _____

FIGURE 6-2   Error Analysis Chart for Oral Reading

ERROR TYPE	NOTATION	EXAMPLE
Omissions	Circle the word, words, or part of a word that is omitted	He did not want to go in(to) his friend's house.
Substitutions	Write the substituted word above the correct word	She put the coins in the bag. *box*
Mispronunciations	Write the mispronounced word above the correct word.	The man is a thief. *thife*
Repetitions	Draw a wavy line under the repeated word or words.	He wants a truck for his birthday.
Insertions	Write in the insertion. Indicate with a caret.	The doll has brown hair. *dark*
Reversals	For a letter reversal within a word, write the substituted word above the corrected word.	They were cooking soup in the pot. *top*
	For reversals of words draw a line indicating the transposition of words.	He looked quickly for his homework.
Hesitations	Indicate with a slash mark.	The park was close/to the school.
Unknown or aided	Underline the word(s) after waiting a sufficient time for a response.	The boys were <u>exhausted</u> from their hike.
Omission of punctuation marks	Cross out the punctuation mark that was omitted.	The little girl put on her coat. X She went outside.
Self-corrected errors	Write the incorrect word and place a check beside it.	He wants a new bike for his birthday. *bike* ✓

FIGURE 6-3   Notation System for Indicating Oral Reading Errors

From S. Evans, W. Evans, and C. Mercer, *Assessment for Instruction.* Copyright © 1986 by Allyn and Bacon, Inc.

ing that the student is using. The last step involves *recording the results of the error analysis.* This could be a simple chart in which the type and number of errors as well as instructional priorities are identified.

Reading Comprehension

Morsink and Gable (1990) suggested the use of the same four-step procedure in evaluating the errors in reading comprehension. For step one, *obtaining the sample,* they suggest a procedure in which the teacher asks the student to read from a passage and then to tell what the story was all about. The teacher then notes the key thought units recalled and separates these into areas such as main ideas, actual details, sequential events, or inferences.

For the second step, *identifying the errors and retesting,* the teacher should probe further if it is noted that the student is having difficulty with a particular aspect of comprehension. This can be accomplished by asking specific detailed questions. Morsink and Gable (1990) also noted that this is a good time to focus on the student's understanding of vocabulary words. They suggest that for each error made during word recognition, the teacher can indicate that word in text and ask, "What does ———— mean?" This might also provide important information. For example, Salvia and Hughes (1990) noted that in literal comprehension, the most important areas are related to vocabulary and grammar. In other words, many errors in literal comprehension may be due to the student's lack of knowledge of the meaning of the words or the grammatical structure used in the passage. They also note that when the student does understand the words and grammar, lack of comprehension could result from such things as slow reading in which the train of thought is lost.

In step three, *interviewing the student,* the student is asked directly about the type of strategies or procedures being used to complete the comprehension exercise. To illustrate, "The student with difficulty in simple literal comprehension may say, 'I just try to remember what it says but when there are so many things, I can't remember them all.' This type of response indicates the absence of a workable strategy for recall." (Morsink & Gable, 1990, p. 58). For the last step, *recording the findings,* they suggest that a chart be developed that includes the type and number of the errors that are made. In the areas of critical reading, making inferences, sequence of events, main idea/summary, and/or recall of factual detail may be addressed. Again, based on this information, prioritized instruction can be identified.

Miscue Analysis.   *Miscue analysis* is an informal process for assessing oral-reading deficits. Specifically, miscue analysis yields information on skills in oral reading, comprehension, and word analysis by providing a systematic method for studying the patterns of reading errors. Although any method of analyzing the errors can be used, the *Reading Miscue Inventory* (Goodman & Burke, 1972) is perhaps the most popular. Goodman, Watson and Burke (1987) described the steps in conducting a miscue analysis. First, an appropriate reading selection is made, the student reads the selection, and the oral reading is audiotaped. Next, the student retells the story. Finally, the pattern of errors are studied both qualitatively and quantitatively. The areas that are addressed are syntactic acceptability, semantic acceptability, meaning change, graphic similarity, sound similarity (does the reading error sound similar to the correct word?), and correction (did the reader attempt to self–correct?).

Mathematics

Error analyses in mathematics are relatively simple, because, as a rule, a written product is available; thus, the teacher has a tremendous amount of potential information from the students' routine math work in school. Several in-depth studies have been conducted to determine the typical extent and types of mathematics errors. Lankford (1972) studied the computational errors of 176 seventh-grade students from various regions in the United States. He found, for example, five major types of errors in addition and seven in subtraction, multiplication, and division. Miller and Milam (1987) specifically looked at the error patterns of learning disabled students in the areas of multiplication and division. They found that poor memory for basic multiplication and addition facts was the most common multiplication error, whereas omitting the remainder was the most common division error. The area of subtraction has been studied relatively extensively. Frank, Logan, and Martin (1982) found that learning-disabled students had a definite pattern to their subtraction errors rather than making random errors. Cebulski and Bucher (1986) reported that borrowing and inversion (subtracting smaller number from larger regardless of their position) were the most common errors.

Ashlock (1990) has written a widely used book that addresses error patterns in arithmetic computation. The problems in Figure 6-4 are examples of the error types discussed by Ashlock.

As can be seen from the examples shown in the box, it is important to do more than just note whether a problem is worked out correctly. The pattern of error can yield meaningful information, particularly in determining the teaching strategy that is most appropriate.

Enright, Gable, and Hendrickson (1988), described a nine-step model for diagnosing and remediating errors in mathematics computation. Each of these steps will be presented with a brief discussion.

Step 1—Obtain samples.   This involves gathering multiple samples of the student's mathematics computation work. Enright et al. recommend that samples should include at least three to five items for each subskill measured.

Step 2—Interview the student.   The diagnostic interview is a very helpful technique in math error analysis. Using this procedure, the examiner asks the students to "talk their way through" the arithmetic problems as they are solving them. In many cases, the examiner will clearly be able to see where and why the student is making an error. Take the following as an example:

$$3\overline{\smash{\big)}\,63}^{\,12} \qquad 4\overline{\smash{\big)}\,124}^{\,13} \qquad 2\overline{\smash{\big)}\,148}^{\,47} \qquad 5\overline{\smash{\big)}\,155}^{\,13}$$

The student commented, "3 into 6 is 2, I put the 2 in the ones column. 3 into 3 is 1, so I put that here." In this situation, the student understands division facts but probably is confused because addition, subtraction, and multiplication problems are all solved from right to left. He inappropriately generalized that procedure to division. The student responded in a

Addition examples:

(1)	82	(2)	68	(3)	45
	+ 41		+ 39		+ 35
	123		917		710

Error pattern: The student is adding the 1s column and the 10s column independently without carrying or noting the place value in the sum.

Subtraction examples:

(1)	63	(2)	49	(3)	81
	− 37		− 27		− 19
	34		22		78

Error pattern: The student is subtracting the smaller number from the larger number in each column regardless of their positions as subtrahend or minuend.

Multiplication examples:

(1)	83	(2)	63	(3)	48
	× 4		× 5		× 2
	362		355		106

Error pattern: The student is adding the carried digit before instead of after multiplying. In the first example, for instance, the student multiplied 3 × 4, wrote the 2, carried the 1, and added this to 8. The student then calculated 4 × 9 rather than (4 × 8) + 1.

Division examples:

$$(1)\ 3\overline{)93}\quad\quad (2)\ 4\overline{)72}\quad\quad (3)\ 6\overline{)138}$$

```
      13              81              32
(1) 3/93        (2) 4/72        (3) 6/138
      9               4               12
      ─               ──              ──
      3               32              18
      3               32              18
      ─               ──              ──
```

Error pattern: The student is dividing correctly but is writing down the answer from right to left.

FIGURE 6-4   **Examples of Math Errors**

similar fashion to the other three problems. Underhill, Uprichard, and Heddens (1982) provide more detailed guidelines for conducting diagnostic interviews in the area of mathematics.

Step 3—Analyze errors and identify error patterns.   A variety of major error types have been used in classification. Salvia and Hughes (1990) summarized five distinct types of computational errors. These were a lack of prerequisite skills; wrong operation (e.g., adding instead of subtracting); an obvious computational error; a defective algorithm (when a student tries to apply the correct operation but makes errors in making the necessary steps); and random responses. Gable and Coben (1990) also included grouping errors (mistake in placing digits in the proper column when regrouping) in addition to those just listed.

To assist in the analysis, Enright et al. suggested the use of a computational error chart (Figure 6-5) that indicates the type and number of errors that are made. As an exercise, try to identify the type of error for each of the following examples using the error chart in Figure 6-5.

EXAMPLE 1

$$\begin{array}{r} 48 \\ +8 \\ \hline 416 \end{array}$$

EXAMPLE 2

$$\begin{array}{r} 91 \\ \times 4 \\ \hline 157 \end{array}$$

EXAMPLE 3

$$\begin{array}{r} 35 \\ -25 \\ \hline 60 \end{array}$$

EXAMPLE 4

$$\begin{array}{r} 43 \\ \times 6 \\ \hline 308 \end{array}$$

EXAMPLE 5

$$\begin{array}{r} 45 \\ +23 \\ \hline 67 \end{array}$$

ANSWERS

#1 Grouping (student correctly added but did not carry)

#2 Random (no apparent pattern)

#3 Wrong operation (student added instead of subtracted)

#4 Defective algorithm (student correctly multiplied but added 1 to 4 before multiplying)

#5 Computational error (student added 5 + 3 incorrectly)

Student _____ Date _____

Material _____ No. of Problems/Digits _____

Problem Class _____

	Error Type/Number	Corrective Strategy
Wrong Operation		
Computa-tional		
Defective Algorithm		
Grouping		
Random		
Other		

Beginning Time_____ Ending Time _____
Corrects Per Minute _____ Errors Per Minute _____

Peer Standards
   High Performer -- Corrects Per Min. ___ Errors Per Min. ___
   Med Performer -- Corrects Per Min. ___ Errors Per Min. ___
   Low Performer -- Corrects Per Min. ___ Errors Per Min. ___

FIGURE 6-5   Computation Error Chart

Step 4—Select priority error pattern and show the precise error to the student.   The information presented in Figure 6-5 might be shared with the student as a means of providing corrective feedback.

Step 5—Demonstrate a correct computational procedure as part of the corrective feedback mechanism.   The teacher should demonstrate the correct computational procedure and leave the completed problem as a permanent model.

Step 6—Select a corrective strategy.   At this point, the error pattern has been determined and feedback has been provided to the student about (1) why the answer was incorrect and (2) how to determine the correct answer. Now it is necessary to determine instructional strategies that might be helpful in teaching the correct procedure. As an example of this, Enright et al. suggested that color coding the signs, such as green for plus, red for minus, when a student is using the wrong operation might help draw attention to the appropriate operation to complete.

Step 7—Introduce appropriate practice.   This involves a structured series of practice exercises that reinforces the correct computational procedure that has been taught.

Step 8—Identify and apply normative standards.   Essentially, this refers to the establishment of criteria that the teacher feels is necessary to indicate that the child has mastered a particular computational procedure. In a sense, this is very similar to establishing criteria for mastery noted in criterion referenced testing.

Step 9—Evaluate performance.   This refers to the ongoing assessment that is necessary in the diagnostic remedial process.

Spelling

A tremendous amount of information can be gleaned from looking at types of spelling errors. As in the analysis of arithmetic errors, spelling-error analysis is relatively easy to do because a written product is usually available. Perhaps the most common types of spelling errors are phonological substitutions (such as "desishun" for "decision") and omissions (such as "namly" for "namely"). Thomas (1977) reported the results of a study that determined types of spelling errors made by 450 students. He found that substitutions and omissions accounted for approximately 38 percent of all errors. Other errors included confused pronunciation (such as "denist" for "dentist"), doubling "such as "citty" for "city"), insertions (such as "biteing" for "biting"), transpositions (such as "freind" for "friend") and homonyms (such as "see" for "sea"), plus some unclassified errors.

The information obtained from a careful look at error types suggests certain remedial strategies. For example, a student with transpositional errors might have difficulty learning or remembering spelling rules. A student with homonym errors might have problems attending to or understanding the meaning of words. Thomas (1979) identified potential causes and remedial procedures for each of these eight types of errors.

The following misspelled words provide an exercise for conducting an error analysis:

ACTUAL WORD	STUDENT'S SPELLING	TYPE OF ERROR
1. Enough	Enuff	_____
2. Believe	Belive	_____
3. Motel	Mottel	_____
4. Nerve	Nerv	_____
5. Has	Haz	_____
6. Good	Goode	_____
7. Carrying	Carring	_____
8. Eight	Ate	_____
9. Towel	Towle	_____
10. Girls	Grils	_____

Answers: (1) PS (2) O (3) D (4) O (5) PS (6) I/A (7) O (8) H (9) T (10) T

Key: PS—phonological substitution   O—omission
         D—doubling   I—insertion
         A—addition   H—homonym
         T—transposition

More recently, Silva and Yarborough (1990) provided a model for understanding and analyzing spelling errors. In their model, they encourage the analysis of actual writing samples rather than isolated spelling words. They use three major areas of errors: language/dialect, orthographic rules/convention, and learned lexicon/visual memory. Each major area has subcategories. For example, a language/dialect error could involve a wrong or missing ending or affix (e.g., irresponsible for unresponsible). An orthographic rule/convention error might include those related to doubling (e.g., skiped for skipped) or the silent e rule (e.g., ninty for ninety). The learned lexicon/visual memory error might involve homonym confusion, compound word errors, reversals, and added or missing syllables as examples.

To conduct a spelling error analysis, Hendrickson and Gable (1990) suggested a five-step process:

Step 1—Obtain a sample.   It is recommended that word lists, paragraphs, or stories be dictated to the student.

Step 2—Interview the student.   This procedure can be used to identify spelling strategies that the student uses. Questions such as, How do you remember how to spell new words that you learn? can be asked to better determine how the student approaches the reading process.

Step 3—Analyze and classify the errors.   The analysis might involve some method of objectively scoring the errors. This is particularly helpful if the number of words sampled remains constant and the student is frequently reevaluated. Hendrickson and Gable summarized five approaches that can be used in scoring spelling errors. These are whole word, syllables, sound cluster, letters in place, and letter sequences. These approaches differ in the extent to which the spelling error is analyzed and scored. For example, using the syllable approach the word "city" would be scored 1/2 if it was spelled "cite" (ci/<u>te</u> note: underline portion is scored as an error). If the word were spelled "site" the score would be 0/2 (<u>si</u>/<u>te</u>). Using the letter in place approach, "cite" would be scored 3/4 (c/i/t/<u>e</u>) and "site" would be scored 2/4 (<u>s</u>/i/t/<u>e</u>). Hendrickson and Gable note that the whole word approach (the word is scored right or wrong) is the most logical for typical classroom use but that the others are more precise and might be helpful for more serious spelling problems.

Regardless of the scoring system used, it is important to look at the *pattern* of the errors. Hendrickson and Gable suggest using a spelling error chart that indicates the *type* of errors (vowels, consonants, or rules/ patterns) and whether the error *tendency* is to omit, delete, substitute letters or to change their order.

Step 4—Select a corrective strategy.   By classifying the words misspelled as regular, irregular, or predictable, instructional strategies can be identified. For example, if a student consistently missed predictable words (those that conform to traditional spelling words), the instructional strategy would be different than for irregular words that might require the use of certain memory strategies. Interested readers are referred to Hendrickson and Gable (1990) for guidelines for selecting and implementing instructional strategies that are beyond the scope of this discussion.

Step 5—Implement strategy and evaluate its impact.   This would involve continuous monitoring to determine the effectiveness of the instructional program.

Instrument or Technique	Suggested Use							Target Population						Educational Relevance for Exceptional Students	Special Considerations
	Prereferral			Postreferral											
	Screening and Initial Identification	Informal Determination and Evaluation of Teaching Programs and Strategies	Determination of Current Performance Level and Educational Need	Decisions about Classification and Program Placement	IEP Goals	IEP Objectives	IEP Evaluation	Mild/Moderate	Severe/Profound	Preschool	Elementary Age	Secondary Age	Adult		
Criterion-Referenced Test	X	X	X		X	X	X	X	X	X	X	X	X	very useful	Can be developed by the teacher on the basis of a student's curriculum; determination of criteria is arbitrary
Error Analysis—Reading	X	X	X					X			X	X		very useful	Provides information on oral-reading and comprehension
Error Analysis—Mathematics	X	X	X					X			X	X		very useful	Relatively easy to do, since written products (math problems) are readily available
Error Analysis—Spelling	X	X	X					X			X	X		very useful	Relatively easy to do, since written products (spelling words) are readily available

7

Curriculum-Based Assessment

AREAS COVERED

CRITERION-REFERENCED CBA
- Development of a CBA Instrument
- Uses and Limitations

CURRICULUM-BASED MEASUREMENT
- Computer-Based CBM
- Uses and Limitations

CBA AND CBM: AN INTEGRATED MODEL

WHY USE?
Determination and evaluation of objectives and teaching strategies; gathering of prereferral information; development and evaluation of IEPs

WHO SHOULD USE?
Teachers

Recently, curriculum-based assessment (CBA) has received widespread attention in the area of special education. The concept of CBA is certainly not new and has been employed in schools for a number of years. The recent emphasis on CBA in special education is more a result of philosophical changes than technological changes regarding test construction. The Regular Education Initiative discussed in Chapter 1, for instance, placed heavy emphasis on the use of CBA. Idol, Nevin, and Paolucci-

Whitcomb (1986) noted that interest in CBA seemed to develop as a means of coping with low-achieving and special-needs learners who were mainstreamed into regular education. They further noted that the CBA model fits nicely into a noncategorical model in which the emphasis is on testing curricular-based skills instead of testing for labeling purposes.

CBA involves the measurement of the level of a student in terms of the *expected curricula outcomes of the school* (Tucker, 1985). In other words, the assessment instrument is based on the content of the student's curriculum (Taylor, Willits, and Richards, 1988). CBA actually refers to a variety of different procedures. Some types of CBA are relatively informal while others are more formal and standardized (Fuchs & Fuchs, 1989). In fact, there has been some confusion as to what professionals are talking about when they refer to the term CBA . Shinn, Rosenfeld, and Knutson (1989) investigated the professional literature regarding CBA procedures and categorized them into four models. The first was *CBA for instructional design* in which the determination of instructional needs is based on students' continuous performance in the existing curriculum. The second, *curriculum-based evaluation,* is characterized by the measurement of specific subcomponents of a curricular task. The other two—*criterion-referenced CBA* and *curriculum-based measurement* (CBM)—are the most widely researched and used and will be discussed in detail.

CRITERION-REFERENCED CBA

Most criterion-referenced or informal CBA procedures are based on a task-analytic model that can be applied to developmental (hierarchical) curricula, spiraling curricula (organized by levels with concepts repeated at later levels), and/or unestablished (individualized to student need) curricula (Spruill, 1990). There are a number of guidelines that have been suggested for developing an informal CBA instrument. Blankenship (1985) suggested that the first step should be to list the skills presented in the curriculum, write an objective for each skill, develop items for each listed objective, and then administer the test before and after a structured program has been initiated. Cohen (1990) identified a five-step process that involved identifying the purpose of the CBA, developing the test specifications for curriculum objectives, constructing and revising the test items, administering the CBA instrument, and finally, graphing the student's performance. Similarly, Salvia and Hughes (1990) expanded somewhat on these previously mentioned steps and suggested the following: (1) specify reasons for decisions; (2) analyze the curriculum; (3) formulate the behavioral objectives; (4) develop appropriate assessment procedures; (5) collect data; (6) summarize data; (7) display the data; (8) interpret data and make decisions. It should be noted that the steps outlined by these various authors are very similar to the steps noted in

Chapter 6 in terms of developing a criterion-referenced test (CRT). In fact, this type of CBA is essentially a CRT with the content of the curriculum dictating the content of the instrument.

CBA instruments can be developed for any type of curriculum. Usually, the content of the test reflects several levels of the curriculum. For example, if the curriculum area were reading, it would be desirable to develop tests that would include passages selected from each level of the reading series. If the test was focused on spelling, items could be randomly chosen from each lesson at each level in a spelling series. A teacher can then choose to give the entire CBA or only portions related to a given skill area.

It is generally recommended that a student be evaluated on three separate days using three separate forms of the test (Idol, Nevin, & Paolucci-Whitcomb, 1986). In other words, three forms should be developed that cover the same content but that have different items. By administering these three forms, one can get a truer picture of the student's true ability and help to control for sporadic performance (White & Liberty, 1976). CBA instruments are also frequently group-administered. By placing the tests on ditto sheets, it is possible to administer them to an entire class to find out where they are in relation to the curriculum.

Development of a Criterion-Referenced CBA Instrument: An Example

Using the procedures outlined for developing a CRT that was noted in Chapter 6, it is possible to give an example of how to develop an informal CBA instrument.

Step 1—Identification of skill to be measured

The curriculum area chosen for the CBA was mathematics. The first step was to look at the mathematics curriculum for the student and determine the skill areas included in that curriculum. Suppose that the mathematics curriculum from Scott, Foresman, and Co. was being used. The teacher would analyze that curriculum and determine what specific skill areas were being covered. (NOTE: For this example, only a portion of the mathematics curriculum was analyzed for ease of discussion.) It was determined that the following skills were included in the part of the mathematics curriculum analyzed:

> digit writing
> place value
> greater than-lesser than concept
> addition
> subtraction
> missing addends

If the entire curriculum had been analyzed, a chart could have been developed that included all of the skill areas covered, the sequence of the skills, and even the page numbers in the curriculum where the skills are taught.

Step 2—Identification of objectives

When breaking down skill areas into objectives, a *summary sheet* is sometimes used that allows the teacher to determine the specific concepts to be tested as well as the number of items that measure each objective and the standards of performance. Table 7-1 shows the summary sheet for this CBA instrument.

TABLE 7-1   Summary Sheet for a Mathematics CBA.

CONCEPTS	PROBLEM NUMBERS	DAY 1	DAY 2	DAY 3	TOTAL SCORE 5/6	MASTERY 5/6
Writing digits	1,2	/2	/2	/2	/6	/6
Place value	3,4	/2	/2	/2	/6	/6
Comparing numbers	5,6	/2	/2	/2	/6	/6
Add basic facts 0–10	7,21	/2	/2	/2	/6	/6
Add basic facts 11–20	8,22	/2	/2	/2	/6	/6
Add 2 digits (no renaming)	9,24	/2	/2	/2	/6	/6
Add 1 renaming	10,26	/2	/2	/2	/6	/6
Add 3 digits (no renaming)	11,28	/2	/2	/2	/6	/6
Add 2 renaming	12,30	/2	/2	/2	/6	/6
Add 3 or more numbers	13,32	/2	/2	/2	/6	/6
Add 4 digits (renaming)	12,30	/2	/2	/2	/6	/6
Subt. basic facts 0–10	15,23	/2	/2	/2	/6	/6
Subt. basic facts 11–20	16,25	/2	/2	/2	/6	/6
Subt. 2 digits (no renaming)	17,27	/2	/2	/2	/6	/6
Subt. 2 digits (1 renaming)	18,29	/2	/2	/2	/6	/6
Subt. 3 digits (no renaming)	19,31	/2	/2	/2	/6	/6
Subt. 3 digits (1 renaming)	20,33	/2	/2	/2	/6	/6
Missing addends (1)	35,36	/2	/2	/2	/6	/6

Adapted from L. Idol, A. Nevin, and P. Paolucci-Whitcomb, *Models of Curriculum-Based Assessment.* Copyright © 1986 by Aspen Publishers, Inc. Reprinted with permission of Aspen Publishers, Inc.

Step 3—Development of test items

Figure 7-1 displays the test developed from the portion of the mathematics curriculum that was analyzed. Note that the *Problem Numbers* heading in Table 7-1 relates to the items in the test itself. The test in

SAMPLE MATH CBA

Math CBA — Day 1

Give the number:

1. 9 tens, 6 ones   2. 3 thousand, 7 hundred forty-one

————   ————

Tell what place 7 holds:

3. 271 ———   4. 8,726 ———

Compare the numbers. Use > or < :

5. 32 ——— 49   6. 2×3 ——— 10

Add:

7. 2	8. 7	9. 42	10. 76	11. 231
+6	+5	+21	+17	+243

12. 373	13. 7+2+5 = ———	14. 3692
+147		+2345

Subtract:

15. 8	16. 11	17. 87	18. 76	19. 588	20. 349
−7	−4	−43	−59	−164	−187

Add or subtract:

21. 4	22. 6	23. 9	24. 55	25. 15
+3	+3	−4	+31	−8

26. 24	27. 79	28. 401	29. 82	30. 242
+36	−25	+296	−37	+369

31. 865	32. 4+4+6 = ———	33. 824	34. 4654
−321		−717	+1975

Fill in the missing number:

35. 3+ ——— = 9   36. 57− ——— = 39

FIGURE 7-1   Sample Math CBA.

Figure 7-1 would be one of the three tests developed that measure the same areas.

Step 4—Determination of standards of performance

Table 7-1 indicates that the student is required to correctly answer five out of six items for each objective to reach mastery. The criteria are based on the student's performance on the three tests together.

Step 5—Administration and interpretation of the CBA instrument

Each of the three tests were administered on consecutive days to the entire class. Table 7-2 shows the results of the testing for one student in the class. These results would indicate that this particular student was having no problems with writing digits, understanding place value and comparing numbers, and addition and subtraction of single- and multiple-digit numbers without remaining. The student, however, apparently had no idea how to "carry" or "borrow" when adding and subtracting and had not mastered how to supply missing addends. It would be possible, therefore, to have a good idea which skill—renaming—to teach this student. Further, the teacher could group the students in the class according to performance, so that students with similar deficits could be taught together.

Uses and Limitations of Criterion-Referenced CBA Instruments

Overall, the research support for CBA procedures has been very positive. Among the strengths of CBA that have been noted are its ability to lead to student improvement (Galagan, 1985) and its use as an effective communication tool with parents (Marston & Magnusson, 1985). Clearly, its primary advantage is in allowing increased instructional decision-making (Howell & Morehead, 1987)

Although the majority of information about CBA is positive, proponents and critics alike agree that there are certain limitations to CBA procedures. For example, Heshusius (1991) argued that the CBA model was simplistic and did not consider the learning process itself. He further argued that the use of CBA results in a situation in which the teacher is virtually teaching the test. He instead argued for holistic evaluation that emphasized process and ecological testing. Taylor, Willits, and Richards (1989) also noted some limitations to CBA and mentioned several issues that CBA users should consider. Among those considerations were that the validity of the curriculum on which the CBA instrument is based will affect the validity of the instrument as well and that the term *CBA* is so broad that many people have interpreted it differently. Shinn (1988) also noted that there was no uniform approach to the development of CBA procedures that incorporated a consistent, identifiable set of objectives.

TABLE 7-2.   Results from the CBA.

CONCEPTS	PROBLEM NUMBERS	DAY 1	DAY 2	DAY 3	TOTAL SCORE 5/6	MASTERY 5/6
Writing digits	1,2	2/2	2/2	2/2	6/6	6/6
Place value	3,4	2/2	2/2	2/2	6/6	6/6
Comparing numbers	5,6	2/2	2/2	2/2	6/6	6/6
Add basic facts 0–10	7,21	2/2	2/2	2/2	6/6	6/6
Add basic facts 11–20	8,22	2/2	2/2	2/2	6/6	6/6
Add 2 digits (no renaming)	9,24	2/2	1/2	2/2	5/6	5/6
Add 1 renaming	10,26	0/2	0/2	0/2	0/6	0/6
Add 3 digits (no renaming)	11,28	2/2	2/2	1/2	5/6	5/6
Add 2 renaming	12,30	0/2	0/2	0/2	0/6	0/6
Add 3 or more numbers	13,32	2/2	1/2	2/2	5/6	5/6
Add 4 digits (renaming)	12,30	0/2	0/2	0/2	0/6	0/6
Subt. basic facts 0–10	15,23	2/2	2/2	2/2	6/6	6/6
Subt. basic facts 11–20	16,25	2/2	2/2	2/2	6/6	6/6
Subt. 2 digits (no renaming)	17,27	1/2	2/2	2/2	5/6	5/6
Subt. 2 digits (1 renaming)	18,29	0/2	0/2	0/2	0/6	0/6
Subt. 3 digits (no renaming)	19,31	2/2	2/2	2/2	6/6	6/6
Subt. 3 digits (1 renaming)	20,33	0/2	0/2	0/2	0/6	0/6
Missing ad-dends (1)	35,36	1/2	1/2	1/2	3/6	3/6

Adapted from L. Idol, A. Nevin, and P. Paolucci-Whitcomb, *Models of Curriculum-Based Assessment.* Copyright © 1986 by Aspen Publishers, Inc. Reprinted with permission of Aspen Publishers, Inc.

CURRICULUM-BASED MEASUREMENT (CBM)

One of the more widely researched models of CBA is CBM, which was developed by Deno and his associates at the University of Minnesota (Deno, 1987; Deno & Fuchs, 1987). While CBA is a more generic term that usually refers to informal and nonstandardized assessment (including the previously discussed criterion-referenced CBA), CBM is a standardized, empirically derived version. CBM differs from informal CBA in at least two ways: First, it focuses measurement on the annual curriculum so that the items represent an entire school year's content. For example, spelling might include a 20-word test drawn randomly from the entire pool of words for the year. Secondly, it uses a standardized methodology with documented reliability and validity (Fuchs, Fuchs, Hamlett, & Allinder, 1989). Shinn et al. (1989) also noted that informal CBA instruments are used primarily as pretests and mastery tests before instruction begins, whereas CBM is an ongoing evaluation process that is used after an instructional program is initiated. Fuchs and Fuchs (1990) noted the following characteristics of the CBM model: (1) a selection of one long-term goal instead of a series of short-term curricular steps; (2) measurement of standard behaviors that have documented reliability, validity, and sensitivity; (3) use of prescribed measurement methods; (4) incorporation of rules that provides systematic procedures for summarizing and evaluating the information; and, (5) accommodation of any instructional paradigm.

One of the hallmarks of the CBM model is the importance of instructional decision-making based on the student's progress within the curriculum. Therefore, when CBM procedures are used, it is important to determine the *trend line or progress line* of the student's performance (based on graphed data points) and compare that with the goal that has been established for the student. If the trend line indicates that the progress is slower than expected (in relation to the goal), an instructional change is suggested. If the trend line indicates that the progress is faster than expected, the goal is modified accordingly. The determination of the progress line can be accomplished informally by visually drawing a line through the data that appears to best fit the trend. The accuracy of this approach has been questioned, however (Tawney & Gast, 1984). There are some relatively simple approaches that can be used to increase the reliability of the trend line. Examples of these approaches are the *quarter-intersect method* and a modification of this procedure called the *split-middle method* (White & Haring, 1980). The following steps describe the two procedures. In addition, the steps are visually depicted in Figure 7-2.

Step 1.   Divide the data into two equal parts. If there is an odd number of data points, the line will be through the middle (median) data point going from left to right. If there is an even number the line will be between two data points.

Step 2.   For each half draw a vertical line at the mid-date. This will be the middle data point from left to right if there is an odd number of data points or between the middle data points if there is an even number.

Step 3.   For each half draw a horizontal line through the mid-rate line (the middle data point or between the two middle data points counting from bottom to top). Note that this line may pass though more than one data point (as depicted in Figure 7-2).

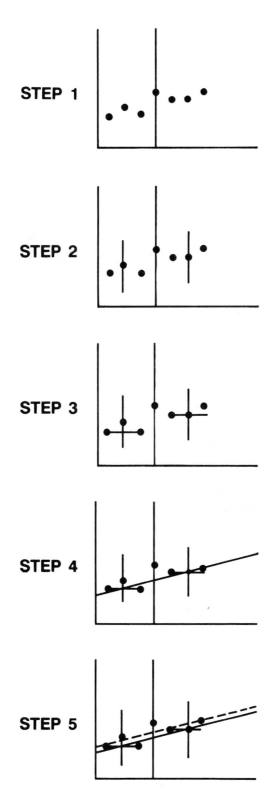

FIGURE 7-2   Determination of Progress Line
Using Quarter-Intersect and Split-Middle Methods.

Step 4.   Draw a line that passes through the intersection created in steps 1 and 2. THIS IS THE QUARTER-INTERSECT METHOD.

Step 5.   Move the line (always in a parallel fashion) up or down until there are the same number of data points on or above the line as there are data points on or below the line. THIS IS THE SPLIT MIDDLE METHOD.

Fuchs and Fuchs (1990) provided an excellent description of the use of CBM in the area of reading. The following example summarizes their description.

1. The teacher determines that by the end of the year the student should be proficient on third-grade level material (proficiency defined as reading at least 90 words per minute correctly with no more than five errors). This constitutes the long-term goal.

2. The teacher assesses the student at least twice weekly, each time on a different passage, randomly sampled in the third-grade curricular text. The teacher states a standard set of directions, has the student read orally for 1 minute from the text, and scores the number of correctly and incorrectly read words.

3. The teacher charts the student's performance on graph paper and the performance criterion of 90 words per minute would be placed on the graph at the intersection of the goal date and criterion level. Then a goal line connecting the baseline level and date and the goal criterion and date will be drawn onto the graph. Figure 7-3 shows an example of such a graph in which the student correctly read 29 words in the first week of September with the goal set at 90 words correct by the end of May.

4. The teacher provides an instructional program and continues to assess and graph the student's performance.

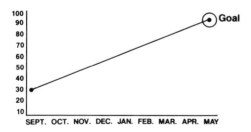

• **Words read correctly per minute**

FIGURE 7-3   Graph Reporting Baseline
Performance and Goal/Date for Student in the
Area of Oral Reading.

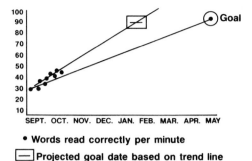

• **Words read correctly per minute**

☐— **Projected goal date based on trend line**

FIGURE 7-4   Graph Indicating that Goal Date
Should Be Changed.

5. Whenever at least eight scores have been collected, the teacher analyzes the adequacy of the student's progress and then draws a line of best fit through the student's data.

6. At this point the teacher determines the effectiveness of the teaching program. If the student's actual progress is steeper than the goal line, the teacher increases the goal (Figure 7-4). This would indicate that the date of the goal could be moved to mid-January. If the student's progress is less steep than the goal line, the teacher changes the instructional program to address the student's instructional needs (Figure 7-5). This figure shows that the student's improvement was not consistent with the projected goal.

Note that in the CBM procedure there is heavy reliance on decision-making based on visual inspection of the data. In other words, the assessment information is used continually to monitor progress and to aid the teacher in instructional decision making.

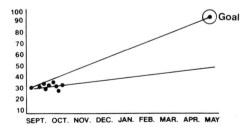

• **Words read correctly per minute**

FIGURE 7-5   Graph Indicating that
Instructional Change Is Necessary.

Computer-Based CBM

More recently, the use of computers to monitor and assist in CBM decision-making has become increasingly widespread. Programs have been designed to help teachers store, graph, and analyze student performance data (Hasselbring & Moore, 1990). An example of a computer-based measurement technique is *Monitoring Basic Skills Progress* (Fuchs, Hamlett, & Fuchs, 1990), a computer program package that is available for reading, spelling, and mathematics.

Monitoring Basic Skills Progress

Monitoring Basic Skills Progress (MBSP) comprises three software programs that were designed using the CBM model. As such, they allow the student to take a series of short tests at a given grade level that are automatically scored by the computer. It also provides feedback to the student and saves the student's scores and responses. Finally, it summarizes the performance for the teacher by providing a graph of the student's scores across the school year and a profile.

The three programs are *Basic Reading, Basic Spelling,* and *Basic Math.* The materials for each program include a Sample Student Disk, a Master Student Disk, and a Teacher Disk. In addition, information related to the reliability and validity of each program is included in the manuals. The Sample Student Disk contains assessment information for several students so that the teacher can get an idea of the types of graphs and skill profiles that will be presented. The Master Student Disk contains the software that allows the students to take the tests. The Master is used to make an individual student disk for each student. The Teacher Disk is used to allow the teacher to examine student assessment information. The MBSP Manuals include guidelines to help teachers make instructional decisions by interpreting the graphs and skill profiles that are generated by the computer. The guidelines include suggestions for monitoring goals, adjusting instructional programs, and comparing the relative effectiveness of different instructional components. The skill profile provides such information as the objectives that the student has mastered, partially mastered, not mastered, or were not attempted. The graphs provide a visual representation of the student's progress over time. Figure 7-6 shows an example of a student's graph where performance indicated that an instructional change was necessary. All disks require an Apple II computer with at least one disk drive and 64K of memory.

Basic Reading Tests. The tests used for Basic Reading are on separate Story Disks (one for each grade level from one to six). The tests use a "maze" procedure (see Chapter 13 for a detailed discussion of this procedure). In the MBSP, the maze procedure is set up so that every

Uh-oh!   Make a teaching change.

FIGURE 7-6   Sample Performance Pattern for Recommended
Teaching Change.

seventh word in a 400-word reading passage is deleted and replaced with
a blank. The students read the story and when they get to a blank they
press the spacebar to get three choices to replace the blank. The student
indicates the correct choice and then goes to the next blank. It is recommended that the student take a test every week (twice a week for special
education students). The test is automatically scored and saved, and a
graph similar to that in Figure 7-7 is created.

FIGURE 7-7   Sample Printed Graph Format to Distribute to Students.

Basic Spelling Tests.   Basic Spelling includes 30 lists of 20 spelling words at each of six grade levels. The words are dictated by the teacher and the student types the responses into the computer. As in the Basic Reading program, the computer then scores the responses, provides feedback to the student, and generates graphs and profiles for the teacher to analyze.

Basic Math Tests.   There are 30, 25-item mathematics tests available for each of six grade levels. The computer automatically administers the tests at the grade level designated by the teacher. The same scoring and feedback features noted in the other programs are available. A separate booklet with the 180 mathematics tests also comes with the package.

Uses and Limitations of CBM

Similar to the research on CBA, the professional literature has generally supported the use of CBM procedures, particularly for enhancing instructional decision-making. For example, Wesson, Vierthaler, and Haubrich (1989) reported that the use of CBM required less than 5 minutes per student to establish reading groups that were similar to those established over a 7-month period based on teacher recommendation. Other research has been conducted to determine ways to improve decision-making based on CBM. For example, it has been reported that the appropriate selection of the long-term goal has been a problem (Fuchs, Fuchs, & Hamlett, 1989) and that teachers need to know the actual student responses and not just the graphed responses to effectively make instructional decisions (Fuchs, Fuchs, Hamlett, & Allinder, 1991). As a result, skill analysis programs such as that noted in the MBSP have been developed to provide more specific information for the teacher. In addition, other refinements and suggestions for maximum decision-making are being made.

There are also some limitations to the CBM procedure noted in the professional literature. Some have criticized it because it emphasizes the isolation of skills rather than the examination of the learning process itself. Also, it tends to view learning in a linear fashion and the use of the graphs may oversimplify the learning process (Coleman, 1990). Gable (1990) also noted that CBM procedures are not always useful for designing interventions. In other words, whereas they can effectively indicate when a program change is needed, they do not provide the type of information that would help in determining the nature of an effective program. As an example of this, Frank and Gerken (1990) found that CBM probes were not sufficient in making program decisions for mildly retarded students.

CBA AND CBM: AN INTEGRATED MODEL

It is clear that there are similarities and differences in the CBA and CBM procedures discussed in this chapter. Both procedures have many advantages over traditional assessment methods. Cohen and Spence (1990) summarized several of these advantages. First, they provide increased communication for parents, teachers, and students about instructional decisions and student progress. Second, they have increased sensitivity and a direct impact on the student's curriculum. Third, they allow for peer referencing. In other words, they allow the teacher to determine the student's growth in comparison to a set of predetermined criteria (CBA) or in comparison to other students' progress (CBM). Finally, they noted that the use of these procedures reduces the bias in teacher referrals.

Should the CBA and CBM procedures discussed in this chapter be viewed and used in isolation? Hopefully not, because each provides important information in the evaluation process. Shapiro (1990), in fact, proposed an integrated model for CBA. He suggested that the first step should be to assess the academic environment through interviews and observation. The second step should be to assess the grade level of the student across the curriculum material. The third step should be to assess the instructional level within the correctly placed grade level. The fourth step should be to determine when instructional modification is necessary as new skills are acquired. The last step should be to assess the student's progress. Given the information presented in this chapter, CBA would be appropriate for Step 3 (as a pretest) and Step 5 (as mastery tests or probes). CBM would be appropriate for Steps 2, 4, and 5.

Instrument or Technique	Suggested Use							Target Population						Special Considerations	Educational Relevance for Exceptional Students
	Prereferral			Postreferral											
	Screening and Initial Identification	Informal Determination and Evaluation of Teaching Programs and Strategies	Determination of Current Performance Level and Educational Need	Decisions about Classification and Program Placement	IEP Goals	IEP Objectives	IEP Evaluation	Mild/Moderate	Severe/Profound	Preschool	Elementary Age	Secondary Age	Adult		
Criterion-Referenced CBA	X	X	X		X	X	X	X		X	X	X		Uses the actual curriculum as the content of the testing	very useful
Curriculum-Based Measurement	X	X	X		X	X	X	X		X	X	X		A more standardized version of CBA	very useful
Monitoring Basic Skills Progress	X	X	X		X	X	X	X			X			A computerized version of CBM; available in reading, math, and spelling	useful

PART THREE

Assessment of Abilities

One of the hallmarks of educational and psychological assessment is the measurement of an individual's abilities. Ability assessment involves the measurement of hypothetical constructs (i.e., underlying abilities) and is distinguished from the assessment of achievement (discussed in Part Four). As will be discussed, however, there is some question whether this ability/achievement distinction represents a true dichotomy. The abilities and their subsequent assessment that are discussed in this section are *intelligence, adaptive behavior, emotional/behavioral status,* and *language.*

As noted in Chapter 4, evaluation of the areas discussed in this section are important to help determine eligibility decisions. For example, the areas of *intelligence* and *adaptive behavior* are measured to help determine the label of mental retardation. In addition, IQ is used as a measure of *aptitude* in many states to help determine the aptitude/achievement discrepancy that is necessary for a label of learning disability. *Language* testing is used to help determine those who are eligible for programs for students with speech and language impairments, whereas *emotional/behavioral* testing is used with students suspected of having problems in those particular areas.

Perhaps more importantly, these types of tests can also be used to provide information about a student's strengths and weaknesses in each of the areas. They might also be used to identify general educational goals for the student and to identify areas that require further assessment. Finally, they are frequently used to make assumptions about an individual's underlying abilities. Often, ability tests are administered by ancillary personnel such as school psychologists, social workers, or speech-language clinicians (depending on the area tested). Teachers, however, do administer some of the tests discussed in this section. Further, it is important that teachers be familiar with these areas because they will see assessment information related to them.

Both formal tests and informal tests and procedures are included in these chapters. For each test described in this section the following information is included:

1. A summary matrix is provided that presents information about specific instruments and techniques in a format that allows easy comparison of the instruments for suggested use and target population. The matrix also includes a statement of any special considerations of which a user should be aware. In addition, for each instrument, the matrix gives the educational relevance for exceptional students. The matrices are directly related to the assessment model proposed in Chapter 2.

2. A thorough review of relevant research is provided for each norm-referenced instrument. The review emphasizes the use of the test with exceptional students.

3. An overview box is provided for each test. The overview summarizes the age range, technical adequacy (for norm-referenced tests), and suggested use for each instrument.

In addition, information related to how each type of test best fits into the overall assessment process is presented.

After reading Part Three you should be able to:

1. *Identify critical issues related to the assessment of intelligence*
2. *Identify alternative methods of measuring intelligence*
3. *Identify the various uses of adaptive behavior testing*
4. *Identify the advantages of using language samples*
5. *Identify the various philosophical approaches of measuring emotional/behavioral status*
6. *Identify the strengths and weaknesses of the major instruments used to measure intelligence, adaptive behavior, language, and emotional/behavioral status*

8

Assessment of Intelligence

INSTRUMENTS/PROCEDURES INCLUDED

ALTERNATIVES TO TRADITIONAL TESTS

INTELLIGENCE TESTS
- Group Tests
- Detroit Tests of Learning Aptitude–3
- Differential Ability Scales
- Kaufman Assessment Battery for Children
- Stanford-Binet–Fourth Edition
- Wechsler Intelligence Scale for Children–III
- Woodcock-Johnson–Revised

ADDITIONAL INSTRUMENTS
- Cognitive Levels Test
- Goodenough-Harris Drawing Test
- Kaufman Brief Intelligence Test
- McCarthy Scales of Children's Abilities
- Slosson Intelligence Test–Revised

For routine screening, Mrs. McMillan decided to give her fourth-grade class a group intelligence test. One of her students, Phillip, scored significantly below the rest of the class. Mrs. McMillan had been concerned about Phillip ever since he transferred into her class from another state. She had been collecting academic information that justified a referral for possible placement in a special-education program. After she referred Phillip, the school psychologist administered an individual intelligence test to help make a decision about Phillip's eligibility for special education.

Intelligence testing is one of the most debated issues in special education. Intelligence tests have both their staunch supporters and their vehement critics. Legal battles have been fought over whether these instruments have their place in the field of education. Suffice it to say that the debate is far from over and that ignoring the issue will not make it go away.

Historically, intelligence has been an enigmatic concept. It is a much-valued construct or quality that is extremely difficult to define. Is intelligence the same as verbal ability? Analytical thinking? Academic aptitude? Strategic thinking? The ability to cope? Different theorists might argue for each, or a combination, of these abilities. Similarly, they might ask whether intelligence is, or should be, defined in the same way for individuals of different cultural, ethnic, or social backgrounds.

As noted in Chapters 1 and 3, intelligence tests have been the focus of considerable debate because of their alleged bias against ethnic minority students. Research on the presence of bias in intelligence testing is fairly straightforward. Individuals from different cultural, ethnic, and socioeconomic groups do score differently on most measures of intelligence, particularly those that are verbal. Empirical investigation of the tests themselves (much of which was conducted as a result of the court cases regarding discriminatory evaluation) suggests that they are not statistically biased. Perhaps educators should be less concerned about whether or not a test is biased and more concerned about the uses of test data for discriminatory purposes. For instance, verbally-oriented intelligence tests have been shown to be valid predictors of school performance (measured by achievement tests), regardless of the racial or ethnic background of the student (Oakland, 1977; Reschly & Reschly, 1979). The use of these tests to predict teachers' ratings of students is somewhat more speculative (Partenio & Taylor, 1985; Reschly & Reschly, 1979). Their use in making major educational decisions is inappropriate (Clarizio, 1982). Certainly, test-based statements regarding "intellectual potential" should be avoided. In other words, intelligence tests have been criticized (probably erroneously) because incorrect or inappropriate decisions have been made from intelligence-test data. The problem is not necessarily inherent in the test itself; it is more a function of what we, as professionals, are doing with the tests.

One reason for this misunderstanding is that a distinction between "potential" and "performance" has not always been made. Many professionals have used intelligence tests as if they measured "intellectual potential." The tests, however, are much more accurate in reflecting what individuals have been taught and the material to which they have been exposed. Even performance on nonverbal analytical tasks is affected by a person's experience with similar tasks.

Several alternatives to traditional intelligence testing, however, are now receiving more and more attention. These alternative approaches will be discussed briefly, and an analysis of several intelligence measures widely used in special education will then follow.

ALTERNATIVES TO TRADITIONAL INTELLIGENCE TESTING

Traditional intelligence testing has been referred to as static assessment; as such, it does not measure the extent to which a student will profit from instruction (Campione, 1989). This static approach has been criticized when used to identify mentally retarded students and to assess culturally different minority-group children. Another criticism of traditional intelligence tests is that they are based on a too-narrowly-defined concept of intelligence (Naglieri, Das, & Jarman, 1990). These criticisms have led to a number of attempts to devise alternative techniques for measuring learning potential. These techniques are usually referred to as *dynamic assessment*. According to Haywood, Brown, and Wingenfeld (1990), dynamic assessment is characterized by (1) use of a test-teach-test paradigm; (2) emphasis on assessment of process not product; (3) attempts to specify obstacles to more effective learning; (4) attempts to specify conditions that will allow more effective performance; and (5) attempts to distinguish between performance and potential. Dynamic assessment procedures have been found to have limited reliability, although they do have validity (Laughon, 1990). Several of these procedures are discussed in the following sections.

Learning Potential Assessment Strategy (Budoff, 1973)

Budoff uses a test-train-retest paradigm to measure an individual's ability to learn from teaching. The procedure was developed initially for adolescents who had been classified as educably mentally retarded (EMR). Using nonverbal measures (for example, Raven's Progressive Matrices, Koh's Block Designs), Budoff pretests the subjects, trains or coaches the subjects on problem solving strategies, and posttests the subjects twice over a 1-month period. He then classifies the subjects as *high scorers* (pretest scores are high—gain little from training); *gainers* (pretest scores are low—gain from training); and *nongainers* (pretest scores are low—gain little from training). Budoff supports such a model to identify those students who are *educationally* as opposed to *mentally* retarded.

Learning Potential Assessment Device (Feuerstein, Haywood, Rand, Hoffman, & Jensen, 1984)

Feuerstein and colleagues' approach, like Budoff's, uses a test-train-retest paradigm. The Learning Potential Assessment Device (LPAD) consists of four nonverbal tasks (including the Raven's Progressive Matrices). The training in the LPAD, however, is somewhat different from Budoff's training. Feuerstein encourages the examiner to interact constantly with the examinee to maximize the probability of solving the problem. Feuerstein suggests that results from his measure can be used to identify appropriate teaching strategies as well as to supply information helpful in classifying a student.

Paired-Associate Learning

Paired-associate learning is certainly not a new technique. In experimental psychology, it has been a commonly used technique to measure memory and other skills. Paired-associate learning requires a subject to learn a novel set of associated items. For instance, a student might be told "ball—chair, brick—curtain, plant—tape, book—tree, plate—roof." The first word of each pair is then told to the subject who, in turn, must provide the associated word. Typically, the number of trials necessary for the subject to complete the associations is used as the measure of learning. Both meaningful and nonmeaningful associations have been used within this paradigm. The use of paired-associate learning is based on the assumption that learning new material is a good indication of learning ability. Kratochwill (1977) pointed out, however, that this technique measures only rote memory, which is merely one of many skills necessary for achievement in school.

Chronometric Techniques

More recently, chronometric techniques such as reaction time and speed of information processing (e.g., speed of memory retrieval) have been suggested as measures of intelligence. Vernon (1990) noted that such approaches place no emphasis on previous learning or acquired knowledge yet are strongly correlated with standardized IQ measures.

INTELLIGENCE TESTS: GENERAL PURPOSE AND DESCRIPTION

WHY USE?
   Screening and identification (group tests); decisions about classification and program placement (individual tests)

WHO SHOULD USE?
   School psychologists, guidance personnel; information also used by teachers

As previously noted, intelligence tests are relatively good predictors of school performance (particularly, of achievement-test scores). They are much less accurate in measuring the "learning potential" of an individual.

Reschly (1979) reported a type of "surgeon general's warning" that can be used to help avoid misinterpretation of results from intelligence tests:

> *IQ tests measure only a portion of the competencies involved with human intelligence. The IQ results are best seen as predicting performance in school, and reflecting the degree to which children have mastered middle class cultural symbols and values. This is useful information, but it is also limited. Further cautions—IQ tests do not measure innate-genetic capacity and the scores are not fixed. Some persons do exhibit significant increases or decreases in their measured IQ. (p. 24)*

Intelligence tests fall into two major categories: group administered and individually administered. Group-administered intelligence tests are very similar in structure and format to group-administered achievement tests. They measure, in fact, very similar areas. Group intelligence tests usually have different levels that are used with individuals in certain grades. Typically, they include some combination of measures of language ability, memory skills, comprehension, analogical reasoning, and reading and mathematics aptitude.

Fields and Kumar (1982) surveyed 90 teachers and found that 30 percent found little or no use for the scores from group intelligence tests. Even though such a relatively large number of the teachers thought the information was limited, approximately 85 percent still used it. These tests, however, should be used for *rough screening only*. The determination and use of IQs on the basis of these group tests is not advised. Table 8-1 summarizes the areas measured by some of the more popular group intelligence tests.

Individual intelligence tests vary tremendously in their format and content. Some intelligence tests (or tests that purportedly measure intelligence) measure only one skill such as vocabulary or visual analogy. Other more popular instruments are multiskilled—that is, they measure many components of the intelligence construct. There are also a number of tests that have been developed for or are used primarily with populations such as blind, deaf, or physically handicapped individuals. For example, the Perkins-Binet Intelligence Scale for blind individuals, the Leiter International Performance Scale for deaf individuals, and more recently, the Test of Nonverbal Intelligence–2 are designed in such a way to circumvent the person's specific handicap (see Appendix B).

Individual intelligence testing, until recently, has been a crucial, even mandatory component in the formal assessment process. It is still required to determine eligibility for special education in the vast majority of states.

This section focuses on six tests that are commonly used in special education. The Wechsler Intelligence Scale for Children–Third Edition (WISC-III) is a recent revision of the most popular instrument. The Detroit Tests of Learning Aptitude–3 (DTLA–3) is the second revision of

TABLE 8-1   Frequently Used Group-Administered Intelligence Tests.

NAME	AREAS MEASURED (SCORES AVAILABLE)[*]
Analysis of Learning Potential (Durost, Gardner, Madden, & Prescott, 1971)	Overall learning potential, mathematics, reading
California Test of Mental Maturity (Sullivan, Clark, & Tiegs, 1970)	Logical reasoning, spatial relationships, numerical reasoning, verbal concepts, memory, language, non-language
Cognitive Abilities Test (Thorndike & Hagen, 1986)	Verbal, quantitative, nonverbal
Kuhlmann-Anderson Test (Kuhlmann & Anderson, 1982)	Verbal, quantitative
Lorge-Thorndike Intelligence Tests (Lorge, Thorndike, & Hagen, 1966)	Verbal, nonverbal, composite
Otis-Lennon School Ability Test (Otis & Lennon, 1989)	Analogies, classifying, reasoning, sequencing
Short Form Test of Academic Aptitude (Sullivan, Clark, & Tiegs, 1970)	Sequences, analogies, memory, verbal reasoning, cognitive skills

[*]All the above instruments have several levels designed to be used with individuals from kindergarten (in some cases prekindergarten) through grade 12.

an old and popular test. The Differential Ability Scales is relatively new and increasingly popular. The Kaufman Assessment Battery for Children (K-ABC) is a widely researched instrument. The Stanford-Binet Intelligence Scale–Fourth Edition is the most recent version of the "grandfather" of intelligence tests. The Woodcock-Johnson–Revised measures cognitive ability and achievement. (The achievement section is discussed in Chapter 12.)

Detroit Tests of Learning Aptitude–3

The Detroit Tests of Learning Aptitude–3 (DTLA-3) (Hammill, 1991) is the second major revision of a test that was originally published in 1935. The original and earlier revised versions were criticized for a number of reasons, including a limited standardization sample and questionable validity. The DTLA-2 (Hammill, 1985) included a more representative normative group, added four new subtests, and dropped many subtests from the earlier versions. The DTLA-2, however, retained (with some format/name changes) seven of the subtests from the earlier versions. The DTLA-3 made further changes, revising six subtests, dropping three subtests, and adding three new subtests. The DTLA-3 takes approximately 1–2 hours to administer, depending on the age and ability level of the examinee. Basal and ceiling rules are used to minimize administration time.

Description of subtests

Word Opposites (50 items)—The examinee is asked to give the opposite of vocabulary words such as *"hot, crooked,* and *remember."*

Design Sequences (12 items)—The student is shown a card with a series of pictures on it. Next, the student is shown another card with the same pictures in a different order and is asked to put them in the same order as before.

Sentence Imitation (30 items)—Sentences such as "In summer, we go north where it is cool" are read to the examinee, who must repeat it exactly.

Letter Sequences (12 items)—The student is shown a card with a series of letters printed on it for a brief period of time and is asked to write them down in the exact order.

Story Construction (3 stories)—The student is asked to look at a picture and make up a story about it. The story is scored according to certain criteria related to conceptual and creative attributes, among others.

Design Reproduction (23 items)—The examinee is shown a geometric figure for 5 seconds and then asked to draw it from memory.

Basic Information (40 items)—The student is asked basic questions, e.g., "What planet is closest to the sun?" and must give an oral answer.

Symbolic Relations (30 items)—This subtest requires the student to use visual reasoning to solve a series of problems in which a series of pictures/designs forms a pattern that would lead to a correct answer to complete the pattern.

Word Sequences (30 items)—The student is asked to repeat a series of words ranging from *"man-horse-song"* to *"ear-pig-skate-rope-wool."*

Story Sequences (8 items)—The student is shown a series of pictures (4–8) and must put them in the correct sequence to tell a story.

Picture Fragments (27 items)—The student is shown an incomplete picture and must identify what it is.

Interpretation of results

Raw scores from each individual subtest can be converted to standard scores (mean = 10; standard deviation = 3), percentile ranks, and age equivalents. In addition, several composite scores are available in three major domains. These are determined by combining various subtest scores. There is also a General Mental Ability Quotient (GMAQ) that consists of all 11 subtests in combination and an Optimal Mental Ability Score that is determined by using the four highest subtest scores. Each of these latter scores have a mean of 100 and a standard deviation of 15. A list of the various composite scores and their respective domains follow:

LINGUISTIC DOMAIN

Verbal Aptitude
Nonverbal Aptitude

ATTENTIONAL DOMAIN

Attention-Enhanced Aptitude
Attention-Reduced Aptitude

MOTORIC DOMAIN

Motor-Enhanced Aptitude
Motor-Reduced Aptitude

Finally, Theoretical Composite scores can be determined that include the subtests most highly associated with various theoretical models of intelligence (e.g., Fluid versus Crystallized). Results from the DTLA-3 can be plotted on a profile sheet for visual interpretation. Also, additional interpretive guidelines can be found in the manual.

Technical characteristics

Normative sample.   A stratified sample of over 2,500 students from 36 states were included in the standardization. Race, ethnicity, sex, residence, and geographic area were matched to the U.S. population.

Reliability.   Limited test-retest reliability coefficients ranged from .77 to .96 for the subtests and .81 to .96 for the composites. Internal consistency ranged from .81 to .94 and .89 to .96 for the subtests and composite scores, respectively.

Validity.   Arguments for content and construct validity are presented in the manual. Concurrent-validity coefficients using the DTLA-2, K-ABC, and Woodcock-Johnson–Revised are reported. DTLA-3 subtest coefficients were low to moderate, whereas the composite coefficients were moderate with those measures. The correlation between the GMAQ and the global IQs from the other tests were in the .80s–.90s range.

Review of relevant research

No research on the DTLA-3 was located. In fact, surprisingly little research has been conducted on the DTLA-2. Information related to the DTLA-2 might be relevant for the DTLA-3, although research on the earlier editions must be interpreted cautiously due to format and standardization differences. Stehouwer (1985) reviewed the DTLA-2 and noted that it appears to be potentially useful for identifying students' strengths and weaknesses, although it is still necessary to determine the test's validity and reliability. In one empirical study, Silverstein (1986) factor-analyzed the test and noted that none of the factors corresponded to any of the composite scores that were yielded. This finding questions the construct validity of the instrument. Further research is obviously needed on the DTLA-3.

OVERVIEW: DETROIT TESTS OF LEARNING APTITUDE–3

- *Age level*—6–18 years old
- *Type of administration*—Individual
- *Technical adequacy*—Limited reliability, questionable validity
- *Scores yielded*—Standard scores, percentile ranks, age equivalents
- *Suggested use*—The DTLA-2 and DTLA-3 are certainly an improvement over the original DTLA. However, validity data that give meaning to the various composite scores are lacking. As noted in the manual, one should not compare composite scores from different domains. It is probably best to acknowledge that the DTLA-3 is an *aptitude* test, not an instrument to determine how an individual processes information. Therefore, the Global Composite score is probably the best to interpret as an overall measure of learning aptitude. At present, the test should be interpreted cautiously until more information is available attesting to its uses and limitations. It should be noted that there is also a DTLA–Primary for children aged 3–9 and a DTLA–Adult.

Differential Ability Scales

The Differential Ability Scales (DAS) (Elliot, 1990) is an individually administered battery of cognitive and achievement tests for individuals aged 2 1/2 through 17. The DAS is an updated revision of the British Ability Scales. The DAS is organized into a cognitive battery that includes two levels, preschool and school-age, and the school achievement tests. Each of these will be discussed separately.

Description

Cognitive battery—preschool level.   The preschool level of the cognitive battery is further broken down into two sub-levels, one suitable for children ages 2 1/2 to 3 1/2, the other for children ages 3 1/2 to 6. For each level there are both core subtests and diagnostic subtests that are used to provide supplemental information. The preschool level 2 1/2 to 3 1/2 includes the following four core subtests:

> *Block Building (12 items)*—Requires the child to copy two- and three-dimensional designs with wooden blocks.
>
> *Verbal Comprehension (36 items)*—Requires the child to point to pictures or manipulate objects in response to oral instructions.
>
> *Picture Similarities (32 items)*—Requires the child to identify pictures that share a common element or concept.

Naming Vocabulary (26 items)—Requires the child to identify objects or pictures by name.

For the 3 1/2 to 6 year-old level the subtests include three of the four previously described subtests (Verbal Comprehension, Naming Vocabulary, and Picture Similarities), plus the following three subtests:

Pattern Construction (26 items)—Requires the child to construct a design using flat squares or solid cubes with black and yellow patterns.

Early Number Concepts (28 items)—Requires the child to answer questions about number, size, or numerical concepts.

Copying (20 items)—Requires the child to reproduce a line drawing provided by the examiner.

As mentioned, there are also diagnostic subtests that are available for testing the preschool child. They are administered for additional probing to gather more comprehensive information. For the 2 1/2 to 3 1/2 year-old level the diagnostic subtests are Recall of Digits and Recognition of Pictures. For the 3 1/2 to 6 year-old level, the same two subtests plus Block Building, Matching Letter-Like Forms, and Recall of Objects are used.

Cognitive battery—school age.   For the school age level, ages 6 through 17, there are six core subtests:

Recall of Designs (21 items)—Requires the individual to reproduce a line drawing that is presented for 5 seconds and then removed.

Word Definitions (42 items)—The individual must tell the meaning of words ranging from "gift" to "hirsute."

Pattern Construction (26 items)—Discussed in preschool battery.

Matrices (33 items)—Requires the individual to select from four or six choices the figure that correctly completes an incomplete matrix of abstract figures.

Similarities (34 items)—The individual must identify how three objects or pictures are similar or go together.

Sequential and Quantitative Reasoning (39 items)—The individual must either complete a series of abstract figures by providing one that is missing or find a relationship within two pairs of numbers and apply that relationship to find a missing number.

There are three diagnostic subtests for the school-age level. Those are Recall of Digits, Recall of Objects, and Speed of Information Processing.

SCHOOL ACHIEVEMENT TESTS

Basic Number Skills (48 items)—Requires the individual to solve computational problems presented on a worksheet.

Spelling (70 items)—Requires the individual to write the correct spelling of words ranging from "in" to "ichthyosaurus."

Word Reading (90 items)—Requires the individual to read orally words ranging from "the" to "tertiary."

Interpretation of results

There are a number of scoring options available on the DAS. The following is a description of those scores as they are presented in the test manual:

Cognitive subtests—Percentile ranks and T-scores (mean = 50, standard deviation = 10) are provided for each of the individual cognitive subtests. These tables used are on the basis of *ability scores* that are obtained by converting the raw scores using information found in the record form.

General Conceptual Ability and Cluster scores—For each level a General Conceptual Ability (GCA) score (similar to an IQ) can be determined using a combination of the core subtests. The GCA is presented as a standard score with a mean of 100 and a standard deviation of 15. In addition, at the 3 1/2 to 6-year-old level a Verbal Ability and Nonverbal Ability Cluster score can be obtained. Similarly, for the school-age level, Verbal Ability, Nonverbal Reasoning Ability, and Spatial Ability Cluster scores can be determined. These scores also are based on a mean of 100 and a standard deviation of 15.

The School Achievement Tests—These individual tests can be interpreted by use of standard scores (mean of 100, standard deviation of 15) and percentiles by both age and grade.

Age Equivalents—These scores are available for all cognitive and achievement subtests.

Score Comparisons—This provides information helpful in profile analysis, including such things as determination of aptitude-achievement discrepancies. Information regarding statistical significance of score differences is also presented.

Technical characteristics

Normative sample.   Approximately 3,500 children were included in the sample. The sample was stratified by sex, race/ethnicity, current education, and geographic region. In addition, for the preschool population, stratification was based on educational preschool enrollment. The technical handbook for the DAS provides extensive descriptions of the tryout and standardization samples. Care was taken to ensure that percentages in the sample were similar to those in the U.S. population.

Reliability.   Internal reliabilities for the preschool level of the cognitive battery were in the .70s and .80s range for subtests and in the high .80s and .90s for the GCA and Cluster scores. A similar pattern but with somewhat higher coefficients was recorded for the school-age level and for the achievement tests.

Test/retest reliabilities for the preschool subtests were low to moderate. Test/retest coefficients for the Cluster scores and GCA were higher, ranging from .79 to .94. For the school-age subtests correlation coefficients were somewhat higher, whereas the Cluster and GCA coefficients were similar to that in the preschool population. Interrater reliability was also determined for four subtests for which that type of reliability would be relevant. Those coefficients ranged from .90 for Copying to .96 for Similarities.

Validity. The author provides a considerable amount of evidence for construct validity, including intercorrelations of subtests and composites and results of a factor analysis that supports the cluster scores. Concurrent validity for the DAS for the preschool level with the Wechsler Preschool and Primary Scale of Intelligence–Revised (WPPSI–R) as the criterion was reported. The overall correlation between the GCA and the Full Scale IQ was .89. Correlations between the subtests of the DAS and the WPPSI–R were considerably lower. Coefficients with the Stanford-Binet–4 were also provided with an overall correlation of .77 with the full-scale scores. Correlations with other intelligence measures were in the .60s to .70s range. At the school-age level correlations with the WISC–R at different age levels ranged from .84 to .91. Coefficients with the Stanford-Binet–4 ranged from .85 to .88; the correlation with the K-ABC was .75. The manual also includes correlations between various subtests and other instruments such as language and measures of nonverbal intellectual functioning.

Correlations between the three achievement tests and the same intellectual measures range from approximately .50 to .70. Correlations between the achievement tests and other achievement measures were higher, generally ranging in the .70 to .80 range. One advantageous feature is the reporting of DAS score profiles of special populations including gifted, mentally retarded, learning disabled, and reading disabled. This information provides the breakdown of the representation of those types of students in the standardization sample and their subsequent performance on the DAS.

Review of relevant research

At the time of the completion of this book, limited research had been reported. It is anticipated that the instrument will be widely investigated, particularly in the school psychology literature. Platt, Kamphaus, Keltgen, and Gilliland (1991) reviewed the DAS and the available research on the instrument. They noted that it has many strong qualities, including good psychometric characteristics and the use of extended norms that allow the calculation of GCAs as low as 25. They had questions, however, about the nonverbal reasoning and spatial factors and whether the individual subtests should be interpreted. In another study reported in the professional literature, Kercher and Sandoval (1991) found that children with reading disabilities displayed a characteristic pattern, performing poorly in achievement and Recall of Digits/Recall of Objects.

OVERVIEW: DIFFERENTIAL ABILITY SCALES

- *Age level*—Ages 2 1/2 through 17
- *Type of administration*—Individual
- *Technical adequacy*—Good standardization, good reliability and validity (particularly construct validity)
- *Scores yielded*—Percentile ranks, standard scores, age equivalents, grade equivalents.
- *Suggested use*—The DAS appears to be one of the better constructed individual intelligence tests. The manuals are thorough, and the technical handbook provides comprehensive descriptions of individual studies regarding its development and subsequent validation. The attention paid to the preschool level is worthy of note. Unlike many other instruments the DAS reports technical characteristics of the preschool level in some detail, and the information is easy to find in the manual. In addition, the preschool subtests can be administered in significantly less time than many other instruments designed for the same age such as the WPPSI–R or the McCarthy Scales. In fact, the school-age level can also be administered relatively quickly (40–65 minutes). Another notable characteristic is the use of both core and diagnostic subtests as well as guidelines for "extended" and "out-of-level" testing when individuals who are performing considerably lower or higher than others of the same chronological age are evaluated. Although research is needed to investigate its usefulness, it appears to be a well-developed instrument that will provide an option to the traditional intelligence measures usually employed.

The Kaufman Assessment Battery for Children

The Kaufman Assessment Battery for Children (K-ABC) (Kaufman & Kaufman, 1983) is a widely researched addition to the available intelligence measures. According to the authors, the K-ABC is a measure of both intelligence and achievement (acquired knowledge) for children of ages 2 1/2 through 12 1/2. The theoretical basis for the instrument is drawn heavily from cognitive psychology and neuropsychology. The authors define and measure intellectual ability as the child's ability to perform problems requiring sequential and simultaneous processing. *Sequential processing* refers to the ability to arrange stimuli in sequential or serial order. *Simultaneous processing* requires an individual to integrate and synthesize spatial or analogic information.

Description

The K-ABC has 16 subtests. Three subtests comprise the sequential-processing scale; seven subtests comprise the simultaneous-processing scale; and six subtests comprise the achievement scale. Certain subtests are appropriate for certain age levels.

SEQUENTIAL PROCESSING

Hand Movements (ages 2 1/2 through 12 1/2)—This subtest requires the child to reproduce a series of hand movements demonstrated by the examiner.

Number Recall (ages 2 1/2 through 12 1/2)—In this subtest, the child must repeat a series of verbally presented digits.

Word Order (ages 4 through 12 1/2)—The child must touch a series of pictures in the same sequence that is verbally presented by the examiner.

SIMULTANEOUS PROCESSING

Magic Window (ages 2 1/2 through 4)—The child must identify a picture that is exposed only partially at any one time.

Face Recognition (ages 2 1/2 through 4)—The child is exposed briefly to a photograph that shows one or two faces and must pick out the faces from a photograph of a group of faces.

Gestalt Closure (ages 2 1/2 through 12 1/2)—The child must name an object that is only partially drawn.

Triangles (ages 4 through 12 1/2)—The child is required to reproduce various models using identical triangle puzzle pieces.

Matrix Analogies (ages 5 through 12 1/2)—The child must choose a picture that best completes a visual analogy.

Spatial Memory (ages 5 through 12 1/2)—The child is shown a page with several pictures placed in certain areas and must remember the placement of the pictures.

Photo Series (ages 6 through 12 1/2)—The child must place several photographs of an event (for example, a candle melting) in chronological order.

ACHIEVEMENT

Expressive Vocabulary (ages 2 1/2 through 4)—The child must name objects in a photograph.

Faces and Places (ages 2 1/2 through 12 1/2)—The child must name a fictional character, place, or well-known person shown in a photograph.

Arithmetic (ages 3 through 12 1/2)—The child must demonstrate school-related mathematics abilities on a number of tasks.

Riddles (ages 3 through 12 1/2)—The child is given a list of characteristics of a concrete or abstract concept and must determine that concept.

Reading/Decoding (ages 5 through 12 1/2)—The child must identify letters and read words.

Reading/Understanding (ages 7 through 12 1/2)—The child must execute commands that he or she reads in sentences.

Interpretation of results

Standard scores (mean = 100; standard deviation = 15) are available for the sequential-processing scale, simultaneous-processing scale, achievement scale, and for a mental-processing composite (sequential and simultaneous). In addition, national percentile ranks and sociocultural percentile ranks are also available for each of these four areas. The sociocultural percentile rank allows a child's scores to be compared with the scores of children of similar ethnic and socioeconomic background. Sociocultural data are obtainable for the subtests in the sequential-processing and simultaneous-processing scales (scaled score mean = 10; standard deviation = 3) and for the achievement subtests (standard score mean = 100; standard deviation = 15). A profile sheet is available to provide direct comparisons of the scores as well as to determine discrepancies between the mental-processing and achievement scores. An interpretation manual is available separately and includes research reports and possible uses with exceptional children.

Technical characteristics

Normative sample.   Two thousand children from 22 states were included; stratified sample based on 1980 census; exceptional children were also included. This normative sample overlapped with that used for the Vineland Adaptive Behavior Scales (see Chapter 9).

Reliability.   Split-half reliability coefficients ranged from .86 to .93 (preschool) and from .89 to .97 (elementary). Test-retest coefficients increased with age, ranging from .77 to .95 for preschoolers to .87 to .97 for a sample of children aged 9–12 1/2.

Validity.   Evidence for construct and criterion-related validity is relatively strong. The interpretation manual summarizes over 40 validity studies with a variety of populations.

Review of relevant research

The K-ABC received a great deal of attention when it first appeared on the market. Entire issues of journals were devoted to reviews of and research related to the K-ABC. The following is a discussion of the major issues that have been addressed.

- Some researchers feel the K-ABC has adequate construct validity (Kaufman & McLean, 1986; Majorski, 1984), but others question the theoretical and psychometric validity claims of the test (Hopkins & Hodge, 1984; Sternberg, 1984; Weibe, 1986).
- There are many questions about the simultaneous and sequencing processing components of the K-ABC (Bracken & Howell, 1989; Strommen, 1988). Some researchers question whether the two components can be specified from achievement and from each other (Hall & Goetz, 1984). Das (1984) indicated that the processes are actually measures of nonverbal and verbal

abilities. Gridley, Miller, Barke, Fischer, and Smith (1990) found no evidence of the two constructs with a preschool population. Swanson, Bradenburg-Ayres, and Wallace (1989) found no evidence with gifted students.

- A lack of long-term reliability data and predictive validity has been noted (Mehrens, 1984); however, one study reports adequate stability when used with at-risk preschool children (Lyon & Smith, 1987). Another study showed that stability improved with the subject's increasing age (Kamphaus & Reynolds, 1984).

- The K-ABC does not provide an adequate data base from which to propose remediation (Weibe, 1986). It has been suggested that the test's components be interpreted as reading achievement and verbal reasoning to facilitate educational decision making (Dunbar & Keith, 1984).

- It is inconclusive whether weak processes can be trained (Hritcko & Salvia, 1984). Kaufman (1984) opposes the ability-training approach, although others are proponents. Simultaneous processing was reported to be more amenable to change in one study (Lyon & Smith, 1987).

- Further research needs to be done in the area of proper interpretation (Dunbar & Keith, 1984). Profiles must be interpreted cautiously (Hopkins & Hodge, 1984); it must be noted that significant processing differences are common in the normal population (Chatman, Reynolds, & Willson, 1984). A microcomputer program, *ASSIST,* is available for scoring and is helpful in increasing scoring accuracy and reducing scoring time (Merz, 1984).

- The K-ABC has moderate positive correlations with WISC-R for learning-disabled, mildly retarded, and normal children (Klanderman, Perney, & Kroeschell, 1985, Naglieri, 1985; Smith, Lyon, Hunter, & Boyd, 1988). There is also some indication that the factor structure for learning-disabled (LD) and non-LD students is similar on the K-ABC (Kaufman & McLean 1986). The K-ABC appears useful in identifying dyslexic readers (Hooper & Hynd, 1986) and other LD children, although a characteristic LD profile was not found (Naglieri, 1985).

- More research is needed to support the K-ABC's claim of being a relatively nondiscriminatory test (Naglieri, 1986). There is some evidence that the reliability of the test is similar for black and white children (Matazow, Kamphaus, Stanton, & Reynolds, 1991) and that the items are not racially biased (Wilson, Nolan, Reynolds, & Kamphaus, 1989). However, Jensen (1986) noted that the reduced difference between black and white scores (compared to the WISC-R) was not the result of greater validity or of a less biased measurement of IQ. In addition, Valencia and Ronkin (1988) reported that the K-ABC is not as good a predictor of achievement for Mexican-American students as it is for white students.

- The nonverbal K-ABC subtests adequately differentiate intellectual functioning in school-age deaf children when either pantomime and gestures or American Sign Language are used (Kirby & Porter, 1986); however, caution should be taken when using it with hearing-impaired preschoolers, because the test provides only three subtests (Telzrow, 1984).

- It has been suggested that the test be supplemented with paper and pencil tasks in such areas as arithmetic, language, and behavior (Telzrow, 1984).

In addition, the Bender-Gestalt has been suggested as a valuable aid to be used with the simultaneous scale (Haddad, 1986).

■ English-speaking Mexican-American children score generally higher on the simultaneous than on the sequential scale and show a restricted range of all scores involved with verbal scales (Valencia, 1984).

■ The test should be used with caution to identify gifted children (Harrison, 1988); many subtests have low ceilings, there is a lack of complex intellectual content in the mental processing scales, and it has low concurrent predictive validity for general academic achievement (Hessler, 1985). In addition, the factor structure for gifted students is different from that reported for the standardization sample (Swanson et al, 1989).

■ The K-ABC is of limited use with preschool children having lower levels of cognitive ability (Bloom et al, 1988). Further, the K-ABC results in lower scores with preschool children than the Wechsler Scale (Wade, Kutsick, & Vance, 1988).

■ There are questions concerning the representativeness of the norms used for the K-ABC (Hopkins & Hodges, 1984).

■ The factor structure for the K-ABC and the WISC-R is very similar. The verbal-comprehension, perceptual-organization, and freedom-from-distractability factors from the WISC-R corresponded to the achievement, simultaneous-processing, and sequential-processing components from the K-ABC, respectively (Kaufman & McLean, 1986).

■ In a review of the K-ABC, Kaufman, Kamphaus, and Kaufman (1985) noted that

1. The sequential processing component is less reliable than the simultaneous component.
2. There is a heavy emphasis on visual stimuli, making the test inappropriate for children with visual problems.
3. The test does not adequately measure verbal reasoning and spontaneous expression.
4. There are too few manipulative tasks for preschoolers and too few easy items for children aged 2–6.

Summary of research findings

Much of the research on the K-ABC has focused on its construct validity. Specifically, the meaning of the simultaneous and sequential processing components has been investigated with unclear results. Criterion-related validity with the WISC-R is generally good. Research on its use with exceptional students is equivocal. There is evidence that it can be helpful with LD and hearing-impaired students, although its use with visually-impaired and gifted students has been discouraged. Its use with young, preschool children also appears to be limited. The nondiscriminatory nature of the K-ABC has also been debated. More research will undoubtedly shed light on a number of issues.

OVERVIEW: KAUFMAN ASSESSMENT BATTERY FOR CHILDREN

- *Age level*—2 1/2 to 12 1/2 years old
- *Type of administration*—Individual
- *Technical adequacy*—Good standardization, adequate reliability, questionable validity (construct)
- *Scores yielded*—Scaled scores, standard scores, national percentile ranks, sociocultural percentile ranks
- *Suggested use*—The K-ABC was a much awaited instrument when it was published a decade ago. As such, it has received much attention in the professional literature. The technical characteristics of the instrument are acceptable, and the addition of the sociocultural percentile ranks is a useful feature. This addition, in fact, helped give the instrument an early favorable reputation as a nondiscriminatory assessment measure. Questions about this as well as other claims (such as usefulness for LD diagnosis because of intelligence-achievement comparisons), however, have not been answered adequately. There is also some question about the interpretation of the various processing components. Further research and continued use will hopefully answer many of the questions regarding the interpretation of the K–ABC.

Stanford Binet Intelligence Scale–Fourth Edition

The fourth edition of the Stanford-Binet Intelligence Scale (SBIS-4) (Thorndike, Hagen, & Sattler, 1986) has retained many of the characteristics of the earlier versions yet has made some significant changes. According to the authors the SBIS-4 was constructed for the following purposes:

1. To help differentiate between students who are mentally retarded and those who have specific learning disabilities.
2. To help educators and psychologists understand why a particular student is having difficulty in school.
3. To help identify gifted students.
4. To study the development of cognitive skills of individuals from ages 2 to adult. (p. 2)

The SBIS-4 includes 15 subtests that fit into a three-level hierarchical model that includes a general intelligence level (g) at the top, three broad factors (crystallized abilities, fluid-analytic abilities, and short–term memory) at the second level, and three narrower factors (verbal reasoning, quantitative reasoning, and abstract-visual reasoning) at the third level (Figure 8-1).

		g		

CRYSTALLIZED ABILITIES			FLUID-ANALYTIC ABILITIES	SHORT-TERM MEMORY

VERBAL REASONING	QUANTITATIVE REASONING		ABSTRACT/VISUAL REASONING	

Vocabulary	Quantitative	Pattern Analysis	Bead Memory
Comprehension	Number Series	Copying	Memory for Sen-
Absurdities	Equation Building	Matrices	tences
Verbal Relations		Paper Folding and	Memory for Digits
		Cutting	Memory for Objects

FIGURE 8-1   Hierarchical Model of the Stanford-Binet Intelligence Scale.

Reprinted with permission of THE RIVERSIDE PUBLISHING COMPANY from page 4 of *Stanford-Binet Intelligence Scale: Guide for Administering and Scoring the Fourth Edition* by R. L. Thorndike, E. P. Hagen, and J. M. Sattler. THE RIVERSIDE PUBLISHING COMPANY, 8240 W. Bryn Mawr Avenue, Chicago, IL 60631. Copyright © 1986.

Description of subtests

Vocabulary (46 items)—This subtest includes 14 picture-vocabulary items and 32 oral-vocabulary items. This subtest is also used to determine the starting point for the other 14 subtests.

Bead Memory (42 items)—This subtest requires the examinee to look at a picture of beads of various sizes and colors that are arranged in a certain pattern and then reproduce the pattern placing beads on a stick.

Quantitative (34 items)—This subtest measures quantitative skills and concepts.

Memory for Sentences (42 items)—In this subtest, the examiner reads a sentence that must be repeated by the examinee.

Pattern Analysis (36 items)—The examinee must reproduce a cube pattern constructed by the examiner or presented in a picture.

Comprehension (42 items)—This subtest includes identification of body parts and questions requiring verbal reasoning.

Absurdities (32 items)—The examinee must indicate why a picture or parts of a picture are absurd.

Memory for Digits (12 items)—The examinee must listen to a series of digits and then repeat them in the same or in reverse order.

Copying (28 items)—The examinee must either duplicate block patterns or copy geometric figures using a pencil and paper.

Memory for Objects (14 items)—The examinee is shown a series of pictures and then must identify the correct sequence.

Matrices (26 items)—The examinee must complete a series of incomplete matrices.

Number Series (26 items)—The examinee must identify the next number in a series of numbers that is presented following a certain rule.

Paper Folding and Cutting (18 items)—The examiner folds and cuts a piece of paper in a certain way and the examinee must identify from several choices how the paper will look unfolded.

Verbal Relations (18 items)—The examinee must look for similarities and differences in a set of words.

Equation Building (18 items)—The examinee must arrange numbers and mathematical signs to form number sentences.

Interpretation of results

Standard scores are available for individual subtests (mean = 50; standard deviation = 8). It is also possible to obtain standard scores for Verbal Reasoning, Abstract/Visual Reasoning, Quantitative Reasoning, Short-Term Memory, and Total Test Composite (mean = 100; standard deviation = 16).

Technical characteristics

Normative sample. Over 5,000 individuals from all 50 states stratified according to ethnic status, geographic region, community size, and sex.

Reliability. Internal consistency coefficients were generally above .90. Test-retest coefficients ranged from .71 (quantitative reasoning) to .91 (total test composite) for a preschool sample and from .51 to .90 for an elementary school sample.

Validity. Data supporting construct validity is presented in the technical manual. Criterion-related validity coefficients with the Wechsler Scales were above .80. The correlation between the total test composite and the K-ABC composite was .89. Criterion-related validity for samples of exceptional students was somewhat lower.

Review of relevant research

- The SBIS-4 had adequate validity with LD students; there was some support for the validity of the fluid/crystallized interpretation model as well (Knight, Baker, & Minder, 1990).
- The SBIS-4 is useful for assessing black students classified as behavior-disordered or mentally retarded but not LD (Greene, Sapp, & Chissom, 1990).
- Gifted students score considerably lower on the SBIS-4 than on the Wechsler Intelligence Scale for Children–Revised (WISC-R) (Carvajal & Weaver, 1989; Phelps, 1989). In addition, gifted students score lower on the Short Term Memory composite than on the other SBIS-4 composites (Carvajal, 1988).
- Factor analysis of the SBIS-4 does not support the presence of the four composites (Gridley & McIntosh, 1991; Reynolds, Kamphaus, & Rosenthal, 1988)

- The SBIS-4 and the K-ABC correlated .70 for a sample of gifted students, although the SBIS-4 yielded higher scores (Hayden, Furlong & Linnemeyer, 1988). The SBIS-4 also had high correlations with the K-ABC for LD students (Smith, Martin, & Lyon, 1989).
- A nonverbal short form of the SBIS-4 for use with individuals with hearing impairments, speech/language impairments, and limited English proficiency has been developed (Glaub & Kamphaus, 1991).
- The SBIS-4 yielded strong correlations with the K-ABC although there was little support for the theoretical structure of either instrument (Rothlisberg & McIntosh, 1991).
- The SBIS-4 has shown some promise for use with the preschool populations (Krohn & Lamp, 1989; Smith & Bauer, 1989).
- A computer program has been developed to aid in the evaluation of subtest scores (Madle, 1989).
- Glutting (1989) in a review of the SBIS-4 reached the following conclusions:

  1. It should not be used with preschoolers suspected of being in the retarded range.
  2. It provides sufficient ceiling for use with gifted students at any age.
  3. There is reasonable construct validity for the composite (the score that psychologists should interpret).
  4. Lack of appropriate factor structure suggests that the four area scores should not be interpreted.
  5. Abbreviated forms of the test should be avoided.

- In a survey of school psychologists, Obringer (1988) reported the following advantages of the SBIS-4:

  1. It is based on current psychological theory.
  2. It has a broad coverage of information-processing capabilities.
  3. It includes subtests that are attractive and challenging to examinees.

  Its disadvantages included the following:

  1. It has factor analyses that do not support the structure of the scale (interpretation of the composite score is the only one that is recommended).
  2. Some of its subtests are difficult to administer and score.
  3. Its standard age scores for subtests are nontraditional and difficult to evaluate.

Summary of research findings

In general, research on the SBIS-4 supports the use of the global score although the validity of the individual area scores has been questioned. There is also research suggesting that the SBIS-4 yields different scores than other traditional IQ measures, particularly with gifted students. More research is necessary to determine its strengths and limitations with preschool children and with different types of exceptional children.

OVERVIEW: STANFORD-BINET INTELLIGENCE SCALE–4

- *Age level*—2 to adult
- *Type of administration*—Individual
- *Technical adequacy*—Good standardization, acceptable reliability and validity
- *Scores yielded*—Standard scores
- *Suggested use*—The fourth edition of the SBIS has the potential to become one of the major individually-administered intelligence tests, although many school psychologists appear to prefer the third edition of the instrument. Certainly the earlier versions of the Stanford-Binet have played an important role in the history of intelligence testing. Data indicate that the SBIS-4 (at least the global composite) is an adequate measure of general intelligence. There is some question whether the four individual composites should be used, however. Several studies have been conducted that do not support the presence of the four specific areas. Users should also be aware that the SBIS-4 yields different scores than other widely used instruments with certain populations, such as gifted students.

Wechsler Intelligence Scale for Children–Third Edition (Wechsler, 1991)

The WISC-III is a recent revision of the WISC-R, which has been one of the most popular, most widely used individual intelligence tests. The WISC-III is one of three scales developed by Wechsler. The others are the Wechsler Preschool and Primary Scale of Intelligence–Revised (used for children 3 to 7 years old) and the Wechsler Adult Intelligence Scale–Revised (used for individuals from age 16 to adult). The WISC-III is used with children from 6 to 16 years old and, therefore, is the most used of the three scales in schools.

The WISC-III, like all of Wechsler's scales, is based on the concept of global intelligence. In other words, intelligence is viewed as a multifaceted concept as opposed to a single entity. Specifically, the WISC-III has both a verbal section and a performance section. Because of the type of information yielded by the WISC-III, as well as the frequency with which this test is administered, it will be one of the most widely researched instruments in special education (based on the "track record" of the WISC-R).

Description

The WISC-III has 10 subtests and three optional subtests. Six subtests comprise the Verbal Section and seven comprise the Performance Section. To avoid the administration of unnecessary items, the subtests have guidelines for discontinuing the testing after the child makes a certain number of consecutive errors. Also, the subtests on the Performance Section are timed.

VERBAL SECTION

Information—This subtest measures the student's knowledge of general information and facts.

Similarities—This subtest measures a student's ability to perceive the common element of two terms.

Arithmetic—This subtest measures the student's ability to solve problems requiring arithmetic computation and reasoning. This is primarily an oral subtest requiring concentration. Additional items were designed to make it more sensitive to the upper and lower age levels,

Vocabulary—In this subtest, the student is told a word and must orally define it. Items range in difficulty.

Comprehension—This subtest measures the social, moral, and ethical judgment of the student, who must answer questions such as "What are you supposed to do if you find someone's wallet or purse in a store?" and "Why do cars have seat belts?"

Digit Span—This subtest includes two parts: Digits Forward and Digits Backward. The student is given a series of digits at a rate of one digit per second. Digits Forward requires the student to say them back exactly. Digits Backward requires the student to say the numbers in reverse order. There are seven progressively longer series of digits for both sections.

PERFORMANCE SECTION

Picture Completion—In this subtest, the student is shown a picture in which an important element is missing. The student must either verbalize or point to the missing element. Color artwork has been added to the WISC-III.

Picture Arrangement—In this subtest, the student is given a series of pictures that represent a story but are in incorrect order. The task is to sequence the pictures in the correct order. Again, color artwork is used.

Block Design—In this subtest, the student must look at pictures of certain designs and reproduce these using red and white blocks. This subtest basically measures visual analysis and synthesis.

Object Assembly—This subtest for visual organization and synthesis requires the student to put together five jigsaw puzzles.

Coding—This subtest requires the student to copy geometric symbols that are paired or coded with other symbols within a certain time limit. There are two parts, A for children under age eight, and B for individuals of age eight and over. Figure 8-2 shows an example of the type of task included in the coding subtest. The coding subtest measures visual-motor speed, coordination, and to a certain extent, memory. It is the only subtest (other than the supplementary mazes subtest) on the WISC-III that uses a pencil-and-paper format.

FIGURE 8-2 Tasks Similar to the Coding Subtest from the WISC-III.
Courtesy of The Psychological Corporation.

Mazes—This subtest requires the child to use skills in visual planning to complete a number of progressively more difficult mazes.

Symbol Search—In this subtest, the student is required to visually scan a group of symbols to determine if a target symbol is present.

Interpretation of results

Each subtest raw score is converted to a scaled score with a mean of 10 and a standard deviation of 3. This allows for direct comparisons between subtests and has led, in part, to the profile analysis of the WISC-R that has been criticized in recent years (see the section on review of relevant research). The WISC-III also yields Full-Scale, Verbal, and Performance IQs, each having a mean of 100 and a standard deviation of 15. Considerable diagnostic emphasis has been placed—perhaps erroneously—on the difference between the Verbal and Performance IQs. In addition to the scoring options that were available for the WISC-R, new user tables are included in the WISC-III. These include tables that allow the interpretation of intersubtest scatter, verbal performance differences, digits forward–digits backward comparisons, and the significance of subtests scores that differ from the mean of all the subtests. Also included are Index Score Equivalents (mean = 100, SD = 15) for four new factors determined through factor analysis. These are Verbal Comprehension (Information, Similarities, Vocabulary, and Comprehension), Perceptual Organization (Picture Completion, Picture Arrangement, Block Design, and Object Assembly); Freedom from Distractability (Arithmetic and Digit Span), and Processing Speed (Coding and Symbol Search).

Technical characteristics

Normative sample. The WISC-III used a nationally representative sample (similar to the 1988 census) of 2,200. Variables considered were geographic region, race/ethnicity, and parent educational level (to determine socioeconomic status). There were an equal number of boys and girls.

Reliability. Split–half reliability coefficients were determined for all subtests except Coding and Symbol Search (test-retest was computed). These coefficients ranged from approximately .60–.95. The coefficients for the three IQs were all .90 or better, whereas the coefficients for the four factors were in the .80–.95 range.

Validity. Construct validity of the WISC-III was established using factor analysis and intercorrelations of the subtests and scales. Correlations with the WISC-R are also presented (approximately .60–.80 for subtests, .80–.90 for IQs). Criterion-related validity studies with other intelligence measures were underway but not available at the time of the completion of this book.

Review of relevant research
Due to the recent publication of the WISC-III, no research was available at the time that this book was completed. Much research is anticipated. Due to the similarity of the WISC-III and the WISC-R, research on the latter instrument may be of some relevance. Interested readers are encouraged to consult *Intelligent Testing with the WISC-R* (Kaufman, 1979) and *Assessment of Intelligence and Other Special Abilities* (Sattler, 1988) for an in-depth analysis of the WISC-R. Several hundred articles have been written about this instrument. The following summary lists the major research trends and findings:

- A recategorization or regrouping of the WISC-R subtests has been proposed, in which certain subtests are clustered to measure some common area. These clusters are *verbal-conceptualization ability* (Similarities, Vocabulary, Comprehension), *spatial ability* (Picture Completion, Block Design, Object Assembly), *sequencing ability* (Arithmetic, Digit Span, Coding), and *acquired knowledge* (Information, Arithmetic, Vocabulary) (Bannatyne, 1974). Several researchers have discouraged the use of the Bannatyne recategorization with LD children, however (Dundon, Sewell, Manni, & Goldstein, 1986; Kaufman, 1981).
- The factor structure of the WISC-R is remarkably similar for LD, emotionally disturbed and mentally retarded students (Schooler, Beebe, & Koepke, 1978), as well as for children from different ethnic backgrounds (Reschly, 1978; Taylor, Ziegler, & Partenio, 1985; Taylor & Ziegler, 1987). The factor structure for gifted students is not as clear, however (MacMann, Plasket, Barnett, & Siler, 1991).
- Kaufman (1981) reviewed the WISC-R and, specifically, its relation to the assessment of LD students. He found that factor-analytic studies of the WISC-R consistently identify two factors: verbal comprehension and perceptual organization. A third factor, freedom from distractibility, is also men-

tioned. This third factor (which includes arithmetic, coding, and digit span) has promise in the assessment of LD children. Kaufman also noted that "normal" children have substantial discrepancies in their verbal and performance scores (for 25 percent, at least 15 points) and substantial subtest scatter (approximately 7 points). Similarly, Taylor, Ziegler, and Partenio (1984) found an average V–P discrepancy of almost 11 points for a large, nonhandicapped sample. These findings minimize the use of a profile analysis in differentiating LD children from non-LD children.

■ Dudley-Marling, Kaufman, and Tarver (1981) reviewed the literature about WISC-R profiles of LD children. They focused on three specific questions that had previously been addressed in the literature: (1) Do LD children have high Performance IQ–low Verbal IQ? (2) Do LD children exhibit greater subtest scatter than non-LD children? and (3) Do LD children exhibit a characteristic profile? They found that the answers to the first two questions were inconclusive. Regarding the third question they concluded that "although there may be a characteristic WISC(-R) profile for LD individuals as a group, few individual LD children may actually conform to this pattern. Therefore, differential diagnosis should not be based on patterns of WISC(-R) performance" (p. 317–318).

■ Gutkin (1979) looked at subtest scatter as a possible aid in differential diagnosis. He found no significant differences among various special-education categories (for example, emotionally disturbed, LD, brain injured). He also found that 40 percent of the non–special-education group exhibited as much or more scatter as the special-education groups. Similarly, Tabachnick (1979) suggested that subtest scatter should not be used as a means of diagnosing learning disabilities.

■ Galvin (1981) also reviewed the literature in learning disabilities and found that the use of WISC-R patterns as a differential diagnosis is not warranted. She suggested that the WISC-R be used as only one step of several in educational planning and that it be considered an indicator of what direction future assessment should take.

■ Research has not supported item bias or psychometric bias for the WISC-R (Sandoval, 1979), although mean difference bias has been well documented for ethnic minority students (for example, Reschly & Ross-Reynolds, 1980; Taylor & Partenio, 1983) and children of low socioeconomic status (Reschly, 1979).

■ Construct validity and reliability of the WISC-R has been supported in the research literature although the long-term stability with mildly handicapped students has been questioned (Bauman, 1991; Stavrov, 1990).

■ In a review of over 100 articles, Quattrochi and Sherrets (1980) concluded the following:

1. The factor-analytic structure, reliability, and other technical characteristics are very similar for the WISC and the WISC-R.
2. The WISC-R appears to be a reliable measure for a number of populations, including minority and deaf children. It also seems to be a valid predictor of achievement for a variety of populations.
3. Several external variables (for example, verbal praise or scoring errors) can affect scores on the WISC-R.

4. In general, scores on the WISC-R are lower than those obtained from other intelligence tests, including the WISC. Eventually such comparisons between the WISC-R and the WISC-III will be possible.

■ Alternate scoring tables (e.g., corrected confidence intervals and significant subtest score differences) have been developed (Lobello, 1991; Silver & Clampit, 1991). In addition, a computerized interpretation package has been developed (Watkins & Kush, 1988). It is anticipated that similar procedures on the WISC-III are forthcoming.

OVERVIEW: WESCHLER INTELLIGENCE SCALE FOR CHILDREN–III

■ *Age Level:* 6 to 16 years old

■ *Type of Administration:* Individual

■ *Technical adequacy:* Good standardization, adequate reliability for subtests, good reliability for IQs, and good validity (limited data at this time)

■ *Scores yielded:* Scaled scores, verbal and performance IQs, full-scale IQ, index score equivalents

■ *Suggested use:* The WISC-R was the most widely used intelligence test for school-age students and was well constructed and widely researched. It is anticipated that the WISC-III will continue that tradition. The WISC-III measures a number of intellectual skills in both the verbal and performance areas. One additional feature of the WISC-III is that it was normed concurrently with the Weschler Individual Achievement Test (WIAT). The WIAT measures basic reading, mathematics, reasoning, spelling, reading comprehension, mathematics computation, listening comprehension, oral expression, and written expression. This co-norming will allow the types of aptitude-achievement comparisons possible with other instruments such as the Woodcock-Johnson–Revised and the K-ABC. Other improvements of the WISC-III include the addition of color to the performance subtests, and the availability of additional interpretative procedures.

Results of the WISC-R were overinterpreted and misused. Hopefully, information learned from the WISC-R will be applied to the WISC-III. For example, the IQ from the WISC-R is a fairly good predictor of school performance but should not be used as a measure of intellectual potential. Profiles from the WISC-R (for example, subtest scatter, verbal-performance discrepancies) have also been used incorrectly. Research has indicated that a considerable amount of variation in intratest scores exists within the "normal" population. The use of variability as basis for diagnostic and classification decisions is therefore not advised.

In summary, the WISC-III is a well–standardized instrument that can be used confidently to determine an individual's performance in a number of intellectual skill areas. The results should not be overused, however.

Profile analyses for diagnostic purposes should be avoided, until research warrants their use. Further, the test should not be the only instrument on which important placement and instructional decisions are made. Obviously, much research is needed to determine if the significant amount of literature on the WISC-R will be relevant for the WISC-III as well.

Woodcock-Johnson–Revised (Cognitive)

The Woodcock-Johnson Psychoeducational Battery–Revised (WJ-R) (Woodcock & Johnson, 1989) is a revision of the original instrument published in 1977. The WJ-R is a wide-range set of individually administered tests designed to measure cognitive abilities, scholastic aptitude, and achievement. One difference between the WJ and the WJ-R is the omission of the Interest Battery in the revised edition. The WJ-R consists of an Achievement Battery (discussed in Chapter 12) and a Cognitive Battery.

According to the authors, the WJ-R can be used for a variety of purposes, including diagnosis or identification of specific weaknesses, determination of psychoeducational discrepancies, program placement, planning IEPs, guidance, assessing growth, program evaluation, and research. Norms are available for individuals aged 24 months to 95 years. There are also separate norms available for college and university students. There are both "standard" and "supplemental" cognitive batteries.

Description

The cognitive tests included in the WJ-R are based on the Horn–Cattell theory, an extension of the fluid/crystallized model of intelligence. There are seven broad cognitive factors included: long-term retrieval, short-term memory, processing speed, auditory processing, visual processing, comprehension-knowledge, and fluid reasoning. A brief description of the tests in the cognitive battery follows.

Standard cognitive battery. Each of the seven tests in the standard battery measures the seven corresponding cognitive factors noted in the previous discussion.

Memory for Names (72 items)—This is an auditory-visual association task using unfamiliar stimuli.

Memory for Sentences (32 items)—This measures the ability to remember and repeat phrases presented auditorily.

Visual Matching (70 items)—This timed test requires the individual to locate and circle the two identical numbers in a row of six numbers.

Incomplete Words (40 items)—This is an auditory closure task in which words with one or more phonemes missing are presented.

Visual Closure (49 items)—This measures the ability to identify pictures that have been altered (e.g., distortions, missing lines).

Picture Vocabulary (58 items)—This requires the individual to name pictured objects.

Analysis—Synthesis (35 items)—This reasoning task involves the presentation of an incomplete logic puzzle for which the individual must present the missing components.

Supplemental cognitive battery.   The supplemental battery consists of 14 subtests. The first seven, described in the following list, coincide with the seven cognitive factors, consistent with the standard battery. The other seven subtests (Delayed Recall–Memory for Names, Delayed Recall—Visual/Auditory Learning, Numbers Reversed, Sound Patterns, Spatial Relations, Listening Comprehension, Verbal Analogies) are used selectively to probe specific cognitive areas.

Visual / Auditory Learning (7 stories)—Measures the ability to associate new visual symbols with familiar words and then "read" sentences consisting of the verbal symbols.

Memory for Words (27 items)—Requires the individual to repeat a series of unrelated words in the correct sequence.

Cross Out (37 items)—A timed task measuring the ability to scan visual information.

Sound Blending (33 items)—An auditory blending task requiring the individual to say whole words after hearing their parts.

Picture Recognition (30 items)—Requires the individual to recognize a subset of previously presented pictures within a field of distracting pictures.

Oral Vocabulary (44 items)—Measures the meaning of words using both synonyms and antonyms.

Concept Formation (35 items)—A controlled learning task requiring categorical reasoning based on principles of logic.

Interpretation of results

Scoring of the WJ-R is somewhat tedious and affords the opportunity for errors, although it is an improvement over the original version of the test. For example, the conversion tables for each subtest (raw scores to W scores, age equivalents, and grade equivalents) are presented on the test record itself. This reduces the number of tables that must be used in the manual. In the test booklet there are sections for summarizing a variety of scores and plotting the scores to provide a visual profile. There is also a computerized scoring program (Compuscore) available for both Apple and IBM. This procedure is recommended to decrease the likelihood of scoring errors.

For all tests but Memory for Sentences (scored 0, 1, or 2), each item is scored as either 0 (incorrect) or 1 (correct). The raw scores for each of the 21 tests in the standard and supplemental batteries can be converted into percentile ranks and standard scores (mean = 100; standard deviation = 15). In addition, those scores are available for a variety of clusters consisting of various combinations of tests from the standard and supplemental batteries. Those clusters are Broad Cognitive Ability (Extended), Long-term Retrieval, Short-term Memory, Processing Speed, Auditory Processing, Visual Processing, Comprehension-Knowledge, Fluid Reasoning, Reading Aptitude, Math Aptitude, Written Language Aptitude, Knowledge Aptitude, Oral Language, and Oral Language Aptitude. An Early Development Scale can also be used with children as young as age 2. The subtests from the standard battery for that scale are Memory for Names, Memory for Sentences, Incomplete Words, Visual Closure, and Picture Vocabulary. All of the seven tests from the standard battery can be combined for a Broad Cognitive Ability (Standard).

Technical characteristics

Normative sample.   Over 6,300 individuals were included. The subjects were selected by a random stratified procedure. The stratification variables were census region, community size, sex, race, funding of college/university, type of college/university, education of adults, occupational stress of adults, and occupation of adults. In general, the similarity of the sample to the 1980 census data for the United States was relatively close (between 1–5 percent difference).

Reliability.   The split-half procedure was used for all tests except for Visual Matching and Cross Out, for which the test-retest coefficients were calculated. For individual tests the median coefficient ranged from .69 (Visual Closure) to .91 (Memory for Names) for the standard battery and from .75 (Cross Out) to .93 (Concept Formation) for the supplemental. The coefficients of the cluster scores were generally above .90 with the notable exception of Fluid Reasoning (.81).

Validity.   The authors provide a description of the content validity and report the concurrent validity through the use of studies at three age levels (using relatively small sample sizes). At the 3-year-old level the Early Development Scale was correlated with the K-ABC, McCarthy Scales General Cognitive Index and the SBIS-4, in addition to several achievement and basic concept measures. The coefficients with the cognitive measures were in the .60s range and in the .50s with the other measures. For the 9-year-old group, coefficients ranged from .57 (K-ABC) to .69 (WISC-R and SBIS-4) for the Standard Battery. In the 17-year age group the coefficients were approximately .64 for the Standard Battery. Tables are also presented that show the correlations of the eight cognitive factor clusters and the cognitive clusters from other tests. Moderate correlations were found for the Short-term Memory, Comprehension-Knowledge, and Fluid Reasoning clusters with several of the criterion measures. These data in their present form, however, make it difficult to adequately address the issue of validity.

The issue of construct validity was primarily addressed through the use of tables showing the intercorrelations of the tests and clusters, along with results of factor analysis that indicated the two tests making up each cluster do, in fact, load on that specific factor.

Review of relevant research

Unfortunately, at this time, there are few studies to substantiate the technical characteristics, particularly the validity and test-retest reliability, of the instrument. Also, as with most relatively new instruments, its clinical uses and limitations have yet to be determined. It should be noted that the validity of the cluster scores was of some concern on the original WJ (e.g., Phelps, Rosso, & Falasco, 1984). In addition, there was some indication that LD students scored lower on the cognitive section than on other intellectual measures (e.g., Reeves, Hall, & Zakreski, 1979).

OVERVIEW: WOODCOCK-JOHNSON–REVISED (COGNITIVE)

- *Age level*—2 through adult
- *Type of administration*—Individual
- *Technical adequacy*—Good standardization, adequate reliability, questionable validity
- *Scores yielded*—Standard scores, percentile ranks (age equivalents and grade equivalents also available)
- *Suggested use*—The WJ-R appears to be a substantial improvement over the original WJ and is different enough that the tests should not be used interchangeably. The cognitive battery was developed within a theoretical framework (Horn-Cattell), making the interpretation more meaningful. Another improvement in the WJ-R is the slightly easier scoring procedures, although a number of tables must still be used, thus increasing the possibilities of errors. Clearly, if possible, the computerized scoring program (Compuscore) should be used.

One advantageous feature of the WJ-R is the use of continuous-year norms. This means that the standardization occurred throughout the year for the school-aged subjects rather than at one or two times. Thus the scores can be compared to individuals of the exact age or grade placement rather than to individuals of an average age or grade. This procedure helps eliminate the error variance associated with grouping students of similar, but not the same, age or grade.

ADDITIONAL INSTRUMENTS

There are several other less frequently used instruments that provide measures of intelligence. Their more limited use is a result of a variety of reasons including extremely questionable validity (Goodenough-Harris Drawing Test), outdated norms (McCarthy Scale of Children's Abilities), and heavy reliance on one aspect of intelligence (Slosson Intelligence Test–Revised). Other tests are a shorter version of the same comprehensive instrument (Kaufman Brief Intelligence Test) or are similar to a more comprehensive instrument (Cognitive Levels Test). A brief description of these instruments follows.

Cognitive Levels Test

- *Age level*—5 to 21 years
- *Type of administration*—Individual
- *Technical adequacy*—Adequate reliability and validity
- *Score yielded*—Standard scores, percentile ranks, stanines, cognitive-age levels.
- *Suggested use*—The Cognitive Levels Test (CLT) (Algozzine, Eaves, Mann, & Vance, 1988) was designed to "mirror" the Stanford-Binet. Its advantage is a short administration time (approximately 20–35 minutes). A Rapid Cognitive Index can be obtained in approximately 15 minutes. The test has a relatively solid technical base and can be used confidently as a screening instrument.

Goodenough-Harris Drawing Test

- *Age level*—5 to 15 years old
- *Type of administration*—Individual or group
- *Technical adequacy*—Very limited
- *Scores yielded*—Standard scores
- *Suggested use*—The Goodenough-Harris Drawing Test (Harris, 1963) is a frequently used instrument that requires the child to draw a picture of a man, a woman, and himself or herself. The quality of the drawings is scored as a measure of "intellectual maturity." Its popularity is due largely to its ease of administration. The scoring, however, is somewhat subjective. This test should not be considered as a measure of intelligence. There are too many factors that could account for low scores. Research indicates that it tends to underestimate the level of a child's actual ability. It should be noted that a revised instrument—Draw-a-Person: A Quantitative Scoring System has been developed (Naglieri, 1988)

Kaufman Brief Intelligence Test

- *Age level*—4 to 90 years old
- *Type of administration*—Individual

- *Technical adequacy*—Good standardization and reliability, adequate validity
- *Scores yielded*—Standard scores, percentile ranks, descriptive categories.
- *Suggested use*—The Kaufman Brief Intelligence Test (K-BIT) (Kaufman & Kaufman, 1990) is a brief screening instrument that uses two subtests (Vocabulary and Matrices) from the K-ABC. The vocabulary subtest measures word knowledge and verbal concept formation. Matrices are nonverbal problem solving tasks. The K-BIT appears to have adequate technical characteristics and can be used confidently as a brief screener of verbal and nonverbal intelligence. Prewett (1992) did report that the K-BIT produced lower scores (6–10 points) than the WISC-R, although its relationship to other intelligence tests has not been established.

McCarthy Scales of Children's Abilities

- *Age level*—2 1/2 to 8 1/2 years old
- *Type of administration*—Individual
- *Technical adequacy*—Good standardization, adequate reliability (motor index, low reliability), and validity
- *Scores yielded*—General cognitive index, scaled scores, percentile ranks, mental ages
- *Suggested use*—The McCarthy Scales (McCarthy, 1972) is a well-standardized (although outdated) instrument for use with young children. It includes 18 subtests that measure Verbal, Quantitative, Memory, Perceptual Performance, and Motor areas. Its limited age range (2 1/2–8 1/2) has both advantages and disadvantages: there are a representative number of items to measure the various areas, but the instrument cannot be used after approximately second grade, making direct comparisons of a child's ability difficult after that time. The McCarthy Scales is a potentially useful instrument. It measures a number of areas associated with cognitive abilities of young children. There is some evidence that the McCarthy Scales might be more sensitive to the actual school-performance level of students than are other intelligence measures. At this time, the instrument should be used primarily to identify strengths and weaknesses and to a lesser extent to determine eligibility for special education. Drawbacks of the test are its outdated norms and the limitations of the types of scores available. A revised version of the McCarthy Scales is being planned, however.

Slosson Intelligence Test–Revised

- *Age level*—Approximately birth to 27 years old
- *Type of administration*—Individual
- *Technical characteristics*—Adequate standardization, limited reliability, adequate validity
- *Scores yielded*—Mean-age equivalent, total standard score
- *Suggested use*—The Slosson Intelligence Test–Revised (SIT-R) (Slosson, 1991) gives a quick estimate of a person's intelligence. The majority of items

are highly verbal, and the scores tend to overestimate a person's IQ as determined from more comprehensive measures. The SIT-R should be used for screening only. It can help to identify students for whom intelligence testing in more depth might be necessary. The inclusion of a total standard score in the revised version allows for more meaningful interpretation than for its predecessors.

Instrument or Technique	Suggested Use							Target Population						Special Considerations	Educational Relevance for Exceptional Students
	Prereferral		Postreferral												
	Screening and Initial Identification	Informal Determination and Evaluation of Teaching Programs and Strategies	Determination of Current Performance Level and Educational Need	Decisions about Classification and Program Placement	IEP Goals	IEP Objectives	IEP Evaluation	Mild/Moderate	Severe/Profound	Preschool	Elementary Age	Secondary Age	Adult		
Group Intelligence Tests	X							X		X	X	X	X	Use for screening only; resemble group-achievement tests in format and, to a certain extent, content	limited
Wechsler Intelligence Scale for Children–III			X	X				X			X	X		Very widely used, well constructed; profile analyses of subtests should be avoided	very useful
Detroit Tests of Learning Aptitude-3			X					X			X	X		Some question about its validity; needs further research	adequate
Differential Ability Scales			X	X	X			X		X	X	X		Well constructed; includes both core and diagnostic subtests; good potential for preschool children	useful
Kaufman Assessment Battery for Children			X	X				X		X	X	X		Some question about its construct validity; includes an achievement component	useful
Stanford-Binet Intelligence Scale–4			X	X				X		X	X	X	X	The "grandfather" of intelligence tests; global composite should be used	useful
Woodcock-Johnson–Revised			X	X				X		X	X	X	X	WJ-R is an improvement over original; more validity data necessary	adequate
Cognitive Levels Test	X		X					X			X	X		"Mirrors" the content of the Stanford-Binet	useful
Goodenough-Harris Drawing Test	X							X		X	X			Very limited technical aspects; should not be used as a sole measure of intelligence	very limited

Instrument or Technique	Suggested Use							Target Population						Special Considerations	Educational Relevance for Exceptional Students
	Prereferral		Postreferral												
	Screening and Initial Identification	Informal Determination and Evaluation of Teaching Programs and Strategies	Determination of Current Performance Level and Educational Need	Decisions about Classification and Program Placement	IEP Goals	IEP Objectives	IEP Evaluation	Mild/Moderate	Severe/Profound	Preschool	Elementary Age	Secondary Age	Adult		
Kaufman Brief Intelligence Test	X							X		X	X	X	X	Brief version of the K-ABC; use for screening only	useful
McCarthy Scales of Children's Abilities			X	X				X		X	X			Well constructed; measures areas that are important to early school success	useful
Slosson Intelligence Test–Revised	X							X		X	X	X	X	Use for screening only; easy to administer; revised version an improvement	adequate

9

Assessment of
Adaptive Behavior

INSTRUMENTS/PROCEDURES INCLUDED

ADAPTIVE BEHAVIOR INVENTORY

ADAPTIVE BEHAVIOR INVENTORY FOR CHILDREN

AAMR ADAPTIVE BEHAVIOR SCALE–RESIDENTIAL AND
COMMUNITY EDITION

AAMR ADAPTIVE BEHAVIOR SCALE–SCHOOL EDITION

SCALES OF INDEPENDENT BEHAVIOR

VINELAND ADAPTIVE BEHAVIOR SCALES

ADAPTIVE BEHAVIOR SCREENING INSTRUMENTS
- Cain-Levine Social Competency Scale
- Camelot Behavioral Checklist
- Normative Adaptive Behavior Checklist
- TARC Assessment System

*Sam, an 8-year-old boy, was referred by his teacher to the school
psychologist. Sam was new to his present school and seemed to be
significantly below his third-grade peers in academic and social
skills. His teacher felt that alternative placement might be most
appropriate for Sam. On the basis of a group-administered intelligence test, he fell in the educable mentally retarded (EMR) range of
intelligence. The school psychologist administered the Wechsler Intel-*

Portions of this chapter were adapted from R. Taylor, "Assessment Instruments," in *Educating Students with Severe or Profound Handicaps* (2nd ed.), edited by L. Sternberg. Austin,
TX: Pro-Ed. Copyright © 1988 by Pro-Ed. Reprinted with permission of Pro-Ed.

ligence Scale for Children-III (WISC-III) and found Sam's IQ to be 65. A further study of Sam's background, however, indicated that he comes from a lower-socioeconomic-status family and that he had been at four schools in the last three years. The school psychologist, therefore, administered an adaptive-behavior scale to help determine the best placement for Sam.

Joanna, a 12-year-old, severely retarded girl, is enrolled in a private day program for physically handicapped students. Her teacher feels that Joanna has potential in a number of areas including self-help and communications but is unclear about how to establish sequential objectives in those areas. She is also interested in monitoring Joanna's progress, which must be measured in small steps. The consulting psychologist recommended that an adaptive-behavior scale specifically designed for severely handicapped children be administered to Joanna as a help in establishing the objectives and in monitoring her progress.

In its broadest sense, adaptive behavior has to do with a person's ability to deal effectively with personal and social demands and expectations. Adaptive behavior, in general, is a difficult concept to define and measure. Although Harrison (1987) reported that adaptive behavior is a multidimensional concept. Witt and Martens (1984) noted that most definitions include such areas as independent functioning and social responsibility.

The two vignettes noted at the beginning of this chapter demonstrate the diverse uses of adaptive-behavior testing. In general, these instruments can be used for three purposes. The specific purpose for an instrument depends largely on its depth, breadth, and technical characteristics, most notably the nature of the standardization sample. Some instruments are used to help make *classification* decisions. With the American Association on Mental Retardation (AAMD) definition of mental retardation requiring a deficit in adaptive behavior, they play an important role in those labeling decisions. Tests used for this purpose usually measure a number of areas and are usually standardized on nonhandicapped populations. Other adaptive-behavior scales are used more for *developing* and *evaluating specific teaching programs.* Tests used for this purpose usually include very specific sequential items that cover functional, independent-living skill areas. Some of these tests are standardized on, and used with, individuals with more severe handicaps (e.g., Balthazar Scales of Adaptive Behavior; Balthazar, 1976), while others are standardized on nonhandicapped individuals and simply include more expanded and detailed items than those instruments used for classification purposes. A final purpose for adaptive-behavior scales is *screening.* Screening in this sense means either identification of those who need further evaluation or the delineation of general program goals. These instruments are not comprehensive enough to be used for classification purposes or for the development of educational programs.

The content of adaptive-behavior instruments will differ depending on the age range for the test. For instance, adaptive behavior for a 3-year-old child primarily includes motor skills, language skills, and self-help skills. On the other hand, adaptive behavior for a 15-year-old might include social skills and prevocational skills (Taylor, 1985).

The technical characteristics of many adaptive-behavior scales have been questioned. Cicchetti and Sparrow (1981) noted, for instance, that many adaptive-behavior scales have deficient reliability and validity estimates and that for many, the standardization sample is small. Similarly, Kamphaus (1987) reported that many of the instruments lacked predictive validity in particular. On the other hand, Harrison (1987), in a review of adaptive-behavior research, concluded that the instruments exhibit adequate reliability and can differentiate individuals with different labels. The format of adaptive-behavior scales has also been scrutinized. Some scales allow for direct observation, whereas others require the use of an interview. These two procedures do not always yield similar information or results.

A discussion of some of the more widely used adaptive instruments follows including a brief overview of several that are used for screening purposes.

ADAPTIVE BEHAVIOR INSTRUMENTS

WHY USE?
Screening and identification; documentation of educational need; decisions about classification and program placement; development and evaluation of IEPs (largely depending on target population)

WHO SHOULD USE?
Teachers or staff members; school psychologists (often using interview with parent)

Adaptive Behavior Inventory

The Adaptive Behavior Inventory (ABI) (Brown & Leigh, 1986) is an individually administered instrument used with individuals aged 6 through 18. It is designed to be completed by the classroom teacher and is relatively simple to score. The respondent must use a four-point scale to indicate the degree to which the examinee can perform certain behaviors (the items).

The primary use of the ABI is to aid in classification decisions regarding mental retardation and to determine general strengths and weaknesses in various adaptive behavior areas. The ABI does not provide specific information that could be used for educational programming. The ABI includes 150 items (30 items in each of five areas). There is also a 50-item ABI–Short Form available for quick screening.

Description

Self-Care Skills—Items in this scale measure areas such as grooming and personal hygiene.

Communication Skills—This scale measures writing ability as well as expressive and receptive oral language skills.

Social Skills—This scale measures a wide range of skills including responsibility, organizational skills, and leadership ability.

Academic Skills—This scale measures both preacademic and academic reading and mathematics skills.

Occupational Skills—This includes such areas as job responsibility and supervisory skills.

Interpretation of results

For each of the five scales, percentile ranks and standard scores (mean = 100; standard deviation = 15) are available. The scales can thus be used independently although a composite quotient (Total Score) is also available.

Technical characteristics

Normative sample.   The ABI was standardized on both a sample of mentally retarded students and a sample of children with normal intelligence. The mentally retarded sample included approximately 1,100 individuals from 24 states. The normal intelligence group included approximately 1,300 individuals from those same locations.

Reliability.   Internal consistency (coefficient alpha) was generally good for all the age ranges for all five scales (.86–.97). The coefficients for the total score all exceeded .90. Test-retest reliability coefficients for the individual scales and the total score were also above .90. In general, reliability data for the ABI–Short Form were similar.

Validity.   In general, evidence of the validity of the ABI is lacking. Some concurrent validity data are presented (moderate coefficients) using the AAMD Adaptive Behavior Scale and Vineland Adaptive Behavior Scales as criteria. There is also a discussion by the authors regarding the test's content and construct validity. For example, they note the significant differences in the scores of the individuals in the two standardization samples.

Review of relevant research

Although no empirical studies were located, several reviews of the ABI were found; those reviews were, in general, relatively positive.

- Hughes (1988) felt that the test was highly useful for diagnosis and placement decisions because of the inclusion of both mentally retarded and normal samples. Ehly (1989) found the instrument attractive as well as quick and easy to administer.
- Smith (1989) felt that the test was best used to identify general strengths and weaknesses as well as areas for which further assessment to determine instructional goals could be pursued. He added that the total score was better to report than the individual scale scores.

OVERVIEW: ADAPTIVE BEHAVIOR INVENTORY

- *Age level*—6 through 18
- *Type of administration*—Individual
- *Technical adequacy*—Good reliability, questionable validity
- *Scores yielded*—Percentile ranks, standard scores
- *Suggested use*—The ABI is relatively quick and easy to administer. It is designed for use by the classroom teacher or other professional who is familiar with the student. As with most adaptive behavior tests, the ABI should be used to supplement other assessment information, particularly when being used to assist in classification and placement decisions. The test appears to be reliable and the use of both mentally retarded and nonhandicapped norms is a good feature. More evidence of the test's validity would be beneficial.

The Adaptive Behavior Inventory for Children

The Adaptive Behavior Inventory for Children (ABIC) (Mercer & Lewis, 1977) is actually a part of a larger evaluation instrument, the System of Multicultural Pluralistic Assessment (SOMPA). The SOMPA attempts to measure an individual's ability using three models: the medical model, social-system model, and pluralistic (intellectual and learning ability) model. Although the SOMPA itself is used infrequently, the ABIC as an individual instrument is still used by many. The authors state that the ABIC provides a multidimensional view of a child's performance in nonschool settings, yields information about a child from the family's perspective, and offers data to satisfy the adaptive-behavior criterion for the AAMD definition of mental retardation. The ABIC is designed for children 5–11 years old and is administered by means of an interview, with the child's mother usually acting as the informant.

Description

The 242 items on the ABIC are broken down into six scales, described below. In addition, a Veracity Scale is included. Twenty-three of the items are included in more than one scale.

Family (52 items)—This scale includes questions such as "gets along with sisters?" "comes when called?" "gets angry often?" and "repairs machines and motors?"

Community (41 items)—This scale includes questions such as "plays near home?" "knows animals' names?" "visits outside of neighborhood?" and "knows names of service persons?"

Peer Relations (36 items)—This scale includes questions such as "gets along with neighborhood children?" "plays rough, hurts others?" "plays with friends after dark?" and "trades comic books, etc.?"

Nonacademic School Roles (37 items)—This scale includes questions such as "often skips school?" "knows pupils' names?" "brings notes home?" and "tries out for plays or shows?"

Earner/Consumer (26 items)—This scale includes questions such as "purchases with money?" "saves money for something?" "buys gifts for family?" and "earns money baby-sitting?"

Self-Maintenance (49 items)—This scale includes questions such as "afraid of things?" "goes off alone?" "orders food in restaurants?" and "uses bike hand signals?"

Veracity (24 items)—The items in this scale were included to determine whether the respondent or informant is inflating the scores by overestimating a child's ability. These items are of sufficient difficulty that few children will have mastered the behaviors at the expected age level. The precise interpretation of these scores, however, awaits further research.

Interpretation of results

Thirty-five items are administered to all children. The remaining items, on a statistical basis, were assigned to an approximate age category. This arrangement allows items to be sequenced from easiest to most difficult, and it indicates a child's approximate starting place according to age.

The interviewer must score each item in one of five ways: *0, 1, 2, N,* or *DK.* A *0* score indicates that the activity is not performed. A *1* score indicates that the activity is emerging and is performed infrequently. A *2* score indicates that the child has mastered the activity. An *N* score indicates that the child has had no opportunity to engage in the activity. A *DK* score indicates that the respondent does not know whether or not the child engages in the activity. A ceiling is reached when eight consecutive questions are scored either *0* or *N*.

The raw scores for the six scales as well as for the overall ABIC can be determined by adding up the scores of the individual items. These raw scores are then converted to scaled scores with a mean of 50 and a standard deviation of 15. Using the profile sheet provided with the SOMPA allows the scaled scores to be expressed in percentile ranks. Scaled scores of 21 or less are considered "at risk" on the ABIC.

Technical characteristics

Normative sample.   The sample was representative of the general population. It included 696 black, 690 Hispanic, and 699 white children; their mothers provided the information.

Reliability.   Split-half reliability coefficients for the overall ABIC ranged from .94 to .98. For the individual scales, all coefficients were above .75.

Validity.   Validity data are generally lacking.

Review of relevant research

- In a review of the ABIC, Capron (1985) noted that among its strengths were empirically derived and unbiased test items and good internal consistency.
- The ABIC and other SOMPA measures greatly reduced the number and percentage of children eligible for mild mentally retarded classes (Reschly, 1981).
- The percentage of Hispanic children in classes for EMR students was reduced after the administration of the SOMPA. The ABIC was shown to be internally consistent (Talley, 1979).
- Local norms are needed for the ABIC (Kazimour & Reschly, 1981), particularly for low-socioeconomic-status Hispanic children (Scott, Mastenbrook, Fisher, & Gridley, 1982).
- ABIC items tend to favor middle-class children. This characteristic might be considered to reflect culture loading rather than test bias (Oakland & Feigenbaum, 1980).
- Parents and teachers generally disagree when asked to give information about a student. Parents tend to provide higher ratings (Heath & Obrzut, 1984; Wall & Paradise, 1981).
- The ABIC has been used to differentiate gifted from normal students (Childs, 1981) and slow learning from mentally retarded students (Heath & Orbzut, 1986).
- A table is available that allows the determination of statistically significant differences between subscale scores and the total mean, a procedure that enhances profile analysis (Reynolds, 1985).
- Stability of the ABIC over a four-year period ranged from a coefficient of .18 (earner/consumer) to .63 (peer relations). In general the coefficients indi-

cated that the ABIC had moderate stability over time (Wilkinson & Oakland, 1982).

Summary of research findings

The ABIC has been studied primarily within the context of the SOMPA model. Therefore, recent research is virtually nonexistent. Past research has indicated that its use results in the declassification of many children labeled as mildly mentally retarded. There is also an apparent need for local norms if the ABIC is used in classification decisions. Users should also be aware that scores will vary, depending on who the informant is. Further studies on the validity and reliability (test-retest) of the ABIC are necessary.

OVERVIEW: ADAPTIVE BEHAVIOR INVENTORY FOR CHILDREN

- *Age level*—5–11 years old
- *Type of administration*—Individual (interview)
- *Technical adequacy*—Adequate reliability, questionable validity
- *Scores yielded*—Scaled scores, percentile ranks
- *Suggested use*—The ABIC is part of the controversial SOMPA assessment model. As such, it has been used primarily as a measure to declassify minority children who have been labeled mentally retarded. The ABIC focuses on nonschool behaviors, a focus that has certain advantages and disadvantages. It certainly helps decrease the number of children labeled as mentally retarded; its ability to predict school performance is less certain, however. Clearly, the ABIC should be used as a classification measure (particularly if one believes in the SOMPA model) and not as an instrument to provide information for making decisions about program development or instruction.

AAMR Adaptive Behavior Scale–Second Edition: Residential and Community Edition and School Edition

The American Association on Mental Retardation (AAMR) Adaptive Behavior Scales (ABS) were revised for 1993. The new scales are the Residential and Community Edition (AAMR ABS:RCE) (Nihira, Leland & Lambert, 1993), designed for use with individuals between the ages of six and 79 years who live in residential and community settings, and the School Edition (AAMR ABS:SE) (Lambert, Leland, & Nihira, 1993), to be used with students ages six through 21 years who are receiving services in the public schools. Both scales are used with individuals who have mental retardation, emotional handicaps, and/or other disabilities. The

School Edition is actually a short form of the Residential and Community Edition, with some items deleted from the longer version because of their inappropriateness for use with school-aged children receiving services in the public schools. According to the authors, the ABS can be used for identifying persons who may be in need of specialized clinical services; identifying adaptive strengths and weaknesses in individuals under different situations; documenting progress in an intervention program; and stimulating research. It should also be emphasized that a deficit in adaptive behavior and cognitive functioning must be documented before an individual is labeled as having mental retardation. The ABS, in part, was developed for that purpose.

The ABS consists of two parts: Part One deals primarily with personal independence in daily-living skills. Part One of the Residential and Community Edition includes 73 items that are divided into 10 areas or domains and three factors. Part One of the School Edition consists of 61 items that contribute to nine domains and three factors. Part Two, which is concerned with the measurement of maladaptive behavior, includes eight domains and two factors. The RCE has 41 items, and the SE contains 37 items. For the most part, items deleted from the RCE involved sexual relations (e.g., "exposes body improperly," "has sexual behavior that is socially unacceptable"). For both parts of the ABS, information is collected by one of two methods. The first is first-person assessment. This method is used when the evaluator is thoroughly familiar with the person who is being evaluated. The second method is third-party assessment. In this approach the evaluator asks another individual (e.g., teacher, parent, or ward attendant) about each item on the scale. This is usually a very time-consuming endeavor.

Description

Part One.   This part includes 10 domains assessing the degree of independence in daily-living skills. Each item in a given domain is scored in one of two ways. For some items, there is a breakdown and description of skills on a dependent-independent continuum. The examiner chooses which behavioral description best fits the individual being evaluated. For the remaining items, a list of behaviors is provided, and the examiner must check all that apply. Descriptions of the 10 domains follow.

> *Independent Functioning (24 items)*—Included in this domain are eating, toilet use, cleanliness, appearance, care of clothing, dressing and undressing, travel, and other independent functioning.
>
> *Physical Development (6 items)*—This domain includes items measuring a person's sensory development (vision and hearing) and motor development (gross-motor and fine-motor skills).
>
> *Economic Activity (6 items)*—Items in this domain measure ability in money handling, banking, budgeting, errands, purchasing, and shopping resources.

Language Development (10 items)—This domain includes measures of language reception and expression, plus two items concerning social language development (e.g., conversational behavior).

Number and Time (3 items)—Items in this domain measure a person's ability to understand and manipulate numbers and to understand time concepts.

Domestic Activity (6 items)—This domain includes items measuring skills in meal preparation and cleaning.

Prevocational/vocational Activity (3 items)—These items measure work/school habits and job performance.

Self-Direction (5 items)—These items measure an individual's initiative, perseverance, and use of leisure time.

Responsibility (3 items)—These items measure an individual's dependability.

Socialization (7 items)—This domain includes measure of cooperation, consideration for others, and social maturity.

Part Two.   This part was designed specifically to measure the degree of an individual's *maladaptive behavior*. It includes eight domains. For each item in a given domain, several behaviors are listed. The examiner must determine whether each behavior occurs frequently (scored as 2), occasionally (scored as 1), or not at all (scored as 0). Unfortunately, no guidelines are provided that operationally define "frequently" and "occasionally." The eight behavioral domains are summarized below.

Violent and Antisocial Behavior (7 items)—This domain includes such items as "threatens or does physical violence" and "reacts poorly to frustration."

Rebellious Behavior (6 items)—This domain includes questions about impudence, resistance to instructions, and absenteeism.

Untrustworthy Behavior (6 items)—These items inquire about the possible presence of lying, cheating, and stealing behavior.

Stereotyped and Hyperactive Behavior (5 items)—These items measure stereotypical and repetitive behaviors, as well as hyperactive tendencies.

Inappropriate Body Exposure (3 items)—This domain measures behaviors that relate to physical exposure and/or masturbation (not included in SE).

Eccentric and Self-Abusive Behavior (4 items)—This domain includes items such as "does physical violence to self" and "has strange and unacceptable habits."

Withdrawal (4 items)—This domain includes measures of inactivity and shyness.

Disturbed Behavior (6 items)—This domain measures such behaviors as "reacts poorly to criticism" and "has hypochondriacal tendencies."

Interpretation of results
Each item on the ABS is scored by the methods previously described. Scores for all the items in a given domain are added together to obtain a

raw score for that domain. Raw scores for various factors can also be obtained. The domain raw scores—or attained scores, as they are referred to—can then be transformed into percentile ranks and standard scores. The standard scores are then plotted on a Profile/Summary Sheet similar to that shown in Figure 9-1 to provide a visual representation of the individual's adaptive behavior functioning. (Note: The Profile sheet for the 1993 ABS was not published at the time of this book's completion.)

One important consideration in using this instrument is that, for the most part, there are too few items in a given domain to provide adequate information for specific educational programming. The authors do address this issue, however.

Technical characteristics

Normative sample.   The RCE sample consisted of over 4000 persons with mental retardation who reside in residential or community settings. The SE sample consisted of over 1000 nondisabled students and over 1000 students with mental retardation. In both instances, the samples' demographic characteristics are representative of the nation as a whole.

Reliability.   Interrater reliability was established in separate studies by having two staff members or a parent and a staff member independently rate clients/students. In most instances, the coefficients for the various domains approach or exceed .80. Internal consistency reliability coefficients for the RCE and SE domains generally exceed .80 across ages. Factor score reliability coefficients exceed .90 across most ages. Stability reliability coefficients, for the most part, also exceed .80 for the domains and factors.

Validity.   Validity for each version of the ABS was examined in a number of ways. For content validity, a description is provided of how the items were selected for inclusion on the scale. Item discriminating powers and item difficulties lend empirical support. Criterion-related validity evidence is explained by comparing the results of each ABS version with other adaptive behavior scales. Construct validity for both versions was explored by demonstrating that the scales (1) are developmental in nature; (2) correlate significantly with measures of intelligence; (3) relate significantly to measures of achievement; (4) differentiate among groups of students with varying disabilities (i.e., mental retardation, emotional handicaps, learning disabilities) and those without disabilities; (5) have factor clustors that are supported through factor analytic research; and, (6) have valid items.

Review of relevant research

Because the ABS is newly revised (the new revision was not published at the time of this book's completion), there is no independent

Identification _____

Age _____

Sex _____

Date of Administration _____

		I	II	III	IV	V	VI	VII	VIII	IX	X
PROFILE SUMMARY **AAMD ADAPTIVE BEHAVIOR SCALE PART ONE**											
Deciles		Independent Functioning	Physical Development	Economic Activity	Language Development	Numbers & Time	Domestic Activity	Vocational Activity	Self-Direction	Responsibility	Socialization
D9 (90)											
D8 (80)											
D7 (70)											
D6 (60)											
D5 (50)											
D4 (40)											
D3 (30)											
D2 (20)											
D1 (10)											
Attained Scores											

FIGURE 9-1   Profile Summary Sheet from the AAMD Adaptive Behavior Scale.

From K. Nihira, R. Foster, M. Shellhaas, and H. Leland, *AAMD Adaptive Behavior Scale*, 1974. Copyright © 1974 by the American Association on Mental Deficiency. Reprinted by permission.

research available. The new scales are very similar to predecessors, however, in the content measured. Thus, a review of the research conducted on the earlier instruments may be of value.

RESEARCH RELEVANT FOR THE ABS:RCE

- The ABS was helpful in discriminating among three groups of mentally retarded individuals: institutionalized, deinstitutionalized, and those referred for discharge (Spreat, 1980).
- Part Two has been severely criticized. The standardization data are markedly skewed, with 40 to 50 percent of the sample displaying no inappropriate behavior (McDevitt, McDevitt, & Rosen, 1977). In addition, the severity of the behavior is not considered.
- The feasibility of adapting the scoring system to include the severity of behavior has been demonstrated (Taylor, Warren, & Slocumb, 1979) and subsequent severity weightings have been developed for the items in Part Two (Clements, Bost, DuBois, & Turpin, 1980). Spreat (1982a), however, found that the severity weightings did not improve the predictive efficiency of Part Two.
- Several factor analytic studies have been conducted. Spreat (1982b) reviewed these studies and found that it was difficult to make any definite statements about their findings. It appeared that there were two factors for Part One (self-care and motivational aspects of personality) and two factors for Part Two (maladaptive behavior towards self and maladaptive behavior towards others).
- Administering the ABS using direct observation yielded different results than administering it through retrospective observation (Millham, Chilcutt, & Atkinson, 1978), although Stack (1984) found that the method of administration made very little difference.
- Scores on the ABS differed when teachers and parents supplied the information (Mealor & Richmond, 1980; Heath & Orbzut, 1984). Further, teachers were more likely to rate children as being eligible for special education programs (Ronka & Barnett, 1986).
- Teachers demonstrate a slight preference for using direct observation rather than interviews to obtain information for the ABS, except for those items that were considered extremely maladaptive (Taylor & Ivimey, 1982).
- Computerization of the ABS results made using them more effective (Malone & Christian, 1975).
- In a review of the psychometric properties of the ABS, Spreat (1982b) concluded that Part One has reasonably adequate reliability, although for Part Two the reliability is low enough to warrant caution in the interpretation of its scores. Spreat also noted that the ABS was adequate in discriminating among various groups who have various behavioral characteristics.
- A short form of the ABS has been developed that uses 17 percent of the Part One items and 49 percent of the Part Two items to accurately predict the total scores (Roszkowski & Bean, 1981). In addition, Part One has been normed on a deaf-blind population (Suess, Dickson, Anderson, & Hildman, 1981).

- When portions of the ABS were completed by several raters, the score was higher than when the entire test was completed by one rater (Vandergriff, Hester, & Mandra, 1987)
- Operational definitions of "occasionally" and "frequently" for Part Two have been developed that subsequently improved reliability (MacDonald, 1988).

RESEARCH RELEVANT FOR THE ABS–SE

- The ABS-SE Part Two was useful in identifying behavior-disordered students aged 7–12 (Cheramie & Edwards, 1990).
- In a review of the ABS-SE, Vallecorsa and Tittle (1985) stated that it had more representative norms and a broader age range than the ABIC. They also noted that it was easier to administer than the Vineland Adaptive Behavior Scales (discussed later in this chapter).
- When scores from the ABS-SE are compared to WISC-R scores, a common factor of verbal comprehension emerges (Huberty, 1986).
- Factor and comparison scores arc not affected by gender or ethnic status of the examinee, thus providing additional data to support its validity (Lambert, 1986).
- The ABS-SE standardization sample did not approximate the national census data (Evans & Bradley-Johnson, 1988).

Summary of research findings

Most of the research on the ABS explored its psychometric characteristics, particularly its reliability and validity. These studies, in general, supported the use of the ABS to identify groups of individuals according to diagnostic category. In other words, there are significant differences among the scores of differently labeled groups of individuals. As with most adaptive behavior instruments, there has been research on the method of gathering the information and the nature of the informant (usually teacher versus parent). Finally, the reliability of the ABS has been questioned, particularly for Part Two. Part Two, in fact, has been criticized for a number of technical inadequacies although many of these inadequacies have been addressed through alternate scoring methods. It should also be noted that many of these inadequacies were addressed in the revised version. The more limited research on the ABS-SE generally supported its use as an instrument to aid in classification decisions. Clearly, research will need to be conducted to determine if this research will be relevant for the revised edition.

OVERVIEW: AAMR ADAPTIVE BEHAVIOR SCALE–RESIDENTIAL AND COMMUNITY EDITION; SCHOOL EDITION

- *Age level*—6 to 79 years old (RCE) and 6 to 21 years old (SE)
- *Type of administration*—Individual
- *Technical adequacy*—Reliability of domains is acceptable, reliability of factors is good, overall validity questionable (limited data available).

- *Scores yielded*—Percentile ranks, standard scores
- *Suggested use*—The ABS was developed primarily as a result of the AAMR's emphasis on adaptive behavior in its definition of mental retardation. Although no research was located on the ABS-RCE or the new ABS-SE it would appear that the instruments are similar enough to the earlier versions to warrant some generalization. For example, the ABS was successful in identifying groups of individuals according to their diagnostic classification. The ABS, however, had several limitations. Generally speaking, the items were not sensitive enough to be useful for severely retarded individuals. Technical inadequacies in Part Two, in particular, were criticized. The revised versions have addressed many of the technical limitations of the previous editions, however.

Overall, the results from the ABS should be used to aid in classification and placement decisions and to identify general areas of programming needs. Important decisions should not be based on the results alone, nor should specific educational plans be developed around the child's adaptive-behavior profile. Obviously, research needs to be conducted to determine the uses and limitations of the two revised versions of the ABS.

Scales of Independent Behavior

The Scales of Independent Behavior (SIB) (Bruininks, Woodcock, Weatherman, & Hill, 1984) is an individually administered instrument that is designed for use with a wide age range (3 months–adult). The SIB uses a very structured format in which the interviewer makes a statement (e.g., "Picks up and eats food such as crackers" to which the respondent must indicate if the examinee exhibits that behavior "never or rarely," "about one-fourth of the time," "about three-fourths of the time," or "almost always." The SIB consists of 14 subscales that can be grouped into four larger clusters. In addition, there is a Problem Behavior Scale (Figure 9-2). Finally, there is a short form consisting of 32 items and an Early Development Scale to use with younger children that also consists of 32 questions. Also available are a shorter version of the SIB called the *Inventory for Client and Agency Planning* (ICAP) and a related criterion-referenced instrument called the *Checklist of Adaptive Living Skills* (CALS). Finally, there is a correlated curriculum called the *Adaptive Living Skills Curriculum* (ALSC) that completes the package.

Description

MOTOR SKILLS CLUSTER

Gross-Motor (17 items)—Items range from "Sits alone for thirty seconds with head and back held straight and steady (with support)" to " Takes part in strenuous physical activities on a regular basis that requires strength and endurance."

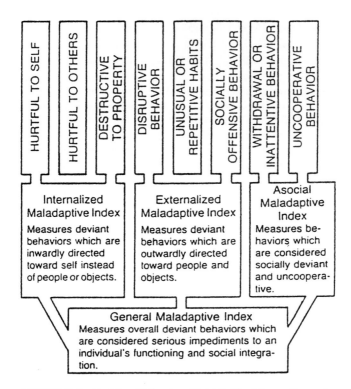

FIGURE 9-2   Problem Behavior: Eight Critical Areas Scored in Three Valid and Useful Indexes

Adapted from R. Bruininks, R. Woodcock, R. Weatherman, and B. Hill, *The Scales of Independent Behavior.* Copyright © 1984 by DLM Teaching Resources, Allen, TX. Used by permission.

Fine-Motor (17 items)—Items range from "Picks up small objects with hand" to "Assembles objects that have at least ten small parts that must be screwed or bolted together."

SOCIAL INTERACTION AND COMMUNICATION CLUSTER

Social Interaction (16 items)—Ranges from "Reaches for a person whom he or she wants" to "Makes plans with friends to attend activities outside the home without needing permission."

Language Comprehension (16 items)—Includes "Turns head toward speaker when name is called" and "Reads one or more articles in a regular newspaper at least weekly."

Language Expression (17 items)—Ranges from "Makes sounds or gestures to get attention" to "Explains the terms of a written contract, such as an installment purchase agreement."

PERSONAL LIVING SKILLS CLUSTER

Eating (16 items)—Ranges from "Swallows soft foods" to "Plans and prepares meals regularly for self and family."

Toileting (14 items)—Items include "Stays dry for at least three hours" and "Closes the bathroom door when appropriate before using the toilet."

Dressing (18 items)—Includes "Removes socks" and "Selects and buys appropriate size and style of clothing."

Personal Self-Care (15 items)—Ranges from "Holds hands under running water to wash them when placed in front of sink" to "Makes appointments for periodic medical or dental examinations."

Domestic Skills (16 items)—Includes "Places his or her empty dish in or near the sink" and "Cleans refrigerator and throws out food that may be spoiled."

COMMUNITY LIVING SKILLS CLUSTER

Time and Punctuality (15 items)—Includes "Points to any number from one to five when asked" and "States the time on a clock with hands to the nearest minute."

Money and Value (17 items)—Items range from "Counts from one to five" to "Invests savings to achieve the most favorable conditions and rate of return."

Work Skills (16 items)—Includes "Indicates when a chore or assigned task is finished" and "Prepares a written summary of work experience."

Home/Community Orientation (16 items)—Includes "Finds toys or objects that are always kept in the same place" and "Locates his or her polling center at election time."

Interpretation of results

There are a variety of derived scores available for each of the four clusters as well as Broad Independence (a global score combining the clusters). Scores for those areas include age equivalents, standard scores (mean = 100; standard deviation = 15), percentile ranks, and normal curve equivalents. Because the SIB is a part of the original Woodcock–Johnson Psychoeducational Battery, the types of scores common to that Battery are also available. They include instructional ranges, relative performance indexes, and functioning levels (e.g., moderate deficit). For the Problem Behavior Scale, stanines, maladaptive behavior indices, and an indication of the level of seriousness are available.

Overall, the SIB is easy to administer; the use of suggested starting points and basal and ceiling rules decreases the number of items that must be given. Scoring, however, can be tedious because of the number of tables that must be used. There is an automated computer scoring program, COMPUSCORE, that is available, however.

Technical characteristics

Normative sample. Over 1,700 individuals were included. The authors intended to include subjects in the same proportion as the U.S.

population regarding sex, community size, race, socioeconomic status, and geographic region.

Reliability.   Split-half reliability coefficients for each subscale for each of 13 age groups were computed. The resulting coefficients were quite varied, ranging from .00 to .95. The coefficients for the cluster scores were higher and more consistent (generally in the .80–.90 range), although Motor Skills and Community Living Skills yielded lower coefficients (.60s) for some age groups. The Broad Independence was the highest (.95 or higher).

Test-retest coefficients are reported for two specific age groups (6–8 and 10–11 years). A similar pattern to the split-half coefficients emerged with the subscale coefficients lower and more variable than the clusters (.70s–.90s) and Broad Independence (.87–.96).

Validity.   Criterion–related validity coefficients with the AAMD ABS ranged from approximately .60 to .90. The Problem Behavior Scale demonstrated moderate coefficients with the Revised Problem Behavior Checklist (discussed in Chapter 10). The authors also present arguments supporting its content validity and the results of several studies that demonstrate its construct validity.

Review of relevant research
- In one review, Camp (1989) noted that the materials (easel kit) were cumbersome when administering the test.
- In another review, Thomas (1990) felt that the SIB was psychometrically stronger than most of the indirect measures of adaptive behavior.
- Similarly, Heifetz (1989) praised several of the instrument's psychometric properties and concluded that it was a better indirect measure of adaptive behavior than the ABI or AAMD ABS but not as good as the Vineland Adaptive Behavior Scales.
- The SIB Broad Independence score correlated .83 with the Vineland Composite score with a sample of 3 to 7 year-old children (Middleton, Keene, & Brown, 1990).
- Scores on the SIB were used to correctly classify 76 percent of subjects according to their level of retardation (Ilmer, Bruininks, & Hill, 1988).
- Factor analysis of the SIB with both retarded and nonretarded samples yielded a large adaptive or personal independence dimension for both samples (Bruininks, McGrew, & Maruyama, 1988).

Summary of research findings
The results of the few studies on the SIB reported in the professional literature have been relatively positive. Overall, the instrument appears to have good validity and can help in making classification decisions.

OVERVIEW: SCALES OF INDEPENDENT BEHAVIOR

- *Age level*—3 months to 44 years
- *Type of administration*—Individual
- *Technical adequacy*—Good standardization, adequate reliability (not for individual subscales), good validity
- *Scores yielded*—Standard scores, age equivalents, percentile ranks, normal curve equivalents, stanines, several descriptive approaches
- *Suggested use*—The SIB appears to be a reasonably valid instrument to aid in classification decisions. The technical characteristics of the instrument indicate that it is more advisable to use the cluster scores or preferably, the Broad Independence score rather than the individual subscale scores. This is particularly true in tests of a very young child or an adult for whom subscales would be of little value (e.g., work skills for infants or gross-motor skills for adults).

There are several features of the test and related materials that are favorable. One is a Spanish version of the SIB that can be purchased from the publisher. The second is the inclusion of the Early Development Scale for a quick estimate of young childrens' adaptive behavior. The third is the computerized scoring system that is recommended to save time and decrease the possibility of making errors. Finally, the availability of the ICAP, CALS, and ALSC provides a total adaptive behavior package to examiners.

Vineland Adaptive Behavior Scales

The Vineland Adaptive Behavior Scales (VABS) (Sparrow, Balla, & Cicchetti, 1984) is a revision and modification of the Vineland Social Maturity Scale (Doll, 1965). Doll made a significant contribution to the overall area of adaptive behavior assessment, and the authors of the VABS incorporated many of his concepts in designing the new instrument. The VABS, however, is a much more comprehensive test than its predecessor.

The VABS, designed for use with individuals from birth to age 18, has three separate editions that can be used individually or in combination. These are the classroom edition, which allows teachers to assess adaptive behavior within the classroom environment, and two interview editions that are administered in a semistructured format with the parents or primary caregiver as the respondent. The Interview Edition–Survey Form is most like the original Vineland and provides an overall measure of an individual's strengths and deficits. The Interview Edition–Expanded Form is more comprehensive and is the edition that has the most relevance for individuals with severe handicaps. Both interview editions measure five domains that are further broken down into 12 subdomains.

Description of sections
Interview editions.   The five areas measured by the interview editions are communication, daily living skills, socialization, motor skills, and maladaptive behavior. There are a total of 574 items on the expanded form and 297 on the survey form.

> *Communication Domain (67 items–survey, 133 items–expanded)*—There are three subdomains in this section. These are the Receptive subdomain, which measures areas such as "beginning to understand" and "listening and attending"; the Expressive subdomain, with areas such as "prespeech sounds" and "articulating"; and the Written subdomain, which measures reading and writing skills.
>
> *Daily Living Skills Domain (92 items–survey; 200 items–expanded)*—The three subdomains in this section are Personal, which measures areas such as eating and toileting; Domestic, measuring such areas as housecleaning and food preparation; and Community, which includes such areas as safety and understanding money.
>
> *Socialization Domain (66 items–survey; 134 items–expanded)*—The three subdomains are Interpersonal Relationships (areas such as "recognizing emotions" and "initiating social communication"), Play and Leisure Time (areas such as "playing with toys" and "sharing and cooperating"), and Coping Skills (such as "following rules").
>
> *Motor Skills Domain (36 items–survey; 71 items–expanded)*—This section includes items broken down into gross-motor and fine-motor areas.
>
> *Maladaptive Behavior (36 items–both editions)*—This optional domain allows for the ratings of a number of maladaptive or inappropriate behaviors.

Classroom edition.   This section of the VABS is designed for use by the classroom teacher and is presented in a checklist format. As such, it assumes that the teacher has had the opportunity to observe directly the adaptive behaviors included on the checklist. The Classroom Edition is designed for children aged 3–13.

Interpretation of results
A variety of scores are available from the VABS. These include standard scores, percentile ranks, stanines, and age equivalents. These are available for the domains, subdomains, and a composite of the Communication, Daily Living Skills, Socialization, and Motor Skills domains. One nice feature is a summary report for parents (Figure 9-3) that is used to provide meaning to the test scores. There is also a computer program called ASSIST that can be used for scoring the VABS Interview Editions.

Technical characteristics
Normative sample.   A nationally representative sample of over 3,000 individuals was used; approximately 10 percent were receiving some type of special education.

Reliability. Test-retest of survey form is very high (.98–.99); interrater reliability ranged from .62 (socialization) to .78 for motor skills.

Validity. Concurrent-validity coefficient between survey edition and original Vineland was .55. Authors also provide arguments for its content and construct validity.

The following chart describes more specific areas of adaptive behavior. Although scores such as percentile ranks and stanines are not given for these specific areas, the chart shows the areas in which your child's performance is above average, average, or below average when compared with the national norm group.

			Above Average	Average	Below Average
COMMUNICATION	**Receptive**	What your child understands			
	Expressive	What your child says			
	Written	What your child reads and writes			
DAILY LIVING SKILLS	**Personal**	How your child eats, dresses, and practices personal hygiene			
	Domestic	What household tasks your child performs			
	Community	How your child uses time, money, the telephone, and job skills			
SOCIALIZATION	**Interpersonal Relationships**	How your child interacts with others			
	Play and Leisure Time	How your child plays and uses leisure time			
	Coping Skills	How your child demonstrates responsibility and sensitivity to others			
MOTOR SKILLS	**Gross**	How your child uses arms and legs for movement and coordination			
	Fine	How your child uses hands and fingers to manipulate objects			

General Summary _____

_____

_____

Recommendations _____

_____

_____

_____

_____

_____

_____

_____

FIGURE 9-3   Portion of Parent Report for the Vineland Adaptive Behavior Scales.

From S. Sparrow, D. Balla, and D. Cicchetti, *Vineland Adaptive Behavior Scales.* Copyright © 1984 by American Guidance Service, Circle Pines, MN.

Review of relevant research

- In a review of the VABS, Kamphaus (1987) summarized several important points:

    1. The VABS is truly a set of scales rather than a single instrument.
    2. The Expanded Form should be used primarily for intervention planning.
    3. There is a general lack of technical data for the Expanded Form. In reality, the norms for this edition were determined through extrapolation of the normative data from the Survey Form.
    4. The Classroom Edition is very different from the Interview Editions. It is somewhat lengthy, and teachers often have not had the opportunity to observe some of the behaviors.

- In another review, Sattler (1989a) noted that many of the items require information that might be beyond the informant's knowledge base.
- The VABS and ABS-SE were highly correlated with a sample of autistic students (Perry & Factor, 1989), although the VABS and the ABS yielded significant differences with a group of developmentally handicapped and learning disabled children (Ronka & Barnett, 1986).
- For a group of 3–7-year-old children, the most valid scales were Personal Living skills, Communication Skills, and Community Living Skills (Middleton, Keene, & Brown, 1990)
- Tables have been developed to indicate the differences necessary between VABS scores and scores from a variety of IQ measures to reach statistical significance (Atkinson, l990a) In addition, tables are available that provide confidence intervals when using the VABS with the same person more than once (Atkinson, 1990b).
- The VABS is of limited use for moderately to severely retarded individuals (Bensberg & Irons, 1986). These researchers also compared the VABS with the ABS-SE and reported high correlations and that teachers voiced no preference over either of the tests.
- The means and standard deviations vary considerably from age group to age group, making comparisons difficult (Silverstein, 1986). Cicchetti and Sparrow (1986) argue, however, that that criticism is based on flawed reasoning and invalid statistical arguments.
- Correlations with the AAMD ABS were in the moderate range (.40 to .70) with a sample of institutionalized mentally retarded adults (Bolen, Childers, & Durham, 1984).
- There were no differences between black and white children on the VABS (Calnon, 1984).
- The VABS was successful in differentiating learning disabled from mentally retarded children (Rainwater-Bryant, 1985) and nonhandicapped children from children with mild personality problems (Sparrow et al., 1986).
- Supplementary tables for educable and trainable mentally retarded children have been developed (Harrison, Schmitt, & Ittenbach, 1990).

Summary of research findings

In general, research on the VABS has supported its use. Most of the research has been conducted on the Survey Form, which seems to be measuring similar constructs as many other adaptive behavior tests.

There is some question about the appropriateness of the norms for the Expanded Form and the practicality of the Classroom Edition. There have been several additional tables developed to aid in the interpretation of the VABS.

OVERVIEW: VINELAND ADAPTIVE BEHAVIOR SCALES

- *Age level*—Birth to 18 years old
- *Type of administration*—Individual
- *Technical adequacy*—Good standardization and test-retest reliability, good validity (Survey Form)
- *Scores yielded*—Standard scores, percentiles, age equivalents, stanines
- *Suggested use*—The VABS is probably the most widely used adaptive behavior instrument. The standardization and technical aspects are generally good, and it is based on a sound theoretical model. The test has its greatest use with mildly and moderately handicapped students, although the Expanded Form contains many items that are appropriate for individuals with severe handicaps. The format of the VABS allows it to be used to aid in making decisions about and placement as well as about educational programming.

ADAPTIVE BEHAVIOR INSTRUMENTS: FOR SCREENING ONLY

As noted earlier in this chapter, there are a number of adaptive behavior instruments that are used more for screening purposes. These instruments are not as comprehensive as those previously discussed, and the majority are used to get a quick overview of the student's adaptive behavior skills so that general program goals can be determined.

Cain-Levine Social Competency Scale

- *Age level*—5 to 13 years old
- *Type of administration*—Individual
- *Technical adequacy*—Limited standardization (trainable mentally retarded), adequate reliability, no validity data
- *Scores yielded*—Percentile ranks
- *Suggested use*—The Cain-Levine (Cain, Levine, & Elzey, 1977) should be used to determine general program objectives for moderately retarded children. The test is not appropriate for severely and profoundly retarded individuals. The scoring system is somewhat subjective, although the reliability is adequate. The lack of validity data for the Cain-Levine seriously

limits the use of the instrument. Overall, it covers four domains—self-help, initiative, social skills, and communication.

Camelot Behavioral Checklist

- *Age level*—Children and adults (no age range given)
- *Type of administration*—Individual
- *Technical adequacy*—Limited standardization, questionable reliability and validity
- *Scores yielded*—Percentiles, item profiles, and score profiles
- *Suggested use*—The Camelot (Foster, 1974) is best thought of as a screening instrument to determine general areas of program need. A profile sheet offers a visual representation of that information. The scoring system, however, does not allow for sensitive discriminations among retarded persons' performances. The technical adequacy of the Camelot is also somewhat questionable. The test includes 10 domains and 40 subdomains.

Normative Adaptive Behavior Checklist

- *Age level*—Infancy–age 21
- *Type of administration*—Individual (questionnaire)
- *Scores yielded*—Standard scores, age equivalents
- *Technical adequacy*—Good reliability, adequate validity; standardized on over 6,000 nonhandicapped individuals
- *Description and suggested use*—The N-ABC (Adams, 1986) includes over 100 items that measure the areas of self-help, home living, independent living, social, sensorimotor, and language and academic skills. It can be used to provide a quick, reliable estimate of a person's adaptive behavior. If a person scores low on the N-ABC, an extended, much longer version, the Comprehensive Test of Adaptive Behavior, can be administered to provide more specific information.

TARC Assessment System

- *Age level*—3 to 16 years old
- *Type of administration*—Individual
- *Technical adequacy*—Limited (standardized on a heterogeneous group of severely handicapped individuals)
- *Scores yielded*—Raw scores are plotted on profile sheet that yields standard scores
- *Suggested use*—The TARC (Sailor & Mix, 1975) should be used for screening purposes only. The normative aspects of the instrument are limited and, therefore, use of the standard scores should be discouraged. The TARC does offer a quick estimate of an individual's strengths and weaknesses in self-help skills, motor skills, communication skills, and social skills.

Instrument or Technique	Suggested Use							Target Population						Special Considerations	Educational Relevance for Exceptional Students
	Prereferral			Postreferral											
	Screening and Initial Identification	Informal Determination and Evaluation of Teaching Programs and Strategies	Determination of Current Performance Level and Educational Need	Decisions about Classification and Program Placement	IEP Goals	IEP Objectives	IEP Evaluation	Mild/Moderate	Severe/Profound	Preschool	Elementary Age	Secondary Age	Adult		
Adaptive Behavior Inventory			X	X	X			X			X	X		Easy to administer and score; there is a shorter version for screening purposes	useful
Adaptive Behavior Inventory for Children				X				X			X			Part of System of Multicultural Pluralistic Assessment; used primarily to "declassify" minority children	adequate
Adaptive Behavior Scale–Residential and Community Edition			X	X	X			X	X	X	X	X	X	Technical aspects of Part Two have been questioned; has limited use for more severely retarded individuals	useful
Adaptive Behavior Scale–School Edition			X	X	X			X		X	X	X		Potentially useful instrument to aid in classification and placement decisions	useful
Scales of Independent Behavior			X	X	X			X	X	X	X	X	X	There is a screening version, criterion-referenced instrument and a curriculum that is associated with the SIB	useful
Vineland Adaptive Behavior Scales			X	X	X	X	X	X	X	X	X	X		A useful instrument for the overall measurement of adaptive behavior	very useful
Cain-Levine Social Competency Scale	X				X			X			X			Does not yield specific information for programming; validity data are lacking	limited
Camelot Behavioral Checklist	X				X			X			X	X	X	Does not yield specific information for programming; limited technical aspects	limited

Instrument or Technique	Suggested Use							Target Population						Special Considerations	Educational Relevance for Exceptional Students
	Prereferral			Postreferral											
	Screening and Initial Identification	Informal Determination and Evaluation of Teaching Programs and Strategies	Determination of Current Performance Level and Educational Need	Decisions about Classification and Program Placement	IEP Goals	IEP Objectives	IEP Evaluation	Mild/Moderate	Severe/Profound	Preschool	Elementary Age	Secondary Age	Adult		
Normative Adaptive Behavior Checklist	X				X			X		X	X	X		Can be used in conjunction with the Comprehensive Test of Adaptive Behavior	useful
TARC Assessment System	X				X				X	X	X	X		Use informally to determine strengths and weaknesses	limited

10

Assessment of Behavioral/Emotional Status

INSTRUMENTS/PROCEDURES INCLUDED

BEHAVIOR RATING SCALES
- Revised Behavior Problem Checklist
- Behavior Rating Profile–2
- Burks Behavior Rating Scales
- Child Behavior Checklist
- Devereux Elementary School Behavior Rating Scale–II
- Social Skills Rating System
- Walker–McConnell Scale of Social Competence and School Adjustment
- Walker Problem Behavior Identification Checklist

MEASUREMENT OF EMOTIONAL STATUS
- Projective Methods
- Self-Concept
- Inventories and Questionnaires

Wendy has had a history of emotional problems. Her parents report that she would have extreme mood swings. One minute she would be depressed and withdrawn and the next, elated, happy, and laughing; no environmental effect seemed to be triggering these changes. At other times, she would become extremely aggressive. When she was 5, she seriously injured her two-year-old brother. At that time she was taken to a psychologist, who attempted to evaluate her emotional state. There was some question whether placing Wendy in a school for emotionally disturbed children would be the most appropriate thing to do for her.

Hector is a fifth-grade student who is constantly getting into trouble. Both his teacher and parents describe him as "very active." Recently, Hector has also been getting into trouble for stealing and destroying property. His teacher decided to administer a behavior-rating scale to document the areas in which Hector was having problems and to help prioritize behavioral goals for him to achieve.

This chapter addresses two areas: the indirect measurement of emotional status and the direct measurement of classroom behavior. Measurement of an individual's emotional state usually requires a great deal of inference and subjectivity on the part of the examiner. On the other hand, standardized measures of classroom behavior usually involve direct observation documented by some type of behavior-rating scale.

BEHAVIOR-RATING SCALES

WHY USE?
Screening and identification, decisions about classification and program placement; establishment of IEP goals

WHO SHOULD USE?
Teachers, school psychologists

Behavior-rating scales are concerned with documenting observable behavior. Typically, these scales are developed for use by the classroom teacher or some other individual who has an opportunity to observe the examinee. Like inventories and questionnaires (discussed later in this chapter), behavior-rating scales usually include items grouped according to some categorical characteristic. Although there are very few similarities across the names of categories in different rating scales (Edelbrock, 1983), many of the categories tend to measure the same behavioral dimensions (Bullock, Wilson, & Campbell, 1990). Theoretically, the grouping of items leads to a profile of a student's behavior patterns. Behavior-rating scales have been criticized, however, on a number of grounds. For example, the technical adequacy of most scales has been questioned. Also, the educational significance of their data is limited.

Revised Behavior Problem Checklist

The Revised Behavior Problem Checklist (RBPC) (Quay & Peterson, 1983) includes 89 items designed for use with students from kindergarten through sixth grade. The instrument is designed for use by teachers, and it is easy to administer and score. The examiner indicates whether each of the 89 items (or behavioral characteristics) represents a problem for the child being evaluated.

Description

The 89 items of the RBPC are divided into four major scales and two minor scales. The major scales are Conduct Disorders (22 items), Socialized Aggression (17 items), Attention Problems-Immaturity (16 items), and Anxiety-Withdrawal (11 items). The minor scales are Psychotic Behavior (6 items) and Motor Excess (5 items). For each of the items (for example, "has temper tantrums") the rater must assign the child a score of 0 (does not constitute a problem), 1 (mild problem), or 2 (severe problem).

Interpretation of results

The scores for each scale are added and then analyzed by looking at a profile that will highlight an individual's behavioral excesses and deficits. It is also possible to compare the scores with "normal" and "clinical" groups. T-scores (standard scores with a mean of 50 and a standard deviation of 10) are available, but the author cautions that more data should be collected before they can be used reliably.

Technical characteristics

Normative sample.   Over 750 children from four separate samples provided information that was factor-analyzed to develop the RBPC. Data regarding the standardization are generally lacking.

Reliability.   A number of limited reliability studies have been conducted. Interrater reliability ranged from .52 (Anxiety-Withdrawal) to .85 (Conduct Disorder). Test-retest coefficients ranged from .49 (Social Aggression) to .83 (Attention Problems-Immaturity).

Validity.   The construct validity has been carefully established through the use of factor analysis to aid in item selection. The authors also report some concurrent validity data and a discussion of the relationship between dimensions of the RBPC and various diagnostic categories.

Review of relevant research

The majority of the literature focuses on the earlier versions of the RBPC. There are considerable similarities in these versions so that these research studies are probably relevant for the RBPC as well. In fact, Heinze (1987) reported high correlations between the BPC and the RBPC. Research on both versions are included.

- Four factors have been identified for the BPC: hyperkinetic, shy-inept, depressed, and dyssocial (Arnold, Barneby, & Smeltzer, 1981).

- The BPC can be used effectively with preschool children (Gayton, Thornton, & Bassett, 1982).
- Three dimensions of problem behavior are typically identified to account for the majority of variance in children classified as deviant. These are conduct disorder, anxiety-withdrawal, and immaturity (Von Isser, Quay, & Love, 1980). The same researchers point out that the BPC measures these three areas.
- Learning-disabled (LD) students scored differently than did non-LD students on items measuring traits such as anxiety, nonparticipation, and poor self-confidence (Cullinan, Epstein, & Lloyd, 1981).
- The conduct-disorder and personality-problem factors best discriminated groups of behaviorally disordered, educable mentally retarded, and LD students (Cullinan, Epstein, & Dembinski, 1979). Educable mentally retarded (EMR), LD, and emotionally disturbed students all scored high on the immaturity-inadequacy factor (Gajar, 1979).
- The BPC can be used confidently with deaf students (Hirshoren & Schnittjer, 1979).

A few studies located looked at the use of the RBPC. Those are listed below.

- Only low-to-moderate correlations were found between two groups of teachers using the RBPC (Simpson, 1989; Simpson & Arnett, 1987).
- Low correlations between mothers' and teachers' ratings were reported (Mattison, Bagnato, & Strickler, 1987; Simpson & Halpin, 1986).
- The Motor Excess Scale was useful in differentiating attention deficit disorders (ADD) with hyperactivity and ADD without hyperactivity (Lahey, Schaughency, Strauss, & Frame, 1984).
- The RBPC was useful in differentiating inattentive versus conduct-disordered preschool children (Hinshaw, Morrison, & Carta, 1987).
- The RBPC was found to have less than acceptable reliability and was criticized for measuring only negative behaviors (Wilson & Bullock, 1988).
- The lack of national norms is a serious drawback (Lahey & Piacentini, 1985).
- There have been several reviews of the RBPC. Cancelli (1985) noted that the increased number of items in the revised version increased its reliability and that the minor subscales did little to add to its predictive validity. Lahey and Piacentini (1985) stated that the RBPC had excellent construct validity and was "perhaps the most valid of all teacher rating scales in terms of factor structure and related measures of validity" (p. 285). Both reviewers noted that local norms should be developed, particularly since nationally representative derived scores are not available. Finally, Simpson (1990) noted that the RBPC had relatively low interrater reliability, although overall it is still judged to be one of the better behavior rating scales.

Summary of research findings

Research on the RBPC and its earlier versions has primarily investigated the instruments' technical characteristics. The careful analysis of the various behavior factors and the subsequent items chosen for each factor makes a profile analysis appropriate. In general the construct validity of the instrument has been supported, although the reliability, particularly interrater reliability has been questioned.

OVERVIEW: REVISED BEHAVIOR PROBLEM CHECKLIST

- *Age level*—Kindergarten–grade 6
- *Type of administration*—Individual
- *Technical characteristics*—Adequate reliability (limited interrater), acceptable validity (based on research data)
- *Scores yielded*—Profile analysis
- *Suggested use*—The RBPC is one of the more popular rating scales. It is easy to administer and score. A growing body of literature is focused on its technical and interpretive characteristics. The RBPC seems to be a valid measure of classroom behavior problems although, like many behavior rating scales, it has some problems regarding reliability. One concern is the limited standardization sample.

Behavior Rating Profile–2

The Behavior Rating Profile–2 (BRP-2) (Brown & Hammill, 1990) is an ecological approach to assessment, in that the information is obtained from a number of sources. The BRP-2 includes four components: Student Rating Scales—Home, School, and Peer; a Teacher Rating Scale; a Parent Rating Scale; and a Sociogram. This allows for the evaluation of the student in a number of settings and by a number of individuals. The test is individually administered (except for the Sociogram) and is appropriate for children 6 1/2–18 1/2 years old.

Description

Student Rating Scales—The three student rating scales consist of 20 items about school, 20 items about home, and 20 items about peers. This section, which is completed by the student, is presented in a true-false format. Examples include "I can't seem to stay in my desk at school" (school item); "Other children are always picking on me" (peer item); and "I don't listen when my parents are talking to me" (home item).

Teacher Rating Scale—This scale can be completed by all school personnel who have significant contact with the student. It consists of 30 items that the teacher must categorize as "very much like the student," "like the student," "not like the student," or "not at all like the student." Examples of items are "doesn't follow class rules" and "tattles on classmates."

Parent Rating Scale—This section can be completed by one or both of the parents. It is similar in format to the Teacher Rating Scale. Examples of items include "is verbally aggressive to parents" and "won't share belongings willingly."

Sociogram—This is a method to get peer perceptions into the evaluation. A pair of questions is given to each student in the class. An example is, "Which of the girls and boys in your class would you most like to have as your friend?" and "Which of the girls and boys in your class would you least like to have as your friend?" Each student must provide three names for each question. Using the scoring procedures noted in the manual, the examiner rank-orders the students according to their acceptance level.

Interpretation of results

Results from each section can be converted to standard scores with a mean of 10 and a standard deviation of 3. These scores can be plotted on a behavior-rating profile sheet. Percentile ranks are also available.

Technical characteristics

Normative sample.   The sample included 2,682 students and 1,452 teachers from 26 states. The 1,948 parents involved came from only 19 states. Demographic information is included in the manual.

Reliability.   Internal consistency was generally acceptable. Most coefficients were above .80. Test-retest coefficients ranged from .78 to .91 with a sample of 36 high school students and from .76 to .97 with approximately 75 disturbed and LD children. In a somewhat larger study (approximately 200 students, teachers, and parents), test-retest coefficients ranged from .43 to .90 (student), .69 to .96 (parent), and .90 to .96 (teacher). The lowest coefficients were for grades one and two.

Validity.   Concurrent validity was established with the Walker Problem Behavior Checklist, the Behavior Problem Checklist, and the Vineland Social Maturity Scale. The authors state that 86 percent of the coefficients were above their acceptable level of .35. Relatively low coefficients with measures of aptitude and achievement are reported, although the authors argue that this is expected. Arguments supporting content and construct validity are also provided.

Review of relevant research

To date, no research has been reported on the BRP-2. The original BRP has received limited attention in the literature. In one review, Posey (1989) noted limitations including response bias and its unidimensionality. Bacon (1989) noted that no interrater reliability was given.

In one empirical study, Ellers, Ellers, and Bradley-Johnson (1989) found that the teacher form had adequate reliability for both screening and eligibility decisions for grades 1–12. They reported that the parent form was suitable for screening for grades 3–12 and eligibility for grades 3–6 and 11–12. They also found that the student form was not reliable enough for use at any age. These data can be generalized to the BRP–2 with some degree of confidence given the slight changes in the revised edition.

OVERVIEW: BEHAVIOR RATING PROFILE–2

- *Age level*—6 1/2–18 1/2 years old
- *Type of administration*—Individual (except for sociogram); small group possible
- *Technical characteristics*—Adequate reliability (except for grades 1 and 2, and for student form), questionable validity
- *Scores yielded*—Standard scores, percentile ranks
- *Suggested use*—The BRP-2 is a somewhat unique instrument in that it measures a student's behavior in a number of settings and with information from a number of individuals. This yields information that, for instance, will help to determine if a student's behavior problem occurs only at home or only at school. Unfortunately, it is difficult to determine whether a difference in behavior is really a difference—or only the way in which the behavior is perceived, since more than one person is rating. (What if, for instance, two teachers and the parents rate the student as average, and one other teacher indicates that a problem exists. Does the student behave differently in that one teacher's class or does that particular teacher have different standards and expectations?) Perhaps using multiple raters in each setting would be the procedure to follow. Alternatively, more interrater-reliability studies might allow examiners to interpret the results more confidently. It does appear to be limited for younger children and the student form has questionable relevance at all age levels.

  In summary, the BRP-2 is a potentially useful tool to determine how a student behaves in different settings, and how different individuals perceive that behavior. Definitive diagnostic decisions should not be based solely on the BRP-2. Clearly, more research should be conducted on the BRP-2.

Burks Behavior Rating Scales

The Burks Behavior Rating Scales (BBRS) (Burks, 1977) is an instrument used to identify certain patterns of inappropriate behaviors demonstrated by children from grades 1–8. According to the author (p. 5), the BBRS has six specific purposes:

1. Identify patterns of disturbed behavior that distinguish between several groups of children.
2. Show changes in behavior patterns over a period of time.
3. Indicate areas in a child's personality where further evaluation might advantageously take place.
4. Provide a source of information useful to school personnel for conferences with parents.
5. Predict which children will do well in special-education classes and which will not.
6. Be of practical value when used by both parents and teachers.

Description

The BBRS consists of 110 items divided into 19 behavior categories or scales. Another version for preschool and kindergarten children has 105 items. Ratings can be obtained from anyone who is thoroughly familiar with a child on a day-to-day basis. Usually, teachers or parents rate the child. The person giving the ratings should not be the one who tabulates the scores because of the possibility of a "halo effect." For each item, the respondent must rate the child on a scale of 1 ("You have not noticed this behavior at all") to 5 ("You have noticed the behavior to a very large degree"). A description of the scales follows.

> *Excessive Self-Blame (5 items)*—Items include "blames self if things go wrong" and "questions indicate a worry about the future."
>
> *Excessive Anxiety (5 items)*—Items include "appears nervous" and "shows many fears."
>
> *Excessive Withdrawal (6 items)*—Items include "is difficult to get to know" and "appears disinterested in classwork of others."
>
> *Excessive Dependency (6 items)*—Items include "seeks constant praise" and "clings to adults."
>
> *Poor Ego Strength (7 items)*—Items include "avoids competition" and "plays the clown of the class."
>
> *Poor Physical Strength (5 items)*—Items include "gets hurt in physical play" and "appears physically lethargic."
>
> *Poor Coordination (5 items)*—Items include "accidentally runs into people and objects" and "has trouble holding onto things."
>
> *Poor Intellectuality (7 items)*—Items include "does not ask questions" and "gives inappropriate responses."
>
> *Poor Academics (5 items)*—Items include "homework is not done or incomplete" and "shows poor spelling."
>
> *Poor Attention (5 items)*—Items include "attention span not increased by punishment or reward" and "attention span is short."
>
> *Poor Impulse Control (5 items)*—Items include "cannot control self" and "is hyperactive and restless."

Poor Reality Contact (8 items)—Items include "makes weird drawings" and "rotates or rocks his body."

Poor Sense of Identity (6 items)—Items include "rejects classmates in a hostile manner" and "will not take suggestions from others."

Excessive Suffering (7 items)—Items include "appears unhappy" and "seems to welcome punishment."

Poor Anger Control (5 items)—Items include "becomes angry quickly" and "flares up at classmates when teased or pushed."

Excessive Sense of Persecution (5 items)—Items include "will not forgive others" and "complains others do not like him."

Excessive Aggressiveness (6 items)—Items include "hits or pushes others" and "is sarcastic."

Excessive Resistance (4 items)—Items include "does things his own way" and "is rebellious when disciplined."

Poor Social Conformity (8 items)—Items include "is truant" and "shows little respect for authority."

Interpretation of results

The individual scores for the various items in each scale are summed. The sums are plotted on a profile sheet. On this profile sheet, the raw score for each scale is simply categorized as "not significant," "significant," or "very significant." The interpretation of the profile sheet centers around information in the manual regarding "patterns of behavior pathology seen in children." These patterns include profiles of children characterized in the following ways: disadvantaged-immature, shy-withdrawn, anxious-neurotic, hyperactive-distractible, aggressive-hostile, socialized delinquent, and schizophrenic. In addition, suggestions are given for remediation for children with high scores in the various scales. No transformation from raw scores to standard scores or any other type of derived score is available.

Extreme caution must be taken not to overemphasize the differential diagnostic profiles included in the manual. Most of the information yielded by this instrument has more relevance for clinicians (as supplemental data) than for teachers.

Technical characteristics

Normative sample.   The sample consisted of 494 primary-school-age children, plus 69 seventh and eighth graders; approximately 70 percent were Mexican-American.

Reliability.   Test-retest coefficients (using 95 emotionally disturbed children) ranged from .60 to .83.

Validity. Several types of validity are discussed in the manual, although the data presented are somewhat limited.

Review of relevant research

A few studies of previous editions exist, and these studies demonstrate that different groups of students have different patterns on the BBRS. The scale, however, has not been studied systematically to determine its strengths and inadequacies. One exception was a study by Burke, Broad, Ryford, and Sims (1983) who reported inadequate interrater reliability between therapists and teachers.

OVERVIEW: BURKS BEHAVIOR RATING SCALES

- *Age level*—Grades 1–8 (preschool version—ages 3–6)
- *Type of administration*—Individual
- *Technical characteristics*—Inadequate standardization, limited reliability and validity
- *Scores yielded*—Raw scores, interpreted as "not significant," "significant," and "very significant."
- *Suggested use*—The BBRS has limited use in the classroom. Although the author suggests that it can be used to predict students who will or will not do well in special education, diagnostic decisions should not be made using this instrument. The technical characteristics, particularly the standardization group, are limited. The scoring system and typical profiles mentioned in the manual are overly simplified and subject to misinterpretation. The use of the BBRS should be limited to an initial screening of students, but even for this purpose, more relevant instruments are available.

Child Behavior Checklist

The Child Behavior Checklist (CBCL) (Achenbach & Edelbrock, 1991) is designed to be used by parents to rate the behavioral competencies and behavioral problems of their child. The CBCL is designed to be used in conjunction with the Revised Child Behavior Profile (RCBP), which provides the interpretive guidelines for the information obtained from the CBCL. There are also supplemental instruments or components called the Teacher Report Form, Direct Observation Form, and a Youth Self-Report that provide a comprehensive behavior rating system. The CBCL can be used for individuals aged 2–16. Although there are some minor changes from earlier editions, the 1991 CBCL can be scored on the same profile as previous editions. A brief description of the components follows.

Description
Child Behavior Checklist and Revised Child Behavior Profile. The CBCL includes items that measure social competence in areas such as involvement with social organizations and relationships with friends. There are also additional items that focus on behavior problems. Results of the CBCL are placed on the RCBP, which consists of three social competency scales and a number of behavior-problem scales identified through factor analysis. There are separate profiles (with differing scales) for both boys and girls for four separate age ranges (2–3, 4–6, 6–11, 12–16). For example, several different scales (factors) were statistically determined for boys aged 4–6 and for girls aged 12–16. In general, the various factors or scales can be classified as internalizing (for example, social withdrawal); externalizing (for example, aggressive); and mixed (for example, immature). Figure 10-1 shows an example of the profile, and subsequent scales, for girls aged 6–11.

The CBCL for ages 2–3 includes 99 items, 59 of which have counterparts on the CBCL for ages 4–16 (Achenbach, 1990). There are six syndrome scales as well as internalizing, externalizing, and total problems.

Teacher Report Form. This component has separate forms for boys and girls aged 5–18. There are items that allow the rating of behavior problems, plus an item on academic performance and an item on adaptive functioning.

Direct Observation Form. This section is somewhat unique; it requires the evaluator to observe the child in 10-minute time samples and then respond to 96 items that yield a behavior problem score and an on-task score. The revised version provides more detailed scoring and item definitions than the original.

Youth Self-Report. This section asks the child to rate himself or herself. There are several general questions (for example, "Please list any jobs or chores that you have") and other items (for example, "I show off or clown") that must be rated on a "not true," "sometimes true," or "very true" basis. Essentially, this section is the same as the CBCL with the wording changed to reflect the first person. There are 16 items from the CBCL that have been replaced with socially desirable items endorsed by most youth. This can be completed by students aged 11–18 with at least a fifth grade reading-level ability.

Interpretation of results
As noted previously, results of the CBCL are interpreted through the use of the RCBP. The profile shown in Figure 10-1 shows the "normal range" of performance that is based on the T-scores (mean = 50; standard

FIGURE 10-1 Example of a Revised Child Behavior Profile for One Age and Sex Group.

From T. Achenbach and C. Edelbrock, *Child Behavior Checklist and Revised Child Behavior Profile.* Copyright © 1983 by T. M. Achenbach. Reprinted with permission.

deviation = 10) yielded. A computer scoring program for the Profile is also available.

Technical characteristics

Normative sample.   The CBCL was normed on 2,368 children. Scales were devised from parents' ratings of 4,455 clinically referred children.

Reliability.   Interrater reliabilities were primarily in the .90s for the CBCL and from the .70s to the .90s for the Direct Observation Form. Test-retest coefficients were in the .80s—.90s range for the teacher report form.

Validity.   Results of several validity studies are reported in the manual. These generally demonstrate moderate correlations with other behavior-rating scales and the instruments' ability to identify children who have been referred for mental health services.

Review of relevant research

- More reliable information can be obtained by adding the Teacher Rating Form to the overall Child Behavior Profile when screening for behavior problems (Edelbrock & Achenbach, 1984).
- The CBCL did not correlate highly with risk factors typically associated with childhood psychiatric problems (Mooney, Thompson, & Nelson, 1987).
- There was generally low agreement between teachers and parents using the CBCL, thus indicating the need for a multiple-rater system (Garrison & Earls, 1985).
- The Direct Observation Form provides valid and reliable information with a minimum of training (Reed & Edelbrock, 1983).
- Elliot and Busse (1990) felt that the Youth Self-Report was useful but not for classification decisions. They also pointed out that whereas the Teacher Form was not user-friendly, it was psychometrically superior to most behavior rating scales.
- The CBCL correlated highly with the RBPC (Heinze, 1987).
- The CBCL scores were dissimilar when administered to both parents. There is a need for separate norms for mothers and fathers (LeBlanc & Reynolds, 1989).
- The CBCL has good internal consistency and construct validity in relation to widely accepted indices of school functioning (Pryor, Wilkinson, Harris & Travato, 1989).
- Christenson (1990), in a review of the CBCL, highly recommended both the Teacher and Self Report form. She noted that the manuals were well written, were reliable and valid, and were based on ongoing research.

Summary of research findings

The majority of published research on the CBCL has focused on establishing the validity and reliability of its various components. In general, the technical characteristics of the CBCL have been favorable. There are also many articles that describe and review the CBCL. A list of over 700 articles in which the CBCL has been used can be obtained from the authors of the instrument.

OVERVIEW: CHILD BEHAVIOR CHECKLIST

- *Age level*—2 to 16 years old
- *Type of administration*—Individual
- *Technical adequacy*—Generally good reliability and validity
- *Scores yielded*—T-scores (type of standard score); results are placed on the RCBP
- *Suggested use*—Overall, the CBCL is one of the better behavior-rating scales available. Items were carefully selected and statistically validated. The idea of separate profiles (with different scales included) for boys and girls at different age levels is an excellent one. In addition, the use of separate forms that allow multiple ratings provides potentially important information. The CBCL and its associated components are continually updated through ongoing research by the authors. This is advantageous but requires test users to keep up with the latest versions of the latest instruments. Overall, the CBCL can be used confidently to document the behavioral status of students in a variety of areas.

Devereux Elementary School Behavior Rating Scale–II

The Devereux Elementary School Behavior Rating Scale (DESB–II) (Swift, 1982) is one of three scales published by the Devereux Foundation. The others are the Devereux Child Behavior Rating Scale (for children 8–12 years old) and the Devereux Adolescent Behavior Rating Scale (for individuals 13–18 years old). The DESB–II is a revision of the 1967 edition and is designed for children in grades 1–6.

Description

The items on the DESB–II are grouped into 10 behavior factors and 4 behavior clusters derived through factor analytic studies. In addition, there are two items that measure the student's achievement compared to the "average" and to the student's own "ability." Approximately half of the items are rated on a 1 (never) to 5 (very frequently) scale and half using a 1 (not at all) to 7 (extremely) scale.

BEHAVIOR FACTORS

Work Organization (4 items)—An item example is "complete assignments on time?"

Creative Initiative/Involvement (5 items)—An item example is "initiate classroom discussion?"

Positive Toward Teacher (4 items)—An item example is "respond positively to praise?"

Need for Direction in Work (3 items)—An item example is "unable to correct errors in his own work?"

Socially Withdrawn (4 items)—An item example is "avoid involvement or communication with others?"

Failure Anxiety (4 items)—An item example is "get upset or angry when having difficulty understanding something?"

Impatience (4 items)—An item example is "hand in work without checking it first?"

Irrelevant Thinking/Talk (4 items)—An item example is "jump from one thought to another when telling something?"

Blaming (4 items)—An item example is "say he doesn't like the work assigned?"

Negative/Aggressive (4 items)—An item example is "poke, torment, or tease classmates?"

BEHAVIOR CLUSTERS

Perseverance (2 items)—An item example is "stay with work until completed?"

Peer Cooperation (2 items)—An item example is "work well with peers?"

Confusion (3 items)—An item example is "forget the directions that are given?"

Inattention (4 items)—An item example is "unable to attend to a task when other activities are going on?"

Interpretation of results

The DESB–II includes a profile sheet (Figure 10–2) that gives a visual representation of the individual's performance in standard–score units. Except for three factors (Work Organization, Creative Initiative/Involvement, Positive Toward Teacher) and two clusters (Perseverence, Peer Cooperation), a score above 1 standard deviation is considered a problem. For those other areas, a score below 1 standard deviation is considered problematic.

Technical characteristics

Normative sample. Two samples—regular education and special education—were included. A total of 121 teachers were involved; 708

FIGURE 10-2 Profile Sheet from the Devereux Elementary School Behavior Rating Scale–II.

From M. Swift, *Devereux Elementary School Behavior Rating Scale–II.* Copyright © 1982 by the Devereux Foundation. Reprinted with permission.

regular-education students and an unspecified number of special-education students were rated.

Reliability.   Test-retest coefficients from a small sample ranged from .64 (Confusion Cluster) to .90 (Work Organization factor).

Validity.   Construct validity is reported in the form of data demonstrating significant differences between the regular and special education students on every factor and cluster except Creative Initiative/Involvement and Positive Toward Teacher.

Review of relevant research

The following research relates to the DESB; no studies on the DESB-II were located.

- The DESB is valid and reliable, although teachers may vary in their use of the instrument (Finkelman, Ferrecase, & Garmazy, 1988).
- The DESB is a valid and reliable measure of inappropriate behavior for visually impaired children (Ross & Gallagher, 1976).
- The reliability of the DESB is satisfactory (Schaefer, Baker, & Zawel, 1975). The researchers identified three factors: (1) classroom-management problem, (2) self-reliant learner, and (3) seeks teacher approval.
- The DESB needs to have separate grade-level and sex norms (Horne & Larrivee, 1979).
- The DESB was not as accurate as the Behavior Problem Checklist in identifying children as aggressive, hyperactive, or withdrawn (Proger, Mann, Green, Bayuk, & Burger, 1975).
- In a longitudinal study of 600 children, eight profile patterns were identified. These profiles roughly corresponded to eight achievement levels (reported in Spivack & Swift, 1973).
- In studying the item validity of the DESB, Willis, Smithy, and Holliday (1979) suggested that the instrument is much more effective in identifying students with severe rather than mild problems. They also suggested a 36-item instrument that eliminates four scales (Irrelevant-Responsiveness, Impatience, Disrespect-Defiance, and External Blame).

Summary of research findings

Although no information was located regarding the DESB-II, the DESB has been widely researched. In general, the instrument seems to be a reliable and valid measure of school-related behaviors. The norms of the test have been criticized, however, and one study found that it did not discriminate group status as well as the Behavior Problem Checklist did. Spivack and Swift (1973), in a review of various behavior-rating scales, concluded that "the DESB as a tool would seem to have specific applicability in school systems when a question arises regarding behaviors that interfere with classroom performance. It was not designed to make clinical diagnosis nor to measure basic personality dimensions" (p. 80). As authors of the DESB, Spivack and Swift should be aware of its strengths and weaknesses; other users of the test should pay attention to the authors' statements. Also, because the DESB–II includes different factors from its predecessors, care should be given not to overgeneralize these results.

OVERVIEW: DEVEREUX ELEMENTARY SCHOOL BEHAVIOR RATING SCALE-II

- *Age level*—Grades 1–6
- *Type of administration*—Individual
- *Technical characteristics*—Adequate reliability and validity
- *Scores yielded*—Standard scores, profile sheet
- *Suggested use*—The DESB-II was once a relatively popular instrument. It should be used to identify behaviors or areas that are interfering with academic progress. The instrument is a reasonably good screening instrument, but it should not be used to make diagnostic decisions. There are more appropriate instruments available.

Social Skills Rating System

The Social Skills Rating System (SSRS) (Gresham & Elliot, 1990) is a multi-rater assessment battery of social behaviors that can affect teacher/student relations, peer acceptance, and academic performance. There are teacher, parent, and student forms, each of which elicit information about the student from various viewpoints. The Teacher and Parent Forms are available for three levels: preschool, K–6, and 7–12, whereas the Student Rating Form is available for grades 3–6 and 7–12. Unlike many other behavior rating scales, the SSRS focuses on positive behaviors as opposed to maladaptive behaviors. It does, however, include a brief assessment of problem behaviors as well. According to the authors, the SSRS can be used for a variety of purposes, including (1) identifying students at risk for social behavior problems; (2) differentiating mildly handicapped students from non-handicapped students; (3) categorizing behavior difficulties; (4) selecting behaviors for school and home interventions; and (5) guiding the selection of intervention strategies. The information can also be used to assist in writing IEPs.

Description

As noted previously, there are three rating scales at three different age levels. In addition, three specific areas are measured: social skills, problem behaviors, and academic competence. The various forms and the corresponding areas that they measure are noted in the following section.

Preschool Level: Teacher Form
  Social Skills (30 items)
  Problem Behaviors (10 items)

Preschool Level: Parent Form
  Social Skills (39 items)
  Problem Behaviors (10 items)

Elementary Level: Student Form
  Social Skills (34 items)

Elementary Level: Teacher Form
  Social Skills (30 items)
  Problem Behavior (18 items)
  Academic Competence (9 items)

Elementary Level: Parent Form
  Social Skills (38 items)
  Problem Behaviors (17 items)

Secondary Level: Student Form
  Social Skills (39 items)

Secondary Level: Teacher Form
  Social Skills (30 items)
  Problem Behaviors (12 items)
  Academic Competence (9 items)

Secondary Level: Parent Form
  Social Skills (40 items)
  Problem Behaviors (12 items)

Interpretation of results

Each rater responds to items such as "has temper tantrums" or "participates in group activities" using a 0 (never), 1 (sometimes), or 2 (very often) scale. In addition, for the Parent and Teacher Forms there is a separate rating on how important each behavior is to the rater (0—not important, 1—important, 2—critical). This information is used to prepare the intervention program for the individual student.

There are a variety of scoring options available for the SSRS. In addition to percentile ranks and standard scores (mean = 100; standard deviation = 15), the behavior level can also be determined. The behavior level is simply a descriptive category that might be used to help identify areas for intervention.

Technical characteristics
Normative sample.   The Student Rating Form was standardized using over 4,000 children stratified by sex, race, region, and community

size. The Teacher Rating Scale included 259 teachers' ratings of 1,335 children. The Parent Form used approximately 1,000 parents and was based on a volunteer sample. The authors note some limitation in the parent and teacher samples compared to the U.S. population; for example, the parent sample was better educated than the population as a whole.

Reliability. Internal consistency coefficients for the social skills area ranged from .93 to .94 for the Teacher Form, .87 to .90 for the Parent Form, and were .83 for the Student Form. For the problem behavior area, the internal consistency coefficients ranged from .82 to .88 for the Teacher Form and .73 to .87 for the Parent Form. The coefficients for academic competence were .95. Test/retest coefficients for the Teacher Form were .85 for social skills, .84 for problem behaviors, and .93 for academic competence. Coefficients for the Parent Form for social skills were .87 and for problem behavior .65. For the Student Form, the coefficient for social skills was .68.

Validity. The authors provide an argument for the assurance of content and social validity (the social significance of the behavior selected for intervention) and provide criterion-related validity coefficients. For the Teacher Form, coefficients for the social skills section with a variety of other rating scales ranged from .64 to .70. The correlations for the problem behavior area were somewhat lower, ranging from .55 to .81. The coefficients for the academic competence area ranged from .59 to .67. For the Parent Form, the coefficients with the CBCL ranged from .37 to .58 for the social skills area and .52 to .70 for the problem behavior area. The Student Form was also correlated with the CBCL (Youth Self-Report Form) and correlations ranged from .23 to .33. A correlation study with a self-concept scale also yielded a low coefficient of .30. The authors spend a considerable amount of time discussing and presenting data to support the construct validity of the instrument. This includes intercorrelations of the scales as well as factor analysis results. In addition, convergent and discriminate validity data are reported.

OVERVIEW: SOCIAL SKILLS RATING SYSTEM

- *Age level*—Preschool through secondary level
- *Type of administration*—Multiple raters (student, parent, teacher)
- *Scores yielded*—Behavior Level, standard score, percentile rank
- *Technical adequacy*—Adequate standardization (Student Form), limited standardization (Teacher and Parent Forms); adequate reliability, questionable validity

■ *Suggested use*—The SSRS allows for multiple ratings (similar to the BRP-2) that can provide important diagnostic information. The SSRS was built on a solid theoretical framework and does have the advantage of looking primarily at the pro-social behaviors as opposed to maladaptive behaviors. An important aspect of the SSRS is the inclusion of an Assessment Intervention Record that allows the development of specific intervention programs based on data obtained on the SSRS. This provides a convenient record to list social skill strengths, social skill performance deficits, social skill acquisition deficits, and problem behaviors. In addition, the record provides a table that links the assessment needs with specific intervention suggestions. The test manual, in fact, devotes a chapter to discussing the development of intervention plans. Although the information presented is cursory, it does emphasize the importance of linking the assessment to a program of intervention strategies. It should be noted that the preschool version of the SSRS is somewhat limited due to the small standardization sample. Clearly, research needs to be conducted on the SSRS, primarily to discover the validity of the instrument. Hopefully, such data will support its use. Its several positive features (multiple ratings, consideration of importance of social behaviors, and assessment-intervention record) make it a viable alternative to other behavior rating scales.

Walker–McConnell Scale of Social Competence and School Adjustment

The Walker–McConnell Scale (W-M Scale) (Walker and McConnell, 1988) was designed for the identification of children with social skill deficits. The instrument is a rapid measure requiring only approximately five minutes to complete. There are three subscales to the W-M Scale: Teacher-Preferred Social Behavior, Peer-Preferred Social Behavior, and School Adjustment Behavior. The instrument is designed to be administered or completed by teachers who have had the opportunity to observe the student for at least 2 months. Although no age range is noted in the manual, norms are provided for children from kindergarten through grade six.

Description
Teacher Preferred Social Behavior (16 items)—Examples include "accepts constructive criticism from peers without becoming angry" and "controls temper."

Peer Preferred Social Behavior (17 items)—Examples include "plays or talks with peers for extended periods of time" and "plays games and activities at recess skillfully."

School Adjustment Behavior (10 items)—These items, which measure adaptive social behavioral competencies, include "displays independent study skills" and "uses free time appropriately."

Interpretation of results

The W–M Scale is completed using a one to five likert-type scale (1 = never, 5 = frequently). The raw score for the total scale is converted to a standard score with a mean of 100 and a standard deviation of 15. In addition, percentile ranks and standard scores for the subscales (mean = 10, standard deviation = 3) are also available. According to the authors, any individual who scores 1 to 1-1/2 standard deviation units below the mean should be considered for further evaluation. They also briefly describe a method of using profile analysis to interpret the results. While the authors also mention that individual items could be used for writing objectives for IEPs, this practice has been questioned by reviewers (Worthington & Harrison, 1990).

Technical characteristics

Normative sample.   Approximately 1,800 individuals were included in the standardization sample. In general, information about the sample is somewhat limited in the manual, although the authors do provide a description of some of the sample characteristics. Information such as socioeconomic status and the intellectual level of the students is not given.

Reliability.   Test/retest reliability ranged from .67 to .97 for the subscales and total score. Internal consistency reliability coefficients were high and all exceeded .90. Interrater reliability coefficients ranged considerably (from .11 to .74.) The Teacher-Preferred Social Behavior subscale had the lowest interrater reliability.

Validity.   The authors describe the rationale for choosing the items that were initially used in the development of the instrument. They also discuss preliminary studies that were used to determine the final items used in the W-M Scale. Evidence of construct validity was provided through the use of confirmatory factor analysis, as well as by the results of studies that differentiated students of known different behavioral status. The concurrent validity of the W-M Scale was established using the Walker Problem Behavior Identification Checklist and the Social Skills Rating System and a self-concept scale. Coefficients were moderate, with most in the .70 range. No evidence of predictive validity was presented.

Review of relevant research

Only one empirical study was found in the professional literature. Merrell (1989) reported that the W-M Scale had moderate-to-high correlations with the Teachers Self-Control Rating Scales. The W-M Scale has been reviewed on several occasions. Worthington and Harrison (1990) felt that the W-M Scale was brief, easily administered, and provided important information about the child's interpersonal social skills. They further noted that the technical characteristics of the instrument were good, although the standardization sample was not adequately described. Lewis (1991) also noted the brevity of administration time and pointed out that the instrument was good for identifying withdrawn, and not just acting out, students.

OVERVIEW: WALKER-MCCONNELL SCALE OF SOCIAL COMPETENCE AND SCHOOL ADJUSTMENT

- *Age level*—Kindergarten through grade six
- *Type of administration*—Teacher rating (individual student)
- *Technical adequacy*—Limited standardization (poorly described), good reliability, adequate validity
- *Scores yielded*—Standard scores, percentile ranks
- *Suggested use*—The W-M Scale appears to be a reliable, relatively valid yet quick measure of social skill development in elementary-aged students. Its use as a screening instrument appears to be justified, and its short administration time (5 minutes) will allow its use in combination with other measures. The W-M Scale is based on a sound theoretical framework. Its use in more comprehensive diagnostic decisions should be avoided, however. Further studies that focus on the predictive validity of the instrument should be forthcoming.

Walker Problem Behavior Identification Checklist

The Walker Problem Behavior Identification Checklist (WPBIC) (Walker, 1983) is a standardized list of 50 behaviors that are typically observed in the classroom. The author states that the checklist should be used as a supplement in the overall assessment process, rather than as an instrument to classify children as emotionally disturbed or socially maladjusted. He further states that the WPBIC can function as a tool for the teacher in initially identifying children who should be referred for further evaluation and for treatment. The items on the list were determined by experienced teachers and are designed for teacher use. A 2-month observation period prior to rating a child is recommended. The 1983 version includes an extension of the norms to include preschool–grade three.

Description

The 50 items of the WBPIC, although numbered consecutively, are broken down into five scales:

Acting Out (14 items)—This scale covers behaviors such as "becomes upset, hysterical or angry when things do not go his way," "has rapid mood shifts—

depressed one moment, manic the next," "does not obey until threatened by punishment," and "displays physical aggression toward objects or persons."

Withdrawal (5 items)—This scale covers behaviors such as "tries to avoid calling attention to himself," "does not engage in group activities," and "does not initiate relationships with other children."

Distractibility (11 items)—This scale covers behaviors such as "has difficulty concentrating for any length of time," "disturbs other children: teasing or provoking fights," "interrupts others," "continually seeks attention," and "frequently stares blankly into space and is unaware of his surroundings when doing so."

Disturbed Peer Relations (10 items)—This scale includes items that are concerned with inadequate social skills, poor self-image, and compulsiveness.

Immaturity (10 items)—This scale covers behaviors such as "is listless and continually tired," "expresses concern about something terrible or horrible happening to him," and "weeps or cries without provocation."

Interpretation of results

The scoring format for the WPBIC is shown in Figure 10-3. If a behavior is observed, the item number for that behavior is circled. For

	SCALE				
	1	**2**	**3**	**4**	**5**
10. Is overactive, restless, and/or continually shifting body positions.			2		
11. Apologizes repeatedly for himself and/or his behavior.					2
12. Distorts the truth by making statements contrary to fact.	1				
13. Underachieving: performs below his demonstrated ability level.				1	
14. Disturbs other children: teasing, provoking fights, interrupting others.			2		
15. Tries to avoid calling attention to himself.		1			
16. Makes distrustful or suspicious remarks about actions of others toward him.	2				
17. Reacts to stressful situations or changes in routine with general body aches, head or stomach aches, nausea.					3
18. Argues and must have the last word in verbal exchanges.	1				
19. Approaches new tasks and situations with an "I can't do it" response.				1	
20. Has nervous tics: muscle-twitching, eye-blinking, nail-biting, hand-wringing.					3

FIGURE 10-3 Excerpt from the Walker Problem Behavior Identification Checklist.

From H. Walker, *Walker Problem Behavior Identification Checklist.* Copyright © 1983, 1976, 1970 by Western Psychological Services, Los Angeles, CA. Reprinted by permission.

behaviors that are not observed, the item numbers are left uncircled. The number of circles for each scale is the raw score for that scale; the raw scores for the five scales are added to yield a total raw score. The total raw score is then transformed into a T-score. A T-score distribution normalizes the data. (Because the WPBIC is composed primarily of negative behaviors, a positive-skewed distribution would be expected.)

Separate T-score conversion tables are available for males and females. The value of the WPBIC, however, is in the use of the profile sheet available on the record form. It allows the plotting of scores within each scale to identify behavioral strengths and weaknesses.

Technical characteristics

Normative sample. Three samples were used; preschool/kindergarten sample included 469 children and 29 teachers. The grade 1–3 sample included 852 children and 35 teachers, while the grade 4–6 sample involved 534 children rated by 21 teachers.

Reliability. The split-half coefficient was .98. Test-retest coefficients from two studies averaged .80 and .86; individual factors were somewhat lower. Reliability for preschoolers was lower than for school-aged children.

Validity. The author discusses several types of validity and also reports the results of studies indicating that on this test the scores of disturbed and nondisturbed children differed significantly. The manual, in addition, includes factor-analysis data; other validity data are generally lacking.

Review of relevant research

Research on the WPBIC has not appeared extensively in the professional literature. In one study, Moon and Marlowe (1987) noted that only the acting-out scale emerged using factor analysis and that the other four scales should be interpreted cautiously. In another, Wilson and Bullock (1988) noted that the test focused on maladaptive behaviors and did not include those that are considered positive.

OVERVIEW: WALKER PROBLEM BEHAVIOR IDENTIFICATION CHECKLIST

- *Age level*—Preschool–grade 6
- *Type of administration*—Individual
- *Technical characteristics*—Adequate reliability (for screening), questionable validity
- *Scores yielded*—T-scores, profile index

■ *Suggested use*—The WPBIC should be considered a quick-screening instrument. Its checklist format makes it easy to administer and score. It can be helpful in identifying areas for which evaluation in more depth may be necessary. The validity of the instrument has not been established adequately, and there is a general paucity of literature on the test. These limitations should caution overgeneralization of the results.

MEASUREMENT OF EMOTIONAL STATUS

WHY USE?
Determination of personality characteristics, self-concept and general emotional status; frequently used in non-school settings for individuals with emotional problems

WHO SHOULD USE?
Psychologists

Ironically, many examiners try to infer a child's emotional state by "analyzing" the observable behavior. For instance, "Because Susan is sitting alone in the back of the classroom, she has a poor self-concept"; or "Because Billy hit his sister, he is having problems with sibling rivalry." Inferences of this type should be avoided; they usually result in some kind of misinterpretation.

Several types of instruments have been used historically to measure emotional status. Most of these procedures are administered only by trained psychologists and psychiatrists. The relevance to special education is minimal at best. These instruments include projective tests, measures of self-concept, and objective inventories.

Projective Methods

Projective methods grew out of psychoanalytic and Gestalt psychology. The concept is very simple. When presented with an ambiguous stimulus, an individual will "project" his "way of seeing life, his meanings, significances, patterns and especially his feelings" (Frank, 1939, p. 403). Theoretically, the ambiguous stimulus will break down the individual's defense mechanisms; further, the more ambiguous the stimulus, the deeper the penetration into the personality (Haley, 1963). Thus, an ink blot, hypothetically, will penetrate "more deeply" into the personality than a picture of people engaging in some activity.

The appropriateness of projective testing has been seriously questioned in recent years. O'Leary and Johnson (1979) noted, for example, that the Society for Projective Techniques and Personality Assessment dropped the words Projective Techniques from their title in 1970. Similarly, that organization's journal also deleted the same words from its title. The use of projective tests in special education particularly has been challenged for a number of reasons. As a general rule, projective tests are lacking in reliability and validity. The subjective way in which they are scored tends to lower their reliability. Because the tests measure abstract hypothetical constructs, validity is difficult to establish.

Even though projective tests have been criticized by many, they are still used in the school and are frequently defended. Sarbaugh (1983) stated, for example, that because of the unique nature of projective instruments, traditional standards of technical adequacy are not important, although others (for example, Peterson & Batche, 1983) take the opposite view. In fact, professionals' views about projectives are generally mixed. In one survey of school psychologists, 63 percent said that projectives would not be important in schools in the future, while 37 percent felt that they had their role.

Another problem with projective tests is insufficient standardization or an insufficient normative group. Many times, in fact, norms are never used—the results are interpreted completely subjectively. This is particularly true if the examiner is highly experienced in projective techniques. It can, however, result in a type of "reverse projection." Consider this hypothetical situation:

> *EXAMINER:*   (*shows examinee a card with an ink blot*) Tell me what you
> see.
> *EXAMINEE:*   A bat.
> *EXAMINER:*   Anything else?
> *EXAMINEE:*   Just a bat, an angry bat.

After several interactions about various ink blots, the examiner determines that the examinee is "a hostile, impulsive person with hyperactive tendencies." In reality, the examiner's own response has been "projected"—the examinee's response was the stimulus! The message, clearly, is to avoid subjective interpretation of the response.

A number of projective tests are still used in special education. Many of these (for example, the Rorschach Ink Blot Test, the Thematic Apperception Test, the Tasks of Emotional Development) are administered by trained psychologists. To administer the Rorschach, for instance, requires about a year or a year and a half of training. Other tests (such as sentence-completion tests, the Human Figure Drawing Test, and the projective adaptation of the Bender-Gestalt) are sometimes administered by teachers and diagnosticians as well; this practice, however, is discouraged. The following is a brief discussion of several projective tests.

Rorschach Ink Blot Test (Rorschach, 1932). The Rorschach Ink Blot Test is the test that typically comes to mind when the term *projective test* is mentioned. The test consists of 10 ink blots that are presented one at a time to the individual. Examinees simply state what they see in each blot. A number of different scoring systems were devised for the Rorschach (for example, Beck, Beck, Levitt, & Molish, 1961; Klopfer & Kelly, 1942). In general, the examiner considers the content of the response, the part of the ink blot that was used, and the determinants (for example, the blot's shape or color) that led to the response. Diagnostic interpretation of Rorschach is based on clinical data. (For example, 75 percent of schizophrenic subjects have a certain pattern. An individual who takes the test and has that pattern will more than likely be considered schizophrenic on the basis of the results.)

Thematic Apperception Test (Murray, 1943). The Thematic Apperception Test (TAT) uses a series of 31 pictures as stimuli to elicit projected stories. The examiner looks for themes in the stories, particularly themes related to the main character. Although quantitative scoring systems have been devised for the TAT, its interpretation is largely subjective.

Children's Apperception Test (Bellak, Bellak, & Haworth, 1974). In the Children's Apperception Test (CAT), as in the TAT, cards with pictures on them are used as stimuli. The CAT consists of two sets of cards: One set of 10 cards has pictures of animals involved in a variety of situations. (Younger children supposedly identify more with animals than with humans.) The other set of 10 cards has pictures of humans. (This set can be used with older children.)

Education Apperception Test (Thompson & Sones, 1973). The Education Apperception Test (EAT) consists of 18 pictures of children engaged in school-related activities. The test supposedly measures a child's emotions in four areas: reaction toward learning, reaction toward authority, peer relations, and home attitude toward school. As with the other apperception tests, the primary scoring procedure for this test is the interpretation of the stories.

Tasks of Emotional Development (Cohen & Weil, 1971). The Tasks of Emotional Development (TED) consists of 13 photographs that are associated with specific areas of emotional development in children and adolescents. Those areas, as designated by the authors (p. 7), are

1. Socialization within the peer group
2. Establishment of trust in people
3. Acceptance and control of aggressive feelings toward peers
4. Establishment of positive attitudes toward academic learning

5. Establishment of a conscience with respect to the property of others
6. Separation from the mother figure
7. Identification with the same-sex parent
8. Acceptance of siblings
9. Acceptance of limits from adults
10. Acceptance of affection between parents (the resolution of the oedipal conflict)
11. Establishment of positive attitudes toward orderliness and cleanliness (the ability to control drives)
12. Establishment of a positive self-concept
13. Establishment of positive heterosexual socialization.

Unlike other projective-story tests, the TED attempts to make the stimulus resemble the person being tested. For this reason, the set of pictures for each of the areas comes in multiple versions showing males and females of different ages. The examiner uses the picture version (for example, adolescent male) that is most similar to the subject.

Sentence completions.   Two tests for this popular technique are the Rohde Sentence Completion Test (Rohde, 1957) and the Rotter Incomplete Sentences Blank (Rotter & Rafferty, 1950). In these tests, based on a popular projective technique, the examinee must fill in incomplete sentences by writing anything that comes to mind.

Hutt Adaptation of the Bender-Gestalt Test (Hutt, 1977).   This adaptation uses the Bender Motor Gestalt Test (see Appendix A) as a projective instrument. Types of errors made and the approach taken in copying the geometric forms are interpreted in terms of personality characteristics. For example, if a person places the figures compactly on one section of the paper, it might be indicative of depression or rigidity.

Human Figure Drawing Test (Koppitz, 1968).   This very popular test is one of many instruments that is designed to use a child's drawing of a human figure as a projective measure. The HFDT is scored according to 30 emotional "indicators" identified by Koppitz. Unfortunately, many unqualified individuals have administered this test and attempted to interpret the results of children's drawings.

Kinetic Drawing System for Family and School (Knoff & Prout, 1985).   This instrument is a combination of the older Kinetic Family Drawing and the Kinetic School Drawing. It is designed for ages 5–20 and includes five diagnostic categories.

Summary of projective techniques
Theoretically, projective tests are able to measure some underlying emotional characteristic of an individual that he or she cannot or will not

verbalize. By using ambiguous stimuli, the individual "projects" his feelings and needs. Unfortunately, evaluating the responses usually requires a great deal of subjective interpretation by the examiner. The use of projective testing should be limited to those examiners who have been trained specifically in projective techniques.

Regardless of the examiner, however, it should be questioned whether projective tests have any relevance at all in the field of special education. Research, in general, has not supported the validity of these instruments. Commonly used projective tests such as the Human Figure Drawing and the Bender-Gestalt have been found, for instance, to add very little in the identification and evaluation of children with behavior problems (studies include Dieffenbach, 1977; Trahan & Strickland, 1979). O'Leary and Johnson (1979) summarized the state of the art for projective testing over a decade ago:

> The data are simply not compelling enough to suggest that projective methods be used for clinical purposes. With a few exceptions, the validity coefficients are either inconsistent or so small as to preclude their use in routine clinical work. Most projective methods require substantial time to administer and score and, as important, they require many hours to learn. Since information gathered on projective techniques can generally be obtained from simpler and less expensive methods, it is incumbent upon advocates of projective methodologies to demonstrate their clinical utility in terms of costs in time and training as well as predictive validity (pp. 218–219).

Measures of Self-Concept

One area that is assessed frequently is a student's self-concept. Because this is a very difficult construct to define, most of the instruments in this area are of questionable validity. Many self-concept instruments use a system of self-evaluation and self-report. In other words, the subject reads a statement such as "I am an unhappy person" and must agree or disagree with that statement. Other self-concept scales are nonverbal and still others are completed by someone other than the subject. One problem with most self-concept scales is that the positive or negative intent of the items is fairly obvious. Many children will answer the way they think others expect them to respond. Brief descriptions of several measures of self-concept follow.

Inferred Self-Concept Scale

Age level—Grades 1–6

Areas measured—General self-concept

Administration and scoring—The Inferred Self-Concept scale (McDaniel, 1973) has 30 items. For each item, teachers or counselors must rate the subject on a scale of 1 (seldom) to 5 (always).

Reading required—No

Technical adequacy—Very limited

Martinek-Zaichkowsky Self-Concept Scale for Children

Age level—Grades 1–8

Areas measured

   Satisfaction and happiness
   Home and family relationships and circumstances
   Ability in games, recreation, and sports
   Personal traits and emotional tendencies
   Behavioral, personal, and social characteristics in school

Administration and scoring—In the Martinek-Zaichkowsky Self-Concept Scale for Children (Martinek & Zaichkowsky, 1977) the subject is shown 25 pairs of pictures and must state, for each pair, which picture he or she identifies with more

Reading required—No

Technical adequacy—Adequate reliability, limited validity

Piers Harris Children's Self-Concept Scale

Age level—Grades 4–12

Areas measured

   Behavior
   Intellectual and School Status
   Physical Appearance and Attributes
   Anxiety
   Popularity
   Happiness and Satisfaction
   Lie Scale

Administration and scoring—The Piers-Harris Children's Self-Concept Scale (Piers & Harris, 1984) includes 80 statements. The subject must read each statement (for example "I am a good person") and score it yes or no.

Reading required—Yes (approximately third-grade level)

Technical adequacy—Adequate reliability, limited validity

Self-Esteem Index

Age level—7–18 years

Areas measured

   Academic competence (self-esteem in school)
   Family acceptance (self-esteem at home)
   Peer popularity (relationships outside the family unit)
   Personal security (Physical appearance and personal attributes)

Administration and Scoring—The Self-Esteem Index (Brown & Alexander, 1991) is administered to individuals or groups. It includes a self-report format using a four-point likert scale.

Reading required—Yes

Technical adequacy—Adequate reliability and validity

Tennessee Self-Concept Scale

Age level—12 and older

Areas measured

Counseling form—Self-criticism; self-esteem (9 areas, including identity, moral-ethical self)

Clinical and research form—Above areas; plus 15 others, including response bias, net conflict, total conflict, empirical scales, and deviant signs

Administration and Scoring—The Tennessee (Fitts, 1984) has 100 items. The subject must rate each item on a scale of 1 (false) to 5 (true).

Reading required—Yes (approximately sixth-grade level)

Technical adequacy—Adequate reliability, limited validity

Inventories and Questionnaires

The intent of inventories and questionnaires is to measure objectively the emotional and personality characteristics of individuals. Most of these instruments are designed for adolescents and adults. One notable exception is the Personality Inventory for Children (PIC) discussed in the following section. They usually include a large number of items that purportedly measure several personality traits or characteristics. (A group of items referring to a given trait is usually referred to as a scale for that trait.) Many times, these items are in the form of a behavioral description (such as "I sometimes hear strange voices") that the examinee must label as true or false. This self-report technique is used in the majority of these instruments, although some of them require a familiar person (such as a parent) to complete the items about the examinee.

In addition to the personality scales themselves, these instruments usually include some type of validity scale to help determine if the examinee is "telling the truth." In general, however, both the reliability and the validity of these instruments have been questioned. Many inventories have also been criticized because the various areas identified for a profile analysis overlap in content. For these and several other reasons, the use of these instruments as tools in the process of education is very limited. A discussion of the PIC follows, in addition to a brief description of three other popular personality inventories.

Personality Inventory for Children

The Personality Inventory for Children (PIC) (Wirt, Lachar, Klinedinst, & Seat, 1984) is one of the few inventories designed specifically for evaluating children. It is often thought of as a downward extension of the very popular Minnesota Multiphasic Personality Inventory (MMPI) and is appropriate for children aged 3–16 years.

Description

The PIC includes 600 items that are grouped into 30 scales. Of these 30 scales, 13 are considered the "profile scales" that have the most clinical relevance. There are also three validity scales to help determine if truthful responses are being given. The remaining scales are called experimental. The items are completed in a true/false format by the child's parent. An example of an item in each of the 13 profile scales follow. The first three scales are known as the cognitive triad, since they measure characteristics related to the child's cognitive ability.

> *Adjustment (74 items)*—"My child loves to make fun of others."
>
> *Achievement (31 items)*—"My child could do better in school if he (she) tried."
>
> *Intellectual Screening (35 items)*—"My child learned to count things by age six."
>
> *Development (25 items)*—"My child could eat with a fork before the age of four years."
>
> *Somatic Concern (40 items)*—"My child seldom has back pains."
>
> *Depression (46 items)*—"Others often remark how moody my child is."
>
> *Family Relations (35 items)*—"During the past few years we have moved often."
>
> *Delinquency (47 items)*—"I have heard that my child drinks alcohol."
>
> *Withdrawal (25 items)*—"Often my child takes walks alone."
>
> *Anxiety (30 items)* —"My child is afraid of animals."
>
> *Psychosis (40 items)*—"My child gets lost easily."
>
> *Hyperactivity (36 items)*—"My child will do anything on a dare."
>
> *Social Skills (30 items)*—"My child tends to be pretty stubborn."

Interpretation of results

Scores from the PIC can be transformed into T-scores and plotted on a visual profile (Figure 10-4).

Technical characteristics

Normative sample.   The sample included 2,390 individuals aged 6–16. Information in the manual describes age, sex, and education and occupation of the parents. A separate preschool sample of 192 children was also used.

Reliability.   Test-retest coefficients from several studies with clinical and normal samples averaged in the .71–.89 range. Internal consistency ranged from .57 (intellectual screening) to .86 (depression). Interrater reliability was somewhat lower, ranging from .34 to .68 for a normal sample and .21 to .79 for a clinical sample.

Validity. The authors attempted to maximize the validity of the PIC through careful, empirically-based item selection.

Review of relevant research

The PIC has been reviewed extensively. On the one hand, Achenbach (1981) criticized the PIC, arguing that it was based on outdated personality theories and was subject to respondent bias. Similarly, DeMoor-Peal and Handal (1983) criticized the PIC, most notably with preschool children because of the small normative sample. On the other hand, Dreger (1982) felt that the PIC was a good child-personality inventory with sound empirical support. Lachar and LaCombe (1983) also noted the technical adequacy of the PIC, and Knoff (1989) reported that the PIC had enormous potential but needed a stratified national restandardization.

The PIC has been used in a number of research studies as a measure of personality status. The following studies, however, are representative of those that focus on its technical characteristics and clinical utility.

- Parents are effective informants on the PIC (Keenan & Lachar, 1988)
- Some researchers have noted high correlations between PIC results and intelligence (Keenan & Lachar, 1985), whereas others have reported low correlations (Beck & Pruill, 1987)
- Because of the possibility of faking responses, profiles on the PIC cannot be considered valid all the time (McVaughn & Grow, 1984)
- Learning disabled and behavior-disordered students were differentiated on the PIC (Goh, 1984). It also discriminated emotionally disturbed with learning problems from emotionally disturbed without learning problems and learning disabled with emotional problems from underachieving emotionally disturbed children (Forbas, 1987)
- The PIC was effective in screening intelligence in a preschool population (Durrant & Porter, 1989)
- The PIC differentiated between conduct disordered and emotionally disturbed children (Kelly, 1988). Also, Clarke, Kehle, and Bullock (1988) reported that learning disabled, mentally retarded, and emotionally disturbed students all had elevated scores in cognitive deficits and maladaptive behavior. They noted that the *degree* of elevation discriminated group status.

Summary of research findings

In general the research on the PIC has supported its use as part of an assessment battery. It has been shown to aid in the differentiation of students with different diagnostic labels. Reviews on the PIC are mixed and are probably based somewhat on the reviewers' theoretical perspective.

FIGURE 10-4 **Example of a Profile from the Personality Inventory for Children.**

From R. Wirt, D. Lachar, J. Klinedinst, and P. Seat, *Personality Inventory for Children.* Copyright © 1977 by Western Psychological Services, Los Angeles, CA. Reprinted with permission.

OVERVIEW: PERSONALITY INVENTORY FOR CHILDREN

- *Age level*—3 to 16 years old
- *Type of administration*—Individual (group possible)
- *Technical adequacy*—Limited standardization for preschool population, questionable interrater reliability, adequate validity
- *Scores yielded*—T-scores, visual profile
- *Suggested use*—The PIC is one of the few available personality inventories designed for children. One must be aware of the possible bias of the respondents (as with any instrument that requires third-party information). The test is more a clinical instrument than an educational instrument; the results will be used more for classification purposes than educational programming. Caution should be taken when using the PIC with a preschool population.

California Psychological Inventory (Gough, 1969). The California Psychological Inventory (CPI) is a popular instrument used with individuals 13 years of age and older. The test consists of 480 true-false items (of which approximately 200 also appear in the Minnesota Multiphasic Personality Inventory). The CPI is organized into 15 personality scales and 3 validity scales. The personality scales are Dominance; Capacity for Status; Sociability; Social Pressure; Self-Acceptance; Sense of Well-Being; Responsibility; Socialization; Self-Control; Tolerance; Achievement via Conformity; Achievement via Independence; Intellectual Efficiency; Psychological-Mindedness; and Femininity. The validity scales are Well-being; Good Impression; and Community. Researchers have generally supported the use of the CPI, even though there is some redundancy among the scales (Lanyon & Goodstein, 1971).

Minnesota Multiphasic Personality Inventory (Hathaway & McKinley 1967). The MMPI is an extremely popular, widely used inventory designed for individuals 16 years of age and older. The MMPI consists of 566 true-false items, and it yields scores for 10 clinical scales and 3 validity scales. Generally, in interpretation, the *pattern* of scores is used. The clinical scales include Hypochondriasis; Depression; Hysteria; Psychopathic Deviate; Masculinity-Femininity; Paranoia; Psychoasthenia; Schizophrenia; and Hypomania. The 3 validity scales are Lie; Infrequency; and Defensiveness.

The MMPI has been criticized for several reasons. It is time-consuming to administer and interpret. Further, the scales tend to correlate highly with one another, thereby limiting somewhat the test's clinical use for discriminating types of emotional problems (Lanyon & Goodstein, 1971). In general, validity data are lacking for the clinical use of the

MMPI. Finally, the MMPI has been criticized because examinees can identify "desirable" and "undesirable" responses to the items. This could lead to invalid test results.

Sixteen Personality Factor Questionnaire (Cattell, Eber, & Tatsuoka, 1970).   Usually referred to as the 16PF, the Sixteen Personality Factor Questionnaire is designed for use with individuals 16 years of age and older. The test was designed on the basis of years of factor-analytic studies by Cattell. Its scores supposedly measure 16 primary factors: Reserved versus Outgoing; Less Intelligent versus More Intelligent; Affected by Feelings versus Emotionally Stable; Humble versus Assertive; Sober versus Happy-go-lucky; Expedient versus Conscientious; Shy versus Venturesome; Tough-minded versus Tender-minded; Trusting versus Suspicious; Practical versus Imaginative; Forthright versus Shrewd; Self-Assured versus Apprehensive; Conservative versus Experimenting; Group-Dependent versus Self-Sufficient; Undisciplined Self-Conflict versus Controlled; and Relaxed versus Tense. The test also includes scores for six second-order factors: Introversion versus Extraversion; Low Anxiety versus High Anxiety; Tenderminded Emotionality versus Tough Poise; Subduedness versus Independence; Naturalness versus Discreetness; and Cool Realism versus Prodigal Subjectivity.

Although the 16PF has several forms, these forms should not be considered interchangeable (Bouchard, 1972). In general, this instrument lacks validity data.

Summary of inventories and questionnaires

Inventories and questionnaires generally lack supportive data that would establish their reliability and validity. The use of these instruments in special education is questionable and is typically limited to providing information to help make classification and placement decisions. Most of these instruments are designed for use with adolescents and adults. The notable exception is the PIC, which has received some attention in special education.

Instrument or Technique	Suggested Use							Target Population						Special Considerations	Educational Relevance for Exceptional Students
	Prereferral			Postreferral											
	Screening and Initial Identification	Informal Determination and Evaluation of Teaching Programs and Strategies	Determination of Current Performance Level and Educational Need	Decisions about Classification and Program Placement	IEP Goals	IEP Objectives	IEP Evaluation	Mild/Moderate	Severe/Profound	Preschool	Elementary Age	Secondary Age	Adult		
Revised Behavior Problem Checklist	X		X		X			X			X			Adequate technical aspects; has some empirical support in the literature	useful
Behavior Rating Profile	X		X		X			X			X			Student is evaluated by a number of individuals in a number of settings; validity data are lacking	adequate
Burks Behavior Rating Scale	X		X		X			X			X			Limited technical aspects; results are subject to misinterpretation	limited
Child Behavior Checklist	X		X		X			X			X	X		Has separate forms for multiple raters; different profiles for boys and girls	useful
Devereux Elementary School Behavior Rating Scale–II	X		X		X			X			X			Somewhat limited technical aspects; relatively popular instrument	adequate
Social Skills Rating System	X		X		X			X		X	X	X		Assessment-intervention record is a nice feature; preschool version limited	useful
Walker–McConnell Scale	X							X			X			A valid screening instrument that can be quickly administered	useful
Walker Problem Behavior Checklist	X							X		X	X			Limited validity data; is a quick screening device	useful
Projective Techniques				X				X			X	X	X	Losing popularity in special education; very little evidence of reliability or validity for most of these instruments	very limited

													Comments	
Self-Concept Scales	X					X			X	X	X		Most lack validity data; many use a self-report system to obtain the scores	limited
Inventories and Questionnaires			X			X			X	X	X	X	Most have limited technical aspects; most are designed for adolescents and adults	limited
Personality Inventory for Children			X					X	X	X	X		One of the few personality inventories for children	adequate

11

Assessment of Language

INSTRUMENTS/PROCEDURES INCLUDED

INFORMAL ASSESSMENT
- Language Sampling (Oral)
- Language Sampling (Written)

FORMAL LANGUAGE TESTS
- Peabody Picture Vocabulary Test–Revised
- Test of Adolescent Language–2
- Test of Language Competence
- Tests of Language Development–2
- Test of Written Language–2

TESTS FOR SPEECH/LANGUAGE CLINICIANS

Bobby is a sixth-grade student who has been making little progress in his weak areas of reading and spelling. Bobby typically does not follow directions, writes very slowly, and uses incorrect grammar when responding to the resource-room teacher. After reviewing Bobby's records, the teacher noted that he had been given a number of tests but that none of the tests measured his ability to process and produce language. She therefore decided to administer a language test to Bobby to provide information that might be incorporated into his educational program.

Although there are many definitions of language, it is generally agreed that communication is its primary function. Bryen (1982) stated that language is "a rule-governed symbol system that is capable of representing one's understanding of the world" (p. 7). Language is usually thought of as the use of spoken or written symbols, although manual symbols should also be considered. In education, language, as a way in which we receive and express information, is important for success in virtually all areas of academic life. Reading, writing, spelling, and following directions are just a few of the areas in which language plays an important part. In special education, language assessment is obviously an important area.

Structurally, language can be viewed as having five components: phonology, morphology, syntax, semantics, and pragmatics. Each of these five components involves both reception (or processing) and expression (or production). *Phonology* involves the use of phonemes, the smallest significant units of sound that are combined into words, or with words, to be meaningful. For example, the word "goes" comprises three phonemes: /g/, /o/, /z/. The assessment of phonology involves both the aural discrimination of speech sounds and the articulation of speech sounds. Examples of instruments that measure these areas are the Tree/Bee Test of Auditory Discrimination (Fudala, 1978) and the Templin-Darley Test of Articulation (Templin & Darley, 1969).

Morphology is concerned with how phonemes are put together to give meaning. A morpheme is the smallest combination of sounds that has a meaning. For instance, the word "displacement" has three morphemes: (dis), (place), (ment). Most assessment instruments measure morphology and syntax together because they are both concerned with grammar; one exception is the Test for Examining Expressive Morphology (Shipley, Stone, & Sue, 1983).

Syntax involves the relational meanings of language—that is, how words are put together to form sentences. Assessment of syntax involves the measurement of the understanding of the meaning of sentences and the ability to formulate sentences. For the most part, syntax measures are designed for younger children. Examples are the Tests of Auditory Comprehension of Language (Carrow-Woolfolk, 1985) and the Developmental Sentence Analysis (Lee, 1974).

Semantics refers to the meaning of words. The assessment of semantics skills usually involves the measurement of a person's receptive and expressive vocabulary skills. Receptive vocabulary can be measured using instruments such as the Peabody Picture Vocabulary Test–Revised (discussed later in this chapter). Expressive vocabulary measures are included on tests such as the Kaufman Assessment Battery for Children (K-ABC) and Wechsler Intelligence Scale for Children–III (WISC-III). There are also quick measures of semantics such as the Receptive One Word Vocabulary Test and the Expressive One Word Vocabulary Test.

Pragmatics refers to the use of language within the communicative context. In a certain sense, pragmatics deals with the most important function of language—that of communication. Although all the other components of language must be intact before communication can occur, it is possible that an individual might have all the necessary skills in the areas of phonology, morphology and syntax, and semantics, yet still have difficulty "communicating with others." This is particularly true with older students. The *assessment* of pragmatics is a relatively new practice.

The Test of Pragmatic Skills (discussed later in this chapter) is one example of the interest in this area.

The overall area of language assessment is a complex process for a number of reasons. As previously discussed, there are a number of language components that are involved; there is also the issue of the processing/production dichotomy, and the fact that language can be transmitted and understood in both the oral and written form (not to mention manual and other forms). Still further, there is the question of whether or not language tests accurately measure the language skills that an individual actually uses. As a result, informal assessment of language is very important; in addition, there are many types of formal tests available. Many of the tests are designed to be used by different professionals for different reasons.

The discussion that follows will focus on the informal areas of oral and written language sampling and the formal oral- and written-language tests that are typically used by special educators. Also included will be a brief discussion of specific language tests that are used more by speech and language clinicians.

INFORMAL ASSESSMENT OF LANGUAGE SKILLS

WHY USE?
Screening and identification of language problems; informal determination of objectives and teaching strategies; analysis of spontaneous use of language

WHO SHOULD USE?
Teachers; speech and language clinicians

Oral Language

Over the past 40 years, the increase in knowledge of language development has resulted in many changes in language assessment with increasing emphasis on evaluating in a naturalistic, interactive context (Lund & Duchan, 1988). Because formal language testing usually occurs in a contrived situation (sometimes requiring the student to imitate language skills), it is possible that many individuals may be able to exhibit certain language skills that they do not produce spontaneously. Conversely, it is possible that they may fail to exhibit certain skills that they might be able to perform within a naturalistic context (e.g., Bloom & Lahey, 1978).

One approach that can be used to evaluate the spontaneous use of language in a naturalistic setting is *language sampling*. This usually involves eliciting (taping, transcribing) and analyzing an individual's language. Language sampling actually refers to a set of possible procedures for gathering information ranging from a spontaneous unstructured sample to a highly structured sample.

Eliciting the sample.   In general, the procedures for obtaining a language sample include (1) a spontaneous sample taken during free play or a conversation; (2) an elicited sample asking the child to tell or retell a story; (3) an elicited imitative sample requiring the child to respond to questions, pictures, or activities that are specifically designed to elicit certain language structures; and/or (4) an imitative language sample asking the child to repeat sentences produced by the examiner.

Each procedure for obtaining a language sample provides different types of evaluation information on the child's language abilities. The decision to use one procedure over another is dependent upon the child who is being evaluated and the behaviors to be examined. As noted previously, however, the most meaningful information regarding the individual's actual use of language will be gathered from the procedure. If this is the procedure chosen, it is important that the sample be representative of the highest level of language of which the student is capable (Smiley, 1991a). Provided below are suggestions for obtaining a language sample regardless of the procedures (Florida Department of Education, 1989):

1. Use a high-quality recorder to assure a good playback. The tape recorder should have a quality microphone that will result in a quality sample. The speakers are also important during playback. For purposes of transcription, a recorder with a counter will be invaluable as you will find you need to stop, rewind a short distance, and listen again many times.

2. Use appropriate stimulus materials (e.g., toys, pictures) based on the interests, intellectual level, and handicaps of the child.

3. Present the stimulus material to the child and ask questions about the material that require more than one- or two-word responses from the child. Try to elicit complete sentences from the child and set a conversational climate conducive to eliciting responses from the child.

4. Try to elicit different grammmatical forms such as past tense, plural, and so on, if possible. Encourage this by using them in your own speech. For example, ask, "What will he do next?" "What did he say then?"

5. Repeat what the child says, if possible. This will aid you later in transcribing the tape. This should be done so that the child is unaware of it. If the repeating becomes distracting, discontinue. For example

CHILD: He don't goes in
EXAMINER: He don't goes in? Why not?

CHILD: He too big.
EXAMINER: He too big. Yes, he is.

6. Take notes while the child is talking, including attempts to write out some of the utterances. These notes help when you go back and transcribe the tape. Also, this gives you a good idea of the number of utterances obtained from the child.

7. Transcribe the tape as soon as possible after the session so that you can make use of your own recall of the sample.

Analyzing the sample.   Once the language sample has been obtained from the child, the examiner needs to determine the level of analysis of the sample. This analysis includes (1) form, including phonology, morphology, and syntax; (2) content, including vocabulary; and (3) use, including pragmatics. In addition, the use of any nonstandard dialect should be noted. The specific guidelines to follow are beyond the scope of this discussion. However, Smiley (1991a; 1991b) provided teacher-oriented suggestions for the analysis of both the quantitative and qualitative aspects of language sampling. For example, she noted that the following information should be included, at least when morphology and simple syntax are analyzed:

1. Plural markers, both regular and irregular
2. Past tense markers, both regular and irregular
3. Third person singular markers, both regular and irregular
4. Articles (a, an, the)
5. Copula (linking verb) and auxiliary (helping verb)
6. Modal auxiliaries and emphatic auxiliary
7. Pronouns
8. Prepositions
9. Comparative and superlative markers

In addition, Smiley provides examples and suggestions for analysis. Interested readers are encouraged to read those two articles that were designed for a teacher audience.

Written Language

Just as important as the evaluation of oral language in the natural setting is the evaluation of written language using the student's actual work products. According to Gable (1990), the analysis of written products should focus on the following types of errors: careless, excessive usage, verbs, nouns, pronouns, punctuation, capitalization, and paragraphs. Much of the analysis should focus on the *T-unit,* which is defined as "an independent clause including any dependent clauses attached to or embedded in it" (Gable, 1990; p. 94). For example, "the batter hit the baseball and the third baseman tried to catch it" is considered two T-units. Table 11-1 provides an example of scoring procedures based on the eight previously mentioned error types.

Other areas of written language have also been recommended for error analysis. Isaacson (1988) suggested that fluency (number of words written), content (e.g., coherence and organization), convention (including spelling and handwriting), syntax, and vocabulary should be evaluated. Salvia and Hughes (1990) suggested that the two major areas of *content* and *style* be evaluated. They noted that the most common errors related to content are incomplete sentences or sentence fragments that might be interpreted as incomplete learning or poor proofreading skills. In the area of style, errors might be located in grammar, mechanics (e.g., punctuation and capitalization), diction (word usage), and/or diversity (e.g., use of grammatical transformations). Identification of errors in these areas can be used to provide feedback about the incorrect aspects of the student's writing (student product) as well as the appropriate aspects (teacher model).

FORMAL LANGUAGE TESTS

WHY USE?
Screening and identification of language problems; informal determination of objectives and teaching strategies; establishment of IEP goals.

WHO SHOULD USE?
Teachers; speech and language clinicians

Oral Language Tests

Peabody Picture Vocabulary Test–Revised

The Peabody Picture Vocabulary Test–Revised (PPVT-R) (Dunn & Dunn, 1981) is an extremely popular individually administered instrument that measures an individual's receptive language ability (semantics: receptive). According to the authors the PPVT-R can be considered both an achievement test and a scholastic-aptitude test for individuals from standard-English-speaking environments. The original 1965 edition of the PPVT was frequently used—actually, misused—as an intelligence measure, primarily because it included a table to transform raw scores to IQs. The authors do point out, however, that the test is not a comprehensive measure of general intelligence. In the manual, the authors also mention

TABLE 11-1   Error Analysis Scoring Instructions.

Enter the name of the *Student, Age* (years and months), *Grade,* and the *Date* the student wrote the sample. *Writing Time:* Record the total number of minutes allowed for writing, and the actual number of minutes the student wrote.

Picture # or Topic #: List the picture or topic number used for the writing stimulus.

1. *Total Words:* Draw a line through the title, sound effects, and end markers such as "The End." Count the total words written. Exclude words marked out.
2. *Garbled Words:* Circle garbled words. Enter the total in the space provided.
3. *Readable Words:* Subtract the number of garbled words from the total words and enter in the space provided.
4. *T-Unit:* Mark the end of each T-unit with a slash mark (/) and number the T-unit. Enter the number of T-units.
5. *Average Number of Words per T-Unit:* Divide the total readable words by the number of T-units. Round off to the nearest hundredth.
6. *Scorer:* Sign your name.

Note: FOR ALL ERROR TYPES BEGINNING WITH *OMITTED* WORDS THROUGH *INAPPROPRIATE CAPITALS* COUNT THE TOTAL ERRORS AND DIVIDE BY THE TOTAL T-UNITS TO FIND THE NUMBER PER T-UNIT.

1. *Careless Errors:*
   Omitted Words: Write omitted words in pencil above the appropriate space. Write only words that are obvious (such as *and, he, the*) and that do not change the meaning of the T-unit.
   Substituted Words: Write *sub* above substituted words.
2. *Excessive Usage:*
   Beginning of T-Unit: Count the number of T-units that begin with conjunctions.
   Within T-Unit: Underline each use of conjunctions if they appear more than once for coordination within the T-unit. Do not count conjunctions at the beginning of the T-unit in this count.
3. *Verbs:*
   Inflections: Write in the correct verb ending.
   Subject-Verb Agreement: Write *s-v* above the verb for every subject-verb error.
   Verb Tense Changes: Place a check mark (✓) at the end of each T-unit in which the verb tense is different from the verb tense in the previous T-unit. If there are tense changes within a T-unit, place a check mark in the margin tor each change. An exception is if the verb tense change occurs with a change from narrative to direct quotation.
4. *Nouns:*
   Number: Underline nouns that show incorrect form for number.
   Possession: Write *NP* above the error.
5. *Pronouns:* Write the correct pronoun above each incorrect use.
6. *Punctuation:*
   End: Write in the correct form for the omitted or incorrect punctuation and circle it.
   Within T-Units: Using a red pencil, write in the correct form for the omitted or incorrect punctuation.
7. *Capitalization:*
   Beginning: Write correct upper-case letters over lower-case letters used at the beginning of T-units.
   Proper Nouns: Write correct upper-case letters over lower-case letters used for proper nouns.
   Inappropriate: Draw an X through the incorrectly capitalized letter.
8. *Paragraphs:*
   Extraneous T-Units: Underline extraneous T-units.
   New Line for Each T-Unit: Circle *Yes* or *No.*

Summary: Count the number of each type of error and enter in the appropriate row under "# per T-unit" on the Error Analysis Form. Divide the number of each error type by the number of T-units, and enter the result in the space provided.

several school, clinical, vocational, and research uses for the PPVT-R. The test is both easy and quick to administer. It has two forms (L and M) that can be used with individuals from ages 2 1/2–40.

Description

The PPVT-R is included in an easel-kit. On each plate four pictures are shown. The vocabulary word is stated and the examinee must indicate the correct picture either verbally or by pointing. Figure 11-1 shows an example for the word *giant*.

Interpretation of results

The PPVT-R offers four types of derived scores: standard-score equivalents, percentile ranks, stanines, and age equivalents. The standard-score equivalents and the age equivalents take the place of the intelligence quotient and the mental ages that were yielded by the 1965 PPVT. The standard-score equivalent is based on a mean of 100 and a standard deviation of 15. The authors also mention that the standard error of

FIGURE 11-1   Example from the Peabody Picture Vocabulary Test–Revised.

From L. Dunn and L. Dunn, *Peabody Vocabulary Test–Revised*. Copyright © 1981 by American Guidance Service, Circle Pines, MN. Reprinted with permission.

measurement (approximately 7 for the standard-score equivalent) should also be considered in the overall interpretation of the score.

Technical characteristics
Normative sample.   The population included 4,200 subjects 2 1/2–18 years old in a representative sample and 828 subjects 19–40 years old in a less representative sample.

Reliability.   Split-half coefficients were .84 for Form L and .81 for Form M. Alternate-form coefficients ranged from .77 to .79.

Validity.   A discussion of content and construct validity is included in the manual. No criterion-related validity data are presented, although an extensive review of the 1965 edition of the PPVT is included.

Review of relevant research
- The PPVT-R yields lower scores than the PPVT for educable mentally retarded (EMR) students (Bracken & Prasse, 1981) and for gifted students (Pedriana & Bracken, 1982), as well as for preschool children (Naglieri & Naglieri, 1981).
- The PPVT-R produced significantly higher scores than did the Cognitive Levels Test with college students (Overton & Apperson, 1989).
- The PPVT-R yielded significantly different scores for boys and girls (Smith, Edmonds, & Smith, 1989).
- The PPVT-R is a useful measure of receptive language of EMR students (Prasse & Bracken, 1981). Its effectiveness in screening for gifted students is limited, however (Wright, 1983).
- The alternate-form reliability is adequate for most preschool children (Bracken & Prasse, 1983). Black preschoolers, however, systematically obtained higher scores on Form M than on Form L (McCallum & Bracken, 1981). The alternate form reliability coefficient was only .65 for learning disabled (LD) students in one study (Breen, 1983). Also, Worthing, Phye, and Nunn (1984) found that the two forms were not equivalent for older special-education students.
- Correlations reported between the PPVT-R and both the Peabody Individual Achievement Test (.53) and the McCarthy Scale GCI (.78) were similar to correlations reported between the PPVT and those tests (Naglieri, 1981).
- The PPVT-R has adequate test-retest reliability for bilingual children (Scruggs, Mastropieri, & Argulewicz, 1983) although its use with Hispanic students has been questioned (Sattler & Altes, 1984).
- The PPVT-R correlated significantly with the Wide Range Achievement Test–Revised (WRAT-R) and the Wechsler Intelligence Scale for Children–Revised (WISC-R), suggesting that it could be used to screen underachievers (Smith, Smith, & Dobbs, 1991).
- Vance and Stone (1990) felt that while the PPVT-R's manual and technical supplement provided much useful information, further research was necessary on its validity with young children.

Summary of research findings

Most research studies on the PPVT-R have compared the revised test with the 1965 edition (which was discussed in hundreds of articles). The results suggest that the two instruments yield similar correlations with various criterion measures. The PPVT-R, however, yields *lower* scores than the 1965 PPVT. There is also some evidence that the two forms (L and M) might not be equivalent. The PPVT-R has also been found to have moderate correlations with a variety of criterion measures including intelligence and achievement tests.

OVERVIEW: PEABODY PICTURE VOCABULARY TEST–REVISED

- *Age level*—2 1/2–40 years old
- *Type of administration*—Individual
- *Technical adequacy*—Limited standardization for individuals 19–40 years of age, adequate reliability, limited validity data
- *Scores yielded*—Standard scores, percentile ranks, stanines, age equivalents
- *Suggested use*—For years, the 1965 edition of the PPVT was used inappropriately as an intelligence measure. In the PPVT-R, the authors carefully excluded the IQ transformation table. The PPVT-R seems to be a reasonable measure of receptive vocabulary, but its use as a basis for serious educational decisions should be avoided. The PPVT-R can be used with individuals with speech and (to a certain extent) motor handicaps. Until its psychometric properties have been more extensively investigated, it should be used primarily as a screening instrument.

Test of Adolescent Language–2

The Test of Adolescent Language–2 (TOAL-2) (Hammill, Brown, Larsen, & Weiderholt, 1987) is an individually administered instrument designed for use with students aged 12–18 1/2 years. Portions of the test can also be group administered. According to the authors, the TOAL-2 can be used

> *(1) to identify those students whose scores are significantly below those of their peers who might profit from interventions designed to improve language proficiency; (2) to determine areas of relative strength and weakness in language abilities; (3) to document progress in language development as a consequence of special intervention programs; and (4) to serve as a measurement device for research efforts designed to investigate language behaviors of adolescents. (p.3)*

The TOAL-2 is one of the few tests available for measuring language skills in older students.

Description

The TOAL–2 is designed to measure the areas of semantics and syntax, both receptively and expressively, as well as in spoken and written form. This design results in eight subtests (Table 11-2).

Listening/Vocabulary (35 items)—In this subtest, the examiner says a word, and the student must choose from four pictures the one that represents its meaning.

Listening/Grammar (35 items)—In this subtest, the examiner reads three sentences, two of which have essentially the same meaning. The student must indicate the two sentences that are similar in meaning. For instance, "(a) He is not someone I know, (b) I know someone who knows him, and (c) Someone who knows him knows me."

Speaking/Vocabulary (25 items)—In this subtest, the examiner says a word to the student who, in turn, must make up a sentence using that word.

Speaking/Grammar (30 items)—In this subtest, the examiner reads a sentence and the student must repeat it verbatim.

Reading/Vocabulary (30 items)—In this subtest, the student is given three stimulus words that are similar in some way. The student is then given four words and is asked to choose two of these words that are similar to the stimulus words. For instance, if the stimulus words were "duke, earl, emperor," the choices might be "knight, military, dazzle, noble."

Reading/Grammar (25 items)—This subtest is similar to the Listening/ Grammar subtest except that the student reads five sentences and chooses the two that mean almost the same thing. For example, "(a) She belonged to the cat, (b) Whose cat was it? (c) It was her cat, (d) The cat was hers, and (e) That is my cat."

Writing/Vocabulary (30 items)—In this subtest, the student is given a stimulus word and asked to write a sentence using that word.

Writing/Grammar (30 items)—In this subtest, the student is given a series of sentences and asked to combine them into one sentence. For instance, "She has two dogs," "One dog is a collie," "One dog is a spaniel," "They perform different duties on the farm."

Interpretation of results

Two types of derived scores are available, subtest and composite. Subtest scores are scaled with a mean of 10 and a standard deviation of 3. The composite scores are obtained by combining certain subtests to form 10 areas: listening, speaking, reading, writing, spoken language, written language, vocabulary, grammar, receptive language, and expressive language. From two to four subtests are combined to form each area. Composite scores (or quotients) are based on a mean of 100 and a standard deviation of 15. There is an overall Adolescent Language Quotient with the same mean and standard deviation. It is somewhat questionable if the combination of only two subtests adequately measures the general areas

TABLE 11-2 Areas Measured by the Test of Adolescent Language–2.

FORM	SYSTEM	FEATURE	TOAL–2 SUBTEST NAME
Spoken	Receptive	Vocabulary	Listening/Vocabulary
Spoken	Receptive	Grammar	Listening/Grammar
Spoken	Expressive	Vocabulary	Speaking/Vocabulary
Spoken	Expressive	Grammar	Speaking/Grammar
Written	Receptive	Vocabulary	Reading/Vocabulary
Written	Receptive	Grammar	Reading/Grammar
Written	Expressive	Vocabulary	Writing/Vocabulary
Written	Expressive	Grammar	Writing/Grammar

From D. Hammill, V. Brown, S. Larsen, and J. L. Wiederholt, *The Test of Adolescent Language–2* (Austin, TX: Pro-Ed, Inc., 1987). Copyright © 1987 by D. Hammill, V. Brown, S. Larsen, and J. L. Weiderholt. Reprinted with permission.

of reading, writing, speaking, and listening. A profile sheet is available for both the subtest scores and the composite scores.

Technical characteristics
Normative sample. In this sample, 2,628 students were used. The race, sex, place of residence, and geographic location of the sample was similar to the 1985 census data.

Reliability. Internal reliability coefficients were generally .90 or above for subtests and composites. Test-retest coefficients ranged from .85 to .98 for the composites.

Validity. Discussions regarding the test's content and construct validity are in the manual. The criterion-related validity coefficients with a wide variety of measures ranged from .59 to .83 for the total score.

Review of relevant research
Research on the TOAL-2 is limited primarily to the validity studies mentioned in the test manual. There is a need for further research on the TOAL-2, particularly with learning- and language-disabled students.

OVERVIEW: TEST OF ADOLESCENT LANGUAGE–2

- *Age level*—12 to 18 1/2 years old
- *Type of administration*—Individual; some portions can be group administered
- *Technical adequacy*—Adequate reliability, questionable validity

- *Scores yielded*—Subtest scale scores, composite quotients
- *Suggested use*—The TOAL-2 is one of the few instruments that measures the language ability of older students. It is therefore a much-needed and potentially useful instrument. The validity of the TOAL-2 is not established adequately and research in this area is necessary. Whether it is meaningful to put a few subtests together to form a general composite score has been questioned. The inclusion of both oral and written language tasks is a positive feature, particularly for the age range for which the test is intended.

Test of Language Competence

The Test of Language Competence (TLC) (Wiig & Secord, 1985) was designed to identify individuals aged 9–19 who have language disabilities. The test focuses on the areas of semantics, syntax, and pragmatics. The test is individually administered and takes about an hour to give. There are four subtests; the examiner can discontinue each subtest when the examinee fails to make *any* response for three consecutive items.

Description of subtests

Understanding Ambiguous Sentences (13 items)—In this subtest, the examinee is read a sentence that could mean more than one thing and is asked to identify the two meanings. For example, "the elephant was ready to lift" could mean either the elephant was ready to lift something or the elephant was ready to be lifted.

Making Inferences (12 items)—In this subtest, the examinee is read related statements and asked to make inferences. For example, the examinee is read:

Mother was happy to have the turkey and all the trimmings in the house.

The family was disappointed when they had to eat at a restaurant on Thanksgiving day.

The examinee must then indicate which two of the four sentences might be the reason that they had to go to a restaurant:

A. The mother got sick with the flu.
B. Mother forgot to buy the turkey.
C. Most people think Thanksgiving dinner is always better at a restaurant.
D. Mother burned the turkey by cooking it too long.

Recreating Sentences (13 items)—In this subtest, the examinee is shown a picture and given three words. He/she must make up a sentence about the picture that uses the three words. For example the words for Figure 11-2 are "sit," "painted," and "because."

Understanding Metaphoric Expression (12 items)—In this subtest, the examinee is told about a situation that includes a metaphoric expression. For example "The situation is two boys talking at a dog show. One of them said

'He is crazy about that pet.'" The examinee must first tell what the statement means and must then indicate from four choices the one that represents its meaning.

Interpretation of results

Standard scores, percentile ranks, age equivalents, and stanines are available for both subtests (mean = 10; standard deviation = 3) and total test (mean = 100; standard deviation = 15). In addition, the authors provide goals and objectives for each subtest that could be used for the development of IEPs. Guidelines are also provided for extension testing that uses an error analysis approach.

Technical characteristics

Normative sample. A representative sample of 1,796 students between the ages of 9–19 from 13 states was used.

Reliability. Internal consistency coefficients ranged from .75 to .82 for the total test; coefficients were somewhat lower for the individual

sit   painted   because

FIGURE 11-2 Example from the Recreating Sentences Subtest from the Test of Language Competence.

From E. Wiig and W. Secord, *Test of Language Compentence.* Copyright © 1985 by The Psychological Corporation. Reproduced by permission. All rights reserved.

subtests. Test-retest coefficients were .78 for the total test and ranged from .34 (Recreating Sentences) to .73 (Understanding Metaphoric Expressions) for the subtests.

Validity. Data from factor analysis and intercorrelations are presented to demonstrate its construct validity. Moderate correlations with the TOAL, WISC-R, and the Educational Abilities Series with both language-learning disabled (LLD) and non-LLD students are reported. Evidence of predictive validity is also reported.

Review of relevant research
No research other than that reported in the *Technical Manual* was located.

OVERVIEW: TEST OF LANGUAGE COMPETENCE

- *Age level*—9–19 years old
- *Type of administration*—Individual
- *Technical adequacy*—Limited reliability, adequate validity
- *Scores yielded*—Standard scores, percentile ranks, age equivalents, stanines
- *Suggested use*—The TLC focuses on language usage and is based on a solid research base suggesting that individuals with language-learning disabilities demonstrate deficits in the use of cognitive and linguistic strategies. The format of the test is unique and interesting and requires the application of linguistic rules. Research is needed to demonstrate that the TLC can efficiently differentiate language-disordered from non-language-disordered individuals.

Tests of Language Development–2

The Tests of Language Development–2 (TOLD-2) (Newcomer & Hammill, 1988) consist of a Primary Edition (TOLD-2 Primary) and an intermediate edition (TOLD-2 Intermediate). According to the authors, the TOLD-2 can be used to identify children who have language disorders and to profile individual strengths and weaknesses in basic language abilities. They add that the test is based on a sound theoretical model. The TOLD-2 Primary, for example, follows the model used by its predecessor, the Test of Language Development–Primary (see Figure 11-3). This model includes semantics, syntax, and phonology through both the receptive and expressive channels. The TOLD-2 Intermediate measures both semantics and syntax.

Linguistic Features	Linguistic Systems	
	Listening (Receptive Skills)	Speaking (Expressive Skills)
Semantics	Picture Vocabulary	Oral Vocabulary
Syntax	Grammatic Understanding	Sentence Imitation
		Grammatic Completion
Phonology	Word Discrimination	Word Articulation

FIGURE 11-3 Theoretical Model for the Test of Language Development–2—Primary.

From P. Newcomer and D. Hammill, *Test of Language Development–2*. Copyright © 1988 Pro-Ed, Inc., Austin, TX. Reprinted with permission

Description

TOLD-2 Primary.   The Primary edition of the TOLD-2 is designed for use with children aged 4–8. It includes five subtests that measure syntax and semantics and two optional subtests that measure phonology. The subtests and what they measure follow.

>*Picture Vocabulary*—understanding words
>*Oral Vocabulary*—defining words
>*Grammatic Understanding*—understanding sentence structure
>*Sentence Imitation*—generating proper sentences
>*Grammatic Completion*—using acceptable morphological forms
>*Word Discrimination (supplemental)*—noticing sound differences
>*Word Articulation (supplemental)*—saying words correctly

TOLD-2 Intermediate.   The Intermediate version of the TOLD-2 is designed for use with children aged 8 1/2–12. The six subtests and what they measure follow.

>*Sentence Combining*—constructing sentences
>*Vocabulary*—understanding word relationships
>*Word Ordering*—constructing sentences
>*Generals*—knowing abstract relationships
>*Grammatic Comprehension*—recognizing grammatical sentences
>*Malapropisms*—correcting ridiculous sentences

Interpretation of scores

The TOLD-2 yields several derived scores. These include language ages, percentiles, and standard scores for the individual subtests. The standard scores have a mean of 10 and a standard deviation of 3. In addition, the subtests can be grouped into the following composites: syntax, semantics, speaking, listening, phonology (Primary only), and overall spoken language. Each of these composites yields quotients with a mean of 100 and a standard deviation of 15. A summary sheet and profile chart are also available that display the scores visually.

Technical characteristics

Normative sample.   The Primary edition was standardized on approximately 2,500 children from 29 states; the Intermediate edition used over 1,200 children from 21 states. The characteristics of the samples were similar to the national population in 1985.

Reliability.   Internal consistency and test-retest coefficients for both editions were generally acceptable.

Validity.   Evidence is presented in the manual to support both editions' content and construct validity. Concurrent validity data with a variety of criterion measures are also presented.

Review of relevant research

The limited literature to date primarily has been on the TOLD and the TOLD-P, predecessors of the TOLD-2 Primary. All three of the tests are similar in format, however. The one study located on the TOLD-2 indicated that both the primary and intermediate forms had adequate reliability with the exception of the eight-year-old level (Fodness, McNeilly, & Bradley-Johnson, 1991). Research on previous editions are included below.

- The TOLD is a reliable and valid measure when used with a language-impaired population (Newcomer & Hammill, 1978).
- Total scores from the TOLD successfully discriminated group status for normal-reading, reading-disabled, and language-delayed children. The Sentence Imitation subtest was the best discriminator (Wong & Roadhouse, 1978).
- On the TOLD, LD students showed a deficit in oral language (Newcomer & Magee, 1977).
- A table has been developed to help determine statistically significant differences among subtests on the TOLD-P (Reynolds, 1983).

Summary of research findings

The limited research on the TOLD suggests that it is a useful instrument for learning-disabled and language-disordered children. Further research is needed in this area, however, particularly with the TOLD-2.

OVERVIEW: TESTS OF LANGUAGE DEVELOPMENT–2

- *Age level*—4 to 8 years (Primary); 8 1/2 to 12 years (Intermediate)
- *Type of administration*—Individual
- *Technical adequacy*—Acceptable reliability and validity
- *Scores yielded*—Standard scores, percentile ranks, age equivalents
- *Suggested use*—The TOLD-2 are very similar to their predecessors, the TOLD Primary and the TOLD Intermediate. Both tests measure a number of language areas in both the receptive and expressive channels. This model allows for a profile of a child's strengths and weaknesses in language, using the same comparison group. The value of the tests depends on the extent to which the subtests actually measure the various language components. Although the authors state that the TOLD-2 has the strongest research base of any currently available language test, little has been published in the professional literature. The limited number of studies has supported its validity and reliability.

Written Language Tests

Test of Written Language–2

The Test of Written Language–2 (TOWL-2) (Hammill & Larsen, 1988) was developed to identify students who have problems with written expression, to indicate strengths and weaknesses in the written-language skills, to document progress, and to aid in research studies related to the writing process. There is also a downward extension called the Test of Early Written Language (Hresko, 1988) for ages 3–7 although its validity has been questioned (Shanklin, 1989). The TOWL-2 can be either individually or group administered and is designed to be used with students ages 7 1/2 through 18. The authors divide the area of written language into three components: conventional, linguistic, and cognitive. They also refer to two formats or methods of eliciting writing samples: contrived and spontaneous. The ten subtests on the TOWL-2 measure the various components in the authors' model (see Table 11-3). There are two equivalent forms—A and B—available.

Description

There are ten subtests on the TOWL-2. The first five are considered contrived, while the second five are considered spontaneous. Although the contrived subtests are administered before the spontaneous ones, a story is first written by the student using the picture depicted in Figure 11-4. This story is the basis for the five spontaneous subtests, which can be scored at a later time.

TABLE 11-3 Component and Format Characteristics of the TOWL-2 Subtests.

	FORMATS	
COMPONENTS	CONTRIVED	SPONTANEOUS
Conventional	Style Spelling	Contextual Style Spontaneous Spelling
Linguistic	Sentence Combining Vocabulary	Syntactic Maturity Contextual Vocabulary
Conceptual	Logical Sentences	Thematic Maturity

From D. Hammill and S. Larson. *Test of Written Language–2.* Copyright © 1988 by Pro-Ed, Austin, TX. Reprinted with permission.

CONTRIVED SUBTESTS

Vocabulary (30 items)—This requires the student to write a sentence using a word (e.g., night, umbrage) supplied by the examiner.

Spelling (25 items)—This subtest is scored along with subtest no. 3, Style.

Style (25 items)—The student is read a series of sentences that must be written with correct spelling, punctuation, and capitalization. Performance on this subtest also results in a score for subtest no. 2, Spelling.

Logical Sentences (25 items)—The student is given sentences that do not make sense and is told to write them so that they do. For example, "John blinked his nose" should be written as "John blinked his eye" or "John blew his nose."

Sentence Combining (25 items)—The student is given several individual sentences and must combine them to make one sentence.

SPONTANEOUS SUBTESTS

Thematic Maturity—The student's freely written story is scored using 30 criteria such as "Does the student write in paragraphs?" and "Is time set for the story?"

Contextual Vocabulary—The raw score for this subtest is simply the number of words in the story that contain seven or more letters.

Syntactic Maturity—The raw score for this subtest is the number of words in the story that are used grammatically correctly. Unacceptable grammar, such as problems in case, tense, or number agreement, is not scored.

Contextual Spelling—The raw score is the number of words that are spelled correctly in the story.

Contextual Style—The student's punctuation and capitalization usage is scored using 34 criteria.

Interpretation of results

The TOWL-2 includes standard scores and percentile ranks for subtests and three composites: Contrived Writing (first five subtests),

Story

FIGURE 11-4   Stimulus for the Spontaneous Writing Sample from the Test of Written Language–2.

From D. Hammill and S. Larson. *Test of Written Language–2*. Copyright © 1988 by Pro-Ed, Austin, TX. Reprinted with permission.

Spontaneous Writing (last five subtests), and Overall Written Language (all ten subtests). The standard scores for the subtests have a mean of 10 and a standard deviation of 3. The composite standard scores have a mean of 100 and a standard deviation of 15. All data are placed on a summary-and-profile sheet that presents a visual display of the scores from all ten subtests.

Technical characteristics
Normative sample. Approximately 2,200 subjects from 19 states were included in the sample. Race, geographic region, ethnicity, sex, and urban or rural residence were considered in the selection of subjects.

Reliability. Interscorer reliability was determined using two examiners' scoring of 20 protocols. Coefficients ranged from .91 (Logical Sentences) to .99 (Vocabulary and Spelling). Internal consistency coefficients for the subtests ranged from .74 (Sentence Combining—Form A; Contextual Style—Form B) to .96 (Contextual Spelling—Form A). Coefficients for the composites and Total Score were all above .90. Test-retest coefficients using the alternate forms were moderate-to-strong.

Validity. A discussion of the test's content and construct validity is provided in the manual. Concurrent validity coefficients with the SRA Language Arts area were low-to-moderate for the subtests. The coefficients for the contrived and spontaneous composites were .70 and .39, respectively, while the Overall Written Language score produced a coefficient of .62.

Review of relevant research
No research on the TOWL-2 was found in the literature. One study on the original TOWL (which was considerably different from the TOWL-2) by Poplin, Gray, Larsen, Banikowski, and Mehring (1980), found that LD students score lower than non-LD students on most subtests, particularly in the areas of spelling, punctuation, and word usage. In a review of the TOWL-2, Poteet (1990) noted that although the revision was a vast improvement over the original instrument, further research investigating the constructs and psychological properties of the TOWL-2 should be conducted.

OVERVIEW: TEST OF WRITTEN LANGUAGE–2

- *Age level*—7 1/2 to 18 years
- *Technical adequacy*—Adequate reliability, questionable validity
- *Scores yielded*—Standard scores and percentile ranks (subtests and composites)

■ *Suggested use*—The capacity to use written language is, unfortunately, often overlooked in educational assessment. The TOWL-2 was developed to offer the special educator a current measure in that area. The TOWL-2 measures several components of written language and appears to be a considerable improvement over its predecessor. The validity of this instrument, however, particularly of the spontaneous subtests, needs to be established before important decisions are based on the scores.

TESTS FOR SPEECH/LANGUAGE CLINICIANS

WHY USE?
Identification, determination of goals and objectives

WHO SHOULD USE?
Speech and language clinicians

There are a number of recently published tests that, although useful to the special educator, are typically administered by speech and language clinicians. These tests focus on various aspects of language and are typically used to identify individuals who might have a language disorder in one or more areas. Many of these tests stress the emphasis on pragmatic skills that has received so much attention. It is recommended that the manuals and test materials be consulted for more information about these tests.

Clinical Evaluation of Language Fundamentals–Revised

The Clinical Evaluation of Language Fundamentals-Revised (CELF-R) (Semel & Wiig, 1987) is a revised edition of the Clinical Evaluation of Language Functions (CELF). The CELF-R, in addition to the name change, revised several subtests from the CELF, added and deleted others, and provides more interpretative guidelines. The CELF-R provides an evaluation of both language processing and production for students from kindergarten through grade 12. The 11 subtests are Formulated Sentences, Listening to Paragraphs, Semantic Relationships, Word Structure, Sentence Structure, Sentence Assembly, Oral Directions, Recalling Sentences, Word Associations, Word Classes, and Linguistic Concepts.

The test can be administered in approximately an hour and can provide standard scores, age equivalents, and percentile ranks. There is also an intervention program called the Clinical Language Intervention Program (CLIP) that can be used with both the CELF and the CELF-R.

Language Processing Test

The Language Processing Test (LPT) (Richard & Hanner, 1985) was designed to measure an individual's ability to attach meaning to language and to effectively formulate a response. Norms are available for individuals aged 5–12, although the authors state that the LPT can be used with older individuals for more informal purposes. The authors further indicated the types of behaviors that might be observed in individuals whose language problems might be identified through the use of the LPT. These include word-retrieval problems, inappropriate word usage, neutral or nonspecific word usage (for example, thing-a-mi-jig), inability to correct recognized errors, seemingly poor memory, avoidance or no response, repeating what has been asked, and pausing.

There are six subtests on the LPT: (1) Associations, (2) Categorization, (3) Similarities, (4) Differences, (5) Multiple Meanings, and (6) Attributes. There are also two pretests called Labeling and Stating Functions. Age equivalents, percentile ranks, and standard scores are available for interpretation purposes. Guyette (1989) suggested that the LPT should be used as a clinical instrument rather than a test whose scores are interpreted rigidly.

Test of Pragmatic Skills

The Test of Pragmatic Skills (TPS) (Shulman, 1986) is used with children aged 3–8 and assesses their use of language for conversational intent. The format of the TPS is somewhat unique. It consists of four guided-play interactions, or tasks, that serve as a basis through which pragmatic behaviors are elicited and recorded. The TPS was designed to provide information on 10 separate categories of communicative intentions. Those are: Requesting Information, Requesting Actions, Rejection/Denial, Naming/Labeling, Answering/Responding, Informing, Reasoning, Summoning/Calling, Greeting, and Closing Conversation. The authors specifically state that the test only focuses on pragmatics and that other tests should be used to identify semantic and/or syntax problems. Although the format of the TPS is unique, there is some question whether or not it provides any more information that might be gathered in a thorough language sample (Fujiki, 1989).

For each of the four tasks there are a number of probes or statements that the examiner makes and to which the examinee responds:

Playing with puppets—10 probes
Playing with pencil and paper—7 probes
Playing with telephones—9 probes
Playing with blocks—8 probes

Each of the tasks and subsequent probes are intended to measure up to 8 of the 10 conversational intentions previously listed. The examinee is rated as a 0 (no response) to a 5 (contextually appropriate response with extensive elaboration) for each of the responses to the probes. Normative data based on 650 children are available in the form of percentile ranks.

Test of Problem Solving

The Test of Problem Solving (TOPS) (Zachman, Jorgensen, Huisingh, & Barrett, 1984) is designed for use with children aged 6–12; it assesses their ability to verbalize reasons, solutions, and justifications in an appropriate manner. According to the authors, the TOPS is an expressive test that is used to determine a child's thinking and reasoning ability related to events of everyday living. The test includes five subtests: (1) Explaining Inferences, (2) Determining Causes, (3) Negative Why Questions, (4) Determining Solutions, and (5) Avoiding Problems. As in the LPT, the authors feel that the test can be used informally for individuals outside the intended age range. Three types of scores are available for the TOPS: age equivalents, percentile ranks, and standard scores. In a study designed to evaluate speech-language clinicians' impressions of the TOPS, it was concluded that the content validity of the instrument is questionable (Bernhardt, 1990).

Test of Word Finding

The Test of Word Finding (TWF) (German, 1986) is designed to measure the word–finding ability of elementary school–aged children. There are two forms, the Primary form for grades 1 and 2 and the Intermediate form for grades 3–6. Norms are provided for children aged 6 1/2–12. The authors state that prior to the development of the TWF, the identification of children with this expressive language disorder was done informally.

There are six sections to the TWF: (1) Picture Naming: Nouns, (2) Sentence Completion Naming, (3) Description Naming, (4) Picture Naming: Verbs, (5) Picture Naming: Categories, and (6) a Comprehension section. This last section is given after the five other sections and involves only the items that are missed on those sections. The TWF provides percentile ranks and standard scores for both age and grade comparisons. There is also considerable information in the manual about the types of word-finding skills that can be identified. Although the TWF appears to be a reliable, technically sound instrument, there has been some question about how useful the test results actually are for classification or instructional decisions (Drum, 1989).

Instrument or Technique	Suggested Use							Target Population						Special Considerations	Educational Relevance for Exceptional Students
	Prereferral			Postreferral											
	Screening and Initial Identification	Informal Determination and Evaluation of Teaching Programs and Strategies	Determination of Current Performance Level and Educational Need	Decisions about Classification and Program Placement	IEP Goals	IEP Objectives	IEP Evaluation	Mild/Moderate	Severe/Profound	Preschool	Elementary Age	Secondary Age	Adult		
Oral Language Sampling	X	X			X			X		X	X	X	X	Very good to use to determine individual's actual spontaneous use of language	very useful
Written Language Sampling	X	X			X			X		X	X	X	X	Very helpful and easy to do because of availability of written products	very useful
Peabody Picture Vocabulary Test–Revised	X							X		X	X	X	X	Can be used with individuals with speech and motor handicaps	useful
Test of Adolescent Language–2	X	X	X		X			X				X		One of a few tests designed to measure language abilities of older students	adequate
Test of Language Competence	X	X	X					X			X	X		Focuses on language usage in older students	useful
Tests of Language Development–2	X	X	X		X			X		X	X	X		Measures a variety of language skills; has a primary and intermediate form	adequate
Test of Written Language–2	X	X	X		X			X			X			Measures an important and often overlooked area; technical aspects are somewhat limited	useful
Clinical Evaluation of Language Fundamentals	X	X	X		X			X			X	X		Measures language processing and production	useful
Language-Processing Test	X	X						X			X			Used to identify children with language processing problems	adequate

Instrument or Technique	Suggested Use							Target Population						Special Considerations	Educational Relevance for Exceptional Students
	Prereferral		Postreferral												
	Screening and Initial Identification	Informal Determination and Evaluation of Teaching Programs and Strategies	Determination of Current Performance Level and Educational Need	Decisions about Classification and Program Placement	IEP Goals	IEP Objectives	IEP Evaluation	Mild/Moderate	Severe/Profound	Preschool	Elementary Age	Secondary Age	Adult		
Test of Pragmatic Skills	X	X								X	X			One of the few tests designed to measure pragmatics	adequate
Test of Problem Solving	X	X						X			X			Measures the use of language related to events of everyday living	adequate
Test of Word Finding	X							X			X			Tests for expressive language problems	adequate

___ PART FOUR ___

Assessment of Achievement

As noted in Part 3, one of the major focuses of educational and psychological assessment is the evaluation of an individual's abilities. Another major focus of assessment is the measurement of achievement. This usually involves the basic skill areas of reading, arithmetic, and spelling. They are sometimes evaluated together (through the use of a general achievement test), whereas at other times they are evaluated separately (through the use of a variety of instruments and techniques).

The assessment of achievement is extremely important in making appropriate educational decisions. Evaluation in this area is necessary to document that an educational need exists (a requirement of Public Law 94-142) and to help make eligibility decisions (e.g., aptitude/achievement discrepancies for learning disabilities). More importantly, information in this area is used to assist in the establishment of relevant goals and objectives and to monitor progress in relation to those goals and objectives. The use of the instruments and procedures discussed in this section (along with the techniques discussed in Part 2) are primarily the responsibility of the teacher.

As in Part 3, both formal and informal tests will be discussed and information provided describing how each type fits into the overall assessment process; the same format will be used to describe the tests. That includes the following elements:

1. A summary matrix that presents information about specific instruments and techniques in a format that allows easy comparison of the instruments for suggested use and target population. The matrix also includes a statement of any special considerations of which a user should be aware. In addition, for each instrument, the matrix gives the educational relevance for exceptional students. The matrices are directly related to the assessment model proposed in Chapter 2.

2. A thorough review of relevant research for each norm-referenced instrument. The review emphasizes the use of the test with exceptional students.
3. An overview box for each test. The overview summarizes the age range, technical adequacy (for norm-referenced tests), and suggested use for each instrument.

After reading Part Four you should be able to:

1. Identify strengths and weaknesses of the major general achievement tests

2. Identify strengths and weaknesses of individual- and group-administered reading tests

3. Identify a variety of informal methods of assessing reading

4. Identify strengths and weaknesses of individual- and group-administered arithmetic tests (formal and informal)

5. Identify strengths and weaknesses of spelling instruments (formal and informal)

__12__

Assessment of General Achievement

INSTRUMENTS/PROCEDURES INCLUDED

NORM-REFERENCED TESTS
- Group-Administered
- Basic Achievement Skills Individual Screener
- Diagnostic Achievement Battery–2
- Diagnostic Achievement Test for Adolescents
- Kaufman Test of Educational Achievement
- Peabody Individual Achievement Test–Revised
- Quick-Score Achievement Test
- Wide Range Achievement Test–Revised

CRITERION-REFERENCED INSTRUMENTS
- The Brigance Inventories
- Multilevel Academic Survey Test
- Mastery: An Evaluation Tool

Mr. Segerson is a sixth-grade teacher in a rural school district. As part of his duties he is required to administer a group achievement test at the end of the year to document the academic level of each of his students. In the most recent testing two of his students scored extremely low in reading and mathematics. He referred the two students to the learning-disabilities specialist, who scheduled them for in depth academic testing. The first step was to administer an individual achievement test. After it was determined that one of the students was eligible for special education, portions of a criterion-referenced inventory was given in his deficient areas to help determine objectives for his IEP.

Probably all individuals have taken some kind of achievement test during their years as students. Typically, group achievement tests are administered annually or semiannually to document both the level of academic ability and the progress of individuals in specific academic areas. Individual achievement tests are sometimes administered to yield more specific academic information and to allow the examiner to observe the student's approach to the individual tasks. Many students perform quite differently on group and individual achievement tests, although individual achievement tests are usually required for students who receive special-education services. There are also a number of criterion-referenced inventories that are used to gather more specific information about certain academic areas.

An extremely important issue in achievement testing is content validity. It is absolutely necessary that an achievement test measure the curriculum to which a student is exposed. This requires that the "appropriate" achievement test be carefully selected. In other words, the content of an achievement test must be appropriate and complete in relation to the behaviors (curriculum) being measured. This can best be achieved by choosing valid instruments that measure the content a student has been taught. This is also one of the reasons that curriculum-based assessment has become so widespread.

Although most norm-referenced achievement tests are not really thought of as screening tests, many are used for this purpose. In fact, most achievement tests are used to gather some basic, preliminary information before more in-depth academic assessment is pursued. Some individually administered achievement tests are also used to document that an educational deficit exists in order to meet that requirement of P.L. 94-142.

NORM-REFERENCED TESTS

Group-Administered Tests

WHY USE?
Screening and identification of students needing further academic testing; informal determination of objectives

WHO SHOULD USE?
Teachers

Group achievement tests usually have different levels for different grades in school. Tests that measure achievement in the elementary grades typically include items related to the basic skill areas of reading, spelling, and arithmetic. The levels for older students are concerned not only with basic skills, but also with content areas such as science and social studies. Therefore, it is important to note that not all of the areas measured by each test are used with students of all ages; certain areas are relevant and designed for students at specific grades. A brief description of the most commonly used group achievement tests follows.

California Achievement Tests

Age range—Kindergarten through grade 12

Standardization—Stratified sample of approximately 300,000

Technical adequacy—Acceptable

Areas measured—Seven major areas are measured: Reading, Spelling, Language, Mathematics, Study Skills, Science, Social Studies

Types of scores obtained—Grade equivalents, stanines, percentile ranks, scaled scores, normal curve equivalents

Special features—The California Achievement Tests (CAT) (CTB/McGraw-Hill, 1985) include a locater test that is used to identify the level of test that is most appropriate to give to an individual. Its value for group administration to exceptional students is questionable, however, due to the heterogeneity of the population. Criterion-referenced objectives are also available.

Iowa Test of Basic Skills

Age range—Kindergarten through grade 9

Standardization—Stratified sample of over 150,000 students

Technical adequacy—Acceptable

Areas measured—The Iowa Test of Basic Skills (ITBS) (Hieronymus, Lundquist, & Hoover, 1986) has 10 levels. The following are the areas measured: Listening, Writing, Vocabulary, Word Analysis, Reading Comprehension, Language, Word Study, Mathematics, Social Studies, and Science.

Types of scores obtained—Percentiles, stanines, standard scores, grade equivalents, age equivalents

Special features—The ITBS was standardized concurrently with the Cognitive Abilities Test (a group-administered intelligence test). Administration of these two tests allows comparisons based on the same normative sample.

Metropolitan Achievement Tests

Age range—Kindergarten through grade 12 (grade 9 for instructional tests)

Standardization—Stratified sample of over 400,000

Technical adequacy—Good

Areas measured—The Metropolitan Achievement Tests (MAT) (Prescott, Balow, Hogan, & Farr, 1987) include two sets of tests: diagnostic and survey. The diagnostic tests cover specific educational objectives in the areas of reading, mathematics, and language, the survey tests give an overall assessment in the skill and content areas of the school curriculum. The survey tests cover the areas of Reading, Mathematics, Language, Science, and Social Studies.

Types of scores obtained—Scaled scores, percentile ranks, stanines, grade equivalents, normal-curve equivalents, performance indicators, instructional mathematics levels, and instructional, independent, and frustration reading levels.

Special features—The inclusion of both diagnostic and survey tests is unique. They provide a complete battery of norm-referenced and criterion-referenced tests.

SRA Achievement Series

Age range—Kindergarten through grade 12

Standardization—Stratified sample of approximately 200,000

Technical adequacy—Good

Areas measured—Reading, Mathematics, Language Arts, Reference Materials, Social Studies, and Science

Types of scores obtained—Grade equivalents, percentiles, stanines, standard scores (two types, normal-curve equivalents and growth-scale values)

Special features—The SRA Achievement Series (Naslund, Thorpe, & Lefever, 1981) was standardized concurrently with the Educational Ability Series. This theoretically allows aptitude-achievement comparisons using the same normative sample. There are also six types of computer-printed report forms.

Stanford Achievement Test and Stanford Test of Academic Skills

Age range
　　Stanford Achievement Test (SAT): Middle of grade 1 to middle of grade 9
　　Test of Academic Skills: Grades 9 through 13 (community college)

Standardization—Stratified sample of over 275,000

Technical characteristics—Good

Areas measured—The SAT (Gardner, Rudman, Karlsen, & Merwin, 1982) measures the following areas: Vocabulary, Reading Comprehension, Word Study Skills, Mathematics Concepts, Mathematics Computation, Mathematics Applications, Spelling, Language, Social Science, Science, and Listening Comprehension

Areas measured—The Stanford Test of Academic Skills measures the following areas for grades 9 through 13:

Reading
Language
Mathematics

Types of scores obtained—Percentile ranks, stanines, grade equivalents, scaled scores, and item-difficulty scores (percent of students that answered each item based on the standardization)

Special features—The Stanford tests, along with the Metropolitan tests, are the most commonly used group achievement tests. The SAT offers a number of profile charts to summarize the data.

Tests of Achievement and Proficiency

Age range—High school (grades 9 through 12)

Standardization—Stratified sample of approximately 60,000

Technical adequacy—Acceptable

Areas measured—For all grades 9 through 12 the following areas are measured: Reading Comprehension, Written Expression, Using Sources of Information, Mathematics, Social Studies, Science, Listening, Writing, Language Skills

Types of scores obtained—Percentiles, stanines, standard scores, grade equivalents

Special features—The Tests of Achievement and Proficiency (TAP) (Scannell, 1986) are an upward extension of the Iowa Test of Basic Skills. This instrument was standardized concurrently with the Iowa Test and the Cognitive Abilities Test.

Individually Administered Tests

WHY USE?
Screening and identification of students needing further academic testing; documentation of educational need; establishment of IEP goals

WHO SHOULD USE?
Teachers; diagnosticians; school psychologists

Until the 1980s, there were only two individually administered norm-referenced tests that were specifically designed to measure overall academic achievement. Those two tests, the Peabody Individual Achievement Test and the Wide Range Achievement Test, were frequently used and constantly scrutinized. Other tests were developed, and the two "old standbys" were revised. A description of these instruments follows.

Basic Achievement Skills Individual Screener

As indicated by its name, the Basic Achievement Skills Individual Screener (BASIS) (The Psychological Corporation, 1983) is designed to be used more as a first step in documenting the performance of students in the basic skill areas. The test is designed to be administered in less than an hour and provides information in the areas of reading, mathematics, spelling, and writing (an optional area). The test is designed for students aged 6–18 and provides criterion referenced as well as norm-referenced information about the student who is tested. As in many tests that cover a wide age range, there are suggested starting levels, as well as basal and ceiling rules, that help eliminate the need to administer unnecessary items. The BASIS incorporates the concept of *grade-referenced clusters* for this purpose. This means that a number of items are clustered together to represent information presented at a certain grade level (readiness, grades 1 through 8 are included). Rather than stopping administration after six consecutive failed items, for example, administration of the BASIS is stopped after all the items in a grade cluster are missed. The description of the areas that are measured follows.

Description

Mathematics—This section includes items related to mathematics readiness (seven items), dictated word problems (two items for each grade level cluster), and mathematics computation (six items for each grade level cluster).

Reading—This section includes reading readiness (letter identification and visual discrimination), beginning reading (word reading and sentence reading), and reading passages. This latter area measures reading comprehension using a cloze procedure. Figure 12-1 gives an example of one of the reading passages.

Spelling—This subtest measures the student's written spelling ability. There are six words per grade cluster (a total of 48 words).

Writing—This optional subtest is only relevant for students in grade 3 or above. The student is asked to take 10 minutes and write a story about his or her favorite place. The quality of the story is then compared to sample stories on the basis of sentence structure, organization, vocabulary, mechanics, and ideas.

Interpretation of results

Results from the Mathematics, Reading, and Spelling sections can be reported as percentiles, standard scores (mean = 100; standard deviation = 15), and age/grade equivalents. The writing sample is judged to be either above average, average, or below average. There is also information included that allows for criterion-referenced interpretation. This information includes suggested grade placement in the different areas (based on performance within the grade-referenced clusters) as well as basic information regarding error analysis.

The Peanut Hunt

My friends and I went on
a peanut hunt. My sister
helped us. She hid the peanuts
in the long grass in the park.
Then she said, "Ready!" We
had to _____ for the
peanuts. It was hard. The
peanuts were very little. We
could not _____ them.

At last, I found two
peanuts. My friend found five.
It was fun after the game
was over too. We put all our
peanuts together. Then
we got to _____ them.

FIGURE 12-1   Example of Cloze Procedure from BASIS.

Technical characteristics
Normative sample.   Over 3,000 individuals were included in the standardization sample. Overall, the sample was poorly described.

Reliability.   Internal consistency coefficients were predominantly in the .90s. Test-retest coefficients were determined from a limited sample at three grade levels and ranged from .74 (math at grade 8) to .95 (spelling at grade two).

Validity. Evidence of validity is primarily supported through the reporting of positive correlations between BASIS scores and school grades/ other achievement data. In general the nature of the criterion variables are poorly described. Several reports of small validity studies with special populations are also included in the manual.

Review of relevant research

BASIS has received mixed reviews in a number of professional journals. For example, Hambleton and DeVries (1985) believed that the test had too few test items per grade level cluster and had too few subjects in the normative group. They also questioned the content validity of the instrument. Similarly, Conley (1986) noted that it was particularly limited for older students. On the other hand, Fitzpatrick (1984) and Ysseldyke (1985) argued that the test was an efficient measure of basic skills. In one empirical study, McGehee (1986) found that there was considerable overlap of the three sections, making a profile analysis inadvisable.

OVERVIEW: BASIC ACHIEVEMENT SKILLS INDIVIDUAL SCREENER

- *Age level*—6 to 18 years old
- *Type of administration*—Individual
- *Technical adequacy*—Adequate reliability, limited validity
- *Scores yielded*—Standard scores, percentiles, age and grade equivalents
- *Suggested use*—The BASIS was intended to be a screening instrument for the basic skill areas. To use it for anything more than screening would be a mistake. Although the mathematics and spelling areas are measured in a traditional fashion, the reading area incorporates a cloze procedure and might not provide a true picture of a student's comprehension skills. The writing section provides little educationally relevant information. There is some question about whether there are a sufficient number of items, particularly for older students.

Diagnostic Achievement Battery–2

The Diagnostic Achievement Battery–2 (DAB-2) (Newcomer, 1990) is an individually administered group of subtests used to measure a number of academic areas. According to the author, the DAB-2 is intended to address four purposes: the identification of students who are having difficulties in the areas of spoken language, written language, and mathematics; the determination of an individual's strengths and weaknesses; the documentation of student progress; and the possible use as a measurement device for research studies regarding academic achievement. The DAB-2 includes 12 subtests that are grouped together in various combinations to provide a number of composite areas. The model followed includes composite scores in spoken language, including the areas of listening and speaking; written language, including the areas of reading and written language generation; and mathematics (Figure 12-2). The test is designed for students aged 6–14.

Description

As noted previously, there are 12 subtests in the DAB-2. A brief description of each follows.

LISTENING

Story Comprehension (35 items)—The student is required to listen to brief stories and then answer several questions about each story. This subtest is essentially a measure of listening comprehension.

Characteristics (35 items)—Requires the student to give true-or-false answers to questions such as "all trees are maples" and "all nails are metal."

SPEAKING

Synonyms (25 items)—The examiner says a word and the student must supply another word that has the same meaning.

Grammatic Completion (27 items)—The student is given an incomplete sentence(s) such as, "I lost one tooth and you lost one tooth. We lost two ———," and asked to supply the missing answer.

READING

Alphabet/Word Knowledge (65 items)—This subtest measures visual discrimination skills, letter recognition and beginning sounds at the beginning of the subtest and word recognition for the majority of the subtest.

Reading Comprehension (45 items)—This subtest includes a series of eight progressively more difficult passages that the student must read and subsequently answer questions asked by the examiner.

WRITING

Capitalization (30 items)—The student is provided a series of sentences that have no capitalization (Figure 12-3). The student must rewrite the sentences, editing appropriate capital letters.

Punctuation (30 items)—The same sentences used in punctuation are used in this subtest. The student must also add the appropriate punctuation to the sentences.

Spelling (20 items)—The words are orally read by the examiner and written by the student.

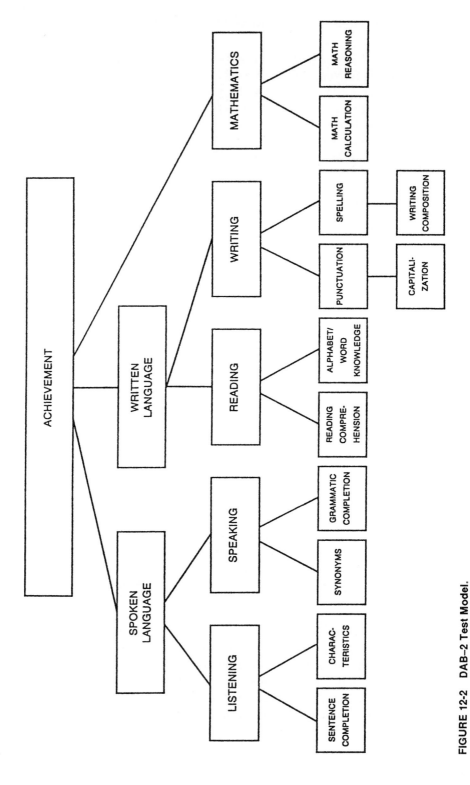

FIGURE 12-2   DAB–2 Test Model.

From: P. Newcomer. *Diagnostic Achievement Battery–2.* Copyright © 1990 by Pro-Ed, Austin, TX. Reprinted with permission.

Writing Composition (see description of subtest)—The student looks at three pictures that depict a car race. The student is instructed to write a story about the picture that has a beginning, middle, and end. The examiner simply counts the number of words with seven or more letters and evaluates the thematic content to determine the raw score.

MATHEMATICS

Mathematics Reasoning (30 items)—This subtest uses pictures at the lower levels in which the majority of the problems are presented orally and the student points to the correct response. The last half of the subtest includes orally presented problems that the student must solve without the use of visual cues or pencil and paper.

Mathematics Calculation (36 items)—This subtest is a series of progressively more difficult mathematics computation problems. The student has 15 minutes to complete as many as possible.

Interpretation of results

Each of the 12 subtests yields grade equivalents, percentile ranks, and standard scores (mean = 10; standard deviation = 3). Further, the subtests are combined as noted above into composites that yield quotients with a mean of 100 and a standard deviation of 15. The five quotients are listening, speaking, reading, writing, and mathematics. In addition, the listening and speaking areas can be combined to form a spoken language quotient, and the reading and writing areas can be combined to form a written language quotient. Finally all of the subtests can be combined to provide a total achievement quotient. All of the quotients have a mean of 100 and a standard deviation of 15. There is a computerized scoring program as well.

Technical characteristics

Normative sample.   The sample consisted of 2,623 children from 40 states. The sample was stratified according to sex, type of residence, race, ethnicity, and geographic region. According to the author, the percentage of individuals included in the standardization sample was similar to the U.S. population in 1985.

Reliability.   The internal consistency reliability was computed using a sample of 450 children for both the individual subtests and the composites. For the most part, the reliability coefficients exceeded .80 and the majority exceeded .90. Synonyms and spelling had the lowest coefficients. Test-retest coefficients ranged from .80 (mathematical reasoning) to .99 (alphabet/word knowledge) for individual subtests and .92 (mathematics) to .99 (writing and written language) for the composites. These data were based on a limited sample of 34 children, however.

Practice Item: the dog is big

1. the man is tall

2. we ate breakfast

3. today is monday

4. where are evans shoes

5. his name is mr a w parker

6. katie lives on main street

7. didnt alan mail the letter

8. christmas comes in december

9. jeffs mother came from canada

10. joan and angela got home at 230 am

11. yes elaine there is a santa claus

12. no she said i dont want to go

13. they sailed around the cape of good hope

14. steve was born on july 6 1985 wasnt he

15. stop the wedding the brides father shouted

16. mickey mouse is my favorite cartoon character

17. the largest dolphins live in the pacific ocean

18. the italian german and russian all spoke english

19. marilyn was elected president of harvard college

20. she works for a good newspaper the daily chronicle

21. isnt your brothers house in philadelphia pennsylvania

22. the teacher asked what have you children been doing

23. there were thirty five ducks swimming in the farmers pond

24. did you read william shakespeares midsummer nights dream

25. among her children were four females sandy kathy dale and marge

26. watch your step jean shouted to the crowd as she waved the sword

27. the chimp after climbing to the top of the oak tree threw an orange at barbara

28. sol and his brothers all six of them played baseball for the new york tigers

29. ednas powerful backhand carried her to the wimbledon championship didn't it

30. marjorie and allen dressed as peter pan and tinker bell for the halloween party

FIGURE 12-3   Capitalization Subtest from the Diagnostic Achievement Battery–2.

From: P. Newcomer. *Diagnostic Achievement Battery–2.* Copyright © 1990 by Pro-Ed, Austin, TX. Reprinted with permission.

Validity.   Criterion-related validity was determined by comparing scores from the DAB-2 with scores from seven other tests. Unfortunately, only 25 third-graders and 21 sixth-graders were included in the analysis. The coefficients ranged from .37 (written vocabulary) to .81 (spelling) for individual subtests and from .46 (speaking) to .73 (reading) for the composites. Another study using 45 students reported coefficients ranging from .36 to .78 with two additional tests. Also, the author provides a theoretical argument supporting the construct validity of the DAB-2.

Review of relevant research

No research articles investigating the DAB-2 or the original DAB were located in the professional literature. There is a definite need for research on this test to determine its potential uses and limitations. Deni (1985) reviewed the DAB and felt that it was a useful tool for screening and evaluating achievement, although the written subtests were limited with younger children. Lewandowski (1985) also gave the DAB a positive review, noting that it was carefully designed.

OVERVIEW: DIAGNOSTIC ACHIEVEMENT BATTERY–2

- *Age level*—6 to 14 years old
- *Type of administration*—Individual; some small group
- *Technical adequacy*—Adequate standardization; adequate reliability and validity, particularly for composite scores; technical data based on limited samples, however
- *Scores yielded*—Percentiles, standard scores
- *Suggested use*—The DAB-2 is a potentially useful instrument to determine individual strengths and weaknesses in a number of academic areas. As with most tests, the composite scores are more stable than the individual subtest scores and should be used for important educational decisions. Research on the DAB-2 is needed before its full potential can be determined. There is a computerized scoring program (PROSCORE) available.

Diagnostic Achievement Test for Adolescents

The Diagnostic Achievement Test for Adolescents (DATA) (Newcomer and Bryant, 1986) is an individually administered instrument designed to evaluate the overall achievement areas for individuals ages 12 through 18. According to the authors, the DATA can be used for four purposes: (1) to identify students who are significantly below their peers in academic areas, (2) to identify strengths and weaknesses, (3) to document student progress, and (4) to serve as a measurement device for research studies. These purposes are essentially the same as those noted by the author of the DAB-2. The DATA has nine subtests and takes between 1 and 2 hours to administer. Basal and ceiling guidelines are used in the DATA in an attempt to decrease the testing time as much as possible.

Description

Word Identification (45 items)—This requires the individual to correctly pronounce words ranging from "transfusion" to "bucolic."

Reading Comprehension (42 items)—This consists of seven short stories that the student reads and six comprehension questions asked about each reading passage.

Mathematics Calculation (45 items)—This includes mathematical problems that must be completed. Pencil and paper are provided to the student.

Mathematics Problem Solving (45 items)—In this subtest, the examiner reads mathematical story problems to the student, who must provide the correct answer. The students may also read the items as the examiner reads them. Again, pencil and paper are provided to the student.

Spelling (45 items)—This requires the student to write the correct spelling of words ranging from "banquet" to "derelict."

Writing Composition—The student is shown three pictures and is instructed to write a story based on those pictures. This test is scored simply by counting the number of words containing seven or more letters. That number becomes the raw score.

Science (45 items)—The student is read questions such as "what are Earth, Pluto, and Mars?" and "what instrument is used to detect earthquakes?" The student must provide an oral response.

Social Studies (45 items)—This subtest uses the same format as science with questions such as "who invented the telephone?" and "what is the formal indictment of a President called?"

Reference Skills—This subtest has six sections. These sections are guide words, alphabetizing, encyclopedia skills, dictionary skills, library catalog skills, and table of contents. Figure 12-4 shows a portion of this subtest.

Interpretation of results

A variety of scores are available for the DATA. These include percentile ranks and standard scores for individual subtests (standard score mean = 10, standard deviation = 3). There are also several composite scores that are available. These composites (Reading, Mathematics, and Writing) are combinations of various subtests and also are reported as standard scores with a mean of 10 and standard deviation of 3. Also available is an Achievement Screener (Word Identification, Math Computation, and Spelling) and Total Achievement, which is combination of all of the subtests. These are reported as quotients (standard scores with a

Guide Words

Directions: Imagine that the words listed below are guide words found at the top of a dictionary page. The page number between each set of words represents the page on which the guide words are found. Using the guide words as a source, write the number of the page that would contain each word.

rabble	625	radiance
radical	626	rampant
rampart	627	ransack
ransom	628	rare
rarefied	629	rate
ratify	630	reach
ready	631	reasonable

Practice: rant   _____

1. radian   _____   5. rancorous   _____

2. rayless   _____   6. rampion   _____

3. rabies   _____   7. rearwards   _____

4. rarefy   _____

Alphabetizing

Directions: Below are sets of four words each. You are to put the four words in alphabetical order by placing a 1, 2, 3, or 4 next to each word, depending on which word comes first, second, third, or fourth.

Practice:		Set 1:		Set 2:	
_____	coerce	_____	revealment	_____	committee
_____	cognitive	_____	retreat	_____	commode
_____	codger	_____	revel	_____	commital
_____	coffee	_____	retrograde	_____	commixture

FIGURE 12-4   Portion of Reference Skills Subtest from the Diagnostic Achievement Test for Adolescents.

From: P. Newcomer and Bryant. *Diagnostic Achievement Test for Adolescents*. Copyright © 1986 by Pro-Ed, Austin, TX. Reprinted with permission.

mean of 100 and a standard deviation of 15). Finally, the authors provide a formula for transforming the standard scores into grade equivalents, although they discourage this practice.

Technical characteristics
Normative sample. Over 1,100 children residing in 15 states were included in the standardization. The demographic characteristics of sex, residence, race, geographic area, and ethnicity were considered, and the percentages of individuals in the standardization sample were similar to the 1985 total U.S. percentages.

Reliability. Internal consistency was determined using coefficient alpha using a sample of 350 students. For the individual subtests all coefficients were above .90. All composites were above .90 as well, with the exception of the writing composite, which averaged .88. Test-retest reliability was determined using a sample of 58 students. The coefficients for individual subtests ranged from Writing Composition (.71) to Spelling (.95). The composite coefficients ranged from .86 for Reading to .89 for Mathematics; both the Achievement Screener Quotient (ASQ) and Total Achievement Quotient (TAQ) were above .90.

Validity. The authors provide a brief discussion of their attempt to ensure content validity at the point of test construction. Regarding criterion-related validity, 234 children from the DATA's normative sample who had been administered other achievement tests were included in a variety of studies. These 234 children had been administered one of five achievement tests or diagnostic academic tests. There is a wide range of correlations mostly in the moderate range. The authors note that 86 percent of the correlation coefficients were at or exceeded .35 although this is relatively low for a validity coefficient. Evidence for construct validity was also presented, including data that showed the interrelationships among the subtests and composites and correlations with the Short Form Test of Academic Aptitude (coefficient for TAQ = .72)

Review of relevant research
Although no empirical studies were located in the professional literature, several reviews were found. The reviewers were generally supportive of the DATA, although several questioned the test's technical characteristics. For example. Kamphaus (1989) noted that the DATA has several appealing features but the standardization was inadequate. Similarly, Ysseldyke (1989) noted that although the DATA was the only individually administered achievement test that measures reading, mathematics, spelling, social studies, as well as science and use of references, the standardization procedures were insufficiently described. Conversely, Schumm (1987) and Stuempfig (1987) felt that the test was well-constructed and had adequate reliability and validity. Stuempfig noted,

however, that the DATA was more a survey instrument of general achievement than a diagnostic test to pinpoint specific learning problems.

OVERVIEW: DIAGNOSTIC ACHIEVEMENT TEST FOR ADOLESCENTS

- *Age level*—12 years through 18 years old.
- *Type of administration*—Individual
- *Technical adequacy*—Limited standardization, adequate reliability and validity.
- *Scores yielded*—Standard score and percentile ranks for subtests, composites, the achievement screener, and total achievement.
- *Suggested use*—The DATA is the only individually administered achievement test designed specifically for adolescents. Therefore, for that age range it includes more appropriate items than many of the other achievement tests that attempt to cover a wide age range—usually from kindergarten to high school. The use of the reference skills subtest is unique; more research, however, is necessary to determine its true utility. The criticism that has been aimed at the DATA is the lack of appropriate description regarding the standardization sample. The test is best thought of as a general achievement test. Until further validity data are generated, the use of individual subtest scores should probably be discouraged.

Kaufman Test of Educational Achievement

The Kaufman Test of Educational Achievement (K-TEA) (Kaufman & Kaufman, 1985) is an individually administered instrument designed to measure a number of achievement areas of students in grades 1–12. There are two forms of the K-TEA, a comprehensive form that measures five areas and a brief form that measures only three. This description focuses on the comprehensive form. The time requirements for administration range from approximately 20–30 minutes for first-grade students to approximately one hour for secondary-level students. According to the authors there are 11 purposes for which the K-TEA would be appropriate, including the identification of individual strengths and weaknesses, the determination of the types of academic errors made, program planning, and making program decisions. The K-TEA is presented in an easel-type format that makes the administration easy. The directions are clear and the manual is comprehensive and easily understood.

Description
Five subtests are included in the comprehensive form of the K-TEA. Of these five, three (reading decoding, spelling, mathematics computation) are included on the brief form.

Mathematics Applications (60 items)—The student is required to answer different types of conceptual and reasoning questions. The items are presented orally, although the student has a visual stimulus (for example, table, graph, or word problem) to act as a cue. In addition, the student can use pencil and paper to aid in the computation required by many of the questions.

Reading Decoding (60 items)—This subtest includes items ranging from letter identification to word identification/pronunciation.

Spelling (50 items)—The student must write the correct spelling of words of increasing difficulty dictated by the examiner.

Reading Comprehension (50 items)—The majority of items require the student to read a passage and subsequent questions and respond orally to the questions. One interesting feature is the inclusion of eight items at the beginning of the subtest that require the student to respond gesturally, such as "make a fist," as well as five items at the end of the subtest in which the student must respond orally to commands presented in printed sentences.

Mathematics Computation (60 items)—The student must solve traditional addition, subtraction, multiplication, and division problems in addition to fractions, algebraic formulae, and other more complex types of problems.

Interpretation of results

The K-TEA provides a variety of interpretative guidelines that helps the examiner get the most out of the results from the test. Each subtest yields standard scores (mean = 100; standard deviation = 15) based on both age and grade norms. In addition, the two reading subtests and the two mathematics subtests can be combined to form a reading and mathematics composite score, respectively. Finally, all five subtests can be combined to provide a battery composite score. All of the composite scores also have a mean of 100 and a standard deviation of 15. There are also tables that allow the transformation of the standard scores into age or grade equivalents, percentile ranks, and stanines.

The authors also provide a number of tables that allow additional interpretation of the results. For instance, it is possible to determine when a specific subtest standard score differs significantly from the average of all the subtest standard scores. This information is very important in determining intraindividual strengths and weaknesses. Another notable feature is the error analysis guidelines provided by the authors. These provide a classification system for the type of errors made on each subtest as well as normative data that indicate whether or not the number of different types of errors are considered significant depending on the age of the examinee. Figure 12-5 shows the types of errors that are noted for the mathematics application subtest.

Technical characteristics

Normative sample.   The K-TEA was involved in two separate standardizations (spring and fall) to provide more specific comparative infor-

Mathematics applications

SKILL CATEGORIES: Elementary Number Concepts, Reading Tables & Graphs, Addition, Subtraction, Multiplication, Division, Fractions, Decimals & Percents, Advanced Number Concepts, Measurement, Money, Estimation, Two-Step Problems

Grade	Item		Response	Score
1-2	1	Identify 4		
	2	Name 12		
	3	Identify 3rd person in line		
	4	9 people − 5 people = ?		
	5	Name 37		
3-4	6	Identify 30		
	7	(a, b) More people or puppets		
	8	(a, b) Read boxtops graph		
	9	6 elephants − 4 elephants = ?		
	10	6 elephants + 5 elephants = ?		
5-6	11	(a-d) Reorder shirt numbers		
	12	Read calendar to find day of week		
	13	6 pages + 8 pages = ?		
	14	3 bags + 8 bags + 4 bags = ?		
	15	Identify cube		
7-10	16	1 dozen = ?		
	17	31 stamps + 58 stamps = ?		
	18	3 boxes × 30¢/box = ?		
	19	24 pictures + 7 pictures = ?		
	20	Read clock		
11-12	21	12 rabbits ÷ 3 = ?		
	22	7 boxes × 100 pencils/box = ?		
	23	2 × 5 = ?		
	24	65 stamps − 43 stamps = ?		
	25	4 × ? = 8		
	26	7 boxes × 30¢/box = ?		
	27	Check with subtraction		
	28	Read table; subtract time		
	29	$1.00 − (2 × 30¢) = ?		
	30	⅞ yd. − ⅜ yd. = ?		

FIGURE 12-5   Error Analysis from the Kaufman-Test of Educational Achievement.

mation based on the time of year that a student is tested. The spring standardization included more than 1400 students from 15 states. The fall standardization included over 1000 students from 16 states. Sampling was based on census reports from 1983–1984 considering geographic region, socioeconomic background, and ethnic group.

Reliability. Split-half reliability coefficients were determined for both subtest and composite scores. In general, these coefficients were greater than .90, with a few in the .80 range. The test-retest coefficients were computed in two separate studies. In the first study (grades 1–6), the coefficients ranged from .83 (Mathematics Computation) to .95 (Spelling). In the second study (grades 7–12) the coefficients ranged from .90 (Reading Comprehension) to .96 (Spelling). For both samples the battery composite yielded a .97 coefficient. Data correlating the Brief form with the Comprehensive form are also reported with the majority above .80.

Validity. The authors detail the steps followed in ensuring the content validity of the test (for example, item selection) and provide empirical support. They also present data supporting construct validity. Concurrent validity was established by reporting correlational data with the Wide Range Achievement Test and Peabody Individual Achievement Test, The Kaufman Assessment Battery for Children, the Peabody Picture Vocabulary Test–Revised, and a number of group achievement tests. More data using more appropriate criterion measures are necessary.

Review of relevant research

Interestingly, relatively little research related to the K-TEA has appeared in the professional literature. One study indicated that the K-TEA yielded scores that were 5–9 points higher than the popular Wide Range Achievement Test–Revised (WRAT-R) (Webster, Hewett, & Crumbacker, 1989). In another, McGehee (1986) found some overlap in the subtests in a group of underachieving students. The K-TEA has received several favorable reviews, however. Henson and Bennett (1986) noted that it is easy to administer, has a well-written manual, and has a good empirical and normative base. Similarly, Worthington (1987) agreed that the K-TEA had good technical characteristics and allowed the maximum analysis of an individual's academic strengths and weaknesses. Miller (1990) noted that the K-TEA should not be used for academically delayed first-grade students but that the instrument had unique features and good psychometric properties that allowed its use for students of other ages. Sattler (1989b) also noted that the K-TEA had good norms and technical characteristics.

OVERVIEW: KAUFMAN TEST OF EDUCATIONAL ACHIEVEMENT

- *Age level*—6–18 years old (grades 1–12)
- *Type of administration*—Individual
- *Technical characteristics*—Good reliability, acceptable validity
- *Scores yielded*—Standard scores, percentile ranks, age and grade equivalents, stanines, error analysis guidelines
- *Suggested use*—The K-TEA is a technically sound, well-constructed general achievement test. It is relatively easy to administer and score. For

the most part, the K-TEA measures achievement in a similar fashion to classroom demands (for example, written spelling and math computation). The error analysis guidelines are a helpful addition and should serve as a constant reminder of the importance of error analysis on any norm-referenced test. In summary, the K-TEA has the potential to be one of the better, if not the best, general achievement tests. More research on the instrument is needed before more definitive statements can be made. The limited data indicate that the test might yield slightly elevated scores compared to other tests.

Peabody Individual Achievement Test—Revised

The Peabody Individual Achievement Test—Revised (PIAT-R) (Dunn & Markwardt, 1988) is designed for use with students from kindergarten through grade 12. The PIAT-R retained many of the features from the original PIAT including quick administration and scoring, use of demonstration and training exercises, and the use of easels for test administration. It also retained the format of the PIAT that includes a visual, multiple-choice stimulus that requires a verbal or motor (pointing) response for the Spelling, Mathematics, and Reading Comprehension subtests. This format makes the test attractive to use with individuals with speech or motor problems because of the optional response requirements. The PIAT-R consists of five subtests: General Information, Reading Recognition, Reading Comprehension, Mathematics, and Spelling as well as an optional subtest of Written Expression. The five subtests were retained from the original PIAT although the item content was updated and approximately 20 percent of the items are new. The Written Expression subtest is a new addition.

Description

General Information (100 items)—This is the only subtest that is given entirely verbally and requires only a verbal response. Questions are asked on subjects ranging from science and social studies to fine arts and sports.

Reading Recognition (100 items)—This subtest includes items ranging from matching letters of the alphabet to orally reading words of increasing difficulty.

Reading Comprehension (82 items)—This subtest requires the student to silently read a sentence on one page and then to choose which one of four pictures presented on another page best represents the meaning of the sentence.

Mathematics (100 items)—This subtest includes items ranging from matching and recognizing numbers to solving geometry and trigonometry problems (where the student must indicate which of four choices is the correct answer).

Spelling (100 items)—This subtest includes items that require the identification of a letter that is presented with three other objects, items that require the identification of one specific letter or word from four choices, and items that require the correct spelling of a word from four choices.

Written Expression (optional)—This subtest has two levels. Level I, designed for kindergarten through grade 2, requires the student to copy letters and words, write his or her name, and write letters and words from dictation. Level II requires the student to write a story about one of two pictures. The story is scored according to criteria such as sentence construction and the use of metaphors.

Interpretation of results

Raw scores from the PIAT-R can be transformed into a variety of derived scores. Standard scores (mean = 100, standard deviation = 15), percentile ranks, grade equivalents, stanines, normal curve equivalents, and age equivalents are available for each of the five subtests. Total Score (combination of the five subtests) and Total Reading (combination of Reading Recognition and Reading Comprehension) are also available. Scores from the optional subtest (Written Expression) are not included in the total score but rather are reported in terms of stanines within grades and developmental scaled scores. The optional subtest is also considerably more difficult to score.

Technical characteristics

Normative sample.   The PIAT-R used a stratified sample of over 1,500 students from kindergarten through grade 12. The stratification variables were geographic region, sex, socioeconomic status, and ethnic background. The sample was similar to the breakdown of census data, although there were some minor deviations for the earlier and later age groups.

Reliability.   Reliability coefficients were calculated for each subtest for each age group in the standardization sample. Split-half coefficients and internal consistency coefficients were good; the vast majority exceeded .90. Test-retest coefficients were somewhat lower, although approximately two thirds of the coefficients also exceeded .90. Coefficients for the Written Expression were calculated and reported separately. The internal consistency coefficients were considerably lower than those of the other five subtests. Interrater reliability was also calculated and found to be in the .50s.

Validity.   In general, validity data on the PIAT-R are lacking. The manual includes a discussion regarding its content validity, and criterion-related validity data are provided. The criterion measure used, however, is the Peabody Picture Vocabulary Test–Revised, a measure of receptive vocabulary only.

Review of relevant research

Surprisingly, very little research has appeared in the professional literature that investigates the PIAT-R. In one study, Robertson, Rengel, and Wang (1989) attempted to refine the Written Expression subtest by adding age-related weights to the scoring system, but found that it did not improve the instrument. Costenbader and Adams (1991) reviewed the PIAT-R and noted the low reliability of the Written Expression Subtest. They also cautioned against its use for ages 5 and 9 and grades 9 and 12 because of norming limitations. Interestingly, research on the original PIAT appears to be continuing, although it has decreased significantly in the past 10 years. In fact, most of the research on the PIAT was conducted in the 1970s. Below is a sampling of some of the findings on the PIAT. While the format of the PIAT and PIAT-R are similar, some caution should be taken in generalizing the research findings from one test to the other.

- The PIAT is not discriminatory against lower socioeconomic or minority-group children (Rodriguez, 1989).
- Validity coefficients between the PIAT and Woodcock Reading Mastery Tests decreased as the age of the subjects increased (Eaves, Darch, & Haynes, 1989).
- The PIAT is a good test to use with secondary-school learning-disabled students (Stoneburner & Brown, 1979) and intellectually advanced preschoolers (Shorr, Jackson, & Robinson, 1980).
- The reliability of the PIAT subtests with emotionally disturbed children is generally lower than the reliabilities reported in the manual (Dean, 1979).
- An alternate method of interpreting the scores has been suggested in which the standard score of a subtest is compared to the mean of the standard score of all the subtests. Statistical tables to facilitate this pattern analysis are available for the original PIAT (Naglieri & Kamphaus, 1981; Reynolds & Gutkin, 1980; Silverstein, 1981). It is anticipated that similar tables will be available for the PIAT-R.
- The overall PIAT has adequate validity with mentally retarded students (Burns, Peterson, & Bauer, 1974; Ysseldyke, Sabatino, & Lamanna, 1973). However, a more suitable reading-vocabulary measure should be substituted for Reading Comprehension, since that subtest and the Reading Recognition subtest measure the same thing in nonreaders (Baum, 1975; Burns, 1975). Also, the validity of the Spelling subtest with mentally retarded students is limited (Ysseldyke, Sabatino, & Lamanna, 1973).
- There is evidence that the PIAT measures two factors: a verbal comprehension and reasoning skills factor and an acquired practical knowledge factor (Reynolds, 1979b).
- The Mathematics subtest can and should be approached using a diagnostic-testing or error-analysis framework. An error-analysis matrix has been developed to facilitate this process (Algozzine & McGraw, 1980).

Summary of research findings

Due to the similarity in format, research on the PIAT might be generalized to the PIAT-R, although this should be done with some degree of caution. In general, there is some evidence that the PIAT can be used reliably with learning-disabled or gifted students, although its reliability with emotionally disturbed students has been questioned. The PIAT also has been found to be useful with mildly retarded students. Alternate interpretation models have been suggested by researchers. It is anticipated that research on the PIAT-R will be forthcoming.

OVERVIEW: PEABODY INDIVIDUAL ACHIEVEMENT TEST–REVISED

- *Age level*—Kindergarten through grade 12
- *Type of administration*—Individual
- *Technical adequacy*—Good standardization; limited validity; adequate reliability
- *Scores yielded*—Age and grade equivalents, percentile ranks, standard scores, stanines, normal curve equivalents
- *Suggested use*—The PIAT-R is a well standardized general achievement test designed for grades K-12. Its appropriateness with special-education students largely depends on the nature of the disability. In language- or motor-impaired individuals, it would be the more appropriate general-achievement test. On the other hand, its use with students with visual or visual-perceptual problems is limited. You must keep in mind the nature of the tasks presented on the PIAT-R. The mathematic and spelling subtests, in particular, measure different aspects of those skills than are measured in typical classroom activities. The addition of the written expression subtest may prove helpful, although Lazarus, McKenna, and Lynch (1990) noted that informal interpretation of the writing samples is probably the best procedure to follow.

Quick Score Achievement Test

The Quick-Score Achievement Test (Q-SAT) (Hammill, Ammer, Cronin, Mandlebaum, & Quinby, 1987) is a relatively new addition to the available general achievement tests. According to the authors, the Q-SAT can be used to determine relative strengths and weaknesses, to identify those individuals who are markedly deficient or superior in achievement, to obtain reevaluation data, and to provide information for research purposes. The Q-SAT can be used with individuals from age 7 through age 17 and takes between 30 minutes and 1 hour to administer. There are four subtests included in the Q-SAT: Writing, Arithmetic, Reading, and Facts. Because of the wide age range for which the test is intended, there are basal and ceiling rules as well as suggested starting points for each subtest. There are also two different forms, A and B.

Description of subtests

Writing (22 items)—In this subtest, the student is read a sentence and must write it correctly, including appropriate spelling, capitalization, and punctuation. The sentences increase in complexity from "he left" to "the campaign, of course, failed; and we began a long, hard retreat."

Arithmetic (40 items)—This subtest measures computation skills. The first two items are read to the student; the other 38 are presented on the test form.

Reading (40 items)—The student is asked to read a word list. The items range in difficulty from "go" to "sagacity." This subtest measures word identification only—there is no comprehension component.

Facts (20 items)—The student is asked a series of general information questions in the areas of science, social studies, humanities, health, and language arts. Examples include "the South Pole is located in which continent?" and "what is another word for cerebrum?"

Interpretation of results

Each of the four subtests yield standard scores (mean = 10; standard deviation = 3). There is also a General Achievement Quotient (GAQ) that can be determined by combining the subtests. The GAQ has a mean of 100 and a standard deviation of 15. All the scores can be plotted on a Q-SAT Profile Sheet.

Technical characteristics

Normative sample.   Sample consisted of 1,495 students from 15 states.

Reliability.   Test-retest, internal consistency and alternate form reliability were computed. The majority of the coefficients were above .80.

Validity.   Criterion-related validity was determined using three group achievement tests. The coefficients ranged from .24 to .66 with a median of .50. The authors also provide arguments for its content and construct validity.

Review of relevant research

Although no research on the Q-SAT was located, two reviews have appeared in the professional literature. Maddux (1989) noted that the instrument had adequate reliability (except for Facts) but little validity data. He also felt that it provided a narrow coverage of the curriculum areas it is intended to measure. Lazarus and Novoa (1987) cautioned against its use with children under 7 or underachievers under 9 years of age.

OVERVIEW: QUICK-SCORE ACHIEVEMENT TEST

- *Age level*—7–17 years old
- *Type of administration*—Individual
- *Technical adequacy*—Adequate reliability, limited validity
- *Scores yielded*—Standard scores, General Achievement Quotient
- *Suggested use*—Until more is known about the Q-SAT, it is best thought of as a screening test. It is easy to administer and score, although there is limited technical data, particularly related to validity. There is also some question about its appropriateness with younger students.

Wide Range Achievement Test–Revised

The WRAT-R (Jastak & Wilkinson, 1984) is an individually administered general achievement test that measures word recognition and pronunciation, written spelling, and arithmetic computation. The WRAT-R is a very popular, widely used instrument that takes a relatively short time to administer and score. The WRAT-R has two levels: Level I, designed for children aged 5–12; and Level II, designed for individuals from age 12 through adulthood (norms extend to age 74). The authors state that the WRAT-R can be used to "measure the codes which are needed to learn the basic skills of reading, spelling, and arithmetic" (p. 1). They also state that the test can be used in conjunction with an intelligence test with the same mean and standard deviation to determine the presence of a learning disability.

Description

LEVEL I

Spelling (45 items)—This section requires the child to spell dictated words that range in complexity from *go, cat,* and *in* to *prejudice, belligerent,* and *occurrence.* This part of the test is discontinued when and if the person misspells 10 consecutive words. If fewer than 6 successes are obtained, the prespelling section is administered. This includes the copying of geometric symbols and the printing or writing of the person's name.

Reading (75 items)—This section includes words that are read aloud by the person taking the test. The words range in difficulty from *cat, see, read,* and *to* to *idiosyncracy, itinerary, pseudonym,* and *aborigine.* This test is discontinued after 12 consecutive failures. If errors occur on the first line of words (first 11 items), the prereading section is administered. This includes the identification and naming of letters of the alphabet and a visual matching component.

Arithmetic (44 items)—This section includes computation problems that are printed on the test form. The child is given 10 minutes to complete the problems. If fewer than 5 problems are answered correctly, the prearithmetic part, which includes counting, reading digits, understanding numerical concepts, and orally adding and subtracting, is administered.

LEVEL II

Spelling (46 items)—This section includes words given in oral dictation. The words range in difficulty from *cat, run,* and *arm* to *acquiesce, charlatan,* and *pusillanimous.* A person who scores 4 or less on the dictation part would also take the prespelling section.

Reading (74 items)—This section includes words ranging in difficulty from *milk, city,* and *tree* to *egregious, heinous, internecine,* and *synecdoche.* If a person reads only 10 or fewer words, the prereading section is given.

Arithmetic (56 items)—This section includes written computation problems. The prearithmetic or oral section is given if fewer than 5 problems are answered correctly.

Interpretation of results

Scores from the WRAT-R can be transformed into grade equivalents, percentiles, and standard scores. The grade equivalents are printed on the test form and give a rough idea of the individual's grade level in reading, arithmetic, and spelling. The authors warn users of the WRAT-R that the grade equivalent is not a statistical score. The authors, in fact, only provide an indication of whether a student scores at the beginning, middle, or end of a certain grade rather than giving precise information (for example, the 3.2 grade level). Thus the scores cannot be compared to give an indication of how many months improvement a student supposedly has made. Grade equivalents do not take into consideration instructional differences, school expectations, or the age of the person taking the test. The authors suggest that the standard scores (mean = 100; standard deviation = 15) are the most appropriate score to use for comparison purposes.

Technical characteristics

Normative sample.   The sample included 200 individuals from each of 28 age groups (5,600) were included. The sample was stratified according to age, sex, geographic region, race, and type of community.

Reliability.   Test-retest coefficients ranged from .94 to .97 for Level I and .79 to .90 for Level 2. Internal reliability coefficients in the .90s for most age groups were reported.

Validity.   Authors provide arguments for the test's content and construct validity. Validity data from previous editions are summarized as well.

Review of relevant research

Most of the information found in the professional literature focuses on previous editions of the test. The format of and items on the WRAT have remained essentially the same through several editions. The norms, however, have been updated in each edition. The WRAT-R has some minor changes from the previous edition. Those are summarized by Reinehr (1984):

1. New recording forms with larger print and more space
2. New and improved norms
3. New method of calculating grade equivalents
4. Minor item changes in math
5. Extension of norms to age 75

Reinehr further stated that the results of previous studies should be applicable to the WRAT-R. Some of that research is noted below.

- The same edition of the WRAT should not be used in test-retest situations, an opinion based on a comparison of the norms of the 1976 and 1978 editions (Silverstein, 1980) and of the 1965 and 1978 editions (Sattler & Feldman, 1981).
- The WRAT is a valid instrument to use with a visually handicapped population (Alford, Moore, & Simon, 1980).
- The WRAT does not accurately identify young underachievers and should be used with caution as a screening or diagnostic device with this population (Grossman, 1981).
- Moderate to high correlations have been reported between scores on the PIAT and WRAT with learning-disabled (LD) students. The PIAT, however, yields significantly higher math scores for older LD students (approximately fourth grade and up). This difference is presumably due to the written worksheet format of the WRAT (Harmer & Williams, 1978; Scull & Brand, 1980).
- The WRAT and the PIAT should not be used interchangeably for educable mentally retarded (EMR) or LD students. Significant differences were noted for both elementary and secondary students (Lindsey & Armstrong, 1984)
- The 1976 and 1978 editions yielded significant differences in the spelling and reading grade equivalents for LD students. The two editions had no significant differences in standard scores, suggesting their use as derived scores in preference to grade equivalents (Breen & Prasse, 1980).
- Test-retest reliabilities with emotionally disturbed and slow-learning children are generally high (.87 to .98) (Woodward, Santa-Barbara, & Roberts, 1975).
- The norms on the WRAT tend to underestimate the true achievement level of individuals (Silverstein, 1978). This finding was based on a large national representative sample.
- The WRAT does meet the minimum reliability and validity requirements with Mexican-American children (Mishra, 1981).

Summary of research findings

Although most available information focuses on the earlier editions, a few studies have investigated the WRAT-R. In one study, Smith and Smith (1986) noted that the correlations between the WRAT-R and the Wechsler Intelligence Scale for Children—Revised (WISC-R) were similar to those of the WRAT and the WISC-R. Also, Spruill and Beck (1986) found that the WRAT-R standard scores were significantly lower than the WRAT standard scores (8–11 points). This information is consistent with the previous findings that the various editions of the WRAT should not be considered interchangeable. The appropriateness of the WRAT-R with lower socioeconomic and minority children has also been reported (Rodriguez, 1989).

The majority of the literature on the WRAT has focused on its relationship with the PIAT. This research indicates high correlations but significant differences between scores from the two tests. Since both of these tests have been revised, there is a need for new research that compares these instruments.

OVERVIEW: WIDE RANGE ACHIEVEMENT TEST–REVISED

- *Age level*—5 to 74 years old
- *Type of administration*—Individual
- *Technical adequacy*—Acceptable reliability, questionable validity
- *Scores yielded*—Standard scores, percentiles, grade equivalents
- *Suggested use*—The WRAT-R is a quick and easily administered achievement test. This is perhaps the primary advantage of the test. The weaknesses of the WRAT-R are numerous. It has been criticized for its lack of a reading-comprehension component, although the authors stated that they intentionally designed the test to eliminate the effects of comprehension. Overall, the lack of validity has been a common criticism. There is also some evidence that earlier editions of the WRAT are not appropriate to use with younger children; previous research has indicated that it provides inflated scores for children approximately 5–7 years old. In reviewing the WRAT-R, Reid (1986) and Reynolds (1986) both agreed that the WRAT-R is not a substantial improvement over previous editions and that there are more appropriate achievement tests available.

  In summary, the WRAT-R should be used for screening purposes only to identify individuals who need more in-depth testing. An analysis of the types of errors might be helpful.

Woodcock-Johnson–Revised (Achievement)

A general description of the Woodcock-Johnson–Revised (WJ-R) (Woodcock and Johnson, 1989) can be found in Chapter 8 in the section that focuses on the cognitive battery. This discussion will address the achievement battery of the WJ-R. There are two forms for the achievement tests (A and B). For both the achievement and cognitive tests there are "standard" and "supplemental" batteries. There are nine tests in the standard achievement battery and five tests in the supplemental achievement battery.

Description

STANDARD ACHIEVEMENT BATTERY

Letter Word Identification (57 items)—This measures the individual's skill in identifying isolated letters and words.

Passage Comprehension (43 items)—This uses a modified cloze procedure to evaluate a person's comprehension and vocabulary skills.

Calculation (58 items)—This uses a traditional format in which problems of varying difficulty are presented in the subject's response booklet.

Applied Problems (60 items)—This requires the subject to solve and analyze practical mathematical problems. This subtest requires decision-making regarding the most appropriate mathematical operations to use.

Dictation (56 items)—This requires the subject to provide written responses to a variety of questions measuring spelling, punctuation, capitalization, and so on.

Writing Samples (30 items)—The subject is required to provide written sentences that are evaluated as to the quality of expression.

Science (49 items)—The subject orally responds to questions regarding the biological and physical sciences.

Social Studies (49 items)—This requires oral responses to questions related to history, geography, government, and economics.

Humanities (45 items)—The subject answers questions about art, music, and literature.

SUPPLEMENTAL ACHIEVEMENT BATTERY

Word Attack (30 items)—This measures the individual's ability to apply phonic and instructional analysis skills using nonsense words.

Reading Vocabulary (69 items)—This measures the individual's knowledge of both synonyms and antonyms.

Quantitative Concepts (48 items)—This measures mathematical concepts and vocabulary but does not require calculation or application decisions.

Proofing (36 items)—This requires the subject to identify a mistake in a typewritten passage and indicate how it should be corrected. The mistakes might be incorrect punctuation or capitalization, inappropriate word usage, or misspelling.

Writing Fluency (43 items)—This timed subtest measures the individual's ability to formulate and write simple sentences quickly.

NOTE: There are four other measures (Punctuation and Capitalization, Spelling, Usage, and Handwriting) that can be obtained through the administration of Dictation and Writing Samples from the Standard Battery and Proofing from the Supplemental Battery.

Interpretation of results

For all tests but Writing Samples, each item is scored either 0 or 1. (Writing Samples is scored 0, 1, or 2.) Through a series of transformations, the raw scores can be converted to percentile ranks or standard scores (mean = 100; standard deviation = 15). The WJ-R also provides a Relative Mastery Index (RMI), a score that is presented as a fraction with a constant denominator of 90. This score indicates the percentage of material that the examinee has mastered that a reference group (by either age or grade) has mastered at 90%. For example, if a 10 year, 6-month-old boy received a RMI of 62/90 in calculation, it would indicate that he has mastered 62% of the content in that area compared to 90% for the average child of the same age. All of these scores (standard scores, percentile ranks, RMIs) are also available for "standard battery clusters" of broad reading, broad mathematics, broad written language, broad knowledge, and skills.

Technical characteristics
Normative sample.   See description of WJ-R–Cognitive in Chapter 8.

Reliability.   For the standard battery, the median internal consistency coefficients ranged from .87 to .93 for the individual tests. The knowledge tests had slightly lower coefficients, as did the supplemental tests (ranging from .76 to .93). For the cluster scores, the median coefficients ranged from .94 to .96 for the Standard Battery and .91 to .96 for the Supplemental.

Validity.   According to the authors, content validity was maximized through careful item design that closely parallels the academic demands of the classroom (i.e., open-ended or open response as opposed to multiple choice). The concurrent validity was determined through a series of studies conducted at three different age groups: 3, 9, and 17. In general, the sample sizes for the studies were small, ranging from approximately 50 to 70. At the three-year level the Knowledge cluster and Skills cluster were correlated with a variety of criterion measures with correlations ranging from .29 to .72 for the Knowledge cluster and .10 to .63 for the Skills cluster. The majority of the coefficients were in the .50s and .60s. For the 9-year-old group, correlations for the Broad Reading, Broad Math, Broad Written Language, and Knowledge clusters were generally in the .60s to .80s range. The correlations for the 17-year-old group were appreciably smaller, particularly in the area of reading. The author also provides evidence of the construct validity of the achievement battery through tables showing the intercorrelation of the various tests at different age levels.

Review of relevant research

There has been little research on the achievement battery of the WJ-R. Mather (1989) found that the writing tests on the WJ-R had relatively high correlation coefficients with other standardized writing tests such as the Test of Written Language. Also, Taylor (1990), in a review of the achievement battery, noted the favorable addition of the writing tests to the WJ-R.

OVERVIEW: WOODCOCK-JOHNSON–REVISED (ACHIEVEMENT)

- *Age level*—2 years–adult
- *Type of administration*—Individual
- *Technical adequacy*—Good standardization, adequate reliability and validity
- *Scores yielded*—Standard scores, percentile ranks, relative mastery index (age and grade equivalents also available)
- *Suggested use*—The WJ-R–Achievement Battery is a comprehensive, wide-range set of tests that measure a variety of areas. The WJ-R is a substantially different instrument from the original WJ. Users of the WJ-R should *not* consider the two instruments interchangeable. In addition, users should make note of the administration differences related to the basal and ceiling items.

There are several changes and improvements in the WJ-R that are worthy of mention . First, there are more tests available with the inclusion of standard and supplemental batteries. This also means that additional planning must be done to determine which tests to administer to an individual. A second change is a much-welcomed addition of actual writing samples to the Written Language cluster. The lack of such a measure on the original WJ was noteworthy.

Another improvement in the WJ-R is the slightly easier scoring procedures, although a number of tables must still be used, thus increasing the possibilities of errors. Clearly, if possible, the computerized scoring program (Compuscore) should be used. In addition, an Early Development Scale (six subtests) can be used for preschool testing programs in light of P.L. 99-457. If both the achievement and cognitive batteries are administered, it is possible to calculate aptitude and achievement discrepancies in the areas of Oral Language, Reading, Mathematics, Written Language, and Knowledge.

CRITERION-REFERENCED INSTRUMENTS

WHY USE?
  Establishment of IEP goals and objectives, monitoring educational progress

WHO SHOULD USE?
  Teachers

Inventories and criterion-referenced tests that measure academic skills are crucial tools for both pre- and postreferral assessment, particularly for mildly handicapped students. Frequently, the use of these instruments (in conjunction with informal techniques) is all that is necessary to evaluate students. Even if a student goes through the formal assessment process, these instruments, typically, are the ones that yield the most functional educational data for instructional purposes. Information from these instruments, for instance, is extremely helpful in developing IEPs. These instruments, usually described as *multicomponent,* are also very comprehensive, so that only selected portions are administered.

Multicomponent Instruments

The Brigance Inventories

Over approximately the last 15 years, a number of inventories developed by Albert Brigance and published by Curriculum Associates have received widespread attention. These Inventories consist of lists of skill sequences that cover a large number of areas. For each skill sequence an objective is provided (Figure 12-6) that can be used for an IEP or as an informal teaching objective. There is, in fact, a computer program available for the Brigance Inventories called the *Talley Goals and Objectives Writer* (Talley, 1985).

   Appropriate use of the Brigance Inventories requires that the teacher/test administrator carefully select those skill sequences that are relevant for a given student. Under no circumstances should any Inventory be given in its entirety. Many people unfortunately have assumed that "since this is a test, I'll administer it." This has led to criticism of the Inventories because of inappropriate use. In reality, the Inventories are not really tests in a literal sense. Robinson and Kovacevich (1984), in reviewing the Brigance Inventories, noted that they could best be described as "an item pool waiting for a test to happen." They go on to say that if the user realizes the Inventories' intentions and limitations, important information can be gathered.

NUMBER OF SYLLABLES AUDITORILY

SKILL: Can tell the number of syllables in a word auditorily.

> **DIRECTIONS:** Pronounce the words in the lists below, one at a time. Pause for the student to indicate the number of syllables.
>
> **Say:** *I'm going to say some words. Listen carefully and tell me how many syllables you hear in each word.*
>
> #### List for Testing One-Syllable Words
>
> 1. *ring* (1)   3. *tested* (2)   5. *must* (1)
> 2. *sounded* (2)   4. *sand* (1)   6. *inform* (2)
>
> #### List for Testing Two-Syllable Words
>
> 1. *refund* (2)   3. *understand* (3)   5. *pretend* (2)
> 2. *shown* (1)   4. *friendly* (2)   6. *referring* (3)
>
> #### List for Testing Three-Syllable Words
>
> 1. *understanding* (4)   3. *innocent* (3)   5. *volcano* (3)
> 2. *labor* (2)   4. *comprehend* (3)   6. *public* (2)

OBJECTIVE: When a word is pronounced by the examiner, the student will verbally indicate the number of syllables the word contains with 100% accuracy for ———— (quantity) syllable words.

DISCONTINUE: If the student does not respond correctly to the three words being tested on any list. Disregard incorrect responses on other words in the lists.

TIME: 10 seconds per response.

ACCURACY: 3/3 for each list. In each list, the student must respond correctly only for the words containing the number of syllables being tested in that list. Disregard incorrect responses on other words. For example, in the first list, score only for correct responses on the words *ring, sand,* and *must.*

FIGURE 12-6 Example of an Objective Provided by the Brigance Inventories.

From A. Brigance, *BRIGANCE® Inventory of Basic Skills.* Copyright © 1977 by Curriculum Associates, Inc. Reprinted with permission. BRIGANCE® is a registered trademark of Curriculum Associates, Inc.

    The Brigance Inventories are often referred to by their color rather than their name. These are yellow (Inventory of Early Development–Revised—discussed in Chapter 15)—blue (Inventory of Basic Skills), green (Comprehensive Inventory of Basic Skills), and red (Inventory of Essential Skills).

Brigance Inventory of Basic Skills (Blue)

The Brigance Inventory of Basic Skills (Brigance, 1977) is a comprehensive instrument that measures basic readiness skills as well as academic skills through grade six. The Inventory specifically measures four major content areas: Readiness; Reading; Language Arts; and Mathematics. The inventory is primarily used to establish educational objectives and monitor progress toward these objectives. The format of the test allows the easy identification of behavioral objectives associated with the various items. The Brigance Inventory of Basic Skills is one of a group of four inventories designed for use with children from birth through grade 12.

Description.   The four content areas of this test include 141 skill sequences. These skill sequences are essentially identifiable abilities for which sequential test items are available. For example, the skill sequence "gross-motor coordination" includes "walks line," "jumps on both feet," "hops on right foot," "hops on left foot," and "steps." The examiner chooses the skill sequences to be administered.

> *Readiness*—This content area includes 24 skill sequences, among them, color recognition; body image; verbal directions; alphabet; and recognition of lowercase and uppercase letters.
>
> *Reading*—This content area is further broken down into four components: word recognition (6 skill sequences); reading (including comprehension level and oral reading level); word analysis (19 skill sequences); and vocabulary (5 skill sequences).
>
> *Language Arts*—This content area is also divided into four components: handwriting (3 skill sequences); grammar mechanics (3 skill sequences); spelling (5 skill sequences); and reference skills (9 skill sequences).
>
> *Mathematics*—This content area is divided into five components: estimated grade level; numbers; operations; measurement (including money, time, calendar, and liquid measurement); and geometry. In all, it includes 64 skill sequences.

Interpretation of results.   As previously mentioned, the primary reason for using the Inventory of Basic Skills is to identify appropriate objectives for a student. The Inventory is designed to facilitate this purpose. Each skill sequence is associated with a stated behavioral objective, so that objectives can be directly determined from a child's performance on the Inventory. Figure 12-7 shows an example of the suggested procedures in using this as well as the other Brigance Inventories.

OVERVIEW: BRIGANCE INVENTORY OF BASIC SKILLS

- *Age level*—Kindergarten–grade 6
- *Suggested use*—The Brigance Inventory of Basic Skills is used with children from kindergarten through grade 6. It covers the basic areas of readiness skills, reading, language arts, and math. It is quickly becoming (along with the other Brigance Inventories) one of the more popular multicomponent instruments. Many school systems have in fact adopted the Brigance as the primary instrument used in developing IEPs. The format of the test also allows for its use in monitoring progress within the various skill areas. The Inventory is comprehensive and is not designed to be used in its entirety; rather, the examiner must identify those areas in need of evaluation and instruction for each individual. This could be viewed as a disadvantage if the examiner is not familiar with the student. For this reason, the Brigance is usually administered by the teacher. It should also be noted that this Inventory, like all the Brigance Inventories, is somewhat cumbersome to administer.

Brigance Inventory of Essential Skills (Red)

The Brigance Inventory of Essential Skills (Brigance, 1981) is designed for use with students in grades 4–12. The Inventory basically measures those minimal competencies commonly accepted as important in lifetime experiences. As such, it is one of the few instruments that includes measures of functional academics at the secondary level. Like the Brigance Inventory of Basic Skills, this inventory is used primarily to establish and monitor educational or prevocational objectives.

Description. The Inventory of Essential Skills includes 26 content areas, with a total of 181 skill sequences. Ten informal rating scales are also included.

Word Recognition Grade Placement—This content area assesses the approximate grade level of the student's word-recognition ability.

Oral Reading—This content area includes 5 skill sequences that give the student's approximate grade level for oral-reading skills.

Reading Comprehension—This content area has 9 skill sequences that measure the student's grade level in reading comprehension.

Functional Word Recognition—This content area includes 6 skill sequences, for example, "basic sight vocabulary," "warning/safety signs," and "informational signs."

Word Analysis—This content area includes 9 skill sequences, for example, "common endings of rhyming words," "suffixes and prefixes," and "syllabication concepts."

MODEL OF FORMAT FOR AN ASSESSMENT PROCEDURE WITH A CHILD PAGE

1. **SKILL:** A general statement of the skill being assessed. When appropriate, the skill sequence in the *Developmental Record Book* is also listed.

2. **DEVELOPMENTAL AGE NOTATION:** The numbers preceding a sequence indicate the year and month the child usually begins to learn or master that skill. Those following indicate when mastery is usually accomplished. Example: for [4-7], read 4 years and 7 months developmental age.

   In addition, the developmental ages are explained or discussed in a separate note where necessary.

3. **DEVELOPMENTAL RECORD BOOK:** The page on which this skill is listed in the *Developmental Record Book*.

4. **ASSESSMENT METHODS:** The means recommended for assessing.

5. **MATERIALS:** Materials which are needed for the assessment.

6. **DISCONTINUE:** Indicates the number of items the child may fail before you discontinue the assessment of skills in this sequence.

7. **TIME:** Time limits suggested for the child's response.

8. **ACCURACY:** Explanation of scoring criteria.

9. **DIRECTIONS:** The recommended directions for assessing the skills sequence. Recommended phrasing of instructions or questions is clearly labeled, indented and printed in bold face type.

10. **OBJECTIVE:** The objective for the skills being assessed is stated, and is a valuable resource for developing individualized education programs (IEP's).

NOTES ON CHILD PAGE:

a. You have the publisher's permission to reproduce the child pages in the *Inventory* for non-profit educational purposes.

b. Some child pages have been designed for copying and cutting so you can present items individually.

c. Screen part of the page if the child finds a whole page visually confusing.

d. You may cover the child's page with acetate to prevent soiling and to make it possible to use an acetate marker.

e. All child pages are designated with a "C" preceding the number, which corresponds to the facing examiner page.

11. **REFERENCES:** the numbers listed correspond to the sources used to establish and validate the skill sequences and developmental ages. References are found in the *Bibliography* on page 246-7.

12. **NOTES:** Helpful notes on observations, resources or diagnosing are listed here.

13. Examiner's page number.

14. Skill assessed.

15. The first letter, "I," indicates the section, where all basic reading skills are located.

16. This number indicates the ninth of the skills sequenced in the basic reading section of the *Inventory*.

CHILD PAGE
(Oriented for the child facing the examiner.)

EXAMINER PAGE

FIGURE 12-7   Format for the Brigance Inventories.

From A. Brigance, *BRIGANCE® Inventory of Basic Skills.* Copyright © 1977 by Curriculum Associates. Reprinted with permission. BRIGANCE® is a registered trademark of Curriculum Associates, Inc.

Reference Skills—This content area includes 5 skill sequences, for example, "uses dictionary" and "uses library card catalogues."

Schedules and Graphs—The 3 skill sequences for this content area are "reads class schedule," "reads television schedules," and "identifies and interprets graphs."

Writing—This content area includes 7 skill sequences, for example, "writing manuscript and cursive letters," "capitalization," and "punctuation."

Forms—The 2 skill sequences for this content area are "school information form" and "computer-based form." These measure the individual's ability to correctly fill out blank forms.

Spelling—This content area includes 8 skill sequences, for example, "spelling number words," "days of the week," and "months of the year."

Math Grade Placement—This content area gives grade levels for computation and math comprehension.

Numbers—This content area has 4 skill sequences, including "writes numerals as dictated" and "rounds off numerals."

Number Facts—This content area measures a student's knowledge of addition, subtraction, multiplication, and division facts.

Computation of Whole Numbers—This content area has 6 skill sequences, including "subtraction of whole numbers," "division of whole numbers," and "computes averages."

Fractions—This content area includes 9 skill sequences related to the comprehension and computation of fractions.

Decimals—This content area includes 6 skill sequences related to the knowledge and understanding of decimals.

Percents—This content area includes 4 skill sequences that require conversion of fractions and decimals into percentages.

Measurement—This content area includes 15 skill sequences, for example, "conversion to units of time," "understanding of a calendar and a ruler," and "conversion to units of measurement."

Metrics—This content area includes 16 skill sequences measuring the understanding of and ability to apply the metric system.

Math Vocabulary—The 3 skill sequences of this content area are "basic mathematics vocabulary," "computational vocabulary," and "basic geometric shapes and concepts."

Health and Safety—This content area includes 4 skill sequences. Examples are "medical vocabulary," "medicine labels," and "warning labels." Two rating scales are also included: "health practices and attitude rating scale" and "self-concept scale."

Vocational—This content area includes 23 skill sequences, for example, "employment signs" and "simple application for employment." Five rating scales are also included, among them, "job-interview rating scale" and "attitude rating scale."

Money and Finance—This content area includes 11 skill sequences, for example, "banking and credit vocabulary," "computes interest on loans," and "comprehends monthly credit statement."

Travel and Transportation—This content area includes 9 skill sequences, for example, "application for driver's-instruction permit," "mileage table," and "road maps." A rating scale, "auto safety," is also included.

Food and Clothing—This content area includes 10 skill sequences, for example, "food preparation vocabulary," "quantity at the best price," and "clothing labels."

Oral Communication and Telephone Skills—This content area has 5 skill sequences, including "listening skills" and "telephone book." Two rating scales are also included: "speaking skills" and "listening skills."

Interpretation of results.   The Inventory of Essential Skills primarily yields information related to behavioral objectives, although grade-placement approximations are given in a number of areas. Results from the Inventory are often used in secondary-level special-education classrooms to identify and help develop prevocational and other survival skills necessary after high school.

The information from the 10 rating scales can be used to identify "specific traits, behavior attitudes and skills that may need to be changed or improved in order to help a student achieve optimal adjustment and success" (p. 373). These scales should be used with caution, since no validity data exist to support their use. They are, in fact, more similar to checklists than rating scales.

OVERVIEW: BRIGANCE INVENTORY OF ESSENTIAL SKILLS

- *Age level*—grades 4–12
- *Suggested use*—The Inventory of Essential Skills is designed for use with students in grades 4–12. The Inventory emphasizes minimal competencies and includes measures of "functional academics." This instrument is, in fact, one of the few that includes items for the secondary-level special-education student. It undoubtedly will become an increasingly popular instrument for IEP development for older students. Objectives from the Essential Skills Inventory also have been correlated with instructional materials from the Janus Company, although no research is available to support or refute their effectiveness. This test, like all Brigance Inventories, should not be administered in its entirety. Rather, the Skill sequences should be carefully chosen by the teacher or other examiner who is familiar with the student to be evaluated.

Brigance Comprehensive Inventory of Basic Skills (Green)

The Brigance Comprehensive Inventory of Basic Skills (Brigance, 1982) is the newest in the Brigance series and is designed for students from kindergarten through grade 9. This Inventory essentially includes skill sequences that are found on the Inventory of Basic Skills and the

Inventory of Essential Skills. In all, 22 content areas are measured, with 185 total skill sequences. Since the content areas of this Inventory have been described in the discussion of the two preceding instruments, a limited description follows.

Readiness (31 skill sequences)
Speech (5 skill sequences)
Word Recognition and Grade Placement (2 skill sequences)
Oral Reading (7 skill sequences)
Reading Comprehension (14 skill sequences)
Listening (6 skill sequences)
Functional Word Recognition (9 skill sequences)
Word Analysis (17 skill sequences)
Reference Skills (8 skill sequences)
Graphs and Maps (5 skill sequences)
Spelling (9 skill sequences)
Writing (9 skill sequences)
Math Grade Placement (2 skill sequences)
Numbers (4 skill sequences)
Number Facts (4 skill sequences)
Computation of Whole Numbers (6 skill sequences)
Fractions and Mixed Numbers (10 skill sequences)
Decimals (6 skill sequences)
Percents (4 skill sequences)
Measurement (18 skill sequences)
Metrics (7 skill sequences)
Mathematical Vocabulary (4 skill sequences)

Interpretation of results. This Inventory is scored in the same manner as the previously discussed Brigance Inventories.

OVERVIEW: BRIGANCE COMPREHENSIVE INVENTORY OF BASIC SKILLS

- *Age level*—Kindergarten–grade 9
- *Suggested use* —The Brigance Comprehensive Inventory of Basic Skills is essentially a combination of parts from the Inventory of Basic Skills and the Inventory of Essential Skills. The instrument covers skills usually taught from kindergarten through middle school. If you are interested in testing students in the late elementary or early secondary grades, this Inventory might be the one of choice, and it might give the continuity missing in the other two instruments. If you are interested in testing students in the early elementary or later secondary grades, the other Brigance Inventories would be more appropriate.

Multilevel Academic Survey Test–Curriculum Level

The Multilevel Academic Survey Test (MAST) (Howell, Zucker, & Morehead, 1985) actually comprises two different types of tests. The first, a *grade-level test,* is a norm-referenced measure of reading and mathematics designed for students from kindergarten to grade eight. The *curriculum-level test* is intended to complement the grade-level test by providing specific information regarding content/skill deficits. Used together, the two provide comparative and curricular information. Much of the information in the MAST evolved from the authors' previous assessment instrument, the Multilevel Academic Skills Inventory (MASI) described in Taylor (1984).

Description of content areas

Reading—This section includes eight levels of graded passages that are read aloud by the student to determine decoding skills. The comprehension part also involves graded passages that the student must read silently and then answer questions about. A series of passages that use the maze procedure are also included.

Mathematics—Included in this section are computation items related to whole numbers, fractions, decimals, ratios, and proportions, as well as a problem-solving test that uses a multiple-choice format.

Interpretation of results

The curriculum-level test from the MAST provides specific information for teaching purposes. There is a Decision/Activity analysis tree on the record form that indicates when a student needs additional testing, instruction, or progression into more difficult content areas.

OVERVIEW: MULTILEVEL ACADEMIC SURVEY TEST

- *Age level*—Kindergarten–grade 8
- *Suggested use*—The MAST is a comprehensive assessment instrument that provides both norm-referenced and criterion-referenced information. The curriculum-level test provides the more specific information for teaching purposes. The grade-level test, however, can be used initially to determine the appropriate starting point in the curriculum-level test. Issacson (1990), in a review of the instrument, felt that the MAST had many desirable features.

Mastery: An Evaluation Tool

Mastery: An Evaluation tool (Science Research Associates, 1980) is a series of criterion-referenced tests in mathematics and reading. The Mastery program is designed for students from kindergarten through grade 9. Objectives have been identified for both reading and mathematics.

Description

By grades, there are 175 math objectives for K–2; 352 mathematical objectives for 3–8; 162 reading objectives for K–2; and 140 reading objectives for 3–9. For each objective, three test items have been developed. For mastery of a specific objective, the criterion is correct answers to all three items. Two options are available for users: custom tests and catalog tests. Custom tests allow you to select the objectives to be measured. The catalog tests include preselected objectives that are most commonly taught at each grade level.

OVERVIEW: MASTERY: AN EVALUATION TOOL

- *Age level*—Kindergarten–grade 9
- *Suggested use*—Mastery: An Evaluation Tool includes criterion-referenced tests of reading and math objectives for curricula in kindergarten through grade 9. The system was designed more for monitoring and documenting progress than for specific educational programming. The custom tests are an attractive feature because they give the teacher or examiner some degree of latitude in determining the content of the test. The system is expensive, however, and its equivalent could be developed in a teacher-made test format. Mastery: An Evaluation Tool can be used with Diagnosis: An Instructional Aid (discussed in the next chapter) to give a comprehensive evaluation package.

| Instrument or Technique | Suggested Use | | | | | | | Target Population | | | | | | Special Considerations | Educational Relevance for Exceptional Students |
| | Prereferral | | | Postreferral | | | | | | | | | | | |
	Screening and Initial Identification	Informal Determination and Evaluation of Teaching Programs and Strategies	Determination of Current Performance Level and Educational Need	Decisions about Classification and Program Placement	IEP Goals	IEP Objectives	IEP Evaluation	Mild/Moderate	Severe/Profound	Preschool	Elementary Age	Secondary Age	Adult		
Group Achievement Tests	X							X			X	X		Stanford and Metropolitan have good technical characteristics; good for initial screening	adequate/useful
Basic Academic Skills Individual Screener	X							X			X	X		Should be used for screening only; writing section probably not helpful	adequate
Diagnostic Achievement Battery-2	X	X	X		X			X			X	X		Provides a profile of strengths and weaknesses; composite scores most useful	adequate
Diagnostic Achievement Test for Adolescents	X	X	X		X			X				X		The only achievement test designed specifically for adolescents	adequate
Kaufman Test of Educational Achievement	X	X	X		X			X			X	X		Good technical aspects; error analysis helpful; overall one of the better achievement tests	very useful
Peabody Individual Achievement Test–Revised	X	X	X		X			X			X	X		Adequate technical aspects; revised version has optional written subtest; unique format	useful
Quick-Score Achievement Test	X							X			X	X		Use for screening only; easy to administer and score	adequate
Wide Range Achievement Test–Revised	X	X	X		X					X	X	X	X	Results often overused; best used as a screening measure	adequate
Woodcock-Johnson–Revised (Achievement)	X	X	X		X			X		X	X	X	X	Part of WJ Battery that also includes a cognitive section	useful

Instrument or Technique	Suggested Use							Target Population						Special Considerations	Educational Relevance for Exceptional Students
	Preferral			Postreferral											
	Screening and Initial Identification	Informal Determination and Evaluation of Teaching Programs and Strategies	Determination of Current Performance Level and Educational Need	Decisions about Classification and Program Placement	IEP Goals	IEP Objectives	IEP Evaluation	Mild/Moderate	Severe/Profound	Preschool	Elementary Age	Secondary Age	Adult		
Brigance Inventory of Basic Skills		X	X		X	X	X	X			X			Includes objectives for each skill measured; used in IEP development	useful
Brigance Inventory of Essential Skills		X	X		X	X	X	X				X		Same as above	useful
Brigance Comprehensive Inventory of Basic Skills		X	X		X	X	X	X			X	X		Most appropriate for students in later elementary grades	useful
Multilevel Academic Survey Test	X	X	X		X	X	X	X			X			Includes both a grade level and curriculum level	useful
Mastery: An Evaluation Tool	X	X	X		X			X			X	X		Used for screening and monitoring progress	adequate

13

Assessment of Reading

INSTRUMENTS/PROCEDURES INCLUDED

INFORMAL PROCEDURES
- Diagnosis: An Instructional Aid
- Informal Reading Inventories
- Cloze and Maze Procedures
- Reading Diagnosis Sheet
- Portfolio Assessment

DIAGNOSTIC READING TESTS
- Gray Oral Reading Tests–Diagnostic
- Stanford Diagnostic Reading Test
- Test of Reading Comprehension
- Woodcock Reading Mastery Tests–Revised
- Durrell Analysis of Reading Difficulty
- Diagnostic Reading Scales

ORAL READING TESTS
- Gray Oral Reading Test–3
- Gilmore Oral Reading Test

Dexter is a 9-year-old boy in the third grade. His teacher has noted that he constantly falls behind on reading assignments, reads very slowly, often sounds out the words orally, and has difficulty remembering what he reads. Dexter was tested to determine which area or areas within the reading process were causing him difficulty.

One certainly cannot minimize the importance of reading to the overall success of the student during the school years. Reading virtually affects all areas of an individual's life. It certainly is not surprising that so much attention is paid to the assessment and subsequent remediation of reading. Reading involves the components of recognition, analysis, and comprehension. Ekwall and Shanker (1988) provided a cohesive framework for the components of reading and its subsequent evaluation or assessment. Figure 13-1 provides a schematic of that framework. Within this model the overall process of reading is broken down into two sub-areas: (1) recognition and analysis of words and (2) understanding words and ideas. This roughly is equivalent to word recognition and reading comprehension. Word recognition can further be broken down into sight word identification and word-analysis skills. Sight word identification involves the immediate identification of a word even though the individual might not understand its meaning. Word analysis skills are used when a reader does not instantly recognize the word and therefore must use a variety of word attack skills to attempt to read it. As noted in Figure 13-1, word attack involves the configuration or the shape of the word, context cues that a person receives from the way a word is used in the sentence, phonetic analysis, structural analysis (ability to derive meaning from word parts), and dictionary skills, such as alphabetizing and using guide words.

The other main area of reading involves the understanding of words and ideas. According to Ekwall and Shanker, this involves (1) vocabulary development or the understanding of the meaning of words and (2) other comprehension skills or the student's ability to make sense from written material. As noted, this involves such things as literal comprehension (e.g., understanding and remembering the facts presented in a passage) and inferential comprehension (e.g., the ability to understand what might happen next in a passage).

READING ASSESSMENT

As in most areas, the evaluation of the reading process can be done either informally or formally. Parker (1990) did note, however, that there is an increased need for the use of informal tests and teacher observation of reading behavior. Information from these sources can be combined with results from criterion-referenced or teacher-made tests to assist in reading diagnosis. One advantage of informal reading assessment is that it provides more of an opportunity to understand the *reading process* rather than simply to analyze the *reading product*. The areas of informal reading assessment that will be discussed in this chapter include criterion-referenced and informal reading inventories, other informal techniques such as the cloze procedure and the maze procedure, and a relatively recent approach called portfolio assessment. The reader is also referred to the information on error analysis presented in Chapter 6. That informal procedure is very helpful in determining instructional strategies.

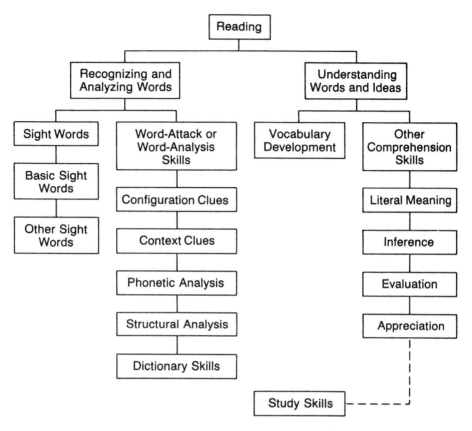

FIGURE 13-1   Components of the Reading Process.

From Eldon E. Ekwall and James L. Shanker, *Diagnosis and Remediation of the Disabled Reader* (3rd ed.) ©
1988 Allyn & Bacon. Reprinted with permission.

Those instruments that are considered more formal tests are usually
called diagnostic reading tests, although the term diagnostic is in a sense
a misnomer. The reasons for administering the test is not to diagnose a
problem in a traditional sense but to gather specific information about
where a problem might exist and how to remediate it. Many of these
diagnostic academic tests actually magnify a particular area to determine
an individual's strengths and weaknesses. In other words, although these
tests are norm-referenced, their primary objective is frequently to obtain
important information for remediation and not to compare the student's
performance to others. Most diagnostic reading tests measure such areas
as oral reading recognition, reading rate, comprehension, word attack
skills, and vocabulary, although not all tests measure all of these areas.

Another type of formal test is the oral reading test. These instruments provide documentation of the child's overall reading ability consid-

ering such areas as speed and accuracy. Some also include measures of comprehension areas.

INFORMAL ASSESSMENT PROCEDURES

WHY USE?
Identification of areas for further evaluation or remediation; informal determination of objectives and teaching strategies; development and evaluation of IEPs

WHO SHOULD USE?
Teachers

Diagnosis: An Instructional Aid in Reading

Diagnosis: An Instructional Aid in Reading (Shub, Carlin, Friedman, Kaplan, & Katien, 1973) is a comprehensive reading skills program for students in grades 1–6. The system is composed of three components: Survey Tests, Probes, and Prescription Guides. The Survey Tests measure general strengths and weaknesses and act as a screening instrument. Alternative forms are available for posttesting. The Probes are a series of specific criterion-referenced measures designed to identify specific learning objectives. In the Prescription Guides, materials for remediation (from workbooks, textbooks, and other resources) are correlated with each learning objective. The program has two levels: A and B.

Description

Level A—This level is designed for students in grades 1–4. It covers phonetic analysis, comprehension, vocabulary, and uses of sources (for example, dictionary use).

Level B—This level is designed for students in grades 3–6. It covers phonetic analysis, structural analysis, comprehension, vocabulary, and study skills.

Interpretation of results
This instrument yields instructional objectives and suggested curriculum materials.

OVERVIEW: DIAGNOSIS: AN INSTRUCTIONAL AID IN READING

- *Age level:* Grades 1–6.
- *Suggested use:* Diagnosis: An Instructional Aid in Reading is a comprehensive assessment package that includes screening, in-depth testing, and specific suggestions for remediation

---

Informal Reading Inventories

Informal reading inventories (IRIs), like many other informal assessment procedures, are sometimes developed and sold commercially. When a teacher or other test user develops an IRI, it is usually necessary to select representative passages from various levels of a student's reading program and generate comprehension questions related to those passages. Newcomer (1985) found, however, that teachers frequently had difficulty selecting representative passages, partly as a function of variations of reading levels within the same text. She also noted that teachers often have problems formulating the comprehension questions. As a result, commercially-prepared IRIs are relatively popular.

Although IRIs differ from one another in format and content, most contain graded reading passages that yield a measure of word-recognition and comprehension skills. Most commercially prepared IRIs construct the reading passages from existing word lists. Among the more popular commercially prepared IRIs are the Analytical Reading Inventory (Woods & Moe, 1989), the Basic Reading Inventory (Johns, 1988), the Classroom Reading Inventory (Silvaroli, 1989), the Informal Reading Inventory (Burns & Roe, 1989), and the Ekwall Reading Inventory (Ekwall, 1986). Table 13-1 shows a comparison of four of these IRIs. The term *graded* refers to the approximate grade level associated with the passages. Typically, three levels of reading are determined from an IRI. The *independent* level is identified as the level at which the student can read alone without any help from another person. The *instructional* level is the teaching level where the student can read relatively comfortably but finds it challenging. The *frustration* level is the level at which the student finds the material difficult and frustrating. In some IRIs, the *listening comprehension* level is also determined. That is the level at which the student can comfortably understand material that is read to him. As in criterion-referenced tests, criteria are established that indicate how much of the material the student must read correctly (oral reading) and understand (comprehension) to be placed at the various reading levels. Although the criteria for these reading levels vary for different IRIs, there is at least some agreement on some general guidelines. The most widely accepted criteria for reading levels are those proposed by Betts (1946). He indicated that recognition of 99, 95, and 90 percent of the words at a specific grade level corresponds to the independent, instructional, and frustration levels. The criteria for *comprehension* for the three levels were 90, 75, and 50 percent, respectively. Several critics, such as Powell (1972) and Spache (1964), however, argued that these levels were too stringent.

Several researchers have compared the strengths and weaknesses of various IRIs and noted certain limitations. Elliott and Piersel (1982), for example, stated that IRIs are not constructed very rigorously and are more prone to measurement error than standardized reading tests. In addition, the usefulness of the comprehension measures have been questioned (Dufflemeyer, Robinson & Squiers, 1989), particularly related to main ideas (Dufflemeyer and Dufflemeyer, 1989).

Newcomer (1985) also noted that there is a general lack of reliability and validity data for most IRIs and that different IRIs do not necessarily yield similar results when administered to the same student. She found, in fact, that in more than 50 percent of the students tested, the two tests (Classroom Reading Inventory and Ekwall Reading Inventory) identified different instructional levels. In a comparison of the Analytic Reading Inventory (ARI), Basic Reading Inventory (BRI), Classroom Reading Inventory (CRI) and Informal Reading Inventory (IRI), Pikulski (1990) made the following recommendations:

ARI—Use when longer passages are preferred to sample reading ability
BRI—Use when information about use and interpretation of IRIs is desired
CRI—Use when quick, less complete evaluation is preferred
IRI—Use for older students (forms available above ninth grade)

Other Informal Techniques

A number of other informal techniques are available. Examples are the *cloze* and the *maze* procedures, the *Reading Diagnosis Sheet,* and *portfolio assessment.*

Cloze procedure

The cloze procedure consists of a reading passage (usually 250–300 words) in which certain words are deleted (usually every fifth or tenth). This "fixed ratio" approach of choosing the deleted words has been criticized, although Jonz (1990) found that such an approach was not erratic in choosing deleted words with similar linguistic and content characteristics.

In the cloze procedure, the student must read the passage and provide the missing words by analyzing the content and its structure. This procedure measures the reader's ability to interpret written pas-

Inventory	Grade levels	Forms of Inventory	Length of passages	Source of passages	Use of pictures	Use of purpose setting questions	Number of comprehension questions per passage	Types of comprehension questions	Criteria for Instructional level	Time needed for administration
Analytic Reading Inventory (ARI)	Primer to 9th, 1st-9th for science and social studies	3 equivalent narrative forms; 1 social studies and 1 science form	varies: 50-352	Written for inventory. Some science and social studies passages from textbooks	No	Discourages discussion before reading, but allows examiner discretion	6 for levels primer-2nd; 8 for levels 3rd-9th	main idea factual terminology cause and effect inferential conclusion	95% for word recognition; 75% comprehension	not stated
Basic Reading Inventory (BRI)	Preprimer to 8th	3 Forms; A for oral, B for silent, C as needed	50 words at preprimer; 100 words primer to 8th grade	Revised from earlier editions; original source not stated	No	Uses prediction from titles	10 for all levels	main idea fact inference evaluation vocabulary	95% for word recognition (only "significant" miscues counted); 75% comprehension	not stated
Classroom Reading Inventory (CRI)	Preprimer to 8th	4 forms in all; A & B for students in grades 1-6; C for junior high students; D for high school and adults	Varies; 24 words to 157 words	Written for inventory based on readability	Yes	Yes	5 for all levels	factual inferential vocabulary	95% for word recognition; 75% comprehension	12 minutes
Informal Reading Inventory by Burns & Roe (IRI-BR)	Preprimer to 12th	4 forms; all interchangeable	Varies; 60 words to 220 words	Primarily from graded materials in basal readers & literature books	No	Yes	8 for all levels	main idea detail inference sequence cause/effect vocabulary	85% word recognition for grades 1 & 2; 95% word recognition for grades 3 & above; 75% comprehension	40-50 minutes

TABLE 13-1 A Comparison of Four Commonly Used Informal Reading Inventories.

From J. Pikulski, Informal Reading Inventories. *Reading Teacher, 43,* 515. © 1990 by The Reading Teacher. Reprinted with permission.

sages and it requires the student to use both comprehension skills and knowledge of linguistic structure. The percentage of correct responses can be determined and can serve as a rough indication of the reading level of the student.

Rankin and Culhane (1969), for example, developed criterion levels for the cloze procedure. They suggested, for instance, that the instructional reading level was the level at which a student could correctly replace 41 percent to 61 percent of the missing words. For a student who read a cloze passage from a third-grade text and correctly replaced 50 percent of the words, the instructional reading level would be the third grade, according to this criteria. If, however, the student correctly replaced only 30 percent of the words, an easier passage would be needed to establish the reading level. Figure 13-2 gives an example of a cloze passage. In this example, the student correctly replaced approximately 45 percent of the words (16 out of 36).

The cloze procedure can also be used to evaluate spelling. For example, the student might be given a series of sentences such as "I hope mother doesn't b——n the food" and asked to supply the missing letters. Obviously the child's reading ability might also affect the results.

Maze procedure

Another technique used to measure a student's reading comprehension and knowledge of linguistic structure is the maze procedure. This procedure is similar to the cloze method, except that vertically presented choices are given instead of blanks. The following sentence is an example of the maze procedure:

store
On Tuesday, John went to the corn
on

Both the cloze and the maze procedures are examples of informal adaptations of curriculum materials into assessment devices. As with the criterion-referenced tests previously discussed, however, it is necessary for the teacher to establish criteria that reflect not only the curriculum and objectives for their students, but also the learning abilities of these students. The criteria that others have established as standards may be too strict or too lenient. Pikulski and Pikulski (1977) found, for instance, that in a study of regular fifth graders, the maze and cloze scores were higher than teachers' judgments of the students' reading abilities.

Reading diagnosis sheet

Another informal procedure for reading evaluation is offered by Ekwall (1981). He developed a *Reading Diagnosis Sheet* (Figure 13-3) that

Sir Walter Raleigh

Four hundred years ago, when Elizabeth I was Queen of England, a young man *called* (named) Walter Raleigh once saw *her* (her) crossing a street. It *was* (was) raining hard and the *streets* (streets) were muddy. He took *down* (off) his rich velvet cape *then* (and) threw it down in *front* (front) of the Queen, so *when* (that) she could step on *it* (it) as on a carpet. *The* (The) Queen was so pleased *when* (that) she made Walter Raleigh *the* (a) knight. From then on, *he* (he) was called Sir Walter *Raleigh* (Raleigh,) and he became one *of* (of) the Queen's special friends.

Sir (Sir) Walter Raleigh was very *very* (much) interested in the new *city* (country) of America. He sent *many* (some) Englishmen to the American *city* (Coast) to found a colony, *then* (which) he named Virginia. They *took* (brought) back potatoes and tobacco *for* (to) England, and Sir Walter *Raleigh* (Raleigh) learned how to smoke *like* (as) the Indians did.

The *dumb* (English) people did not know *about* (about) tobacco and they didn't *know* (know) how to smoke. One *time* (day) while he was smoking *a* (his) pipe, a servant saw *much* (the) smoke coming out of *his* (his) master's mouth and thought *Walter* (he) was on fire. He *went* (ran) for a bucket of *water* (water) and dumped it on *his* (his) master's head.

FIGURE 13-2 Example of the Cloze Procedure.

From William H. Rupley and Timothy R. Blair, *Reading Diagnosis and Remediation*, 1979, p. 116. Copyright © 1979 by Houghton Mifflin Company, Boston, MA. Reprinted with permission.

breaks down the reading process into 28 areas. Ekwall gives information on how to recognize a problem in each of the 28 areas and provides a discussion of possible causes for the problem. He also offers recommendations for remediation.

One approach that has been used to measure reading comprehension is the "think-aloud" procedure. According to Meyers and Lytle (1986) this involves having the student read a passage (a sentence or clause at a time), and tell what he or she is thinking about or what might happen next. This procedure has been used primarily with older students but recently has been tried with younger children.

NAME ——————

GRADE ——————

TEACHER ——————

SCHOOL ——————

	1st Check	2nd Check	3rd Check		
1				Word-by-word reading	ORAL READING
2				Incorrect phrasing	
3				Poor pronunciation	
4				Omissions	
5				Repetitions	
6				Inversions or reversals	
7				Insertions	
8				Substitutions	
9				Basic sight words not known	
10				Sight vocabulary not up to grade level	
11				Guesses at words	
12				Consonant sounds not known	
13				Vowel sounds not known	
14				Blends, digraphs or diphthongs not known	
15				Lacks desirable structural analysis	
16				Unable to use context clues	
17				Contractions not known	
18				Fails to comprehend	ORAL SILENT DIFFICULTIES
19				Unaided recall scanty	
20				Response poorly organized	
21				Low rate of speed	SILENT READING
22				High rate at expense of accuracy	
23				Voicing-lip movement	
24				Inability to skim	
25				Inability to adjust reading rate to difficulty of material	
26				Written recall limited by spelling ability	OTHER RELATED ABILITIES
27				Undeveloped dictionary skill	
28				Inability to locate information	

The items listed above represent the most common difficulties encountered by pupils in the reading program. Following each numbered item are spaces for notation of that specific difficulty. This may be done at intervals of several months. One might use a check to indicate difficulty recognized or the following letters to represent an even more accurate appraisal:

D—Difficulty recognized
P—Pupil progressing
N—No longer has difficulty

FIGURE 13-3 The Reading Diagnosis Sheet.

From Eldon Ekwall, *Locating and Correcting Reading Difficulties*, 3rd ed. Columbus, Ohio: Charles E. Merrill, 1981, p. 5. Copyright © 1981 by Bell and Howell Company. Reprinted with permission.

Portfolio assessment

One relatively recent approach to informal reading assessment involves the formulation and analysis of a student reading portfolio. The reading portfolio can serve as an excellent means of discussing progress with the student or with parents. The approach moves away from a skill-by-skill approach to assessment toward a more holistic evaluation that focuses on the process of reading as well as the product of reading (Mathews, 1990; Valencia, 1990). Valencia (1990) compared a reading portfolio to an artist's portfolio in which samples of his or her work are used to exemplify the depth and breadth of their expertise. Included in a typical reading portfolio are samples of student work such as classroom tests or audiotapes, teacher's observational notes, the student's self-evaluation, and progress notes. Mathews (1990) described a district-wide portfolio assessment procedure that was initiated. Included in the portfolio was the following:

1. A reading development checklist (measuring attitudes toward reading, concepts about print, strategies for word identification and comprehension)
2. Writing samples
3. Lists of books read by the student
4. A reading comprehension test
5. Other information such as anecdotal records and student self-evaluation.

DIAGNOSTIC READING TESTS

WHY USE?
Screening and identification; informal determination of objectives and teaching strategies; documentation of educational need; establishment of IEP goals

WHO SHOULD USE?
Teachers; diagnostic specialists

Gray Oral Reading Test–Diagnostic

The Gray Oral Reading Test–Diagnostic (GORT-D) (Bryant & Wiederholt, 1991) is an individually administered set of reading tasks designed for children 5-1/2 through 12. There are two forms of the GORT-D, A and B, each of which can be administered in approximately 50–90 minutes. There are seven subtests included in the instrument; each subtest has designated entry points, basals, and ceilings.

Description of subtests

Paragraph Reading (9 stories)—In this subtest students are scored according to rate (time in seconds), accuracy, number of mistakes made in oral reading, as well as responses to comprehension questions.

Decoding (15 subtests)—The student is shown a letter followed by a space and more letters (e.g., C——AL). The child must sound out and blend the sounds to form a word. This particular subtest uses nonsense words.

Word Attack (8 items)—In this subtest the student is shown a word such as "potato" and is asked to identify as many small words that are in the bigger word as they can (e.g., pot, at, to, and tat).

Word Identification (30 items)—For each item, a series of four words is presented. The student must correctly read each of the four words and indicate which two words go together in order to receive credit. For example, "if, car, train, and goat" must all be read correctly and the student must indicate that car and train go together.

Morphemic Analysis (36 items)—This subtest is broken down into three sections. In section 1, *Inflectional Ending,* the student is shown a sentence in which a word is missing and is asked to choose one of four responses that best fits the sentence. In the second section, *Contractions,* the student must look at a series of contractions and indicate the two words that make up the contraction. For example, the student is shown "here's" and must indicate that it is the contraction of "here is." In the last section, *Compound Words,* the student is again shown a series of sentences where part of the compound word is missing and the student must complete the compound word. For example, the student is shown "I must finish my home —— before I can play" and must indicate the correct missing word.

Contextual Analysis (30 items)—The student is again shown series of sentences in which a word is missing, however, this time the missing word has its beginning letter or letters shown to act as a contextual cue for the student.

Word Ordering (25 items)—The student is given a series of words out of order and must put them together in the correct order to make a good sentence. For example, "big Tom is" could be placed together to form "Tom is big" or "Is Tom big?"

Interpretation of scores

The raw scores from the GORT-D can be transformed into percentiles, subtest standard scores (mean of 10, standard deviation of 3), composite quotients (mean of 100, standard deviation of 15), and grade equivalents. The use of grade equivalents, however, is discouraged by the authors. The composite quotients available are for Total Reading (TRQ), which is a combination of all the subtests; Meaning Cues (paragraph reading, word identification); Graphic Phonemic Cues (decoding, word attack); and Function Cues (morphemic analysis, contextual analysis, and word ordering). A profile sheet is available to visually plot the scores from all the subtests as well as the individual quotients.

Technical characteristics

Normative sample. The GORT-D was standardized on 831 students from 13 states. Demographic characteristics related to sex, geographic region, race, ethnicity, and type of residence was controlled to approximate that of the 1985 U.S. population.

Reliability. Internal consistency reliability coefficients ranged from .88 to .96 for individual subtests and .96 to .99 for composites. Other than the one correlation of .88, all coefficients were above .90. Test-retest reliability using alternate forms was also determined. This procedure allows for the determination of both alternate form and stability estimates. The alternate-form coefficients for composites ranged from .75 (Function Cues) to .89 (Meaning Cues). Stability coefficients ranged from .75 (Function Cues) to .92 (Meaning Cues).

Validity. The authors provide a discussion for the content validity of the instrument and provide data related to construct validity such as age differentiation (scores increasing with age) and intercorrelation among the GORT-D subtest scores. Criterion-related validity was established in a study of 67 students. Correlations between the TRQ of the GORT-D and the reading quotient for the Diagnostic Achievement Battery–2 (DAB-2) was .84, and for the TRQ of the GORT-D and the total score from the GORT-R it was .42.

Review of relevant research
Because of the recency of the publication of the GORT-D, no information in the professional literature was located.

OVERVIEW: GRAY ORAL READING TESTS–DIAGNOSTIC

- *Age level*—5-1/2 through age 12
- *Type of administration*—Individual
- *Technical adequacy*—Adequate reliability; questionable validity
- *Scores yielded*—Standard scores (total, composite, subtest); percentiles; grade equivalents
- *Suggested use*—The GORT-D is a relatively new diagnostic reading test. It covers the main areas of oral reading and comprehension, although it contains a large number of structural analysis tasks as well. The theo-

retical rationale of the various composite scores is sound, although research on the reliability and validity of those scores should be pursued. One should be aware of the large percentage of "nontraditional" reading subtests that make up the Total Reading Score. This is not an indictment of the test; rather it is a caution that the total score might not reflect the student's classroom performance on traditional classroom measures.

Stanford Diagnostic Reading Test

The Stanford Diagnostic Reading Test (SDRT) (Karlsen & Gardner, 1985) is a group-administered and individually administered instrument designed to measure a student's strengths and weaknesses in reading. It is used with students from the end of first grade through junior college. The authors suggest that the results from the SDRT can be used to help in grouping students and in developing appropriate instructional strategies. The SDRT places special emphasis on the low-achieving student, and it contains more easy items than many reading-achievement tests. The SDRT measures four major components of reading: vocabulary, decoding, comprehension, and rate. The SDRT has four levels, each designed for different age ranges:

> *Red Level*—Used with students at the end of grade 1, grade 2, and low-achieving students in grade 3
>
> *Green Level*—Used with students in grades 3 and 4 and low-achieving students in grade 5
>
> *Brown Level*—Used with students from grades 5 through 8 and with low-achieving high-school students
>
> *Blue Level* (sometimes referred to as the SDRT Level III)—Designed for use with students from grades 9 through 12 and also with community-college students

For each level, several tests are given that measure performance in such areas as auditory vocabulary, auditory discrimination, comprehension, reading rate, and phonetic and structural analysis. Each level has two forms: A and B.

Description

Red Level.   The Red Level includes five tests that generally measure decoding, vocabulary, and comprehension:

> *Auditory Vocabulary (36 items)*—This test requires a student to recognize the meaning of words found in the primary-grade curriculum.
>
> *Auditory Discrimination (30 items)*—This test requires a student to identify the similarities and differences among consonant and among vowel sounds.

Phonetic Analysis (40 items)—This test requires a student to identify consonant and vowel sounds by their common spellings.

Word Reading (42 items)—This test requires a student to identify words commonly seen in primary-grade reading materials.

Reading Comprehension (48 items)—This test measures a child's understanding of sentences and paragraphs.

Green Level.   The Green Level also includes five tests:

Auditory Vocabulary (40 items)

Auditory Discrimination (30 items)

Phonetic Analysis (30 items)

Structural Analysis (48 items)—This test requires a student to divide two-syllable words into their component parts and to blend sounds to form words.

Reading Comprehension (48 items)—This test includes a measure of both literal and inferential understanding of passages.

Brown Level.   The Brown Level includes five tests that measure all four aspects of reading (decoding, vocabulary, comprehension, and rate):

Auditory Vocabulary (40 items)

Reading Comprehension (60 items)—This test includes both literal and inferential comprehension.

Phonetic Analysis (30 items)

Structural Analysis (78 items)—This test measures word division and blending of three-syllable words.

Reading Rate (33 items)—This test measures the student's ability to combine speed and comprehension in reading easy material.

Blue Level.   The Blue Level includes seven tests. The formats of tests 1, 4, and 5 (Reading Comprehension, Phonetic Analysis, and Structural Analysis) have been discussed under the previous levels. The remaining tests are these:

Vocabulary (30 items)—This test requires the student to recognize the meaning of words in context.

Word Parts (30 items)—This test requires the student to demonstrate the understanding of affixes, root words, and word roots.

Scanning and Skimming (32 items)—This test requires the student to recall information after quickly reading a passage.

Fast Reading (30 items)—This test includes a 500-word passage presented in a modified cloze procedure and requires the student to demonstrate both speed and comprehension.

Interpretation of results

The SDRT can be either hand scored or machine scored. The raw scores from each test can be transformed into a number of norm-referenced scores. The manual for each level includes tables for percentile ranks, stanines, grade equivalents, and scaled scores. Computer scoring can also provide stanines and percentile ranks compared to both local and national norms. In fact, the computer scoring profile provides much valuable information (Figure 13-4). The SDRT also includes progress indicators, which are essentially cutoff points that were determined by the authors and that document whether a student has demonstrated competence in various reading skills. The authors suggest that the cut-off points be used only as guides and that they may need to be modified according to the individual's instructional program. Also included with the SDRT is an instructional-placement report that summarizes the results of an entire class by using the scores that are viewed as the most relevant.

Technical characteristics

Normative sample.   A nationally stratified sample of over 30,000 was used.

Reliability.   Internal reliability coefficients were generally above .80; many were .90 or above.

Validity.   A discussion of content validity can be found in the manual. Construct and criterion-related data are available from the Psychological Corporation.

Review of relevant research

Although the SDRT has not been studied extensively, Lewandowski and Martens (1990) reviewed the test and noted that it was very useful as a screening instrument. They did point out, however, that some of the subtests were inappropriately named and there was little rationale presented for its theoretical base.

OVERVIEW: STANFORD DIAGNOSTIC READING TEST

- *Age level*—Grade 1 through community college
- *Type of administration*—Group
- *Technical adequacy*—Good
- *Scores yielded*—Percentile ranks, stanines, grade equivalents, scaled scores, progress indicators
- *Suggested use*—The SDRT is a well-constructed diagnostic reading test. Its standardization sample was representative and the reliability and the validity good. It can therefore be used as a reasonable measure of vocabulary, decoding skills, comprehension, and reading rate, particularly for screening purposes. It gives more normative information but less informal information (for example, error analysis) than other diagnostic reading tests.

FIGURE 13-4   Computer Scoring Profile from the Stanford Diagnostic Reading Test.

From B. Karlsen, R. Madden, and E. Gardner, *Stanford Diagnostic Reading Test*, 3rd ed. Copyright © 1984 by the Psychological Corporation. Reprinted with permission.

Test of Reading Comprehension

The Test of Reading Comprehension (TORC) (Brown, Hammill, & Wiederholt, 1986) is an individually administered instrument designed for students between the ages of 7 and 18. It can also be used with small groups of students. The test measures the comprehension of *silent* reading; therefore, individuals who have articulation or other oral-reading problems are not penalized. Six uses are specifically mentioned in the manual.

1. To determine a student's relative reading comprehension in relation to a normative group
2. To determine how well a student or group of students can comprehend written language when a program-independent measure is needed
3. To examine strengths and weaknesses from one subtest to another for diagnostic purposes
4. To compare relative performance in reading comprehension with other conceptual abilities when appropriate measures are available
5. To compare TORC performances with other language behavior to determine relative strengths and weaknesses
6. To investigate behaviors related to reading comprehension and to study the construct itself (p. 15).

Description

Eight subtests are included in the TORC. Subtests 1–3 are called the General Reading Comprehension Core. Subtests 4–7 are called Diagnostic Supplements, and Subtest 8 is optional.

General Vocabulary (25 items)—This subtest measures the student's conceptual understanding of sets of vocabulary items. For instance, the words *sausage, pancake,* and *hamburger* are given as stimulus items. The student must choose which two of a group of four—such as *tortilla, salad, salute, fragrant*—are most like the stimulus words.

Syntactic Similarities (20 items)—This subtest measures the child's understanding of syntactically different sentences. For instance, the following sentences are shown to the student: "A. We ran yesterday," "B. We run daily," "C. We will run tomorrow," "D. We run," and "E. We run every day." The student must indicate which two sentences have the same meaning.

Paragraph Reading (30 items)—Six paragraphs are read silently, and five multiple choice questions are answered from each.

Content-Area Vocabularies (three subtests: Mathematics, Social Studies, and Science) (75 items)—These three subtests use the same format as subtest 1. The vocabulary tests, however, are associated with mathematics, social studies, and science content.

Reading the Directions of Schoolwork (25 items)—This subtest is used for younger or remedial readers. The student must read and follow simple directions.

Sentence Sequencing (10 items)—Five sentences are presented to the reader. The task is to sequence the sentences to make a meaningful story.

Interpretation of results

Raw scores from the TORC can be transformed into scaled scores, percentile ranks, and a Reading Comprehension Quotient (RCQ) The scaled scores for all subtests have a mean of 10 and a standard deviation of 3. The RCQ is based on the total scaled scores of the Reading Comprehension Core and has a mean of 100 and a standard deviation of 15.

Technical characteristics

Normative sample. Two thousand four hundred and ninety-two subjects were tested. Information regarding sex, age, grade level, and geographic region is included in the manual. Many of the subjects were also a part of the normative sample from the 1978 edition.

Reliability. Internal consistency is adequate; coefficients were generally above .80. Test-retest consistency ranged from .64 to .91 (based on a limited sample).

Validity. Data from several concurrent validity studies are presented in the manual. These correlations range from .22 to .87 (depending on the TORC subtest and the particular criterion measure).

Review of relevant research

Few studies of the TORC are to be found in the professional literature. In one study, Brown and Sherbenou (1981) found that the TORC results correlated between .40 and .66 with teachers' evaluations of the students' reading abilities. In another, Eaves and Simpson (1986) provided a table that allows an examiner to determine statistically significant differences between subtest scores for a more precise analysis of intraindividual strengths and weaknesses. It should be noted that these were based on the 1978 edition, although the two versions are essentially the same test (Misulis, 1989). There have been several reviews of the revised TORC. Poteet (1989) suggested that potential users should become familiar with the theoretical rationale of the TORC to determine if this matches the curricular demands. Tierney (1989) questioned the limitation or narrowness of the TORC in measuring traditional reading comprehension. On the other hand, Misulis (1989) pointed out that the TORC is interesting, unique, and represents a valuable contribution to the reading profession.

OVERVIEW: TEST OF READING COMPREHENSION

- *Age level*—7–18 years old
- *Type of administration*—Individual (small group is possible)
- *Technical adequacy*—Adequate standardization, questionable reliability and validity
- *Scores yielded*—Scaled scores, percentile ranks, Reading Comprehension Quotient
- *Suggested use*—The TORC is theoretically a measure of *silent reading comprehension*. Only a small part of the test actually focuses on traditional comprehension measures (that is, on reading a passage and answering questions about the content). Most of the test is concerned with vocabulary and syntax. This is not necessarily a criticism of the test, although you should be aware of the test's content if you use the results exclusively to assess a student's comprehension. The TORC is most appropriate for students aged 8–14.

Woodcock Reading Mastery Tests–Revised

The Woodcock Reading Mastery Tests–Revised (WRMT-R) (Woodcock, 1987) kept many but also added and/or changed several of the features of the popular WRMT. The WRMT-R includes six individually administered tests and a two-part supplementary checklist designed for individuals aged 5–75+. There are two forms of the test—form G contains all six tests and the supplementary checklist, whereas form H contains only four tests. According to the author, the WRMT-R can be used for a variety of reasons including diagnosis of reading problems, program planning, and program evaluation. The tests are designed for both criterion-referenced and norm-referenced purposes, although their use as a criterion-referenced tool is somewhat limited.

Description

Visual-Auditory Learning (Form G only; 133 items)—This subtest requires the examinee to associate new visual symbols with familiar words and then translate sentences using those new symbols.

Letter Identification (Form G only; 51 items)—This subtest requires the student to identify lower- and upper-case letters presented in common styles (such as cursive) and uncommon styles (such as special type styles).

Word Identification (106 items)—This subtest includes words arranged sequentially according to level of difficulty. The examinee simply has to read the word.

Word Attack (45 items)—This subtest measures the ability to pronounce nonsense words (for example, "gnouthe") through the use of structural and phonetic analysis.

Word Comprehension (146 items)—This test is comprised of three separate subtests. Antonyms (34 items) requires the examinee to say a word that is opposite of a vocabulary word, while Synonyms (33 items) requires the examinee to say a word that means the same thing as a vocabulary word. Analogies (79 items) requires the person to read a pair of analogous words (for example, cowboy-horse) and then complete a second analogy (for example, pilot - ————).

Passage Comprehension (68 items)—This subtest uses a modified cloze procedure. The examinee must read a passage in which a key word is missing and must identify the missing word.

Supplementary Letter Checklist (Form G only; 63 items)—This checklist includes both a capital letter (27 items) and lower-case letter section (36 items). These letters are presented in the sans serif type style that is common in many beginning reading programs.

Interpretation of results

The subtests of the WRMT-R can provide specific information about the examinee or can be combined into various clusters for interpretation. Age equivalents, grade equivalents, percentile ranks, and standard scores (mean = 100; standard deviation = 15) are available in the following areas: Readiness (Visual-Auditory Learning and Letter Identification); Basic Skills (Word Identification and Word Attack); Reading Comprehension (Word Comprehension and Passage Comprehension); Total Reading-Full Scale (Word Identification, Word Attack, Word Comprehension, and Passage Comprehension); and Total Reading-Short Scale (Word Identification and Passage Comprehension). A Relative Performance Index (RPI) is also available that gives an indication of the relative mastery of content at a specific grade level. Scoring of the WRMT-R, although easier than its predecessor, is still rather cumbersome. Several interesting and potentially valuable additions are a word attack error inventory and tables that allow for the determination of aptitude-achievement discrepancies. Scores can also be placed on a diagnostic profile, a percentile rank profile, and/or an instructional level profile. The diagnostic profile allows the interpretation of scores from other tests as well as the WRMT-R. Figure 13-5 shows the percentile rank profile.

Technical characteristics

Normative sample.   Over 6,000 subjects were used in the standardization. The kindergarten–grade 12 population was over 4,000 of the total. The sample was stratified according to geographic region, race, occupation (for adult subjects), and community type.

Reliability.   Split half coefficients were above .90 for all subtests and clusters. A coefficient of .99 was reported for the total reading.

FIGURE 13-5   Percentile Rank Profile from the Woodcock Reading Mastery Tests–Revised.

From R. Woodcock, *Woodcock Reading Mastery Tests–Revised.* Copyright © 1987 by American Guidance Service. Reprinted with permission.

Validity.   Concurrent validity coefficients with the reading tests from the Woodcock-Johnson Psychoeducational Battery ranged from .25 to .91. Total reading scores from one test correlated .85 or above with total reading from the other test. Arguments for the test's content and construct validity are also reported in the manual.

Review of relevant research

Surprisingly, little research on the WRMT-R was found. Reviews and critiques of the instrument have appeared in the reading literature, however. Cooter (1988) felt that it was a substantial improvement over the 1973 WRMT although it still evaluated the reading process in fragments rather than holistically. Lewandowski and Martens (1990) noted several problems, including the lack of information related to the validity of the profiles and lack of alternate form reliability data. Jaeger (1989) questioned the diagnostic and instructional planning value of the instrument, suggesting that it should be used to develop tentative hypotheses that should be confirmed through more extensive assessment. Eaves (1990) reported that the available validity for the WRMT-R is weak (primarily because there are so little data) and that more research needs to be conducted in this area.

Because of the similarity between the WRMT-R and its predecessor, some of the research on the WRMT has relevance for the new edition as well.

- Learning-disabled and non-learning-disabled students performed similarly on the WRMT. The reliability of scores for the two groups was high (McCollough & Zaremba, 1979).
- The WRMT has a unique format that might be helpful in evaluating learning-disabled students (Coleman & Harber, 1982).
- The word-identification test is the most accurate single predictor of the total reading scores for adolescent learning-disabled students (Williamson, 1976).
- The WRMT is a valid instrument for slow learning and underachieving individuals (Haines, 1977).
- For a group of reading-disabled students, the word-identification test yielded scores approximately one year lower than did sight-vocabulary tests from other reading instruments (Memory, Powell, & Calloway, 1980).
- The analogy format of the word-comprehension test has been challenged (Laffey & Kelly, 1979).

Summary of research findings

The limited research on the original WRMT suggests that it is a reasonably valid instrument with a variety of students, including the learning disabled. The format of the test has been questioned, however. Research on the WRMT-R is needed to substantiate prior findings and explore further issues related to its potential uses and limitations. Reviews of the WRMT-R also note the need for additional technical data.

OVERVIEW: WOODCOCK READING MASTERY TESTS–REVISED

- *Age level*—Ages 5–75+
- *Type of administration*—Individual
- *Technical adequacy*—Adequate standardization, good but limited reliability (only split-half), somewhat limited validity
- *Scores yielded*—Standard scores, percentile ranks, age and grade equivalents, Relative Performance Index
- *Suggested use*—The original WRMT was probably the most popular norm-referenced diagnostic reading test used in special education and the WRMT-R has continued the popularity. The tests are easy to administer and cover a number of abilities. The WRMT-R, however, is tedious to score, requiring the use of a number of tables that could lead to scoring errors. It is important that examiners practice the scoring several times before administering it in a real test situation. The meaning and interpretation of the visual-auditory learning subtest and the aptitude-achievement discrepancy tables need to be established. The error inventory is a nice addition. In summary, it appears that the WRMT-R has improved many of the shortcomings of the original test. It should probably be thought of as a screening test or a measure to gather pretest-posttest data until more information is available regarding its potential uses.

Other Diagnostic Reading Tests

In addition to the previously discussed norm-referenced reading tests, there are two others that deserve mention. These two, the Durrell Analysis of Reading Difficulty and the Diagnostic Reading Scales, are best used informally and are often administered by reading specialists.

Durrell Analysis of Reading Difficulty

Age level—Preprimary through grade 6

Type of administration—Individual

Technical adequacy—Adequate standardization, questionable reliability and validity

Scores yielded—Independent, instructional, capacity reading levels, informal checklist

Description—The DARD (Durrell & Catterson, 1980) includes nine subtests ranging from oral and silent reading to listening comprehension, visual memory of words, and sounds in isolation. The strength of the DARD is its use as an informal instrument. The checklist of instructional needs can be a very helpful tool to analyze errors. It does, however, require the examiner to have a certain amount of knowledge in the area of reading. The reading levels yielded should be used as rough estimates only. The DARD should probably be used by experienced reading teachers to maximize its potential diagnostic ability. There is very limited information on its use with exceptional students.

Diagnostic Reading Scales

Age level—Grade 1 through grade 8

Type of administration—Individual

Technical adequacy—Adequate (based on limited data)

Scores yielded—Error analysis; instructional, independent, and potential reading levels

Description—The DRS (Spache, 1981) includes word lists and reading passages that measure oral reading and comprehension. There are also measures of word analysis and phonics. The reading levels determined from the DRS should be used as estimates only. There is also evidence that the reading levels determined from the 1981 edition and the 1972 edition are markedly different. Thus, the various editions should not be used interchangeably. One special feature of the DRS is the section focusing on concerns in administering the test to children who speak non-standard-English dialects. (No information is included regarding exceptional students, however.) In addition, the error analysis can be helpful for experienced reading teachers.

ORAL READING TESTS

WHY USE?
Screening and identification; informal determination of objectives and teaching strategies; documentation of educational need; establishment of IEP goals

WHO SHOULD USE?
Teachers; diagnostic specialists

Oral reading tests are used to measure a student's rate and accuracy of reading and, in some cases, the comprehension of orally read material. Most oral reading tests use graded passages to determine the level of reading and to identify the types of errors made. The two most common oral reading tests are the Gray and the Gilmore. A brief discussion of each follows.

Gray Oral Reading Test–3

Alternate forms—This test has two forms.

Age level—7–18 years

Technical adequacy—Normed on 1,485 students from 18 states. Evidence for content, criterion-related and construct validity, as well as alternate-form and internal reliability, is reported in the manual.

Areas measured—Rate (how long it takes the student to read a passage) and deviations from print (how many and what types of errors are made)

Types of scores—Standard scores, percentile ranks, grade equivalents, miscue analysis

Suggested use—The error analysis yields the most important information, although an examiner with a strong diagnostic reading background would get the most usable information from the test.

The GORT–Revised (Wiederhold & Bryant, 1986) technical characteristics were a considerable improvement over the original GORT (Hickman, 1989). It appears that the GORT-3 (Wiederholt & Bryant, 1991) is even more improved.

Gilmore Oral Reading Test

(Gilmore & Gilmore, 1968)

Alternate forms—Two forms, C and D, are available

Age level—Grades 1–8

Technical adequacy—Normed on over 2,200 children. Alternate form reliability coefficients were moderate at best; no validity data mentioned.

Areas measured—Accuracy (number and type of errors), comprehension, reading rate

Types of scores—Performance ratings (poor through superior), grade scores (based on accuracy)

Suggested use—Clearly, the informal use (error analysis) is the primary advantage of this instrument. Normative use is discouraged.

Instrument or Technique	Suggested Use							Target Population						Special Considerations	Educational Relevance for Exceptional Students
	Prereferral			Postreferral											
	Screening and Initial Identification	Informal Determination and Evaluation of Teaching Programs and Strategies	Determination of Current Performance Level and Educational Need	Decisions about Classification and Program Placement	IEP Goals	IEP Objectives	IEP Evaluation	Mild/Moderate	Severe/Profound	Preschool	Elementary Age	Secondary Age	Adult		
Diagnosis: An Instructional Aid in Reading	X	X	X		X	X	X	X			X			Test items are correlated with instructional materials	very useful
Informal Reading Inventories	X	X	X		X			X			X	X		Most measure word recognition and comprehension skills	useful
Cloze Procedure	X	X						X			X	X		The reading levels that are determined should be used only as guidelines	adequate
Maze Procedure	X	X						X			X	X		The reading levels that are determined should be used only as guidelines	adequate
Reading Diagnosis Sheet	X	X						X			X	X		This procedure is included in a book that also suggests remedial strategies	useful
Portfolio Assessment	X	X						X			X	X		Focuses on the entire process of reading; helpful at parent conferences	useful
Gray Oral Reading Test-Diagnostic	X		X		X			X			X			Includes a number of "nontraditional" reading tasks	useful
Stanford Diagnostic Reading Test	X		X		X			X			X	X		Well constructed; can be group administered; does not give specific instructional information	useful
Test of Reading Comprehension	X				X			X			X	X		Heavily weighted toward vocabulary and syntax	adequate

Instrument or Technique	Suggested Use		Postreferral					Target Population						Special Considerations	Educational Relevance for Exceptional Students
	Prereferral														
	Screening and Initial Identification	Informal Determination and Evaluation of Teaching Programs and Strategies	Determination of Current Performance Level and Educational Need	Decisions about Classification and Program Placement	IEP Goals	IEP Objectives	IEP Evaluation	Mild/Moderate	Severe/Profound	Preschool	Elementary Age	Secondary Age	Adult		
Woodcock Reading Mastery Tests–Revised	X		X		X			X			X	X		Earlier version widely used; some improvements in revision; tedious scoring system	adequate
Durrell Analysis of Reading Difficulty		X	X		X			X			X			Normative data are limited; should be used informally	adequate
Diagnostic Reading Scales		X	X		X			X			X			Best used informally; error analysis could be helpful	adequate
Gray Oral Reading Test–3	X	X						X			X	X		Error analysis yields the most information	adequate
Gilmore Oral Reading Test	X	X						X			X			Very limited technical aspects; should be used informally	limited

14

Assessment of Mathematics and Spelling

INSTRUMENTS/PROCEDURES INCLUDED

DIAGNOSTIC ARITHMETIC TESTS
- Key Math–Revised
- Stanford Diagnostic Mathematics Test
- Test of Mathematical Abilities

CRITERION-REFERENCED INSTRUMENTS
- Diagnosis: An Instructional Aid in Mathematics
- Enright Inventory of Basic Arithmetic Skills
- Mathematics Concept Inventory

DIAGNOSTIC SPELLING TESTS
- Test of Written Spelling–2

CRITERION REFERENCED INSTRUMENTS
- Spellmaster

Albert is a fourth-grade student who has always been "scared of numbers." He often confuses the mathematics signs and will add instead of subtract or subtract instead of divide. He also has great difficulty with time and number concepts. He still has problems reading and understanding a clock. His teacher felt that a sequential list of objectives in the deficient mathematics areas would be very beneficial. Albert was referred for testing to evaluate his overall mathematics ability and to identify appropriate educational objectives.

Sarah is in the sixth grade in a private school. Her spelling ability is very weak and she frequently avoids any tasks requiring her to spell. Her teacher and parents have noted that when she does spell, she does so phonetically (for example, "posishun" for "position"). Often she will spell difficult words correctly and misspell much easier words. Further diagnostic testing in spelling was recommended.

Compared to the area of reading, less attention is given to the assessment of mathematics and spelling. Evaluation of these academic areas is very important, however, and should be included when conducting a comprehensive basic skill assessment. A look at the general achievement tests discussed in Chapter 12 will reveal that subtests that measure mathematics and spelling are included in virtually every instrument.

The assessment of mathematics usually involves the areas of mathematical concepts, computation, application, and problem-solving. *Mathematical concepts* focuses on basic information such as the understanding of numeration, mathematical operations, number concepts, and place value. *Computation* involves such areas as addition, subtraction, multiplication, and division of whole numbers, fractions, and decimals. *Application* includes such areas as measurement skills, money skills, and time concepts, whereas *problem-solving* involves the ability to (1) determine how to solve a given problem (frequently a word problem) and (2) perform the necessary operation(s) to determine the correct answer.

Norm-referenced tests for the mathematical areas are sometimes referred to as *diagnostic* tests. Similar to diagnostic reading tests, however, these instruments are used to determine strengths and weaknesses and to identify areas for remediation rather than "diagnosing" in a traditional sense. Criterion-referenced instruments in the area of mathematics are used to identify more specific information that might be incorporated into an IEP.

Spelling is an important academic area that is crucial for written communication. In fact, spelling is sometimes included in discussions of written language because of its important role in that area. Language instruments such as the Test of Written Language–2 (discussed in Chapter 11) even include a spelling subtest. In this text, however, spelling will be discussed separately because both norm-referenced and criterion-referenced instruments have been developed specifically for this area.

For both the areas of mathematics and spelling, it is crucial to consider the use of the error analysis procedures that were discussed in Chapter 6. The ease of obtaining written products in these two areas adds to the benefits of using error analysis. Many of the tests presented in this chapter, particularly the criterion-referenced instruments, are based on an error analysis approach.

DIAGNOSTIC ARITHMETIC TESTS

WHY USE?
Screening and identification; informal determination of objectives and teaching strategies; documentation of educational need; establishment of IEP goals

WHO SHOULD USE?
Teachers; diagnostic specialists

Key Math–Revised

The Key Math–Revised (Key Math-R) (Connolly, 1988) is the new edition of the very popular Key Math Diagnostic Arithmetic Test. The Key Math-R, like its predecessor, is contained in an easel kit; most of the items are presented orally by the examiner, using colored plates as a visual stimulus. The Key Math-R has two forms, A and B, and has extended the age range of the test from kindergarten through grade seven to kindergarten through grade nine.

Description

The Key Math-R contains 13 subtests that measure the general areas of basic concepts, operations, and applications. Items within each subtest can be clustered into domains. The subtests and their respective domains are listed next.

BASIC CONCEPTS

Numeration (24 items)—Numbers 0–9, numbers 0–99, numbers 0–999, multidigit numbers

Rational Numbers (18 items)—Fractions, decimals, percents

Geometry (24 items)—Spatial/attribute relations, two–dimensional shapes, coordinates/transformations, three–dimensional shapes

OPERATIONS

Addition (18 items)—Models and basic facts, algorithms: whole numbers, adding rational numbers

Subtraction (18 items)—Models and basic facts, algorithms: whole numbers, subtracting rational numbers

Multiplication (18 items)—Models and basic facts, algorithms: whole numbers, multiplying rational numbers

Division (18 items)—Models and basic facts, algorithms: whole numbers, dividing rational numbers

Mental Computation (18 items)—Computation chains, whole numbers, rational numbers

APPLICATIONS

Measures (24 items)—Comparisons, non–standard units, standard units: length, area, standard units: weight, capacity

Time and Money (24 items)—Identifying passage of time, using clocks and clock units, monetary amounts to $1, monetary amounts to $100

Estimation (18 items)—Whole and rational numbers, measurement, computation

Interpreting Data (18 items)—Charts and tables, graphs, probability and statistics

Problem Solving (18 items)—Solving routine problems, understanding non–routine problems, solving non–routine problems.

Interpretation of results

Four levels of diagnostic information are available—total test, area, subtest, and domain. Domain-related information provides insight into the student's specific strengths and weaknesses. Standard scores (mean = 100; standard deviation = 15), grade and age equivalents, percentile ranks, and stanines are available for the three area composites and the total test. Standard scores (mean = 10; standard deviation = 3), percentile ranks, and stanines are available for the subtests. A computer software package is also available that provides a scoring summary and a score profile.

Technical characteristics

Normative sample.   Approximately 1,800 students were included. The sample was stratified by geographic region, grade, sex, socioeconomic status, and racial/ethnic background. Separate fall and spring norms are available.

Reliability.   Alternate-form coefficients are reported. Total score was the only acceptable coefficient. Area and subtest coefficients were below .85. Split-half coefficients were acceptable for the total test and for the areas after approximately grade two.

Validity.   Very little validity data are presented. A brief discussion of content validity was included in the manual.

Review of relevant research

Even though the Key Math-R is a relatively new instrument, it is surprising that no research was located on the revised version. The Key Math-R is similar to the original Key Math in format. Therefore, the research on the original might be relevant.

- The Key Math is a useful instrument with learning disabled students for several reasons: (1) It measures current curricula; (2) it requires neither reading nor writing; (3) it offers a simplified visual presentation; and (4) it allows the examiner to observe the child during the testing (Tinney, 1975).
- The Key Math is a good test to use with adolescent learning-disabled students. The test discriminated between learning-disabled and non-learning-disabled students. Further, the learning-disabled students demonstrated a specific pattern of computational errors (Greenstein & Strain, 1977).
- The Key Math has moderate predictive validity. It correlated .67 with Metropolitan Achievement Test scores obtained 1 year later (Kratchowill & Demuth, 1976).
- The Key Math should be used as a screening test rather than as a diagnostic test with mentally retarded students. While the difficulty level of the basal items was generally acceptable (except for multiplication and missing elements), the children tended to reach the ceiling rapidly (Goodstein, Kahn, & Cawley, 1976).
- The Key Math and Wide Range Achievement Test arithmetic sections yielded comparable scores for educable mentally retarded students. Therefore, you must weigh the additional diagnostic features of the Key Math against the shorter administration time of the WRAT when you select either of these instruments (Powers & Pace, 1976).
- Because of the relatively low reliabilities of the individual subtests, the standard error of measurement for each should be plotted on the diagnostic record (Van Etten & Watson, 1978).

Summary of research finding

Surprisingly few studies have been reported for a test that was as widely used as the Key Math. The available research suggests that the Key Math is a potentially useful instrument for learning-disabled students, although its use with mentally retarded students is limited. Learning-disabled students tend to have a specific pattern with a relatively high number of computation errors. Several studies have also noted the technical inadequacies of the Key Math. Research on the Key Math–R should indicate whether these findings will be true for the newer edition as well. Bachor (1990) did note that the Key Math–R was a substantial improvement over its predecessor.

OVERVIEW: KEY MATH–REVISED

- *Age level*—Kindergarten–grade 9
- *Type of administration*—Individual
- *Technical adequacy*—Adequate reliability (total score); limited validity.
- *Scores yielded*—Standard scores, age and grade equivalents, percentile ranks, stanines.
- *Suggested use*—The Key Math–R should be used either informally as a criterion-referenced test, or normatively as a screening device. Users of

the Key Math–R must keep in mind the visual (and largely nonwritten) format of the test. This has its advantages and disadvantages. It might be appropriate to measure the mathematical skills of a student with reading problems. On the other hand, the format requires skills that are dissimilar to the majority of skills required of students during classroom activities. To date, validity data are limited.

Stanford Diagnostic Mathematics Test

The Stanford Diagnostic Mathematics Test (SDMT) (Beatty, Madden, Gardner, & Karlsen, 1985) is a group-administered or individually administered instrument designed to measure basic arithmetic concepts and skills from grade 1 through grade 12. The SDMT is divided into four levels.

Red Level—Designed for mathematics concepts usually taught in the first and second grade and is used with children at the end of first grade, second grade, third grade, and students in the fourth grade having problems in the mathematics area. Also included is a practice test that familiarizes the student with general test-taking skills.

Green Level—Measures those concepts and skills usually taught in grades 3 and 4 and is used with students in grades 4 and 5 and some students in grade 6.

Brown Level—Covers those skills usually taught by the end of the sixth grade and is used with sixth and seventh graders and lower-achieving eighth-grade and high-school students.

Blue Level—Overlaps some of the content of the Brown Level and includes mathematics information usually taught by the end of the eighth grade. This level is used with students in grades 8–12 and with community-college students.

Each level contains three tests that measure a student's knowledge in the following areas: Number Systems and Numeration, Computation, and Applications. The tests themselves are used as diagnostic instruments to determine a student's strengths and weaknesses in math.

Description
RED LEVEL

Number System and Numeration (30 items)—This test measures the child's knowledge of whole numbers, decimal-place value, and operations and properties.

Computation (30 items)—This test includes addition facts, addition with no renaming, subtraction and subtraction with no renaming.

Applications (30 items)—This test includes items measuring problem solving, reading and interpreting graphs, and geometry and measurement.

GREEN LEVEL

Number System and Numeration (33 items)—This subtest covers whole numbers, decimal-place value, rational numbers and numeration, and operations and properties.

Computation (45 items)—This test includes addition, subtraction, multiplication, and division of whole numbers.

Application (30 items)—This test covers problem solving, reading and interpreting tables and graphs, and geometry and measurement.

BROWN LEVEL

Number System and Numeration (36 items)—This test includes items in the areas of whole numbers and decimal-place value, rational numbers and numeration, and operations and properties.

Computation (45 items)—This test includes items measuring addition, subtraction, multiplication, and division of whole numbers, fractions, and decimals, as well as equations.

Application (33 items)—This test involves problem-solving, reading and interpreting tables and graphs, and geometry and measurement.

BLUE LEVEL

Number System and Numeration (36 items)—This test measures whole numbers and decimal-place value, rational numbers and numeration, and operations and properties.

Computation (48 items)—This test includes items measuring the addition, subtraction, multiplication, and division of whole numbers, fractions, and decimals; the calculation of percentages and equations.

Application (33 items)—This test involves problem-solving, reading and interpreting tables and graphs, and geometry and measurement.

Interpretation of results

Raw scores from the SDMT can be transformed into a number of norm-referenced measures. Tables for percentile ranks, stanines, grade equivalents, and scaled scores can be found in the manuals for each level. Like the SDRT, computer scoring can also provide percentiles and stanines compared to both local and national norms. In addition to these, the SDMT offers a progress-indicator (Pi) score that, essentially, is a cutoff point. Its purpose is to help teachers identify students who have reached the level of competence necessary to achieve success in the instructional goals of the individual classroom. Each test can be either hand scored or machine scored. Each level includes an instructional-placement report that summarizes the results for an entire class. The authors also endorse a three-step process of test-plan-teach and provide services and materials to facilitate this process (Figure 14-1).

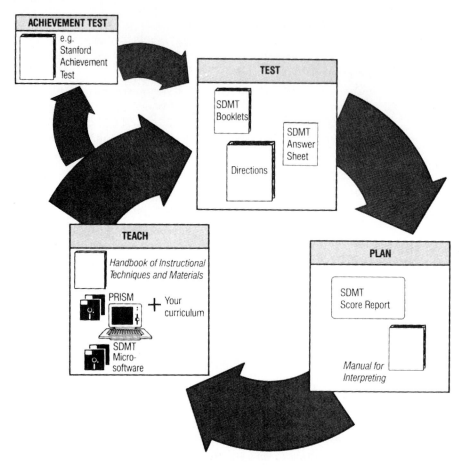

FIGURE 14-1 **Three-step Process Recommended for Users of the Stanford Diagnostic Mathematics Test.**

From L. Beatty, R. Madden, E. Gardner, and B. Karlsen, *Stanford Diagnostic Mathematics Test.* Copyright © 1984 by the Psychological Corporation. Reproduced with permission. All rights reserved.

Technical characteristics

Normative sample. A large, stratified, nationally representative sample was used.

Reliability. Internal consistency was generally good; coefficients were mostly above .90.

Validity. Information related to content and concurrent validity is available from the Psychological Corporation.

Review of relevant research

The SDMT has not been studied extensively. Two reviewers of the 1976 SDMT had different opinions about the diagnostic utility of the instrument. Sowder (1978) indicated that it gave a "not too specific" indication of strengths and weaknesses and that it should be used for comparison rather than for educational programming. Lappan (1978), on the other hand, felt that it was adequate to identify strengths and weaknesses and to group students for instructional purposes. The format and items of the 1976 and the 1985 versions are very similar.

OVERVIEW: STANFORD DIAGNOSTIC MATHEMATICS TEST

- *Age levels*—Grades 1 through 12, plus community college
- *Type of administration*—Group
- *Technical adequacy*—Good
- *Scores yielded*—Percentile ranks, stanines, grade equivalent, scaled scores, progress indicator
- *Suggested use*—The SDMT is a well-constructed test. It can be used to identify general strengths and weaknesses in the areas of number concepts, computation, and application. The SDMT is more appropriate as a general comparative test than as a specific test to determine instructional goals and objectives.

Test of Mathematical Abilities

The Test of Mathematical Abilities (TOMA) (Brown & McEntire, 1984) includes five subtests that provide standardized information about two major skill areas—story problems and computation—and related information about attitude, vocabulary, and the general application of information. It is a norm-referenced test designed for use in grades 3 through 12. The General Information subtest must be administered individually, whereas the other subtests may be group or individually administered. Administration takes between 45 minutes to 1 hour and 45 minutes, although no time limits are imposed.

Description

Attitude Toward Math (15 items)—The subtest requires the subject to decide how he feels about each math-related sentence. The student indicates "agree," "disagree," or "don't know." Sentences are usually read to the subject, but good readers may proceed independently.

Vocabulary (20 items)—This subtest lists math-related vocabulary words that the subject must briefly define in writing.

Computation (25 items)—This subtest is a paper-and-pencil test of math computation. Problems are arranged in order of difficulty.

General Information (30 items)—This is an orally administered subtest of general mathematical knowledge. It requires some subjectivity in the scoring.

Story Problems (17 items)—This subtest includes problems that the subject must read and complete. Nonreaders' scores should not be included, although the problems can be read aloud as part of a separate diagnostic analysis.

Interpretation of results

The TOMA provides standard scores for all subtests, as well as percentiles, and a quotient that incorporates standard scores for all subtests. The manual includes suggestions for proper interpretation and use, as well as a list of resources for further assessment and programming of mathematical difficulties.

Technical characteristics

Normative sample. The sample included 1,560 students from Alabama, California, Vermont, Washington, and Wisconsin. The characteristics of the sample compare favorably with those of the general U.S. population. Mainstreamed handicapped students were included.

Reliability. Coefficient Alpha for all subtests showed adequate internal consistency, ranging from .78 to .97. Test-retest reliability was not as strong among subtests with coefficients ranging from .71 to .80 (total score yielded .87). Learning-disabled students' coefficients were somewhat lower.

Validity. Criterion-related validity was demonstrated through correlations with the original Key Math, Peabody Individual Achievement Test (PIAT), and Wide Range Achievement Test (WRAT). Construct validity was reported using age and grade differentiation, relationship of TOMA to IQ tests, and subtest interrelationships.

Review of relevant research

No empirical studies on the TOMA were located. Howell (1990) in a review of the TOMA noted, "The TOMA seems more notable for what it attempts to do than for what it actually does. For example, while a major strength of the test is its innovative conceptualization of mathematics, a major weakness is the attempt to validate this conceptualization through correlations with more typical measures" (p. 216).

OVERVIEW: TEST OF MATHEMATICAL ABILITIES

- *Age level*—8-1/2 through 18 years old
- *Type of administration*—Individual for general information subtest, all others individual or group
- *Technical adequacy*—Adequate standardization, questionable reliability and validity
- *Scores yielded*—Standard scores, percentiles, and an overall quotient
- *Suggested use*—Properly used, the TOMA can be a useful tool to diagnose mathematical abilities and disabilities, but results should be followed by additional study of mathematical abilities (testing, observation, interview, etc.). The scores do not provide a sufficient basis for planning instructional programs on IEPs. Individual subtests are not appropriate for certain subjects (nonreaders, deaf, etc.) and should be eliminated from their assessments. Further validity data are necessary before its potential use can be determined.

CRITERION-REFERENCED INSTRUMENTS

WHY USE?
Identification of areas for further evaluation or remediation; informal determination of objectives and teaching strategies; development and evaluation of IEPs

WHO SHOULD USE?
Teachers

Diagnosis: An Instructional Aid in Mathematics

Diagnosis: An Instructional Aid in Mathematics (Guzaitis, Carlin, & Juda, 1972) is designed to pinpoint strengths and weaknesses in mathematics. The instrument is also used to identify instructional objectives and appropriate instructional materials. Two levels are included: Level A (kindergarten through grade 3) and Level B (grades 3 through 6). Each level has three major components: Survey Tests, Probes, and a Prescriptive Guide.

Description of components

Survey Tests—The survey tests serve as a screening device to determine general strengths and weaknesses in mathematical abilities. In addition, they identify specific areas that need further assessment.

Probes—This component consists of 32 probes, or individual criterion-referenced tests. Each probe measures a specific area (for example, addition, division, problem solving), and each item in a probe is correlated with an instructional objective.

Prescription Guide—This component correlates the instructional objective with appropriate sections of available mathematical curricula.

Interpretation of results

The interpretive value of Diagnosis: An Instructional Aid in Mathematics is in the careful selection of appropriate instructional objectives and concomitant suggested curriculum materials.

OVERVIEW: DIAGNOSIS: AN INSTRUCTIONAL AID IN MATHEMATICS

- *Age level*—Kindergarten–Grade six
- *Suggested use*—Diagnosis: An Instructional Aid in Mathematics is a comprehensive diagnostic-prescriptive instrument that offers the teacher a model from screening through instruction and remediation. The survey tests serve as screening devices, the probes are a series of criterion-referenced tests, and the prescription guide offers alternative methods and materials for teaching the identified instructional objectives.

Inventory of Basic Arithmetic Skills

The Enright Diagnostic Inventory of Basic Arithmetic Skills (Enright, 1983) is designed for elementary-, middle-, and junior-high-school students who have specific problems with mathematics. The Inventory consists of 13 sections, including basic computation (adding, subtracting, multiplying, dividing) with whole numbers, fractions, and decimals, as well as conversions of fractions. Items in the Inventory are based on a task analysis of each computational skill area. The Inventory can be either individually or group-administered. It includes three types of tests: basic facts, wide-range placement, and skill placement.

Description of tests

Basic Facts—This section includes two forms that each measure basic arithmetic facts in the areas of addition, subtraction, multiplication, and division.

Wide-Range Placement—This section includes two forms that each include two items from each of the 13 computation sections. This can be administered to determine a starting place for the more in-depth skill placement test.

Skill Placement—This section includes 13 tests, each with two forms, that measure the computation sections. A total of 144 skill sequences are included. A brief description follows.

> *Addition of Whole Numbers*—Twelve skill sequences ranging from "two-digit numbers with sum less than 10" to "two 3-digit numbers, regrouping ones and tens."

> *Subtraction of Whole Numbers*—Fifteen sequences ranging from "1-digit number from a 1-digit number" to "3-digit number from a 3-digit number with zeros in the ones and tens places."

> *Multiplication of Whole Numbers*—Eighteen sequences ranging from "two 1-digit numbers" to "3-digit number with zero in the tens place by a 2-digit number."

> *Division of Whole Numbers*—Twenty-two sequences ranging from "1-digit number by a 1-digit number with no remainder" to "5-digit number by a 3-digit number with remainder."

> *Conversion of Fractions*—Eight sequences ranging from "improper fraction to a whole number" to "three fractions to the lowest common denominator (LCD) with the LCD not included."

> *Addition of Fractions*—Ten sequences ranging from "two like fractions" (in horizontal form) to "two mixed numbers."

> *Subtraction of Fractions*—Nine sequences ranging from "fraction from a like fraction" to "mixed number from a mixed number, with regrouping (in horizontal form)."

> *Multiplication of Fractions*—Six sequences ranging from "fraction by a like fraction" to "mixed number by a mixed number."

> *Division of Fractions*—Six sequences ranging from "fraction by a like fraction" to "mixed number by a mixed number."

> *Addition of Decimals*—Eleven sequences ranging from "two tenths decimals with no regrouping" to "two mixed decimals with regrouping (in horizontal form)."

> *Subtraction of Decimals*—Eleven sequences ranging from "tenths decimal from a tenths decimal with no regrouping" to "mixed decimal from a mixed decimal, with regrouping."

> *Multiplication of Decimals*—Six sequences ranging from "whole number times a tenths decimal" to "mixed number times a mixed number with regrouping."

> *Division of Decimals*—Ten sequences ranging from "tenths decimal by a 1-digit number with no regrouping" to "mixed number by a mixed number."

Interpretation of results

According to the author, the Inventory of Basic Arithmetic Skills provides three types of information. First, it provides specific information on which computational skills the student has mastered. A criterion level of 80 percent (four out of five items for each of the skills) is suggested for assuming mastery. Second, each of the 144 skill areas are correlated with the grade levels in which they are taught in five separate basal mathematics series. Finally, a valuable feature is the inclusion of guidelines to perform an error analysis. The author identified 233 discrete error patterns that could be grouped together into seven error clusters: regrouping; process substitution; omission; directional; placement; attention to sign; and guessing. Figure 14-2 shows an example of some of the process-substitution error patterns.

OVERVIEW: ENRIGHT INVENTORY OF BASIC ARITHMETIC SKILLS

- *Age level*—Elementary–Junior high
- *Suggested use*—The Enright Inventory of Basic Arithmetic Skills is a comprehensive, well-constructed instrument. The Inventory includes items related to basic computation of whole numbers, fractions, and decimals. The skill areas are sequential, so that information from the test can be used to identify appropriate objectives for an IEP. The error analysis also yields information important in choosing teaching strategies. Individual progress-report sheets and class-record sheets are available to summarize and clarify the test data. Although the level and detail of information provided by this instrument might not be necessary for the average student, it is quite appropriate for those for whom more complete information is warranted (Smith, 1989).

Mathematics Concept Inventory

The Mathematics Concept Inventory (MCI) (Cawley, Fitzmaurice, Goodstein, Lepore, Sedlak, & Althaus, 1977) is a comprehensive assessment device that is a part of Project MATH. Also included in Project MATH is a multiple-option curriculum that contains prescriptive guides and activity books. The MCI can be used as a measure to determine appropriate objectives and subsequent teaching strategies and as a method of monitoring progress towards reaching the objectives.

Description
The MCI has four levels. Level 1 (58 items) includes content usually covered from prekindergarten through grade one. Level 2 (63 items) is appropriate for grades 1 and 2. Levels 3 (60 items) and 4 (59 items) can be used to measure concepts and skills taught in grades 2.5–4 and grades 5–6, respectively.

FIGURE 14-2 **Example of Error Patterns from the Enright® Diagnostic Inventory of Basic Arithmetic Skills.**

From B. Enright, ENRIGHT® *Diagnostic Inventory of Basic Arithmetic Skills.* Copyright © 1983 by Curriculum Associates, Inc. Reprinted with permission. ENRIGHT® is a registered trademark of Curriculum Associates, Inc.

Interpretation of results

Each item for each level is associated with a strand, an area, a concept, and the prescriptive guides to teach the item. Figure 14-3 shows an example of the student page and examiner page for an item from Level 3. For that item, the administration guide would also indicate the appropriate prescriptive guides and learning activities to use to develop that skill. A class record and individual progress records are also available to summarize data from the MCI.

OVERVIEW: MATHEMATICS CONCEPT INVENTORY

- *Age level*—Prekindergarten–Grade six
- *Suggested use*—The MCI is part of a comprehensive program called Project MATH. Its 240 items cover material normally taught from

---

Look at the four multiplication examples on the card. Point to the correct answer for each problem. (Learner may use scratch paper.)

	946		1358
312	926	321	1284
× 3	1036	× 4	1248
	936		1344

	1259		3252
453	1269	5 4 2	3052
× 3	1349	× 6	3042
	1359		3242

Answers:

936	1284
No Regrouping	Regrouping 100's to 1000
1359	3252
Regrouping 10's and 100's	Regrouping All

Strand—NUMBERS
Area—MULTIPLICATION
Concept—ONE–DIGIT MULTIPLIER

FIGURE 14-3   Example from the Mathematics Concept Inventory: Project Math.

prekindergarten through grade six. Each item is associated with both a general and a specific mathematics area, and also with curriculum materials appropriate for that skill. As in any test of this type, content validity is of the utmost importance.

DIAGNOSTIC SPELLING TESTS

WHY USE?
Screening and identification; informal determination of objectives and teaching strategies; documentation of educational need; establishment of IEP goals

WHO SHOULD USE?
Teachers; diagnostic specialists

Test of Written Spelling–2

The Test of Written Spelling–2 (TWS-2) (Larsen & Hammill, 1986) is an individually administered and group-administered test designed to pinpoint a child's written spelling level and to specify the types of words with which a child is having problems. Its use as a group-administered instrument is somewhat limited, however. It is designed for use with children aged 6–18.

Description
The TWS-2 is comprised of 100 spelling words divided into two categories: predictable and unpredictable. The "predictable" subtest includes 50 words; these conform to usual spelling rules and generalizations (for example, *bed, tardy, signal*). The "unpredictable" subtest also includes 50 words; these words do not follow the usual rules and, therefore, primarily have to be memorized (for example, *myself, eight, knife, enough*). Each word is said in isolation, used in a sentence, and repeated in isolation. The student spells the word on the form provided. Suggested starting points are provided and the testing is terminated after five consecutive errors in each section so that the student will not become frustrated.

Interpretation of results
The raw scores for the predictable subtest, the unpredictable subtest, and the total (predictable and unpredictable) test can all be converted to percentile ranks and standard scores or quotients (mean = 100; standard deviation = 15).

Technical characteristics

Normative sample. The sample included 3,805 children from 15 states. Geographic location, grade, sex, residence, and social status of the sample are described in the manual.

Reliability. Internal consistency was good; coefficients ranged from .86 to .97 (predictable); from .88 to .97 (unpredictable); and from .92 to .98 (total test). Test-retest coefficients (for a limited sample) were also good with almost all above .90.

Validity. Concurrent validity coefficients (with 63 fourth graders) with the spelling subtest of the Durrell Analysis of Reading Difficulty, the WRAT, the California Achievement Tests, and the SRA Achievement Series are reported. Coefficients ranged from .63 to .86 (predictable), from .76 to .92 (unpredictable), and from .69 to .90 (total test). These data come from the original 1976 TWS, although the authors provide evidence that the two versions are comparable. Information related to content and construct validity of the TWS-2 is also provided.

Review of relevant research

No empirical studies on the TWS-2 were located. In reviews of the TWS-2, Erickson (1989) reported that it was an excellent screening instrument and Noyce (1989) noted that it was well constructed and easily administered. Based on the authors' data and statements regarding the equivalence of the two tests, research on the TWS might be considered relevant for the TWS-2.

■ Subjects' scores from the TWS were more accurate in predicting their California Achievement Test language scores than their spelling, mathematics, or reading scores. The correlation coefficients between these two tests were small, however (from .20 to .38) (Carpenter & Carpenter, 1978).

■ A computerized version of the TWS has been developed to decrease the examiner's time spent and the number of scoring errors (Hasselbring & Crossland, 1982).

OVERVIEW: TEST OF WRITTEN SPELLING-2

■ *Age level*—6 through 18 years old

■ *Type of administration*—Individual (small group possible)

■ *Technical adequacy*—Good reliability; more validity data needed

■ *Scores yielded*—Standard scores (quotients), percentiles

■ *Suggested use*—Although the TWS-2 yields normative data, its real value lies in the informal use of the word lists. The idea of having predictable and unpredictable word lists is a good one. The reliability of the revised version has been improved over the original TWS, however, making the normative use more acceptable. No matter how the results are used, an error analysis should also be conducted to provide additional information.

CRITERION-REFERENCED INSTRUMENTS

WHY USE?
Identification of areas for further evaluation or remediation; informal determination of objectives and teaching strategies; development and evaluation of IEPs

WHO SHOULD USE?
Teachers

The Spellmaster Assessment and Teaching System

The Spellmaster (Greenbaum, 1987) is a criterion-referenced assessment instrument consisting of three sets of tests: Diagnostic, Irregular Word, and Homonym. The Spellmaster was field-tested on more than 2,500 students and is designed for use with pupils in kindergarten through grade 8, although it can be used through adult age. The Spellmaster was developed to assist in the identification of strengths and weaknesses in spelling. It is also useful in grouping students according to their spelling needs. There are three sets of tests at eight levels that include specific types of spelling words. There are also entry-level tests that can be used to determine the most appropriate level of test to use for a particular student.

Description of tests

Diagnostic (8 tests)—These tests include regular words, that is, words that use rules that generalize to the spelling of the majority of the words in the English language.

Irregular Words (8 tests)—These tests include words whose spelling violates basic phonics rules, thus requiring a person to master or memorize each rule and not rely on generalization.

Homonym (8 tests)—The spelling of the words on these tests can be either regular or irregular, but the correct spelling has to do with its meaning.

Interpretation of results

Results of the Spellmaster can be used to identify strengths and weaknesses in spelling and can be used to group students according to their spelling needs. The value of the Spellmaster is in its ability to pinpoint specific types of errors that are made. Techniques and activities are described that can be used to remediate the spelling problems that are identified. The name of the instrument reflects its pragmatic approach to testing and teaching spelling.

OVERVIEW: SPELLMASTER ASSESSMENT AND TEACHING SYSTEM

- *Age level*—Kindergarten–grade 8
- *Suggested use*—The Spellmaster offers a series of word lists that can assist a teacher in determining the type of words a student is having difficulty spelling. Care should be taken to analyze the types of errors made and not simply to group students according to spelling ability. The information related to teaching the identified spelling problems is valuable. Harrison (1990) noted that although the Spellmaster may be useful in some classrooms, there is no evidence that the tests adequately sample spelling skills needed in schools. Wiese (1990) also noted that the tests lacked technical adequacy.

Instrument or Technique	Screening and Initial Identification	Informal Determination and Evaluation of Teaching Programs and Strategies	Determination of Current Performance Level and Educational Need	Decisions about Classification and Program Placement	IEP Goals	IEP Objectives	IEP Evaluation	Mild/Moderate	Severe/Profound	Preschool	Elementary Age	Secondary Age	Adult	Special Considerations	Educational Relevance for Exceptional Students
	Prereferral / Suggested Use			Postreferral				Target Population							
Key Math–Revised	X		X		X			X			X			A revised version of a very popular test; the format should be considered in its interpretation	adequate
Stanford Diagnostic Mathematics Test	X	X	X		X			X			X	X		Good technical aspects; computer scoring available	useful
Test of Mathematical Abilities	X							X			X	X		Has sections on attitude toward math and math vocabulary	adequate
Diagnosis: An Instructional Aid in Mathematics	X	X	X		X	X	X	X			X			Can be used for screening and programming; test items are correlated with instructional materials	very useful
Inventory of Basic Arithmetic Skills	X	X	X		X	X	X	X			X			Used to determine specific math objectives; error analysis is recommended	very useful
Mathematics Concept Inventory		X	X		X	X	X	X			X			Includes curriculum materials for each of the 240 items	adequate
Test of Written Spelling–2	X	X	X		X			X			X			One of the few tests that yields normative information in spelling	useful
Spellmaster	X	X	X		X			X			X			Information from error analysis is most valuable	useful

___PART FIVE___

Special Assessment Considerations

In this section, assessment concerns related to three populations will be addressed. These are *infant assessment, early childhood assessment*, and *transitional/vocational assessment*. These areas have become increasingly important because of legislation that has mandated educational services for infants and toddlers (Public Law 99-457) and transitional services for secondary students (P.L. 101-456). The Carl D. Perkins Act also brought increased attention to vocational services for handicapped students.

In addition to a description of a variety of instruments (formal and informal) used with these populations, discussions will also center around the type of assessment process (e.g., team assessment) and alternative procedures (e.g., play assessment, analysis of work samples) that should be considered. The format for describing instruments will be similar to the chapters in Parts Three and Four. That includes the following:

1. A summary matrix that presents information about specific instruments and techniques in a format that allows easy comparison of the instruments for suggested use and target population. The matrix also includes a statement of any special considerations of which a user should be aware. In addition, for each instrument, the matrix gives the educational relevance for exceptional students. The matrices are directly related to the assessment model proposed in Chapter 2.
2. A thorough review of relevant research for each norm-referenced instrument. The review emphasizes the use of the test with exceptional students.
3. An overview box for each test. The overview summarizes the age range, technical adequacy (for norm-referenced tests), and suggested use for each instrument.

After reading Part Five you should be able to:

1. *Identify the reasons for needing team assessment for infants and toddlers*
2. *Identify the importance of using play assessment for young children*
3. *Identify the strengths and weaknesses of a variety of screening and developmental tests*
4. *Identify the importance of developing transitional programs for secondary students*
5. *Identify the need for analyzing work samples and "on the job" assessment*
6. *Identify the strengths and weaknesses of a variety of vocational interest and attitude measures*

__15__

Infant Assessment

INSTRUMENTS/PROCEDURES INCLUDED

DEVELOPMENTAL TESTS (NORM-REFERENCED)
- Battelle Developmental Inventory
- Denver II
- Developmental Profile II

DEVELOPMENTAL TESTS (CRITERION-REFERENCED)
- Assessment Log and Developmental Progress Chart
- Ordinal Scales of Psychological Development
- Brigance Inventory of Early Development–Revised
- Callier–Azusa Scale
- Uniform Performance Assessment System
- Vulpé Assessment Battery

Interest in the area of early childhood assessment has been increasing. This popularity is partly due to legislation that has provided increased awareness of, and has mandated increased responsibility for, the educational needs of children from birth to 5 years old. For example, Public Law 98-199 (the Education of the Handicapped Amendment Act of 1983) targeted the expansion and improvement of services to preschool handicapped children as one of its primary initiatives. P.L. 99-457 (discussed in Chapter 1) outlined specific responsibilities for the identification and appropriate educational programming for children from birth.

It is important that young children be evaluated by a team approach. Frequently, for example, infants who are handicapped or suspected of being handicapped will have medical problems that will require evaluation from appropriate medical personnel. Others who might be involved are parents, psychologists, speech-language pathologists, audiologists, and physical/occupational therapists. It is important that these professionals, in conjunction with the teacher, work together to coordinate assessment results into the most viable overall educational plan. For older preschool children, evaluation might be conducted for many purposes, including screening and eligibility decisions when a less severe problem is suspected. Subsequently it is paramount that communication be optimized among the various team members so that appropriate decisions can be made. Again, the teacher should be an active member of that team. Given the multidisciplinary nature of the assessment procedures used with young children, the instruments and techniques discussed in the next two chapters will focus on those used by teachers and other educational personnel.

The instruments used (norm-referenced and criterion-referenced) for infants and toddlers can be primarily considered *developmental* while those for preschool children can be considered *developmental* (both norm-referenced and criterion-referenced), *screening,* or *pre-academic.* It should be noted that many tests used in early childhood extend the entire preschool age range (usually birth to age 6 or 7). For ease of discussion, however, tests and techniques for infants and toddlers (birth to 3 years) will be presented separately from those for preschool children ages 4–6. The reader should recognize that there is an overlap in age ranges and skills measured for many of the instruments discussed in the next two chapters.

DEVELOPMENTAL TESTS: INFANTS AND TODDLERS

Until recently, few norm-referenced developmental instruments were available. The majority of infants and toddlers were evaluated by either intelligence tests such as the Bayley Scales of Infant Development or a wide variety of developmental checklists and inventories. Many norm-referenced developmental instruments were used only for screening purposes. In this chapter, the Battelle Developmental Inventory (which provides a general overview of the child's developmental profile) and two developmental screening instruments, the Developmental Profile II and the Denver II, are discussed.

There have been many criterion-referenced instruments designed for informal use with infants and toddlers. These tests are usually concerned with what developmental skill the child can or cannot exhibit rather than how they perform compared to others. In other words, results of these types of instruments are used to determine educational objectives and not to document developmental levels. These tests are extremely comprehensive and frequently follow a task analytic model. A number of specific skill areas are identified, and the items tested in each skill are essentially the steps of the task analysis. Because of many items included, only portions of the test are administered, depending on the reason for evaluation. Neisworth and Bagnato (1988) referred to these instruments as either curriculum-imbedded (e.g., the Assessment Log and Developmental Progress Chart) or curriculum-referenced (e.g., the Brigance Inventory of Early Development-Revised). Still other tests have been developed following Piaget's theory of development (e.g., The Ordinal Scales of Infant Development). Peterson (1988) classified this type of instrument as one based on the cognitive-stages perspective. Finally, there are instruments that are designed specifically for children with handicaps, particularly, sensorimotor handicaps. These instruments, such as the Callier–Azusa, are sometimes called adaptive to handicap measures (Neisworth & Bagnato, 1988) because they provide or allow certain adaptations. It should be noted that while many of the criterion-referenced tests are designed for use with infants and toddlers, they are sometimes used with older, severely handicapped students for whom these developmental items would be appropriate. A discussion of the norm-referenced and criterion-referenced developmental instruments follows.

DEVELOPMENTAL TESTS (NORM-REFERENCED)

WHY USE?
Screening, establishment of educational need (developmental lag), establishment of IEP goals

WHO SHOULD USE?
Teachers, school psychologists, social workers

Battelle Developmental Inventory

The Battelle Developmental Inventory (BDI) (Newborg, Stock, Wnek, Guidubaldi, & Svinicki, 1984) is an individually administered battery of tests that measure developmental skills of children from birth to age 8 years. According to the authors, the BDI can be used for four purposes. These are (1) the assessment and identification of handicapped children, (2) the assessment of nonhandicapped children, (3) the planning and provision of instruction (that is, the development of IEPs), and (4) the evaluation of groups of handicapped children. This latter purpose refers to the monitoring of progress of students who are placed in special education programs. The BDI uses three procedures for obtaining the information: traditional administration, observation, and interview. The manual indicates what type(s) of procedures are relevant for the given items.

Description

The BDI consists of 341 items that are grouped within five domains: Personal-Social, Adaptive, Motor, Communication, and Cognitive. These domains are further broken down into areas or subdomains. There is also a screening version of the BDI that consists of 96 items that can be used as a quick assessment of the skills covered in the five domains.

Personal-Social (85 items)—Includes the areas of adult interaction, expression of feeling/affect, self-concept, peer interaction, coping, and social role.

Adaptive (59 items)—Includes the areas of attention, eating, dressing, personal responsibility, and toileting.

Motor (82 items)—Includes the areas of muscle control, body coordination, locomotion, fine-muscle, and perceptual-motor.

Communication (59 items)—The areas of receptive and expressive communication are included.

Cognitive (56 items)—Includes the areas of perceptual discrimination, memory, reasoning and academic skills, and conceptual development.

Interpretation of results

Scores from the BDI can be translated into a variety of standard scores (including developmental quotients), percentile ranks, and age equivalents. Overall, there are 10 major areas for which scores are available. These are the five domains, plus fine-motor, gross motor, expressive communication, receptive communication, and total. In addition, a score summary sheet is available that provides a visual representation of the child's developmental strengths and weaknesses (Figure 15-1). Information is also available regarding suggested cutoff points to aid in educational decision-making.

Technical characteristics

Normative sample.   A total of 800 children from 24 states were included. Breakdown by age, race, and sex is available in the manual.

Reliability.   Test-retest coefficients were generally high (.81–.97). Interrater reliability coefficients were .95 or higher.

Validity.   Concurrent validity coefficients with a variety of criterion measures are reported in the manual. These ranged from .41 with a verbal intelligence quotient to .94 with an adaptive behavior measure. In general, these coefficients were determined from small samples. The authors also report data and provide arguments for the tests' construct and content validity.

SCORE SUMMARY

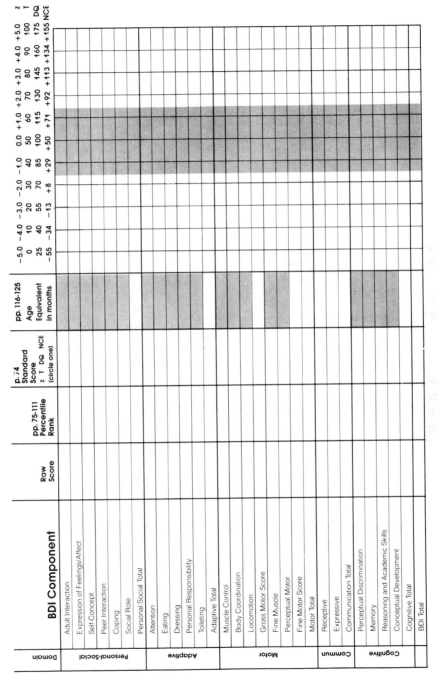

FIGURE 15-1   Summary Sheet from the Battelle Developmental Inventory.

From J. Newborg, J. Stock, L. Wnek, J. Guidubaldi, and J. Svinicki, *Battelle Developmental Inventory*. Allen, TX: DLM Teaching Resources. Copyright © 1984 by LINC Associations. Reprinted with permission.

Review of relevant research

- The pattern and strength of the correlations between the BDI and the Bayley Scales support the use of the BDI to measure development in infants with known or suspected handicaps (Boyd, Welge, Sexton, & Miller, 1989).
- Guidubaldi and Perry (1984) reported that the BDI had both high concurrent validity and predictive validity coefficients with a variety of criterion measures. They particularly noted that it was a favorable predictor of first-grade achievement when administered during kindergarten.
- Mott (1987) investigated the validity of the communications domain with speech and language-disordered children using a variety of language measures as criteria. She found that the total and expressive communication scores correlated highly with the language measures but that the receptive communication scores did not.
- Because of the way the tables are presented, a child could receive radically different scores from one day to the next despite identical performance (Boyd, 1989).
- The screening version of the BDI tends to overidentify. In one study, 22 of 35 children were identified as needing further assessment on the basis of the BDI screen. In reality only three needed extensive assessment based on results from the full BDI (McLean, McCormick, Baird, & Mayfield, 1987).
- Sheehan and Snyder (1990) noted that the BDI should not be used with young handicapped children because of the lack of appropriate items for children under two years of age. They also noted that the cutoff scores suggested in the manual should be used cautiously.
- The BDI had good test-retest reliability, ranging from .81 to .97 (McLinden, 1989). Boyd et al. (1989) reported slightly lower coefficients.
- Teachers were moderately positive about the usefulness of the BDI. They noted, however, that many of the suggested test adaptations were not appropriate (Bailey, Vandiviere, Dellinger, & Munn, 1987).

Summary of research findings

In general, research on the BDI has supported its use as a valid and reliable measure of developmental skills. The screening version of the BDI, however, has been shown to significantly overidentify children as needing further evaluation. Questions related to the tables, its usefulness with very young children, and the suggested adaptations have also been brought up by researchers.

OVERVIEW: BATTELLE DEVELOPMENTAL INVENTORY

- *Age level*—Birth–8 years old
- *Type of administration*—Individual
- *Technical adequacy*—Good reliability, adequate validity
- *Scores yielded*—Standard scores, percentile ranks, age equivalents

■ *Suggested use*—The BDI is a well-constructed developmental inventory. It provides a helpful profile of a child's developmental strengths and weaknesses. The manual is easy to follow and there are guidelines for adapting the test items for the evaluation of handicapped children. There is some question, however, of whether those adaptations are useful. Overall, in fact, the test is more useful for toddlers than infants, and with children with mild, rather than severe, handicaps. Although the authors describe procedures for calculating lower standard scores from the raw scores obtained, the tables themselves do not provide low enough standard scores to differentiate performance of severely handicapped children.

The reliability and validity of the instrument is good. Harrington (1985), in reviewing the BDI, noted that it is rare that a developmental test meets all of the standards for test construction that are outlined in the *Standards for Educational and Psychological Tests* but that the BDI, in fact, does. Overall, it appears that the BDI can be used confidently to identify developmental strengths and weaknesses of both handicapped and nonhandicapped children. The use of the screening edition of the BDI is more questionable.

Denver II

The Denver II (Frankenburg, Dodds, Archers, Bresnick, Maschka, Edelman, & Shapiro, 1990) is an individually administered instrument designed to detect developmental deviations in young children. It is a revision of perhaps the most widely used norm-referenced developmental screening test—the Denver Developmental Screening Test (DDST). The authors state that the Denver II should be used only for screening, not as a definitive predictor of current or future adaptive behavior or intelligence. They further state that the test should not be used to generate a diagnostic label. The test is used with children from birth to 6 years old. The items are arranged in four sections: Personal-Social, Fine Motor-Adaptive, Language, and Gross Motor. The test items are designed to measure skills that correlate with normal child development. Some test materials are meant to elicit responses in the child, although many other items can be administered through an interview with the parents.

Description

Personal-Social (25 items)—Essentially, these tasks measure a child's ability to take care of himself or herself and to relate to other people. The section includes such tasks as playing pat-a-cake, imitating activities, and dressing and undressing.

Fine Motor-Adaptive (29 items)—This section measures fine-motor dexterity, drawing ability and recognition, and manipulation of objects. It includes tasks such as building a tower with blocks, reaching for objects, and scribbling.

Language (39 items)—This section measures a child's ability to perceive, understand, and express language. It includes tasks such as turning to a spoken voice, imitating speech sounds, and naming pictures.

Gross Motor (32 items)—This section measures the child's ability to sit, stand, walk, and jump.

Interpretation of results

Each item on the Denver II is presented on the test form in a developmental sequence (Figure 15-2). A developmental age is reported at which 25 percent, 50 percent, 75 percent, and 90 percent of "normal" children passed each item. For instance, the item "Bangs 2 cubes held in hands" is passed by 25 percent of "normal" children at 6.7 months, by 50 percent at 7.5 months, by 75 percent at 10 months, and by 90 percent at 10.9 months. Each item is scored as "advanced," "normal," "caution," "delayed," or "no opportunity" and provides a developmental profile. The Denver II profile is then interpreted on the basis of advanced, caution, and/or delayed items. The greater the number of cautions and/or delayed items, the greater the probability that the child should be further evaluated. Referrals should be based on the child's past rate of development, Denver II profile, clinical picture, and the availability of further evaluation resources. A child who refuses to perform a majority of the items is considered "untestable."

Technical characteristics

Normative sample.   The sample included 2,096 children between the ages of 2 weeks and 6.5 years; only nonhandicapped children from Colorado were included.

Reliability.   The test-retest coefficient with 38 children was .90. Interrater reliability (having more than one examiner score the results) was .99.

Validity.   The validity of the test is the accuracy with which it measures what it purports to measure—the precision in item placement. Thus it should be used like a growth curve as a basis of comparison of a given child with other children.

Review of relevant research

Because of the relative recency of the Denver II no research was located. Research on its predecessor (the DDST) is widespread. The authors argue, however, that the two instruments are sufficiently different to warrant caution in applying these findings to the Denver II.

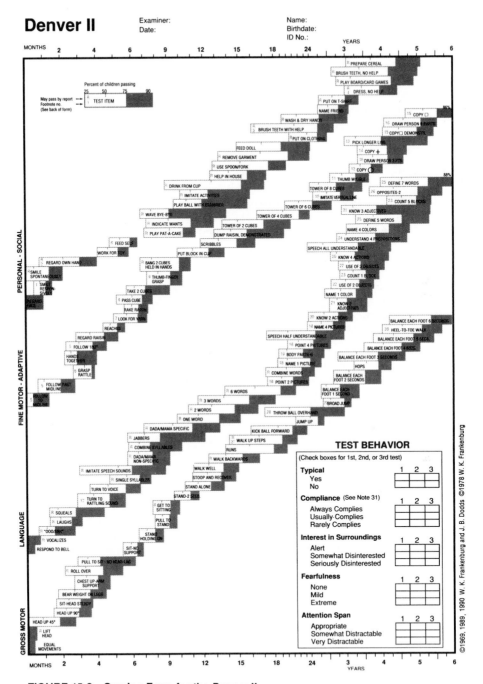

FIGURE 15-2   Scoring Form for the Denver II

- The DDST failed to identify the majority of children who had failed expressive language screening even when more rigorous cutoffs were used (Glascoe & Borowitz, 1988).
- The DDST was relatively inefficient in identifying children with IQs between 50 and 70 (Nugent, 1976). In fact, Diamond (1987) found that the DDST failed to identify the majority of children who had subsequent school problems.
- The DDST was not effective in screening for children with neurological problems. It identified only 17 percent of the children found by physical examination to have organic neurologic problems. Furthermore, 56 percent of the children with neurological problems successfully passed all four DDST sections (Sterling & Sterling, 1977).
- The DDST underidentifies children needing further evaluation (McLean, McCormick, Baird, & Mayfield, 1987).
- A second level of screening should be used for children who fail the DDST (Testa & Stoneburner, 1980)
- The DDST has questionable applicability with disadvantaged children (Harper & Walker, 1983) particularly in the language areas.
- Preschool children with behavior problems scored lower on the DDST than did children without such problems (Garrity & Servos, 1978).
- Several shorter versions of the DDST have been developed. Frankenburg, Van Doorninck, Liddell, and Dick (1976) report the Preschool Developmental Questionnaire in which the parents answer 10 questions about their child. An abbreviated DDST has also been developed that can be administered in less than half the time of the entire test (Frankenburg, Fandal, Sciarillo, & Burgess, 1981).
- The DDST correlates highly (.84 to .95) with various intelligence measures (Frankenburg, Camp, & Van Natta, 1971), although there are no data to support its predictive validity (Miller & Sprong, 1986).

Summary of research findings

Most literature on the DDST has questioned its applicability to a number of populations. It does not seem to be appropriate in the early age limits or with mildly handicapped children. Its concurrent validity seems to be adequate, although it was established by using intelligence measures as criteria. There are also shorter versions of the DDST available, although there is little evidence supporting their validity. It should be noted, however, that many of the criticisms of the DDST were based on inappropriate uses of the instrument (e.g., predicting achievement). In addition, the Denver II has attempted to address many of these criticisms (e.g., increasing language items). Research on the Denver II should be forthcoming to determine the relevance of the information available on the DDST.

OVERVIEW: DENVER II

- *Age level*—Birth through 6 years old

- *Type of administration*—Individual
- *Technical adequacy*—Adequate standardization, questionable validity, acceptable reliability
- *Scores yielded*—Profile that is interpreted as "normal," "questionable," "abnormal," or "untestable"
- *Suggested use*—The Denver II is an updated version of DDST. The DDST was criticized for several reasons including its lack of predictive validity, particularly for children with milder problems. Specifically, the DDST appeared to underidentify children in need of further evaluation. These limitations suggested that the DDST should be used cautiously. The Denver II does provide updated norms and slightly different scoring procedures. Research on this instrument is necessary.

Developmental Profile–II

The Developmental Profile II (DP-II) (Alpern, Boll, & Shearer, 1986) is designed to evaluate children from birth through age 9. It is meant to be used as a parent interview, which can be given in approximately 20–40 minutes. The DP-II, however, can also be used as a self-interview that is usually completed by the teacher. The DP-II uses an age scale in which there are approximately three items per age level. An age level can encompass a 5–6-month interval (e.g., 25–30 months) to a 1-year interval (e.g., 79–90 months). There are five subscales on the DP-II. An example of items (and associated age level) from each subscale follows.

Description

Physical Developmental Age Scale (39 items)—Examples of items are "can the child roll from his/her stomach to his/her back and from back to stomach without help?" (0–6-month level) and "can the child run fast enough to compete with a normal eight-year-old child in a race or game of tag?" (79–90-month level).

Self-help Developmental Age Scale (39 items)—Examples are "does the child try to get objects that are near but beyond reach?" (0–6-month level) and "does the child take off his/her coat without help when buttons or zippers are undone?" (19–24-month level).

Social Developmental Age Scale (36 items)—Examples are "does the child come when called at least 25% of the time?" (7–12-month level) and "is the child interested in exploring new places such as a friend's house or a neighbor's yard?" (19–24-month level)

Academic Developmental Age Scale (34 items)—Examples are "does the child use pencils or crayons in definite attempts to make marks on any surface?" (13–18-month level) and "in the child's play, are things ever grouped together by color or form or size?" (25–30-month level)

Communication Developmental Age Scale (38 items)—Examples include "does the child use at least 15 different words in the right way?" (19–24-

month level) and "does the child name, not just repeat, at least 20 things seen in pictures?" (25–30-month level).

Interpretation of results

As noted previously, the DP-II uses age scores that compare a person's performance on the test to a "typical performance" by a person of the same age. These types of scores are generally discouraged for use with standardized tests. On the DP-II, items are scored as passed, failed, or no opportunity, with items from each subscale grouped together to provide an age score. The age scores are thus interpreted as either advanced or delayed, based on the actual chronological age of the child. There are also tables included in the manual that provide methods of interpreting the significance of delays based on the point at which various percentages of the children in the standardization sample passed the various item. Overall, the interpretive procedures for the DP-II are less than adequate.

Technical characteristics

Normative sample.   A total of over 2,300 non-handicapped children, ages birth through 9-1/2, were included. Overall, the sample is not representative of the U.S. population, having significant restrictions both geographically and in terms of socioeconomic status. The normative sample for the DP-II was the same for that of the original Developmental Profile normed in 1972.

Reliability.   Overall, little reliability data are offered in the test manual. More information is necessary before evaluating the reliability of the test.

Validity.   The authors provide an argument for content validity of the instrument although it is somewhat unclear how the items were chosen. There is also limited evidence of concurrent validity, primarily with the Stanford-Binet Intelligence Scale (Form LM).

Review of relevant research

There is limited research focusing on the DP-II, although there are some studies on the original DP published in 1972. As mentioned, there were very few changes made in the DP-II. There is some evidence that the original DP was a better predictor of language delays than the Denver Developmental Screening Test (German, Williams, Herzfield, and Marshall, 1982) and that the DP, when used in conjunction with a battery of instruments, resulted in consistent clinical judgment among evaluation between members (Bagnato, 1984). In one study of the DP-II, Harris and Fagley (1987) reported significant positive correlations with later measures of self-help, physical development, and communication with a group of 29 autistic children evaluated 4–7 years later.

The DP-II has also been reviewed negatively in the professional literature. Huebner (1989) noted its technical inadequacy, whereas Hightower (1989) suggested that the norm-referenced uses of the test be downplayed.

OVERVIEW: DEVELOPMENTAL PROFILE II

- *Age level*—Birth–9-1/2 years
- *Type of administration*—Individual (interview)
- *Technical adequacy*—Limited normative sample, reliability, and validity
- *Scores yielded*—Age score, descriptive categories
- *Suggested use*—The DP-II should be used for screening purposes only. Because of the interview format, the DP-II can be given to parents to provide some basic information and can often act as an "ice breaker." The technical inadequacy of the instrument limits its use. Further, the use of age scales is questionable and results in less than adequate interpretive value. Clearly, the DP-II should be used only in conjunction with other instruments to provide supplemental data from parental input.

DEVELOPMENTAL TESTS (CRITERION-REFERENCED)

WHY USE?
Development of IEP goals and objectives; IEP evaluation

WHO SHOULD USE?
Teachers

Assessment Log and Developmental Progress Chart–Infants

The Assessment Log and Developmental Progress Chart–Infants (Johnson-Martin, Jens, & Attermeier, 1986) is part of the Carolina Curriculum for Handicapped Infants and Infants at Risk. It includes items that are correlated with 24 curriculum sequences and is presented in a checklist format. In general, the areas of cognition (using primarily a Piagetian approach), language/communication, self-help/social skills, fine motor, and gross motor are included. Within each of the 24 areas, a number of sequential items are included.

Description
The 24 areas and examples of the first and last item in each area follow.

Tactile Integration and Manipulation (11 items)—"Responds differently to warm/cold, rough/smooth" to "pokes or plays with clay."

Auditory Localization and Object Permanence (10 items)—"Quiets when noise is presented" to "turns head and looks back for two sounds." In this area, there are also alternative items for visually impaired children.

Visual Pursuit and Object Permanence (7 items)—"Visually fixates for at least three seconds" to "looks at cover under which object has disappeared."

Object Permanence-Visual Motor (12 items)—"Pulls cloth from face" to "finds object after systematic search under 3 covers."

Spatial Concepts (14 items)—"Shifts attention from one object to another" to "uses tools to deal with spatial problems (e.g., extends reach with a stick)."

Functional Use of Objects and Symbolic Play (12 items)—"Moves hand to mouth" to "talks to dolls or animals or makes them interact with one another."

Control over Physical Environment (9 items)—"Repeats activity that produces an interesting result" to "uses tools to solve problems."

Readiness Concepts (7 items)—"Matches simple geometric shapes" to "understands concept of big."

Responses to Communication from Others (23 items)—"Quiets to voice" to "follows 3 different 3-part commands."

Gestural Imitation (10 items)—"Looks at person talking and gesturing" to "imitates sequence of 2 signs that stand for words."

Gestural Communication (15 items)—"Shows anticipation of regularly occurring events in everyday care" to "combines signs to communicate."

Vocal Imitation (12 items)—"Vocalizing in response to person talking" to "imitates 3-syllable words."

Vocal Communication (22 items)—"Differentiates cries" to "combines 2 or more words in sentences."

Social Skills (19 items)—"Can be comforted by talking to, holding, or rocking" to "shares spontaneously with peers."

Self-Direction (6 items)—"Moves away from Mom in same room" to "explores unfamiliar places with mother present."

Feeding (19 items)—"Sucks from nipple smoothly" to "distinguishes between edible and nonedible substances."

Grooming (4 items)—"Cooperates in hand-washing" to "wipes nose if given a handkerchief."

Dressing (6 items)—"Cooperates in dressing and undressing" to "puts on loose shoes or slippers."

Reaching and Grasping (11 items)—"Moves arms actively when sees or hears object" to "uses neat pincer grasp."

Object Manipulation (9 items)—"Looks at hand (or toy) to one side" to "looks toward object and visually directs reach or adjusts reach to get noisy object." This section has modifications for visually impaired children.

Object Manipulation (continued) (30 items)—This section includes items related to form manipulation, block patterns, drawing, placing pegs, and putting in and taking out objects.

Bilateral Hand Activity (14 items)—"Bats at objects at chest level" to "strings 3 large beads."

Gross-Motor Activities: Prone (16 items)—"Lifts head, freeing nose; arms and legs flexed" to "crawls down stairs backward."

Gross-Motor Activities: Supine (7 items)—"Turns head from side to side in response to visual and/or auditory stimuli while in supine position" to "rolls from back to stomach."

Gross-Motor Activity: Upright (10 items)—"Head steady when held" to "moves from hands and knees, to hands and feet, to standing."

Gross-Motor Activities: Upright (continued) (15 items)—Measures areas of stair climbing, balance, jumping, posture, and locomotion.

Interpretation of results

The authors suggest that an individual be evaluated in each of the 24 areas, usually beginning with the first item and continuing until he or she fails three consecutive items. The obvious exceptions are those areas that cannot be measured because of the nature of an individual's handicap (for example, auditory localization for a person with a significant hearing impairment). The results are then placed on the Developmental Progress Chart (see Figure 15-3). Items are scored as passed, failed, or emerging. Determination or prioritizing of instructional goals can then be accomplished. In addition, general age ranges for the various items can be determined from the results placed on the Developmental Progress Chart. These are grouped in 3-month clusters from birth to 24 months. These age ranges, particularly when interpreted with students with severe or profound handicaps, must be viewed with caution.

OVERVIEW: ASSESSMENT LOG AND DEVELOPMENTAL PROGRESS CHART

- *Age level*—Birth to 24 months
- *Suggested use*—The Assessment Log and Developmental Progress Chart is used in conjunction with the Carolina Curriculum. It is a well-researched model that shows promise in determining instructional goals as well as providing instructional procedures. It should be noted that the entire model was designed for *infants,* although there is information related to use with older individuals mentioned in the manual. In general, that information suggests that many of the items might need to be adapted and that care should be taken to choose areas that are adaptive (functional) for the individual. There is a general lack of data available about the use of the curriculum and, subsequently, the assessment component with older students with severe or profound handicaps. There is mention in the manual of field-test data that did not find the use of the curriculum effective with this population on a short-term (3–6 months) basis. Clearly, more research on the model is necessary.

Developmental Progress Chart

Name: _____

Dates: _____

▨ No norms available.   ■ Items beyond this point are necessary only for certain populations (see Assessment Log).

	Sequence	0 – 3 mo.	3 – 6 mo.	6 – 9 mo.	9 – 12 mo.	12 – 15 mo.	15 – 18 mo.	18 – 21 mo.	21 – 24 mo.
Cognition	1. Tactile Integration and Manipulation	a	b c	d e f	g h	i	j	k	▨
	2. Auditory Localization and Object Permanence	a b c	d e	f	g ■ h	■	j	k	
	3. Visual Pursuit and Object Permanence	a b c d e	f	g	h	■ i	k	k	▨ l
	4. Object Permanence (Visual-Motor)		a b c	d e f g	h	i j	j k	l m	n
	5. Spatial Concepts	a b	c	e	g	h	j	l	l
	6. Functional Use of Objects and Symbolic Play	a b	c d	e f g	g	h	h	h	i
	7. Control over Physical Environment	a	c d e	d	e	f	g		
	8. "Readiness" Concepts	a b					a b	c d	e f g
Communication/Language	9. Responses to Communication from Others	a b	c d e f g	h	j k	l m	n o p	q r s	t u v w
	10. Gestural Imitation	a	b	c d e	f	g h	i	q r s t	
	11. Gestural Communication	a b	c d e f	g h i	j	k	j	j	o
	12. Vocal Imitation		e f g h		g	h i	k	k	
	13. Vocal Communication	a b c d	e f g h	i j	k	l m n	o p	q r s t	t u v
S.S./A.	14. Social Skills	a b c	d e f	g h	i j k l	l m	n o	p q	r s
	15. Self-Direction	a b c	d e f g	h	a b	c	d	e	f
Self-Help	16. Feeding	a	b c	g	m	n o	p q	r	s
	17. Grooming				a	a	b	c	d
	18. Dressing	b	c	c	a	b	c	d e	f
Fine Motor	19. Reaching and Grasping	a b	c d e f	g h i j k	a	a b	c d	d e	e f g
	20. Object Manipulation	a b c d	e f	g h i	III	a b c	d e	d e	e f g
				IV	v a b	c d	e	f	g
	21. Bilateral Hand Activity	a b	c d e	f	g	h i	j k	l m	n
Gross Motor	22. Gross Motor Activities: Stomach	a b	c d e f g h	i j k l	m n	o p	II a b	c	d
	23. Gross Motor Activities: Back	a b c d	e f g		III		a	b	b
	24. Gross Motor Activities Upright	a	b	c	IV de f g h i	j	IV a b	c d	e

*S.S./A. = Social Skills/Adaptation.

FIGURE 15-3   The Developmental Progress Chart.

From N. Johnson-Martin, K. Jens, and S. Attermeier, *Assessment Log and Developmental Progress Chart for the Carolina Curriculum for Handicapped Infants and Infants at Risk.* Baltimore: Paul H. Brookes. Copyright © 1986 by Nancy Johnson-Martin, Kenneth Jens, and Susan Attermeier.

Assessment in Infancy: Ordinal Scales of Psychological Development

The purpose of the Ordinal Scales of Psychological Development (Uzgiris & Hunt, 1975) is to provide a measure of an individual's cognitive and perceptual development using a Piagetian approach. The Scales are based on the assumption that individuals go through specific identifiable sequences of development. Rather than using a norm-referenced model of assessment, the ordinal model focuses on the determination of the developmental level of an individual regardless of age. In other words, the ordinal model is based on the assumption that there is an invariant sequence of behaviors, not linked with a specific age. Although the Ordinal Scales were originally developed for use with infants, it has been used with older mentally retarded individuals. In fact, a manual has been provided by Dunst (1980) that offers additional items (called steps) to make the Ordinal Scales more sensitive to the intermediate levels that individuals with severe or profound handicaps pass through during development.

Description

The Ordinal Scales assess development in the following six areas: (1) Development of Visual Pursuit and the Permanence of Objects, (2) Development of Means for Obtaining Desired Environmental Events, (3) Development of Vocal and Gestural Imitation, (4) Development of Operational Causality, (5) Construction of Object Relations in Space, and (6) Development of Schemes for Relating to Objects. These areas are further broken down into *steps,* or test items. The steps involve an activity, or directions for eliciting the responses including the location for the activity and the materials to be used (a list of 34 items such as stacking rings and string is included in the manual). The behavior that is necessary to meet the criteria for passing each step is also specified. A description of the six scales follows:

> *The Development of Visual Pursuit and the Permanence of Objects (15 items)*—Requires the individual to perform tasks ranging from "following a slow-moving object through a 180-degree arc" to "finding object following a series of invisible displacements by searching in reverse of the order of hiding."
>
> *The Development of Means for Obtaining Desired Environmental Events (12 steps)*—Includes items ranging from "appearance of hand-watching behavior" to "foresight in the problem of the solid ring."
>
> *The Development of Imitation: Vocal and Gestural (10 steps)*—Items range from "use of vocalization other than crying" to "imitation of new words" (vocal), and "systematic imitation of familiar simple schemes" to "imitation of unfamiliar gestures invisible to the infant" (gestural).

The Development of Operational Causality (7 steps)—Items include "behavior in a familiar game situation" and "behavior to a spectacle created by an agent."

The Construction of Object Relations in Space (11 steps)—Items range from "observing two objects alternately" to "indicating absence of familiar persons."

The Development of Schemes for Relating to Objects (3 steps)—The items are "acting on simple objects," "acting on several objects available together," and "acting on objects with social meaning."

Interpretation of results

For each item or step, several behaviors are possible. For example, for the item "follows a slowly moving object through a 180-degree arc," the following behaviors are possible: "does not follow object," "follows jerkily through part of arc," "follows smoothly through part of arc," and "follows smoothly through complete arc." A student's performance is scored using the following categories: (+) critical behavior is exhibited, (✓) critical behavior is exhibited after demonstration, (≠) critical behavior is emerging, and (−) critical behavior is not demonstrated. Only the (+) and the (✓) are counted in determining an individual's highest developmental attainment in each scale. Perhaps the most valuable use of the test results is provided in Dunst's manual, in which intervention activities are suggested. These activities are based on the assumption that consideration of the relationships between sensorimotor domains and the development of general cognitive functioning is more important than the development of an isolated skill.

OVERVIEW: ASSESSMENT IN INFANCY: THE ORDINAL SCALES

- *Age level*—Birth–24 months
- *Suggested use*—The Ordinal Scales of Psychological Development can provide important information regarding the cognitive functioning of infants or with older individuals with severe or profound handicaps, especially when used in conjunction with the Dunst (1980) manual. A major limitation, however, involves the reliance within some test areas on the individual's intact gross- and fine-motor capabilities. Major adaptations are then necessary for students with severe motor limitations.

Brigance Inventory of Early Development–Revised

The Brigance Inventory of Early Development-Revised (Brigance, 1991) was designed for use with individuals below developmental age 7. It can be used to identify strengths and weaknesses, to determine instructional objectives, and to indicate the individual's approximate developmental level in a number of areas. It can also be used as an ongoing evaluation system to monitor progress. The test items were cross-referenced with texts and other tests to determine developmental-age equivalents that should be used cautiously.

Description

The Inventory of Early Development–Revised measures abilities in 11 content areas. These 11 areas include 84 skill sequences, which, essentially, are task analyses of the skill areas. A number of supplemental sequences are also available. One feature of the revised Inventory is the inclusion of *comprehensive skill sequences*. These are more detailed sequences that can be used with more severely handicapped children or others for whom the need for smaller steps is apparent. For example, the skill sequence of feeding/eating consists of 37 items, whereas the comprehensive sequence includes 67. The author notes that the regular sequences are adequate for use with the majority of children.

> *Preambulatory Motor Skills and Behaviors (46 items)*—This content area includes 4 skill sequences: supine position, prone position, sitting position, and standing position.
>
> *Gross-Motor Skills and Behaviors (94 items)*—This content area includes 10 skill sequences, beginning with standing, walking, and climbing stairs, and ending with rolling and throwing. There are three supplemental skill sequences: ball bouncing, rhythm, and wheel toys.
>
> *Fine-Motor Skills and Behaviors (96 items)*—This content area includes 9 skill sequences, such as general manipulative skills, prehandwriting skills, and cutting with scissors. Three supplemental sequences are also available.
>
> *Self-Help Skills (137 items)*—This content area includes 8 skill sequences, such as feeding and eating skills, undressing, dressing, toileting, and grooming.
>
> *Speech and Language Skills (179 items)*—This content area includes 10 skill sequences, such as pre-speech, receptive language, picture vocabulary, and sentence memory, and one supplemental sequence (singing).
>
> *General Knowledge and Comprehension (218 items)*—This content area includes 11 skill sequences, such as knowledge of body parts, colors, classifying, and knowing where to go for service.
>
> *Social and Emotional Development (122 items)*—This section includes three skill sequences including play skills and work-related skills.
>
> *Readiness (168 items)*—This content area measures 4 aspects of reading readiness: visual discrimination; reciting alphabet; and matching, identifying, and naming uppercase and lowercase letters.
>
> *Basic Reading Skills (78 items)*—This content area includes 10 skill sequences, such as auditory discrimination, initial consonants with pictures, short vowel sounds, long vowel sounds, and reading level.

Manuscript Writing (125 items)—This content area measures 7 areas, including the printing of uppercase and lowercase letters sequentially and from dictation, and the printing of simple sentences.

Basic Math (open-ended number of items)—This content area includes 12 skill sequences, such as number concepts, rote counting, numerical comprehension, addition combinations, subtraction combinations, recognition of money, and time concepts.

Interpretation of results

Figure 15-4 shows the record-keeping system for the Inventory of Early Development–Revised. Most notable in the interpretation of results are the objectives that are spelled out according to the student's performance. These are designed for use with IEPs. Developmental-age equivalents are also assigned to certain items to give a rough estimate of the student's ability level.

OVERVIEW: BRIGANCE INVENTORY OF EARLY DEVELOPMENT–REVISED

- *Age level*—Birth–6 years
- *Suggested use*—The Brigance Inventory of Early Development–Revised is a comprehensive test measuring 11 major skill areas. The test should not be given in its entirety; rather, the evaluator should choose the most appropriate areas to measure. The developmental age equivalents yielded should be considered only as estimates. The addition of the comprehensive sequences is a nice feature.

  The test is not norm-referenced in the traditional sense. No reliability data are mentioned in the manual. Like the other Brigance inventories (described in Chapter 12) this one is somewhat cumbersome to administer.

Callier–Azusa Scale

The Callier–Azusa Scale (Stillman, 1978) is an individually administered instrument designed to assess the developmental level of deaf-blind and severely or profoundly handicapped children. It is designed to be administered by teachers or other individuals who are thoroughly familiar with the child. The author states that the child should be observed for at least two weeks, preferably in a classroom setting. The age range for the Scale is from birth through approximately age 9.

Description

The Callier-Azusa Scale is comprised of 18 subscales in five major areas. Each major area is organized into several subscales that contain

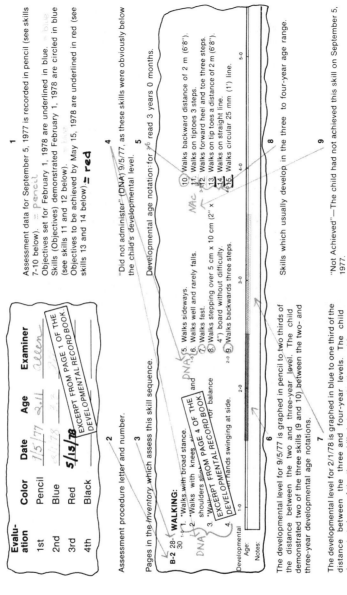

FIGURE 15-4   Illustration of the Record-Keeping System of the Brigance® Inventory of Early Development.

From A. Brigance, *BRIGANCE® Inventory of Early Development.* Copyright © 1978 by Curriculum Associates, Inc. Reprinted with permission. BRIGANCE® is a registered trademark of Curriculum Associates, Inc.

sequential steps measuring the particular developmental milestones included in that subscale. In some cases the step is further broken down into as many as five separate items.

Motor Development—This area includes the subscales of postural control (18 steps), locomotion (17 steps), fine-motor skills (20 steps), and visual-motor skills (21 steps).

Perceptual Development—This area includes the subscales of visual development (15 steps), auditory development (6 steps), and tactile development (13 steps).

Daily Living Skills—This area includes the subscales of undressing and dressing (16 items), personal hygiene (13 steps), feeding skills (16 steps), and toileting (13 steps).

Cognition, Communication, and Language—This area includes the subscales of cognitive development (21 steps), receptive communication (18 steps), expressive communication (20 steps), and development of speech (10 steps).

Social Development—This area includes the subscales of interaction with adults (16 steps), interactions with peers (17 steps), and interactions with environment (10 steps).

Interpretation of results

To obtain credit for a particular step, a child must attain all the behaviors described in all items within that step. If a behavior is emerging, occurs only infrequently, or occurs only after prompting or in specific situations, credit is not given. Some items in the subscales are starred (*). These items can be omitted if a "child cannot be expected to exhibit behavior because of a specific sensory or motor deficit" (p. 4). To score the Scale, the examiner notes each subscale step that the child exhibits (a certain format for scoring is discussed in the manual). Each subscale score can be converted to a "rough" age equivalency. The author notes, however, that the behavior sequences for a child, not the age norms, provide the most important information.

OVERVIEW: CALLIER–AZUSA

- *Age level*—Birth–9 years
- *Suggested use*—The Callier–Azusa is one of a few scales specifically designed to use with individuals with sensory or motor deficits. Also, a number of its items are designed for low-functioning individuals. The test should be used to determine strengths and weaknesses and to identify general educational goals, rather than to assess an individual's developmental level.

Uniform Performance Assessment System

The Uniform Performance Assessment System (UPAS) (Haring, White, Edgar, Affleck, & Hayden, 1981) is an individually administered instrument used with persons who are functioning at the developmental level between birth and age 6. The test can be adapted for small-group use. According to the authors, "UPAS is a curriculum-referenced test in that the majority of items represent a reasonable outline of what most people would teach young or low-functioning pupils. Rather than simply helping to discriminate handicapped from nonhandicapped individuals, therefore, the items on UPAS help teachers and parents select which skills and behaviors should probably be targeted for instruction" (p. 1). The UPAS contains approximately 250 items (or criterion tests) in four major areas: Preacademic, Communication, Social/Self-Help, and Gross Motor. In addition to the criterion tests, there are stimulus cards to use for some of the items. The UPAS also includes a coding system to allow the items to be adapted for physically handicapped individuals. Figure 15-5 shows an example of a criterion test.

Description of areas

Preacademic (76 items)—These criterion tests measure fine-motor skills, visual-perceptual skills, and beginning reading and beginning mathematics ability.

Communication (69 items)—These items range from basic response to the environment to receptive and expressive language abilities.

Social/Self-Help (45 items)—These criterion tests measure an individual's functional skills such as eating, dressing, and toileting.

LEVEL __4–5 mo.__   **BEHAVIOR CATEGORY** __Motor__

I. SKILL

The subject emits spontaneously produced consonant-vowel combinations.

II. EQUIPMENT AND MATERIALS

1. Record Form

III. TEST/OBSERVATION PROCEDURE

Tester notes whether the subject spontaneously produces consonant-vowel combinations, e.g., "ba ba, ga ga," during the normal course of the day.

IV. CRITERIA FOR SCORING

1. Tester records + on the Record Form if the subject utters at least one consonant-vowel combination, repeated at least twice in a row, e.g., "ba ba" or "ga ga."
2. Tester records − on the Record Form if the subject does not utter at least one consonant-vowel combination repeated at least twice in a row.

FIGURE 15-5   Criterion Test from the Uniform Performance Assessment System.

Gross Motor (93 items)—This section includes 66 items that measure preambulatory or ambulatory skills, as well as 27 items measuring wheelchair use skills.

Interpretation of scores

Results from the UPAS should be used to develop IEPs and to monitor progress. The UPAS includes a method of determining the percentage of items passed (with and without adaptation for physical handicap) in each area. Even though each criterion test is associated with an age range, the authors warn against using this association to evaluate developmental ages. In addition to the specific items passed or failed, the adaptation coding-information can be helpful, because it can indicate what adaptation, if any, is necessary to allow the individual to pass a given item.

OVERVIEW: UNIFORM PERFORMANCE ASSESSMENT SYSTEM

- *Age level*—Birth–6 years
- *Suggested use*—The UPAS could be a helpful tool in planning educational objectives for younger or moderately handicapped students. The number of items in each area is too small to allow for the monitoring of progress in more severely handicapped students. The developmental ages associated with these items should not be used.

Vulpé Assessment Battery

The Vulpé Assessment Battery (Vulpé, 1979) is a developmentally-based system for measuring behaviors of children from birth to age 6. Information from the Vulpé can be used to determine an appropriate specific teaching approach, to indicate program goals and objectives, and to provide an accountability system for individual programs. The author states that the Assessment Battery is applicable to all children, including multihandicapped, at-risk, and "normal." She further states that the battery is extremely comprehensive, individualized, and competency-oriented. The Vulpé is divided into eight developmental skill areas or sections, and further divided into subskill areas or subsections. Each developmental skill area is sequentially based. There is also an appendix that includes a developmental reflex test and functional tests of muscle strength, motor planning, and balance.

Description

Many of the items on the Vulpé Assessment Battery appear in more than one of the instrument's eight skill areas or sections. In order to eliminate the need to administer an item more than once, those that are included in more than one section are cross-referenced on the assessment form. In addition, all the equipment necessary and the instructions for administering each item are included on the record form. The skill areas are as follows:

Basic Senses and Functions (16 items)—This section deals with the central nervous system functions that are considered important in performing basic activities. Included are the areas of vision, hearing, smell, balance, muscle strength, range of motion, and reflex status.

Gross-Motor Behaviors (206 items)—Included in this section are items that measure such behaviors as standing, jumping, lying down, sitting, kneeling, skipping, and running.

Fine-Motor Behaviors (177 items)—The items in this section deal with behaviors requiring small-muscle movements, such as eye coordination, eye-hand coordination, reaching, manipulation, and use of toys and utensils.

Language Behaviors (241 items)—This section is divided into two subsections.

Auditory Expressive Language (160 items)—This subsection includes items ranging from vocalizing noises to saying one-word sentences to using free expression.

Auditory Receptive Language (81 items)—Items in this subsection range from hearing sounds in the environment to comprehending full sentences.

Cognitive Processes and Specific Concepts (245 items)—This section is divided into 13 subsections.

Object Concepts (17 items)—This subsection measures a child's understanding of objects. Measurement is within a developmental (for example, Piagetian) framework.

Body Concepts (32 items)—This subsection supplies information about self-image and knowledge of body parts.

Color Concepts (9 items)—This subsection includes items ranging from matching and sorting to naming and discriminating colors.

Shape Concepts (22 items)—This subsection includes items that require a child to identify shapes and to discriminate three dimensional objects and parts of objects.

Size Concepts (6 items)—This subsection measures the child's understanding of concepts such as "bigger," "longer," and "shorter."

Space Concepts (36 items)—This subsection includes items related to the child's understanding of the relationship of his or her own body to objects in space as well as the abstract understanding of space not directly related to self.

Time Concepts (16 items)—This subsection includes items measuring a child's understanding of events occurring in the immediate present as well as the understanding of more abstract concepts of past and future.

Amount and Number Concepts (22 items)—This subsection includes counting and items that measure understanding of quantitative concepts.

Visual Memory (12 items)—This subsection includes items requiring a child to use rote memory and more complex sequential memory.

Auditory Discrimination (12 items)—This subsection requires a child to discriminate consonants, words, sounds, and tones.

Auditory Attention, Comprehension, and Memory (25 items)—This subsection includes items such as "follows one-step command," "repeats four words," "follows three-step commands," and "repeats four digits."

Cause/Effect or Means/End Behavior (12 items)—This subsection includes items such as "understands relationship of adult's presence to being lifted" and "uses parts of objects for specific purposes."

Categorizing/Combining Scheme (24 items)—This subsection includes items requiring a child to integrate information and to organize it into meaningful thoughts and actions.

Organization of Behavior (79 items)—This section is divided into four subsections.

Attention and Goal Orientation (18 items)—This subsection deals with the ability of the child to orient and react to sensory stimuli, to selectively pay attention, to focus attention, and to maintain attention.

Internal Control to Environmental Limits (20 items)—This subsection deals with recognition of boundaries of behavioral limits within the environment and the desire and ability to control behaviors in order to function effectively within the environment.

Problem Solving and Learning Patterns (17 items)—This subsection includes items measuring a child's ability to react appropriately to the environment, to imitate others, and to solve problems of different complexity.

Dependence/Independence (24 items)—This subsection measures a child's behavior along a dependence-independence continuum.

Activities of Daily Living—The items in this section are similar to those in most adaptive behavior scales measuring daily living skills. The section has seven subsections.

Feeding (47 items)
Dressing (32 items)
Social-Interaction (48 items)
Playing (50 items)
Sleeping (16 items)
Toileting (17 items)
Grooming (12 items)

Assessment of Environment (44 items)—This section is somewhat unusual for a developmental-skill instrument such as the Vulpé. It measures the interaction of the child with the environment to discover whether the child's physical and emotional needs are met by the physical and social environment.

Interpretation of results

Each item on the Vulpé is given one of seven possible scores. A *no* score is given if the child has no apparent interest or motivation to participate in the task or cannot attend to the task. An *attention* score is given when a child shows any interest in any part of the activity but does not actively participate, whether because of physical incapacity or insufficient attention. A *physical assistance* score is used if a child actively participates in the activity when the task or environment is modified. A *social-emotional assistance* score is given when the child participates in the task when given more feedback, reinforcement, or reassurance. A *verbal assistance* score is given when the child's performance changes if verbal cues are given or the instructions repeated. An *independent* score is assigned when the student succeeds with no assistance within familiar surroundings. Finally, a *transfer* score is given when the student can perform tasks of similar complexity in different environments.

These scores can be marked directly on the Performance Analysis/ Developmental Assessment scoring pad (Figure 15-6). In addition, comments about a child's performance (such as "did not perform due to sensory impairment") can be included. Age levels are provided for the items, but they represent gross indicators and should be used only to evaluate relative strengths and weaknesses.

OVERVIEW: VULPÉ ASSESSMENT BATTERY

■ *Age level*—Birth–6 years

■ *Suggested use*—The Vulpé offers a highly comprehensive assessment of developmental skills of children between birth and age 6. Its comprehensiveness, in fact, might be considered one of its faults. It takes a good deal of time to administer and score all the appropriate items using the Vulpé system. The results, however, are more meaningful than those yielded from most developmental tests, particularly for use in educational programming. On the other hand, the relatively few items in certain subsections is a limitation. Venn (1987) in a review of the Vulpé, noted that it is useful for interdisciplinary assessment because of both its traditional developmental and learning content and its areas covering neurological development.

VULPE ASSESSMENT BATTERY * SCORING PAD
PERFORMANCE ANALYSIS/DEVELOPMENTAL ASSESSMENT

Name: . . . . Birthdate:. . . . .

Developmental Area:. . . . .

Date:. . . . . Manual page:. . . . .

| | COMMENTS |
| SCALE SCORE | INFORMATION PROCESSING AND ACTIVITY ANALYSIS |

No	Attention	Phys. Assis.	Soc./Emot. Assis.	Verbal Assis.	Independent	Transfer	1. Analyse activities considering component parts of each and relationship to: Basic Senses & Functions Organizational Behaviors Cognitive Processes & Specific Concepts Auditory Language Gross & Fine Motor	2. Information Processing Consider: Input Integration Feedback Assimilation Output
1	2	3	4	5	6	7		

Activity (Item number)

2 3 4 5 6 7

Activity (Item number)

1 2 3 4 5 6 7

Activity (Item number)

1 2 3 4 5 6 7

Activity (Item number)

1 2 3 4 5 6 7

Activity (Item number)

1 2 3 4 5 6 7

©NIMR, 1977 For use with the Vulpé Assessment Battery, by Shirley German Vulpé. NIMR, 4700 Keele St., Downsview, Ont. Canada M3J 1P3

FIGURE 15-6 Scoring Sheet from the Vulpé Assessment Battery.

From S. Vulpé, *Vulpé Assessment Battery.* Copyright © 1979 by the National Institute on Mental Retardation, Ontario, Canada. Reprinted with permission.

398

Instrument or Technique	Suggested Use							Target Population						Special Considerations	Educational Relevance for Exceptional Students
	Prereferral		Postreferral												
	Screening and Initial Identification	Informal Determination and Evaluation of Teaching Programs and Strategies	Determination of Current Performance Level and Educational Need	Decisions about Classification and Program Placement	IEP Goals	IEP Objectives	IEP Evaluation	Mild/Moderate	Severe/Profound	Preschool	Elementary Age	Secondary Age	Adult		
Battelle Development Inventory	X	X			X			X	X	X	X			Well constructed; includes adaptations for handicapped; limited with very young children	useful
Denver II	X							X	X	X				Limited technical aspects. Revision of the popular DDST	limited
Developmental Profile–II	X	X						X	X	X	X			Uses interview format; technical characteristics are limited	limited
Assessment Log and Developmental Progress Chart–Infant			X		X	X	X	X	X	X				Used in conjunction with the Carolina curriculum	useful
Ordinal Scales of Psychological Development			X		X			X	X	X				Follows Piaget's model; helpful when used with Dunst manual	adequate
Brigance Inventory of Early Development–Revised			X		X	X	X	X	X	X				Includes objectives for each item; developmental age equivalents should be used informally only	adequate
Caller–Azusa Scale			X		X				X	X				Designed for use with deaf-blind children	adequate
Uniform Performance Assessment System			X		X	X	X	X	X	X				Includes a code for any test adaptations that are necessary	adequate
Vulpé Assessment Battery			X		X	X	X	X	X	X				Has a tedious scoring system that yields important programmatic information	useful

_16_

Early Childhood Assessment

INSTRUMENTS/PROCEDURES INCLUDED

TEAM ASSESSMENT: A COLLABORATIVE EFFORT
- Natural Assessment Model
- System to Plan Early Childhood Services

PLAY ASSESSMENT

SCREENING INSTRUMENTS
- AGS Early Screening Profiles
- Developmental Indicators for the Assessment of Learning–Revised
- Miller Assessment for Preschoolers

PREACADEMIC INSTRUMENTS
- Basic School Skills Inventory–Diagnostic
- Boehm Test of Basic Concepts–Revised
- Bracken Basic Concept Scale

INSTRUMENTS FOR EDUCATIONAL PROGRAMMING
- Assessment Log and Developmental Progress Chart
- Behavior Characteristics Progression
- Learning Accomplishment Profile–Revised

ADDITIONAL TESTS
- First-Grade Screening Test
- Gesell School Readiness Test
- Meeting Street School Screening Test
- Metropolitan Readiness Tests
- Test of Early Reading Ability–2
- Test of Early Mathematics Ability–2

As noted in Chapter 15, there has been an increased interest in the evaluation of young children, including those ages 3 through 5, who might have mild disabilities or at risk for becoming disabled. Also noted in Chapter 15 is the importance of a team approach to evaluate this population. There are, in fact, a number of specific guidelines that should be followed when preschool children are evaluated (Florida Department of Education, 1989). First, reevaluations and continuous monitoring are extremely important due to the rapid developmental changes that occur during the preschool years. Also, it is necessary to address environmental variables that have a significant impact on young children and to evaluate the home environment.

Other guidelines relate to the testing session itself. First, it should be structured in a way that allows for optimal responding on the child's part. Subsequently, issues such as length of testing, establishing rapport, nature of instructions, and type of directions must be given extra consideration. Also, if possible, the child should not be subjected to multiple testing sessions with a number of different examiners. This may require that more than one person see the child at the same time. Finally, it might be advantageous to make the testing sessions more playlike to sustain the child's attention. In fact, it is important to observe play behavior as part of the evaluation process.

In response to the very important issue of evaluating preschool children, the National Association for the Education of Young Children presented a position paper in 1988. Those points are summarized below.

1. Standardized tests used in early childhood programs must be reliable and valid.
2. Decisions that have a major impact on young children should be based on multiple scores and should never be based on any single test score. (This includes other sources of information, such as systematic observation, samples of child's work, and input from family.)
3. Standardized tests should only be used for the purposes for which they are intended.
4. Test results should be interpreted cautiously and accurately to parents.
5. Tests should be chosen that match the theory, philosophy, and objectives of the available educational program.
6. Testing should be conducted by someone who is sensitive to the developmental needs of young children.
7. Testing must be sensitive to individual diversity.

Although these suggestions should be considered best practice for *all* individuals, it emphasizes the importance of carefully planning and conducting an evaluation with young children.

In this chapter, the first area to be discussed will be general assessment procedures, including those areas such as team assessment models, the assessment of play behavior, and the assessment of social behavior and interactions of young children. As noted previously, these areas are extremely important to evaluate at some point during the assessment process when working with young preschool children.

Next, the specific area of developmental screening will be discussed. Developmental screening tests provide a brief assessment of a child's abilities that are highly associated with future school success. These tests are usually administered to identify children that may need early intervention or special education services. Because of the nature of the decision being made, the issue of predictive validity is very important since those decisions related to a child's future performance are made on the basis of the test results. Most developmental screening tests are quick and easy to administer and include typical developmental skills such as gross motor, fine motor, language, and conceptual skills. It should be noted that two possible erroneous outcomes can result from using developmental screening tests. These are (1) identifying as high risk a child who does not have a problem; and (2) identifying as low risk a child that does have a problem. The first type of error can lead to a waste of time and money and might result in undue anxiety for the parents and the child. The second type of error results in the lack or postponement of a necessary prevention or remediation program.

The third area that will be discussed is that of preacademic/readiness testing. These tests include items specifically designed to measure skills that are necessary to perform adequately in the early school years. Obviously the content of many of these instruments will overlap with developmental screening tests, particularly regarding perceptual and fine motor skills that are normally developing in the preschool years. Preacademic and readiness tests, however, are more concerned with curriculum-related skills that a child has already acquired and are prerequisite for specific instructional programs (Meisels, 1987).

The last area to be discussed will be testing for educational programming. The available tools are primarily criterion-referenced inventories that have been developed specifically for the preschool-age range. Like many tests discussed in Chapter 15, these instruments provide detailed skill sequences in a variety of developmental areas. It is important that those using these instruments focus only on those areas in which educational programming is necessary. In other words, the entire instrument is not administered; rather, based on the data gathered from the home environment, observation, and formal test results, the appropriate curriculum areas are identified and subsequently evaluated.

It should also be noted that many of the instruments and techniques discussed in other chapters in this book are also applicable to young children. Obviously, such areas as observation, criterion-referenced testing, and curriculum-based assessment have direct relevance. Similarly, in many norm-referenced tests young children are represented in the standardization sample so that it is possible to obtain scores that can be applied to that age group. Examples of this are the Kaufman-Assessment Battery for Children, the Scales of Independent Behavior, and the Differential Ability Scales. Still other instruments include a separate preschool version (usually a downward extension). Examples are the Test of Language Development–Primary and the Detroit Tests of Language Aptitude–Primary. There are, however, assessment devices that are designed specifically for use with infants, toddlers, and preschool children.

TEAM ASSESSMENT: A COLLABORATIVE EFFORT

As noted previously, the evaluation of preschool children involves a number of professionals. It is extremely important that these individuals work as a team, communicating with each other to streamline the evaluation and to coordinate decision making. In some situations the child might be evaluated by an entire team, whereas in other situations the child might be evaluated by individual members although team decisions will be made. An example of each of these approaches, the Natural Assessment Model and the System to Plan Early Childhood Services, is discussed next.

Natural Assessment Model

The Natural Assessment Model was developed and implemented in the Schaumburg, Illinois, school district. In this model, the evaluation team is composed of members from different disciplines who observe the child's performance in a variety of developmental domains. Each team member receives training in the areas of intellectual, language, social/emotional, and motor development. The assessment is carried out in a play setting and involves interaction with peers, thus focusing on the child's natural interaction with the environment. Four or five children are observed simultaneously by the evaluation team for 1 hour. At the same time, the parent is interviewed and histories are obtained. The observation room is supplied with a variety of toys and large motor equipment.

Each team member completes a developmental checklist called the "Mini-wheel of Developmental Milestones." The areas on the Mini-wheel are primarily based on Piaget's work and measure the four major areas of intellectual, language, motor, and social-emotional development. Each area is further broken down into 12 specific skills that have accompanying definitions. The team is trained in each of the areas. Other notes are also taken by the team members related to the child's quality of performance. There is an ongoing communication between team members to ensure that each area on the wheel is being evaluated for each child. The usual team members and their respective roles are noted below.

Speech-language pathologist—Interacts with the child and records a spontaneous language sample, observes phonological processing, and is primarily responsible for language scores on the Mini-wheel.

Preschool teacher—Observes the child's interactions, problem-solving abilities, and drawing/fine-motor ability and is primarily responsible for the social, emotional, and motor scores on the Mini-wheel.

Psychologist—Assists in the determination of the intellectual score on the Mini-wheel and meets with the parents, acting as the school district liaison.

Teacher assistant—Collects information from the parent and engages in motor activities with the child.

Social worker—Meets with the parents to explain the Mini-wheel and the evaluation procedures, interview them, and obtains developmental histories.

Nurse—Conducts initial screening for vision and hearing prior to the evaluation.

After the evaluation there is a 20- to 30-minute meeting with the team and parents to gather and share information. Each team member relates his or her observations and ratings on the Mini-wheel, and a consensus on the child's performance is reached.

System to Plan Early Childhood Services

Another approach to team assessment uses the System to Plan Early Childhood Services (SPECS; Bagnato & Neisworth, 1990). SPECS was developed to provide a mechanism for multiple professionals to communicate results from assessment and other sources of information. There are three sections or components of SPECS: Developmental, Team, and Program. *Developmental SPECS* provides the opportunity for parents, teachers, psychologists, therapists, and other professionals to convert a variety of assessment information into mutually understood ratings regarding the child's development and educational status in 19 areas. *Team SPECS* allows the team to compare ratings and arrive at a consensus regarding the child's level of functioning across the 19 important areas. The 19 areas can be clustered into developmental dimensions. Those are communication, sensorimotor, physical, self-regulation, cognition, and self/social. Finally, *Program SPECS* includes over 40 items to consider when planning a child's educational program. Each of these items is accompanied by a set of service options so that a program plan is generated. The amount of intensity required for specific services is also indicated when Program SPECS is completed. In other words, by completing all other components of SPECS, a team will have consensus on child assessment, a blueprint for the child's service plan, and an idea of the extent or intensity of needed services.

The advantage of using a system such as SPECS is that it allows each individual on the team to gather data using their preferred instruments and techniques and provides a common ground for discussing and agreeing upon the meaningfulness of those data. Figure 16-1 shows the steps that are followed in using SPECS.

PLAY ASSESSMENT

The area of play assessment is extremely important when considering the overall developmental status of young children. Although many states require the use of standardized tests (particularly for eligibility decisions), play assessment should be incorporated into any evaluation. Linder (1989) in her book, *Transdisciplinary Play Assessment,* provides a comprehensive and meaningful discussion of the informal and formal guidelines to follow when conducting a play assessment. For example, Linder suggests the following sequence of activities (although she notes that flexibility is a key to a successful assessment):

> *Phase I—Unstructured Facilitation:* This 20–25-minute period allows the child to take the lead and to choose his or her own activities.

> *Phase II—Structured Facilitation:* This 10–15-minute period allows the evaluator to observe such skills as puzzle-making, drawing, or other areas not exhibited during the unstructured situation.

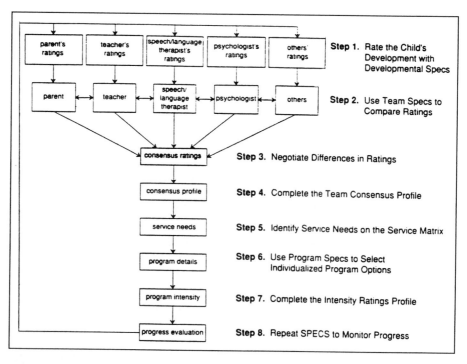

FIGURE 16-1   Steps to Follow in Using the SPECS System.

From S. Bagnato and J. Neisworth, *System to Plan Early Childhood Services.* © 1991 American Guidance Service. Reprinted with permission.

Phase III—Child–Child Interaction: In this 5–10-minute period two children are allowed to play in an unstructured situation. If no interaction occurs, more structure (e.g., toys, prompts) are added.

Phase IV—Parent–Child Interaction: In this phase the parent interacts with the child for 5 minutes in an unstructured situation. At that point, the parent is asked to leave, and the child's reaction to the separation is observed. Finally, the parent is brought back for another 5 minutes in a more structured situation.

Phase V—Motor Play: This involves a 10–20-minute session of both structured and unstructured play.

Phase VI—Snack: The final phase allows for additional observation of social interaction, self-help skills, adaptive behavior, and motor skills.

Linder also provides observational guidelines as well as checklists for the areas of cognitive development, social/emotional development, communication and language development, and sensorimotor development. Interested readers are encouraged to consult her book for more detailed information regarding this area.

There are also specific play assessment instruments that might be used by the practitioner. These include the *Play Observation Scale* (Rogers, 1986), which allows for the assessment of sensorimotor and symbolic stages of play and includes items related to social communication, and the *Symbolic Play Checklist* (Westby, 1980), which describes a 10-step hierarchy that focuses on language, cognitive, and social aspects of play. Other examples are the *Play Assessment Checklist for Infants* (Bromwich, Fust, Khokha, and Walden, 1981), which also uses observation during free play, and *A Manual for Analyzing Free Play* (McCune-Nicholich, 1980), which provides an organized format for analyzing play using Piaget's theories. In many of these observational instruments, a specified toy set is used to structure the free play.

Other instruments are designed to evaluate the more specific area of social behaviors and interactions of young children. Table 16-1 provides a brief description of several of these instruments that are based upon direct observation.

SCREENING INSTRUMENTS

WHY USE?
Screening

WHO SHOULD USE?
Teachers, social workers, school psychologists, parent input (often a team approach)

TABLE 16-1 Assessment of Social Behavior and Interaction of Young Children with Handicaps through Direct Observation.

From D. Bailey and M. Wolery, *Assessing Infants and Preschoolers with Handicaps.* © 1989 Merrill Publishing Co. Reprinted with permission.

Instruments	Age Range	Behaviors Assessed	Description
Systematic Anecdotal Assessment of Social Interaction (Odom, McConnell, Kohler & Strain, 1987)	Open	Behaviors generated by the teacher	A structured anecdotal recording system for collecting social interaction information
Social Interaction Scan (Odom et al., 1988)	Preschool	Isolate/unoccupied Proximity Interactive Negative Teacher Interaction	A system for scanning classrooms of children. Designed to measure both interaction play and social integration.
Observation Assessment of Reciprocal Social Interaction (McConnell, Sisson, & Sandler, 1984)	Preschool	Initiations (five behaviors listed) Response (four behaviors listed) Summative (four behaviors listed) Teacher behavior (two behaviors listed	An interval-sampling system designed to measure components and durations of social interaction of peers
Scale of Social Participation (Parten, 1932)	Preschool	Unoccupied Onlooker Solitary Parallel Associative Cooperative	An interval-sampling system designed to measure young children's participation in social interaction
Parten/Smilansky Combined Scale (Rubin, 1983)	Preschool	Unoccupied Onlooker Solitary Parallel Associative Cooperative Functional Constructive Dramatic Games with rules	An interval-sampling system designed to measure cognitive play within a social context
Guralnick & Groom (1987)	Preschool	Gains peer attention Uses peer as resource Leads peer in activity-positive Leads peer in activity-negative Imitates peer Expresses affection to peer Expresses hostility to peer Competes for adult attention Competes for equipment Shows pride in product Follows peer's activity without specific direction	Event-recording system for measuring peer interactions
Odom, Silver, Sandler, & Strain (1983); Strain (1983); Tremblay, Strain, Hendrickson, & Shores (1980)	Preschool	Play organizer Share request Share Assistance Assistance request Affection Complimentary Negative Motor Gestural Negative Vocal Verbal	Event-recording system for measuring peer social interactions

AGS Early Screening Profiles

The AGS Early Screening Profiles (ESP) (Harrison, 1991) is designed for use with children ages 2 through 6. Its primary purpose is to aid in the identification of those children with possible handicaps or, conversely, those who might be potentially gifted. The ESP uses an ecological approach to screening whereby numerous areas are measured and several individuals are involved in the assessment process. Both the child and the parent and/or teacher are evaluated in the ESP. The evaluation time for children ranges from 15–30 minutes, while the parent and teacher questionnaires can be completed in approximately 15 minutes. There are seven sections included (Figure 16-2). These are the Cognitive/Language, Motor, and Self-help/Social Profiles, and the Articulation, Home, Health History, and Behavior Surveys. Each of these will be discussed.

Description

Cognitive/Language Profile (78 items)—This profile includes four subtests that are administered directly to the child. Those are verbal concepts, visual discrimination, logical relations, and basic school skills.

Motor Profile (8 items)—This section includes both gross motor and fine motor areas. There are, however, a limited number of items that are used in this profile (five in gross motor, three in fine motor).

Self-help/Social Profile (120 items)—This information is gathered through both parent and teacher reports and measures four domains. Those are communication, daily living skills, socialization, and motor skills.

Articulation Survey (20 items)—In this survey the child is required to identify 20 common objects. The examiner notes the initial, medial, and final sounds of those words.

Home Survey (12 items)—This questionnaire is completed by the parent and addresses such issues as types of play materials available, numbers of books in the home, and the amount of responsibility that is given to the child.

Health History Survey (12 items)—This also is completed by the parent and simply provides a general indication of the child's medical history, including information related to the birth of the child.

Behavior Survey (13 items)—This survey is completed by the test administrator after the cognitive/language and their motor profiles have been administered. This section can be completed in approximately 2 minutes and provides information related to such areas as attention span, activity level, and cooperativeness.

Interpretation of results

The ESP has two levels of scoring. In Level I, the individual profiles and total screening are reported in screening indexes that range from one to six. Each index represents a range of performance expressed in various standard deviation units from the mean. For example, a screening index

Components

ESP's three basic components, called Profiles, are supplemented by four Surveys. For most children, the total time needed for the three Profiles is under <u>30 minutes</u>. The Surveys, completed by a parent, teacher, or screening examiner, require an additional <u>15-20 minutes</u>.

Profiles

• The Cognitive/Language Profile is administered individually to the child. Tasks assess reasoning skills, visual organization and discrimination, receptive and expressive vocabulary, and basic pre-academic and school skills. The Profile can be separated into Cognitive (nonverbal) and Language (verbal) subscales, a useful feature for screening children with language difficulties, hearing problems, or limited English proficiency.

• The Motor Profile, also individually administered, assesses both gross and fine motor skills.

• The Self-Help/Social Profile is a questionnaire that is completed by the child's parent, teacher, or daycare provider. It assesses the child's typical performance in the areas of communication, daily living skills, socialization, and motor skills.

Surveys

• The Articulation Survey measures the child's ability to pronounce 20 words selected to test common articulation problems in the initial, medial, and final positions of words.

• The Home Survey is completed by the parent and asks nonintrusive questions about the child's home environment.

• The Health History Survey, also completed by the child's parent, is a brief checklist summarizing any health problems the child has had.

• The Behavior Survey is used by the examiner to rate the child's behavior during administration of the Cognitive/Language and Motor Profiles. The child is rated in categories such as attention span, frustration tolerance, and response style.

FIGURE 16-2   Components of the AGS Early Screening Profile.

From P. Harrison, *AGS Early Screening Profile.* Circle Pines, MN: American Guidance Service, 1991 © 1991 American Guidance Service. Reprinted with permission.

of one represents performance that is two standard deviations or more below the mean, whereas a screening index of five represents a performance 1 to 2 standard deviations above the mean. For Level II, a variety of derived scores are available, including standard scores (mean = 100; standard deviation = 15); percentile ranks; normal curve equivalents; stanines; and age equivalents. Scores for the individual subtests and domains and the profiles are also available (both Level I and Level II scoring). Scoring of the surveys result in descriptive categories of "above average," "average," and "below average." The Health History Survey is not scored. The manual provides a number of suggestions on ways of combining profiles and the effect this has on the referral rate. Overall, the manual discusses the issue of interpretation to a significant extent.

Technical Characteristics

Normative sample.   Over 1,100 children, ages 2 through 6, were included in the standardization. The sample was stratified based on sex, geographic region, socioeconomic status, and race or ethnic group. The percentage of children in the sample was very similar to the 1990 U.S. census data.

Reliability.   Internal consistencies using coefficient alpha were reported in the .80s and .90s range for all Profiles and Surveys with the exception of the Motor Profile (.60s and .70s), the Home Survey (.30s to .50s), and the Behavior Survey (primarily .70s). Test-retest reliability was determined for the profiles and total screening excluding the teacher-completed Self-help/Social Profile. Again, the coefficients were in the .80s to .90s range except for Motor, which was reported at .70. Delayed test-retest reliability coefficients were somewhat lower than expected and were primarily in the .70s and .80s range except for Motor, which was .55. Interrater reliability was determined for the Motor Profile. Those correlations were acceptable, ranging from .80 to .99 for the various items.

Validity.   A thorough discussion of validity can be found in the manual. Results of concurrent validity studies indicated moderate-to-good correlations with a variety of criterion measures. Results of predictive validity studies generally indicated good correlations (usually .60s and .70s). Statistical evidence of construct validity is also provided.

Review of relevant research

Because of the recency of this instrument, no research was located at the time this book was completed. Interested readers are referred to the Examiner's Manual for a summary of a number of unpublished technical reports.

OVERVIEW: AGS EARLY SCREENING PROFILES

- *Age level*—2 through 6 years
- *Type of administration*—Individual (child is tested, parent and teacher interviewed)

■ *Suggested use*—The AGS ESP provides an ecological screening that involves direct testing of the child and input from the parent and/or teacher. A close inspection of the technical data indicates that the correlations between the teacher-completed and the parent-completed Self-help/Social Profiles were relatively low. Subsequently, the choice of informant might affect screening decisions. Another technical issue is the low correlations between the motor domain of the Self-help/Social Profile and the Motor Profile. The relatively poor reliability of the Motor Profile adds to its questionable use.

There are several features that make the ESP a valuable instrument. These include the use of multiple domains and sources of information; ease of administration and scoring; overall sound psychometric qualities; and compatibility with more inclusive instruments such as the K-ABC, the Vineland Adaptive Behavior Scales, and the Bruininks-Oseretsky Test of Motor Proficiency. (The individual authors of many of the Profiles and Surveys are the same as those of these more comprehensive instruments.) The idea of receiving multiple sources of information on which to base screening decisions is a good one. One limitation of the ESP is the use of the Motor Profile based on the limited number of items and its relatively low reliability. Also, when interpreting the results of the ESP, the use of subtest scores (using Level II scoring) should probably be discouraged because of the lack of supportive reliability data.

The Developmental Indicators for the Assessment of Learning–Revised

The AGS version of the Developmental Indicators for the Assessment of Learning Revised (DIAL-R) (American Guidance Service, 1990) is a revision of the 1983 DIAL-R (Mardell-Czudnowski & Goldenberg, 1983). It represents an attempt to improve on the scoring and technical characteristics of the DIAL-R. These areas were the source of criticism in a number of reviews (e.g., Linder, 1985). Harrison (1990) noted six major changes from the 1983 addition to the 1990 AGS addition. Those were (1) a more comprehensive manual; (2) a greater variety of methods to use in making the overall screening decisions; (3) a reanalysis of the original DIAL-R normative data using statistical weights; (4) norms for census, white, and minority groups; (5) standard errors of measurement; and (6) a wide variety of validity data. The DIAL-R is quick (20–30 minutes) and easy to administer and can be used to identify a wide variety of children, from those with severe problems to those who are potentially advanced.

Description
The DIAL-R consists of 24 items that measure the areas of language, concepts, and motor skills. The eight items in the language area require the child to do things such as classify food and name nouns. Examples of

the eight items on the concepts section are counting and naming letters. The motor section includes items such as catching and writing. Each of the three areas also includes a checklist of social and emotional behavior.

Interpretation of Results

A five-point scale (0–4) is used to obtain item scores. These can be combined to determine area scores and a total score. Percentile ranks and standard scores are available for both the total test and for the three areas of motor, concepts, and language. One advantage of the AGS Edition is the use of cutoff scores for plus and minus 1, 1-1/2, and 2 standard deviations as well as the 5th and 95th and 10th and 90th percentiles for the total and the area scores. These provide flexible alternatives for making screening decisions.

Technical Characteristics

Normative sample.   A stratified sample of 2,447 children was used. The AGS Edition carefully reanalyzed the normative data to match the 1990 census data related to sex, geographic region, community size, ethnic background, and parents' education.

Reliability.   Internal consistency coefficients were in the .70s for the areas and .86 for the total test. Test-retest coefficients were .76 (Motor), .77 (Language), .90 (Concepts), and .87 (Total Test).

Validity.   Results of several studies determining the criterion-related validity of the DIAL-R are reported in the manual. These studies generally show a moderate correlation with a variety of criterion measures, including achievement tests and readiness tests. In addition, higher coefficients are reported with other developmental instruments such as the Learning Accomplishment Profile. The manual also includes discussions regarding the content validity and construct validity of the instrument as well. Some statistical analyses are also reported that did not support the uniqueness of the three areas suggesting that the total score is the most valid to report.

Review of relevant research

Due to the recency of publication of the AGS Edition, no studies were located. There are, however, a few empirical studies and reviews on the 1983 edition of the DIAL-R.

Linder (1985) noted that the DIAL-R was one of the few tests that purportedly identifies young gifted students. She also noted that local school districts can choose the normative sample that is the most similar to theirs for comparison purposes. Barnett (1989) felt that the DIAL-R relied too much on the child's actual test performance and did not take advantage of parent input. Mardell-Czudnowski and Goldenberg (1987), in a longitudinal study of approximately 300 children, found that the DIAL-R had good sensitivity and specificity but did not correspond well with subsequent special education placement. In another study, Barnett, Fowst, and Sarmir (1988) found that the profiles could not be interpreted separately with confidence, emphasizing that the total score was the best to report. Sven, Mardell-Czudnowski, and Goldenberg (1989) also reported that the total score could be used reliably but suggested that the separate profiles should not be interpreted.

OVERVIEW: DEVELOPMENTAL INDICATORS FOR THE ASSESSMENT OF LEARNING–REVISED (AGS EDITION)

- *Age level*—2 to 6 years
- *Type of administration*—Individual
- *Technical adequacy*—Good standardization; acceptable reliability and validity (particularly for total score).
- *Suggested use*—The AGS DIAL-R is a quick screening device for the identification of handicapped and gifted children. The items on the DIAL-R are a typical sample of those found on most developmental tests. Overall, this edition appears to be an improvement over the original DIAL-R, particularly in relation to technical characteristics and scoring options. The availability of separate norms for white and minority children is a nice feature. There is some evidence that the individual areas lack the technical adequacy to be interpreted separately and that the total score is the best to report. There is much discussion in the manual concerning guidelines that school districts can use to determine both screening procedures and cutoffs. In fact, there is considerable discussion regarding how to set up the screening station to administer the test. As with most screening tests, local districts should make the important determination of what cutoffs to use to indicate further evaluation.

Miller Assessment for Preschoolers

The Miller Assessment for Preschoolers (MAP) (Miller, 1988) is designed to evaluate children ages 2 years, 9 months to 5 years, 8 months. According to the author, the MAP can be used to assess developmental status across a broad range of domains including behavioral, motor, and cognitive. The instrument can be administered in approximately 30 minutes and is used to identify mild, moderate, and severe developmental delays. The MAP includes 27 norm-referenced test items and a supplemental observations sheet that can be used to make appropriate use of subjective observations made during the testing session.

Description

The 27 test items are categorized into five performance indices, although some test items are included in more than one index.

Foundations Index (10 items)—These items measure basic sensory and motor abilities such as sense of position and movement and sense of touch.

Coordination Index (7 items)—These items also measure sensory and motor abilities including gross motor and fine motor tasks.

Verbal Index (4 items)—These items measure memory, sequencing, comprehension, association, and expression.

Nonverbal Index (5 items)—These items measure memory, sequencing, visualization, and mental manipulations without a language component.

Complex Tasks Index (4 items)—This index includes items that require both sensorimotor and cognitive abilities that require the interpretation of visual spatial information.

Supplemental Observations (5 areas)—The supplemental observation sheet is found in the record booklet and is divided into five sections: Vision, Touch, Speech and Language, Draw a Person, and Movement. Each section is designed to help the examiner assess behaviors that might influence test performance.

Interpretation of results

Percentile ranks are available for the MAP total score and performance index scores. In addition, cutoff scores are used on a color-coded basis. *Red* indicates that the child is functioning at or below the 5th percentile rank and needs further evaluation, *Yellow* means the child is functioning between the sixth and 25th percentile rank and should be monitored closely for developmental delays, whereas *Green* indicates that the child is above the 25th percentile and appears to be functioning at an average or above-average level. There is also a "Behavior During Testing" checklist that is not scored but simply notes whether the child's behavior was within normal limits during the testing.

Technical characteristics

Normative sample.   Approximately 1,200 children were included in the standardization sample. The sample was stratified by age, sex, race, community size, and socioeconomic status. Prior to the standardization the test was administered to a tryout sample of approximately 500 children.

Reliability.   Interrater reliability was determined using a sample of 40 children. Coefficients ranged from .84 (Coordination) to .99 (Nonverbal). The total MAP yielded a coefficient of .98. Test-retest reliability was determined using a sample of 81 children. Those coefficients ranged from .72 to .94. The total score had a test-retest coefficient of .81. Internal reliability coefficients using the split-half method were approximately .80.

Validity. The author discusses the content validity of the instrument by providing a thorough review of the theoretical literature on child development. Concurrent validity was determined by administering the MAP and one of four standardized instruments, including intelligence tests and other screening tests, to a group of 30 children. These correlations were variable and low. For example, the correlations between total score on the MAP with an IQ measure and language measure were .27 and .31, respectively. The correlations with a sensory integration test ranged from .02 to .17. When compared to the Denver Developmental Screening Test, the MAP identified 24 percent more children as being at risk. Predictive validity was determined by following approximately one-fourth of the children in the standardization sample and correlating their scores with later standardized instruments and school performance criteria. The coefficients were low to moderate, ranging from .17 (report card mathematics) to .50 Wechsler Intelligence Scale for Children–Revised (WISC-R full-scale IQ). Other data regarding construct validity and classification accuracy are discussed in the manual.

Review of relevant research

- In a review of the MAP, Padget (1985) concluded that the test's overreliance on visual-motor tasks limits its usefulness in screening for possible learning problems. Linder (1985) also noted its heavy emphasis on sensory and motor functioning.
- The MAP can consistently and correctly identify the majority of children who have later school problems (Miller, 1986) and can differentiate children with subsequent school problems from those without (Miller, 1988).
- The Foundations Index was found to be a psychometrically valuable contributor to the total MAP score (Miller & Lemerand, 1986).
- The MAP Verbal Index is less culturally biased against older preschool children than certain language tests such as the Peabody Picture Vocabulary Test–Revised (Wilderstrom, Miller, & Marzano, 1986).

Summary of research findings

Research on the MAP has generally supported the predictive validity of the instrument (although it should be noted that the majority of the research was conducted by the test author). Reviews of the MAP have noted its neurological base and its heavy emphasis on sensorimotor tasks.

OVERVIEW: MILLER ASSESSMENT FOR PRESCHOOLERS

- *Age level*—2 years, 9 months–5 years, 8 months
- *Type of administration*—Individual

- *Technical adequacy*—Adequate reliability, questionable validity
- *Scores yielded*—Percentile ranks, cutoff scores
- *Suggested use*—The MAP offers an alternative to traditional developmental screening tests. It was developed by an occupational therapist and the content is heavily weighted toward sensorimotor and sensory integration tasks. It attempts to measure specific motor, language, and cognitive skills, as well as underlying neurological processing. More research is needed to determine the instrument's validity. The test should not be used for diagnostic purposes.

READINESS/PREACADEMIC INSTRUMENTS

WHY USE?
   Screening, establishment of IEP goals, grouping for instruction

WHO SHOULD USE?
   Teachers

Basic School Skills Inventory–Diagnostic

The Basic School Skills Inventory-Diagnostic (BSSI-D) (Hammill & Leigh, 1983) is described as a "new approach to readiness assessment" by the authors of the test. The BSSI-D was designed to be used as both a norm-referenced and a criterion-referenced test. Its purpose is to identify both general and specific readiness skills that might need remedial attention for children aged 4 to 7 1/2.

Description
   The BSSI-D includes 110 items that measure six major areas: daily living skills, spoken language, reading readiness, writing readiness, math readiness, and classroom behavior. The format of the test is somewhat unique in that it includes a mixture of teacher and student responses. For example, in the reading area, the teacher answers a series of questions about the child's letter knowledge, word recognition skills, and so on, while in the writing area the child must copy words and write dictated words. There is also a screening version—*Basic School Skills Inventory–Screen* that includes 20 items from the diagnostic version put in checklist form.

Interpretation of results
   Scores from the BSSI-D can be transformed into percentile ranks and standard scores for both the individual areas and the total test (called

the skill quotient). The mean and standard deviation for the individual areas and the skill quotient are 10 and 3, and 100 and 15, respectively.

Technical characteristics

Normative sample. The sample included 813 children residing in 18 states and was based on the representation of the population noted in the 1980 census.

Reliability. The majority of the internal consistency coefficients were in the .80 and .90 range.

Validity. Concurrent validity coefficients using teacher ratings as criteria were somewhat low (.22–.42). The authors provide arguments for the test's content and construct validity.

Review of relevant research

Although no research studies focusing on the BSSI-D were located, the test has been reviewed in the professional literature. In general, these reviews have not been particularly favorable. Webster (1985) noted, for example, that there was a general lack of both standard administration procedures and clear scoring criteria. Bacon and Carpenter (1985) pointed out that the test was not appropriate for children above age 6. They in fact indicated that a child of that age could have a perfect performance but would only receive an average score.

OVERVIEW: BASIC SCHOOL SCREENING INVENTORY–DIAGNOSTIC

- *Age level*—4 to 7 1/2 years old
- *Type of administration*—Individual
- *Technical adequacy*—Limited validity and reliability
- *Scores yielded*—Percentile ranks, standard scores
- *Suggested use*—The BSSI-D needs further validation before it can be used confidently. There are little data available to support its use as a readiness test. The criticism of its lack of clear scoring criteria and standard administration procedures would also imply that further reliability data should be collected. At the present time, the test should be used only informally to determine the child's strengths and weaknesses in the six areas that are measured.

Boehm Test of Basic Concepts–Revised

The Boehm Test of Basic Concepts–Revised (Boehm-R) (Boehm, 1986) is a group-administered instrument designed to measure a child's mastery of concepts that are necessary for successful performance early in school. It is used with children from kindergarten and first and second grades. The author states that the tests can be used both to identify children who have problems in the tested area and to identify specific concepts that need to be emphasized or taught. There is also a separate preschool version called the Boehm Test of Basic Concepts–Preschool Version (BTBC-PV) that includes 26 items designed for children ages 3–5.

Description

The Boehm-R has two equivalent forms, Form C and Form D, each containing 50 items, presented in separate booklets. The items are arranged in order of difficulty, and each booklet has three sample questions. The administration is straightforward: The examiner reads a passage such as, "Look at the beads and strings. Mark the bead that has a string *through* it." The child is then required to look at three pictures. One has the string around the bead, one has the string under the bead, and one has the string through the bead.

In general, the concept categories of space (24 items), quantity (18 items), and time (6 items) are measured, as well as a miscellaneous category (2 items). One interesting addition to the Boehm-R is an *application booklet* that allows for the assessment of concepts used in combination, in sequences, or in making comparisons. Except for this addition, the Boehm-R is similar to the original test (7 new items were added and 2 old items were deleted).

The BTBC-PV is a downward extension of the Boehm-R that should be administered individually. The results of the BTBC-PV are best used informally because of the limited standardization sample on which the normative scores are based.

Interpretation of results

Two types of scores can be derived from the Boehm-R. First, an examiner can compare to others of the same grade and socioeconomic status the percentage of students that pass each item. For instance, an average of 86 percent of the lower-socioeconomic status kindergarten children passed item 1, Form C. This information allows the examiner to make gross comparisons of the class's concept knowledge with the normative sample. The Boehm-R also yields percentiles for comparing individual raw scores. The author states, however, that the test should be used for teaching and screening rather than for prediction or administration; these norms, therefore, need not always be used. A class-record form is available that allows data for the entire class to be recorded on a single sheet. This record form can be used to assign students to groups or to look for concepts that the majority of the class missed.

Technical characteristics

Normative sample.   Field testing was conducted using approximately 1,500 students. Standardization sample was broken down by geographic region, size of school, and socioeconomic status. Size of sample is unclear.

Reliability.   Alternate-form reliability coefficients ranged from .65 (grade 2) to .82 (kindergarten). Split-half coefficients ranged from .64 to .85 for form C and .73 to .83 for form D. Test-retest coefficients ranged from .75 to .88 and .55 to .85 for forms C and D, respectively.

Validity.   A detailed discussion of steps taken to ensure content validity can be found in the manual. Predictive validity coefficients ranged from .38 to .64 in a series of studies.

Review of relevant research
Because of the similarity in format and structure, research related to the Boehm Test of Basic Concepts (BTBC) might have relevance for the Boehm-R.

- The BTBC demonstrated good predictive validity with language, mathematics, and reading as assessed by teachers (Smith, 1986)
- The BTBC is potentially beneficial as an indicator of receptive language in developmentally delayed children (Hutcherson, 1978).
- The BTBC has been used successfully in a battery of tests to identify gifted students (Hardman & Croyle, 1979).
- The BTBC should be used cautiously with hard-of-hearing individuals. In one study, 18 of 24 hard-of-hearing students scored below the 10th percentile (Davis, 1974).
- Poor performance on the BTBC could be due to any number of factors, including the inability to focus on key words in the directions, the complexity of the directions, deficits in spatial perception, vocabulary deficits, problems with abstraction, difficulty with negative concepts, and inadequate auditory memory (Spector, 1979).
- Learning-disabled students scored lower and with greater variability on the BTBC than did students without learning disabilities. The learning-disabled group scored lowest in the quantity, space, and miscellaneous categories, in that order (Kavale, 1982).
- The BTBC measures an overlap of cognitive and linguistic factors best described as a language-comprehension factor (Beech, 1981).
- The BTBC has low reliability with rural children and should be used cautiously with that population (Houck, Biskin, & Regetz, 1973).

■ There is some evidence that the BTBC has moderate predictive validity for subsequent achievement (Estes, Harris, Moers, & Wodrich, 1976).

Summary of research findings

As noted previously, the similarity between the Boehm-R and the original test suggests that research on the original can be cautiously generalized to the revised version. Schwarting (1987) reviewed the Boehm-R and noted the similarities between it and the BTBC. Earlier research suggests that the BTBC has a positive relationship with academic achievement and that it can be used with a variety of special-education populations. Two studies located on the Boehm-R are supportive of the previous research. In one study with black urban children the Boehm-R had appreciable test-retest reliability and moderate-to-substantial predictive validity (Glutting, Kelly, Boehm, & Burnett, 1989). In the other, Zucker and Riordan (1988) found significant correlations between the Boehm-R and the Bracken Basic Concept Scale. Clearly, more research is needed to replicate and extend those findings. No research was located on the BTBC-PV.

OVERVIEW: BOEHM TEST OF BASIC CONCEPTS–REVISED

■ *Age level*—Kindergarten through grade 2 (preschool version available)

■ *Type of administration*—Group

■ *Technical adequacy*—Limited

■ *Scores yielded*—Percentiles

■ *Suggested use*—As a norm-referenced test, the Boehm-R would have to be judged technically inadequate. The reliability for some age groups is extremely low, and only minimal data support its validity. Furthermore, the items are too easy for children in the upper age limit of the test. After first grade, it definitely loses its sensitivity for normative decisions. The value of this test lies in its use as an informal measure. On the assumption that development of basic concepts is essential or at least important in establishing a foundation for later learning, the Boehm-R can be helpful. If used as a norm-referenced device, its purpose should primarily be as a screening instrument (Fitzmaurice & Witt, 1989). In general, these statements about the Boehm-R are relevant for the BTBC-PV as well.

Bracken Basic Concept Scale

The Bracken Basic Concept Scale (BBCS) (Bracken, 1984) is a comprehensive measure of basic concepts designed for preschool and early elementary-aged children (ages 2–6 through 7–11). There are two scales—a diagnostic scale that can be administered in approximately 20–30 minutes and a screening test. The screening test has two alternate forms (A and B) and is designed for children ages 5–7. The screening test can be given to small groups in approximately 10–15 minutes. The BBCS has also been translated into Spanish. Information on this translation and subsequent validation is available (Bracken & Fouad, 1987).

Description of diagnostic scale

The diagnostic scale includes 258 items that measure 11 different conceptual areas. Those areas are color, letter identification, numbers/counting, comparisons, shape, direction/position, social/emotional, size, texture/material, quantity, and time/sequence. The format of the test involves the presentation of a page that has four pictures on it. The examiner states the concept, and the child must indicate which of the four pictures represents the concept. The BBCS uses basal and ceiling rules to avoid administering unnecessary items.

Interpretation of scores

Raw scores from the BBCS can be transformed into a variety of derived scores including standard scores, percentile ranks, stanines, and age equivalents. The first five subtests (color, letter identification, numbers/counting, comparisons, and shape) are combined to form a School Readiness Composite. Each of the other six individual subtests are scored separately. A Profile Summary is also available to provide a visual representation of the child's strengths and weaknesses in the various conceptual areas.

Technical characteristics

Normative sample.   A sample of 1,109 children was included. The makeup of the sample was relatively close to the 1980 census regarding demographic variables.

Reliability.   Test-retest on a small sample ranged from .67 (size) to .98 (School Readiness Composite). Median split-half reliability coefficients were .96 for the total test and .85 for the subtests.

Validity.   Concurrent validity coefficients were determined using a variety of criterion measures and ranged from .68 to .88. The author does an excellent job in describing the steps that were taken to ensure content validity.

Review of relevant research

- Estabrook (1984) reviewed the test and felt that it was the most comprehensive basic concept measure available.
- Turco (1989) reviewed the test and noted that it could provide a link between assessment and remedial interventions.

- The BBCS is a better predictor of achievement than the Gesell Developmental Exam (Sterner & McCallum, 1988).
- Low-to-moderate correlations were reported between the BBCS and the Preschool Language Scale and Slosson Intelligence Test, suggesting that they do not measure the same abilities (Pecyna-Rhyner & Bracken, 1988).
- Deaf children score significantly lower than non–hearing-impaired children on the BBCS (Bracken & Cato, 1986).
- The BBCS has been translated into Spanish (Bracken & Fouad, 1987).
- Bracken, Sabers, and Insko (1987) found that black children scored approximately one half standard deviation below white children on the test, although the pattern of their performance was similar. They also discuss the possibility that the BBCS is also an intelligence measure since most intelligence tests include the assessment of basic concepts.
- Naglieri and Bardos (1990) noted that the BBCS was a well-designed instrument that had good psychometric properties and could be used confidently as a measure of basic concepts.

Summary of research findings

Although the research on the BBCS is limited, there is some evidence that the test can be used to predict achievement. Limited data indicate that individuals with different characteristics (e.g., different handicaps, ethnic status) perform differently on the test. There is conflicting information regarding its relationship with general intelligence.

OVERVIEW: BRACKEN BASIC CONCEPT SCALE (DIAGNOSTIC)

- *Age level*—2 1/2–8 years old
- *Type of administration*—Individual
- *Technical adequacy*—Adequate standardization, adequate validity and reliability
- *Scores yielded*—Standard scores, percentile ranks, age equivalents
- *Suggested use*—The BBCS is a well-constructed, comprehensive instrument designed to measure a variety of concepts. Because of the general paucity of reliability and validity data, it is probably best used to identify strong and weak areas to aid in teaching the appropriate concepts. Further research might indicate that it could also be used for comparison purposes as well. The Spanish translation is also a nice feature.

INSTRUMENTS FOR EDUCATIONAL PROGRAMMING

WHY USE?
Determination of IEP goals and objectives, monitoring progress

WHO SHOULD USE?
Teachers

Assessment Log and Developmental Progress Chart–Preschool

The Assessment Log (Johnson-Martin, Attermeier, & Hacker, 1990) is designed for use with the Carolina Curriculum for Preschoolers with Special Needs. It is an extended version of the Assessment Log for Infants described in Chapter 15. Similar to the Assessment Log for Handicapped Infants, the Assessment Log for Preschoolers divides the associated curriculum into major domains and teaching sequences. Similarly, the authors suggest that once the Assessment Log has been administered, the Developmental Progress Chart should be completed to provide a profile of skills. The Assessment Log measures five major domains broken down further into 25 specific skill sequences. An example of the first and last item in each of the skill sequences follow:

Description

DOMAIN 1—COGNITION

1. Attention and Memory (24 items)—"Anticipates parts of rhymes or sounds" and "remembers the place in an array where a picture was seen only briefly."

2a. Concepts: General (26 items)—"Sorts objects by color form or name" and "identifies an object that does not belong in a set and finds the one that does not belong using up to three characteristics."

2b. Concepts: Size and Number (21 items)—"Uses or understands size words (e.g., big/little)" and "recognizes repeating pattern in a sequence and can continue it."

3. Symbolic Play (11 items)—"Engages in adult role playing" and "engages in complex adult role playing (e.g., plays house with other children, solving problems as adults would solve them)."

4. Reasoning (10 items)—"Experiments with cause and effect in play" and "reasons about future events."

5a. Visual Perception: Block Designs (7 items)—"Imitates block train" and "copies horizontal block patterns."

5b. Visual Perception: Puzzles and Matching (11 items)—"Places round, square and triangular forms in form board" and "matches name and short words."

DOMAIN 2—COMMUNICATION

6. Expressive Vocabulary (12 items)—"Names most common objects when seen" and "defines 10 simple words."

7. Interest in Sounds and Language Functions (8 items)—"Identifies objects, people and events by their sounds" and "soon after hearing the meaning of a new word, uses it in his or her own speech."

8. Receptive Skills (19 items)—"Understands look" and "responds appropriately to questions involving time concepts."

9. Conversation Skills (24 items)—"Requests objects or activities with words or signs" and "tells two familiar stories without pictures for help—includes all important parts."

10. Sentence Construction (23 items)—"Uses two word utterances to indicate possession (e.g., Mommie's sock, my dog) and action (e.g., eat cookie and tie shoes)" and "uses comparatives (e.g., big, bigger, biggest)."

DOMAIN 3—SOCIAL ADAPTATION

11. Responsibility (10 items)—"Avoids common dangers" and "answers telephone appropriately and delivers message."

12. Self-Concept (15 items)—"Expresses feelings of interest, pleasure, surprise, excitement, warning, and complaint (4 or more)" and "seeks activities that challenge skills."

13. Interpersonal Skills (21 items)—"Greets familiar adults spontaneously" and "asserts in socially acceptable ways."

14a. Self-Help: Eating (12 items)—"Independently eats entire meal with spoon" and "fixes sandwich independently."

14b. Self-Help: Dressing (8 items)—"Removes shoes" and "zips front opening clothing such as jacket."

14c. Self-Help: Grooming (6 items)—"Dries hands" and "blows nose independently upon request."

14d. Self-Help: Toileting (6 items)—"Usually indicates need to toilet; rarely has bowel accidents" and "wipes self after bowel movement."

DOMAIN 4—FINE-MOTOR

15. Fine Motor Skills: Hand Use (7 items)—"Plays with missing materials such as clay—patting, pinching, and fingering" and "places ten pellets in a bottle in 30 seconds."

16. Fine Motor Skills: Manipulation (10 items)—"Turns doorknob with forearm rotation" and "places paperclips on paper."

17. Fine Motor Skills: Bilateral Skills (7 items)—"Strings large beads" and "folds 8-1/2" x 11" paper in half."

18. Fine Motor Skills: Tool Use (6 items)—"Transfers material with a spoon" and "uses clothespin to transfer small objects."

19a. Visual Motor Skills: Pencil Control and Copying (11 items)—"Makes a crayon rubbing" and "copies asterisk."

19b. Visual Motor Skills: Representational Drawing (5 items)—"Draws a person with a head and one feature" and "draws a person with a head and eight features."

19c. Visual Motor Skills: Cutting (6 items)—"Snips with scissors" and "cuts out pictures following general shape."

DOMAIN 5—GROSS-MOTOR

20a. Locomotion: Walking (3 items)—"Walks backward ten feet" and "uses heel-toe walking pattern, arms swinging at side or free to carry objects."

20b. Locomotion: Tiptoe Walking (3 items)—"Walks three to four steps with heels off the ground" and "walks ten feet on tiptoes on a one-inch line."

20c. Locomotion: Galloping, Skipping (4 items)—"Gallops five cycles" and "skips ten plus steps with rhythmical weight transfer landing on toes."

20d. Locomotion: Running (5 items)—"Runs five to ten feet without falling" and "runs changing direction 180 degrees within four to eight steps."

20e. Locomotion: Hopping (6 items)—"Hops once in place" and "hops forward sixteen inches on preferred foot, twelve inches on non-preferred foot."

21a. Stairs: Upstairs (6 items)—"Walks up three steps using same-step placement, holding railing" and "walks up ten steps using alternate-step placement without holding railing."

21b. Stairs: Downstairs (7 items)—"Walks down three steps using same-step placement holding railing" and "walks down ten steps using alternate-step placement without holding railing."

22a. Jumping: Jumping Up (7 items)—"Jumps off floor with both feet" and "jumps completing a half turn in one jump."

22b. Jumping: Jumping Down (5 items)—"Jumps from 8 inch height, one foot leading" and "jumps from 32 inch height possibly leading with one foot."

22c. Jumping: Broad Jumping (4 items)—"Broad jumps 4 inches to 14 inches" and "broad jumps 36 inches or more."

23a. Balance: Static Balance (8 items)—"Stands on one leg for one to two seconds" and "stands on each leg with hands on hips and opposite knee bent for 10 seconds each."

23b. Balance: Dynamic Balance (14 items)—"Walks along a ten foot line from a general direction" and "kicks ball six feet to twelve feet in the air."

24a. Balls: Throwing (6 items)—"Throws 8 inch ball to an adult underhand five feet" and "throws an 8 inch ball overhand to an adult."

24b. Balls: Catching Balls (5 items)—"Catches 8 inch ball from five feet, arms straight in front of body" and "catches three inch ball from seven feet, arms bent and held at sides."

25. Outdoor Equipment (7 items)—"Propels riding toy with feet, ten feet" and "rides bicycle with training wheels."

Interpretation of results

The authors note that prior to the administration of the Assessment Log the child should be observed for a short period of time. They note that after 20 minutes of observation, many of the items on the Assessment Log can be completed without formal assessment. In fact, the majority of the Assessment Log can be used as an observation instrument; again the authors note that because the assessment is criterion-referenced, it does not matter if the test is completed in one day or over several weeks.

The Assessment Log is essentially a checklist of skills that is correlated with the areas on the Carolina Curriculum. After the checklist is completed, the Developmental Progress Chart is filled out to reveal the profile of skills.

OVERVIEW: THE ASSESSMENT LOG AND DEVELOPMENTAL PROGRESS CHART–PRESCHOOL

- *Age level*—3 to 5 years
- *Suggested Use*—The Assessment Log and Developmental Progress Chart–Preschool is used with the Carolina Curriculum of Preschoolers with Special Needs. Each item on the Assessment Log is correlated with a curriculum area for which the following information is available: materials necessary, procedure, group activities possible, and criterion for mastery. Through observation and direct testing the Assessment Log and the Developmental Progress Chart are completed, appropriate areas in the curriculum are identified and progress is monitored as the child progresses through the teaching sequences. Overall, the Assessment Log and the Developmental Progress Chart, in conjunction with the Carolina Curriculum, provide a helpful package for the assessment and programming of preschoolers with handicaps. One interesting feature of the manual is a separate chapter that focuses on selected handicapping conditions and their effects. Such areas as tactile defensiveness and hyperactivity/attention deficit disorders and their effects in the classroom as well as suggested teaching practices are discussed.

Behavioral Characteristics Progression

The Behavioral Characteristics Progression (BCP) (VORT Corporation, 1973) is a continuum of behaviors in chart form. It contains 2,400 observable traits referred to as *behavioral characteristics*. These behavioral characteristics are grouped into 56 criterion-referenced categories called *strands*.

This tool was intended to assist teachers of exceptional children to structure into a more coherent and manageable sequence the teaching of the various areas they are asked to cover. Particular care was taken to address the self-help, emotional, and practically-oriented academic skills that are commonly needed by the special-education student. Although the BCP does include some "higher-functioning" areas, many of the strands are appropriate for severely and profoundly handicapped individuals as well.

As an *assessment* tool, the BCP provides the teacher with a comprehensive chart of pupil behaviors to aid in identifying which behavioral characteristics a pupil displays or does not display. As an *instructional* tool, the BCP assists the teacher in developing individualized, appropriate learner objectives for each student. As a *communication* tool, the BCP offers a historical recording device that, throughout the education of the student, can be used to indicate progress.

Description

Strands 1–22 deal with self-help skills. Strands 23–45 include items related to social, academic, and recreational skills. Strands 46–56 involve skills specifically needed by blind, deaf, and orthopedically handicapped individuals.

The evaluator should choose the strand or strands that are most appropriate for the person being evaluated. This choice is facilitated by observing the *identifying behaviors* listed in the test materials; the evaluator can use these identifying behaviors as a checklist to determine and assign priorities to the most appropriate strands.

Interpretation of results

For each student, the strands selected are noted in an individual record booklet. A baseline for each strand is determined by measuring the behavior characteristics. The behavior characteristics are scored according to the following system: (–), behavior not displayed; (1/2), behavior exhibited, but less frequently than the recommended 75 percent required incidence level; (✓), behavior displayed at the 75 percent level with no assistance; (H), physical handicap prevents demonstrations of behavior. From this information, objectives can be delineated, and progress toward them can be monitored.

OVERVIEW: BEHAVIOR CHARACTERISTICS PROGRESSION

- *Age level*—No age provided
- *Suggested use*—The BCP is a comprehensive criterion-referenced instrument. Although it is designed for individuals with a wide range of abilities, a number of its items deal with lower-level skills. Booklets of instructional suggestions that are correlated with the strands are also

available. One potential disadvantage of the test is that it could be cumbersome if the number of strands is not limited.

Learning Accomplishment Profile–Revised

The Learning Accomplishment Profile (LAP) (Sanford & Zelman, 1981) is an individually administered test used with handicapped individuals up to developmental age 6. The LAP uses a task-analytic model to offer a hierarchy of sequential skills. The LAP is specifically designed to help the teacher identify behavioral objectives and to evaluate the student's progress in attaining those objectives. The items on the LAP were chosen from existing developmental and intellectual scales.

Description

Six areas of ability are measured on the LAP. In each area, the items are sequential. In addition, the test includes checklists that allow precise measurement of a number of skill areas.

> *Gross-Motor (37 items)*—Items in this section range from "sits without support" and "pulls self to stand" to "jumps from height of 12 inches landing on toes only."
>
> *Fine-Motor (47 items)*—These items measure general fine-motor skills such as "transfers cube hand-to-hand" and writing skills such as "scribbles spontaneously" and "copies circle."
>
> *Social Skills (38 items)*—Items in this section range from "smiles spontaneously" and "reaches for familiar persons" to "gets along in small groups" and "conforms to adult ideas."
>
> *Self-Help (38 items)*—These items measure the overall areas of eating, dressing, and toileting.
>
> *Cognitive Skills (35 items)*—Items in this section range from "fetches or carries familiar objects" and "uses names of familiar objects" to "can tell how a crayon and pencil are the same and how they are different" and "understands numbers up to ten."
>
> *Language Development (53 items)*—Items in this section range from "makes small, throaty noises" and "responds to bell" to "speaks fluently and correctly except for confusions of s, f, and th" and "asks meaning of abstract words."

Interpretation of results

For each item on the LAP, a developmental-age equivalent is given. In many instances in the test, different numbers of items are given for different developmental ages. Also, the developmental-age increments are not always consistent; for example, the items in the gross-motor section are given for 5, 8, 11, 12, 14, 21, 24, 30, 36–48, 48–60, 56, and 60–72 months. The record sheet provides space for writing comments and for noting the date of achievement for each item.

OVERVIEW: LEARNING ACCOMPLISHMENT PROFILE–REVISED

- *Age level*—36–72 months
- *Suggested use*—The LAP-R is an individually administered criterion-referenced instrument. It is appropriate for individuals up to developmental age 6. Although it is appropriate for children with mild disabilities, it has too few items at the lower ranges to be an effective aid in developing programs for severely and profoundly handicapped children. There is also some question about the sequence of items in each area. Finally, scoring of many of the items, particularly at the upper levels, is rather subjective, and this would tend to decrease the test's reliability. The LAP-R is, nevertheless, a comprehensive instrument that might help in educational programming and progress-monitoring. There is also an Early LAP (for children birth to 36 months), a LAP Diagnostic edition, and a booklet of learning activities that correspond to the LAP-R test items. Thus, a LAP total-evaluation system is available.

ADDITIONAL TESTS

There are also a number of other tests that have been used to identify children who are lagging behind in developmental areas or to identify children who might have potential problems. These tests (the First Grade Screening Test, Gesell School Readiness Test, and the Meeting Street School Screening Test), although outdated and lacking in acceptable technical characteristics, are nonetheless used in many schools. Other tests (e.g., Metropolitan Readiness Tests) are frequently administered to large groups of students to identify readiness for the early grades.

First Grade Screening Test

Age level—End of kindergarten through beginning of first grade

Type of administration—Group

Technical adequacy—Adequate reliability, moderate predictive validity

Scores yielded—Percentiles, cutting scores

Description—The FGST (Pate & Webb, 1969) is heavily weighted towards vocabulary and language. It seems to have adequate reliability, and the limited data on its validity support its use as a screening and readiness test. The scoring format, however, seems to be overly rigid. For instance, the children are shown a page with six pictures on it. They are instructed to circle "all the things that you use a needle with." Some pictures must be circled, some pictures cannot be circled, and some pictures can either be circled or not. A child must have the right responses for all six pictures in order for the item to be considered correct. This system could lead to a large number of children being considered "at risk" if they make several slight errors.

Gesell School Readiness Test

Age level—4 1/2 to 9 years old

Type of administration—Individual

Technical adequacy—Questionable reliability and validity

Scores yielded—Developmental age

Description—The GSRT (Ilg, Ames, Haines, & Gillespie, 1978) is based largely on the work of Arnold Gesell and is tied into a theory of development "which openly addresses and recommends retention" (Carstens, 1985; p. 55). In other words, if a child scores low on the GSRT, it indicates that the child is developmentally young and should not be promoted. The GSRT includes items requiring the child to copy and write, manipulate cubes, name animals, identify left and right, answer basic interview questions, and demonstrate visual-memory skills. There is considerable controversy surrounding the GSRT and what it actually measures. The construction of the test leaves a lot to be desired. The value of the test depends on one's philosophical orientation towards Gesell's theories. It has both strong advocates and vocal critics.

Meeting Street School Screening Test

Age level—5 to 7-1/2 years old

Type of administration—Individual

Technical adequacy—Limited standardization, adequate reliability, questionable validity

Scores yielded—Scaled scores

Description—The MSSST (Hainsworth & Sigueland, 1969) was designed to identify children with learning disabilities. Although the test has been shown to have adequate predictive validity for achievement, it should not be used as the only instrument to identify learning-disabled children. The test is heavily weighted towards sequencing ability and is based on the authors' concept of learning disabilities (primarily language and motor). In summary, the MSSST has some limited potential as a predictor of achievement and as a rough screening device for the identification of learning disabilities.

Metropolitan Readiness Tests

Age level—Preschool–beginning first grade

Type of administration—Group

Technical adequacy—Excellent standardization, adequate reliability, questionable validity

Scores yielded—Percentile ranks, stanines, Performance Ratings, scaled scores, normal curve equivalents

Description—The MRT (Nurss & McGavran, 1986) is the oldest and most widely used readiness test. The 1986 edition has maintained many of the features of earlier editions. It is heavily weighted toward preacademic skills (e.g., beginning consonants) as opposed to perceptual or developmental skills. The standardization sample was large and representative, although the predictive validity of the instrument has yet to be established. The predictive usefulness of the test, of course, depends on the specific first-grade curriculum.

Many other tests purport to measure the early academic abilities of very young children, although they have questionable validity for the preschool child.

Test of Early Reading Ability–2

Age level—3–9 years

Type of administration—Individual

Technical adequacy—Adequate reliability, questionable validity (for preschool children)

Scores yielded—Standard score, percentile ranks, normal curve equivalent

Description—The TERA-2 (Reid, Hresko, and Hammill, 1989) was designed to measure the actual reading ability of young children. Areas such as knowledge of contextual meaning, alphabet, and reading conventions are measured. There are two equivalent forms of the TERA-2, form A and form B, which would allow examiners to test with one form and retest with another after the initiation of an intervention program. There is some question of the validity of the instrument before the age of 4 or after the age of 7. The authors, in fact, note this limitation and suggest that anyone using the instrument with those age groups establish its suitability before administration .

Test of Early Mathematics Ability–2

Age level—3 through 8 years

Type of administration—Individual

Technical adequacy—Adequate reliability, questionable validity

Scores yielded—Standard scores, percentiles, age equivalents

Description—The TEMA-2 (Ginsberg & Baroody, 1990) is a norm-referenced instrument that can also be used informally to determine specific strengths and weaknesses. According to the authors, the test can be used to monitor progress, evaluate programs, screen for readiness, identify gifted students, and guide instruction and remediation. It measures four formal areas, Knowledge of Convention (reading and writing numerals), Number Facts, Calculation (algorithms), and Base Ten Concepts, and three informal areas of Mathematics, Concepts of Relative Magnitude, Counting, and Calculation. The TEMA-2 was standardized on a somewhat limited sample, and the validity of the instrument is generally lacking. One potential advantage of the TEMA-2 is the availability of a book of remedial techniques for improving the skills that are measured.

Instrument or Technique	Suggested Use							Target Population						Special Considerations	Educational Relevance for Exceptional Students
	Prereferral		Postreferral												
	Screening and Initial Identification	Informal Determination and Evaluation of Teaching Programs and Strategies	Determination of Current Performance Level and Educational Need	Decisions about Classification and Program Placement	IEP Goals	IEP Objectives	IEP Evaluation	Mild/Moderate	Severe/Profound	Preschool	Elementary Age	Secondary Age	Adult		
AGS Early Screening Profiles	X							X		X				Uses a team approach including information from the parent; motor section limited	useful
Developmental Indicators for the Assessment of Learning–Revised (AGS)	X							X		X				Has been used for early identification of handicapped and gifted; quick to administer	adequate
Miller Assessment for Preschoolers	X							X		X				More time-consuming to administer; heavily weighted to sensorimotor and sensory integration tasks	adequate
Basic School Skills Inventory	X							X		X	X			Limited technical aspects; unclear scoring criteria	limited
Boehm–R		X			X			X		X	X			Best used informally; normative information of questionable relevance	useful
Bracken Basic Concept Scale	X	X			X			X		X	X			Well constructed; potentially very useful basic concept scale	useful
Assessment Log and Developmental Progress Chart–Preschool			X		X	X	X	X	X	X				Used with the Carolina Curriculum; infant edition available	useful
Behavior Characteristics Progression			X		X	X	X	X	X	X				Books of instructional suggestions that are correlated with each item are available	useful
Learning Accomplishment Profile			X		X	X	X	X	X	X				Not appropriate for more severely handicapped; sequencing of some items is questionable	limited

Test							Comments	
Gesell School Readiness Test	X			X	X	X	Very limited technical aspects; used to make retention decisions	very limited
First Grade Screening Test	X			X	X	X	Overly rigid scoring system; heavily weighted toward vocabulary skills	limited
Meeting Street School Screening Test	X			X	X	X	Heavily weighted toward perceptual-motor skills	limited
Metropolitan Readiness Tests	X			X	X	X	Good technical aspects; is very comprehensive	useful
Test of Early Reading Ability–2	X			X	X	X	Limited for preschool children	limited
Test of Early Mathematics Ability–2	X			X	X	X	Limited for preschool children	limited

_17_

Vocational/Transitional Assessment

INSTRUMENTS/PROCEDURES INCLUDED

INFORMAL PROCEDURES
- Informal Checklists and Rating Scales
- Work Samples
- Curriculum-Based Vocational Assessment
- Direct Observation and Ecological Assessment

FORMAL PROCEDURES

INTEREST AND APTITUDE INSTRUMENTS
- Differential Aptitude Tests
- Gordon Occupational Checklists–III
- Kuder Occupational Interest Survey–Revised
- Occupational Aptitude Survey and Interest Schedule–2
- Reading-Free Vocational Interest Inventory–Revised
- Strong Campbell Interest Inventory
- Vocational Preference Inventory–Revised
- Wide Range Interest-Opinion Test

In recent years, the emphasis on vocational/transitional programs, particularly for secondary-level students, has increased dramatically. Along with increased emphasis on vocational programming comes an increased emphasis on vocational assessment. While in the past the focus of vocational assessment was on the use of formal instruments, current trends in the field have led to the use of more informal techniques that help to develop a more encompassing data-base that can and should stretch across a student's school career. Although traditional assessment procedures have not been abandoned, this recent shift has led to a more transdisciplinary approach to vocational assessment. In turn, this has led to shared responsibilities and cooperative planning and programming that are necessary to achieve successful post-school adjustments for students with handicaps. While the specific role that vocational assessment and education specialists might play is dictated by funding and various state and local program needs, the special education teacher can and should be familiar with the techniques included in this chapter. Aside from some of the specific tests and inventories, virtually all other procedures can be implemented by classroom teachers. If vocational assessment is conducted and the information is used appropriately, it is logical to assume that vocational programming goals and objectives on IEPs, vocational programs, and curricula and the quality of transition services will improve. With these improvements, we should also see much more positive post-school outcomes for students with disabilities.

Vocational assessment is an activity that has evolved from and employs the talents of several professional discipline areas (Stodden, 1986). Not surprisingly then, vocational assessment has traditionally involved a wide variety of procedures. These have included describing overt skills, drawing inferences about student abilities, predicting student job performance, assessing interests and aptitudes, and providing suggestions for instruction (Gaylord-Ross, 1986). More specifically, vocational assessment may rely on the use of interviews and rating scales, psychometric testing, the use of work samples, and situational assessment (Meehan & Hodell, 1986). In fact, it has been suggested that vocational assessment that relies on a single summative evaluation is probably not sufficient for accurate appraisal of the interests and attitudes of students with handicaps (Buschner, Watts, Siders, & Leonard, 1989). Others have noted that there should be increased reliance on the use of work samples (Peterson, 1986), curriculum-based vocational assessment (Conaway, 1987), and ecological assessment strategies (Falvey, 1989).

In this chapter, the current trends in transition planning and programming will be discussed with particular reference to federal mandates that have an impact on vocational assessment and education for students with handicaps. The steps in developing transition plans and the role of vocational assessment in that process will also be addressed. The development and use of work samples are included, as well as the basis and strategies for the use of curriculum-based vocational assessment and direct observation of students on the job. Finally, information concerning a number of relevant and commonly used psychometric instruments used in assessing students' vocational interests and aptitude will be provided.

It is worth noting that some experts differentiate between vocational assessment (i.e., gathering data) and vocational evaluation (i.e., reviewing and interpreting assessment information) (Stodden, 1986). In this chapter, the terms will be used interchangeably and are intended to include both of the above processes.

NEED AND SUPPORT FOR TRANSITION SERVICES

Over the past decade there has been increased interest in and requirements for the provision of transition services for handicapped students that will better prepare them for the world of work. In 1984, Madeleine Will, then Director of the Office of Special Education and Rehabilitative Services, wrote a position statement concerning the delivery of transition services to individuals with handicaps. She noted that the transition period includes high school, graduation, post-secondary placement, and initial years of employment. Transition planning and programming is a process that requires sound preparation and adequate support. Finally, Will stated that successful transitions require an effort that emphasizes shared responsibilities among service agencies.

Several legislative acts have supported the need for cooperative planning and service delivery to ensure successful transition programs. Such legislation has been necessary because the assimilation of people with handicaps into the mainstream workforce has yet to reach an optimal level (Rusch & Phelps, 1987). It should be noted, however, that many educators believe that in addition to legislative mandates, actual transition planning and programming will be required to provide better opportunities for individual students with handicaps who are leaving school and entering the "real world."

In 1983, Public Law 98-199, Section 626, "Secondary Education and Transitional Services for Handicapped Youth," was enacted specifically to increase the likelihood of successful school-to-work transitions for students with disabilities. Other legislative acts such as the Americans with Disabilities Act (P.L. 101-336) provide protection against discrimination and require reasonable accommodations in the workplace for people with handicaps (Linthicum, Cole, & D'Alonzo, 1991). In 1984, the Carl D. Perkins Vocational Education Act expanded the services provided to students with disabilities through vocational education and assessment to include transition planning and programming. More recent mandates and amendments to the Carl D. Perkins Act (e.g., Carl D. Perkins Vocational and Applied Technology Education Act of 1990, P.L. 101-392), have, however, made unclear the magnitude of the role vocational assessment personnel eventually may play within specific state and local transition programs for students with handicaps (Kochhar, 1991). Nevertheless, this law is important in understanding the relationship between vocational assessment and transition planning and programming. A more in-depth analysis of this law follows.

Carl D. Perkins Vocational Education Act

Specifically, the Carl D. Perkins Act provided for an increase in the accessibility to vocational education services for special education students. Wehman, Moon, Everson, Wood, and Barcus (1988) outlined the following provisions of the Act that affect services to youths with handicaps: (1) 10 percent of a state's grant allotment be used to provide services to students with handicaps; (2) each student and his/her parents be informed of vocational opportunities available at least 1 year prior to the provision of vocational education services (or by the time the student reaches ninth grade); and (3) equal access be provided to vocational educational services as deemed appropriate through the IEP process. These services may include (1) vocational assessment; (2) guidance and career counseling and development; (3) adaptation of curriculum and provision of special services to meet individual needs; and/or (4) staff and counseling services to facilitate successful transitions. It is clear from the above summary that Congress intended that special education students be afforded access to those same vocational services available to non-handicapped peers. Amendments to the Carl D. Perkins Act enacted in 1990 (P.L. 101-392) may, however, have some negative impact on provision of vocational services to students with handicaps (Kochhar, 1991). Kochhar asserted that the language of the law appears to ensure that services such as those just mentioned remain intact but that program or personnel cuts due to funding changes for vocational education programs may result in changes in the provision of these services, in particular state or local programs. Interestingly, however, the importance of transitional planning was reiterated in recent legislation such as P.L. 101-476.

Public Law 101-476

Among the many provisions of P.L. 101-476 (discussed in Chapter 1), was one for a new state grant program that authorized state education and vocational rehabilitation agencies to apply jointly for funds to develop, implement, and improve transition services for students with disabilities from age 14 through their exiting school (National Association of State Directors of Special Education [NASDSE], 1990). NASDSE reported that these funds must be used to (1) increase availability, access, and quality of transition services through development or improvement in policies, procedures, systems, and other mechanisms; (2) improve ability of professionals, parents, and advocates to work with such youth to improve transition outcomes; and (3) improve relationships among education agencies, adult service providers, families, and the private sector to identify and reach consensus on what transition services are needed and how they are to be applied. Additionally, the law mandates that transition plans be developed for all students with handicaps by age 16.

For the purposes of this chapter, it will be assumed that vocational assessment and education services will continue to be widely available. Even if this should prove not to be the case, the reader should be familiar with many of the techniques discussed for assessing vocational performance. Special education teachers should be capable of implementing, modifying, or adapting many of these practices in order to obtain vocational assessment data.

GUIDELINES FOR ESTABLISHING TRANSITION SERVICES: IMPORTANCE OF VOCATIONAL ASSESSMENT

Repetto, White, and Snauwaert (1990) reported on results of a state survey concerning the provision of transition services. These authors discovered considerable variance among states concerning the use of an Individualized Transition Plan (ITP) form, the relationship between the IEP and ITP, the age at which transition planning should begin, those to be involved in the planning, the issues to be addressed, and the expected outcomes to be emphasized. Nevertheless, general guidelines and procedures will be offered that should serve as a model for effective vocationally related transition programming.

Transition planning and programming should begin no later than a student's first year in high school.   The more barriers a student faces (e.g., behavioral difficulties, limited employment skills), the earlier this process should begin. Planning for students with severe disabilities may begin as early as middle school. Parents might be encouraged to "brainstorm" about desired adult outcomes from a student's earliest years.

The assessment aspect of transition planning and programming may begin prior to the first year of high school.   Interest inventories, aptitude tests, work samples, curriculum-based vocational assessment, and even on-the-job assessment may be administered prior to the high school years. For example, Elrod, Isbell, and Braziel (1989) noted that vocational assessment may be conducted throughout the student's school career through inexpensive and easily administered procedures. Specifically, teachers and other personnel should assess prevocational competencies and relate those competencies to the basic skills curriculum (Elrod et al., 1989). For example, Elrod et al. suggested the use of short student self-evaluation scales with clear, easily understood, and brief item statements with open-ended or yes/no response requirements. Sample items requiring a yes/no response might include "I like to keep my desk neat," "I like to think about what I will be when I grow up," "I like people to count on me," and "I like to earn money" (Elrod et al., 1989, p. 253). Teachers might also evaluate their efforts to improve transition/vocational outcomes through similar rating scales (Elrod et al., 1989). These authors suggested possible items using a 1–5 scale that included "I integrate transition-related skills within basic skills objectives," "I select classroom activities which are applicable to real-life settings," and "I assign class-room duties to promote proper work attitudes" (p. 254). Elrod et al. suggested that targeted competencies might be derived from the Life-Centered Career Education curriculum (Brolin, 1983). Because there should be emphasis on career awareness for elementary-aged students, assessment at this stage of schooling should not be ignored.

Vocational assessment becomes critical to the transition process as the student prepares for postsecondary adjustment. During IEP and ITP discussions, a written vocational assessment report may be reviewed if available; otherwise relevant vocational assessment data should be discussed. That information should be used in deciding on vocationally related goals and objectives, daily classroom activities implemented, vocational education, and/or vocational training placements (Meehan & Hodell, 1986; Wisniewski, Alper, & Schloss, 1991). Wisniewski et al. also stressed that systematic assessment by a transition specialist may assist in guiding community-based instruction, as well as ensure that the vocational curriculum is functional and relevant. Vocational assessment data are combined with that of other assessment specialists and educators to provide a total picture of the student's abilities, interests, and skills that might affect his/her postschool performance. According to Elrod and Sorgenfrei (1988), information collected from various personnel might include (1) psychoeducational information involving areas such as intelligence, perception, psycholinguistics, and psychomotor skills; (2) sociobehavioral information including direct observation of social conduct, personality, and psychiatric evaluation; (3) academic information including the areas of reading, mathematics, and language arts; and (4) career vocational/assessment information involving interests, needs, aptitudes, and abilities that relate to all areas of life adjustment. This latter area might include a consideration of the roles of the student in home/family, community, and workplace (Kokaska & Brolin, 1985), as well as specific vocational interests and skills. Furthermore, the specific emphasis on career/vocational assessment should increase substantially as the student enters junior and senior high school, whereas academic assessment is emphasized less (Elrod & Sorgenfrei, 1988).

Developing and Implementing the Transition Plan

Vocational assessment information is brought to the transition team meeting for sharing, discussion, and use in planning for desired outcomes and specific goals and objectives. During these meetings, the transition team will formulate an ITP that is separate from the IEP and in some cases may be part of an Individualized Written Rehabilitation Plan (IWRP) (Repetto et al., 1990). The following are the suggested steps of Wehman et al. (1988) for implementing the transition plan and program. First, organize the ITP teams for all transition-age students. This step includes *identifying the students according to some criteria* (e.g., age and severity of barriers to postschool adjustment), identifying appropriate school personnel (i.e., individuals from different disciplines who have had recent meaningful contact with the individual), and identifying adult service agencies that may be involved in the transition process (e.g., vocational rehabilitation or Association for Retarded Citizens). Wehman et al. further noted that many adult service agencies will not have sufficient staff to participate in transition team meetings until perhaps the final 2 years of school. The vocational assessment specialist (or special or vocational education teacher involved in gathering relevant career/vocational assessment data) may well be the individual most qualified to suggest possible employment options, postsecondary training options, and potential employers or adult service providers. Step two involves *conducting the actual ITP meeting.* Typically, these meetings are scheduled simultaneously with the IEP for convenience and to increase the likelihood of parental and staff participation. During the actual meeting, the following procedures should be followed to formulate the ITP:

1. Open the transition meeting by introducing all present and establishing an informal, comfortable atmosphere.
2. Generate a discussion of desired outcomes and what support services are available.
3. Identify transition goals.
4. Determine steps/objectives to accomplish those goals.
5. Devise a checklist to ensure that responsible persons and time lines are identified for providing various services (e.g., referral to vocational rehabilitation, investigating application for food stamp assistance).
6. End the meeting by having all participants sign the plan.

The third step is to actually *implement the plan.* This will likely involve interagency cooperation and the terms of state or local interagency agreements. The fourth step involves *ensuring that the ITP is updated at least annually* (and conceivably more frequently in the actual transition year). Follow-up procedures are also necessary to ensure goals and objectives are being addressed. The fifth and final step is to *schedule an exit meeting* just prior to the student's leaving school to discuss the continued provision of services and follow-up as necessary. Those individuals involved in vocational assessment should be prepared to be responsible for assisting in referrals to appropriate agencies/programs (e.g., vocational rehabilitation), providing ongoing assessment, and providing follow-up assessment services after graduation. It is important to note that the IEP and ITP are related but somewhat different documents. Unlike the IEP, the transition plan typically spans a multiyear period, stresses the involvement of both educators and adult service providers serving on a single team, and is broader in scope in that vocational, residential, leisure, social, and com-

Student _____   Current Classroom Placement_____

Date of Plan_____   Projected Graduation Date_____

Concerns	Objective	Activities	Personnel Responsible	Completion Date
Income: Ability of person to support himself/herself				
Job & Job Training: Ability of person to hold a job on his/her own				
Living Arrangements: Ability to live independently				
Recreation & Leisure: Ability to participate in community recreation and leisure activities				
Transportation: Ability to travel from home to work, postsecondary programs, community activities, etc.				
Medical Needs: Person's medical needs are met				
Friends/Advocates: Ability to develop and maintain friendships with peers and advocates				
Long-Term Planning: Adequate provision made for long-term care/supervision needs				
Family Relationships: Person can maintain contact with his/her family				
Insurance: Adequate provision made for health and other types of insurance				

FIGURE 17-1   Transition Plan.

From B. Cobb and S. Hasazi, School-aged transition services: Options for adolescents with mild handicaps. *Career Development for Exceptional Individuals, 10,* 17. © 1987 by Council for Exceptional Children. Reprinted with permission.

munity living skills are addressed (Stowitschek & Kelso, 1989). The ITP is developed to facilitate entry into and maintain adult working and community life situations and to coordinate educational and postsecondary efforts toward this goal (Stowitschek & Kelso, 1989). A sample ITP is shown in Figure 17-1. The possible forms and formats for an ITP are many and varied (Repetto et al., 1990).

Assessment information used to develop ITPs and to make other vocational programming decisions is gathered through a variety of procedures. Informal procedures such as the use of checklists or rating scales may assist the teacher in gathering preliminary information. Direct approaches such as work samples, curriculum-based vocational assessment, and observation of students on the job provide meaningful information about students' vocational skills. Finally, instruments such as career interest inventories and vocational aptitude tests might provide important information for determining career options.

INFORMAL PROCEDURES

Checklists and Rating Scales

WHY USE?

Screening for vocational/career preferences/interests and vocational aptitudes, developing educational/vocational programs

WHO SHOULD USE?
Teachers

A variety of informal procedures might be used to evaluate vocational skills. Elrod et al. (1989) suggested that observational data and anecdotal records might be compiled and informal interviews conducted. Sample questions might include "What job would you like to have when you finish your education?" "Do you like to work alone or with others?" and "Would you prefer a desk job or a job where you can use your physical skills?" Elrod et al. pointed out that the *Brigance Diagnostic Inventory of Essential Skills* (discussed in Chapter 12) includes components in the vocational subtest that might serve as bases for either individual or group paper-pencil tasks or for interviewing. They also suggested that informal assessment of prevocational aptitudes (for grades 7–12) might involve the use of rating scales completed by the teacher that include items related to placement in vocational education or in private employment. An example of such a rating scale is included in Figure 17-2. Similar rating scales might be employed at actual job placements. (This use is discussed later in the chapter.) Furthermore, while these techniques are easily employed by classroom teachers, the information gleaned from such assessments may not provide a complete portrait of a student's aptitudes and abilities. Work samples, both commercially produced and locally validated, are an example of a more formal technique that might also prove useful.

Work Behavior		Rating			
1. Dresses appropriately	1	2	3	4	5
2. Is well groomed	1	2	3	4	5
3. Attends class regularly	1	2	3	4	5
4. Is punctual	1	2	3	4	5
5. Demonstrates initiative	1	2	3	4	5
6. Works well independently	1	2	3	4	5
7. Works well with peers	1	2	3	4	5
8. Works well with authority figures	1	2	3	4	5
9. Is receptive to constructive criticism	1	2	3	4	5
10. Shows pride in work	1	2	3	4	5
11. Keeps neat work area	1	2	3	4	5
12. Completes tasks on time	1	2	3	4	5
13. Asks questions, if needed	1	2	3	4	5
14. Accepts new responsibilities	1	2	3	4	5
15. Solicits additional duties when finished with a task	1	2	3	4	5

Rating Scale: 1 = Never observed; 2 = Observed sometimes; 3 = Observed about half of the time; 4 = Observed often; 5 = Always observed.

FIGURE 17-2   Prevocational Aptitude Rating Scale.

From G. Elrod, C. Isbell, and P. Braziel, Assessing transition-related variables from kindergarten through grade 12. *Diagnostique, 14,* 259. © 1989 by Council for Exceptional Children. Reprinted with permission.

Work Samples

WHY USE?
Evaluate performance of specific and general work skills and worker traits and characteristics

WHO SHOULD USE?
Vocational assessment personnel

Work samples are a situational assessment tool used to simulate tasks that are associated with jobs in the labor market. Work samples are defined in the Vocational Evaluation and Work Adjustment Association–Commission on the Accreditation of Rehabilitation Facilities (VEWAA-CARF) Vocational Evaluation and Work Adjustment Standards (1978) as

> A well-defined work activity involving tasks, materials, and tools which are identical or similar to those in an actual job or cluster of jobs. It is used to assess an individual's vocational aptitude, worker characteristics, and vocational interests (p. 20).

Work samples incorporate the tools and the standards associated with the actual job. Ideally, the activities associated with work samples should be as realistic as possible (i.e., as similar as possible to the community-based work). Work samples are a common component in the vocational assessment process because they emphasize performance skills and approximate work more closely than traditional psychometric instruments. Activities performed on a work-sample task give the evaluator an opportunity to observe work behavior in a controlled environment.

Data gathered during the work-sample activities assist the vocational evaluator in identifying strengths and weaknesses, determining a practical and realistic career goal, and assessing interest areas. They also provide the evaluator with information concerning work habits, dexterity and manipulative skills, physical abilities, interpersonal skills, and work capacity. This information may be helpful to the evaluator in analyzing vocational potential, selecting appropriate training programs, and identifying program modifications. Results obtained from the work sample approach assist personnel in providing vocational counseling, program development, and job placement (Sarkees & Scott, 1985).

Work sample activities may be provided through the use of a wide variety of commercial and locally developed batteries (Peterson, 1986). Many commercial work samples provide normative data as well as information on validity and reliability. Work samples may attempt to simulate the complete range of activities associated with a single job or they may provide selected activities designed to represent a number of related

tasks. There are five different types of work samples defined by the
VEWAA-CARF (1978):

> *Cluster Trait Work Sample*—A single work sample developed to assess a
> cluster of worker traits. This type of sample is based on an analysis of an
> occupational area and the traits necessary for successful performance. The
> student's potential to perform various tasks is assessed.
>
> *Indigenous Work Samples*—This type provides activities that are used to
> assess the essential factors affecting performance in an occupation as it
> presently exists in the community.
>
> *Job Sample*—This type precisely replicates actual industrial jobs and in-
> cludes the equipment, tools, raw materials, procedures, and standards used
> on the job.
>
> *Simulated Work Sample*—This type is similar to the Job Sample, but only a
> segment of the essential work is replicated as well as work-related factors
> and the use of the tools required on the job.
>
> *Single Trait Work Samples*—This type focuses assessment on a single
> worker trait. This trait or characteristic may be relevant to either a specific
> job or to a variety of jobs, but only this single isolated factor is assessed.

Sitlington and Wimmer (1978) cited eight advantages of using commercial work sample systems versus other assessment approaches. First,
work samples provide the student with the opportunity for job exploration. Given actual simulations of work activities, individuals often begin
to think seriously about the type of work they might enjoy. Second, they
allow actual job simulations to be brought into the evaluation setting,
where they can be conducted without the pressure that might be experienced in an actual job setting. Third, work samples are motivating. Not
only do they provide an alternative to traditional testing procedures, but
they also often provide the types of tasks at which a person with a
disability can be successful. Fourth, they may provide motivation for
classroom learning by establishing relevance for certain academic skills
that are related to the task. Fifth, work samples allow habilitation personnel to compare an individual's abilities to those of workers employed in
particular occupations. Sixth, they may be used as behavioral change
instruments, allowing assessment and training of work habits and personal social skills. Seventh, work samples allow determination of an
individual's strengths and weaknesses on work-related tasks. Finally,
work samples can build confidence by providing successful experiences.

Regardless of the advantages of work samples, their exclusive use in
vocational assessment has significant limitations (Sax, 1973). Some of the
disadvantages of the exclusive use of work samples include (1) a tendency
to emphasize quality and quantity of production rather than personality
factors, (2) difficulty in developing work samples for the many different
jobs in the labor market, (3) problems in comparing the working environment in industry and the more controlled environment in which the work

sample is collected, (4) lack of assurance that the sample is measuring the actual job skills, (5) the risk of developing a good appraisal instrument for jobs that no longer exist because work technology change is so rapid, and (6) lack of reliability and validity information for many work-sampling approaches. Sarkees and Scott (1985) specifically noted the disadvantages of using commercial work samples, among which were that the systems are often expensive and time-consuming to administer and that some work samples are too simple and do not present a realistic view of the job. In addition, the norms provided for work-sample performance may not relate to the population being evaluated. Sitlington and Wimmer (1978) identified a series of questions to ask when a commercial system is considered:

1. Does the system take into account expectancy to fail?
2. Does the system take into account academic limitations?
3. Does the system take into account verbal limitations?
4. Does the system take into account experience limitations?
5. Does the system allow for more than one trial on tasks?
6. Does the system allow for repeated instructions and check for comprehension?
7. Does the system have face validity (i.e., is it an accurate assessment of the content presented)?
8. Does the system allow for appropriate conditions for testing (i.e., does it offer pleasant surroundings, orderly administration, and considerations for fatigue of individuals)?
9. Is the system adequately normed on handicapped individuals and the workers who are doing the various types of tasks?

Selection of appropriate commercial systems should also take into consideration the following factors: (1) range of jobs available in the community and scope of jobs represented in the work sample, (2) validity and reliability for the client population to be served, and (3) purpose of the evaluation including occupational information through hands-on experience, assessment of present skills and aptitudes without relating information to career functions, a thorough evaluation of student aptitude and work behaviors, occupational information and dissemination, and occupational exploration (Revell, Kriloff, & Sarkees, 1980, p. 80).

Locally developed work samples can provide a more appropriate means of assessment because they are more closely associated with the limitations and demands of the local labor market than commercially developed work samples (Peterson, 1986; Sitlington, 1979). Work-sample activities can be developed by vocational personnel to evaluate the abilities of an individual to perform a specific task—activities that usually reflect proficiencies necessary for entry-level vocational courses associated with the program. These work samples may not always sample the total classroom curriculum, but they include tasks that suggest a potential for successful performance in the classroom and may help to point out areas for remediation (Sarkees & Scott, 1985). Pruitt (1977) pointed out that informal work samples can be used to provide career exploration; assess work habits, coordination, physical capacity, and interpersonal skills; assess abilities and limitations; and evaluate skills of the individual prior to placement in a job situation. An example of how a work sample might be evaluated is presented in Table 17-1. This example was taken from the Albuquerque, New Mexico, public schools.

Table 17-1   Example of an Evaluation of a Work Sample. (Written Direction Test)

PURPOSE	Practical assessment of functional reading ability. May also measure organizational skills of students with adequate reading comprehension.
PERTINENT REFERRAL QUESTIONS	1. How does this student learn best?
	2. This student has poor reading comprehension skills. Can he/she work from written directions at all?
	3. McDonald's Restaurant requires their manager trainees to read manuals. Is this an appropriate placement?
READING LEVEL	5th or 6th grade level
TIME TO ADMINISTER	Takes about 10 or 15 minutes to complete.
STRENGTHS	1. Practical and quick measure of ability to follow written directions.
	2. Students seem to dislike this instrument less than other reading tests.
	3. Provides a comparison to other short tests of learning style.
WEAKNESSES	1. Limited norm base.
	2. Does not include a speed measure.
POSSIBLE INTERPRETATIONS	*High*
	1. Student may be able to work from written directions on a job.
	Low
	1. Student may lack experience in working from written directions.
	2. Student should avoid jobs requiring the use of written directions.
	3. Other methods of instruction may be appropriate.

Work samples continue to play an important role in vocational assessment programs in school and rehabilitation settings. As Peterson (1986) pointed out, the use of work (real or simulated) as a focal point in vocational assessment is both a valid and valuable process. Many programs use a combination of commercial work-sample systems and locally developed work samples. Care must be taken to ensure that the work samples selected are appropriate for the population being served. Carelessness in work-sample selection can result in instruments that are unrelated to the local labor market or unrealistic for the targeted population given their capabilities and limitations (McCray, 1982). Recently, some schools have implemented curriculum-based vocational assessment as another means of measuring students' vocational skills.

Curriculum-Based Vocational Assessment

WHY USE?
Evaluate acquisition of vocational and related skills embedded within content and applied courses

WHO SHOULD USE?
Teachers, vocational assessment personnel

Historically, vocational assessments have been conducted without appropriate collaboration between vocational and special education personnel and without a single, unifying funding source (Ianacone & Leconte, 1986). As a result, many programs experienced the following problems: (1) lack of expertise to assist in setting up vocational services; (2) the use of a rehabilitation model rather than a career exploration, planning and programming, and vocational training model; (3) overreliance on the use of commercial assessment systems insensitive to local job market needs; (4) assessment in isolated settings that failed to obtain critical information concerning social and work-related behaviors; (5) emphasis on career exploration activities as opposed to more relevant assessment services; (6) lack of planning and release time for developing relevant, locally valid work samples; (7) lack of use of assessment information in making programmatic decisions; (8) lack of a uniform system for referrals, with some students being referred too early to have developed adequate motivation or concern over career goals and some too late for the assessment to have programmatic impact; (9) prohibitive transportation costs when assessments were conducted in a Center; and (10) lack of trained personnel with knowledge concerning vocational assessment as well as both vocational and special education (Ianacone & Leconte, 1986). As a result of these problems, curriculum-based vocational assessment (CBVA) was offered as an alternative. This process is very similar to the curriculum-based assessment procedures discussed in Chapter 7. CBVA focuses on students' career development and vocational needs based upon actual and ongoing performance within the existing course content (Ianacone & Leconte, 1986). Conaway (1987) noted that CBVA may occur in vocational exploration or special education classrooms as well as through integrated services provided by counselors, teachers, and vocational education staff.

One model for CBVA, described by Porter and Stodden (1986), includes three levels of data collection. The first encompasses junior high school prevocational courses and activities. At this level, readiness and awareness skills are assessed during exploratory classes and activities. The second level begins in high school and addresses performance in vocational coursework. The third level includes assessment of work-related behaviors and both generalized vocational outcomes and specific skills in actual job placements obtained through cooperative work-experience programs (Porter & Stodden, 1986). Included in Figure 17-3 are the key steps to developing a CBVA model listed by Ianacone & Leconte (1986). Included in Figure 17-4 is a vocational assessment rating form used in the CBVA model proposed by Porter & Stodden (1986). It is important to note that CBVA, as curriculum-based assessment in general, is only as valid as the curriculum itself (Taylor, Willits, & Richards, 1988). That is, if the career/vocational course content is not meeting the needs of students, the assessment information may prove to be of little use. Additionally, students with more severe handicaps may not be participants in vocational education as experienced by students with milder disabilities. For these students (and for students with mild disabilities as noted earlier), direct observation of student performance at community-based work-experience sites yields data that may require fewer inferences about actual vocational interests, strengths, and weaknesses. Direct observation also provides information concerning behaviors (e.g., social interaction) that affect employability as well as the specific performance of the job itself.

Direct Observation and Ecological Assessment

WHY USE?
Evaluate performance of specific and general work skills, work-related behaviors; determine modifications for instruction

WHO SHOULD USE?
Teachers, vocational assessment personnel, transition personnel

The first step involved in direct observation involves activities in the actual worksite and matching the requirements of the job to the individual student. This process is referred to as the "job match" (Falvey,

1. Identify key development personnel.

   - Who are the key personnel needed to conceptualize, develop, and validate a curriculum-based vocational assessment model?
   - Who are the key personnel needed to operate and develop the vocational assessment model?
   - What disciplines and administrative personnel are critical to implementation and need to be represented?

2. Conduct a comprehensive search of program models, research literature, vocational evaluation/assessment instrumentation, and pertinent legislation.

   - What research is available concerning the efficacy of vocational assessment services in school-based settings?
   - What program models currently exist and what factors have influenced their effectiveness within the local education community and employment settings?
   - What factors influence validity and reliability in the collection of assessment data?

3. Establish basic considerations for the model based on previous research; analyze and synthesize the programmative needs. These considerations include tenants, i.e., vocational assessment:

   - Should be an integrated part of the total delivery of career/vocational services.
   - Should reflect pre-assessment readiness needs of the student and provide developmental growth information.
   - Should be a student-centered process with a career development orientation consisting of experiences to increase one's awareness, exploration, and understanding rather than a strict predictive procedure providing isolated ability data.
   - Should be based on the assessed employment needs of the local community and the applicable skills of the student to insure key validity and efficacy factors contributing to the structure of the model.
   - Should measure key situational factors specific to work roles that can be critical determinants of interest and performance.
   - Should produce a wide variety of demonstratively useful information that can be assessed and used by several disciplines, the student, and the parents.
   - Who should coordinate and use the assessment information to make placement and programming decisions?
   - How will this information be applied to the development of individualized educational and vocational planning and program development?

4. Establish an operational plan to implement the process.

   - Where will vocational assessment activities occur?
   - Who will be assessed?
   - What information will be collected?
   - How will vocational assessment information be collected (instruments, activities, techniques)?
   - Who will conduct vocational assessment activities?
   - How will the vocational assessment information be gathered and organized?

(continued)

- Who will be responsible for coordinating information gathering, which includes facilitating, providing support, and monitoring?
- Who will analyze, synthesize, and interpret vocational assessment findings to appropriate decision-making groups?
- What time frame will be used for vocational assessment activities?
- How will data collection be integrated and formalized as part of the instructional process?
- How will the vocational assessment instrumentation be developed?
- What specific competencies and specific related behaviors will be assessed?
- How should the collected data be formatted and displayed for optimal application and use?
- What evaluation criteria will be used to measure competency attainment and behaviors?

5. Pilot and evaluate the CBVA implementation activities.

- What school(s) and personnel should be involved in field testing?
- What steps need to be taken (additional inservice training, technical assistance, and ongoing support) to insure the appropriate climate and expertise for full integration and application of the vocational assessment process in the pilot sites?
- What criteria will be used to evaluate the process, instrumentation, and overall impact at the pilot site?
- What modifications need to be made to the process, instrumentation, or support mechanisms as a result of the pilot test?
- Who will make the modifications?

6. Implement, evaluate, and expand options.

- What additional steps need to be taken on a systemwide basis for full integration and application of the curriculum-based vocational assessment model and process?
- What specific evaluation data will be collected?
- What implementation and evaluation checkpoints need to be established?
- What additional course and activity settings would yield relevant career and vocational assessment information?
- What additional steps are needed to assist teachers to view their instructional processes and outcomes in a career or vocational context?

FIGURE 17-3   Key Steps to Curriculum-Based Vocational Assessment.

From R. Ianacone and P. Leconte, Curriculum-based vocational assessment. *Career Development for Exceptional Individuals, 9,* 117. © 1986 by Council for Exceptional Children. Reprinted with permission.

1989). As Falvey noted, it is critical that the student's abilities be adequate to the demands of the employment situation. This includes not only the specific skill requirements, but a host of other variables that may impact upon successful employment. A work-site analysis is then con-

DODDS	VOCATIONAL ASSESSMENT RATING FORM		INDUSTRIAL ARTS - WOODS

Entry _____ Exit _____

STUDENT: LAST NAME   FIRST   M.I.   GRADE   LENGTH OF TERM

9 weeks _____ 18 weeks _____

SCHOOL

DATES ATTENDED

I WORK RELATED BEHAVIORS	P	M	II GENERALIZED OUTCOMES	P	M	III SPECIFIC SKILL OUTCOMES	P	M
1 Display initiative			1 Understands oral directions			1 Compare/select products		
2 Exhibit a desire to improve			2 Can give oral directions			2 Identify product assembly processes		
3 Display integrity			3 Understand written directions			3 Follow systematic production planning		
4 Exhibit self-confidence			4 Apply related terminology			4 Use mixing processes in production		
5 Display frustration tolerance			5 Apply related measurement functions			5 Apply coating processes		
6 Exhibit flexibility			6 Apply related math computations			6 Use bonding processes		
7 Make judgements and decisions			7 Apply related science concepts			7 Prepare template		
8 Relate with peers/co-workers			8 Practice related hygienic requirements			8 Prepare a jig		
9 Relate with teachers/supervisors			9 Demonstrate safety procedures			9 Prepare a fixture		
10 Cooperate as a team member			10 Demonstrate problem solving technique			10 Identify object by shape/size		
11 Accept constructive criticism			11 Shows interest in occupational area			11 Bore hole with hand brace		
12 Work unsupervised			12 Perform equipment maintenance			12 Bore hole with portable hand drill		
13 Complete tasks accurately			13 Understand employer-employee roles			13 Cut hole with keyhole saw		
14 Complete tasks in a timely manner			14 Understand function of a supervisor			14 Select proper hammer and drive nails		
15 Seek assistance appropriately			15 Understand role of employee evaluation			15 Level and plumb installations		
16 Display appropriate habits/manners			16 Understand business enterprise function			16 Apply stains/shellac/varnish		
17 Display appropriate appearance						17 Operate portable drill		
18 Comply with attendance regulations						18 Operate portable sander		
19 Practice punctuality						19 Operate drill press		
20 Display appropriate conduct						20 Operate grinder		
21 Use and care of materials/equipment						21 Operate vertical band and table saw		
						22 Perform precision cutting		
						23 Operate horizontal saw		
						24 Set up and operate lathe		
						25 Demonstrate hand sawing		
						26 Demonstrate planning procedures		
						27 Demonstrate abrading procedures		

DIRECTIONS

As related to your course, CIRCLE the student's overall: INTEREST....High   Medium   Low
                                                            APTITUDE....High   Medium   Low

- Please check the appropriate category.
  P = Proficient--can perform with *80% accuracy
  M = Proficient with modification--can perform with instructor assistance at *80% accuracy

ADDITIONAL INFORMATION   **COMMENTS**

- Circle the number when information was taught in class but student did not achieve proficiency.

- Do not check or circle when information was not evaluated/covered.

- List additional behavior/competencies. Use the blank spaces in each column for additional behaviors/competencies relevant to your curricular area.

*This standard of proficiency may vary in relation to course content, instructional level and degree to which competitive employment standards are used in your classroom.

INSTRUCTOR'S SIGNATURE — DATE

FIGURE 17-4   Vocational Assessment Rating Form.

From M. Porter and R. Stodden, A Curriculum-based vocational assessment procedure: Addressing the school-to-work transition needs of secondary schools. *Career Development for Exceptional Individuals, 9,* 125. © 1989 by Paul Brookes. Reprinted with permission.

ducted where more in-depth information is gathered (Falvey, 1989). Figure 17-5 includes a sample job-site analysis form. Once this information is gathered, the job coach (the individual providing direct training at a job) or teacher may then proceed with breaking down activities and skills into teachable components as required by the student's rate of learning.

Although originally developed for students with severe handicaps, the use of ecological and student repertoire inventories (Brown et al., 1979; Brown et al., 1980; Falvey, Brown, Lyon, Baumgart, & Schroeder, 1980) are applicable to this type of training situation and with students with handicaps in general. During this process, the teacher/assessment specialist analyzes the environment in terms of what skills are required to be successful in the activities occurring in that environment and then assesses the student's performance of those skills. For example, when performing an ecological inventory, Brown et al. (1979) outlined the following general steps. First, delineate the environment itself (e.g., McDonald's restaurant). Second, delineate subenvironments where the student will be required to function successfully (e.g., up front where orders are to be taken, in the cooking area, in the storeroom, outside on the restaurant grounds and parking area). Third, the specialist delineates the activities that occur in each of those environments (e.g., taking orders, filling orders, cooking french fries and sandwiches, assembling and wrapping sandwiches, stocking shelves, picking up trash). Fourth, the specialist delineates the particular skills required to participate in each activity (e.g., greeting the customer, listening to the order, inspecting to see if the items are available or must be ordered from the cooks, telling the customer the cost, ringing up items on the cash register, giving change). The similarity between the process and task analysis discussed in Chapter 6 should not be overlooked. In fact, a completed ecological inventory may resemble an assortment of task analyses related to each of the activities/skills involved in the job. Also noted in Chapter 6, the degree to which activities/skills would be broken down would depend on the severity of the student's disability. For example, a student with mild handicaps may require fewer and "larger" steps than would an individual with a moderate or severe disability.

Falvey et al. (1980) stressed that once the ecological inventory is completed, a student repertoire inventory must be implemented. The student repertoire inventory is used to assess the student's performance compared to that of nonhandicapped peers on the ecologically inventoried skills. Falvey (1989) listed the following steps in conducting the student repertoire inventory. First, complete the ecological inventory delineating the skills performed by nonhandicapped individuals. Second, observe and record whether the student is able to perform the skills exhibited by the nonhandicapped individuals for a given activity. These observations should be systematic and the recording procedures suggested in Chapter 5 may be used (e.g., event recording, duration recording). Third, conduct a dis-

Job Site Analysis

Job site: _____

Address: _____

Telephone number: _____

Supervisor(s): _____

Significant co-workers: _____

_____

Teacher/vocational specialists: _____

_____

Job placement staff: _____

Student(s): _____

_____

Work days/hours: _____

Relevant Information (obtain prior to student training)

1. Location of time clock, lounge, lockers, restrooms, pay telephone, etc.:

   _____

   _____

   _____

2. Location of work area and specific set up instructions: _____

   _____

   _____

   _____

3. Location of materials and supplies: _____

   _____

   _____

4. Required paperwork, production forms, documents, etc.: _____

   _____

   _____

5. Procedure for obtaining required job task assignments, materials, and task priorities/sequence: _____

   _____

   _____

6. Variations within the task sequence or within the job task: _____

   _____

   _____

7. Procedure for handling finished goods and completing tasks: _____

   _____

   _____

8. Expected work/break behavior (e.g., you can sit, eat, leave business):

   _____

   _____

   _____

(continued)

Job Site Analysis

9. Person(s) to ask for answers to work questions: _____
   _____
   _____

10. Clean up, maintenance, or repair responsibilities: _____
   _____
   _____

11. The names of all things involved with the job: _____
   _____
   _____

12. Procedure for what to do when you run out of work or the equipment breaks down: _____
   _____
   _____

13. Proper clothing and safety equipment: _____
   _____
   _____

14. Production and quality expectations: _____
   _____
   _____

15. Schedule for pay days: _____
16. Initial pay rate: _____
17. Details of benefits, work schedule, and procedures for notification of vacation/sick days: _____
   _____
   _____
   _____

18. Channels of communication: _____
   _____

19. Job description: _____
   _____
   _____
   _____

20. Procedure to ensure employer communication of problems: _____
   _____

Job Tasks (in prioritized order): _____
   _____
   _____
   _____
   _____

FIGURE 17-5 A Sample Job Site Analysis Form.

From K. Bishop and M. Falvey, Employment Skills. In M. Falvey, *Community-based curriculum: Instructional strategies for students with severe handicaps* (2nd ed.), p. 178–179. © 1989 by Paul Brookes.

crepancy analysis. This step involves analyzing whether the student is or is not able to perform the inventoried skills. If not, the assessment specialist should observe and analyze all aspects of that skill (e.g., antecedents, consequences, criteria). The student's performance is further analyzed to determine which aspects of the skill are presenting difficulty. Finally, the teacher provides intervention for these same skills using one of the following three options: teaching the skill directly, making adaptations in the skill or in how the student performs the skill, or teaching the student to perform a related skill. Suppose a student working at a fast-food restaurant is having difficulty with the skills necessary for cooking french fries. The student might be taught how to cook the potatoes through direct instruction and task analysis. The student might be provided with some adaptive device (e.g., to assist in emptying the fry basket) or taught to perform another skill that would free another worker to fry potatoes.

The advantages to using ecological and student repertoire inventories are that they assess functional skills in the actual environment where those skills will be used and that the performance is assessed in the presence of naturally occurring conditions. It should be added that this type of assessment may be used to evaluate student performance in other areas related to successful functioning such as home-living and community-living skills. This type of assessment is not, however, the only type of assessment that might be used in a vocational setting. Clearly, in an actual paid work or community-based training situation, input from the employer would also be desirable and might be obtained from a simple, 1–5 scale that is completed by the supervisor and the employee together. Figure 17-6 includes such a scale. Obviously, the teacher/trainer could adapt this scale or develop a new one to suit the particular needs of the student, employer, and teacher. It may be necessary for the teacher/trainer to spend some time with the employer/supervisor to ensure the scale is filled out as objectively as possible. It is certainly not unheard of for an employer/supervisor to either underrate or overrate a student's performance due to unduly low or high expectations. Additional types of information that might be gathered could include production rates, accuracy rate, or rate at which new skills are learned. This information could be obtained using the same observational techniques discussed in Chapter 5.

FORMAL PROCEDURES: VOCATIONAL INTEREST AND APTITUDE INSTRUMENTS

WHY USE?

Screening for vocational/career interests and vocational aptitudes, developing educational/vocational programs

WHO SHOULD USE?
Vocational assessment personnel

There are a number of formal instruments that have been designed to evaluate an individual's vocational interests and/or aptitude. These instruments are usually administered by a guidance counselor, school psychologist, or other professional involved in helping students determine their best career options. Whereas most of these instruments were designed for use with regular education students (e.g., Kuder Occupational Interest Survey), some were developed specifically for students receiving special education (e.g., the Reading-Free Vocational Interest Inventory). The tests designed for handicapped students usually do not require reading, and the format is easy to follow. Below is a brief description of several instruments that are used for career guidance purposes. Please note that this is only a very brief sampling of the many instruments available.

Differential Aptitude Tests (DAT)

Age level—Grades 7–12 (can be used with young adults not in school).

Technical adequacy—Validity and reliability have been supported in the technical manual and in the professional literature.

Areas measured—Verbal Reasoning, Numerical Ability, Abstract Reasoning, Clerical Speed and Accuracy, Mechanical Reasoning, Space Relations, Spelling, and Language Use.

Types of scores—Percentile ranks, stanines, and standard scores for males, females, and combined.

Suggested use—The DAT (Bennett, Seashore, & Wesman, 1990) is currently among the most widely used measures of multiple abilities. The battery is intended primarily for use in educational and vocational counseling with students in grades 7–12, although it is also appropriate for young adults not in school. There are two levels of the test—Level I for students in grades 7–9, and Level II for students in grades 10–12. A special large-print edition is available for the visually impaired, and several different versions have been developed in other languages for use outside the United States.

The battery is designed for group administration, and it is recommended the testing be carried out in two or more sessions because the total procedure takes approximately 2–3 hours. A supplemental test, the *Career Interest Inventory*, is designed to be used with the DAT to allow the students to explore their interest in various fields of employment. The battery yields nine scores, one for each test, with an additional combined score of Verbal Reasoning and Numerical Reasoning. This combined score is used as a measure of scholastic ability and correlates highly with measures of intelligence. There is also a computerized adaptive version of the DAT that has been shown to yield scores similar to the conventional battery (Henly, Klebe, McBride, & Cudeck, 1989).

Name: _____

Job Title: _____

Externship Site: _____

Beginning Date: _____

Completion Date: _____

Please circle the number that best represents your opinion.

1. I arrive and leave work on time.

1	2	3	4	5
Much too Seldom	Not Often Enough	Undecided	Usually	Always

2. I maintain good attendance.

1	2	3	4	5
Much too Seldom	Not Often Enough	Undecided	Usually	Always

3. I take my break and/or meals appropriately.

1	2	3	4	5
Much too Seldom	Not Often Enough	Undecided	Usually	Always

4. I maintain a good appearance.

1	2	3	4	5
Much too Seldom	Not Often Enough	Undecided	Usually	Always

5. My performance compares favorably with other worker's performance.

1	2	3	4	5
Much too Seldom	Not Often Enough	Undecided	Usually	Always

6. Communication with my coworkers is not a problem.

1	2	3	4	5
Much too Seldom	Not Often Enough	Undecided	Usually	Always

7. Communication with my supervisor is not a problem.

1	2	3	4	5
Much too Seldom	Not Often Enough	Undecided	Usually	Always

8. I attend to my job tasks consistently.

1	2	3	4	5
Much too Seldom	Not Often Enough	Undecided	Usually	Always

9. I take responsibility for obtaining work.

1	2	3	4	5
Much too Seldom	Not Often Enough	Undecided	Usually	Always

10. I am performing my job as accurately as my coworkers.

1	2	3	4	5
Much too Seldom	Not Often Enough	Undecided	Usually	Always

11. I am performing my job at the same speed as my coworkers.

1	2	3	4	5
Much too Seldom	Not Often Enough	Undecided	Usually	Always

12. I am treated the same as my coworkers.

1	2	3	4	5
Much too Seldom	Not Often Enough	Undecided	Usually	Always

13. My coworkers and I get along well together.

1	2	3	4	5
Much too Seldom	Not Often Enough	Undecided	Usually	Always

14. I would like to use adaptive equipment to improve my performance.

1	2	3	4	5
Much too Seldom	Not Often Enough	Undecided	Usually	Always

15. I enjoy my job and would like to continue working at my present job.

1	2	3	4	5
Much too Seldom	Not Often Enough	Undecided	Usually	Always

18. I would rate my overall performance at this time as:

Please make additional comments below.

FIGURE 17-6 Joint Evaluation by Employee and Supervisor.

From P. Wehman, J. Everson, R. Walker, et al., Transition services for adolescent-age individuals with severe mental retardation. In R. Ianacone and R. Stodden (Eds.), *Transition Issues and Directions.* © 1987 by the Council for Exceptional Children. Reprinted with permission.

Gordon Occupational Checklists–II

Age level—Persons seeking job training below the college level.

Technical adequacy—Limited reliability and validity data; this checklist is not normed in the traditional sense.

Areas measured—Business, Outdoor, Arts, Services, Technical (subdivided into Mechanical and Industrial).

Types of scores—Each item is keyed to a job title and its corresponding work group listed in the U.S. Department of Labor's *Guide for Occupational Exploration.*

Suggested use—These checklists (Gordon, 1981) provide informal information related to occupational interests. Individuals must simply underline those occupational activities that they would "like to do" and circle those that they would "like to do the very most." As noted previously, each item is correlated with a specific job title and occupational group. The items can be read to those examinees who do not read at the sixth-grade level.

Kuder Occupational Interest Survey–Revised (KOIS)

Age level—Grade 10–adult.

Technical adequacy—Support is generally lacking; predictive validity studies have indicated that approximately 50 percent of the students followed found work in high-interest occupations identified by the KOIS. Relatively small studies have indicated satisfactory reliability.

Area measured—Scores are available in four areas: Dependability, Vocational Interest Estimates, Occupational, and College Majors.

Types of scores—Percentile ranks, Lambda scores (similarity of response between examinee and those in various reference groups).

Suggested use—The 1985 revision of the KOIS (Kuder & Diamond, 1985) is very similar to previous editions. The examinee is presented with a variety of occupational activities that he or she must mark as most preferred or least preferred. Those responses are subsequently compared to a normative group who are in 119 occupational groups. The KOIS also allows the comparison of examinee's responses to a normative group with various college majors. The Dependability scale is used to determine if the test should be considered a valid estimate of the examinee's interests (considering such things as random or omitted responses). The Vocational Interest Estimates provide a ranking of the examinee's occupational preferences. The Occupational and College Major Scales provide a comparison of the examinee's responses to various normative groups. Tenopyr (1989) noted that the revised version has a much improved report form, although the reliability and validity of the instrument need to be investigated further.

Occupational Aptitude Survey and Interest Schedule–2

Age level—Grades 8–12.

Technical adequacy—Validity coefficients of the Aptitude Survey range from .60s to .80s. Reliability coefficients were mostly in the .80s. Reliability coefficients for the Interest Schedule ranged from middle .80s to middle .90s. The validity was determined using factor analysis to support the interest factors.

Areas measured—Aptitude Survey (General Ability, Verbal, Numerical, Spatial, Perceptual, Manual Dexterity); Interest Schedule (Artistic, Scientific, Protective, Mechanical, Industrial, Nature, Business Detail, Selling, Accommodating, Humanitarian, Leading-Influencing, Physical Performing).

Types of scores—Standard scores, percentiles.

Suggested use—The OASIS-2 (Parker, 1991) measures both aptitude and interest. The six aptitude scales are related to over 20,000 jobs listed in the *Dictionary of Occupational Titles* and the interest factors are related to jobs listed in the *Guide of Occupational Exploration*. Profile forms are available to provide a visual summary of the student's aptitude and interests. The instrument is easy to administer; the student booklets have been reformatted in the revised edition to improve their readability. Machine scoring options are available.

Reading-Free Vocational Interest Inventory–Revised

Age level—Ages 13–adult (1987 update includes additional norms for children and adults).

Technical adequacy—Normed on both mentally retarded and learning-disabled individuals; good test-retest reliability (adequate for mentally retarded); adequate validity.

Areas measured—Automotive, Building Trade, Clerical, Animal Care, Food Service, Patient Care, Horticulture, Housekeeping, Personal Services, Laundry Service, Materials Handling.

Types of scores—T-scores, percentile ranks, profile chart is available.

Suggested use—An individual completing the Reading-Free Vocational Interest Inventory–Revised (Becker, 1987) is not required to read or give a verbal response. Rather, pictorial illustrations of individuals engaged in a variety of activities such as pumping gas or folding laundry are presented in a forced-choice format. This instrument was designed for and normed on a special education population. It is easy to administer and can be adapted for group use. The use of the profile chart provides a visual representation of the individual's interests in the 11 measured areas. Although the test was partially normed on a mentally retarded population, there has been some evidence suggesting that it was not particularly helpful for students with moderate to severe retardation (Wilgosh & Barry, 1983).

Strong-Campbell Interest Inventory

Age level—Ages 16 and above.

Technical adequacy—Test-retest coefficients were moderate to strong; validity data supportive of its use.

Areas measured—Occupational Themes; Basic Interests; Occupational Scales; Special Scales (academic comfort, introversion, extroversion); Administrative Indexes.

Types of scores—A variety of scores including T-scores are generated (through computer scoring only) for a variety of scales such as Basic Interest and Occupation.

Suggested use—The Strong-Campbell (Strong, Campbell, & Hansen, 1984) is intended to measure an individual's interest (not aptitude or intelligence) in various occupations. The theoretical foundation for developing the test is based on the assumption that individuals with the same occupations will have similar interests and personality characteristics. The instrument is easy to administer and can be given individually, in groups, or by mail. It takes an average of 25–35 minutes to complete. A computerized version is also available.

The Strong-Campbell is considered by many to be one of the best interest inventories available and is also one of the most widely used instruments for adult assessment (Harrison, Kaufman, Hickman, & Kaufman, 1988). There have been some weaknesses described, however. Tzeng (1985) for example, noted that there were some inconsistencies between the Basic Interest and

Occupational Scales and that more data supporting its construct validity are needed. Also, care should be taken when different editions of the Strong-Campbell are used because they yield considerably different profiles (Creaser & Jacobs, 1987).

Vocational Preference Inventory–Revised (VPI-R)

Age level—Ages 14–adult.

Technical adequacy—Limited; available data support validity and reliability of earlier versions; more current research is needed to establish its technical characteristics.

Areas measured—Personality and Vocational Interests, Realistic, Investigative, Artistic, Social, Enterprising, Conventional, Self-Control, Masculinity-Femininity, Status, Infrequency, Acquiescence.

Types of scores—Standard scores (T-scores).

Suggested use—The VPI-R (Holland, 1985) was designed to measure an individual's personality and vocational interests. It is based on Holland's six work typologies (first six scales listed above). The instrument is easy to administer and score. Shepard (1989) noted that it was one of the more time- and cost-efficient inventories, although it lacked current technical data. In general, support for its claim as a vocational interest inventory is greater than its claim as a personality measure.

Wide Range Interest-Opinion Test (WRIOT)

Age level—Kindergarten–adult.

Technical adequacy—Large normative sample (approximately 9,000); limited reliability and validity data available.

Areas measured—Four-hundred-fifty pictures are used to determine examinee's preferences in 18 interest and 8 attitude areas.

Types of scores—T-scores, profile analysis.

Suggested use—The WRIOT (Jastak & Jastak, 1979) is a reading-free instrument of occupational/leisure activities in which examinees must indicate among a series of three pictures that which they like least and like most. It covers a very wide range of activities primarily because of the very wide age range that it covers. The instrument can be individually or group administered. (A film strip is available.) Organist (1985) noted that although it is appealing for use with a variety of populations, including those with intellectual limitations or learning disabilities, its technical characteristics limit its value.

Instrument or Technique	Screening and Initial Identification	Informal Determination and Evaluation of Teaching Programs and Strategies	Determination of Current Performance Level and Educational Need	Decisions about Classification and Program Placement	ITP Goals	ITP Objectives	ITP Evaluation	Mild/Moderate	Severe/Profound	Preschool	Elementary Age	Secondary Age	Adult	Special Considerations	Educational Relevance for Exceptional Students
Checklists and Rating Scales		X						X			X	X		An informal technique that provides preliminary data but requires additional techniques for complete data	Adequate
Work Samples			X		X	X						X	X	Combination of commercial and locally developed instruments is suggested although cost is a concern	Useful
Curriculum-Based Vocational Assessment		X	X		X	X	X	X				X		Validity of vocational curriculum must be considered	Very useful
Direct Observation Ecological Assessment		X	X		X	X	X	X	X		X	X	X	Probably most adaptable and widely applicable technique	Very useful
Differential Aptitude Tests						X		X				X	X	Widely used instrument; time-consuming; computerized version available	Adequate
Gordon Occupational Checklists–II						X		X				X	X	Not normed in the traditional sense; easy to administer	Limited
Kuder Occupational Interest Survey						X		X				X	X	Limited technical characteristics	Limited
Occupational Aptitude Survey and Interest Schedule–2						X		X				X		Measures aptitude and interests	Adequate
Reading-Free Vocational Interest Inventory						X		X				X	X	Normed on mentally retarded and learning disabled students	Adequate

Instrument or Technique	Suggested Use							Target Population						Special Considerations	Educational Relevance for Exceptional Students
	Prereferral		Determination of Current Performance Level and Educational Need	Decisions about Classification and Program Placement	Postreferral			Mild/Moderate	Severe/Profound	Preschool	Elementary Age	Secondary Age	Adult		
	Screening and Initial Identification	Informal Determination and Evaluation of Teaching Programs and Strategies			ITP Goals	ITP Objectives	ITP Evaluation								
Strong-Campbell Interest Inventory						X		X				X	X	A very popular instrument that is widely researched	Adequate
Vocational Preference Inventory												X	X	Based on Holland's six work typologies	Limited
Wide Range Interest-Opinion Test						X		X			X	X	X	Includes occupational and leisure activities; limited technical data	Limited

PART SIX

Examples

In Chapter 2, a pragmatic approach to the assessment process was discussed and an assessment model provided. Throughout this book, a variety of assessment procedures have been described that can be used to implement that model. This has included both informal and formal procedures that are used for a variety of purposes. Also included has been a description of a number of assessment instruments that are used to evaluate a variety of areas.

In this section (Chapter 18), two examples of the assessment process (from initial identification through the development and evaluation of the IEP) are presented. Both examples use a case study approach; one follows a student with mild disabilities and includes prereferral assessment data and test scores and their interpretation for documentation of educational need. The use of those test scores for labeling and classification is also discussed (noting the caveats mentioned in Chapter 4). Finally, the use of assessment data for the development of the IEP is presented. The other case study involves a student with severe disabilities, so that the similarities and differences of the assessment process with that of the mildly disabled student can be compared.

After reading Part Six you should be able to:

1. *Identify the appropriate use of prereferral assessment data for a student with a mild disability*
2. *Identify the appropriate use of an assessment profile to determine areas for which educational goals and objectives should be developed*
3. *Identify the appropriate use of assessment data to develop goals and objectives*
4. *Compare and contrast the assessment procedures used with students with mild disabilities to those with severe disabilities*

18

Examples: Putting It All Together

FRANK: A STUDENT WITH MILD DISABILITIES
- Step One: Initial Identification
- Step Two: Informal Assessment
- Step Three: Referral
- Step Four: Obtain Parent Permission
- Step Five: Formal Assessment
  Interpreting Results
  Making Decisions
  Writing the IEP

JAMES: A STUDENT WITH SEVERE DISABILITIES
- Step One: Initial Identification
- Step Two: Referral
- Step Three: Obtain Parent Permission
- Step Four: Formal Assessment
  Making Decisions
  Writing the IEP

This chapter includes two case studies that follow a student with mild disabilities and a student with severe disabilities from the beginning of the assessment process (initial identification) through the development of the IEP. The procedures and instruments are typical of those used in many states (although some variation, of course, will exist). These examples are meant to show the uses, as well as the limitations, of various types of assessment instruments and data.

CASE STUDY: FRANK

Frank, a 10-year-old fourth-grader, could not concentrate on many things for more than 2 or 3 minutes at a time. Every 10 minutes or so he would turn around and talk to and bother the student behind him. His teacher had to stand over him and tap his desk every time he began to be disruptive. Writing was painstakingly difficult for Frank. It took him 5 minutes to write a five-word sentence. Most of the time he began sentences in the middle of the page. The letters were usually written very small, and some were written backwards. His script e looked like an l, and he did not dot his i's or cross his t's. When doing tasks of this type, he often got frustrated and tore his paper up. His teacher noted that Frank was a "different boy" when he was working on his science lessons. He would sit quietly, read his assignment, and wait for his turn to present the information to the rest of the class. His teacher wanted an evaluation to determine why Frank performed so well in some areas and so poorly in others. She felt that Frank had the ability to do well in all subjects and wanted information that might help her to motivate him or accommodate his learning style. In addition, she felt that his use of a resource room might help him in his weak areas.

Step One: Initial Identification

Routine curriculum-based assessment indicated that Frank was having considerable difficulty in the language-arts area. He was significantly behind the rest of the class regarding the appropriate placement within the school's language-arts curriculum. Through the use of the CBA results, observation, and evaluation of Frank's work products, his teacher decided that further assessment was needed. One thing she noted was that Frank appeared to be off-task quite often, and he frequently failed to complete assignments.

Step Two: Informal Assessment to Develop and Evaluate Teaching Programs and Strategies

Frank's teacher decided to use informal techniques to collect information prior to a formal referral. Specifically, she used observational data to document his off-task behavior and to evaluate various intervention strategies. She decided to use momentary time sampling, twice a day (during language arts and during science) for a 10-minute period. She took the following steps: (1) Define off-task behavior (no eye contact during verbal tasks, not working at written task); (2) determine schedule for time samples (every 15 seconds); (3) develop charts; (4) collect baseline data; (5) implement intervention programs; (6) observe behavior to evaluate program.

After 3 days, a specific pattern emerged for Frank; the baseline data are shown in Figure 18-1. This information indicated that Frank was off-a – 40 sessions (every 15 seconds for 10 minutes)

x – off-task behavior

FIGURE 18-1   Baseline Data for Frank's Off-Task Behavior.

task approximately 30 percent of the time during the language arts sessions and only about 7 percent of the time during the science sessions. Further, it appeared that he was off-task primarily near the end of the sessions.

On the basis of these observations, Frank's teacher decided to initiate an intervention program during the language-arts period. This consisted of changing the task (from spelling exercises to dictionary work). Figure 18-2 shows the results of that intervention. This had some effect, but he was still off-task approximately 15 percent of the time. His teacher then initiated a reinforcement system, whereby Frank received extra privileges for increasing his on-task behavior each day. While this decreased his off-task behavior, Frank's teacher noted that he still was not completing the tasks. Further, his written assignments in other subjects were not being completed. She decided, therefore, to refer Frank for further evaluation.

Step Three: Referral

Frank's teacher completed the required referral form and attached the observational data that she had collected, as well as results from the CBA and examples of his work in language arts.

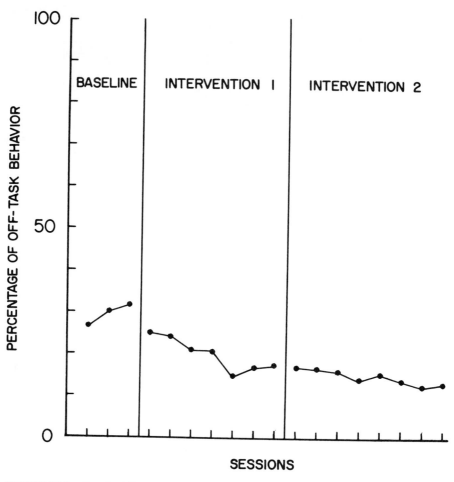

FIGURE 18-2   Graph of Prereferral Data for Frank.

Step Four: Obtaining Parental Permission

Step Five: Formal Assessment Procedures—The IEP Process

Formal evaluation was initiated to document Frank's educational need and to provide information for classification and placement decisions. The following tests were administered initially: Wechsler Intelligence Scale for Children–III, Kaufman Test of Educational Achievement, Vineland Adaptive Behavior Scales, Test of Visual Motor Integration–3, Test of Written Spelling–2, and the Test of Written Language–2. The following data were collected.

Wechsler Intelligence Scale for Children–Third Edition (WISC-III)
(Discussed in Chapter 8)

Full Scale IQ—105
Verbal IQ—111
Performance IQ—96

SUBTEST	SCALED SCORES	SUBTEST	SCALED SCORES
Information	9	Picture Completion	12
Comprehension	13	Picture Arrangement	8
Similarities	13	Block Design	11
Vocabulary	9	Object Assembly	10
Arithmetic	13	Coding	6
Digit Span	7	Mazes	7

Kaufman Test of Educational Achievement (K-TEA)
(Discussed in Chapter 12)

SUBTEST/AREA	STANDARD SCORE
Mathematics Concepts	101
Reading Decoding	97
Spelling	73
Reading Comprehension	96
Mathematics Application	90
Reading Composite	96
Mathematics Composite	95
Battery Composite	90

Vineland Adaptive Behavior Scales (Survey Form)
(Discussed in Chapter 9)

DOMAIN	STANDARD SCORE
Communication	104
Daily Living Skills	110
Socialization	91
Motor Skills	99
Composite	102

Test of Visual Motor Integration–Third Edition (VMI-3)
(Discussed in Appendix A)

Percentile rank—18th

Test of Written Language–2 (TOWL-2)
(Discussed in Chapter 11)

SUBTESTS/COMPOSITE SCALED SCORES

Vocabulary	7
Spelling	6
Style	9
Logical Sentences	9
Sentence Combining	9
Thematic Maturity	8
Contextual Vocabulary	8
Syntactic Maturity	7
Contextual Spelling	5
Contextual Style	7
Overall Written Language	77

Test of Written Spelling–2 (TWS-2)
(Discussed in Chapter 14)

SECTION	SPELLING QUOTIENT	SPELLING AGE	GRADE EQUIVALENT
Predictable	72	7–5	2.1
Unpredictable	79	8–1	2.7
Total	74	7–8	2.3

Interpretation of results

The WISC-III and the K-TEA were administered by the school psychologist. She stated, "On the basis of the WISC-III data, the following comments are warranted. Frank is performing within the average range of intelligence. On the tests, he generally had more difficulty with visual-motor and visual-perceptual tasks than with verbal tasks. Specifically, Frank demonstrated relative strengths in areas requiring abstract thinking and social judgment. His relative weaknesses are in areas requiring sequencing and fine-motor ability. There is also some evidence of a memory problem. His K-TEA scores indicate that he is slightly above average in math concepts and slightly below average in reading recognition and comprehension and in arithmetic computation, but almost 2 standard deviations below in spelling. These results indicate a discrepancy between his overall intellectual performance and his academic achievement, most notably in spelling."

The Vineland was administered by the school counselor to Frank's mother. The counselor reported, "Frank's overall adaptive behavior is consistent with the average student of his age in regular education. Frank shows strengths in the areas of daily living skills. His lowest scores are in areas of socialization."

The learning-disabilities specialist administered the VMI-3, TOWL-2, and TWS-2. She noted that Frank "scored at a level that is approximately 2 years below his chronological age on visual-perceptual tasks involving a motor component. The results from the TOWL-2 indicate that the overall quality and quantity of his written-language production was below average. He scored particularly low in the area of spelling. The TWS-2 confirms his deficit in this area. He was well below average in all areas of spelling."

Use of evaluation data in making decisions.   A case-study conference was held that included the school psychologist, the counselor, the learning-disabilities specialist, Frank's parents, and the regular classroom teacher. On the basis of the test data and information from Frank's teacher, it was concluded that evidence was sufficient to warrant special-education placement for Frank. The following profile was noted:

INTELLIGENCE—Average performance

ACHIEVEMENT—Variable performance; low in some areas

ADAPTIVE BEHAVIOR—Average performance

CLASSROOM BEHAVIOR—Variable performance

OTHER DATA (perceptual motor)—Low performance

On the basis of this available information, it was decided that Frank qualified to be in a resource room part of the day as a learning-disabled student (see Chapter 4 for a critical discussion of the issues and problems in making classification decisions). The next step in developing an IEP for Frank was to determine goals and objectives, timelines, types of services, and IEP-evaluation procedures (see Chapter 2 for a discussion of IEPs). First, however, it was necessary to give Frank a criterion-referenced test to gather more specific educational information. Portions of the Brigance Inventory of Basic Skills were therefore administered to him.

Brigance Inventory of Basic Skills
(Discussed in Chapter 12)

AREA MEASURED	RESULTS
Writing cursive letters—lower case	Wrote every letter except *i, t,* and *e* correctly.
Writing cursive letters—upper case	Wrote eight letters correctly (A, B, C, D, E, I, O, and P), but missed all the others.
Spelling dictation— grade-placement test	Second grade. His spelling for the sentence for second grade was "we found a blue coat and red dress." His spelling for

	the sentence for third grade was "the klown cood not cach th horse."
Spelling—initial consonants	Correctly wrote the beginning consonant for 19 of 21 words presented. He wrote *k* for *car* and *c* for *quit*.
Spelling—initial clusters	Missed 3 of 26 two-letter initial blends. He wrote su for *swell*, sc for *sky*, and *kr* for *crack*. He missed 7 out of 7 three-letter initial blends. Examples include *trl* for *thrill* and *stg* for *string*.
Spelling—suffixes	Missed 25 out of 36 different suffix additions. Basically, he correctly answered only those suffixes that could be added without applying rules.
Alphabetical order	He was able to alphabetize the letters and words with 100 percent accuracy. He did, however, take a long time to complete the task.

Decisions about the IEP.   During the IEP conference, the following observations and decisions were made:

From teacher's input and observational data—Frank is a distractible student, particularly during certain activities. These activities seem to be related to language arts, particularly when some type of written response is required. It is possible to increase his on-task behavior using reinforcement procedures, but he still does not complete the tasks.

From formal evaluation data for eligibility—Frank's profile is most consistent with that of a learning disabled student. He has average overall intelligence but has some significant academic weaknesses, most notably in spelling and other aspects of written language. Further, his problems seem to be related to the production of written language (for example, handwriting) rather than to a visual-perceptual problem. *(Note: These data alone were insufficient in establishing relevant educational objectives necessary for an IEP.)*

From criterion-referenced testing—Frank was able to write all but two lower-case letters cursively. He had more difficulty with upper-case letters (he missed 18 of 26). In terms of spelling, two patterns emerged. First, he made phonetic substitutions (for example, *k* for *c* and vice-versa). Second, he had difficulty with spelling rules (for example, he wrote *hoping* for *hopping*). On a specific language-arts task of alphabetizing letters and words, Frank performed at 100 percent accuracy, although it took him a long time to complete the task. This could explain why, during the prereferral observation, he was able to decrease off-task behavior yet still not complete the task.

In Frank's IEP, therefore, the following goals and objectives were included:

ANNUAL GOALS

1. The student will increase his spelling grade level score from a grade level of approximately 2.5 to approximately 4.0.

2. When presented with pencil and paper and requested to write the lower-case and upper-case cursive letters, the student will correctly and legibly write all 26 letters (upper-case and lower-case) in cursive script.

EVALUATION SCHEDULE

Once a year/use a norm-referenced test

Once a year/use a criterion-referenced test

GENERAL OBJECTIVES

1. *Objective:* When the examiner pronounces words that begin with consonants, the student will demonstrate his ability to recognize initial consonant sounds auditorily by writing the correct initial consonant for 21 out of 21 different consonants.

Every 3 months/use a criterion-referenced test

2. *Objective:* When the examiner pronounces words with initial blends and digraphs (clusters), the student will demonstrate his ability to recognize the initial blend and digraph sounds auditorily by writing the letters that make up the cluster for 33 out of 33 different blends and digraphs.

Every 3 months/use a criterion-referenced test

3. *Objective:* When the examiner presents the student with a printed stimulus root word and requests the student to write the same root word plus a designated suffix, the student will correctly write the altered word. This task will be performed correctly for 27 out of 36 different suffix additions (75 percent accuracy).

Every 3 months/use a criterion-referenced test

IMMEDIATE SHORT TERM OBJECTIVES

(Note: This section includes examples of teaching objectives. Objectives of this type are changed and updated frequently, and they are typically found in lesson plans.)

When the examiner pronounces 15 words with the initial consonants *k, g,* and *c,* the student will demonstrate his ability to recognize initial consonant sounds by writing the correct initial consonant with 100 percent accuracy.

Weekly/use a criterion-referenced test

When the examiner pronounces 15 words with initial blends *sw, sk,* and *cr,* the student will demonstrate his ability to recognize the initial blend by writing the correct two letters with 100 percent accuracy.

Weekly/use a criterion-referenced test

When the examiner pronounces 10 words with initial three-letter blends (for example, *thr, str*), the student will demonstrate his ability to recognize each blend by writing the correct three letters with 50 percent accuracy.

Weekly/use a criterion-referenced test

When presented with three printed stimulus root words and requested to add a designated suffix (*ing* with doubled consonants; *ed* with doubled consonant; *ed* to words ending in silent *e)* to that root word, the student will correctly write the requested word with 100 percent accuracy.

Weekly/use a criterion-referenced test

When presented with pencil and paper, the student will correctly write all the lowercase letters in cursive script.

Weekly/use a criterion-referenced test

When presented with pencil and paper, the student will correctly write the uppercase letters A, B, C, D, E, F, G, H, I, J, K, L, M in cursive script.

Weekly/use a criterion-referenced test

In addition to adopting these goals and objectives, the decision was made to place Frank in the resource room for one hour a day. During this time, he would receive structured one-to-one tutoring in handwriting (using stencils that would be faded gradually) and in spelling rules. Initially, he would be requested to complete the tasks with no time limit. After he met the criteria for mastering the skill, however, he would be required to gradually decrease the time he needed to complete the task. After 1 year, his progress toward the goals would be evaluated, and decisions about further steps would be made on the basis of the evaluation.

CASE STUDY: JAMES

James is a 6-year-old boy who has a medical diagnosis of "severe brain damage from anoxia at birth." James is nonambulatory and blind, and he has an extremely limited range of motion. He is also on heavy medication for control of seizures. James has been enrolled in a preschool program for handicapped children for the past 4 years. He is no longer eligible for this program because of his age.

Step One: Initial Identification

James was identified as having severe disabilities shortly after birth. Extensive documentation from physicians, physical therapists, and other medical personnel accompanied him when he was accepted into his preschool handicapped program. That information, as well as assessment data gathered during his 4 years in preschool, indicated the need for James to continue in some type of special program.

Step Two: Referral

James was referred for evaluation so that the appropriate placement and educational program could be determined and carried out.

Step Three: Obtaining Parental Permission

Step Four: Formal Assessment Procedures— The IEP Process

A formal evaluation was conducted to determine James's ability level in a number of cognitive, social, self-help, motor, and communication areas. The following instruments were administered.

Perkins-Binet Scale of Intelligence
(Discussed in Appendix B)
The psychologist reported that James was "untestable." He would not respond to the test items.

Vineland Adaptive Behavior Scales (Survey Form)
(Discussed in Chapter 9)

DOMAIN	PERCENTILE
Communication	2
Daily-Living Skills	3
Socialization	4
Motor Skills	1
Maladaptive Behavior	2
Total Adaptive Behavior	2

TARC Assessment System
(Discussed in Chapter 9)

AREA	STANDARD SCORE (MEAN, 50; SD, 20)
Self-Help	12
Motor	10
Communication	32
Social	24
Total	15

Callier-Azusa
(Discussed in Chapter 15)

On the basis of the data from the preceding tests, the IEP team determined that a full-day program in a class for severely and profoundly handicapped students would be appropriate. Additional information was needed, however, to determine the goals and objectives for James. The psychologist decided to administer the Callier-Azusa. James was able to do the following:

MOTOR DEVELOPMENT

1. Postural Control—Holds head up for indefinite periods; turns head from side to side
2. Locomotion—Rolls from stomach to back and from side to back
3. Fine-Motor—Has a reflex grasp of small objects
4. Visual-Motor—Does not respond to any visual stimulus

PERCEPTUAL DEVELOPMENT

1. Visual Development—Does not respond to any visual stimulus
2. Auditory Development—Turns head and eyes in the direction of an auditory stimulus
3. Tactile Development—Reacts to tactile stimulation but does not localize the source

DAILY-LIVING SKILLS

1. Undressing and Dressing—Resists being undressed or dressed
2. Personal Hygiene—Plays with toys, soap, and washcloth while being bathed
3. Feeding Skills—Allows being fed from spoon
4. Toileting—Reacts negatively to wet pants

COGNITION, COMMUNICATION, AND LANGUAGE

1. Cognitive Development—Recognizes and reacts to familiar objects (tactilely)
2. Receptive Communication—Understands simple signals that are tactilely presented

3. Expressive Communication—Nonverbally signals to indicate needs (for example, holds out arms to be picked up)

SOCIAL DEVELOPMENT

1. Interaction with Adults—Differentiates familiar and unfamiliar adults (auditorily)
2. Interaction with Peers—Responds to peers' presence
3. Interaction with Environment—Differentiates familiar and unfamiliar environments

Setting goals, objectives, and time tables.   At this point, James's current performance level has been documented, and the IEP goals and objectives, timelines, types of services, and evaluation schedule could be determined. It was decided that James would benefit from physical therapy and speech-and-communication therapy as part of his overall educational program. The following goals were adopted:

ANNUAL GOALS	EVALUATION SCHEDULE
1. The student will sit when supported. His head will be in midline and erect with upper trunk rounded and shoulders forward.	Once a year/observation by physical therapist or teacher
2. The student will crawl forward or backward on his stomach by pulling with his forearm and pushing with his foot from the opposite side.	Once a year/observation by physical therapist or teacher
3. The student will eat from spoon (independently with considerable spilling) after food has been placed on it.	Once a year/observation by teacher
4. The student will respond appropriately to simple one-word commands.	Once a year/observation by teacher
5. The student will use simple gestures, signs, or vocalizations to indicate his needs (situation-specific and probably will not generalize).	Once a year/observation by speech therapist or teacher

Brigance Inventory of Early Development–Revised
(Discussed in Chapter 15)
Once the goals had been adopted, portions of the Brigance Inventory of Early Development–Revised were administered to obtain more information. On the basis of results of this and the previously mentioned tests,

the following objectives were determined in relation to James's annual goals:

OBJECTIVES	EVALUATION SCHEDULE
1a. When placed in a sitting position, the student remains momentarily but head sags forward.	Once a week/observation by the physical therapist or teacher
1b. When placed in a sitting position, the student remains momentarily; head bobs forward, but student demonstrates some evidence of support or control.	Every 3 months/observation by the physical therapist or teacher
1c. Same as above; head steady but not erect.	Same as above
1d. Same as above; head erect and steady.	Same as above
2a. When placed in a prone position, the student will raise chest with arm support.	Weekly/observation by the physical therapist or teacher
2b. When placed in a prone position, the student will support most body weight with hands rather than arms.	Every 3 months/observation by the physical therapist or teacher
2c. When placed in a prone position, the student will turn on his stomach to face in a different direction.	Same as above
3a. The student will feed himself a cracker or cookie.	Weekly/observation by the teacher
3b. The student will feed himself small pieces of food such as raisins.	Every 3 months/observation by the teacher
3c. The student will hold a spoon independently.	Same as above
3d. The student will put spoon to mouth (with physical guidance)	Same as above
4a. The student will respond to a few simple commands that are tactilely presented.	Weekly/observation by the teacher
4b. The student will imitate a gesture with objects present (for example, rolling a ball if the teacher makes a pushing motion).	Every 3 months/observation by the teacher
4c. The student will understand a gesture without objects present	Same as above

(for example, will find a ball to roll if teachers makes a pushing motion).

5a. The student will imitate a gesture *while* the teacher is gesturing.	Weekly/observation by the teacher
5b. The student will imitate a gesture after the teacher stops (prompting necessary).	Every 3 months/observation by the teacher
5c. The student will initiate a gesture without a prompt.	Same as above

Appendix A*

Process Instruments (Instruments Used for Measuring Processing Skills)

VISUAL-MOTOR/VISUAL-PERCEPTUAL TESTS

Bender Visual-Motor Gestalt Test (BVMGT)
(Bender, 1938)

Age level—Ages 5 to 11 years old (Koppitz system)

Type of administration—Individual (group is possible)

Technical adequacy—Limited reliability, questionable validity

Scores yielded—Standard scores, percentiles, age equivalents

Description—The BVMGT requires the child to reproduce (copy) a series of nine geometric figures. Each figure is presented on a separate 3" by 5" index card. The Koppitz scoring system is used to determine the number of developmental errors. The BVMGT has the dubious distinction of being one of the oldest tests used by special educators. This means that the test is well researched and has both strong supporters and harsh critics. The test has been used as a measure of nonverbal intelligence, brain damage, emotional status, and academic readiness as well as visual-motor ability. In general, the BVMGT might be considered a *screening device* for identifying groups of children with various problems (particularly those that have been previously identified). Its use as a clinical screening instrument should be limited to experienced trained examiners. It should not be used as a diagnostic device for any of these purposes by anyone. Special educators should note that, in general, scores on the test do not correlate significantly with reading achievement, particularly with children over 8 years old. We have almost forgotten that the BVMGT is a test of visual-motor ability. It is probably best to remember this and use it as such.

*NOTE: These tests encompass a wide variety of areas but have also been used as a measure of "processing." The suggested use section addresses each test's strengths and limitations. In general, their use as a process measure is discouraged.

484

Developmental Test of Visual-Motor Integration–
Third Revision (VMI-3)
(Beery, 1989)

Age level—Ages 2 to 15 years

Type of administration—Individual (group possible)

Technical adequacy—Adequate standardization, adequate validity and reliability

Scores yielded—Standard scores, percentiles

Description—The VMI-3 also requires the individual to copy geometric figures. The VMI-3 is an extremely easy test to administer, although some degree of subjectivity is required to score the responses. There is a short form (ages 2–8) that requires the child to copy 15 geometric figures. The long form uses 24 figures. Its primary function should be as a screening test for visual-motor integration problems. Like other perceptual-motor instruments, the VMI-3 should not be used as an instrument for identifying learning-disabled or low-achieving students. The results from the VMI-3 should not be used as a basis for a remedial program to improve academic skills.

Developmental Test of Visual Perception (DTVP)
(Frostig, Lefever, & Whittlesey, 1966)

Age level—Ages 4 to 8 years old

Type of administration—Individual or group

Technical adequacy—Very limited reliability and validity

Scores yielded—Perceptual-age, perceptual-quotient, scale scores

Description—The DTVP supposedly measures five areas: Eye-Motor Coordination, Figure-Ground, Form Constancy, Position in Space, and Spatial Relations. The DTVP was a very popular instrument when it first appeared on the market. Its popularity in later years significantly decreased. This decline was partially related to research suggesting that (1) it does not measure five areas of visual perception as it is supposed to; and (2) its relationship to academic skills (particularly reading) is practically nonexistent. The DTVP does have an associated training program, but this program does not improve academic skills. The DTVP seems to have little practical use. Its use as a measure to determine relative strengths and weaknesses and to predict achievement has been seriously questioned. There are more reliable tests of both visual-motor ability and visual-perceptual ability.

Motor Free Visual Perception Test (MVPT)
(Colarusso & Hammill, 1972)

Age level—Ages 4 to 8 years old

Type of administration—Individual

Technical adequacy—Adequate reliability, questionable validity

Scores yielded—Perceptual age, perceptual quotient

Description—The MVPT measures five areas: spatial relationships, visual discrimination, figure-ground skills, visual closure, and visual memory. The MVPT is the only visual-perceptual instrument without a motor component. It can, therefore, be used in conjunction with a visual motor test to obtain needed information. If, for instance, a child performed poorly on a test such as the VMI-3 but scored average or above on the MVPT, a fine-motor or coordination problem could be the reason. Information should be used in this way only very carefully, because the two tests have questionable validity and were standardized on different populations. Another concern is that although the MVPT measures five areas of visual perception, these areas are unevenly represented; for instance, 14 items measure discrimination skills, but only 5 items measure perception of spatial relations.

Purdue Perceptual Motor Survey (PPMS)
(Roach & Kephart, 1966)

Age level—Grades 1 to 4

Type of administration—Individual

Technical adequacy—Very limited data to support reliability and validity

Scores yielded—Raw scores for comparative purposes

Suggested use—There are 11 subtests on the PPMS that measure the three major areas of directionality, laterality, and perceptual-motor matching. The PPMS should really be used only for informal purposes. The scoring system is highly subjective, and the standardization sample was notably restricted. The value of the test largely depends on the user's attitudes toward and knowledge about Kephart's theory of perceptual-motor match. Like the DTVP, the PPMS has a training program that is aimed at improving scores on the test. If this is the examiner's purpose (for example, improve balance and posture or ocular tracking ability), the test has some use. It should not he used, however, to identify children with academic problems or to develop remedial programs for academically deficient students.

AUDITORY-PERCEPTUAL/LANGUAGE TESTS

Auditory Discrimination Test (ADT)
(Wepman, 1973)

Age level—Ages 5 to 8 years old

Type of administration—Individual

Technical adequacy—No information regarding the normative sample; limited data on reliability and validity

Scores yielded—Raw score, transformed into one of the five levels of auditory-discrimination ability

Description—This test requires the child to listen to pairs of words presented by the examiner and say if the words are the same or different. Because the ADT is extremely easy to administer and score, it is a fairly popular instrument. The ADT should be used for screening purposes only. Several limitations (such as effect of dialect; child's knowledge of same or different concept) make its use as a diagnostic device inadvisable. Its use with children who speak nonstandard English should be discouraged.

Goldman-Fristoe-Woodcock Auditory Discrimination Test (GFW)
(Goldman, Fristoe, & Woodcock, 1970)

Age level—Ages 3 1/2 to 80 years old

Type of administration—Individual

Technical adequacy—Limited standardization, questionable reliability and validity

Scores yielded—Percentile ranks, T-scores

Description—The GFW uses a multiple-choice format. For example, a plate with four pictures (depicting "sack," "pack," "tack," and "shack") is shown. A tape is played in which the subject is instructed "point to tack." There is both a quiet subtest and a noisy subtest, in which the word is presented with background noise. The technical adequacy of the GFW is questionable. The evidence for its validity and reliability is very limited. The idea of including a noise subtest is a good one, although the background noise supplied by the tape is so noisy that the subtest yields extremely variable scores (probably because the individual is guessing). Like the ADT, the GFW is affected by language and dialect differences of the examiners and students. The two tests should not be used interchangeably. If the GFW is used, it should be for screening purposes only.

Illinois Test of Psycholinguistic Abilities (ITPA)
(Kirk, McCarthy, & Kirk, 1968)

Age level—Ages 2 1/2 to 10 years old

Type of administration—Individual

Technical adequacy—Extremely limited

Scores yielded—Scaled scores, psycholinguistic ages, psycholinguistic quotients, and percentage scores

Description—The ITPA includes 12 subtests that measure three hypothetical components of communication. These are channels of communication (input-output modalities), psycholinguistic processes (reception, association, expression) and levels of organization (representational and automatic). The ITPA was once one of the more widely used (and abused) instruments in special education. It is based on a legitimate theoretical model, although the test does not validly measure the components of that model. The ITPA should not really be considered a measure of psycholinguistic constructs. Some research suggests that it closely resembles a measure of verbal intelligence.

Results from this test have been used in the past in a number of ways. Some have used the results to identify modality strengths and weaknesses for teaching purposes; this procedure in general has been questioned. Others have used the ITPA as a screening and diagnostic device for academic ability; this purpose is also inappropriate.

In defense of the authors, it should be noted that they, too, are critical of the way many examiners are using ITPA results. It was designed to help identify areas in need of remediation. While its use for this purpose must also be questioned, examiners should keep the authors' purpose in mind and not "overinterpret" the results. In summary, the technical inadequacy of the ITPA seriously limits its use as a norm-referenced test.

Appendix B

Cognitive Measures for Special Populations

VISUALLY IMPAIRED

Blind Learning Aptitude Test (BLAT)
(Newland, 1969)

> *Age range*—Ages 6 to 20 (6 to 12 is recommended)
>
> *Standardization*—Sample included 961 blind students
>
> *Technical adequacy*—Acceptable
>
> *Description*—The BLAT yields a learning-aptitude test age as well as a learning-aptitude test quotient. The test measures abilities such as discrimination, generalization, and sequencing using tactile stimulus items.

Haptic Intelligence Scale
(Shurrager & Shurrager, 1964)

> *Age range*—Adult
>
> *Standardization*—Approximately 700 blind adults
>
> *Technical adequacy*—Acceptable reliability, limited validity
>
> *Description*—Six subtests are included that require the subject to solve problems using tactile input. These subtests (Digit Symbol, Object Assembly, Block Design, Object Completion, Pattern Board, and Bead Arithmetic) are somewhat similar to those found on the Wechsler Scales.

Perkins-Binet Intelligence Scale
(Davis, 1980)

> *Age range*—Ages 2 to 22
>
> *Standardization*—Sample included 2,153 blind and partially sighted students from day and residential programs

Technical adequacy—Good

Description—This adaptation of the Stanford-Binet has two forms: N (for those with nonusable vision) and U (for those with usable vision). Approximately 25–30 percent of the items are performance-related. The test yields both mental age and intelligence quotients.

HEARING IMPAIRED

Arthur Adaptation of the Leiter International Performance Scale
(Arthur, 1950)

Age range—Ages 2 to 12

Standardization—The sample included 289 nonhandicapped children

Technical adequacy—Limited norms and validity, no reliability data

Description—The Arthur Adaptation of the Leiter is a nonverbal, untimed instrument that uses tactile stimulus items and requires motor responses. Tasks involving sequencing, analogies, and matching to sample are included. Mental ages and intelligence quotients can be determined.

Hiskey-Nebraska Test of Learning Aptitude (NTLA)
(Hiskey, 1966)

Age range—Ages 3 to 16

Standardization—The sample included 2,153 individuals (1,079 deaf and 1,074 hearing)

Technical adequacy—Limited reliability and validity

Description—The NTLA can be administered either through pantomime to deaf children or verbally to hearing children. Twelve subtests are included (for example, Memory for Color; Picture Identification; Spatial Reasoning). A learning age and a learning quotient can be determined.

NONVERBAL AND PHYSICALLY DISABLED

Columbia Mental Maturity Scale (CMMS)
(Burgemeister, Blum, & Lorge, 1972)

Age range—Ages 3 1/2 to 10

Standardization—The sample included 2,600 children (stratified sample)

Technical adequacy—Acceptable reliability, limited criterion-related validity

Description—The CMMS measures the child's ability to classify visually presented items. The test yields percentile ranks, standard scores, and a maturity index (similar to a mental age).

Pictorial Test of Intelligence (PTI)
(French, 1964)

Age range—Ages 3 to 8 (3 to 6 is recommended)

Standardization—Sample included 1,830 children (stratified sample)

Technical adequacy—Adequate reliability and validity

Description—The PTI has a multiple-choice format that requires only a pointing or looking response. Six areas are measured: Picture Vocabulary; Form Discrimination; Information and Comprehension; Similarities; Size and Number; and Immediate Recall.

Progressive Matrices
(Raven, 1956)

Age range—Ages 5 and older

Standardization—Sample included 567 Veterans' Administration Hospital patients

Technical adequacy—Limited norms, acceptable reliability and validity

Description—Three separate tests are included: the Standard Progressive Matrices; the Colored Progressive Matrices (for young children); and the advanced Progressive Matrices (for adults of average to above-average ability). The tests require a person to complete visual-analogy problems that vary in complexity. Percentiles can be derived from the raw scores.

Test of Nonverbal Intelligence–2
(Brown, Sherbenou, & Johnsen, 1990)

Age range—Ages 5 to adult

Standardization—Over 2,500 subjects from 30 states

Technical adequacy—Adequate reliability and validity

Description—There are two equivalent forms. The items essentially measure abstract problem-solving, and responses do not require writing or verbalization. The areas of shape, position, direction, rotation, contiguity, shading, size, movement, and pattern are used as the basis for the problem-solving task.

References

Achenbach, T. (1981). A junior MMPI? *Journal of Personality Assessment, 45,* 332.

Achenbach, T., & Edelbrock, C. (1991). *Manual for the Child Behavior Checklist and Revised Child Behavior Profile.* Burlington, VT: Queen City Printers.

Adams, G. (1986). *Normative Adaptive Behavior Checklist.* San Antonio, TX: The Psychological Corporation.

Alberto, P., & Troutman, A. (1990). *Applied Behavior Analysis for Teachers* (3rd ed.). Columbus, OH: Charles E. Merrill.

Alessi, G. (1980). Behavioral observation for the school psychologist: Responsive discrepancy model. *School Psychology Review, 9,* 31–45.

Alford, D., Moore, M., & Simon, J. (1980). A preliminary assessment of the validity and usefulness of the WRAT with visually handicapped residential school students. *Education of the Visually Handicapped, 11,* 102–108.

Algozzine, B., Eaves, R., Mann, L., & Vance, H. B. (1988). *Cognitive Levels Test.* Opelika, AL: Arete, Inc.

Algozzine, B., & Sutherland, J. (1977). The "learning disabilities" label: An experimental analysis. *Contemporary Educational Psychology, 2,* 292–297.

Algozzine, B., & McGraw, K. (1980). Diagnostic testing in mathematics: An extension of the PIAT? *Teaching Exceptional Children, 12,* 71–77.

Alpern, G., Boll, T., & Shearer, M. (1986). *The Developmental Profile–II.* Los Angeles: Western Psychological Services.

American Guidance Service (1990). *Developmental Indicators for the Assessment of Learning–Revised* (AGS Edition). Circle Pines, MN: American Guidance Service.

American Psychological Association. (1985). *Standards for educational and psychological testing.* Washington, D.C.: American Psychological Association.

Anastasi, A. (1988). *Psychological testing* (5th ed.). NY: Macmillan.

Anderegg, M. L., & Vergason, G. (1988). An analysis of one of the cornerstones of the Regular Education Initiative. *Focus on Exceptional Children, 20,* 1–7.

Armstrong, B., & Knopf, K. (1982). Comparison of the Bender-Gestalt and Revised Developmental Test of Visual-Motor Integration. *Perceptual and Motor Skills, 55,* 164–166.

Arnold, L., Barneby, N., & Smeltzer, D. (1981). First grade norms, factor analysis and cross correlation for Conners, Daniels, and Quay-Peterson Behavior Rating Scales. *Journal of Learning Disabilities, 14,* 269–275.

Arter, J., & Jenkins, J. (1977). Examining the benefits and prevalences of modality considerations in special education. *Journal of Special Education, 11,* 281–298.

Arthur, G. (1950). *The Arthur Adaptation of the Leiter International Performance Scale.* Chicago: C. H. Stoelting.

Atkinson, L. (1990a). Intellectual and adaptive functioning: Some tables for interpreting the Vineland in combination with intelligence tests. *American Journal on Mental Retardation, 95,* 198–203.

Atkinson, L. (1990b). Standard errors of prediction for the Vineland Adaptive Behavior Scales. *The Journal of School Psychology, 28,* 355–359.

Ashlock, R. (1990). *Error patterns in computation* (5th ed.). Columbus, OH: Charles E. Merrill.

Bachor, D. (1990). Review of Key-Math–Revised. *Diagnostique, 15,* 87–98.

Bacon, E. (1989). Review of Behavior Rating Profile. In J. Conoley & J. Kramer (Eds.). *Tenth Mental Measurements Yearbook.* (pp. 84–86). Lincoln, NE: University of Nebraska Press.

Bacon, E., & Carpenter, D. (1985). Basic School Skills Inventory–Diagnostic. In D. Keyser and R. Sweetland (Eds.), *Test Critiques* (v. 4) (pp. 68–75). Kansas City, MO: Test Corporation of America.

Bagnato, S. (1984). Team congruence in developmental diagnosis and intervention: Comparing clinical judgment and child performance measures. *School Psychology Review, 13,* 7–16.

Bagnato, S., & Neisworth, J. (1990) *System to Plan Early Childhood Services.* Circle Pines, MN: American Guidance Service.

Bailey, D. B., Vandivere, P., Dellinger, J., & Munn, D. (1987). The Battelle Developmental Inventory: Teacher perceptions. *Journal of Psychoeducational Assessment, 3,* 271–226.

Balla, D., & Zigler, E. (1979). Personality development in retarded persons. In N. Ellis (Ed.), *Handbook of mental deficiency, pychological theory and research* (2nd ed.). Hillsdale, NJ: Lawrence Erlbaum Associates.

Balthazar, E. (1976a). *Balthazar Scales of Adaptive Behavior.* Palo Alto, CA: Consulting Psychologists Press.

Bannatyne, A. (1974). Diagnosis: A note on recategorization of the WISC scaled scores. *Journal of Learning Disabilities, 7,* 272–274.

Barnett, D. (1989) Review of Developmental Indicators for the Assessment of Learning–Revised. In J. Conoley & J. Kramer (Eds.). *Tenth Mental Measurements Yearbook.* (pp. 244–246). Lincoln, NE: University of Nebraska Press.

Barnett, D. W., Faust, J., & Sarmir, M. A. (1988). A validity study of two preschool screening instruments: The LAP-D and DIAL-R. *Contemporary Educational Psychology, 13,* 26–32.

Baum, D. (1975). A comparison of the WRAT and the PIAT with learning disabled children. *Educational and Psychological Measurement, 35,* 487–493.

Bauman, E. (1991). Stability of WISC–R scores in children with learning difficulties. *Psychology in the Schools, 28,* 95–100.

Beatty, L., Madden, R., Gardner, E., & Karlsen, B. (1985). *Stanford Diagnostic Mathematics Test.* New York: Harcourt Brace Jovanovich.

Beck, S., Beck, A., Levitt, E., & Molish, H. (1961). *Rorschach's Test.* New York: Grune & Stratton.

Beck, B., & Spruill, J. (1987). External validation of the cognitive triad of the Personality Inventory for Children: Cautions on interpretation. *Journal of Consulting and Clinical Psychology, 55,* 441–443.

Becker, R. (1987). *Reading Free Vocational Interest Inventory.* Columbus, OH: Elbern Publications.

Beech, M. (1981). Concurrent validity of the Boehm Test of Basic Concepts. *Learning Disability Quarterly, 4,* 53–60.

Beery, K. (1989). *Developmental Test of Visual-Motor Integration–Third Edition.* Austin, TX: Pro-Ed.

Bellak, L., Bellak, S., & Haworth, M. (1974). *Children's Apperception Test.* Larchmont, NY: C.P.S., Inc.

Bender, L. (1938). A Visual Motor Gestalt Test and its clinical use. *American Orthopsychiatric Association Research Monograph,* No. 3.

Bennett, G., Seashore, H., & Wessman, A. (1990). *Differential Aptitude Tests* (5th ed.). San Antonio: Psychological Corporation.

Bensberg, G., & Irons, T. (1986). A comparison of the AAMD Adaptive Behavior Scale and the Vineland Adaptive Behavior Scales within a sample of persons classified as moderately and severely retarded. *Education and Training of the Mentally Retarded, 21,* 220–228.

Berk, R. (1981). What's wrong with using grade equivalent scores to identify LD children? *Academic Therapy, 17,* 133–140.

Berk, R. (1984). *A guide to criterion-referenced test construction.* Baltimore: Johns Hopkins Press.

Bernhardt, B. (1990). A review of the Test of Problem Solving (TOPS). *Language, Speech, and Hearing Services in Schools, 21*(2), 98–101.

Betts, E. (1946). *Foundations of reading instruction.* New York: American Book Co.

Blankenship, C. (1985). Using curriculum–based assessment data to make instructional decisions. *Exceptional Children, 52,* 233–238.

Bloom A. S., Allard, A. M., Zelko, F., Brill, W., Topinka, C. W., & Pfohl, W. (1988). Differential validity of the K–ABC for lower functioning preschool children versus those of higher ability. *American Journal on Mental Retardation, 93,* 273–277.

Bloom, L., & Lahey, M. (1978). *Language development and language disorders.* New York: John Wiley & Sons.

Boehm, A. (1986). *Boehm Test of Basic Concepts–Revised.* San Antonio: Psychological Corporation.

Boehm, A., & Weinber strengths and *weaknesses. Journal of* Learning Disabilities, 22, 151–165.

Cancelli, A. (1985). Review of the Revised Behavior P*roblem Checklist. In J. Mitchell (Ed.), Ninth Mental Measurements Yearbook (pp. 1274–1276). Lincoln, NE: University of Nebraska Press,*

Capron, E. (1985). Review of the Adaptive Behavior Inventory for Children. In D. Keyser and R. Sweetland (Eds.) Test Critiques (v.3). (pp 13–29). Kansas *City, eventh Mental Measurements Yearbook.* (pp. 329–333). Highland Park, NJ: Gryphon Press.

Bower, E. (1969). Early Identification of Emotionally Handicapped Children in School (2nd ed.). Springfield, IL: Charles Thomas.

Boyd, R. (1989). What a difference a day makes: Age-related discontinuities and the Battelle Developmental Inventory. *Journal of Early Intervention, 13,* 114–119.

Boyd, R., Welge, R., Sexton, D., & Miller, L. (1989). Concurrent validity of the Battelle Developmental Inventory: Relationship with the Bayley Scales in young children with known or suspected disabilities. *Journal of Early Intervention, 13,* 14–23.

Bracken, B. (1984). *The Bracken Basic Concept Scale.* San Antonio: The Psychological Corporation.

Bracken, B., & Cato, L. (1986). Rate of conceptual development among deaf preschool and primary children as compared to a matched group of nonhearing impaired children. *Psychology in the Schools, 23,* 95–99.

Bracken, B., & Fouad, N. (1987). Spanish translation and validation of the Bracken Basic Concept Scale. *School Psychology Review, 16,* 94–102.

Bracken, B. A., & Howell, K. K. (1989). K–ABC subtest specificity recalculated. *Journal of School Psychology, 27,* 335–345.

Bracken, B., & Prasse, D. (1981). Comparison of the PPVT, PPVT–R and intelligence tests used for the placement of black, white and Hispanic EMR students. *Journal of School Psychology, 19,* 304–311.

Bracken, B., & Prasse, D. (1983). Concurrent validity of the PPVT–R for "at risk" preschool children. *Psychology in the Schools, 20,* 25–26.

Bracken, B., Sabers, R., & Insko, R. (1987). Performance of black and white children on the Bracken Basic Concept Scale. *Psychology in the Schools, 24,* 22–27.

Bradley-Johnson, S., Graham, D., & Johnson, C. (1986). Token reinforcement on WISC–R performance for white low socioeconomic upper and lower elementary school aged students. *Journal of School Psychology, 24,* 73–79.

Breen, M. (1983). A correlational analysis between the PPVT–R and Woodcock–Johnson achievement cluster scores for nonreferred regular education and learning disabled students. *Psychology in the Schools, 20,* 295–298.

Breen, M., & Prasse, D. (1982). A comparison of the 1976 and 1978 Wide Range Achievement Test: Implication for the learning disabled. *Journal of Learning Disabilities, 15,* 15–16.

Breuning, S., & Zella, W. (1978). Effects of individualized incentives on norm-referenced IQ test performance of high school students in special education classes. *Journal of School Psychology, 16,* 220–226.

Brigance, A. (1977). *Brigance Inventory of Basic Skills.* North Billerica, MA: Curriculum Associates.

Brigance, A. (1981). *Brigance Diagnostic Inventory of Essential Skills.* North Billerica, MA: Curriculum Associates.

Brigance, A. (1982). *Brigance Comprehensive Inventory of Basic Skills.* North Billerica, MA: Curriculum Associates.

Brigance, A. (1991). *Inventory of Early Development-Revised.* North Billerica, MA: Curriculum Associates.

Brolin, D. (1978). Vocational assessment: What can be gained from it? In R. L. Sitlington and D. Wimmer. Vocational Assessment Techniques for the Handicapped Adolescent. *Career Development for Exceptional Individuals, 1,* 78–87.

Brolin, D. (1983). *Life-centered Career Education: A Competency-Based Approach.* Reston, VA: Council for Exceptional Children.

Bromwich, R. M., Fust, S., Khokha, E., & Walden, M. H. (1981). *Play Assessment Checklist for Infants.* Unpublished document. Northridge, CA: State University, Northridge.

Brown, L., & Alexander, J. (1991). *Self-Esteem Index.* Austin, TX: Pro-Ed.

Brown, L., Branston, M. B., Hamre-Nietupski, S., Pumpian, I., Certo, N., & Gruenwald, L. (1979). A strategy for developing chronological age appropriate and functional curricular content for severely handicapped adolescents and young adults. *Journal of Special Education, 13,* 81–90.

Brown, L., Falvey, M., Vincent, L., Kaye, N., Johnson, F., Ferrara-Parrish, P., & Gruenwald, L. (1980). Strategies for generating comprehensive, longitudinal, and chronological-age-appropriate individualized education programs for adolescent and young-adult severely handicapped students. *Journal of Special Education, 14,* 199–215.

Brown, L., & Hammill, D. (1990). *Behavior Rating Profile–2.* Austin, TX: Pro-Ed.

Brown, L., & Leigh, J. (1986). *Adaptive Behavior Inventory.* Austin, TX: Pro-Ed.

Brown, L., & Sherbenou, R. (1981). A comparison of teacher perceptions of student reading ability, reading performance and classroom behavior. *The Reading Teacher, 34,* 557–560.

Brown, L., Sherbenou, R., & Johnsen, S. (1990). *Test of Nonverbal Intelligence–2.* Austin, TX: Pro-Ed.

Brown, V., Hammill, D., & Wiederholt, J. L. (1978). *Test of Reading Comprehension.* Austin, TX: Pro-Ed.

Brown, V., & McEntire, E. (1984). *Test of Mathematical Abilities.* Austin, TX: Pro-Ed.

Bruininks, R., McGrew, R., & Marvyama, G. (1988). Structure of adaptive behavior in samples with and without mental retardation. *American Journal on Mental Retardation, 92,* 381–384.

Bruininks, R., Woodcock, R., Weatherman, R., & Hill, B. (1984). *The Scales of Independent Behavior.* Allen, TX: DLM Teaching Resources.

Bryan, J., & Bryan, T. (1988). Where's the beef? A review of published research on the Adaptive Learning Environment Model. *Learning Disability Quarterly, 4,* 9–14.

Bryant, B., & Wiederholt, L. (1991). *Gray Oral Reading Tests–3.* Austin, TX: Pro-Ed.

Bryen, D. (1982). *Inquiries into child language.* Boston: Allyn & Bacon.

Budoff, M. (1973). *Learning potential and educability among the educable mentally retarded* (Progress report, Grant No. OEG-0-8-080506-4597 from the National Institute of Education, HEW). Cambridge, MA: Research Institute for Educational Problems.

Bullock, L., Wilson, M., & Campbell, R. (1990). Inquiry into the commonality of items from seven behavior rating scales: A preliminary examination. *Behavioral Disorders, 15,* 87–99.

Burgemeister, B., Blum, L., & Lorge, I. (1972). *Columbia Mental Maturity Scale,* (3rd ed.). New York: Harcourt Brace Jovanovich.

Burke, J., Broad, J., Byford, S. R., & Sims, P. (1983). Use of Burks Behavior Rating Scale with a referred population. *Psychological Reports, 53,* 491–496.

Burks, H. (1977). *Burks Behavior Rating Scales.* Los Angeles: Western Psychological Services.

Burns, E. (1975). An evaluation of the Peabody Individual Achievement Test with primary age retarded children. *Psychology in the Schools, 12,* 11–14.

Burns, E. (1982). The use and interpretation of standardized grade equivalents. *Journal of Learning Disabilities, 15,* 17–18.

Burns, E., Peterson, D., & Bauer, L. (1974). The concurrent validity of the Peabody Individual Achievement Test. *Training School Bulletin, 70,* 221–223.

Burns, P., & Roe, B. (1989). *Informal Reading Inventory.* Boston: Houghton-Mifflin.

Bursuk, L. (1971). Sensory mode of lesson presentation as a factor in the reading comprehension improvement of adolescent retarded readers. (ERIC Document Reproduction Service No. ED 047 435).

Buschner, P. C., Watts, M. B., Siders, J. A., & Leonard, R. L. (1989). Career interest inventories: A need for analysis. *Career Development for Exceptional Individuals, 12,* 129–137.

Cain, L., Levine, S., & Elzey, F. (1977). *Cain-Levine Social Competency Scale.* Palo Alto, CA: Consulting Psychologists Press.

Calnon, M. K. (1984). *Contributions of race and grade level to domain scores on the Vineland Adaptive Behavior Scales.* Unpublished manuscript. University of North Carolina, Chapel Hill.

Camp, B. (1989). Review of Scales of Independent Behavior. In J. Conoley & J. Kramer (Eds.). *Tenth Mental Measurement Yearbook* (pp. 712–713). Lincoln, NE: University of Nebraska Press.

Campione, J. (1989). Assisted assessment: A taxonomy of approaches and an outline of strengths and weaknesses. *Journal of Learning Disabilities, 22,* 151–165.

Cancelli, A. (1985). Review of the Revised Behavior Problem Checklist. In J. Mitchell (Ed.), *Ninth Mental Measurements Yearbook* (pp. 1274–1276). Lincoln, NE: University of Nebraska Press,

Capron, E. (1985). Review of the Adaptive Behavior Inventory for Children. In D. Keyser and R. Sweetland (Eds.) *Test Critiques* (v.3). (pp 13–29). Kansas City, MO: Test Corporation.

Carpenter, D., & Carpenter, S. (1978). The concurrent validity of the Larsen-Hammill Test of Written Spelling in relation to the California Achievement Test. *Educational and Psychological Measurement, 38,* 1201–1205.

Carrow-Woolfolk, E. (1985). *Test of Auditory Comprehension of Language.* McAllen, TX: DLM Resources.

Carstens, A. (1985). Retention and social promotion for the exceptional child. *School Psychology Review, 14,* 48–63.

Carter, J., & Sugai, G. (1989). Survey on prereferral practices: Responses from State Departments of Education. *Exceptional Children, 55,* 298–302.

Cartwright, C., & Cartwright, G. (1984). *Developing observational skills* (2nd ed.). New York: McGraw-Hill.

Carvajal, H. (1988). Relationship between scores of gifted children on the Stanford-Binet IV and the Peabody Picture Vocabulary Test–Revised. *Diagnostique, 14,* 22–25.

Cattell, R., Eber, H., & Tatsuoka, M. (1970). *Sixteen Personality Factor Questionnaire.* Champaign, IL: Institute for Personality and Ability Testing.

Cawley, J., Fitzmaurice, A., Goodstein, H., Lepore, A., Sedlak, R., & Althaus, V. (1977). *Mathematic Concept Inventory.* Tulsa, OK: Educational Development Corp.

Cebulski, L., & Bucher, B. (1986). Identification and remediation of children's subtraction errors: A comparison of practical approaches. *Journal of School Psychology, 24,* 163–180.

Chatman, S., Reynolds, C., & Willson, V. (1984). Multiple indexes of test scatter on the Kaufman Assessment Battery for Children. *Journal of Learning Disabilities, 17,* 523–531.

Cheramie, G., & Edwards, R. (1990). The AAMD Adaptive Behavior Scale, Part Two: Criterion related validity in a behavior disorder sample. *Psychology in the Schools, 27,* 186–195.

Childs, R. (1981). A comparison of the adaptive behavior of normal and gifted five and six year old children. *Roeper Review, 4,* 41–43.

Christenson, S. (1990). Review of Child Behavior Checklist. In J. Conoley & J. Kramer (Eds.). *Tenth Mental Measurements Yearbook* (pp. 40–41). Lincoln, NE: University of Nebraska Press.

Ciardi, E. (1990). Reading comprehension and the SAT. *Journal of Reading, 33,* 558–559.

Cicchetti, D., & Sparrow, S. (1981). *Some recent research on adaptive behavior scales: Toward resolving some methodologic issues.* Paper presented at the 105th meeting of the American Association on Mental Deficiency, Detroit.

Cicchetti, D., & Sparrow, S. (1986). False conclusions about Vineland standard scores: Silverstein's Type I errors and other artifacts. *American Journal of Mental Deficiency, 91,* 5–9.

Clarizio, H. (1982). Intellectual assessment of Hispanic children. *Psychology in the Schools, 19,* 61–71.

Clark, E., Kehle, T. J., & Bullock, D. S. (1988). Personality Inventory for Children: Profiles for learning disabled, emotionally disturbed, and intellectually handicapped children. *School Psychology International, 9,* 43–48.

Clements, P., Bost, L., Dubois, Y., & Turpin, W. (1980). Adaptive Behavior Scale, Part Two: Relative severity of maladaptive behavior. *American Journal of Mental Deficiency, 84,* 465–469.

Cobb, N., & Ray, R. (1975). *Manual for coding discrete behaviors in the school setting.* Oregon Research Bulletin.

Cohen, H., & Weil, G. (1971). *Tasks of Emotional Development.* Lexington, MA: Heath.

Cohen, L., & Spence, S. (1990). Fundamental considerations of curriculum-based assessment. In L. Cohen & J. Spruill (Eds.) *A practical guide to curriculum-*

based assessment for special educators (pps. 3–14). Springfield, IL: Charles Thomas.

Colarusso, R., & Hammill, D. (1972). *The Motor-Free Test of Visual Perception.* San Rafael, CA: Academic Therapy Publications.

Coleman, M., & Harmer, W. (1982). A comparison of standardized reading tests and informal placement procedures. *Journal of Learning Disabilities, 15,* 396–398.

Conaway, C. (1987). Transition: A vocational education perspective. In R. N. Ianacone & R. H. Stodden (Eds.), *Transition Issues and Directions* (pp. 120–124). Reston, VA: Council for Exceptional Children.

Congressional Record, October 10, 1978, H-12179

Conley, M. (1886). Test review: BASIS. *Reading Teacher, 39,* 418–420.

Connolly, A. (1988). *Key Math–Revised.* Circle Pines, MN: American Guidance Service.

Cooter, R. (1988). Woodcock Reading Mastery Test–Revised. *Reading Teacher, 42,* 154–155.

Costenbader, V., & Adams, J. (1991). A review of the psychometric and administrative properties of the PIAT-R: Implications for the practitioner. *Journal of School Psychology, 29,* 219–228.

Creaser, J., & Jacobs, M. (1987). Score discrepancies between the 1981 and 1985 editions of the Strong–Campbell Interest Inventory. *Journal of Counseling Psychology, 34,* 288–292.

CTB/McGraw-Hill. (1985). *The California Achievement Tests.* Monterey, CA: CTB/McGraw-Hill.

Cullinan, D., Epstein, M., & Dembinski, R. (1979). Behavior problems of educationally handicapped and normal pupils. *Journal of Abnormal Child Psychology, 7,* 495–503.

Cullinan, D., Epstein, M., & Lloyd, J. (1981). School behavior problems of learning disabled and normal girls and boys. *Learning Disability Quarterly, 4,* 163–169.

Das, J. (1984). Simultaneous and successive processes and the K-ABC. *Journal of Special Education, 18,* 229–238.

Davis, C. (1980). *Perkins-Binet Intelligence Scale.* Watertown, MA: Perkins School for the Blind.

Davis, J. (1974). Performance of young hearing impaired children on a test of basic concepts. *Journal of Speech and Hearing Disorders, 17,* 342–351.

Dean, R. (1979). Use of the PIAT with emotionally disturbed children. *Journal of Learning Disabilities, 12,* 629–631.

Demoor-Peal, R., & Handal, P. (1983). Validity of the Personality Inventory for Children with four-year-old males and females: A caution. *Journal of Pediatric Psychology, 8,* 261–271.

Deni, J. (1985). Review of the Diagnostic Achievement Battery. In D. Keyser and R. Sweetland (Eds.) *Test Critiques* (v.2). (pp. 235–240). Kansas City, MO: Test Corporation of America.

Deno, S. (1985). Curriculum-based measurement: The emerging alternative. *Exceptional Children, 52,* 219–232.

Deno, S. (1980). Direct observation approach to measuring classroom behavior. *Exceptional Children, 46,* 396–399.

Deno, S., & Fuchs, L. (1987). Developing curriculum-based measurement systems for data based special education problem solving. *Focus on Exceptional Children, 19,* 1–16.

Diamond, K. (1987). Predicting school problems from preschool developmental screening: A four year follow-up of the Revised Denver Developmental Screening Test and the role of parent report. *Journal of the Division for Early Childhood, 11,* 247–253.

Dieffenbach, E. (1977). *Koppitz Human Figure Drawing (HFD): The reliability and clinical validity of its emotional indicators.* Ann Arbor, MI: University Microfilms International, No. 7804261.

Doll, E. (1965). *Vineland Social Maturity Scale.* Circle Pines, MN: American Guidance Service.

Dreger, R. (1981). First-, second-, and third-order factors for the children's classification project instrument and an attempt at reproachment. *Journal of Abnormal Psychology, 90,* 242–260.

Dreisbach, M., & Keogh, B. (1982). Test wiseness as a factor in readiness test performance of young Mexican-American children. *Journal of Educational Psychology, 74,* 224–229.

Drum, P. (1989). Review of Test of Word Finding. In J. Conoley & J. Kramer (Eds.). *Tenth Mental Measurements Yearbook.* (pp. 857–858). Lincoln, NE: University of Nebraska Press.

Dudley-Marling, C., Kaufman, N., & Tarver, S. (1981). WISC and WISC–R profiles of learning disabled children: A review. *Learning Disability Quarterly, 4,* 307–319.

Duffey, L., Salvia, J., Tucker, J., & Ysseldyke, J. (1981). Nonbiased assessment: A need for operationalism. *Exceptional Children, 47,* 427–434.

Dufflemeyer, F., & Dufflemeyer, B. (1989). Are informal reading inventories passages suitable for assessing main idea comprehension? *The Reading Teacher, 42,* 358–363.

Dufflemeyer, F., Robinson, S., & Squier, S. (1989). Vocabulary questions on informal reading inventories. *The Reading Teacher, 43,* 142–148.

Dunbar, S., & Keith, R. (1984). Hierarchical factor analysis of the K-ABC: Testing alternate models. *Journal of Special Education, 18,* 367–375.

Dundon, W., Sewell, T., Manni, J., & Goldstein, D. (1986). The Bannatyne recategorization assessment procedure: Is it valid for individual diagnosis of L.D. children? *Learning Disability Quarterly, 9,* 208–213.

Dunn, L., & Dunn, L. (1981). *Peabody Picture Vocabulary Test-Revised.* Circle Pines, MN: American Guidance Service.

Dunn, L., Markwardt, F. (1988). *Peabody Individual Achievement Test-Revised.* Circle Pines, MN: American Guidance Service.

Dunst, C. (1980). *A Clinical and Educational Manual for Use with the Uzgiris-Hunt Scales of Infant Psychological Development.* Baltimore: University Park Press.

Durost, W., Gardner, E., Madden, R., & Prescott, G. (1971). *Analysis of Learning Potential.* New York: Harcourt Brace Jovanovich.

Durrant, J. F., & Porter, J. F. (1989). Screening ability of the broad-band versus narrow-band intellectual scales of the Personality Inventory for Children (PIC). *Educational and Psychological Measurement, 49*(3), 681–688.

Durrell, D., & Catterson, J. (1980). *Durrell Analysis of Reading Difficulty* (3rd ed.). New York: The Psychological Corporation.

Dusek, J., & O'Connell, E. (1973). Teacher expectancy effects on the achievement test performance of elementary school children. *Journal of Educational Psychology, 65,* 371–377.

Eaves, R. (1990). Review of Woodcock Reading Mastery Tests. *Diagnostique, 15,* 277–298.

Eaves, R. C., Darch, C., & Haynes, M. (1989). The concurrent validity of the Peabody Individual Achievement Test and Woodcock Mastery Test among students with mild learning problems. *Psychology in the Schools, 26,* 261–266.

Eaves, R., & Simpson, R. (1986). Statistically significant differences between subtest scores on the Test of Reading Comprehension. *Psychology in the Schools, 23,* 255–258.

Edelbrock, C., & Achenbach, T. (1984). The teacher version of the Child Behavior Profile: Boys aged 6–11. *Journal of Counseling and Clinical Psychology, 52,* 207–217.

Ehly, S. (1989). Review of Adaptive Behavior Inventory. In J. Conoley & J. Kramer (Eds.). *Tenth Mental Measurements Yearbook.* (pp. 20–21). Lincoln, NE: University of Nebraska Press.

Ekwall, E. (1986). *Ekwall Reading Inventory.* Boston: Allyn & Bacon.

Ekwall, E. (1981). *Locating and correcting reading difficulties* (3rd ed.). Columbus, OH: Charles E. Merrill.

Ekwall, E., & Shanker, J. (1988). *Diagnosis and remediation of the disabled reader* (3rd ed.) Boston: Allyn & Bacon.

Ellers, R., Ellers, S., & Bradley-Johnson, S. (1989). Stability reliability of the Behavior Rating Profile. *Journal of School Psychology, 27*(3), 257–263.

Elliot, C. (1990). *Differential Ability Scales.* San Antonio: The Psychological Corporation.

Elliot, S., & Busse, R. (1990). Review of Child Behavior Checklist. In J. Conoley & J. Kramer (Eds.). *Tenth Mental Measurement Yearbook (Supplement).* (pp. 41–45). Lincoln, NE: University of Nebraska Press.

Elliott, S., & Piersel, W. (1982). Direct assessment of reading skills: An approach which links assessment to intervention. *School Psychology Review, 11,* 267–280.

Elrod, G., Isbell, C., & Braziel, P. (1989). Assessing transition-related variables from kindergarten through grade 12: Practical applications. *Diagnostique, 14,* 247–261.

Elrod, G., & Sorgenfrei, T. (1988). Toward an appropriate assessment model for adolescents who are mildly handicapped: Let's not forget transition! *Career Development for Exceptional Individuals, 11,* 92–98.

Enright, B. (1983). *The Enright Diagnostic Inventory of Basic Arithmetic Skills.* North Billerica, MA: Curriculum Associates.

Erickson, D. (1989). Review of Test of Written Spelling-2. In J. Conoley & J. Kramer (Eds.). *Tenth Mental Measurements Yearbook.* (pp. 858–859). Lincoln, NE: University of Nebraska Press.

Estabrook, G. (1984). Review of Bracken Basic Concept Scale. In D. Keyser & R. Sweetland (Eds.), *Test Critiques* (v. 1) (pp. 125–129). Kansas City, MO: Test Corporation of America.

Estes, G., Harris, J., Moers, F., & Wodrich, D. (1976). Predictive validity of the Boehm Test of Basic Concepts for achievement in first grade. *Educational and Psychological Measurement, 36,* 1031–1035.

Evans, L. (1990). A conceptual overview of the regression discrepancy model for evaluating severe discrepancies between IQ and achievement scores. *Journal of Learning Disabilities, 23,* 406–412.

Evans, L., & Bradley-Johnson, S. (1988). A review of recently developed measures of adaptive behavior. *Psychology in the Schools, 25,* 276–287.

Evans, S., Evans, W., & Mercer, C. (1986). *Assessment for instruction.* Boston: Allyn & Bacon.

Falvey, M. (1989). *Community-Based Curriculum* (2nd ed.). Baltimore: Brookes.

Falvey, M., Brown, L., Lyon, S., Baumgart, D., & Schroeder, J. (1980). Strategies for using cues and correction procedures. In W. Sailor, B. Wilcox, & L. Brown (Eds.), *Methods of Instruction for Severely Handicapped Students.* (pp. 109–133). Baltimore: Brookes.

Federal Register. (1977). Washington, D.C.: U.S. Government Printing Office, August 23, 1977.

Feuerstein, R., Haywood, H., Rand, Y., Hoffman, M., & Jensen, B. (1984). Examiner manuals for the Learning Potential Assessment Device. Jerusalem: Hadassah-WIZO-Canada Research Institute.

Fields, J., & Kumar, V. (1982). How teachers use group IQ test scores. *Journal of School Psychology, 20,* 32–38.

Finkelman, D., Ferrarese, M. H., & Gamezy, N. (1989). A factorial reliability and validity study of the Devereux Elementary School Behavior Rating Scale. *Psychological Reports, 64*(2), 535–547.

Fitts W. (1984). *Tennessee Self-Concept Scale.* Nashville: Counselor Recordings and Tests.

Fitzmaurice, C., & Witt, J. (1989). Review of Boehm Test of Basic Concepts-Revised. In J. Conoley & J. Kramer (Eds.). *Tenth Mental Measurement Yearbook.* (pp. 101–102). Lincoln, NE: University of Nebraska Press.

Fitzpatrick, A. (1984). Test review: BASIS. *Journal of Educational Measurement, 21,* 309–311.

Florida Department of Education. (1989). *Prekindergarten assessment and training of the handicapped.* Tallahassee, FL: Florida Department of Education.

Fodness, R., McNeilly, J., & Bradley-Johnson, S. (1991). Relationship of the Test of Language Development–2 Primary and the Test of Language Development–2 Intermediate. *Journal of School Psychology, 29,* 167–176.

Forbes, G. R. (1987). Personality Inventory for Children: Characteristics of learning disabled children with emotional problems and of emotionally disturbed children with learning problems. *Journal of Clinical Child Psychology, 17*(9), 541–544.

Foster, R. (1974). *Camelot Behavioral Checklist.* Lawrence, KS: Camelot Behavioral Systems.

Frank, A. (1973). Breaking down learning tasks: A sequence approach. *Teaching Exceptional Children, 6,* 16–21.

Frank, A., & Gerken, K. (1990). Case studies in curriculum based measurement. *Education and Training in Mental Retardation, 25,* 113–119.

Frank, A., Logan, H., & Martin, D. (1982). LD students' subtraction errors. *Learning Disability Quarterly, 5,* 194–196.

Frank, L. (1939). Projective methods for the study of personality. *Journal of Psychology, 8,* 389–413.

Frankenberger, W., & Fronzaglio, K. (1991). A review of states' criteria and procedures for identifying children with learning disabilities. *Journal of Learning Disabilities, 24,* 495–500.

Frankenburg, W., Camp, B., & Van Natta, P. (1971). Validity of the Denver Developmental Screening Test. *Child Development, 42,* 475–485.

Frankenburg, W., Dodds, J., Archers, P., Bresnick, B., Maschka, P., Edelman, N., & Shapiro, H. (1990). *Denver-II.* Denver, CO: Denver Developmental Materials, Inc.

Frankenburg, W., Fandel, A., Sciarillo, W., & Burgess, D. (1981). The newly abbreviated Denver Developmental Screening Test: Its accuracy as a screening instrument. *The Journal of Pediatrics, 79,* 988–995.

Frankenburg, W., Van Doorninck, W., Liddell, T., & Dick, N. (1976). The Denver Prescreening Developmental Questionnaire (PDQ). *Pediatrics, 57,* 744–753.

French, J. (1964). *Pictorial Test of Intelligence.* Boston: Houghton-Mifflin.

Frostig, M., Lefever, W., & Whittlesey, J. (1966). *Administration and scoring manual: Marianne Frostig Developmental Test of Visual Perception.* Palo Alto, CA: Consulting Psychologists Press.

Fuchs, D., & Fuchs, L. (1989). Effects of examiner familiarity on black, Caucasian, and Hispanic children: A metanalysis. *Exceptional Children, 55,* 303–308.

Fuchs, L., & Fuchs, D. (1988). Curriculum-based measurement: A methodology for evaluating and improving student programs. *Diagnostique, 14,* 3–13.

Fuchs, L., & Fuchs, D. (1990). Traditional academic assessment: An overview. In R. Gable & J. Hendrickson (Eds.). *Assessing Students with Special Needs* (pp. 1–13). New York: Longman.

Fuchs, L., Fuchs, D., & Hamlett, C. (1989). Computers and curriculum based measurement: Effects of teacher feedback systems. *School Psychology Review, 18,* 112–125.

Fuchs, L., Fuchs, D., Hamlett, C., & Allinder, R. (1991). The contribution of skills analysis to curriculum-based measurement in spelling. *Exceptional Children, 57,* 443–452.

Fuchs, L., Fuchs, D., Hamlett, C., & Allinder, R. (1989). The reliability and validity of skills analysis within curriculum based measurement. *Diagnostique, 14,* 203–221.

Fuchs, L., Hamlett, C., & Fuchs, D. (1990). *Monitoring Basic Skills Progress.* Austin, TX: Pro-Ed.

Fudala, J. (1978). *Tree/Bee Test of Auditory Discrimination.* Novato, CA: Academic Therapy Publications.

Fujiki, M. (1987). Review of Test of Problem Solving. In J. Conoley & J. Kramer (Eds.). *Tenth Mental Measurements Yearbook.* (pp. 847–848). Lincoln, NE: University of Nebraska Press.

Gable, R., & Coben, S. (1990). Errors in arithmetic. In R. Gable & J. Hendrickson (Eds.). *Assessing students with special needs.* (pp. 30–45). New York: Longman.

Gable, R., & Hendrickson, J. (1990). *Assessing Students with Special Needs.* New York: Longman.

Gajar, A. (1979). Educable mentally retarded, learning disabled and emotionally disturbed: Similarities and differences. *Exceptional Children, 45,* 470–472.

Galagan, J. (1985). Psychoeducational testing: Turn out the light the party's over. *Exceptional Children, 52,* 288–299.

Gall, M. (1990). *Tools for learning: A guide to teaching study skills* (ED 320126). Alexandria, VA: Association for Supervision and Curriculum Development.

Galvin, G. (1981). Uses and abuses of the WISC-R with the learning disabled. *Journal of Learning Disabilities, 14,* 326–329.

Gardner, E., Rudman, H., Karlsen, B., & Merwin, J. (1982). *Stanford Achievement Test.* New York: Harcourt Brace Jovanovich.

Garrison, W., & Earls, F. (1985). The Child Behavior Checklist as a screening instrument for young children. *Journal of the American Academy of Child Psychiatry, 24,* 76–80.

Garrity, L., & Servos, A. (1978). Comparison of measures of adaptive behaviors in preschool children. *Journal of Consulting and Clinical Psychology, 46,* 288–293.

Gaylord-Ross, R. (1986). The role of assessment in transitional, supported employment. *Career Development for Exceptional Individuals, 9,* 129–134.

Gayton, W., Thornton, K., & Bassett, J. (1982) Utility of the Behavior Problem Checklist with preschool children. *Journal of Clinical Psychology, 38,* 325–327.

German, D. (1986). *Test of Word Finding.* Allen, TX: DLM Teaching Resources.

German, M. L., Williams, E., Herzfield, J., & Marshall, R. M. (1982). Utility of the Revised Denver Developmental Screening Test and the Developmental Profile II in identifying preschool children with cognitive, language, and motor problems. *Education and Training of the Mentally Retarded, 17,* 319–324.

Giacobbe, G., & Traynelis-Yurck, E. (1989). Undergraduate students' errors in the administration of standardized tests. *Diagnostique, 14,* 174–182.

Gilmore, J., & Gilmore, E. (1968). *Gilmore Oral Reading Test.* New York: Harcourt Brace Jovanovich.

Ginsburg, H., & Baroody, A. (1990). *Test of Early Mathematics Ability–2.* Austin, TX: Pro-Ed.

Glascoe, F. P., & Borowitz, K. C. (1988). Improving the sensitivity of the language section of the Denver Developmental Screening Test. *Diagnostique, 13,* 76–85.

Glaub, V., & Kamphaus, R. (1991). Construction of a nonverbal adaptation of the Stanford-Binet Fourth Edition. *Educational and Psychological Measurement, 51,* 231–241.

Glutting, J. (1989). Introduction to the structure and approach of the Stanford-Binet Intelligence Scale-Fourth Edition. *Journal of School Psychology, 27,* 69–80.

Glutting, J., Kelly, M., Boehm, A., & Burnett, T. (1989). Stability and predictive validity of the Boehm Test of Basic Concepts–Revised among black kindergarteners. *Journal of School Psychology, 27,* 365–371.

Goh, D. (1984). PIC profiles for learning disabled and behavior disordered children. *Journal of Clinical Psychology, 40,* 837–841.

Goldman, R., Fristoe, M., & Woodcock, R. (1970). *Goldman-Fristoe-Woodcock Test of Auditory Discrimination.* Circle Pines, MN: American Guidance Service.

Good, T., & Brophy, J. (1972). Behavioral expression of teacher attitudes. *Journal of Educational Psychology, 63,* 617–624.

Goodman, K. (1977). *Miscue analysis.* Urbana, IL: ERIC, Clearinghouse on Reading and Communication Skills, National Council of Teachers of English.

Goodman, Y., & Burke, C. (1972). *Reading Miscue Inventory.* New York: Macmillan.

Goodman, Y., Watson, D., & Burke, C. (1987). *Reading miscue inventory: Alternative procedures.* New York: Richard C. Owen, Publisher.

Goodstein, H., Kahn, H., & Cawley, J. (1976). The achievement of educable mentally retarded children on the Key Math Diagnostic Arithmetic Test. *Journal of Special Education, 10,* 61–70.

Gordon, L. (1981). *Gordon Occupational Check List II.* San Antonio: Psychological Corporation.

Gough, H. (1969). *California Psychological Inventory.* Palo Alto, CA: Consulting Psychologists Press.

Graziano, W. (1982). Race of the examiner effects and the validity of intelligence tests. *Review of Education Research, 52,* 469–497.

Green, D. (1987). Interpreting grade scores from standardized tests. *National Association of Secondary Schools Bulletin, 71,* 23–35.

Greene, A. C., Sapp, G., & Chissom, B. (1990). Validation of the Stanford-Binet Intelligence Scale: Fourth Edition with exceptional black male students. *Psychology in the Schools, 27*(1), 35–41.

Greenbaum, C. (1987). *The Spellmaster Assessment and Teaching System.* Austin, TX: Pro-Ed.

Greenstein, J., & Strain, P. (1977). The utility of the Key Math Diagnostic Arithmetic Test for adolescent learning disabled students. *Psychology in the Schools, 14,* 275–282.

Gresham, F., & Elliot, S. (1990). *Social Skills Rating System.* Circle Pines, MN: American Guidance Service.

Gridley, B., & McIntosh, D. (1991). Confirmatory factor analysis of the Stanford-Binet Intelligence Scale-Fourth Edition. *Journal of School Psychology, 29,* 237–248.

Gridley, B., Miller, G., Barke, C., Fischer, W., & Smith, D. (1990). Construct validity of the K-ABC with an at-risk preschool population. *Journal of School Psychology, 28,* 39–49.

Gronlund, N. (1973). *Preparing criterion-referenced tests for classroom instruction.* New York: Macmillan.

Gronlund, N. (1988). *How to construct achievement tests* (4th ed.). Englewood Cliffs, NJ: Prentice-Hall.

Gronlund, N., & Linn, R. (1990). *Measurement and evaluation in teaching* (6th ed.). NY: Macmillan.

Grossman, F. (1981). Cautions in interpreting WRAT standard scores as criterion measures of achievement in young children. *Psychology in the Schools, 18,* 144–146.

Grossman, H. (Ed.). (1983). *Classification in mental retardation.* Washington, D.C.: American Association on Mental Deficiency.

Guidubaldi, J., & Perry, J. (1984). Concurrent and predictive validity of the Battelle Developmental Inventory at the first grade level. *Educational and Psychological Measurement, 44,* 977–985.

Gutkin, T. (1979). WISC–R scatter indices: Useful information for differential diagnosis? *Journal of School Psychology, 17,* 368–371.

Guyette, T. (1989). Review of Test of Language Competence. In J. Conoley & J. Kramer (Eds.). *Tenth Mental Measurements Yearbook.* (pp. 432–434). Lincoln, NE: University of Nebraska Press.

Guzaitis, J., Carlin, J., & Juda, S. (1972). *Diagnosis: An Instructional Aid in Mathematics.* Chicago: Science Research Associates.

Haddad, F. (1986). Performance of learning disabled children on the K–ABC and Bender-Gestalt. *Psychology in the Schools, 23,* 342–345.

Haines, H. (1977). *A study of the construct validity of the Woodcock Reading Mastery Tests with underachieving and slow learning fourth, fifth and sixth grade pupils.* Ann Arbor, MI: University Microfilms International, No. 7810802.

Hainsworth, P., & Siqueland, M. (1969). *Early identification of children with learning disabilities: The Meeting Street School Screening Test.* Providence, RI: Crippled Children and Adults of Rhode Island.

Haley, J. (1963). *Strategies of psychotherapy.* New York: Grune & Stratton.

Hall, R., & Goetz, E. (1984). Evaluation of the Kaufman Assessment Battery for Children from an information processing perspective. *Journal of Special Education, 18,* 280–296.

Hallahan, D., & Cruickshank, W. (1973). *Psychoeducational foundations of learning disabilities.* Englewood Cliffs, NJ: Prentice-Hall.

Hallahan, D., & Kauffman, J. (1976). *Introduction to learning disabilities.* Englewood Cliffs, NJ: Prentice-Hall.

Hallahan, D., & Kauffman, J. (1991). *Exceptional children* (5th ed.). Englewood Cliffs, NJ: Prentice-Hall.

Hallahan, D., Keller, C., & Ball, D. (1986). A comparison of prevalence rate variability from state to state for each of the categories of special education. *Remedial and Special Education, 7,* 8–14.

Hambleton, R., & DeVries, D. (1985). Review of the Basic Achievement Skills Individual Screener. *Journal of Counseling and Development, 63,* 383–384.

Hammill, D. (1985). *Detroit Tests of Learning Aptitude–2,* Austin, TX: Pro-Ed.

Hammill, D. (1990). On defining learning disabilities: An emerging consensus. *Journal of Learning Disabilities, 23,* 74–84.

Hammill, D. (1991). *Detroit Tests of Learning Aptitude–3.* Austin, TX: Pro-Ed.

Hammill, D., & Larsen, S. (1988). *Test of Written Language–2,* Austin, TX: Pro-Ed.

Hammill, D., Ammer, J., Cronin, M., Mandlebaum, L., & Quinby, S. (1987). *Quick-Score Achievement Test.* Austin, TX: Pro-Ed.

Hammill, D., Brown, V., Larsen, S., & Weiderholt, L. (1987). *Test of Adolescent Language–2.* Austin, TX: Pro-Ed.

Hammill, D., & Larsen, S. (1974). The relationship of selected auditory perceptual skills and reading ability. *Journal of Learning Disabilities, 7,* 429–435.

Hammill, D., & Larsen, S. (1983). *The Test of Written Language.* Austin, TX: Pro-Ed.

Hammill, D., & Leigh, J. (1983). *Basic School Skills Inventory–Diagnostic.* Austin, TX: Pro-Ed.

Hammill, D., Leigh, J., McNutt, G., & Larsen, S. (1981). A new definition of learning disabilities. *Learning Disability Quarterly, 4,* 336–342.

Hardman, J., & Croyle, G. (1979). A kindergarten screening procedure for the identification of potentially exceptional children. Paper presented at the 26th annual convention of the National Association for Gifted Children. Baltimore.

Hardman, M., Drew, C., Egan, M., & Wolf, B. (1990). *Human Exceptionality* (3rd ed.). Boston: Allyn & Bacon.

Hare, B. (1977). Perceptual deficits are not a cue to reading problems in second grade. *The Reading Teacher, 30,* 624–628.

Haring, N., White, O., Edgar, E., Affleck, J., & Hayden, A. (1981). *Uniform Performance Assessment System.* Columbus, OH: Charles E. Merrill.

Harker, W. J. (1990). Testing reading: We need a new perspective. *Reading Horizons, 30,* 309–319.

Harmer, W., & Williams, F. (1978). The Wide Range Achievement Test and the Peabody Individual Achievement Test: A comparative study. *Journal of Learning Disabilities, 11,* 65–68.

Harper, D. C., & Walker, D. P. (1983). The efficiency of the Denver Developmental Screening Test with rural disadvantaged preschool children. *Journal of Pediatric Psychology, 8,* 273–283.

Harris, D. (1963). *Children's Drawings as Measures of Intellectual Maturity.* New York: Harcourt Brace Jovanovich.

Harris, S., & Fagley, N. (1987). The Developmental Profile as a predictor of status for autistic children: Four to seven year follow up. *School Psychology Review, 16,* 89–93.

Harrison, P. (1981). Mercer's Adaptive Behavior Inventory, the McCarthy Scales, and dental development as predictors of first-grade achievement. *Journal of Educational Psychology, 73,* 78–82.

Harrison, P. (1990) *New prekindergarten assessment instruments.* Unpublished manuscript.

Harrison, P. (1991). *Early Screening Profiles.* Circle Pines, MN: American Guidance Service.

Harrison, P., Kaufman, A., Hichman, J., & Kaufman, N. (1988). A survey of tests used for adult assessment. *Journal of Psychoeducational Assessment, 6,* 188–198.

Harrison, P., Kaufman, A., & Naglieri, J. (1980). Subtest patterns and recategorized groupings of the McCarthy Scales for EMR children. *American Journal of Mental Deficiency, 85,* 129–134.

Harrison, P., & Naglieri, J. (1978). Extrapolated general cognitive indexes on the McCarthy Scales for gifted and mentally retarded children. *Psychological Reports, 43,* 1291–1296.

Harrison, P. L. (1987). Research with adaptive behavior scales. *The Journal of Special Education, 21,* 37–68.

Harrison, P. L. (1988). *K-ABC mental processing profiles for gifted referrals.* Paper presented at the Mid-South Educational Research Association Meeting, Louisville, KY.

Hartlage, L., & Lucas, D. (1972). Scaled score transformations of Bender-Gestalt expectancy levels for young children. *Psychology in the Schools, 8,* 76–77.

Hasselbring, T., & Crossland, C. (1982). Application of microcomputer technology to spelling assessment of learning disabled students. *Learning Disabilities Quarterly, 5,* 80–82.

Hasselbring, T., & Moore, P. (1990). Computer-based and error analysis. In R.

Gable & J. Hendrickson (Eds.). *Assessing Students with Special Needs* (pp. 102–116). New York: Longman.

Hathaway, S., & McKinley, J. (1967). *Minnesota Multiphasic Personality Inventory*. New York: Psychological Corporation.

Hathaway, S., & Meehl, P. (1951). *An Atlas for the Clinical Use of the MMPI*. Minneapolis: University of Minnesota Press.

Hayden, D. C., Furlong, M., & Linnemeyer, S. (1988). A comparison of the Kaufman Assessment Battery for Children and the Stanford-Binet IV for the assessment of gifted children. *Psychology in the Schools, 25,* 239–243.

Haynes, S. (1978). *Principles of behavioral assessment*. New York: Gardner.

Haywood, H. C., Brown, A., & Wingenfeld, S. (1990). Dynamic approaches to psychoeducational assessment. *School Psychology Review, 19*(4), 411–422.

Heath, C., & Obrzut, J. (1984). Comparison of three measures of adaptive behavior. *Americal Journal of Mental Deficiency, 89,* 205–208.

Heifetz, L. (1989). Review of Scales of Independent Behavior. In J. Conoley & J. Kramer (Eds.). *Tenth Mental Measurements Yearbook*. (pp. 713–718). Lincoln, NE: University of Nebraska Press.

Heinze, A. (1987). Assessing general psychopathology in children and youth with visual handicaps. *Australia and New Zealand Journal of Developmental Disabilities, 13*(4), 219–226.

Hendrickson, J., & Gable, R. (1990). Errors in spelling. In R. Gable & J. Hendrickson (Eds.). *Assessing Students with Special Needs*. (pp. 78–88). New York: Longman.

Henkin, P. (1977). *Concept attainment and reading achievement in normal disadvantaged and high risk first grade children*. Ann Arbor, MI: University Microfilms International, No. 7800494.

Henley, S., Klebe, K., McBride, J., & Cudeck, R. (1989). Adaptive and conventional versions of the DAT: The first complete test battery comparison. *Applied Psychological Measurement, 13,* 363–371.

Henson, F., & Bennett, L. (1986). The Kaufman Test of Educational Achievement. In D. Keyser & R. Sweetland (Eds.) *Test Critiques* (v. 4). (pp. 368–375). Kansas City, MO: Test Corporation of America.

Heshusius, L. (1991). Curriculum based assessment and direct instruction: Critical reflections on fundamental assumptions. *Exceptional Children, 57,* 315–328.

Hessler, G. (1985). Review of the Kaufman Assessment Battery for Children: Implications for assessment of the gifted. *Journal for the Education of the Gifted, 8,* 133–147.

Heward, W., & Orlansky, M. (1992). Exceptional children (4th ed.). Columbus, OH: Charles Merrill.

Hickman, J. (1989). Review of the Gray Oral Reading Test-Revised. In J. Conoley & J. Kramer (Eds.). *Tenth Mental Measurements Yearbook*. (pp. 335–337). Lincoln, NE: University of Nebraska Press.

Hieronymus, A., Lindquist, E., & Hoover, H. (1986). *Iowa Tests of Basic Skills*. Lombard, IL: Riverside Publishing Company.

Hickman, J., & Bevins, S. (1990). *Learning Disability Discrepancy Analysis*. Austin, TX: Pro-Ed.

Hightower, A. (1989). Review of Developmental Profile-II. In J. Conoley & J. Kramer (Eds.). *Tenth Mental Measurements Yearbook*. (pp. 249–250). Lincoln, NE: University of Nebraska Press.

Hirshoren, A., & Schnittjer, C. (1979). Dimensions of problem behavior in deaf children. *Journal of Abnormal Child Psychology, 7,* 221–228.

Hiskey, M. (1966). *Hiskey-Nebraska Test of Learning Aptitude*. Lincoln, NE: Union College Press.

Hobbs, N. (1975). *Issues In the Classification of Children* (2 vols.). San Francisco: Jossey-Bass.

Holland, J. (1985). *Vocational Preference Inventory–Revised*. Odessa, FL: Psychological Assessment Resources.

Hooper, S., & Hynd, G. (1986). Performance of normal and dyslexic readers on the Kaufman Assessment Battery for Children: A discriminant analysis. *Journal of Learning Disabilities, 9,* 206–209.

Hopkins, K., & Hodge, S. (1984). Review of the Kaufman Assessment Battery for Children. *Journal of Counseling and Development, 63,* 105–107.

Horne, M., & Larrivee, B. (1979). Behavior rating scales: Need for refining normative data. *Perceptual and Motor Skills, 49,* 383–388.

Houck, C., Biskin, D., & Regetz, J. (1973). A comparison of urban and rural reliability estimates for the Boehm Basic Concept Test. *Psychology in the Schools, 10,* 430–432.

Howell, K. (1990). Review of Test of Mathematical Abilities. *Diagnostique, 15,* 210–217.

Howell, K., & Morehead, M. (1987). *Curriculum-based evaluation for special and remedial education.* Columbus, OH: Charles E. Merrill.

Howell, K., Zucker, S., & Morehead, M. (1982). *Multilevel Academic Skill Inventory.* Columbus, OH: Charles E. Merrill.

Howell, K., Zucker, S., & Morehead, M. (1985). *Multilevel Academic Skills Test.* San Antonio: The Psychological Corporation.

Hresko, W. (1988). *Test of Early Written Language.* Austin, TX: Pro-Ed.

Hritcko, T., & Salvia, J. (1984). The K-ABC and ability training. *Journal of Special Education, 18,* 345–356.

Huberty, T. (1986). Relationship of the WISC-R factors to the Adaptive Behavior Scales School Edition in a referral sample. *Journal of School Psychology, 24,* 155–162.

Huebner, S. (1989). A comparison of school psychologists' interpretations of grade equivalents, percentiles, and deviation IQs. *School Psychology Review, 18,* 51–55.

Huebner, S. (1989). Factors influencing the decision to administer psychoeducational tests. *Psychology in the Schools, 26,* 365–370.

Huebner, S. (1989). Review of Developmental Profile-II. In J. Conoley & J. Kramer (Eds.). *Tenth Mental Measurements Yearbook.* (pp. 250–251). Lincoln, NE: Unversity of Nebraska Press.

Hughes, S. (1988). Adaptive Behavior Inventory. In D. Kayser & R. Sweetland (Eds.) *Test critiques (v. 7).* Kansas City, MO: Test Corporation of America.

Hunnicutt, L., Slate, J., Gamble, C., & Wheeler, M. (1990). Examiner errors on the Kaufman Assessment Battery for Children: A preliminary investigation. *Journal of School Psychology, 28,* 271–278.

Hutcherson, R. (1978). Correlating the Boehm and PPVT. *Academic Therapy, 13,* 285–288.

Hutt, M. (1977). *The Hutt Adaptation of the Bender-Gestalt Test* (3rd ed.). New York: Grune & Stratton.

Ianacone, R. N., & Leconte, P. J. (1986). Curriculum-based vocational assessment: A viable response to a school-based service delivery issue. *Career Development for Exceptional Individuals, 9,* 113–120.

Idol, L., Nevin, A., & Paolucci-Whitcomb, P. (1986). *Models of curriculum-based assessment.* Rockville, MD: Aspen Publishers, Inc.

Ilg, F., Ames, L., Haines, J., & Gillespie, C. (1978). *Gesell School Readiness Test.* New York: Harper and Row.

Ilmer, S., Bruininks, R. J., & Hill, B. K. (1988). Discriminant analysis of intellectual ability groups with measures of adaptive behavior. *Journal of School*

Psychology, 26, 293–296.

Isaacson, S. (1988). Assessing the writing product: Qualitative and quantitative measures. *Exceptional Children, 54*(b), 528–534.

Isett, R., & Spreat, S. (1979). Test-retest and interrater reliabilities of the AAMD Adaptive Behavior Scale. *American Journal of Mental Deficiency, 84,* 93–95.

Jacobs, W. (1978). The effect of learning disability label on classroom teachers' ability objectively to observe and interpret child behaviors. *Learning Disability Quarterly, 1,* 50–55.

Jaeger, R. (1989). Review of Woodcock Reading Mastery Tests-Revised. In J. Conoley & J. Kramer (Eds.). *Tenth Mental Measurements Yearbook.* (pp. 913–916). Lincoln, NE: University of Nebraska Press.

Jastak, J., & Jastak, S. (1979) *Wide Range Interest-Opinion Test.* Wilmington, DE: Jastak Associates.

Jastak, S., & Wilkinson, G. (1984). *Wide Range Achievement Test–Revised.* Wilmington, DE: Jastak Associates.

Jensen, A. (1986). The black-white difference on the K-ABC: Implications for future tests. *Journal of Special Education, 18,* 377–408.

Johns, J. (1988). *Basic Reading Inventory.* Dubuque, IA: Kendall/Hunt.

Johnson, D., & Harlow, S. (1989). Using the computer in educational assessment: Can it be of any help? *Diagnostique, 14,* 274–282.

Johnson, D., & Myklebust, H. (1967). *Learning Disabilities: Educational Principles and Practices.* New York: Grune & Stratton.

Johnson-Martin, N., Attermeier, S., & Hacker, B. (1990). *Assessment Log and Developmental Progress Chart–Preschool.* Baltimore: Paul Brooks.

Johnson-Martin, N., Jens, K., & Attermeier, S. (1986). *Assessment Log and Developmental Progress Chart.* Baltimore: Paul Brooks.

Jonz, J. (1990). Another turn in the conversation: What does Cloze measure? *TESOL Quarterly, 24,* 61–83.

Kamphaus, R. (1987). Conceptual and psychometric issues in the assessment of adaptive behavior. *The Journal of Special Education, 21,* 27–35.

Kamphaus, R. (1989). Review of the Diagnostic Achievement Test for Adolescents. In J. Conoley & J. Kramer (Eds.). *Tenth Mental Measurements Yearbook.* (pp. 253–254). Lincoln, NE: University of Nebraska Press.

Kamphaus, R., & Reynolds, C. (1984). Development and structure of the Kaufman Assessment Battery for Children. *Journal of Special Education, 18,* 213–228.

Karlsen, B., & Gardner, E. (1985). *Stanford Diagnostic Reading Test.* New York: Harcourt Brace Jovanovich.

Kass, R., & Fish, J. (1991). Positive reframing and the test performance of test anxious children. *Psychology in the Schools, 28,* 43–52.

Kauffman, J. (1989). *Characteristics of children's behavior disorders* (4th ed.). Columbus, OH: Charles E. Merrill.

Kaufman, A. (1979). *Intelligent testing with the WISC–R.* New York: John Wiley.

Kaufman, A. (1981). The WISC–R and learning disabilities assessment: State of the art. *Journal of Learning Disabilities, 14,* 520–526.

Kaufman, A. (1984). K-ABC and controversy. *Journal of Special Education, 18,* 409–444.

Kaufman, A., & Doppelt, J. (1976). Analysis of WISC-R standardization data in terms of stratification variables. *Child Development, 47,* 165–171.

Kaufman, A., & Kaufman, N. (1990). *Kaufman Brief Intelligence Test.* Circle Pines, MN: American Guidance Service.

Kaufman, A., Kamphaus, R., & Kaufman, N. (1985). The Kaufman Assessment Battery for Children. In C. Newmark (Ed.), *Major Psychological Assessment Instruments.* Boston: Allyn & Bacon.

Kaufman, A., & Kaufman, N. (1983). *The Kaufman Assessment Battery for Children.* Circle Pines, MN: American Guidance Service.

Kaufman, A., & Kaufman, N. (1985). *The Kaufman Test of Educational Achievement.* Circle Pines, MN: American Guidance Service.

Kaufman, A., & McLean, J. (1986). K–ABC/WISC-R factor analysis for a learning disabled population. *Journal of Learning Disabilities, 19,* 145–153.

Kavale, K. (1982). A comparison of learning disabled and normal children on the Boehm Test of Basic Concepts. *Journal of Learning Disabilities, 15,* 160–161.

Kavale, K., & Mattson, D. (1983). One jumped off the balance beam: Metaanalysis of perceptual-motor training. *Journal of Learning Disabilities, 16,* 165–173.

Kazimour, K., & Reschly, D. (1981). Investigation of the norms and concurrent validity for the Adaptive Behavior Inventory for Children (ABIC). *American Journal of Mental Deficiency, 85,* 512–520.

Keenan, P. A., & Lachar, D. (1988). Screening preschoolers with special problems: Use of the Personality Inventory for Children (PIC). *Journal of School Psychology, 26,* 1–11.

Keller, H. (1980). Issues in the use of observational assessment. *School Psychology Review, 9,* 21–30.

Kelly, E. J. (1988). Personality Inventory for Children: Selected scales in differentiating conduct-disordered and emotionally-disturbed students. *Psychological Reports, 63,* 395–401.

Kercher, A., & Sandoval, J. (1991). Reading disability and the Differential Ability Scales. *Journal of School Psychology, 29,* 293–307.

Kerlinger, F. (1980). *Foundations of Behavioral Research* (3rd ed.). New York: Holt, Rinehart and Winston.

Kirby, E., & Porter, L. (1986). Effects of two instructional sets on the validity of the Kaufman Assessment Battery for Children-nonverbal scale with a group of severely hearing impaired children. *Psychology in the Schools, 23,* 37–43.

Kirk, S., & Gallagher, J. (1988). *Educating Exceptional Children* (6th ed.). Boston: Houghton-Mifflin.

Kirk, S., McCarthy, J. & Kirk, W. (1968). *Illinois Test of Psycholinguistic Abilities.* Urbana, IL: University of Illinois Press.

Klanderman, J., Perney, J., & Kroeschell, Z. (1985). Comparisons of the K-ABC and WISC–R for LD children. *Journal of Learning Disabilities, 18,* 524–527.

Klein, E. (1981). Communication dysfunctions. In R. Smith & J. Neisworth, *Exceptional Child: A Functional Approach.* New York: McGraw-Hill.

Klopfer, B., & Kelly, D. (1942). *The Rorschach Technique.* New York: World Book Co.

Knight, B., Baker, E., & Minder, C. (1990). Concurrent validity of the Stanford-Binet: Fourth Edition and the Kaufman Assessment Battery for Children with learning disabled students. *Psychology in the Schools, 27,* 116–125.

Knoff, H. (1989). Review of Personality Inventory for Children. In J. Conoley & J. Kramer (Eds.). *Tenth Mental Measurements Yearbook.* (pp. 625–630). Lincoln, NE: University of Nebraska Press.

Knoff, H., & Prout, H. (1985). *Kinetic Drawing System for Family and School: A Handbook.* Los Angeles: Weston Psychological Services.

Kochhar, C. A. (1991). Capitol connection. *Division on Career Development Network, 15.*

Kokaska, C. J., & Brolin, D. E. (1985). *Career Education for Handicapped Individuals* (2nd ed.). Columbus, OH: Charles E. Merrill.

Koppitz, E. (1968). *Human Figure Drawing Test.* New York: Grune & Stratton.

Koppitz, E. (1975). *The Bender Gestalt Test for young children* (v. II). New York: Grune & Stratton.

Kratochwill, T. (1977). The movement of psychological extras into ability assessment. *Journal of Special Education, 11,* 299–308.

Kratochwill, T., & Demuth, D. (1976). An examination of the predictive validity of the Key Math Diagnostic Arithmetic Test and the Wide Range Achievement Test in exceptional children. *Psychology in the Schools, 13,* 404–406.

Krohn, E. J., & Lamp, R. E. (1989). Concurrent validity of the Stanford Binet Fourth Edition and K-ABC for Head Start children. *Journal of School Psychology, 27,* 59–67.

Kuder, F., & Diamond, E. (1985). *Kuder Occupational Interest Survey (Form DD).* Chicago: Science Research Associates.

Kuhlmann, F., & Anderson, R. (1982). *Kuhlmann-Anderson Test.* Columbus, OH: Personnel Press.

Lachar, D., & LaCombe, J. (1983). Objective personality assessment: The Personality Inventory for Children and its application in the school setting. *School Psychology Review, 12,* 399–406.

Laffey, J., & Kelly, D. (1979). Test review: Woodcock Reading Mastery Tests. *Reading Teacher, 33,* 335–339.

Lahey, B., & Piacentini, R. (1985). An evaluation of the Quay-Peterson Revised Behavior Problem Checklist. *Journal of the American Academy of Child Psychiatry, 23,* 285–289.

Lahey, B., Schaughency, E., Strauss, C., & Frame, C. (1984). Are attention deficit disorders with and without hyperactivity similar or dissimilar disorders? *Journal of the American Academy of Child Psychiatry, 23,* 302–309.

Lambert, N. (1986). Evidence on age and ethnic status bias in factor scores and the comparison score for the AAMD Adaptive Behavior Scale–School Edition. *Journal of School Psychology, 24,* 143–153.

Lambert, N., Windmiller, M., Tharinger, D., & Cole, L. (1981). *AAMD Adaptive Behavior Scale, School Edition.* Washington, D.C.: American Association on Mental Deficiency.

Lankford, F. (1972). Some computational strategies of seventh grade pupils. (Grant number OE6-3-72-0035.) University of Virginia: Center for Advanced Study.

Lanyon, R., and Goodstein, L. (1971). *Personality assessment.* New York: John Wiley.

Lappan, G. (1978). Review of Stanford Diagnostic Mathematics Test. In O. Buros (Ed.), *The Eighth Mental Measurement Yearbook.* (pp. 436–437). Highland Park, NJ: Gryphon Press.

Larry P. et al. v. Wilson Riles et al. (1979). United States District Court, Northern District of California, Case No. C-71-2270-RFP.

Larsen, S., & Hammill, D. (1975). The relationship of selected visual perceptual abilities to school learning. *Journal of Special Education, 9,* 281–291.

Larsen, S., & Hammill, D. (1986). *Test of Written Spelling-2.* Austin, TX: Pro-Ed.

Larsen, S., & Poplin, M. (1980). *Methods for Educating the Handicapped: An Individualized Approach.* Boston: Allyn & Bacon.

Laughon, P. (1990). The dynamic assessment of intelligence: A review of three approaches. *School Psychology Review, 14,* 459–470.

Lazarus, B., McKenna, N., & Lynch, D. (1990). Peabody Individual Achievement Test-Revised. *Diagnostique, 15,* 135–148.

Lazarus, P., & Novoa, L. (1987). Test review: Quick Score Achievement Test. *Journal of Reading, 31,* 78–83.

Leblanc, R., & Reynolds, C. (1989). Concordance of mothers' and fathers' ratings of children's behavior. *Psychology in the Schools, 26,* 225–229.

Lee, L. (1974). *Developmental Sentence Analysis.* Evanston, IL: Northwestern University Press.

Lewandowski, L. (1985). Test review: Diagnostic Achievement Battery. *Reading Teacher, 39,* 306–309.

Lewandowski, L., & Martens, B. (1990). Selecting and evaluating standardized reading tests (test review). *Journal of Reading, 33,* 384–388.

Lewis, T. (1991). Review of the Walker–McConnell Scales of Social Competence. *Behavioral Disorders, 16,* 159–160.

Lidz, D. (1979). Criterion-referenced assessment: The new bandwagon? *Exceptional Children, 46,* 131–132.

Linder, T. (1985). Review of the Developmental Indicators for the Assessment of Learning-Revised. In D. Keyser and R. Sweetland (Eds.). *Test Critiques* (v. 4) (pp. 220–228). Kansas City, MO: Test Corporation of America.

Linder, T. (1989). *Transdisciplinary Play Assessment.* Baltimore: Paul Brookes.

Lindquist, G. (1982). Preschool screening as a means of predicting later achievement scores. *Journal of Learning Disabilities, 15,* 331–332.

Lindsey, J., & Armstrong, S. (1984). Performance of Educably Mentally Retarded and Learning Disabled on the Brigance, Peabody and Wide Range Achievement Tests. *American Journal of Mental Deficiency, 89,* 197–201.

Lindsley, O. (1964). Direct measurement and prosthesis of retarded behavior. *Journal of Education, 14,* 62–81.

Linthicum, E., Cole, J. T., & D'Alonzo, B. (1991). Employment and the Americans with Disabilities Act of 1991. *Career Development for Exceptional Individuals, 14,* 1–13.

Lobello, S. (1991). Significant differences between individual subtest scale scores and average scale scores on the Weschler Preschool and Primary Scale of Intelligence–Revised. *Psychology in the Schools, 28,* 15–18.

Lorge, I., Thorndike, R., & Hagen, E. (1966). *Lorge-Thorndike Intelligence Tests.* Boston: Houghton-Mifflin.

Lund, N., & Duchan, J. (1988). *Assessing children's language in naturalistic contexts* (2nd ed.). Englewood Cliffs, NJ: Prentice-Hall.

Lyon, M., & Smith, D. (1987). Stability of the K-ABC for a sample of at risk preschool children. *Psychology in the Schools, 24,* 111–115.

Macmillan, D., Jones, R., & Aloia, G. (1974). The mentally retarded label: A theoretical analysis and review of research. *American Journal of Mental Deficiency, 79,* 241–261.

MacDonald, L. (1988). Improving the reliability of a maladaptive behavior scale. *American Journal on Mental Retardation, 92,* 381–384.

MacMann, G., Plasket, C., Barnett, D., & Siler, R. (1991). Factor structure of the WISC-R for children of superior intelligence. *Journal of School Psychology, 29,* 19–36.

Maddux, C. (1989). Review of the Quick Score Achievement Test. In J. Conoley and J. Kramer (Eds.). *Tenth Mental Measurements Yearbook.* (pp. 412–413). Lincoln, NE: University of Nebraska Press.

Madle, R. (1989). An Apple II series program for evaluating Stanford-Binet IV subtest scores. *Journal of School Psychology, 27,* 233–236.

Majorski, L. (1984). The K-ABC: Theory and applications for child neuropsychological assessment and research. *Journal of Special Education, 18,* 257–268.

Malone, D., & Christian, W. (1975). Adaptive Behavior Scale as a screening measure for special education placement. *American Journal of Mental Deficiency 79,* 367–371.

Mardell-Czudnowski, C., & Goldenberg, D. (1988). Predictive validity of the DIAL–R. *Diagnostique, 14,* 55–62.

Marlaire, C., & Maynard, D. (1990). Standardized testing as an interactional phenomenon. *Sociology of Education, 63,* 83–101.

Marston, D., & Magnusson, D. (1985). Implementing curriculum based measurement in special and regular education settings. *Exceptional Children, 52,* 266–276.

Martinek, T., & Zaichkowsky, L. (1977). *The Martinek-Zaichkowsky Self-Concept Scale for Children.* Jacksonville, IL: Psychologists and Educators, Inc.

Matazow, G., Kamphaus, R., Stanton, H., & Reynolds, C. (1991). Relationship of the Kaufman Assessment Battery for Children for black and white students. *Journal of School Psychology, 29,* 37–41.

Mathews, J. (1990). From computer management to portfolio assessment. *The Reading Teacher, 43,* 420–421.

Mattison, R. F., Bagnato, S. J., & Strickler, E. (1987). Diagnostic importance of combined parent and teacher ratings on the Revised Behavior Problem Checklist. *Journal of Abnormal Child Psychology, 15,* 617–628.

McCallum, R., & Bracken, B. (1981). Alternate form reliability of the PPVT–R for white and black preschool children. *Psychology in the Schools, 18,* 422–425.

McCarthy, D. (1972). *Manual for the McCarthy Scales of Children's Abilities.* New York: Psychological Corporation.

McCollough, B., & Zaremba, B. (1979). Standardized achievement tests used with learning disabled and non-learning disabled adolescent boys. *Learning Disability Quarterly, 2,* 65–70.

McCray, P. (1982). *Vocational Evaluation and Assessment in School Settings.* Menomonie, WI: University of Wisconsin-Stout, Stout Vocational Rehabilitation Institute, Materials Development Center.

McCune-Nicholich, B. (1980). *A Manual for Analyzing Free Play.* New Brunswick, NJ: Douglas College, Rutgers University.

McDaniel, E. (1973). *Inferred Self-Concept Scale.* Los Angeles: Western Psychological Services.

McDermott, P. (1981). Sources of error in the psychoeducational diagnosis of children. *Journal of School Psychology, 19,* 31–44.

McDevitt, S., McDevitt, S., & Rosen, M. (1977). Adaptive Behavior Scale, Part II: A cautionary note and suggestions for revisions. *American Journal of Mental Deficiency, 82,* 210–212.

McGhee, T. (1986). *Structural Analysis of the BASIS and K–TEA.* Proceedings of the Mid South Educational Research Association, Memphis, TN (ED 289895).

McLean, M., McCormick, K., Baird, S., & Mayfield, P. (1987). Concurrent validity of the Battelle Developmental Inventory Screening Test. *Diagnostique, 13,* 10–20.

McLinden, S. (1989). An evaluation of the Battelle Developmental Inventory for determining special education eligibility. *Journal of Psychoeducational Assessment, 7,* 66–73.

McVaugh, W., & Grow, R. (1984). Detection of faking on the Personality Inventory for Children. *Journal of Clinical Psychology, 39,* 567–573.

Mealor, D., & Richmond, B. (1980). Adaptive behavior: Teachers and parents disagree. *Exceptional Children, 46,* 386–389.

Meehan, K. A., & Hodell, S. (1986). Measuring the impact of vocational assessment activities upon program decision. *Career Development for Exceptional Individuals, 9,* 106–112.

Mehrens, W. (1984). A critical analysis of the psychometric properties of the K-ABC. *Journal of Special Education, 18,* 297–310.

Meisels, S. (1987). Uses and abuses of developmental screening and school readiness testing. *Young Children, 19,* 4–8.

Memory, D., Powell, G., & Calloway, B. (1980). A study of the assessment characteristics of the Woodcock Reading Mastery Tests. *Reading Improvement, 17,* 48–52.

Mercer, C., King-Sears, P., & Mercer, A. (1990). Learning disability definitions and criteria used by state education departments. *Journal of Learning Disabilities, 23,* 141–152.

Mercer, J. (1972). IQ: The lethal label. *Psychology Today, 6,* 44–47, 95–97.

Mercer, J. (1973). *Labeling the Mentally Retarded: Clinical and Social System Perspectives on Mental Retardation.* Berkeley: University of California Press.

Mercer, J., & Lewis, J. (1977). *System of Multicultural Pluralistic Assessment.* New York: Psychological Corporation.

Merrell, K. (1989). Concurrent relationships between two behavioral rating scales for teachers: An examination of self-control, social competence, and school behavioral adjustment. *Psychology in the Schools, 26,* 267–271.

Meyers, J., & Lytle, S. (1986). Assessment of the learning process. *Exceptional Children, 53,* 138–144.

Merz, W. (1984). Review of Kaufman Assessment Battery for Children. In D. Keyser and R. Sweetland (Eds.), *Test Critiques* (v. 1) (pp. 393–405). Kansas City, MO: Test Corporation of America.

Middleton, H. A., Keene, R., & Brown, G. (1990). Convergent and discriminant validities of the Scales of Independent Behavior and the Revised Vineland Adaptive Behavior Scales. *American Journal on Mental Retardation, 94,* 669–673.

Miller, J., & Milam, C. (1987). Multiplication and division errors committed by learning disabled students. *Learning Disabilities Research, 2,* 119–122.

Miller, L. (1990). Review of the Kaufman Test of Educational Achievement. *Diagnostique, 15,* 75–86.

Miller, L., & Sprong, T. (1986). Psychometric and qualitative comparison of four preschool screening instruments. *Journal of Learning Disabilities, 19,* 480–484.

Miller, L. J. (1988). Differentiating children with school-related problems after four years using the Miller Assessment for Preschoolers. *Psychology in the Schools, 25,* 10–15.

Miller, L. J., & Lemerand, P. A. (1986). Neuromaturational variables within the Miller Assessment for Preschoolers. *Occupational Therapy Journal of Research, 6,* 123–125.

Miller, W. (1986). *Reading Diagnosis Kit.* West Nyack, NY: The Center for Applied Research in Education, Inc.

Millham, J., Chilcutt, J., & Atkinson, B. (1978). Comparability of naturalistic and controlled observation assessment of adaptive behavior. *American Journal of Mental Deficiency 83,* 52–59.

Mishra, S. (1981). Reliability and validity of the WRAT with Mexican-American children. *Psychology in the Schools, 18,* 154–158.

Misulis, K. E. (1989). Test of Reading Comprehension (TORC)–Revised Edition (test review). *Journal of Reading, 33,* 228–229.

Moon, C., & Marlowe, M. (1987). Construct validity of the Walker Problem Behavior Identification Checklist. *Educational and Psychological Measurement, 47,* 249–252.

Mooney, K., Thompson, R., & Nelson, J. (1987). Risk factors and the Child Behavior checklist in a child mental health center setting. *Journal of Abnormal Child Psychology, 15,* 67–73.

Morsink, C., & Gable, R. (1990). Errors in reading. In R. Gable & J. Hendrickson (Eds.). *Assessing students with special needs.*(pp. 46–62). New York: Longman.

Mott, S. (1987). Concurrent validity of the Battelle Developmental Inventory for speech and language disordered children. *Psychology in the Schools, 24,* 215–220.

Motto, J., & Wilkins, G. (1968). Educational achievement of institutionalized emotionally disturbed children. *Journal of Educational Research, 61,* 218–221.

Murray, H. (1943). *Thematic Apperception Test.* Cambridge, MA: Harvard University.

Naglieri, J. (1981). Concurrent validity of the revised Peabody Picture Vocabulary Test. *Psychology in the Schools, 18,* 286–289.

Naglieri, J. (1985). Use of the WISC–R and K-ABC with learning disabled, borderline mentally retarded, and normal children. *Psychology in the Schools, 22,* 133–141.

Naglieri, J. (1986). WISC–R and K-ABC comparison for matched samples of black and white children. *Journal of School Psychology, 24,* 81–88.

Naglieri, J. (1988). *Draw-a-Person: A Quantitative Scoring System.* San Antonio: The Psychological Corporation.

Naglieri, J., & Bardos, A. (1990). Review of Bracken Basic Concept Scale. *Diagnostique, 15,* 41–50.

Naglieri, J., Das, J., & Jarman, R. (1990). Planning, attention, simultaneous, and successive processes as a model for assessment. *School Psychology Review, 19,* 423–442.

Naglieri, J., & Kamphaus, R. (1981). Interpretation of academic strengths and weaknesses on the Peabody Individual Achievement Test. *Psychology in the Schools, 18,* 417–419.

Naglieri, J., & Naglieri, D. (1981). Comparison of the PPVT and PPVT–R for preschool children: Implications for the practitioner. *Psychology in the Schools, 18,* 434–436.

Naslund, R., Thorpe, L., & Lefever, D. (1981). *SRA Achievement Series.* Chicago: Science Research Associates.

National Association for the Education of Young Children. (1988). NAEYC position statement on standardized testing of young children 3 through 8 years of age. *Young Children, 43,* 42–47.

National Association of State Directors of Special Education. (1990). *Education of the Handicapped Act Amendments of 1990 (P.L. 101-476): Summary of Major Changes in Parts A through H of the Act.* Washington, DC: National Association of State Directors of Special Education.

Neisworth, J., & Bagnato, S. (1988). Assessment in early childhood special education. In S. Odom & M. Karnes (Eds.). *Early intervention for infants and children with handicaps* (pp. 23–49). Baltimore: Paul Brookes.

Newborg, J., Stock, J., Wnek, L., Guidubaldi, J., & Svinicki, J. (1984). *Battelle Developmental Inventory.* Allen, TX: DLM Teaching Resources.

Newcomer, P. (1985). A comparison of two published reading inventories. *Remedial and Special Education, 6,* 31–36.

Newcomer, P. (1990). *Diagnostic Achievement Battery-2.* Austin, TX: Pro-Ed.

Newcomer, P., & Bryant, B. (1986). *Diagnostic Achievement Test for Adolescents.* Austin, TX: Pro-Ed.

Newcomer, P., & Hammill, D. (1978). Using the Test of Language Development with language-impaired children. *Journal of Learning Disabilities, 11,* 521–524.

Newcomer, P., & Hammill, D. (1988). Test of Language Development–2. Austin, TX: Pro-Ed.

Newcomer, P., & Magee, P. (1977). Predictive indices of reading failure in learning disabled children. *Educational Research Quarterly, 2,* 17–23.

Newland, T. E. (1969). *Manual for the Blind Learning Aptitude Test: Experimental Edition.* Urbana, IL: T. Ernest Newland.

Nihira, K., Foster, R., Shellhaas, M., & Leland, H. (1975). *AAMD Adaptive*

Behavior Scale. Washington, D.C.: American Association on Mental Deficiency.

Noyce, R. (1989). Review of Test of Written Spelling–2. In J. Conoley & J. Kramer (Eds.). *Tenth Mental Measurements Yearbook.* (pp. 860–861). Lincoln, NE: University of Nebraska Press.

Nugent, J. (1976). A comment on the efficiency of the revised Denver Developmental Screening Test. *American Journal of Mental Deficiency, 80,* 570–572.

Nurss, J., & McGauvran, M. (1986). *Metropolitan Readiness Tests, Teacher's Manual, Part II: Interpretation and Use of Test Results.* New York: Harcourt Brace Jovanovich.

Oakland, T. (1977). *Pluralistic Norms and Estimated Learning Potential.* Paper presented at the annual meeting of the American Psychological Association, San Francisco.

Oakland, T., & Feigenbaum, D. (1980). Comparisons of the psychometric characteristics of the Adaptive Behavior Inventory for Children for different subgroups of children. *Journal of School Psychology, 18,* 307–316.

Obringer, J. (1988). A survey of perceptions by school psychologists of the Stanford-Binet IV. *Diagnostique, 13,* 120–122.

O'Leary, K., & Johnson, S. (1979). Psychological assessment. In H. Quay and J. Werry (Eds.). *Psychopathological disorders of childhood.* New York: John Wiley.

O'Reilly, C. (1989). The confirmation bias in special education eligibility decisions. *School Psychology Review, 18,* 126–135.

Organist, J. (1985). Review of Wide Range Interest–Opinion Test. In D. Keyser and R. Sweetland (Eds.). *Test Critiques (v.4).* (pp. 673–676). Kansas City, MO: Test Corporation of America.

Otis, A., & Lennon, R. (1989). *Otis-Lennon School Ability Test.* New York: Harcourt Brace Jovanovich.

Padget, S. Y. (1985). Test Review: Miller Assessment for Preschoolers (MAP). *The Reading Teacher, 39,* 184–188.

Padilla, A., & Garza, B. (1975). IQ tests: A case of cultural myopia. *National Elementary Principal, 54,* 53–58.

Parker, R. (1991). *Occupational Aptitude Survey and Interest Schedule–2.* Austin, TX: Pro-Ed.

Parrish, B. (1982). A test to test test-wiseness. *Journal of Reading, 25,* 672–675.

Partenio, I., & Taylor, R. (1985). The relationship of teacher ratings and IQ: A question of bias? *School Psychology Review, 14,* 79–83.

Pase v. Hannon, 506 F. Supp. 831 (N.D. Ill. 1980).

Pate, J., & Webb, W. (1969). *First Grade Screening Test.* Circle Pines, MN: American Guidance Service.

Patterson, G., Reid, J., Jones, R., & Conger, R. (1975). *A Social Learning Approach to Family Intervention, V. 1: Families with Aggressive Children.* Eugene, OR: Castalia Publishing Co.

Pecyna-Rhyner, P. M., & Bracken, B. A. (1988). Concurrent validity of the Bracken Basic Concept Scale with language and intelligence measures. *Journal of Communication Disorders, 21,* 479-489.

Pedriana, A., & Bracken, B. (1982). Performance of gifted children on the PPVT and PPVT-R. *Psychology in the Schools, 19,* 183–185.

Pennypacker, H., Koenig, C., & Lindsley, O. (1972). *Handbook of the Standard Behavior Chart.* Kansas City, KS: Precision Media.

Perry, A., & Factor, D. C. (1989). Psychometric validity and clinical usefulness of the Vineland Adaptive Behavior Scales and the AAMD Adaptive Behavior Scale for an autistic sample. *Journal of Autism and Developmental Disorders, 19,* 41–55.

Peterson, D., & Batsche, G. (1983). School psychology and projective assessment: A growing incompatibility. *School Psychology Review, 12,* 440–445.

Peterson, D., Steger, A., Slate, J., Jones, C., & Coulter, C. (1991). Examiner errors on the WRAT-R. *Psychology in the Schools, 20,* 205–208.

Peterson, M. (1986). Work and performance sample for vocational assessment of special students: A critical review. *Career Development for Exceptional Individuals, 9,* 69–76.

Peterson, N. (1988). *Early Intervention for Handicapped and At-Risk Children.* Denver: Love Publishing.

Phelps, L. (1989). Comparison of scores for intellectualy gifted students on the WISC–R and the fourth edition of the Stanford-Binet. *Psychology in the Schools, 26,* 126–129.

Phelps, L., Rosso, M., & Falasco, S. (1984). Correlations between the Woodcock-Johnson and the WISC-R for a behavior-disordered population. *Psychology in the Schools, 21,* 442–446.

Piers, E., & Harris, D. (1984). *The Piers-Harris Children's Self-Concept Scale.* Nashville: Counselor Recordings and Tests.

Pikulski, J. (1990). Informal reading inventories. *Reading Teacher, 43,* 514–516.

Pikulski, J., & Pikulski, E. (1977). Cloze, maze, and teacher judgment. *Reading Teacher, 30,* 766–770.

Plass, J., & Hill, K. (1986). Children's achievement strategies and test performance: The role of time pressure, evaluation anxiety, and sex. *Developmental Psychology, 22,* 31–36.

Platt, L., Kamphaus, R., Keltgen, J., & Gilliland, F. (1991). Overview and review of the Differential Ability Scales: Initial and current research findings. *Journal of School Psychology, 29,* 271–278.

Poplin, M., Gray, R., Larsen, S., Banikowski, A., & Mehring, T. (1980). A comparison of written expression abilities in learning disabled and nonlearning disabled students at three grade levels. *Learning Disability Quarterly, 3,* 46–53.

Porter, M. E., & Stodden, R. A. (1986). A curriculum-based vocational assessment procedure: Addressing the school-to-work transition needs of secondary schools. *Career Development for Exceptional Individuals, 9,* 121–128.

Posey, C. (1989). Review of Behavior Rating Profile. In J. Conoley & J. Kramer (Eds.). *Tenth Mental Measurements Yearbook.* (pp. 86–88). Lincoln, NE: University of Nebraska Press.

Poteet, J. (1989). Review of the Test of Reading Comprehension. In J. Conoley & J. Kramer (Eds.). *Tenth Mental Measurements Yearbook.* (pp. 850–854). Lincoln, NE: University of Nebraska Press.

Poteet, J. (1990). Review of Test of Written Language–2. *Diagnostique, 15,* 228–242.

Powell, W. (1972). The validity of the instructional reading level. In R. Wilson & J. Geyer, (Eds.). *Readings for Diagnostic and Remedial Reading.* Columbus, OH: Charles E. Merrill.

Powers, D., & Pace, T. (1976). A concurrent validity study of the Key Math Diagnostic Arithmetic Test. *Mental Retardation, 4,* 48.

Prasse, D., & Bracken, B. (1981). Comparison of the PPVT-R and WISC-R with urban educable mentally retarded students. *Psychology in the Schools, 18,* 174–177.

Prescott, G., Balow, I., Hogan, T., & Farr, R. (1987). *Metropolitan Achievement Tests: Survey Battery.* New York: Psychological Corporation.

Prewett, P. (1992). The relationship between the Kaufman Brief Intelligence Test and the WISC-R with referred students. *Psychology in the Schools, 29,* 25–27.

Proger, B., Mann, L., Green, P., Bayuk, R., & Burger, R. (1975). Discriminators of clinically defined emotional maladjustment: Predictive validity of the Behavior Problem Checklist and Devereux Scales. *Journal of Abnormal Psychology, 3,* 71–82.

Pruitt, W. A. (1977). *Vocational (Work) Evaluation.* Menomonie, WI: Walt Pruitt Associates.

Pryor, C., Wilkinson, S., Harris, J., & Trovato, J. (1989). Grade repetition and psychological referrals in relation to Child Behavior Checklist scores for students in elementary schools. *Psychology in the Schools, 26,* 230–242.

Psychological Corporation. (1983). *Basic Achievement Skills Individual Screener.* San Antonio: Psychological Corporation.

Public Law 99-457. (Washington, D.C.: H.R. 5520, Sept. 16, 1986).

Quattrochi, M., & Sherrets, S. (1980). WISC-R: The first five years. *Psychology in the Schools, 17,* 297–312.

Quay, H., & Peterson, D. (1983). *Revised Behavior Problem Checklist.* Miami: Author.

Rainwater-Bryant, B. J. (1985). *Comparisons of Parent-Obtained and Teacher-Obtained Adaptive Behavior Scores for Handicapped Children.* Unpublished doctoral dissertation, Memphis State University, Memphis.

Rankin, E., & Culhane, J. (1969). Comparable cloze and multiple choice comprehension test scores. *Journal of Reading, 13,* 193–198.

Raven, J. (1956). *Progressive Matrices.* London: H. K. Lewis & Co., Ltd.

Reed, M., & Edelbrock, C. (1983). Reliability and validity of the Direct Observation Form of the Child Behavior Checklist. *Journal of Abnormal Child Psychology, 11,* 521–530.

Reeve R., Hall, R., & Zakreski, R. (1979). The Woodcock-Johnson Tests of Cognitive Ability: Concurrent validity with the WISC–R. *Learning Disability Quarterly, 2,* 63–69.

Reid, N. (1986). Wide Range Achievement Test, 1984 Revised Edition. *Journal of Counseling and Development, 64,* 538–539.

Reid, K., Hresko, W., & Hammill, D. (1989) *Test of Early Reading Ability–2.* Austin, TX: Pro-Ed.

Reinehr, R. (1984). Review of the Wide Range Achievement Test–Revised. In D. Keyser and R. Sweetland (Eds.). *Test Critiques* (v. 1) (pp. 758–761). Kansas City, MO: Test Corporation of America.

Repetto, J. B., White, W. J., & Snauwaert, D. T. (1990). Individualized transition plans (ITP): A national perspective. *Career Development for Exceptional Individuals, 13,* 109–119.

Repp, A., Nieminen, G., Olinger, E., & Brusca, R. (1988). Direct observation: Factors affecting the accuracy of observers. *Exceptional Children, 55,* 29–36.

Reschly, D. (1978). WISC-R factor structure among Anglos, Blacks, Chicanos and Native American Papagos. *Journal of Consulting and Clinical Psychology, 46,* 417–422.

Reschly, D. (1979). Nonbiased assessment. In G. Phye & D. Reschly (Eds.), *School Psychology: Perspectives and Issues.* New York: Academic Press.

Reschly, D. (1980). *Nonbiased Assessment.* Ames, IA: Iowa State University, ERIC Document Reproduction Service No. ED 209810 and ERIC EC 140324.

Reschly, D. (1981). Evaluation of the effects of SOMPA measures on classification of students as mildly mentally retarded. *American Journal of Mental Deficiency, 86,* 16–20.

Reschly, D. (1991). The effects of placement litigation on psychological and educational classification. *Diagnostique, 17,* 6–20.

Reschly, D., Kicklighter, R., & McKee, P. (1988). Recent placement litigation part III: Analysis of differences in *Larry P. v. Marshall and S-1* and implications for future practices. *School Psychology Review, 17,* 39–50.

Reschly, D., & Lamprecht, M. (1979). Expectancy effects of labels: Fact or artifact?

Exceptional Children, 46, 55–58.

Reschly, D., & Reschly, J. (1979). Validity of WISC-R factor scores in predicting teacher ratings of achievement and attention among four groups. *Journal of School Psychology, 17,* 355–361.

Reschly, D., & Ross-Reynolds, J. (1980). *Report: Iowa Assessment Project.* Unpublished manuscript, Department of Psychology, Iowa State University.

Revell, W., Kriloff, L., & Sarkee, M. (1980). Vocational evaluation. In P. Wehman and P. McLaughlin (Eds.), *Vocational Curriculum for Developmentally Disabled Persons.* Baltimore, MD: University Park Press.

Reynolds, C. (1979). Factor structure of the Peabody Individual Achievement Test at five grade levels between grades one and 12. *Journal of School Psychology, 17,* 270–274.

Reynolds, C. (1983). Statistics for the enhancement of profile analysis on the Test of Language Development-Primary. *Psychology in the Schools, 20,* 5–9.

Reynolds, C. (1985a). Critical measurement issues in learning disabilities. *Journal of Special Education, 18,* 451–476.

Reynolds, C. (1985b). Evaluating subscale performance on the Adaptive Behavior Inventory for Children. *Psychology in the Schools, 22,* 14–18.

Reynolds, C. (1986). Review of the Wide Range Achievement Test–Revised. *Journal of Counseling and Development, 64,* 540–541.

Reynolds, C., & Gutkin, T. (1980). Statistics related to profile interpretation of the Peabody Individual Achievement Test. *Psychology in the Schools, 17,* 316–319.

Reynolds, C. R., Kamphaus, R. W., & Rosenthal, B. L. (1988). Factor analysis of the Stanford-Binet Fourth Edition for ages 2 years through 23 years. *Measurement and Evaluation in Counseling and Development, 21,* 52–59.

Richard, G., & Hanner, M. (1985). *Language Processing Test.* Moline, IL: Linguisystems, Inc.

Rivers, D., & Smith T. (1988). Traditional eligibility criteria for identifying students as specific learning disabled. *Journal of Learning Disabilities, 21,* 642–644.

Robinson, J., & Kovacevich, D. (1984). Review of the Brigance Inventories. In D. Keyser and R. Sweetland (Eds.), *Test Critiques* (v. 3) (pp. 79–98). Kansas City, MO: Test Corporation of America.

Robinson, N., & Robinson, H. (1976). *The Mentally Retarded Child* (2nd ed.). New York: McGraw-Hill.

Rodriguez, R. F. (1989). *The Effect of Sociocultural Factors on the Achievement of Minority Children.* Proceedings of the ACRES/NRSSC Symposium, Albuquerque, NM (ED 315251).

Rogers, S. J. (1986). *Play Observation Scale.* Denver, CO: University of Colorado Health Sciences Center.

Rohde, A. (1957). *Rohde Sentence Completion Test.* Los Angeles: Western Psychological Services.

Ronka, C. S., & Barnett, D. (1986). A comparison of adapative behavior ratings: Revised Vineland and AAMD ABS-SE. *Special Services in the School, 2,* 87–96.

Rorschach, H. (1932). *Psychodiagnostik: Methodik und Ergebnisse eines Wahrnehmungsdiagnostischen Experiments* (ed. 2). Bern, Switzerland: Huber.

Ross, L., & Gallagher, P. (1976). Devereux Scales as behavioral measures of visually impaired residential students. *New Outlook for the Blind, 70,* 251–256.

Roszkowski, M., & Bean, A. (1981). Abbreviated procedure for obtaining sum scores on the Adaptive Behavior Scale. *Exceptional Children, 48,* 265–267.

Rothlisberg, B. (1987). Comparing the Stanford-Binet Fourth Edition to the WISC-R: A validity study. *Journal of School Psychology, 25,* 193–196.

Rothlisberg, B., & McIntosh, D. (1991). Performance of a referred sample on the Stanford Binet IV and the K-ABC. *Journal of School Psychology, 29,* 367–370.

Rotter, J., & Rafferty, J. (1950). *The Rotter Incomplete Sentences Test.* New York: Psychological Corporation.

Rupley, W., & Blair, T. (1988). *Reading Diagnosis and Remediation.* Columbus, OH: Charles E. Merrill.

Rusch, F. R., & Phelps, L. A. (1987). Secondary special education and transition from school to work: A national priority. *Exceptional Children, 53,* 487–492.

Sailor, W., & Mix, B. (1975). *TARC Assessment System.* Lawrence, KS: H and H Enterprises.

Salvia, J., & Hughes, C. (1990). *Curriculum-based Assessment: Testing What Is Taught.* NY: Macmillan.

Salvia, J., & Ysseldyke, J. (1991). *Assessment in Special and Remedial Education* (5th ed.). Boston: Houghton-Mifflin.

Samuda, R. (1975). *Psychological Testing of American Minorities: Issues and Consequences.* New York: Dodd, Mead.

Sandoval, J. (1979). The WISC–R and internal evidence of test bias with minority groups. *Journal of Consulting and Clinical Psychology, 47,* 919–927.

Sandoval, J. & Miille, M. (1980). Accuracy of judgments of WISC–R item difficulty for minority groups. *Journal of Consulting and Clinical Psychology, 48,* 249–253.

Sanford, A., & Zelman, A. (1981). *Learning Accomplishment Profile.* Winston-Salem, NC: Kaplan Press.

Sarbaugh, M. (1983). *Kinetic Family Drawing-School (KFD-S) Technique.* Illinois School Psychologists Association Monograph Series, 1.

Sarkees, M. D., & Scott, J. L. (1985). *Vocational Special Needs* (2nd ed.). Oxford, IN: American Publishers.

Sattler, J. (1988). *Assessment of Intelligence and Other Special Abilities* (3rd ed.). San Diego: J. Sattler.

Sattler, J. (1989a). Review of Vineland Adaptive Behavior Scales. In J. Conoley & J. Kramer (Eds.). *Tenth Mental Measurements Yearbook.* (pp. 879–881). Lincoln, NE: University of Nebraska Press.

Sattler, J. (1989b). Review of the Kaufman Test of Educational Achievement. In J. Conoley and J. Kramer (Eds.). *Tenth Mental Measurements Yearbook.* (pp. 412–413). Lincoln, NE: University of Nebraska Press.

Sattler, J., & Altes, L. (1984). Performance of bilingual and monolingual Hispanic children on the Peabody Picture Vocabulary Test–Revised and the McCarthy Perceptual Performance Scale. *Psychology in the Schools, 21,* 313–316.

Sattler, J., Andres, J., Squire, L., Wisely, R., & Maloy, C. (1978). Examiner scoring of ambiguous WISC-R responses. *Psychology in the Schools, 15,* 486–488.

Sattler, J., & Feldman, G. (1981). Comparison of 1965, 1976, and 1978 Wide Range Achievement Test norms. *Psychological Reports, 49,* 115–118.

Sattler, J., & Gwynne, J. (1982). White examiners generally do not impede the intelligence test performance of black children: To debunk a myth. *Journal of Consulting and Clinical Psychology, 50,* 196–208.

Sax, A. (1973). Work samples. In W. Crow (Ed.), *Positions on the Practice of Vocational Evaluation.* Washington: Vocational Evaluation and Work Adjustment Situation.

Scannell, D. (1986). *Tests of Achievement and Proficiency.* Lombard, IL: Riverside Publishing Company.

Schaefer, C., Baker, E., & Zawel, D. (1975). A factor analytic and reliability study of the Devereux Elementary School Behavior Rating Scale. *Psychology in the Schools, 12,* 295–300.

Schooler, D., Beebe, M., & Koepke, T. (1978). Factor analysis of WISC–R scores for children identified as learning disabled, educable mentally impaired, and emotionally impaired. *Psychology in the Schools, 15,* 478–485.

Schuman, J. (1987). Test review: Diagnostic Achievement Test for Adolescents. *Journal of Reading, 31,* 186–189.

Schwarting, G. (1987). Boehm Test of Basic Concepts–Revised. In D. Keyser & R. Sweetland (Eds.). *Test critiques* (v.6). (pp. 56–59). Kansas City, MO: Test Corporation of America.

Scott, L., Mastenbrook, J., Fisher, A., & Gridley, G. (1982). Adaptive Behavior Inventory for Children: The need for local norms. *Journal of School Psychology, 20,* 39–44.

Scruggs, T., & Lifson, S. (1986). Are learning disabled students "test-wise"?: An inquiry into reading comprehension tests. *Educational and Psychological Measurement, 46,* 1075–1082.

Scruggs, T., & Mastropieri, M. (1986). Improving the test-taking skills of behavior-disordered and learning disabled children. *Exceptional Children, 53,* 63–68.

Scruggs, T., Mastropieri, M., & Argulewicz, E. (1983). Stability of performance on the PPVT-R for three ethnic groups attending a bilingual kindergarten. *Psychology in the Schools, 20,* 433–435.

Scruggs, T., Mastropieri, M., & Tolfaveit, D. (1986). The effects of coaching on the standardized test performance of learning disabled and behavior disordered students. *Remedial and Special Education, 7,* 37–41.

Scull, J., & Brand, L. (1980). The WRAT and the PIAT with learning disabled children. *Journal of Learning Disabilities, 13,* 64–66.

Semel, E., & Wiig, E. (1987). *Clinical Evaluation of Language Fundamentals–Revised.* San Antonio: The Psychological Corporation.

Shanklin, N. L. (1989). Test of early written language. *Reading Teacher, 42,* 630–631.

Shapiro, E. (1990). An integrated model for curriculum-based assessment. *School Psychology Review, 19,* 331–349.

Sheehan, R., & Snyder, S. (1990). Review of Battelle Developmental Inventory. *Diagnostique, 15,* 16–30.

Shepard J. (1989). Review of the Vocational Preference Inventory. In J. Conoley & J. Kramer (Eds.). *Tenth Mental Measurements Yearbook.* (pp. 882–883). Lincoln, NE: University of Nebraska Press.

Sherrets, S., Gard, G., & Langner, H. (1979). Frequency of clerical errors on WISC protocols. *Psychology in the Schools, 16,* 495–496.

Shinn, M. (1988). Development of curriculum-based local norms for use in special education. *Journal of Special Education, 17,* 61–80.

Shipley, K., Stone, T., & Sue, M. (1983). *Test for Examining Expressive Morphology.* Tucson, AZ: Communication Skill Builders.

Shinn, M., Rosenfeld, S., & Knutson, N. (1989). Curriculum based assessment: A comparison of models. *School Psychology Review, 18,* 299–316.

Shorr, D., Jackson, N., & Robinson, H. (1980). Achievement test performance of intellectually advanced preschool children. *Exceptional Children, 46,* 646–648.

Shub, A., Carlin, J., Freidman, R., Kaplan, J., & Katien, J. (1973). *Diagnosis: An Instructional Aid in Reading.* Chicago: Science Research Associates.

Shulman, B. (1986). *Test of Pragmatic Skills.* Tucson, AZ: Communication Skill Builders, Inc.

Shurrager, H., & Shurrager, P. (1964). *Haptic Intelligence Scale.* Chicago, IL: Institute of Technology.

Siegel, L. (1989). IQ is irrelevant to the definition of learning disabilities. *Journal of Learning Disabilities, 22,* 506–546.

Silva, C., & Yarbrough, R. (1990). Help for young writers with spelling difficulties.

The Reading Teacher, 34, 48–53.

Silvaroli, N. (1989). *Classroom Reading Inventory.* Dubuque, IA: Wm. C. Brown.

Silver, S., & Clampit, M. (1991). Corrected confidence intervals for quotients on the WISC–R, by level of quotient. *Psychology in the Schools, 28,* 8–14.

Silverstein, A. (1978). Note on the norms for the WRAT. *Psychology in the Schools, 14,* 152–153.

Silverstein, A. (1980). A comparison of the 1976 and 1978 norms for the WRAT. *Psychology in the Schools, 17,* 313–315.

Silverstein, A. (1981). Pattern analysis on the PIAT. *Psychology in the Schools, 18,* 13–14.

Silverstein, A. (1986a). Non-standard standard scores on the Vineland Adaptive Behavior Scales: A cautionary note. *American Journal of Mental Deficiency, 91,* 1–4.

Silverstein, A. (1986b). Organization and structure of the Detroit Tests of Learning Aptitude (DTLA-2). *Educational and Psychological Measurement, 46,* 1061–1066.

Simpson, R. (1990). Review of the Revised Behavior Problem Checklist. *Diagnostique, 15,* 161–173.

Simpson, R., & Arnett, K. (1987). Relationship between teacher ratings using the Revised Behavior Problem Checklist. *Diagnostique, 13,* 36–41.

Simpson, R. G. (1989). Agreement among teachers in using the Revised Behavior Problem Checklist to identify deviant behavior in children. *Behavioral Disorders, 14,* 151–156.

Simpson, R. G., & Halpin, G. (1986). Agreement between parents and teachers in using the Revised Behavior Problem Checklist to identify deviant behavior in children. *Behavioral Disorders, 12,* 54–59.

Sitlington, R., & Wimmer, D. (1978). Vocational assessment techniques for the handicapped adolescent. *Career Development for Exceptional Individuals, 1,* 78–87.

Slate, J., & Jones, C. (1990). Identifying students' errors in administering the WAIS–R. *Psychology in the Schools, 27,* 83–87.

Slosson, R. (1991). *Slosson Intelligence Test–Revised.* Austin, TX: Pro-Ed.

Smiley, L. (1991a). Language assessment: Part one. *Learning Disability Forum, 16,* 23–26.

Smiley, L. (1991b). Language assessment: Part two. *Learning Disability Forum, 17,* 17–21.

Smith, C. (1989). Review of Adaptive Behavior Inventory. In J. Conoley & J. Kramer (Eds.). *Tenth Mental Measurements Yearbook.* (pp. 21–24). Lincoln, NE: University of Nebraska Press.

Smith, D. (1989). Review of the Enright Diagnostic Inventory of Basic Arithmetic Skills. In J. Conoley and J. Kramer (Eds.). *Tenth Mental Measurements Yearbook.* (pp. 292–293). Lincoln, NE: University of Nebraska Press.

Smith, D. K., & Bauer, J. J. (1989). *Intelligence Measures in a Preschool Sample: SB: FE and K-ABC Relationships.* Paper presented at the 97th meeting of the American Psychological Association, New Orleans, LA.

Smith, D. K., Lyon, M., Hunter, E., & Boyd, R. (1988). Relationship between the K-ABC and WISC-R for students referred for severe learning disabilities. *Journal of Learning Disabilities, 21,* 509–513.

Smith, D. K., Martin, M., & Lyon, M. (1989). A validity study of the Stanford-Binet: Fourth Edition with students with learning disabilities. *Journal of Learning Disabilities, 22,* 260–261.

Smith, T., & Smith, B. (1986). The relationship between the WISC-R and WRAT-R for a sample of rural referred children. *Journal of School Psychology, 23,* 252–254.

Smith, T. C., Edmonds, J., & Smith, B. (1989). The role of sex differences in the referral process as measured by the Peabody Picture Vocabulary Test–Revised and the Wechsler Intelligence Scale for Children–Revised. *Psychology in the Schools, 26,* 354–358.

Smith, T., Smith, B., & Dobbs, K. (1991). Relationship between the Peabody Picture Vocabulary Test–Revised, Wide Range Achievement Test–Revised, and Weschsler Intelligence Scale for Children–Revised. *Journal of School Psychology, 29,* 53–56.

Sowder, L. (1978). Review of Stanford Diagnostic Mathematics Test. In O. Buros (Ed.). *The Eighth Mental Measurement Yearbook.* (pp. 437–439). Highland Park, NJ: Gryphon Press.

Spache, G. (1964). *Reading in the Elementary School.* Boston: Allyn & Bacon.

Spache, G. (1981). *Diagnostic Reading Scales.* Monterey, CA: CTB/McGraw-Hill, Inc.

Sparrow, S., Balla, D., & Cicchetti, D. (1984). *Vineland Adaptive Behavior Scales.* Circle Pines, MN: American Guidance Service.

Sparrow, S. S., Rescorla, L. A., Provence, S., Condon, S. D., Goudreau, D., & Cicchetti, D. V. (1986). A follow-up of "atypical" children. *Journal of the American Academy of Child Psychiatry, 25,* 181–185.

Spector, C. (1979). The Boehm Test of Basic Concepts: Exploring the test results for cognitive deficits. *Journal of Learning Disabilities, 12,* 564–567.

Spivack, G., & Swift, M. (1973). The classroom behavior of children: A critical review of teacher-administered rating scales. *Journal of Special Education, 7,* 55–89.

Spreat, S. (1980). The Adaptive Behavior Scale: A study of criterion validity. *American Journal of Mental Deficiency, 85,* 61–68.

Spreat, S. (1982a). An empirical analysis of item weighting on the Adaptive Behavior Scale. *American Journal of Mental Deficiency, 87,* 159–163.

Spreat, S. (1982b). The AAMD Adaptive Behavior Scale: A psychometric review. *Journal of School Psychology, 20,* 45–56.

Spruill, J. (1990). Applications of CBA to P.L. 94-142. In L. Cohen & J. Spruill (Eds.). *A Practical Guide to Curriculum-based Assessment for Special Educators.* (pp. 25–52). Springfield, IL: Charles Thomas.

Spruill, J., & Beck, B. (1986). Relationship between the WRAT and WRAT–R. *Psychology in the Schools, 23,* 357–360.

Stack, J. (1984). Interrater reliability of the Adaptive Behavior Scale with environmental effects controlled. *American Journal of Mental Deficiency, 88,* 396–400.

Stallings, J. (1977). *Learning to look: A handbook on classroom observation and teaching models.* Belmont, CA: Wadsworth.

Stavrov, E. (1990). The long-term stability of WISC–R scores in mildly retarded and learning disabled children. *Psychology in the Schools, 27,* 101–110.

Stehouwer, R. (1985). Review of the Detroit Tests of Learning Aptitude–2. In D. Keyser and R. Sweetland (Eds.). *Test Critiques,* (v. 2) (pp. 223–230). Kansas City, MO: Test Corporation of America.

Sterling, H., & Sterling, P. (1977). Experiences with the DDST. *Academic Therapy, 12,* 339–342.

Sternberg, R. (1984). The Kaufman Assessment Battery for Children: An information-processing analysis and critique. *Journal of Special Education, 18,* 269–279.

Sterner, A. G., & McCallum, R. S. (1988). Relationship of the Gesell Developmental Exam and the Bracken Basic Concept Scale to academic achievement. *Journal of School Psychology, 26,* 297–300.

Stillman, R. (1978). *Callie-Azusa Scale.* Dallas: University of Texas at Dallas Center of Communication Disorders.

Stodden, R. A. (1986). Vocational assessment: An introduction. *Career Develop-*

ment for Exceptional Individuals, 9, 67–68.

Stoneburner, R., & Brown, B. (1979). A comparison of the PIAT and WRAT performances of learning disabled adolescents. *Journal of Learning Disabilities, 12,* 631–634.

Stowitschek, J. J., & Kelso, C. A. (1989). Are we in danger of making the same mistakes with ITPs as were made with IEPs? *Career Development for Exceptional Individuals, 12,* 139–151.

Strickland, B., & Turnbull, A. (1990). *Developing and Implementing IEPs* (3rd ed.). Columbus, OH: Charles E. Merrill.

Strommen, E. (1988). Confirmatory factor analysis of the Kaufman Assessment Battery for Children: A reevaluation. *Journal of Special Education, 23,* 342–352.

Strong, E., Campbell, D., & Hansen, J. (1984). *Strong–Campbell Interest Inventory.* Palo Alto, CA: Consulting Psychologists Press.

Stuempfig, D. (1988). Review of Diagnostic Achievement Test for Adolescents. In D. Keyser & R. Sweetland (Eds.). *Test Critiques* (v. 7). (pp. 177–184). Kansas City, MO: Test Corporation of America.

Suess, J., Dickson, A., Anderson, H., & Hildman, L. (1981). The AAMD Adaptive Behavior Scale for deaf-blind individuals: Applications and implications. *American Annals of the Deaf, 126,* 814–818.

Sullivan, E., Clark, W., & Tiegs, E. (1970). *California Test of Mental Maturity.* New York: CTB/McGraw-Hill.

Sullivan, E., Clark, W., & Tiegs, E. (1970). *Short Form Test of Academic Aptitude.* Monterey, CA: CTB/McGraw-Hill.

Sven, H., Mardell-Czudnowski, C., & Goldenberg, D. (1989). Classification reliability of the DIAL-R preschool screening test. *Educational and Psychological Measurement, 49,* 673–680.

Swanson, B., Payne, D., & Jackson, B. (1981). A predictive validity study of the Metropolitan Readiness Tests and the Meeting Street School Screening Test against first grade Metropolitan Achievement Test scores. *Educational and Psychological Measurement, 41,* 575–578.

Swanson, H., Bradenburg-Ayres, S., & Wallace, S. (1989). Construct validity of the K-ABC with gifted children. *Journal of Special Education, 23,* 342–352.

Swartz, J. (1986). Comprehensive Test of Adaptive Behavior. In D. Keyser & R. Sweetland (Eds.). *Test Critiques (v. 5).* (pp. 73–75). Kansas City, MO: Test Corporation of America.

Swezey, R. (1981). *Individual Performance Assessment.* Reston, VA: Reston Publishing Company.

Swift, M. (1982). *Devereux Elementary School Behavior Rating Scale–II.* Devon, PA: The Devereux Foundation.

Swift, M., & Spivack, G. (1968). The assessment of achievement-related behavior. *Journal of Special Education, 2,* 137–154.

Tabachnick, B. (1979). Test scatter on the WISC–R. *Journal of Learning Disabilities, 12,* 626–628.

Talley, M. (1985). *Talley Goals and Objectives Writer.* North Billerica, MA: Curriculum Associates.

Talley, R. (1979). Evaluating the effects of implementing the System of Multicultural Pluralistic Assessment: A qualitative perspective. *School Psychology Digest, 8,* 71–78.

Tamkin, A. (1960). A survey of educational disability in emotionally disturbed children. *Journal of Educational Research, 53,* 313–315.

Tawney, J., & Gast, D. (1984). *Single Subject Research in Special Education.* Columbus, OH: Charles E. Merrill.

Taylor, R. (1980). Use of the AAMD classification system: A review of recent research. *American Journal of Mental Deficiency, 85,* 116–119.

Taylor, R. (1984). *Assessment of Exceptional Students: Educational and Psychological Procedures*. Englewood Cliffs, NJ: Prentice-Hall.

Taylor, R. (1985). The measurement of adaptive behavior: Issues and instruments. *Focus on Exceptional Children, 18,* 1–12.

Taylor, R. (1988). Assessment instruments. In L. Sternberg (Ed.). *Educating Students with Severe or Profound Handicaps* (pp. 103–153). Austin, TX: Pro-Ed.

Taylor, R. (1990). *Larry P.* a decade later: Problems and future directions. *Mental Retardation, 28,* iii–vi.

Taylor, R. (1990). Review of the Woodcock-Johnson–Revised. *Diagnostique, 15,* 264–276.

Taylor, R., & Ivimey, J. (1980). Diagnostic use of the WISC-R and McCarthy Scales: A regression analysis approach to learning disabilities. *Psychology in the Schools, 17,* 327–330.

Taylor, R., & Ivimey, J. (1982). Considering alternate methods of measurement on the Adaptive Behavior Scale. *Psychology in the Schools, 85,* 116–119.

Taylor, R., Kauffman, D., & Partenio, I. (1984). The Koppitz developmental scoring system for the Bender-Gestalt: Is it developmental? *Psychology in the Schools, 21,* 425–428.

Taylor, R., & Marholin, D. (1980). A functional approach to the assessment of learning disabilities. *Education and Treatment of Children, 3,* 271–278.

Taylor, R., & Partenio, I. (1983). *Florida Norms for the SOMPA*. Tallahassee, FL: Department of Education.

Taylor, R., Smiley, L., & Ziegler, E. (1983). The effects of labels and assigned attributes on teacher perceptions of academic and social behavior. *Education and Training of the Mentally Retarded, 18,* 45–51.

Taylor, R., & Sternberg, L. (1989). *Exceptional Children: Integrating Research and Teaching*. New York: Springer–Verlag.

Taylor, R., Warren, S., & Slocumb, P. (1979). Categorizing behavior in terms of severity: Considerations for Part Two of the Adaptive Behavior Scale. *American Journal of Mental Deficiency, 83,* 411–414.

Taylor, R. L., Willets, P., & Richards, S. B. (1988). Curriculum-based assessment: Considerations and concerns. *Diagnostique, 14,* 14–21.

Taylor, R., & Ziegler, E. (1987). A comparison of the first principal factor of the WISC–R across ethnic groups. *Educational and Psychological Measurement, 47,* 691–694.

Taylor, R., Ziegler, E., & Partenio, I. (1984). Investigation of WISC–R verbal-performance discrepancies as a function of ethnic status. *Psychology in the Schools, 21,* 436–444.

Taylor, R., Ziegler, E., & Partenio, I. (1985). Factor structure of the WISC–R across ethnic groups: An investigation of construct validity. *Diagnostique, 11,* 9–13.

Telzrow, C. (1984). Practical applications of the K–ABC in the identification of handicapped preschoolers. *Journal of Special Education, 18,* 311–324.

Templin, M., & Darley, F. (1969). *Templin-Darley Test of Articulation*. Iowa City Bureau of Educational Research and Service, University of Iowa.

Tenopyr, M. (1989). Review of the Kuder Occupational Interest Survey. In J. Conoley & J. Kramer (Eds.). *Tenth Mental Measurements Yearbook*. (pp. 427–429). Lincoln, NE: University of Nebraska Press.

Terman, L. (1925). *Genetic Studies of Genius, vol. 1, Mental and Physical Traits of a Thousand Gifted Children*. Stanford, CA: Stanford University Press.

Terman, L., & Oden, M. (1959). *Genetic Studies of Genius, vol. 5, The Gifted Group at Midlife*. Stanford, CA: Stanford University Press.

Teska, J. A., & Stoneburner, R. L. (1980). The concept and practice of second level screening. *Psychology in the Schools, 17,* 192–195.

Thomas, P. (1990). Review of Scales of Independent Behavior. *Diagnostique, 15,* 174–182.

Thomas, V. (1979). *Teaching Spelling* (2nd ed.). Calgary, Canada: Gage Publishing Ltd.

Thompson, J., & Sones, R. (1973). *Education Apperception Test.* Los Angeles: Western Psychological Services.

Thorndike, R., & Hagen, E. (1986). *Cognitive Abilities Test.* Boston: Houghton-Mifflin.

Thorndike, R., Hagen, E., & Sattler, J. (1986). *Stanford-Binet Intelligence Scale.* Chicago: Riverside Publishing Company.

Tierney, R. (1989). Review of Test of Reading Comprehension. In J. Conoley & J. Kramer (Eds.). *Tenth Mental Measurements Yearbook.* (pp. 854–855). Lincoln, NE: University of Nebraska Press.

Tinney, F. (1975). A comparison of the Key Math Diagnostic Arithmetic Test and the California Arithmetic Test with learning disabled students. *Journal of Learning Disabilities, 8,* 57–59.

Trahan, D., & Strickland, A. (1979). Bender-Gestalt emotional indicators and acting out behavior in young children. *Journal of Personality Assessment, 43,* 365–375.

Tucker, J. (1985). Curriculum-based assessment: An introduction. *Exceptional Children, 52,* 199–204.

Tukey, J. (1977). *Exploratory Data Analysis.* Reading, MA: Addison-Wesley.

Turco, T. (1989). Review of Bracken Basic Concept Scale. In J. Conoley & J. Kramer (Eds.). *Tenth Mental Measurements Yearbook.* (pp. 102–104). Lincoln, NE: Unversity of Nebraska Press.

Tymitz–Wolf, B. (1982). Guidelines for assessing goals and objectives. *Teaching Exceptional Children, 14,* 198–201.

Tzeng, O. (1985). Review of the Strong–Campbell Interest Inventory. In D. Keyser & R. Sweetland (Eds.). *Test Critiques, v. II* (pp. 737–749). Kansas City, MO: Test Corporation of America.

Ulissi, S. M. (1989). Use of the Kaufman Assessment Battery for Children with the hearing impaired. *American Annals of the Deaf, 134*(4), 283–287.

Underhill, R., Uprichard, A., & Heddens, J. (1982). *Diagnosing Mathematical Difficulties.* Columbus, OH: Charles E. Merrill.

Uzgiris, I., & Hunt, J. (1975). *Ordinal Scales of Psychological Development.* Urbana: University of Illinois Press.

Valencia, R. (1984). Concurrent validity of the Kaufman Assessment Battery for children in a sample of Mexican-American children. *Educational and Psychological Measurement, 44,* 365–372.

Valencia, R. R., & Rankin, R. J. (1988). Evidence of bias in predictive validity on the Kaufman Assessment Battery for Children in samples of Anglo and Mexican American children. *Psychology in the Schools, 25,* 257–263.

Valencia, S. (1990). A portfolio approach to classroom reading assessment: The why's, what's, and how's. *The Reading Teacher, 43,* 142–148.

Vallecorsa, A., & Tittle, C. (1985). Adaptive Behavior Scale–School Edition. *Journal of Counseling and Development, 63,* 532–534.

Vance, B., & Stone, J. Review of Peabody Picture Vocabulary Test–Revised. *Diagnostique, 15,* 149–160.

Vandergriff, D. V., Hester, J., & Mandra, D. (1987). Composite ratings on the AAMD Adaptive Behavior Scale. *American Journal of Mental Deficiency, 92,* 203–206.

VanEtten, C., & Watson, B. (1978). Arithmetic skills: Assessment and instruction. *Journal of Learning Disabilities, 11,* 155–162.

VanRoekel, B. (1978). Review of Stanford Diagnostic Reading Test. In O. Buros (Ed.). *The Eighth Mental Measurements Yearbook.* Highland Park, NJ: The Gryphon Press.

Venn, J. (1987). Vulpé Assessment Battery. In D. Keyser & R. Sweetland (Eds.). *Test Critiques* (v. 6). (pp. 622–628). Kansas City, MO: Test Corporation of America.

Vernon, P. (1985). Review of the Wechsler Intelligence Scale for Children–Revised. In D. Keyser and R. Sweetland (Eds.). *Test Critiques* (v. 1) (pp. 740–749). Kansas City, MO: Test Corporation of America.

Vernon, P. (1990). An overview of chronometric measures of intelligence. *School Psychology Review, 19,* 399–410.

Vocational Evaluation and Work Adjustment Association–Committees on Accreditation of Rehabilitation Facilities (VEWAA–CARF). (1978). *Vocational Evaluation and Work Adjustment Standards with Interpretation Guidelines and VEWAA Glossary.* Menomonie, WI: University of Wisconsin-Stout, Stout Vocational Rehabilitation Institute, Materials Development Center.

Von Isser, A., Quay, H., & Love, C. (1980). Interrelationships among three measures of deviant behavior. *Exceptional Children, 46,* 272–276.

VORT Corporation. (1973). *Behavioral Characteristics Progression.* Palo Alto, CA: VORT Corporation.

Vulpé, S. (1979). *Vulpé Assessment Battery.* Toronto, Canada: National Institute on Mental Retardation.

Wade, H. L., Kutsick, K., & Vance, B. (1988). A comparison of preschool children's performance on the Kaufman Assessment Battery for Children–Nonverbal Scale and the Wechsler Preschool and Primary Scale of Intelligence Performance Scale. *Diagnostique, 13,* 98–104.

Walker, H. (1983). *Walker Problem Behavior Identification Checklist.* Los Angeles: Western Psychological Services.

Walker, H. (1978). Observing and recording child behavior in the classroom. In Smith (Ed.), *Iowa Perspective.* Des Moines: Iowa Department of Public Instruction.

Walker, H., & Hops, H. (1976). Use of normative peer data as a standard for evaluating classroom treatment effects. *Journal of Applied Behavior Analysis, 9,* 159–168.

Walker, H., & McConnell, S. (1988). *Walker-McConnell Scale of Social Competence and School Adjustment.* Austin, TX: Pro-Ed.

Wall, S., & Paradise, L. (1981). A comparison of parent and teacher reports of selected adaptive behaviors of children. *Journal of School Psychology, 19,* 73–77,

Wang, M., & Birch, J. (1984). Comparison of a full-time mainstreaming program and a resource room approach. *Exceptional Children, 51,* 33–40.

Wang, M., & Zollers, N. (1990). Adaptive instruction: An alternative service delivery model. *Remedial and Special Education, 11,* 7–21.

Watanabe, A., & Algozzine, B. (1989). Who discovered America? How many seeds in a watermelon? Tips for modifying teacher made tests. *Diagnostique,* 191–197.

Watkins, M., & Kush, J. (1988). *Manual for Rational WISC–R Analysis.* Phoenix, AZ: Southwest Educational Psychology Services, Inc.

Webster, R. E., Hewett, H., & Crumbacker, H. (1989). Criterion related validity of the WRAT–R and K–TEA with teacher estimates of actual classroom academic performance. *Psychology in the Schools, 26,* 243–248.

Webster, W. (1985). Review of the Basic School Skills Inventory–Diagnostic. In J. Mitchell (Ed.). *The Ninth Mental Measurements Yearbook.* (pp. 144–145). Lincoln, NE: University of Nebraska Press.

Wechsler, D. (1974). *Manual for the Wechsler Intelligence Scale for Children–*

Revised. San Antonio: Psychological Corporation.

Wechsler, D. (1991). *Manual for the Wechsler Intelligence Scale for Children–Third Edition.* San Antonio: Psychological Corporation.

Wehman, P., Moon, M. S., Everson, J. M., Wood, W., & Barcus, J. M. (1988). *Transition from School to Work.* Baltimore, MD: Brookes.

Weibe, M. (1986). Test review: The Kaufman Assessment Battery for Children. *Education and Training of the Mentally Retarded, 3,* 76–79.

Wepman, J. (1967). The perceptual basis for learning. In E. C. Frierson & W. B. Barbe (Eds.), *Educating Children with Learning Disabilities: Selected Readings.* New York: Appleton-Century-Crofts.

Wepman, J. (1973). *Auditory Discrimination Test.* Chicago: Language Research Associates.

Wesson, C., Vierthaler, J., & Haubrich, P. (1989). The discriminant validity of curriculum-based measures for establishing reading groups. *Reading Research and Instruction, 29,* 23–32.

Westby, C. E. (1980). Assessment of cognitive and language abilities through play. *Language, Speech, and Hearing Services in the School, 11,* 154–168.

White, O., & Haring, N. (1980). *Exceptional teaching* (2nd ed.). Columbus, OH: Charles E. Merrill.

White, O., & Liberty, K. (1976). Behavioral assessment and precise educational measurement. In N. Haring & R. Schiefelbusch (Eds.), *Teaching Special Children.* New York: McGraw-Hill.

Wiederholt, L., & Bryant, B. (1986). *Gray Oral Reading Test–Revised.* Austin, TX: Pro-Ed.

Wiig, E., & Secord, W. (1985). *Test of Language Competence.* San Antonio: The Psychological Corporation.

Wilderstrom, A. H., Miller, L. J., and Marzano, R. J. (1986). Sex and race differences in the identification of communicative disorders in preschool children as measured by the Miller Assessment for Preschoolers. *Journal of Communication Disorders, 19,* 219–226.

Wilgosh, L., & Barry, M. (1983). Assessment of vocational interests of TMH students. *Mental Retardation and Learning Disability Bulletin, 11,* 79–84.

Wilkinson, C., & Oakland, T. (1982). *Stability of the Adaptive Behavior Inventory for Children.* Paper presented at the annual meeting of the American Psychological Association, Washington, D.C.

Will, M. C. (1984). *OSERS Program for the Transition of Youth with Disabilities: Bridges from School to Working Life.* Washington, DC: Office of Special Education and Rehabilitative Services, U.S. Department of Education.

Will, M. (1986). Educating children with learning problems: A shared responsibility. *Exceptional Children, 52,* 411–416.

Williams, R. (1972). *Black Intelligence Test of Cultural Homogeneity.* St. Louis, MO: Williams and Associates.

Williamson, A. (1976). *An analysis of error patterns of disabled readers at secondary level.* Ann Arbor, MI: University Microfilms International, catalogue no. 77-764.

Willis, J., Smithy, D., & Holliday, S. (1979). Item level difficulty of the Devereux Elementary School Behavior Rating Scale. *Journal of Abnormal Child Psychology, 7,* 327–336.

Wilson, M. J., & Bullock, L. M. (1988). Agreement among teachers in using the Revised Behavior Problem Checklist to identify deviant behavior in children. *Behavioral Disorders, 14,* 186–200.

Willson, V. L., Nolan, R., Reynolds, C., & Kamphaus, R. (1989). Race and gender effects on item functioning on the Kaufman Assessment Battery for Children. *Journal of School Psychology, 27,* 289–296.

Wirt, R., Lachar, D., Klinedinst, J., & Seat, P. (1984). *Manual for the Personality*

Inventory for Children. Los Angeles: Western Psychological Services.

Wisniewski, L. A., Alper, S., & Schloss, P. (1991). Work-experience and work-study programs for students with special needs. *Career Development for Exceptional Individuals, 14,* 43–58.

Witt, J., & Martens, B. (1984). Adaptive behavior: Tests and assessment issues. *School Psychology Review, 13,* 478–484.

Wolfram, W. (1990). *Dialect Differences and Testing*. Washington: Office of Educational Research and Improvement (ED 323813).

Wong, B., & Roadhouse, A. (1978). The Test of Language Development: A validation study. *Learning Disability Quarterly, 1,* 48–61.

Wood, D. (1991). Discrepancy formulas and classification and identification issues that affect diagnoses of learning disabilities. *Psychology in the Schools, 28,* 219–225.

Woodcock, R. (1987). *Woodcock Reading Mastery Tests–Revised*. Circle Pines, MN: American Guidance Service.

Woodcock, R., & Johnson, W. B. (1989). *Woodcock-Johnson–Revised*. Allen, TX: DLM Teaching Resources.

Woods, M., & Moe, A. (1989). *Analytical Reading Inventory*. Columbus, OH: Charles E. Merrill.

Woodward, C., Santa-Barbara, J., & Roberts, R. (1975). Test-retest reliability of the Wide Range Achievement Test. *Journal of Clinical Psychology, 31,* 81–84.

Worthing, R., Phye, G., & Nunn, G. (1984). Equivalence and concurrent validity of the PPVT-R Forms L and M for school age children with special needs. *Psychology in the Schools, 21,* 296–299.

Worthington, C. (1987). Kaufman Test of Educational Achievement, Comprehensive and Brief Form. *Journal of Counseling and Development, 65,* 325–327.

Worthington, L., & Harrison, P. (1990). Review of the Walker-McConnell Scale of Social Competence and School Adjustment. *Diagnostique, 15,* 243–253.

Wright, D. (1983). The effectiveness of the PPVT-R for screening gifted students. *Psychology in the Schools, 20,* 25–26.

Ysseldyke, J. (1985). Basic Achievement Skills Individual Screener. *Journal of Counseling and Development, 64,* 90–91.

Ysseldyke, J. (1989). Review of the Diagnostic Achievement Test for Adolescents. In J. Conoley & J. Kramer (Eds.). *Tenth Mental Measurements Yearbook*. (pp. 254–256). Lincoln, NE: University of Nebraska Press.

Ysseldyke, J., Algozzine, B., Regan, R., & McGue, M. (1981). The influence of test scores and naturally occurring pupil characteristics on psychoeducational decision making with children. *Journal of School Psychology, 19,* 167–177.

Ysseldyke, J., & Christenson, S. (1987a). *The Instructional Environment Scale*. Austin, TX: Pro-Ed.

Ysseldyke, J., & Christenson, S. (1987b). Evaluating students' instructional environments. *Remedial and Special Education, 8,* 17–24.

Ysseldyke, J., Sabatino, D., & Lamanna, J. (1973). Convergent and discriminant validity of the Peabody Individual Achievement Test with educable mentally retarded children. *Psychology in the Schools, 10,* 200–204.

Zachman, L., Jorgensen, C., Huisingh, R., & Barrett, M. (1984). *Test of Problem Solving*. Moline, IL: Linguisystems, Inc.

Zucker, S., & Riordan, J. (1986). Concurrent validity of new and revised conceptual language measures. *Psychology in the Schools, 25,* 252–256.

Author Index

Subject Index

Test Index